ANTKIND

A Novel

Charlie Kaufman

4th ESTATE · London

4th Estate
An imprint of HarperCollins*Publishers*
1 London Bridge Street
London SE1 9GF

www.4thEstate.co.uk

HarperCollins*Publishers*
1st Floor, Watermarque Building, Ringsend Road
Dublin 4, Ireland

First published in Great Britain in 2020 by 4th Estate
This 4th Estate paperback edition published in 2021

1

Book design by Simon M. Sullivan

A catalogue record for this book is
available from the British Library

ISBN 978-0-00-831950-2

Set in Janson MT Pro
Printed and bound in Great Britain by
CPI Group (UK) Ltd, Croydon

CHARLIE ⟨...⟩ including *Anomalisa* ⟨...⟩ *hine of the Spotless M*⟨...⟩ ⟨...⟩my Award for his work on *Eternal Sunshine of the Spotless Mind* and has been nominated ⟨...⟩ ⟨...⟩n is also a three-time BAFTA w⟨...⟩ ⟨...⟩writing, ⟨...⟩ he has been nomi⟨...⟩ three Golden Globe Awards, among many other film honours.

'*Antkind* is Kaufman pushing himself to every formal and social limit, no holds barred, bleak and devastating, yet marvellous'
Los Angeles Review of Books

'This is a whopper of a book, bursting with the driest of humour, the strangest of scenarios and the most brilliant of observations. It is wholly original, maddening and marvellous'
SUSAN ORLEAN, author of *The Library Book*

'*Antkind* is unbridled Kaufman energy and wit coming up against the limits of the imagination itself: discursive, subversive and genuinely funny
JOSHUA FERRIS, author of *Then We Came to the End*

'Each page is so stuffed with invention, audacity and hilarity, it feels like an act of defiance. *Antkind* is a fever dream you don't want to be shaken awake from, a thrill ride that veers down stranger and stranger alleys until you find yourself in a reality so kaleidoscopic you will question your own sanity'
MARIA SEMPLE, author of *Where'd You Go, Bernadette*

'Magnificent, genius, enraging, mysterious, joyous, terrifying and, above all, hilarious! *Antkind* might contain the universe'
ANDREW SEAN GREER, Pulitzer Prize-winning author of *Less*

'A tribute to the absurdity of story and ego and obsession that manages to criticise all of this as fiercely as it embraces it all, *Antkind* is as funny and brilliant and utterly idiosyncratic as you could ever hope. I couldn't put it down, which is saying a lot, because holy shit, is it heavy' MAT JOHNSON, author of *Pym*

'[It commands] attention from start to finish for its ingenuity and narrative dazzle. Film, speculative fiction and outright eccentricity collide in a wonderfully inventive yarn – and a masterwork of postmodern storytelling' *Kirkus Reviews* (starred review)

'Pynchonesque ... Kaufman's debut brims with screwball satire and provocative reflections on how art shapes people's perception of the world' *Publishers Weekly* (starred review)

'This novel is magnificently imaginative, bringing to mind Beckett, Pynchon, and A. R. Moxon's more recent *The Revisionaries*. With this surprisingly breezy read, given its length, Kaufman proves to be a masterful novelist, delivering a tragic, farcical and fascinating exploration of how memory defines our lives' *Booklist*

'*Antkind* is majestic, Nabokovian, labyrinthine. A cathedral of self-pity and hubris you visit on your lunch break and then quit your job so as to spend more time in. The story folds endlessly in on itself as it spreads outwards into your mind. Deeply, horrifically funny; spiritually desolating, and thereby consoling. The voice, in all its absurdity, humanity and desperation, sabotages your own interior monologue forever. It's like the worst dream I've ever had, but one that I desperately didn't want to end'

LUKE KENNARD, author of *The Transition*

It is so American, fire. So like us.
Its desolation. And its eventual, brief triumph.
—LARRY LEVIS, "My Story in a Late Style of Fire"

Smoke gets in your eyes
Smoke gets in your eyes
Smoke gets in your eyes
Smoke gets in your eyes
—"Smoke Gets in Your Eyes"

IT LANDS WITH a *thunk*, from nowhere, out of time, out of order, thrown from the future or perhaps from the past, but landing here, in this place, at this moment, which could be any moment, which means, you guess, it's no moment.

It appears to be a film.

HERBERT AND DUNHAM RIDE BICYCLES (1896)

HERBERT 'N' ME is ridin' bi-cycles over to Anastasia Island. They got that new bridge now. It's November 30, 1896, and almost dark but not just yet. I don't know 'zactly the weather because they don't got records this far back, but it's Florida, so it's probably warm, no matter when. Anyways, we's yippin' an' hollerin' and whatnot, the things young boys do, on account of us being just that, and full of beans to boot. I'm about to tell a tall tale to Herbert about a ghost on account of I know he spooks easy and it's always fun to try 'n' get a rise outta him. Herbert an' me, we met on account of the Sisters taking us both in when we was real little cuz we was orphan babies that got found right in the Tolomato grave yard, no lie, which is itself pretty spooky, if ya think about it. So the Sisters, they took us in and that's how we met, and now we're both adopted by the Widow Perkins, who is old and lonesome and she wanted some boys around to make her feel young again an' not so alone, she says. But that's not here nor there as we ride our bi-cycles toward Crescent Beach on account of the fishin' is good there for croakers. It's still not dark and we grab our poles and leave our bi-cycles and make our way down to the water.

"What's that?" says Herbert.

I don't rightly know, but since I been plannin' on spookin' him anyways, I say, "Maybe a spook, Herbert."

Now, Herbert wants to hightail it back to town when he hears that, so I tell him I'm only just foolin' and t'ain't no such thing as a spook in truth, and that seems to convince him it might could be worthwhile to get closer and investigate.

Herbert agrees with some trepidatiousness to proceed to the lump, for that's what it appears to be, a lump.

Well, sir, it is large! I'm no measurin' expert, but I'm guessin' it has to be twenty feet long and ten feet wide. It has four arms. It's white and feels rubbery hard like the soles of the Colchester athletic shoes Widow Perkins bought me for my last birthday at which I was ten. Herbert won't touch the thing, but I can't keep my hands off it.

"What do you s'pose it is?" Herbert says.

"I don't know, Herbert," I say. "What has the mighty sea thrown up to us? Who can know what lurks in the inky dark, black murkiness of the sea? It's kind of like a, what do you call it, metaphor for the human mind in all its unknowability."

Herbert nods, bored. He's heard this all before. Even though we're close as real brothers, we are very different. Herbert is not interested in matters of the spirit or mind. One might say he's more of a pragmatis', truth be told. But he puts up with my speculatin', and I love him for indulgin' me. So I continue: "The Bible that the Sisters learnt us at the orphanage is chock-full of fish symbolism, and from what I heared, there's fish in almost all mythological traditions, be they from the Orient or otherwise. Fact, from what I been told, there's a young Swizzerland feller name of Carl Young, who believes fish is symbolic of the unconscious—is it unconscience or unconscious? I can never remember."

Herbert shrugs.

"Anyhow," I continue, "makes me think of that feller Jonah from the Jew Bible. He gets himself swallowed by a giant fish on account of he's shirkin' what God wants of him. After a spell, God has that fish vomit him out on the shore. Now we have this fish vomited out here on our shore. Is this the opposite of Jonah? Did God have some giant human feller swallow this fish just to throw him up here? I know the Bible is not s'posed to be read literal-like but more like, what do you call it, allegorical and what have you. But here we are with a giant mysterious fish-thing. And it has four arms! Like a fish dog. Or half a octopus. Or two-thirds a ant. It's mysterious!"

I look at Herbert. He's absently poking the monster with a stick.

"C'mon," I say. "Let's tie it to our bi-cycles with seaweed strands and pull it to town."

Now, Herbert likes a task as much as anyone, so his eyes light up and we set to work. Once the whole thing is secured, we get on our bi-cycles and try to ride away. The seaweed snaps pretty quick, causing Herbert and me to fly off our bi-cycles into a ditch, which tells me the sea monster is heavier than we originally figgered. I'm no expert on weights or measurements, as I told you.

It's Herbert's idea to go an' get Doc Webb from town. He's the educatedest man in St. Augustine and an expert in the workings of the natural world. He's also the doctor at the Blind and Deef School, and that's where we find him, taking the temperchers of two little boys with no eyes.

"What's up, fellas?" he asks, to us, not the blind boys, which I guess he already knows the answer to.

"We thought you might wanna know we discovered a sea monster just now on the Crescent Beach," I say, all puffed up and such.

"Is this true, Herbert?" Doc Webb asks Herbert.

Herbert nods, then adds, "We believe it's from the Jew Bible and such."

This isn't exactly true, but I'm surprised Herbert heared even that much.

"Well, I can't investigate till tomorrow. There's an entire dormitory of eyeless children whose vital signs need measuring and recording. Not to mention the earless children across campus."

An' as Doc Webb hurries off to attend to his duties, sumthin' strikes me an' it strikes me so hard it damn near knocks me off my feet.

"Herbert," I say. "What if that mound of stuff was us?"

"Like how?" asks Herbert.

"Like, say there was many of us—"

"Of you and me?"

"Yes. You and me, but 'cept babies of us from the future, that get all jammed up together in their travel back in time to now, all jammed together into one, single unholy monstrosity of flesh. So that maybe it ain't no sea monster on the beach at all, but just us?"

"You and me?"

"Just a notion. But it makes a feller wonder."

CHAPTER 1

My beard is a wonder. It is the beard of Whitman, of Rasputin, of Darwin, yet it is uniquely mine. It's a salt-and-pepper, steel-wool, cotton-candy confection, much too long, wispy, and unruly to be fashionable. And it is this, its very unfashionability, that makes the strongest statement. It says, I don't care a whit (a *Whit*-man!) about fashion. I don't care about attractiveness. This beard is too big for my narrow face. This beard is too wide. This beard is too bottom-heavy for my bald head. It is off-putting. So if you come to me, you come to me on my terms. As I've been bearded thusly for three decades now, I like to think that my beard has contributed to the resurgence of beardedness, but in truth, the beards of today are a different animal, most so fastidious they require more grooming than would a simple clean shave. Or if they are full, they are full on conventionally handsome faces, the faces of faux woodsmen, the faces of home brewers of beer. The ladies like this look, these urban swells, men in masculine drag. Mine is not that. Mine is defiantly heterosexual, unkempt, rabbinical, intellectual, revolutionary. It lets you know I am not interested in fashion, that I am eccentric, that I am serious. It affords me the opportunity to judge you on your judgment of me. Do you shun me? You are shallow. Do you mock me? You are a philistine. Are you repulsed? You are . . . conventional.

That it conceals a port-wine stain stretching from my upper lip to my sternum is tertiary, secondary at most. This beard is my calling card. It is the thing that makes me memorable in a sea of sameness. It is the feature in concert with my owlish wire-rim glasses, my hawkish nose, my sunken blackbird eyes, and my bald-eagle pate that makes me caricaturable, both as a bird and as a human. Several framed examples from various small but prestigious film criticism publications (I refuse to be photographed for philosophical, ethical, personal, and scheduling reasons) adorn the wall of my home office. My favorite is an example of what is commonly known as the inversion illusion. When hung upside down, I appear to be a Caucasian Don King. As an inveterate boxing enthusiast and scholar, I am amused by this visual pun and indeed used the inverted version of this illustration as the author photo for my book *The Lost Religion of Masculinity: Joyce Carol Oates, George Plimpton, Norman Mailer, A. J. Liebling, and the Sometimes Combative History of the Literature of Boxing, the Sweet Science, and Why.* The uncanny thing is that the Don King illusion works in reality as well. Many's the time, after I perform sirsasana in yoga class, that the hens circle, clucking that I look just like that "awful boxing man." It's their way of flirting, I imagine, these middle-aged, frivolous creatures, who traipse, yoga mat rolled under arm or in shoulder-holster, announcing their spiritual discipline to an uncaring world—from yoga to lunch to shopping to loveless marriage bed. But I am there only for the workout. I don't wear a special outfit or listen to the mishmash Eastern religion sermon the instructor blathers beforehand. I don't even wear shorts and a T-shirt. Gray dress pants and a white button-down shirt for me. Belt. Black oxfords on feet. Wallet packed thickly into rear right pocket. I believe this makes my point. I am not a sheep. I am not a faddist. It's the same outfit I wear if on some odd occasion I find myself riding a bicycle in the park for relaxation. No spandex suit with logos all over it for me. I don't need anyone thinking I am a serious bicycle rider. I don't need anyone thinking anything of me. I am riding a bike. That is it. If you want to think something about that, have at it, but I don't care. I will admit that my girlfriend is the one who has gotten me on a bike and into the yoga classroom. She is a well-known TV actress, famous for her role as a wholesome but sexy mom in a 1990s sitcom and many television movies. You would certainly know who she is. You might say I, as an older, intellectual writer, am not "in her league," but you'd be mistaken. Certainly when we met at a book signing of my prestigious small-press critical biography of—

Something (deer?) dashes in front of my car. Wait! Are there deer here? I feel like I've read that there are deer here. I need to look it up. The ones with fangs? Are there deer with fangs? I think there is such a thing—a deer with fangs—but I don't know if I've imagined it, and if I haven't, I don't know why I associate them with Florida. I need to look it up when I arrive. Whatever it was, it is long gone.

I AM DRIVING through blackness toward St. Augustine. My mind has wandered into the beard monologue, as it so often does on long car trips. Trips of any kind. I've delivered it at book signings, at a lecture on Jean-Luc Godard at the 92nd Street Y Student Residence Dining Hall Overflow Room. People seem to enjoy it. I don't care that they do, but they do. I'm just sharing that piece of trivia because it's true. Truth is my master in all things, if I can be said to have a master, which I cannot. Ninety degrees, according to the outside temperature gauge on my car. Eighty-nine percent humidity, according to the perspiratory sheen on my forehead (at Harvard, I was affectionately known as the Human Hygrometer). A storm of bugs in the headlights, slapping the windshield, smeared by my wipers. My semiprofessional guess is a swarm of the aptly named lovebug—*Plecia nearctica*—the honeymoon fly, the double-headed bug, so called because they fly conjoined, even after the mating is complete. It is this kind of postcoital cuddling I find so enjoyable with my African American girlfriend. You would recognize her name. If the two of us could fly through the Florida night together thusly, I would in a second agree to it, even at the risk of splattering against some giant's windshield. I find myself momentarily lost in that sensual and fatal scenario. An audible *splat* wakes me from this diversional road trip reverie, and I see that a particularly large and bizarre insect has smashed into the glass, smack in the center of what I estimate is the northwest quadrant of the windshield.

The highway is empty, the nothingness on either side of me interrupted by an occasional fluorescent fast-food joint, open but without customers. No cars in the parking lots. The names are unfamiliar: Slammy's. The Jack Knife. Mick Burger. Something sinister about these places isolated in the middle of nothing. Who are they feeding? How do they get their supplies? Do frozen-patty trucks come here from some Slammy's warehouse somewhere? Hard to imagine. Probably a mistake to drive here from New York. I thought it would be meditative, would give me time to think about the book, about Marla, about Daisy, about Grace, about how far I seem to be from anything I'd ever envisioned for myself. How does that happen? Can I even know who I was before the world got its hands on me and turned me against myself into this . . . *thing*?

Anyway, it's ancient history, to quote every schmo and his brother. There is no way to know. Random speculation after a meager archaeological dig. Where does this anger come from? Why am I crying? Why do I love that woman at Whole Foods? Even after they were acquired by Amazon, I still love her, even though I know Amazon is all that is wrong with this world. Well, not all. Bezos is still working on *all*. What am I trying to prove? What the fuck am I trying to prove? And I move further into the future, further from when this cracked clay vessel was new, when its purpose was clear, when it was designed to hold a specific long-forgotten thing. What hurt was it made to hold? What embarrassment? What loss? What, dare I speculate, joy? What unmet need forever put away? Here I am on the far side of fifty with no hair on my head and an unkempt gray beard, driving through the night to research a book about gender and cinema, a book that will pay me nothing and be read by no one. Is this what I want to be doing? Am I who I want to be? Do I really want this ridiculous face, which, according to the wags, I deserve? No. And yet, here it is. What I want is to be whole. I want to not hate myself. I want to be pretty. I want my parents to love me a million years ago in ways that they probably didn't. Maybe they did. I think they did, but I can find no other explanation for this constant need, this unfillable hole, this conviction that I am repulsive, pathetic, disgusting. I search every face for some indication to the contrary. Pleadingly. I want them to look at me the way I look at those women, the ones who walk by not seeing me. Haughty and autonomous. Maybe this is why I have the beard. It is protesting too much. It says, I don't need you to love me, to be attracted to me, and here's how I will demonstrate that. I will look like a ridiculous intellectual. I will look dirty, as if perhaps I smell. When I was younger, I held out some hope that I would transform into something attractive. The ugly duckling lie they force-feed sad, unattractive children the way they force-feed corn to the pâté geese. I went to the gym. I ran. I bought some hip clothing. Wide belts were in fashion. I bought the widest belts I could find. I had to go all the way to Lindenhurst to procure them. I had my loops specially enlarged by a tailor in Weehawken who did similar work for David Soul. But the hair disappeared and the face got old and there was no point in denying it, so I went the other way. Maybe I could look wise. Maybe my rheumy eyes behind thick magnifying lenses would appear thoughtful and even kind. This was the best I could hope for. And it certainly got me seen. No doubt there were snickers behind my back, but my persistence illustrated my defiance of the standard model, my independence.

And it worked in some small ways. My current girlfriend, the one who ended my marriage, is an actress, beautiful, the star of a nineties sitcom, you'd definitely know her. I believe she was attracted to my rebellious, intellectual look. And to my last book. She is African American, not that that's important, but I certainly never expected it to happen. I never imagined there'd be any interest in me from an African American woman. I am in no way, shape, or form a supermasculine menial, and she is quite beautiful and fifteen years my junior. She read my book on William Greaves and his film *Symbiopsychotaxiplasm*. She wrote a fan letter. You'd know who she is. She's very beautiful. I won't say her name. We met, and suddenly my difficult marriage became an unbearable one. This African American woman was everything I had ever wanted and didn't think possible. She's been in several movies as well. Movies I've explored in my own writings. Movies in which I've given her favorable mention. She is obviously well-read. She is funny, and our conversation is like lightning: witty, intense, emotionally naked. Often we talk through the night, fueled by coffee, cigarettes (which I gave up years ago but inexplicably find myself smoking when with her), and sex. I didn't know I could get erections like this anymore. The first night I couldn't get it up because I imagined she was comparing me to the stereotypical African American man's anatomy and I was self-conscious and ashamed. But we talked through that. She explained to me that she'd been with both meagerly and well-endowed black men, that there was something inherently racist about my assumption, that I needed to investigate it straight on. She went on to say that size is not important anyway. It is how a man uses his penis, his mouth, his hands. It is the love with which he engages that is the ultimate aphrodisiac, she explained. She ended by saying I needed to check my privilege, which did not seem to be the issue at hand, but about that she was undoubtedly correct. She is a wise African American woman and exceedingly sensual. Everything she does in the world, from tasting, to bathing, to looking, to sex, is done with the most immediacy I've ever witnessed from another human. I have much to learn from her.

Over the decades, I have erected walls that must be torn down. She's told me this, and I am trying. I'm taking yoga with her and I always make sure to position myself behind her so I can watch her amazing African American ass. It's hard to believe I get to touch that. And she's enrolled us in some sort of tantric weekend retreat, which happens in July and about which I am nervous. Ejaculatory mastery is important, but I'm not certain how comfortable I will be engaging tantrically with strangers. My girlfriend has participated in this workshop before and says it is life-changing, but I am not comfortable being naked among strangers. It is not only my penis-size issue, which I'm working on (that is to say, I'm working on my concern), but it is my body-hair issue. It is not considered attractive these days for men (or women, let's not get started on that sexist double standard, on that adult-woman-pretending-to-be-prepubescent societal nightmare) to have body hair at all, let alone excessive body hair. I refuse to participate in the culture of waxing or depilation. I view it as vain and unmanly, so consequently I am left self-conscious. My girlfriend says the workshop will do wonders for our sex life and that is a good thing, but I can't help thinking this means she is dissatisfied. She says she is not, that this is about spiritual communion and freedom from fear, and I guess I accept that. It's just this relationship means the world to me due to its newness and, I admit, its exotic nature. There's a lot to think about and the lovebugs keep slapping the windshield. The wipers don't seem to be working anymore. They just spread the bugs around. I look for a gas station or even a Slammy's where I could get some water and a napkin. But there is nothing. Just blackness.

Tell me how it begins.

In a car. I am driving. Me but not me. You know what I mean? Night. Dark. Black, really. An empty black highway lined with black trees. Constellations of moths and hard-shelled insects in my headlights smack the windshield, leave their insides. I fiddle with the radio dial. I'm nervous, jittery. Too much coffee? First Starbucks, then Dunkin' Donuts. Of course Dunkin' Donuts makes the better coffee. Starbucks is the smart coffee for dumb people. It's the Christopher Nolan of coffee. Dunkin' Donuts is lowbrow, authentic. It is the simple, real pleasure of a Judd Apatow movie. Not showing off. Actual. Human. Don't compete with me, Christopher Nolan. You will always lose. I know who you are, and I know I am the smarter of us. Nothing on the dial for a long span. Then staticky Cuban pop. My fingers tap the wheel. Out of my control. Everything is moving, alive. Heart pounding, blood coursing. Sweat beading on brow, sliding. Then a preacher: "You will keep on hearing but not understand, and you will keep on seeing but not perceive." Then nothing. Then the preacher. Then nothing. Bugs continue to splat in the staticky nothing. Then the preach— I turn off the preacher. The tires hum. It is so dark. Starting to drizzle. How is that done? How does he make the rain fall? A miracle of craft. Another illusion. The beauty of the world created through practice, over decades, through trial and error. Up ahead, a fluorescent blast of light. Fast-food joint. Slammy's. Slammy's in the middle of nothing. In the middle of nowhere. In the middle of drizzle and windshield wipers and bugs and black. Slammy's. The parking lot is empty; the restaurant is empty. Open but empty. I've never heard of Slammy's in the real world. There's something disquieting about unfamiliar fast-food places. They're like off-brand canned goods on a supermarket shelf. Neelon's Genuine Tuna Fish scares me whenever I see it. I never get used to it. I can never bring myself to buy Neelon's Genuine Tuna Fish, even though it promises it's line caught, dolphin safe, canned in spring water, new and improved texture. There have been several of these mystery fast-food places along this road: The Jack Knife. Morkus Flats. Ipp's. All empty. All glowing. Who eats there? Maybe these restaurants are less foreboding during daylight.

In any event, I slow and pull into the lot. The bugs on my windshield have almost completely obscured my vision. I see but do not perceive anything—but bugs. I hear but do not understand—bugs. I need napkins and water. An African American teenager in a carnival-colored uniform pokes her head suspiciously out from the kitchen at the sound of my tires on their gravel. I park and make my way toward her. She watches me, heavy-lidded.

"Welcome to Slammy's," she says, clearly meaning nothing of the kind. "How may I help you?"

"Hello. I just need to use the facilities," I say as I head for the head.

I chuckle at my mental play on words. I make a note to use this somewhere, perhaps at my upcoming lecture for the International Society of Antique Movie Projector Enthusiasts (ISAMPE). They're a fun crowd.

The men's room is a nightmare. One wonders what people do in public restrooms that results in feces spread on the walls. And it is not an uncommon occurrence. Yet how? The stench is unbearable, and there are no paper towels, only one of those hand-blower machines, which I despise because it means there is no way for me to turn the doorknob without touching the doorknob, which I never want to touch.

I turn it using my left hand's thumb and pinkie.

"Left thumb and pinkie," I say, to cement in my brain which fingers I should not rub my eyes with or stick in my mouth or nose until I can find proper soap and water.

"I was just hoping for some water and paper towels. For my windshield," I say to the African American teenager.

"You gotta purchase something."

"OK. What do you recommend then?"

"I recommend you gotta purchase something, sir."

"All right. I'll have a Coke."

"Size?"

"Large."

"Small, Medium, Biggy."

"Biggy Coke? That's a thing?"

"Yes. Biggy Coke."

"Biggy Coke, then."

"We don't have Coke."

"OK. What do you have?"

"Slammy's Original Boardwalk Cola. Slammy's Original Board-walk Root—"

"OK. Cola."

"What size?"

"Large."

"Biggy?"

"Yes, Biggy. Sorry."

"What else?"

I want her to like me. I want her to know I'm not some privileged asshole racist Jew northerner. First of all, I have an African American girlfriend. I want her to know that. I don't know how to bring it up in the context of this conversation, this early in our relationship. But I feel her loathing and want her to know I'm not the enemy. I also want her to know I am not Jewish. There is an historical tension between the African American and Jewish communities. It has been my curse to look Jewish. It's why I use my credit card whenever I can. I will use it to buy the Slammy's cola. Maybe then my wallet can accidentally open to the photo of my African American girlfriend. And she'll see my last name is Rosenberg. Not a Jewish name. Well, not *only* a Jewish name. Will she even know that it's not only? It's wrong for me to assume she's uneducated. That's racist. I need to check my privilege at the door, as my African American girlfriend is fond of saying. Still, I have come across many people of various racial and ethnical makeups who have not known that Rosenberg is not a Jewish name, well, not only. I've assumed they knew. But later in conversation, they would bring up the Holocaust or dreidels or gefilte fish, trying to be nice, to connect. And I use that opportunity to tell them that Rosenberg is in fact a German—

"What else?" she repeats.

"Do I need to purchase something else to get paper towels?"

"Five-dollar minum," she says and points to some imaginary sign.

I want to tell her the word is *minimum*, but I hold my tongue. There will be time enough for that once we become friends. I look above her at the menu: "How's the Slammy's burger?"

She looks at her nails, waiting.

"I'll have that."

"Anything else?"

"No. That'll do it."

"$5.37."

I take out my wallet, photo of my girlfriend on display. You'd recognize her. She starred as a wholesome yet sexy young mother on a 1990s sitcom. I won't say her name, but she's beautiful and smart and funny and wise and African American. She prefers to be referred to as black, but I can't bring myself to go against my training like that. I'm working on it. The girl behind the counter doesn't look at my wallet. I hand her the credit card. She takes it, studies it, then hands it back to me.

"No credit cards," she says.

Why did she take it? I hand her six dollars. She counts out the change, counts it out again, then puts it on the counter. Why won't she touch my hand?

"Can I also get some paper towels and a cup of water?"

She sighs as if I have asked her to help me move this weekend and disappears into the back, which I guess is where they keep the water and paper towels. A young African American man in the same carnival suit sticks his head out and looks at me. I smile and nod. He disappears. The girl returns with a bag, two small paper cups of water, and three sheets of paper towel.

"Could I have some more paper towels? There's a lot of bugs on the windshield."

She looks at me incredulously for a very long time—I want to say five minutes?—then turns and disappears into the back. I really need her to like me. What can I do to change her mind? Does she know I wrote an entire book about the work of groundbreaking African American filmmaker William Greaves, whose documentary/narrative *Symbiopsychotaxiplasm* was so ahead of its time, I dubbed Greaves the Vincent van Gogh of American cinema? Although I realize now there is something inherently racist in validating an African American artist by comparing him to a white European male artist. Dead, too. I forgot to think *dead* and also *heterosexual*. And there's one more . . . *cis*. Does she even know that I wrote that book, though? Is there any way to bring it up here? I am not a racist. Far from it. She returns with three more paper towels. They must come out of the dispenser in threes.

"Do you know who William Greaves is?" I say, testing the waters.

The young man sticks his head out again, threateningly, as if I'd just propositioned the girl.

"Never mind," I say. "Thanks for the towels and water."

I turn to leave. Someone releases a long whistling sigh. Either she or the guy. Maybe there is a third African American in the back who's in charge of sighing. I don't look back to see. I am hurt. I am lonely. I want to be loved. The instant I exit Slammy's, the door locks behind me. The interior lights turn off, leaving the parking lot a dim red. I look back. A neon CLOSED sign in the window. Where did they go? Don't they need light to pack up? Do they have cars?

CHAPTER 2

IT'S EERIE OUT here. Buzzing bugs. Frogs. I put my food and drink in the car and scrub at the windshield with wet paper towels. The bugs spread like Vaseline. Soon the paper towels are useless. The windshield is worse now than it was before. I make the somewhat frantic decision to use my shirt. The large northwest quadrant insect is hard-shelled and stuck fast. I scrape it with my left doorknob pinkie fingernail, the one I paint red in solidarity with Australia's Polished Man movement and also to cover a minor but horribly unsightly fingernail abnormality called *sailor nail*. I suggest you do not look it up. The insect comes off in pieces, its insides black and shiny. The inner portion is still alive somehow, like a just-flayed man, but only barely, and I experience one of those profound moments of communion with the natural world. It's like we acknowledge each other, this insect and I, across species, across time. I feel like he wants to say something to me. Do I see tears in his eyes? What is this creature? As an amateur entomologist, I am fairly conversant in insect varieties, but of course Florida is, in so many ways, its own thing, unlike anywhere else. Even its insects are eccentric and, I suspect, racist. I squash it in my shirt. He was suffering, as are we all. It was the right thing to do.

Then it occurs to me: Perhaps this was a drone. Not an insect at all. A miniature, crying drone. There are such things, I hear. All around us, CCTV monitoring everything. Monitoring everyone. Am I being targeted or was it just an accidental collision? Why would the government want to watch me? Or is it perhaps some nongovernmental organization? Or an individual? Would a fellow critic be able to secure or even afford such technology? Could it be Armond White? Manohla Dargis? One of my enemies? Someone who wishes me ill, who wants to "scoop" me, as it were. I have often sensed that there are forces acting against me, keeping me down. It could be that I am a thorn in the side of the machine. The entertainment industry is a trillion-dollar-a-year enterprise. This is big business, folks. And in addition to the money made, this business has a vast influence on public opinion, cultural shifts, miseducation, not to mention the entire bread and circuses aspect of it. It does not want to be exposed. I've often speculated as to why my career gets stalled again and again. Perhaps it is not chance. I pull the drone from my shirt, examine it, peel away the black "flesh." Inside, I find a tiny, bony skeleton. What fresh hell is this? I ask myself, paraphrasing the great (yet embarrassingly overrated by certain teenage girls) Dorothy Parker, as I speculate as to what our society's unholy synthesis of electronics and animal technology has wrought. Armond White is a monster. This has Armond written all over it.

I crush this nightmare drone under my foot to make certain it cannot, even in this compromised state, still record my doings, then place it in my glove box for later inspection. I am not an electronics expert, although I did take a six-week course on Atomic Layer Deposition, a thin-film application technique, because I misread the Learning Annex catalog description and thought it was a pro-ana filmmaking seminar.

I see I have been, in the end, left with a driver's side circle about the size of a medium pizza to see through. It'll do. I don't want to be here anymore. I climb shirtless back into the rental car and pull onto the highway. Surprisingly, the cola isn't bad. Not as sweet as Coke and with more of a citrus kick. I want to say grapefruit but I'm not sure. Pomelo? I perform a good deal of that lip-smacking, tongue-tapping-the-roof-of-my-mouth action to try to determine the flavor. It seems an essential component of identifying flavors, but my wife didn't do it, and after twenty years of me doing it, she lost all sense of humor about it. What can I say, it's how I do it. Everyone in my family tastes things this way. Three different Thanksgivings ended in the car ride home with my wife telling me she wanted a divorce. She eventually changed her mind each time, and the subsequent divorce came at my request. This mostly had to do with meeting the African American woman at a book signing for my biography *William Greaves and the African American Cinema of African American Identity*. She had been greatly affected by the book and had been surprised to discover I am not African American, so insightful (she said!) were my musings on her race and culture. I make a point of including neither my photograph nor my first name on my film writings. The neutral B. Rosenberg (sometimes B. Ruby Rosenberg, in tribute to the *essential* B. Ruby Rich) allows readers to experience the work free of preconceptions about the source. Granted, she was familiar with the groundbreaking work of celebrated African American Ultimate Frisbee champion Jalen Rosenberger, so she had read the book with a racial assumption about me. But to her credit (not as a credit to her race!), she was able to continue to appreciate the book even after she discovered my race. Even after her second assumption, that I was Jewish. She is an educated woman. I was surprised she did not know that Rosenberg (considering she knew Rosenberger is not necessarily a Jewish name!) is not necessarily a Jewish name. I mentioned that to her. And she said, "Of course I know that, but Jews are matrilineally Jewish, so it seemed conceivable to me you had a Rosenberg father and a Weinberg mother, for example." First of all, I was in love. Secondly, I told her, no, my mother's maiden name is not Weinberg, but rather it is Rosenberger, like Jalen, although sadly no relation according to Genealogy.com. Or the fifteen other sources I checked. I needed her to know. Yes, it can also be a Jewish name but is not in this case. I point out that famed Nazi Alfred Rosenberg was in fact a virulent anti-Semite and I believe I am related to him distantly. So there's that on my side, in terms of not being Jewish.

"You look Jewish," she said.

"I've been told. But I need you to know I'm not."

"OK. Your Greaves book is amazing."

She was amazing. She was all the positive African American characters on TV rolled into one, characters created to combat the negative black stereotypes we see on the news every day. She was articulate, educated, athletic, beautiful, charming, enormously sophisticated. And I suspected I had a chance with her. This would do amazing things for my self-worth, as well as my stature in the academic community. I asked her out to coffee. It's not that I thought of her as a prop or a thing to obtain or something for my résumé. Well, I did think those things, but I wanted *not* to think those things. I planned to work on those unappealing thoughts, to make them go away. I knew they were wrong. And I knew they weren't the entirety of my thoughts. So I would keep them secret and instead focus on the feelings of genuine attraction I felt for this woman. Eventually, the novelty of her African Americanness would recede, and I knew I would be left with a pure love for her, as a woman of any color, of no color: a clear woman. Although I understood that even my feelings for women in general were not pure. Attractiveness was a determining factor, which is wrong. And of course any exotic racial, cultural, or national characteristics were appealing to me. I would be as excited to show off my Cambodian or Maori or French or Icelandic or Mexican or Inuit girlfriend as I would my African American one. Almost. It was something I needed to better understand about myself. I needed to fight my instincts at every turn.

Left thumb and pinkie.

Left thumb and pinkie.

I have often felt that I am being watched. That my life is being witnessed by unseen forces, that adjustments are made as these forces see fit, to thwart me, to humiliate me. I worry that the disabled drone might still have a functioning tracking device smeared on the bottom of my shoe.

I drive to the beach and blow the drone through my Slammy's soda straw, like a pea, into the ocean. Then I scrub my shoe with seawater. I feel suddenly so very lonely. Maybe it is the sea. The vast ocean. Maybe it is the sea that brings on these feelings. I have often felt a certain melancholic homesickness looking out at it. Am I remembering when I once lived there, forty trillion years ago, next to a hydrothermal vent, when I was just a sea slug or whatever?

I arrive in downtown St. Augustine. It's early and still closed up.

The city is, as is everything now, just more Disneyland. Magic castles. Quaint architecture. That the buildings are authentic somehow does not change the sense of falseness, of fetishization. I grieve for us, a world of tourists, for cities in drag, for our inability to be real in a real place. It is 5:00 A.M. The Slammy's burger sits uneaten on the passenger seat. The car smells of onions and sweat. I dial my girlfriend's cell. It'll be 10:00 A.M. in Tunisia. Seems a safe time to call. She's filming a movie there with a director you've heard of. I won't say his name. Suffice to say, he's a serious filmmaker and this is an important career milestone for her. So although I miss her with a heretofore unexperienced fierceness, I respect and even applaud her decision to take this role. Although I will admit I was hurt. There were some words exchanged. I am not proud of that. But our relationship is new and consequently fragile. To force an extended separation at this point is worrisome to me. That it was not worrisome to her did not go unnoticed by me. Undoubtedly, there are some very handsome African American actors from all over the world cast in this movie. She is young and beautiful and sexually liberated, so even though I am supportive of her career, even proud of it, I have insecurities. I hate myself for them, I do. But I have them. I call her often. Often she cannot pick up. They shoot at all hours. I won't tell you the subject of the film, but it is a well-known historical event that took place at all hours. For the sake of cinematic verisimilitude, of which I am certainly one of the foremost champions, by the way—just look at my monograph *Day for Day: The Lost Art of Verisimilitude in Cinema* for evidence of my strong feelings on this issue—they must shoot at all hours. So it is a delightful surprise when she picks up.

"Hi, B." (I don't use my Christian name so as to maintain a gender-neutral identity for my work.)

"Hi, L." (Not her real initial, to protect her privacy.) "I'm glad I caught you."

"Yeah."

"How's it going? I just arrived in St. Augustine. Long drive."

"I'm well," she says.

She never says "I'm well." It sounds formal somehow. Distant.

"Good," I say. "How's the shoot?"

"It's going well."

Two wells.

"Good, good."

I say good twice. I don't know why. I do realize the second good modifies the first good to make the whole thing less good. I know that much. It was not intentional. Is anything ever?

"So," she says, "what's on the agenda for today?"

"I'll check in to the apartment. Maybe grab a few hours' sleep. Then head down to the historical society. I have an appointment at three with the curator."

"Cool," she says.

She does not use the word "cool." Cool equals this doesn't interest me and I can't think of anything else to say.

"I miss you," I try.

"Miss you, too."

Too quick. No pronoun.

"OK," I say.

"OK?" she says.

She knows I'm upset and she's calling me on it.

"Yeah," I say. "Just wanted to say hi. Should probably get some shut-eye."

No pronouns back at her and the term shut-eye. I don't say "shut-eye." What am I going for with that? I don't even know. It sounds casual, tough, maybe, like I'm a gumshoe? I don't know. I'll have to look up the etymology later. All I know now is I hate those handsome, young African American actors over there, with their cocky bravado, their cool confidence, their meaty appendages, their well-muscled bodies. How incredibly narcissistic to spend that kind of time and energy on one's body. Doesn't she see that about them? Maybe not. After all, she does that herself, with her yoga and triathlons and Pilates, her boxing lessons and modern dance classes. But it's different for women, isn't it? We don't like to acknowledge that in our steady societal slog toward genderlessness. But it's the truth. Women are celebrated and rewarded for that type of preening. And now even men, more and more. Certainly the traditional American masculine ideal is strength and muscles, but not for show, not for the sake of muscles. We admired men whose muscles came from work or sport, not muscles that came as a result of the self-conscious pursuit of muscles. Is it any accident that bodybuilding has been, historically, by and large, the domain of the homosexual male? Muscles as adornment. Muscles as drag. Now, however, you're as likely to see a well-muscled heterosexual leading man, shirtless, manicured, depilated. I'd like to pause here to say that I fully recognize that my attitudes toward the gay community are not without stereotyping and that I'm working on that. It's complicated to be a male, especially a white male, with all this lack of sympathy, with all this incessant talk of privilege, with this constant admonition to "Sit down. You've had your turn. Now it is time for you to step aside and adopt the attitude of self-loathing," an attitude I have all along been prone to anyway, by the way. Only now that it is insisted upon, I bristle. If I am to self-loathe, I want it to be my choice, or at least the result of my own psychopathology.

"OK," she says. "Sleep well, B. Talk soon."

Vague. Indeterminate. Formal. Passive-aggressive.

"I'll call tomorrow," I say. Aggressive. "Tell you how it's going."

"OK," she says.

But the timing of the OK is wrong. There's a sweet spot. Too quick, it's forced, jumping the gun, covering for something. Too slow, annoyed, exasperated, communicating a silent sigh.

"Cool," I say.

I never say "cool."

"Cool," she says.

She never says "cool."

"Get some sleep," she adds.

"I will. Love you."

"Love you."

I click off my phone, furious. A stew of heartache, jealousy, resentment, loneliness, and impotent zugzwang. I know if I were a handsome, successful, young African American gentleman, everything would be so simple. If only I were her, even. I would be beautiful and everyone would love me and be sympathetic to my plight, impressed with all I'd overcome as an African American woman in this racist society. If only, I think. Think about being able to admire myself in the mirror whenever I want, how confident I would be in social interactions. How the Slammy's woman would smile at me, give me hundreds of free paper towels because I am a sister. Maybe we'd even sleep together. I feel a tightness in my pants. A horniness has come over me at the thought of this transformation and an affair with the sullen Slammy's woman. I catch sight of my actual self in the rearview mirror: old, bald, scrawny, long unwieldy gray beard, glasses, hook nose, Jewish-looking. The horniness evaporates, leaving me despondent and alone.

My side hurts. A stitch? Kidney disease? Appendicitis? Cancer? It's been hurting for some time now. On and off. When it stops hurting, I forget about it, focus on some other pain. Then it comes back and I think, Why is it coming back? I should go to a doctor but I don't want to know if something is wrong. It would only hasten my demise. I would feel hopeless, give up. I know this. I wouldn't be able to work. I need to work. It is the thing that keeps me alive, this hope that the next thing will be the one to get me noticed. It is always the next one.

I find the apartment building. It's in a complex outside of town. I'm not sure what the building style would be called, but basically it looks like a giant house, three stories high, maybe eight units wide. And there are many of them on a campus of some sort, and they're all pale yellow. There's an empty, pitted tennis court. No net. It's cheap. I didn't get much of an advance on this book. On TripAdvisor, the single review of this place read: *Close to walk to work to and cloe* (sic) *to bus route since I don't have a car and close to restaurants.* The review made me sad for this man (Woman? Trans woman? Trans man?) but also worried I'd end up as his (her, thon) neighbor and driving him (her, thon) to work and restaurants. *Thon* is, of course, my favorite of the available gender-neutral pronouns, probably because it has a certain pedigree, a history, an impressive prescience in that it was created in the gendered wasteland that was the middle of the nineteenth century. I have adopted thon as my own personal pronoun, but other than when I refer to myself in the third person, which happens but infrequently, it gets very little use. Of course I use it in my book-flap biography: "B. Rosenberger Rosenberg writes about film. Thon received the Milton Bradley Film Criticism Certificate of Excellence in 1998, 2003, and 2011. Thon teaches a cinema studies elective at the Howie Sherman Zoo Worker Institute in Upper Manhattan. Thon loves to cook and considers thonself a pretty decent chef. Some of the world's greatest chefs are women." I threw in the last sentence because, sadly, it's still necessary to point out.

CHAPTER 3

IT'S EIGHT O'CLOCK. I knock on the super's door. An old man, reed thin and ramrod straight, answers. By way of greeting, he hands me a stained xeroxed sheet of paper. *I read lips,* it says. *Please enunciate and don't turn away from me or cover your mouth while talking. You don't need to talk loudly or slowly. If you have a foreign accent, indicate which one in the space provided below, as the accent will affect the way your lips move while forming certain words. I am adept at Spanish accents (Cuban and Mexican only), Mandarin, Hebrew, French, Vietnamese, and Dutch. All other accents will make lipreading almost impossible for me and might require paper and pencil, which I am happy to provide for a small fee.*

I write *American accent* on the page and hand it back to him.

He studies it for an oddly long time. I have time to count to thirty in my head and I do this, with all the Mississippis attendant. He looks up, nods. I tell him I am B. and I am here for the apartment. He nods. That's when I come up with my experiment. I don't know why I come up with it. Perhaps it is due to some residual hostility I'm feeling from my phone call—but I decide to see what will happen if I just mouth the words to him. I mouth, "Is the apartment ready?" He nods, walks away, returns with a key, and points me upstairs. It works just fine. I mouth, "Thank you." He nods, smiles, then writes on his paper, *Why are you just mouthing?*

Taken aback, I hesitate, then mouth, "As an experiment. How can you tell?"

You are not breathing when you talk.

25

"Interesting!" I smile. Interesting, indeed. I am learning a great deal about the deaf community already.

Later, I'll practice breathing while I mouth things to him. It'll take some work, but I think I can do it. Practice makes perfect.

The apartment is as expected. Nondescript. Pale yellow bedspread and curtains. It seems clean. Lysol. There's a single brown egg in the refrigerator. I pull the curtains. Sunlight makes the room golden.

Left thumb and pinkie!

The bathroom is clean. I unwrap the hotel-sized bar of Ivory soap, wash my hands. Relief. Finding a decent bathroom on the road is always an ordeal.

ON MY BACK on the still-made bed, I stare at the ceiling while practicing simultaneous mouthing and breathing. I discover mouth-breathing while mouthing creates a voice, a whisper-like sound: a deaf person whispering. I experiment with nose-breathing and mouthing words. It's silent. Takes a little practice. Puts me in mind of learning, as a child, to rub my abdomen and pat my head. I was so goddamn proud of that. I was an idiot, I think. Just like all the other idiot kids. Not the exception. A good student but never the top student. Number two. Number three. I was not a chess prodigy. No one ever approached my mother in a mall and said they were a casting agent and I should be in movies. No adult ever sexually abused me. Only one girl ever sent me a mash note and she was a second-tier girl, not the prettiest or smartest, not even that quirky brooding artistic girl Melliflua Vanistroski. No, the girl who loved me was nondescript. Unloved, certainly. She seemed unsure of herself. She had no discernible personality. Her hair was brown. Her eyes were brown. Her skin was white. Her nose was not cute.

This reminds me and I try the nose-breathing mouthing once again. This time on the exhale, I notice smoke pouring from my nostrils. Odd. I look at my right hand and see a cigarette there. Odd. I did not light a cigarette. I did not have a cigarette. I gave up smoking five months ago. Odd. How did this thing get into my hand? I must admit it does taste good. But quitting was so difficult that I must have somehow unconsciously started up again. I have no recollection of buying cigarettes, lighting one up, inhaling its smoke. Addiction is a powerful beast. I will tear the cigarettes up, throw them out. After I finish this one. It was a tough night and I need to relax. Now fully aware of my little white paper-tubed friend, I suck the smoke deep into my lungs, release it, watch it meander and curl toward the ceiling.

The last cigarette I consciously had was 9 August 1995. The day Jerry Garcia died. Smoker. Heart attack.

The other last cigarette was Christmas 1995 (December). Dean Martin's death. Lung cancer. Dean Martin, whose astounding, mold-breaking turn in Billy Wilder's masterpiece *Kiss Me, Stupid* preceded Charlie Kaufman's "novel" idea of having an actor lampoon himself by only thirty years.

I feel myself dozing to neuronal strains of "That's Amore."

I'M IN MY apartment but it's a hospital but I live there but it's piled with clothing. It's dark. I'm writing something. A book? I write the word *unvicissitudinously* in a sentence. I stare at the word. I can't remember the meaning. I attempt to dissect it into its Latinate components to figure it out. Unvic. Issit. Udinou. Sly. These are not words. Well, *sly* is. But the other words are not words. I am almost positive. A doctor enters with photos pasted on foam core. They are me in profile with different noses.

"These are your options," he says.

I study the labeled photos. Pug. Button. Roman. Greek. African American. Japanese.

"I don't know," I say. "Do I need a new nose? Is the African American nose different from the African African nose?"

Suddenly, I realize—within the dream—that I have been calling the actors in my girlfriend's movie African Americans, even though they are from other countries. I am mortified. Did she hear me say this? I am a horrible racist!

"Why do I need a new nose?" I say. "Won't that make me a lie?"

27

"The surgery is scheduled," he explains. "It will be a hardship for many people if you cancel. The staff has made time. The noses have been ordered. Think of others for once."

He is right. I need to think of others. For once.

"Which nose do you favor?" I ask.

"For you? The Fabray."

He rifles through the cards, pulls out the photo of me with a Nanette Fabray nose.

I like it. It's small. It's cute. I don't think it fits my face, though.

He tells me that this could be the first of many procedures, that over time it would make sense as I was transformed.

"Um . . ."

"Your face is the face you present to the world," he says. "Make sure it's right."

I nod, although with uncertainty. He puts a check mark on the Fabray nose profile and hands it off to a man in surgical scrubs and a mask.

I'm walking in the woods. My face is bandaged. Completely, except for my eyes. I wonder how I'm going to eat. Or breathe. My hand is in my pocket fiddling with my keys. I realize my key chain is my old nose. I recognize it by feel. That small mole on the wing of the nostril. I think, It's nice of them to give me a souvenir. On the path, a dog runs toward me. I panic, tense my body. It's a German shepherd. He is followed at some distance by a jogging woman. She sees my panic, says nothing to me, does not smile apologetically or even acknowledge me. In fact, she seems angry.

"B.," she says. "Come." The dog's name is the same as mine. We share a highly unusual name. She runs past me without any acknowledgment. Her dog is off leash, which I'm sure must be illegal. She is in the wrong and I could call the authorities, if I were so inclined. I have the power. She is in the wrong.

"Thank you for that," I say, bitingly, as she passes. As sarcastically as I can. She doesn't even turn. Does she have earphones in? I think back to seeing her from the front. No. She does not have earphones in. She heard me and ignored me.

"How about a sorry? Fucking cunt," I say, not loud enough for her to hear probably. But so angry. I feel invisible. I hope she didn't hear me. She does not care about me. She thinks I'm unattractive, not worth the flirt or even common courtesy. I hate her. Then I hate myself for hating her. For caring. For being angry. Why couldn't she be decent, though? Why are people so awful? I hate people. I hope she didn't hear me. Why am I not attractive to her? At least she should have sympathy for me because of my bandaged face. People with bandaged faces get sympathy; that's the societal rule. She was pretty, in that female runner sort of way, that taking care of business, women are tough kind of way. That running bra, tank top way. Maybe the long gray beard sticking out from beneath the bandages made her dislike me. Should I have made the first move to be friendly? I might have said, as an icebreaker, that her dog and I share the same highly unusual name. Why is she nice to her dog and not me? I could easily be her dog. Then she would love me. Then I could stick my nose into her crotch and she would just giggle and push me away. Or let me have a little sniff. All in good fun, if one is a dog. My new nose. The Nanette Fabray. I imagine her dog with a Fabray nose as I fixate on her sweating runner's crotch. Women sweat from their crotches more than do men; I read that. Looking back at her running along the trail, I watch her ass. I am lonely. She would never love me. I continue my walk. A woodpecker lands on the trunk of a tree near me. I stop and we look at each other. I speak to him in that baby voice reserved for babies and animals.

"Hello, woodpecker. Hi there. Hi there. How are you today? Hello. Hello."

He hops onto the far side of the tree. Nothing. Asshole.

EVELYN, WHOM I loved once upon a time, who is gone, with whom there was a chance of something human, if such a thing was ever possible in my existence—Evelyn, who is long gone, who, even now, I think perhaps today will call, but she doesn't, she won't, she can't, she doesn't want to, she's no longer interested, she's dead, she's laughing right now with somebody else, she's old and unattractive, she's still amazingly youthful, she doesn't think of me at all, she went back to school and now she's a psychologist, a lawyer, the head of acquisitions for an art museum. There's no way to know. She has no online presence. Maybe she is dead, goes by a different name, a married name. I could hire a private detective, but to what end? Haven't I done enough damage? Shouldn't there come a time when I shrivel into a less egregious presence in the world? Perhaps I should consider meditation. I've always found myself most aligned with the Eastern religious philosophies. And as one becomes less focused on the I, one would probably become more attractive. The wrinkles won't go away, but they will become attractive wrinkles. George Clooney billion-dollar eye crinkles.

CHAPTER 4

I PULL UP TO the St. Augustine Society for the Preservation of St. Augustine Film History (SASFPSAFH) building, which is a minor monstrosity, figuratively as well as literally, designed to resemble a mash-up of the requisite Spanish architecture and the head of the Creature from the Black Lagoon, perhaps the most famous of the St. Augustine–associated cinema; in actuality, it was almost entirely shot in nearby Palatka. The building has no windows other than the Creature's eyes, which are on the third floor, so it's dark in the lobby when I meet the Society's curator, Euridice Snaptem, a roly-poly little woman with a disproportionately small head and fingers.

"So you're a man," is the first thing she says to me. "I've read your work, of course, but your gender has always been a mystery to me. Truth is, I figured you for a woman."

"Well, I take that as a compliment," I say, to say something, and because no one respects women more than I.

"I'm not sure I meant it that way, but . . ." she says and performs some vague and impatient "no matter" gesture with her hands. "Anyway, this way."

And she leads me down the hall and some stairs.

"The vault is in the chin," she says. "We say it's in the chin because it's in the chin of the Creature. You may have noticed that the building is in the form of the head of the Creature from the Black Lagoon; the movie was filmed in nearby Palatka. Anyway, your materials are already set up. Nothing can be removed from the chin. When you're ready to screen the print, make your way from the chin to the first floor, left gill. Follow the signs. Don't forget to lock the chin. Left gill is Screening Room One. It's the left side from the Creature's POV, so, in other words, as if you are the Creature. But everything is clearly marked. If you get lost, call me on my cell and I'll come fetch you. You shouldn't have to, though. Everything is clearly marked. The left gill is always left unlocked. Don't lock it when you're through. For fire safety reasons."

She unlocks the chin, I enter, and she closes the door behind me, leaving me alone with the requested materials. I see three CCTV cameras mounted on the walls. This place means business.

My monograph, which is to be entitled *At Last, I Am Becoming: Gender and Transformation in American Cinema*, will be, perhaps self-evidently, a critical examination of the history of transgenderism in American cinema. The first documented film to explore this terrain was, surprisingly, 1914's *A Florida Enchantment*, shot right here in St. Augustine. The film's logline: *Young woman ingests a magic seed that transforms her into a cisgender heteronormative man—or at least cisgender heteronormative manlike, with all the attendant cisgender heteronormative mannerisms (man-nerisms!) and desires. Her fiancé eventually tries a magic seed as well and finds himself mincing about in a bonnet and a dress, chased by angry townsfolk.* The film is a fascinating time capsule and will set the tone for my entire book.

I get down to business, poring over the notebooks of director Sidney Drew. *What is it to be a woman and why?* he wrote, presciently, one hundred years ago to the day. *This is the thing we must uncover with this motion picture. Is it a simple accident of fate or is it a calling, perhaps the highest calling, to be a woman? That a simple magical seed can alter this biological marvel we call the human female, is all the evidence one needs that human nature is malleable. It is imaginable that in some distant future time, scientists will devise such a seed, although they will likely call it a tablet or perhaps it will come in the form of an unction. How many of those fortunate enough to be on Earth at that time will partake of that tablet or unction or maybe poultice? I believe many will champ at the bit to find out for themselves how the other half experiences the world. Tiresias, of ancient Grecian mythological renown, had just such a transformation thrust upon him by the goddess Hera and lived as a woman for many years, after which he concluded that the female enjoys nine times the sexual pleasure of the male. I would certainly ingest this tablet, or spread this unction within my anus, or drape this poultice over the root of my phallus or wherever was advised by my primary care physician. My curiosity would drive me to do so.*

I pinch my nasal bridge between thumb and forefinger. Drew's notebook is feeling like a disappointment, muddled, incoherent, and fetishizing. I find it telling that Sidney Drew performed a stage act as half of the team Mr. and Mrs. Sidney Drew, with his wife's identity as Gladys Rankin completely erased. After Rankin's death, she was replaced in the act by Drew's second wife, Lucille McVey, who became (drumroll, please!) Mrs. Drew in the act, herself erased as was her predecessor. Did Drew hope to be erased himself by taking the pill, to become nothing more than an extension of a man? I suspect he didn't think that far into his new fantasy female incarnation. I sift through the documents on the desk until I come upon Edith Storey's notebook. She was the female actor (I prefer the nongendered "actist," but according to my editor, the time has not yet come for that) who played Miss (Ms.) Lillian Travers, the FTM in the film. I open it at random to find: *I have discreetly studied the movements of men. They have a tendency to swing their broad shoulders as they walk. It is quite unlike we ladies, who sashay. I will attempt to adopt that masculine gait, for it strikes me as confident and strong, in other words masculine.*

I worry that Ms. Storey might be as unenlightened as her director. I sigh and treat myself to a smallish break to check email. To check Facebook. To check Twitter. To check the various Internet sites I frequent: Clipboard, Chapstick, Nimrod, William's Anomalies, Punching Bag, The Clerk Report, Peptide, Hollywood Blabb, Pimbleton's, Work-a-Doodle, Chim-Chim-Cheree, Poli-Techs, Boop Archives, and Ladies Only.

I write in my journal:

Dear Diary, I am 58 years old today and no one has sent an email. My girlfriend may be shooting and there is a significant time difference, so I am not at this moment without hope. Only 43

Facebook Happy Birthdays. An average number of Facebook
Happy Birthdays is 79. I am down 36, the age of Jesus when he
died, plus 3. Coincidence? I feel alone.

This reductionistic approach of Drew and Storey to the understanding of gender is a bugbear of mine. Can we truly boil our musings on gender down to what amounts to a skeletal distinction?
What about the hippy men among us? Are we not men, those of
slightly wider hippage? What about women with broad shoulders?
Can we reduce gender designation to genitalia? What about the inter-
sexed? Can we reduce it to XY vs. XX? What about the XXY among
us? The XYY? The YYY? The XYXYX? Those rare but no less
human Z's? Current scientific evidence teaches us there is no clear
demarcation and that any attempt to regiment gender is nothing
more than biological Fascism. Hitler would be proud.

Email break.

Facebook break.

Nothing.

I know that if I were to have a child today, I would raise it as a
theyby—no gender announcements; the gender would not be dis-
closed to anyone including the theyby itself. This wonderful option
was not available when we had our children, and I believe my children suffered greatly.

MY LAVISHLY HAIRED brother, Lavoisier, has once again neglected
to offer me a simple "Happy birthday." Has he ever been with an
African American woman? I seriously doubt it. So for all his obvious
success and sexual flag planting, which is in itself a problematic treatment of women, he is not a rebel. He has remained safely within the
prescribed racial confines. Has he ever been with a man, even? Not
him! Despite his full head of hair and an extremely successful wine
distributorship. I am the rebel. Not that I have been with a man, but
I would. I fall in love with people, not body parts. I would be with a
man! Or even, I wouldn't even ask. Let it be a surprise.

In order to suppress my rage, I dig deeper into the pile of documents. I bury my rage in research. My time will come if only I stick to the path. The vault, I discover, contains director Drew's sketched diagrams, handwritten excerpts from the poetry of Whitman, hip-to-shoulder ratios for both males and females. One must consider the possible motivations of Drew. Was he (she) (thon) wrestling him(her)(thon)self with issues of gender dysmorphia, dysphoria, distransia, distendia? This *dis* list within which we all must sadly live goes on, sadly. Such is the human animal. What a pathetic existence. We are none of us fully aligned with our physical selves, with our assigned identities. Our face is the face we show to the world, as my dream doctor said. Our body is also the face we show to the world. As is our genitalia. If, in my heart, I see myself or at least believe myself to be a waifish twenty-year-old waifu with freakishly large, soulfully sad eyes, pouty lips, perhaps an adorable "boy" haircut, smallish perky breasts—my breast size might well vary depending on my mood—then am I not that? Perhaps some days I feel voluptuous and soft, hippy even (more so than I currently am), with an ample, grabbable (but only with my consent!) ass. Perhaps some days I'm a runner, lithe and small breasted. Perhaps on those days I'm a tomboy. I call men "buddy" and it charms them. Perhaps I'm a secretary, making sure everyone is taken care of. Getting coffee. Baking cookies to bring to the office. If these are the ways I see myself, then these are the ways I insist on being seen. Shouldn't we all be seen as we want to be seen? What kind of culture does not allow people the freedom to be seen as they wish? This is the transgender struggle. And Western culture has, throughout its history, forced it underground, into the sewers and dark alleys. Why do those townspeople in *A Florida Enchantment* chase the husband? Why are they threatened by a person's choice of clothing, by thon's mannerisms? Of course the movie is not fully enlightened. In addition to the unenlightened gender explorations, the movie features a troubling racial component. Each of the African American characters is portrayed by a white actor in African American face. In addition, there is a troubling inconsistency in makeup application. Whereas most of the characters are simply wearing dark makeup and wigs, there are some who seem to be painted as minstrel characters, accentuating the lips with lighter makeup. But even that is not the most fascinating and disturbing aspect of racial depiction. When Lillian (now Lawrence) decides she (he) wants a valet instead of a maid, and she (he) forces (!) a pill on her (his) maid, Jane, the maid's transformation (albeit with an added alcoholic component) is violent. She doesn't become a man, the movie tells us, she becomes a *black* man, a savage. Whereas Lawrence flirts and sweet-talks his female conquests, the masculinized Jane beats a male competitor nearly to death to win the woman in whom he is now interested.

I INHALE ITS velvety smoke deep into my lungs. Wait. I have no recollection of lighting this cigarette. And there are No SMOKING signs everywhere. Of course there can be no smoking in a film library. I know that. It would be obvious to the smallest of children, even those with no background in filmic studies or oxidation-reduction reactions. I stub the cigarette out, but only after I finish it and another one.

I take a break to add to my running list of words (and/or concepts) to be included in this or future monographs:

coterie
playful
insouciance
hausfrau
endemic
nervous onion
emotional tourniquet
Guy Debord
cultural priapism
societal zugzwang
Magister Ludi
impish neglect

Why can't I focus on the task at hand? I need to get back to it.

dendroarchaeology
pilgarlic
Shooty Babitt
theybies
Leiomy Maldonado
2008 Passover margarine shortage

CHAPTER 5

Back in my St. Augustine rental, hard at work writing about the wardrobe design in *Enchantment*. I'm whimsically entitling this section "Return to Gender, a Dress Unsewn," which is a play on the song "Return to Sender"—written by the great African American songwriters Scott and Blackwell—which contains the lyric: "Return to sender, address unknown." I am not above being playful in my work.

A violent yelling comes from the apartment of my neighbor directly across the hall.

"Fucking fuck. You fucking little bastard. You sheeny kike little fucker. Do what I tell you to!"

I am taken aback. What poor Jewish soul is the recipient of this abuse? As much as I am not a Jew, I will not tolerate anti-Semitism in any of its many forms. Should I summon the police? Should I mind my business? Certainly a domestic squabble is not a cause for police intervention. And certainly we each of us lose our temper at times. I am new in town. Do I want a 911 call to be my introduction to the neighborhood? Furthermore, due to the general belief that I am a Jew myself, perhaps my interference will be seen as "a Jew protecting a Jew," which many see as Jews sticking together and therefore frown upon. In that way, it might do more harm than good to the local Jewish community. I must carefully consider all of the potential repercussions.

Then there is a *thwack*. Then breaking glass. Then a *thwack*.

I cannot in good conscience not get involved. Remember Kitty Genovese. Or, more to the point, remember Harlan Ellison calling the do-nothing witnesses "thirty-six motherfuckers." I don't want to be called a motherfucker by Ellison, even though it turns out he was wrong and the Genovese witnesses were misrepresented and besides by all accounts Ellison was an obnoxious fellow. The point is everyone still thinks the witnesses were not misrepresented, that Ellison was right. And as we all know, perception is everything. Just ask anyone ever wrongly accused of child molestation. Do they ever get their lives back? The answer is no, and I say that as a sympathizer. To be clear, I say it as a sympathizer of the wrongfully accused, not of child molesters, and certainly not as a Nazi sympathizer, if that's what you're thinking for some reason. Although I will say that there is a witch hunt mentality in our society in regard to any and all perceived aberrations. We have become a country of politically correct sheep. I realize this view opens me up to criticism from others and, more important, even from myself. Then again, perhaps the definition of courage is forging ahead in the face of self-criticism. But let me take this opportunity to reiterate that I do not support any form of abuse of children, physical, emotional, or sexual. However, I would just add, as a matter of fact, that there is a popular misunderstanding of the term pedophilia. It specifically and only refers to sexual attraction to prepubescent children. Interest in young teens is hebephilia and interest in teens older than fifteen is ephebophilia. Look it up.

I decide I will wait for one more indication of my neighbor's violent abuse and, if it happens, act.

"FUCK YOU, HEBREW!" he screams.

I grab my key, leave my room, knock on his door.

A very old man answers.

"Oh, it's you," he says, quietly.

"Excuse me, I could not help but hear some commotion through our common wall. Is everything all right with everyone over here?" I say, trying to look past him into the dark apartment. I am worried that perhaps someone is abusing this elderly Jew standing before me.

"I am alone," he tells me. "I live alone. I have always lived alone. I am an old man," he adds, as if it were germane, as if this were not obvious.

"I heard yelling, someone called a kike. Who were you talking to, if not someone? Or who was talking to you, if you were the one not talking to someone?"

"I was talking to you," he says, enigmatically.

"First of all, I am not a Jew," I say, reflexively, defensively. "And besides, I was not in your apartment when you were or someone was calling someone or you a one."

"I know," he says. "I'm glad we're able to finally talk in a civilized manner."

"I'm sure I do not know what you are saying," I say. "You and I have never before met. In fact, this is my first visit to St. Augustine."

"I am old and lonely," he asserts once more, for no apparent reason.

Then it hits me: OK, here we go. Old man wants a friend. How many times have I found myself in this situation? There should be a psychiatric term for old people.

"I am old and lonely and I do not have much time," he continues. "Perhaps I have wasted my life in isolation. As a young man, I did not have the confidence to speak to the ladies. Then the years passed, as they must, as they will. And here I am today, never having known the love of a woman, never even having had a friend. And here you are in the flesh, finally. Someone to talk to, someone with whom to share my life and work."

"Listen," I say, "I'm in Florida for a very short period and I have a lot of work to do while here. I understand and appreciate your loneliness. Certainly I am on the road to old age myself, as are we all, and, consequently, I just don't have the time to take away from my writing."

"Oh? What are you writing about?" he asks, an odd, obnoxious little smile on his odd and uniformly pale face.

"I'm researching a little-known silent movie shot in St. Augustine in 1914."

"*A Florida Enchantment*," he says. It is not a question.

"How do you know?" I ask.

"I was the little boy in it. Ingo Cutbirth. My name is in the credits."

"There is no little boy in it," I say, racking my brain to make certain. I am an expert on the film, of course, having viewed it several thousand times, not only forward, but backward, something I do with films that interest me. It allows me to look at the film as a formal construction rather than a story, of course, much like copying a face upside down so that one's preconceptions of "nose" and "eyes" and *et chetera* don't get in the way of following the actual lines. But in addition, I, as contemporary physics teaches us, believe the arrow of time is illusory, cause and effect a story we tell ourselves. The truth is there are infinite versions of each story, the first the simple narrative convention: This happens, then this happens because of it. The second version is that events are quantized and separate and occur independently and can, nay must, be viewed in every conceivable order to understand their full implication. Of course the great intellectual of cinema Rene Chauvin explored this very notion in its most simple iteration in his film *Moutarde*, which must be viewed in both directions and centers on a pivotal moment located in the very center of the film between husband Gerard and wife Claire. In the "forward" version of the film, Claire serves Gerard a plate of sausages. He asks if there is any mustard in the house, and Claire says, "Oh, I am so sorry, Gerard. I went to the market today, but I forgot to pick up mustard. I will get some tomorrow." "Don't worry, my dear," he says, and they kiss. The next shot finds Claire at the market, with a sweet smile on her face, lovingly choosing a jar of mustard for her husband. In the reverse juxtaposition, we see Claire lovingly picking up a jar of mustard followed by denying to her husband that she bought any. A devious Claire. Why is she denying her husband his mustard? Of course everything that happens after (or before) these two scenes is colored by this treachery or, in reverse, this act of kindness. That the movie ends (or begins) with the death of Claire, making her a ghost in the reverse version of the movie, only serves to further complicate the story. Chauvin's experiment, which shook the film world to its very core, should in theory work if the scenes were rearranged at random, allowing for even more complex and varied interpretations of this quantized world. In any event (I'll stop nattering), I view all worthwhile films this way, as well as once with the monitor upside down, which forces me to not take gravity for granted as a force in the film. For when we talk about figurative gravity in a film, we often forget that literal gravity is essential to truly understanding the human condition. We are none of us immune to the burden it imposes on us, nor should we be ungrateful for its gift of keeping us from flying off into space and exploding in the cosmic vacuum, or whatever happens in space (I am not a scientist, although I did minor in horror vacui studies at Harvard). The truly great and introspective characters in cinema have an awareness of this duality, and it is only revealed to us by watching them move while upside down, where every step is both a prayer and a commination.

The old man is staring at me.

"I am unseen," he says. "In the *Enchantment* film. It is from my point of view. The director was experimenting with form. I stood under the camera for every shot. I was a smallish boy with a flattish head, so I easily fit. I'm in the credits. Unseen Boy—Ingo Cutbirth."

"Of course!" I say.

Suddenly the movie makes sense. The boy! Of course! The unseen boy! The narrator! The dreamer of the dream. How this changes everything! How many new questions there now are. Why a boy? Why did the director choose a—

"Wait. How old were you in 1914?"

"Six," he says.

Why did the director choose a six-year-old, a boy clearly not yet sexually developed, to have this dream, this fantasy, about an adult woman? This seems—

"Wait. You were born in 1908?"

"Nineteen-fourteen was a time of change," the old man says, ignoring my question. "We knew we had three years left before we would enter the First World War and that the Second World War was scheduled to begin shortly thereafter. The Germans are nothing if not punctual. So—"

"How did you know what the future would bring?" I ask.

"There were prognosticators," he tells me. "Those who understood the quantized nature of time. Physics was a burgeoning field and everyone was jumping on the bandwagon. Painters, writers, even fortune-tellers. Things are not as they seem."

"I know that," I say. "I just told *you* that! Have you read my book on *Mustard*?"

"I'm not much of a foodie."

"The film *Moutarde*."

"Oh," he says. "Not yet, but it's on my night table."

"Really?"

"Of course."

"Why of course?" I ask.

He hesitates, then says a little too quickly: "I have a long-standing interest in film. Anyhoo, my point is that the world was changing. Women were questioning their societal roles. Men were soon to be dying on foreign battlefields. The art of cinema, while not in its infancy, was certainly in its young adolescence, the *Hebe* period, as it was called, I believe."

"Hebe? As in a Jewish slur?"

"As in hebephilia," he says.

"Ah. Yes. Love of Jews? No, that's not it. But the term is familiar. I simply can't put my finger on it."

"And because of that there was all sorts of exploration, growing pains, testing the limits imposed by theater and literature, the mother and father of film, respectively."

"Are you a cinephile?" I ask, suddenly impressed with this withered, white papery Jew (?) before me.

"If by cinephile you mean someone sexually excited by film or film stock, then yes."

"I didn't mean that. I meant a lover of the art of film."

"I am that as—"

"In the platonic sense, I mean."

"Oh. I am that as well. Some films I love as friends, some in a deeper way."

Although I had never put it that way for myself, I understand what he means. And I feel a sudden kinship. I should add here that I have always been violently repulsed by the elderly. I know this is not a societally acceptable reaction and therefore I have kept it to myself. So now as I approach my own doddery, I find that repulsion more and more directed inwardly. Rather than discovering empathy for them, I find I hate them and myself all the more and that I look longingly and jealously at the young, at the taut of skin, at the sharp of mind, at the perfect of form, at the cocky of spirit, at the tattooed of arm, at the pierced of wherever. Granted I see them as stupid and shallow, in their baseball caps with factory-flat bills, stickers still adhered, in their ignorance of international affairs, in their inability to see me, to be sexually attracted to me, to admire me. "You, too, will get old and die," I have on occasion screamed at groups of teens who have called out "baldy" or "beardy" or "baldo" or "beardo" or "baldhead" or "beard face" at me from the safety of the 7-Eleven parking lot. At times I have screamed it at teens who have said nothing to me. Whom I am not repulsed by are the elderly genius directors amongst us. The Godards, the Melvilles, the Renaiseseses. Although I am not homosexual by inclination, I do feel a certain romantic interest in these men. Perhaps because I see them as father figures, as godlike, as paterfamiliases, if you will. Perhaps because I would like them to see me, to love me and admire me the way I love and admire them. How to achieve that? Well, certainly if I could write a monograph elucidating their work in ways never before elucidated in the history of film history that would help. Perhaps if I could even show them things about their work they themselves had never considered. But this has not happened, and as they have died off one by one, the possibility of it happening has diminished greatly. I have often thought it unfair that pulchritudinous young women can gain access to older, successful, brilliant male artists for no reason other than the artist's wanting to fuck them. Whereas I have sweated and strained to understand their work, to shed light on it. I have, in my highly insightful way, adored them, and yet nothing. This is the height of sexism. Why can't they love me? Why couldn't my father love me just for being me? It was always about proving my worth to him. Never because I was cute or sexy. And as a child, I was both, I believe. Imagine a holy synthesis of Brandon Cruz from *The Court-ship of Eddie's Father* and Mayim Bialik of *Blossom* fame and you're imagining me as a boy. I was the epitome of pulchritudinous. I know it's impolitic to celebrate Man-Boy love, but the Greeks, the great-est generation (with apologies to those of you who fought the Nazis), with the most geniuses per square foot in the history of the world, seemed to do all right with it. To be clear, I am not condoning such an uneven power dynamic in any relationship, and I fully believe children must be protected from predators. The only thing I am saying is that if Alain Resnais had taken an interest in me as a little boy, I would have been flattered. Obviously that ship sailed a long time ago.

It pops into my mind, for no clear reason, that sometimes I imag-ine myself as solid through and through. No bones, no blood. No organs. Rubber perhaps, with a skeleton of metal. It would be an ideal construction for a being. No longer any worry about kidney disease, for my kidneys would be solid rubber and solid rubber is impervious to kidney disease. I have looked this up. Just as when I have dental issues, I consider how much better a world it would be if people had beaks, and I mean instead of teeth, not in addition to them as have Hegel and Schlegel. Beaks in addition to teeth would solve no problems, obviously.

I refocus on my previous train of thought: The old man is still old, however, and, let's face it, no Alain Resnais. If I am to cozy up to an old man, he must be a certified genius, a poet, an artist. As I in my youth had hoped to be as an old man in my own future and still do in the future from now, but with less time to get there. But as of now, I am simply a celebrator of geniuses, an apologist for great men who are anti-Semites and racists, for brilliant artists who abuse women. These quirks of character must be forgiven in our geniuses is my unpopular opinion. Artists must have the freedom to express and explore the darkest regions of their psyches. As Persephone must spend half the year in the underworld, so must these men delve deep within themselves (and young women sometimes!) to bring us the fruit we so need for our sustenance. The pomegranate—symbol of life, of death, of royalty, of fecundity, of Jesus's suffering, of virility, and so much more—is of course the fruit associated with Persephone. It chains her forever, albeit intermittently, to the underworld. Do we despise her for this? No, we celebrate her, because when she emerges, she brings us the spring. A field must lie fallow sometimes if we are to have any hope of an eventual renewal. A genius must sometimes be a racist if we are to hope for elucidation. History is generously peppered with geniuses who despised the Jews, who dismissed the blacks, who objectified women. Are we to bury their great works because of this? The answer is a resounding no, we are not to. We are, all of us, human. We are, all of us, imperfect. Prejudice is evolutionarily implanted in our genes. We need to know The Tiger is a dangerous animal. We need *not* know that all tigers are not. Identifying the personalities of individual tigers does not serve our need to survive. Granted, it might make us more enlightened individuals and friends with some tigers, and I am all for that. I applaud that, but one must recognize that there is a tribal instinct in humans and it is at its base an instinct for survival. So accept that, mourn it, decry it, rail against it, but recognize it is a very human trait and have patience with it. Have compassion. Thank you and good night. This is an impromptu speech I delivered to a great deal of heckling in the Bates College copier room when I was a visiting critic in their film department, where my job was to sit in the back during student film screenings, tap my pen impatiently against my notebook, and sigh.

The old man stares. I am not certain how long we have been in his doorway. I search for clues: Was it light before? It is dark now. I don't recall. Perhaps it was light before. Certainly it was light at some point today. Of this I am almost certain.

"Anyhoo," I say.

He asks if I would like to come in. He tells me again that he has spent his life in isolation, brimming with social anxiety, and that he has decided to change his ways at this very late stage. He realizes now that his phobias greatly limited his *joie de vivre*. Never has he felt the embrace of a woman, shared a beer with a male buddy, seen a football match with a buddy, had a buddy, played pool with a buddy. This is actually, he confides with some embarrassment, the first time he's even said the word *buddy*. He likes the word, it turns out, he tells me. It's friendly, he explains. It's got a nice nose to it, as they say about those wines with nice noses to them.

I tell him I'm busy.

He nods sadly.

Then I think, Be nice; he's an old man. Then I think, Not too nice; I don't want him to think every time I bump into him, I'm going to stop for a long conversation. Then I think, Someday I'll be old, what if no one wants to talk to me. Then I think, Oh no, karma: What if I'm not nice to him, maybe something bad will happen to me. Then I think of that movie where Meg Ryan turns into an old man. Not that I believe in that sort of magical nonsense, but the movie does make some valid points. And not that Meg Ryan is by any stretch of the imagination old now, but it does make one remember about how she was once the girl next door and how we as a society keep trading in our old models for new ones. Then I think, This old man was once young—as young as Meg Ryan used to be. But no one can see that now. We are stuck in the present. An old man is old. A young man is young. A boy is a boy. We can't see life as a journey. Where we are now is not where we started. It is not where we're going. It is essential to see this old man not just as a reminder of my own mortality, but as a person, someone who might have had or might still be having a fascinating life with fascinating thoughts.

"I have errands," I say.

"OK. I wasn't sure you were going to say anything. It's odd the way you keep staring at me for so long."

"I had fallen into a fugue state," I say, covering. Then I think, That movie was called *A Kiss to Remember*. Then I think, No, that's not it.

"I envy you young people your fugue states and jelly bracelets. Your Eyebobs."

"Our what?"

"Eyebobs? No Eyebobs yet?"

"I don't even know what that sentence means."

"Sometimes I get ahead of things. See, I have these dreams."

47

Oh boy, I think.

"Why do you say that?" he asks.

"What?"

"Oh boy."

"I said that? I thought I thought it."

"You both thought it and said it, if we are to be completely accurate."

You cagey bastard, I think (say?). I'd best be off.

I am about to turn and go, am actually in process. I am literally turning, but slowly for some reason, in slow motion it seems, for some reason, very, very slowly, when I notice something.

He massages his temples and it occurs to me that his face might be covered with makeup. On his smudged temples, darker skin is revealed. Suddenly I suspect perhaps he is African American and wearing Caucasian American makeup, more commonly called whiteface or paleface or cracker countenance or trash visage or clown white.

"Are you African American?" I ask.

"No!" he screams and slams his door.

But I believe he is. And now I want to know him. More than anything, I want to know him. I pound on his door.

"I want to visit," I say. "I've changed my mind. Helloooo?"

"Go away, kike," he yells.

"I am not Jewish," I explain to the wood between us.

There is no response. He doesn't believe me. It has been said that people are only really seeing themselves when looking at others. Perhaps because he is in denial regarding his own ethnic heritage, he assumes I am in denial about my own. But I am not Jewish. I am not. I will put together a slideshow for him of those who appear to be Jewish but are not. Ringo Starr will be featured. Ringo Starr is not Jewish even though he has a prominent nose. It occurs to me his name is almost the same name as Ingo's name, which is Ingo. The difference is the R, which is the first letter of my surname. R + Ingo = Ringo. I imagine it inside a heart on a tree. I explain all this to him through the door.

"R plus Ingo equals Ringo," I repeat. It feels almost cosmic, somehow meant to be. Perhaps our eventual communion will form a new star in the firmament. I go on to explain that Ringo's last name is Starr and that is why I suggested our relationship might form a new star.

Damn. I should have agreed to visit with him in the first place. When I had the chance. What was I thinking? Even if he had been white, humoring him would have been such a small price to pay to get in his good graces, so I could interview him about his experience on *Enchantment*. Sometimes I don't know what I am thinking or why or even when. My mind travels a thousand miles an hour, careening wildly from topic to topic. It is a thing I must work on, stilling this monkey mind, as the Buddhists call my mind, even though its monkey-ness is a by-product of my intelligence. But due to this intellect, I am a monkey on a string, the butt of some constant cosmic joke of the gods.

"Go away," he says.

CHAPTER 6

I GIVE UP FOR now. Back in my apartment, I find I cannot focus on work. I write a poem for my blog *Poems and Curios*:

> *Home.*
> *Finally home.*
> *Suddenly home.*
> *Never home.*
> *Always home.*
> *Without home.*
> *Going home.*
> *Goodbye home.*
> *Broken home.*
> *Leaving home.*
> *O, Home, where did you go?*
> *O, Homo.*
> *Oh.*
>
> *Conclusion: Home is a word of great power.*
> *Research: Is this so in other languages? Is there a language in*
> *   which there is no word for home? How might a person from*
> *   such a culture think? Where would they say they live? Reread*
> *   Whorf!!! This could be important!!!*

I watch the screen for several hours, constantly refreshing, waiting for the comments to appear. They do not.

I knock on his door again, prepared to make my case. It opens. Now without makeup, I see he is ancient and African American. Oh, the lessons I could learn from him, the places we'll go. But he is odd and distant minus his makeup, even odder and distanter. I attempt to show him I mean him no harm. Oh, the things he must have seen as an African American. The places he must've gone in his long and relentlessly African American lifetime. He was born in 1908. Perhaps his parents had even been slaves. Certainly his grandparents. He is a frail, hunched giant. He wears those new beige orthopedic Nikes everybody is going on about. Air Garry Marshalls. Several elderly people have been killed by several other elderly people down here in Florida for these shoes.

"I mean you no harm," I explain.

He says nothing. Perhaps he didn't hear me.

"I mean you no harm," I tell him again, this time louder.

He bares his gums at me.

"Perhaps I could have you over for tea," I say.

No response.

"I have written a monograph on William Greaves. The great avant-garde African American filmmaker."

I'm grasping at straws. It is not fair to me that he is suspicious of all white people. I understand from whence that instinct comes, but still. I am not that guy, as the kids say, and I am making every effort.

"I have an African American girlfriend," I tell him as the door closes.

I spend hours at my peephole. It is not healthy. He never leaves his apartment. I hatch and discard plan after plan. Might I borrow some ingredient or other for a pie? I'm going to the grocery store, does he need anything? Does he know a good barber? When is trash day again? Do you smell that?

Then his door opens. He peeks out into the hall, looks directly at my door. Is he trying to avoid me? It seems almost cruel at this point. But I remain hidden, watching. I don't want to step out until he is well into the hall, until he has closed his door behind him and cannot get back into his apartment in time if I happen to appear. He emerges, closes his door. I do as well.

"Oh, hello," I say. "I'm B. We've met. When you were wearing your costume. We even chatted."

He doesn't respond.

"I'm the fellow with the African American girlfriend. Perhaps you recall me."

He shuffles slowly toward the staircase in his beige boat-like orthopedic kicks.

"Anyway, I was thinking since we are neighbors, we should exchange keys. In case of emergency."

I fear this is too much too soon. I attempt to backpedal.

"Or just tea. Not saying we should exchange tea, but rather enjoy a cup together."

Nothing.

Then something miraculous happens. He falls down the stairs. It's a brutal tumble as if he has been pushed, and I worry someone will think he was pushed and then think that I pushed him. Which I did not and would never. I would never do that. I make a mad dash back into my apartment and close the door, waiting for another tenant, alerted by the noise of his tumble, his moans, to come to the old man's aid. I will arrive second. That's my alibi. Then I realize the other tenants in the building are either deaf or blind or some combination of the two. It is my great good fortune that the sad man with no car (deaf) happens to enter the building at this very moment.

"I'll take him to the hospital!" I scream from my doorway. "I have a car!"

He doesn't hear me of course and begins dragging Ingo toward what I assume is the nearest bus stop. I run down the stairs and roughly shake the neighbor by the arm to get his attention. He looks up at me.

"I'll take him to the hospital. I have a car," I mouth (using my now-perfected nose-breathing technique). He nods. I worry that this carless sad man will in the future ask for car favors now that he has been made aware of my carfulness, but this is my only opportunity and I must seize it, as Saul Bellow (Jewish and wonderful!) teaches us in his book *Seize Today*.

On the road to urgent care, I try to engage again.

"I am B.," I tell him. "Perhaps you recall we chatted."

I explain that B. is my first initial, which I use professionally as well as personally so as not to clutter my film writings with the gender assumptions of my multitudinous readers, or of those in my personal life, either.

He says nothing.

"I didn't push you," I say, almost shrieking it. In case there is some confusion about that.

I need him to know.

"My girlfriend is African American," I fully shriek.

I need him to know that as well.

He glances over at me, then looks straight ahead and speaks:

"And he went up from thence unto Beth-el; and as he was going up by the way, there came forth little children out of the city, and mocked him, and said unto him: 'Go up, thou baldhead; go up, thou baldhead.' And he looked behind him and saw them, and cursed them in the name of the LORD. And there came forth two she-bears out of the wood, and tore forty and two children of them. 2 Kings 2:23–24."

"Jesus. That's the Bible?" I say. "Jesus. What the hell?"

I wonder if he is mocking my baldness. Or threatening me with bears.

AT THE DESK I watch as he fills out the forms. He is 119! Wasn't he just 116? No matter, a fall at either of those ages is understandable, and not anyone's fault, certainly not mine. I did not push him. Truly, the miracle is that he is at his age still ambulatory. It is remarkable, and he should be grateful I saved him, rather than pointing fingers.

I put myself down as his emergency contact while he is distracted searching for his Medicare card. The attendant asks if I am his son. This thrills me. I am vindicated. Wait till I tell my girlfriend.

"No," I say. "Just a friend."

Not that an interracial friendship is a small thing.

In the car ride home, Ingo has become oddly chatty. Perhaps it is the painkillers. Perhaps it is that I saved his life, but in either case, I am happy to at long last be his friend. As an amateur Franz Boas in the making, cultural anthropology has long been my great passion, and here, practically dropped into my lap, is a receptacle of history. I turn on (with Ingo's permission) my Nagra II reel-to-reel audio recorder, from 1953, itself a piece of history.

"November 4, 2019. I'm here in St. Augustine, Florida, with Ingo Cutbirth, an African American gentleman. What year were you born, Mr. Cutbirth?"

"I was born 1900."

"So you're 119 years old," I say.

"Yes sir."

"I thought you said 1908?"

"Nineteen hundred."

"OK. What are some of your earliest memories?"

"From the past or from the future?" he asks.

"What do you mean, 'from the future'?"

"Well, memories go either way."

"Either way?"

"Yes. Rememorying the future is more or less the same thing as past rememorying; it gets foggy the more far you go away from the time you're at. In either direction."

I am at a crossroads here. Do I want to go down the path of this man's craziness or steer him toward a more reasonable discussion? I have to say, as a student of fabulism, I am, at least presently, feeling the pull of Ingo's future memories. And of course that his speech patterns have again changed is not lost on me. I am, after all, also a student of speech patterns, having studied with Roger K. Moore of the University of Sheffield while penning my monograph *Patterns of Speech, from Stammer to Yammer, from Stutter to Mutter, from Drone to Intone*.

Oh, also, *From Mumble to Grumble*.

"Can you give me an example of something you remember that hasn't yet happened?"

"In the future, everybody talking about Brainio. That's a for example, if you must know."

"Brainio?"

"Yeah."

"Can you elaborate?"

"Can I *a-what-ah-late*?"

"What is Brainio?"

"Brainio everywhere you look. Brainio. Brainio."

"But what is it?"

"Brainio. It's like a radio or a TV set, except it's in a person brain."

"Oh, like shows are broadcast directly into a person's head?"

"Everybody talking about Brainio."

"In the future."

"Yeah."

"Do you have Brainio in your head in the future?" I ask.

"No. I'm dead when there's Brainio."

"Oh."

"I'm a hunnerd twenny-nine now. What the fuck you think?"

"Yes. Right. So you can remember things that happen after you die?"

"Just a few and not very good. Brainio is what they call it. Evy'body talkin' 'bout it."

"Yes. What other things can you remember from the future?" I ask.

"Future cars."

"What do they look like?"

"Silver. Evy'body talkin' 'bout them silver cars all the time. Silver cars this. Silver cars that."

"What do they say about them?"

"I got me a future car, that sort of thing. Look, it's silver. It's all a little foggy. Because it's the future."

"Do these future cars have any unusual characteristics or abilities?"

"Fly. Also they be a boat, too, if you want."

I suddenly suspect this avenue of inquiry will go nowhere, so I back up.

"How about we talk about your past for a bit now."

"Makes no nevermind to me."

"OK, good. Are you still working, Ingo?"

"Retired."

"And what type of work did you do?"

"Janitor at the School for the Blind, Deaf, and Dumb right here in St. Augustine."

"When did you start work there?"

"Six A.M. Evvy day. Rain an' shine."

"No, I'm sorry, I meant what year?"

"Oh. Gosh. Nineteen twenty, I believe. Thereabouts."

"And you worked there your whole life?"

"Till 1995."

"That's seventy-five years."

"I never counted."

"It is," I say.

"If you say."

"It is."

"I'll take your word."

"It is."

"OK then."

"You want me to show you on a calculator?"

"Forgot my Eyebobs at the bottom of them stairs."

"Did you like your job?"

"Sure. Nice people. Treat me nice."

"Good. That's good."

"I like being around the blinds and the deafs."

"Why is that?"

"Hard to explain," he says.

"Could you try?"

"I like the deafs and the blinds because they don't use their eyes and ears what to judge a man."

"I see."

"Though I gotta say, the blinds judge a man's sound and the deafs judge a man's looks. The deaf/blinds are the best in that regard, but the halfsies are still better than all those that can see *and* hear. The wholies. Those are the ones make me most uncomf'able."

"So you're self-conscious?"

"What's that? Self-*what*-sis?"

"You worry about people judging you?"

"I don't care for judging. 'Ceptin' the Lord doin' it."

"Who *does*?"

"What's that?"

"I'm agreeing with you that it's unpleasant to feel judged."

"I see."

"Have you ever been married? Had children?"

"No. I been pretty busy. And anyway, the gals never cared much for me, it seem. I'm not saying I blame 'em. There's no explaining why someone likes someone. Some say it's chemicals, how a person smell because of certain chemicals he got. But I don't know. I've never smelled any chemicals and yet I have liked certain gals. So I don't know."

"Did you ever ask any of them on a date?"

"No. I can tell they don't want me to. With their eyes they're saying, please don't ask me on a date. The ones that ain't blind. The blind ones say it with their ears. And so I just keep walking when I see that look or those ears. But it doesn't mean I don't like them. It's just a secret. And I think about them to myself. Make up stories about them."

"Do you write stories?"

"Not 'zactly."

"What do you mean, not exactly?"

"Well, I do make up stories but they're just for me. They keep me company. I get lonely. Always have. I have my television set and my *TV Guide*, but sometimes I make up stories just for me. Too bad Brainio don't exist yet. I'll be dead 'fore there's Brainio. You know how Brainio works?"

"Um, no. I just heard of it for the first time a few minutes ago," I say.

"Brainio goes into a person brain through invisible rays and the like."

"Like radio waves?"

"That sounds right, though I'm no science-tist. And these invisible rays they tell you a story that you get to see in your brain. But it's not like the television set where you have one story and evy'body watches. Brainio mixes up with your own ideas, and then the story you watch is like you and Brainio making it up together."

"Like a custom-made story."

"What's that?"

"Making it up together."

"That's what I said. And you're in it, too. Did I say that part? You can be in the story. If that's what you want."

"That sounds like a fascinating invention. And not a little terrifying," I say.

"Yeah. I wish I could be alive for Brainio."

"Would you be in your Brainio stories?"

"No. I don't much like looking at myself."

"Even in Brainio?"

"Even there, I expect."

"But you could make yourself look like anything you want in Brainio."

"Yeah. But then it's not me."

"That makes sense."

"I do wish I would be alive when Brainio comes about. It would be so much faster and easier."

"Faster and easier than what?"

"Than the story I'm making up now. Brainio makes stories fast. That's one of the things everyone is saying in the future about Brainio," Ingo says.

"Can you tell me the story you're making up?"

He grows silent and stares off as he had yesterday. I wait. Is he considering telling me? I feel he might be. He licks his lips as if about to talk, but he remains staring off.

"I can't tell it to you."

I am crestfallen.

"Maybe I can show it to you," he says.

"Are you a painter, then? You'll show me pictures?"

"I do some painting. And building. And other arts and crafts and such. Sewing. And many such arts and crafts as is necessary."

"Fascinating! I'd love to see this work! Is it on display in a gallery or—"

"In my apartment. I have to project it for you."

"It's a film?"

"Yes, I'm making a motion picture."

This is too good to be true: ancient, reclusive, eccentric, likely psychotic African American filmmaker. Outsider art, undoubtedly. I have stumbled upon something magnificent. Visions of Darger dance in my head. Now for the sixty-four-thousand-dollar question:

"Have many people seen your film?"

"What's that now?"

"Have you shown your film to a lot of people?"

Please say no.

"It's not for other people. It just for me. Nobody else ever seen it," he says.

How could I have stumbled upon this? No matter how crude, how amateurish, no matter how painful to watch, I can spin this into anthropological gold. I can dine out on this for the rest of my life. Finally I can pry open the prudish legs of *Cahiers du Cinéma*.

CHAPTER 7

BACK HOME, I help Ingo into his apartment (just a sprain, thank God!). His place, the mirror image of mine, is dark and stuffy and crammed to the ceiling with cardboard boxes. He's a hoarder! Too perfect! The boxes are dated and seem to stretch back many decades, with labels such as *Buildings* and *Old Men* and *Storm Clouds* and *The Unseen*. It's spectacular! Who is Ingo Cutbirth? What upon have here I stumbled?

"A lot of boxes," I say, hoping he'll be encouraged to explain.

He isn't. I take a different tack.

"So, anyway, what's in the boxes?"

He won't budge. I try again.

"Is it OK if I look in the boxes?"

"Take the ark of the LORD and place it on the cart; and put the articles of gold which you return to Him as a guilt offering in a box by its side. Then send it away that it may go. Watch, if it goes up by the way of its own territory to Beth-shemesh, then He has done us this great evil. But if not, then we will know that it was not His hand that struck us; it happened to us by chance. Then the men did so, and took two milch cows, hitched them to the cart, and shut up their calves at home. They put the ark of the LORD on the cart, and the box with the golden mice and the likenesses of their tumors. And the cows took the straight way in the direction of Beth-shemesh; they went along the highway, lowing as they went, and did not turn aside to the right or to the left. And the lords of the Philistines followed them to the border of Beth-shemesh. Now the people of

Beth-shemesh were reaping their wheat harvest in the valley, and they raised their eyes and saw the ark and were glad to see it. The cart came into the field of Joshua the Beth-shemite and stood there where there was a large stone; and they split the wood of the cart and offered the cows as a burnt offering to the LORD. The Levites took down the ark of the LORD and the box that was with it, in which were the articles of gold, and put them on the large stone; and the men of Beth-shemesh offered burnt offerings and sacrificed sacrifices that day to the LORD. 1 Samuel 6:8–15," he says.

"Is that a yes?"

He stares at me through bloodshot ancient eyes.

"OK. Maybe later then. Because I'm curious is all. You're an enigma, Ingo Cuthbert. You're an enigma."

"Cutbirth."

"What'd I say?"

"Cuthbert."

"And what is it?"

"Cutbirth."

"Got it. Like *cut* plus *birth*. Got it."

As I head to the door to let myself out, I catch sight of something in an adjacent room. It's an exquisitely crafted miniature scene: a heavily populated city street with perfect little puppets. What's more, I recognize it as my neighborhood. It is West 44th and 10th. There's Dunkin' Donuts. There's H&R Block. It's extraordinary. I can't breathe. Ingo limps to the bedroom door and shuts it.

"May I look in there?" I ask.

He stares at me anciently through rheumy old bloodshot eyes.

"Maybe later then," I say, and I leave.

IN MY APARTMENT, I check *Poems and Curios*. No comments. Then, for the purpose of convincing him, I try to google biblical passages about a black man letting a white man see a miniature city. There's not that much. I do find a thing in Luke saying you should give to anyone who asks, but it's not specific enough (not to mention it's from Luke, the most namby-pamby of the gospels). Ideally, the passage would say something like, *Show thy crafts to those in need of seeing them, so sayeth the Lord.* But there is nothing even close. So much for finding all the answers in the Bible. I call my friend Ocky Marrocco, a biblical scholar at Stanford, but he doesn't pick up. I leave a message, though I'm not hopeful since Ocky and I had a falling-out years ago after I told him the Bible is complete garbage, magical thinking from primitive desert-dwelling nomads. As an atheist, I have that obligation.

I bang hard on Ingo's door. When he answers, I offer to do his shopping now that it will be difficult for him to get around. He sighs and nods, and I step in. The bedroom door is still closed.

"Have you given any thought to my petition?" I ask.

Ingo doesn't respond but simply limps to a notepad on the cluttered kitchen table and begins to write. I scan the room, hoping for elucidation. Boxes. Perhaps hundreds of them, maybe thousands, possibly millions—all marked: *Automobiles, Firemen, Weather, Natives, Pastries, Trees (Palm, Spruce)* . . .

Ingo returns with his list: *Whole Milk, Whole Chicken, Whole Wheat Bread, Hole Puncher, Peach Halves (in syrup), Halvah, Half and Half, Anne Hathaway Havoc DVD, Black Thread, Black-eyed Peas, Ketchup, Mucilage, Carrots, Peanut Butter (chunkless), 150 packages of Ramen (assorted), 50 cans of Neelon's Tuna Fish (improved texture), 80 cans of Nimby's Chicken Noodle Soup, 10 pounds of Bolton's Powdered Eggs, 5 pounds of Fripp's Powdered Milk, 1 pound of Prochnow's Powder (talcum), a thousand boxes (empty).*

I nod.

"So what would you say that little New York City street scene in there is for, if you were to say? If I were to ask?" I ask.

He says nothing.

"The reason I would ask," I say, "if I were to, is that it looked so familiar to me, which I thought you might find amusing. Ha ha. In fact, from my cursory glance before you so aggressively slammed the door, it looked much like the very block on which I myself live at this very time. Well, not at this time, because I live next door now, but where my apartment is, where I live when I don't live here, which is usually. And that is why I ask. That is why hence my curiosity, as it were, if you must know. Coincidence or no, *I* might be of some value to *you* in checking for accuracy. Also, in addition, I might be a *little* curious as to the why of this *particular* miniature set. That is why . . . I ask . . . of you . . . this . . . at this . . . time."

After a protracted period of what I can only characterize as loud nose-whistle breathing, Ingo speaks:

"Nothing is covered up that will not be revealed, or hidden that will not be known. Therefore whatever you have said in the dark shall be heard in the light, and what you have whispered in private rooms shall be proclaimed on the housetops. Luke 12:2–3."

Actually, that is pretty much the type of biblical passage I was searching for earlier. And it was right there all along in namby-pamby Luke. But Ingo got to it first and used it against me. Damn him to hell.

ON THE WAY to the supermarket, I amuse myself by ticking off all the possible narrative conflicts available to filmic storytellers:

Man vs. Man (Woman, Nonbinary, Child)
Man vs. Self
Man vs. Nature
Man vs. Society
Man vs. Machine
Man vs. Supernatural
Man vs. God(dess)
Man vs. Two Men (and *et chetera*)
Man vs. Everything
Man vs. Nothing
Man vs. A Few Things
Man vs. Disease
Man (Sick) vs. Healthy Person of Any Gender
Man vs. Idiocy
Man vs. Memory (Memory is a map of sorts, but hand drawn, incomplete, and full of errors. It can let you know a place exists, but you cannot trust it to get you there. To get you

there, you need a computer. A computer is precise. A computer does not think your mother is more important than the chair, or the space that's not your mother is more important than the space that is, or the glass of water on the table, or the sun pouring through the window, or the velvet drapes, or your mother's love for her father, or the front stoop, or the cracks in the front stoop. This is why Man must fight it.)

Man vs. Computer
Man vs. Time
Man vs. Fate
Man vs. Marketing
Man vs. Clone

Um . . .

Man vs. Smell

Um . . .

Man vs. No Smell

Um . . .

Man vs. Some Smell

Um . . .

I'm certain there are others, but I am preoccupied. The Winn-Dixie supermarket is as big as a football field, and I mean a king-size football field, not a queen-size. While in the produce section, looking at carrots, I once again ponder the tiny re-creation of my neighborhood. I am not a person who believes in destiny. But how could my world be in that elderly African American gentleman's apartment? I choose a bag of carrots. It seems as if I have stumbled upon something dangerous, perhaps even otherworldly. I, an avowed atheist who believes in reason and the rule of law, am not a person who accepts an unseen spirit realm, but something is amiss here. Who is Ingo Cutbirth? I find the mucilage aisle. So many choices! Should I be disturbed that Neelon's also makes a mucilage? Is it Cutbirth or Cuthbert? Either way, he is most likely a giant elderly African American gentleman. Unless this is just more makeup. Shandy's Eco-Mucilage looks good. Oh, the experiences he most certainly has had. It would behoove me to engage him. My privilege shelters me, and Ingo is the ax with which to hack away at the shelter that is the privilege which I have had. Halvah is hard to find. I should train my eyes to look at him with the awe I would afford one of my old white man heroes. Halvah is filed alphabetically under chalva (I had to ask a stockperson). I will imagine he is Godard, the great French filmmaker and talented anti-Semite, and then look at him as if he is the part of Godard that is a genius and not a talented anti-Semite. I think that will work. That is what I have done with Godard himself. Chunkless, it turns out, is not the same thing as smooth, it turns out.

"It's a southern thing," a second stockperson explains.

ON THE DRIVE back, I find myself obsessed with the following cinematic predicament: It is nearly impossible in a motion picture to effectively communicate odor to an audience. And yet a film for blind and deaf people must be all smell all the time. How to accomplish this? I must ask my friend Romeo Quinoa, who is a nasal artist.

Then this: I wonder if there is the possibility of smelling the future. Second smell, I would call it, were the government to assign me the job of naming it. My thoughts are popping like lightning. It is a sign that I am finally excited about something.

As Ingo unpacks his groceries, I attempt to get into his eyeline. His old rheumy bloodshot eyes become glassy. Is he about to cry? Perhaps he has never in his entire life been looked at as though he were an anti-anti-Semitic Godard. I would imagine not, especially as an African American. Such is the lot of African Americans in America. Was he a Pullman porter? A sharecropper? Oh, wait, he told me what he was, but I don't recall. I think I have it on tape. In any event, the things I might learn from Ingo if only I can persuade him to open up. But he is a taciturn man. No one can know the trouble he's seen, certainly not I, with my milk-white skin and my degree from Harvard, which I went to. Sure I have tramped, ridden the rails, lived in a hobo jungle, but that was part of a summer program at The New School, sanctioned by Union Pacific, our hobo jungles simulated, the hobos improvisational actors from Upright Citizens Brigade. Granted it gave us the flavor of the rootless life, but there was at least a hint of a safety net. When Derek Wilkinson had an allergic reaction one day during hobo luncheon (the beans had been prepared in a factory that processed nut products), there was a nurse (dressed as a yard bull) with an EpiPen at the ready. One can assume that an actual hobo with a nut allergy would be on his own in such dire circumstances. Or her own. The assumption of male gender in hobos has hindered the dreams of more female hobos than I as a white man can imagine. Perhaps it is best to refer to all hobos as thon.

"Well," I over-enunciate, "I must bid you *adieu* as I have work to which I must presently attend."

Nodding in a folksy manner, I turn to the door, my right shoulder inching back slightly as it anticipates Ingo's gentle touch, beseeching me to stay for just a bit. "Don't go!" he'd say. But it is not to be, and I must follow through, cross the hall, fumble for my key, enter, and close the door behind me. I do my trick of the sound of receding footsteps, while standing in place and watching Ingo through my security peephole. I am not certain what I am hoping to learn, but I have discovered through my research into the underrated and trailblazing work of filmmaker Allen Albert Funt that a person who believes thonself to be unobserved will act in a manner different from a person who believes thonself to be observed.

Ingo stays put.

CHAPTER 8

DEFEATED, I RETURN to my work on *Enchantment*, but with little enthusiasm. Certainly there is important, essential work to be done here. It is likely that Ingo's film is rubbish, not because he's African American, but rather because most everything everyone does is. Rubbish is the rule, genius the exception, my father always said. Still, it might've offered a window into Ingo's struggles as an African American. I can imagine his little film explores issues of racism in the way Micheaux did in *Within Our Gates*, but with considerably less skill. The film would most likely be a curio of some sort (maybe to be posted on *Poems and Curios*!). One does not discover buried geniuses willy-nilly. If Ingo is unknown, there is certainly a very good reason. There are cases, such as my own, in which the reasons are not valid and come down to simple bad luck and possible conspiracies against me because I have consistently spoken truth to power, and because the cabal of Jew—

My phone rings. It is a number both unfamiliar and local. I do not know anyone in town except the small-headed curator at the film society, the building manager, and—

"This is Ingo Cutbirth."

"Ingo!"

"From across the hall."

"Yes!"

"I'm your neighbor."

"Uh-huh," I say.

"I saw your film," he says.

This takes me aback. No one has seen my film.

"*Gravity in Essence*?" I ask, needing to be certain.

"I believe the critics to be wrong," he says. "The film is not, as they have written, incompetent, pretentious, unrelatable, sophomoric, unbearable, precious, completely unrelatable—"

"You said unrelatable already."

"I said unrelatable the first time, not *completely* unrelatable. Those are from different reviews. And it is neither. I was profoundly moved by the plight of the protagonist, B. Rosenstock Rosenzweig, as he, like his personal heroine, Bisadora Runcan, struggles to make one authentic gesture, albeit not in the world of dance, but in the realm of ideas."

"The critics were unkind," I say. "Thank you."

"I, too, am a filmmaker," he says.

"Yes. I know!"

"And I was hoping," he continues, "perhaps you might be willing to assess my first effort. No one has seen it."

"Thank you! Yes!"

"I will not share my reasons with you, but I do have them."

"I understand."

"Perhaps those reasons will become evident to you at some point in your life."

"OK."

"That I cannot and will not say," he says.

"Time will tell," I agree.

"I can tell you this: No man is one thing. Only a fool believes that. And a fool is also not only one thing, either."

"That makes a lot of—"

"For sometimes a fool can be the wisest of men. 'If one does not understand a person, one tends to regard him as a fool.' Carl Jung said that. There's a great deal of truth in that sentiment. And of course Jung was such a great influence on my work, indeed on the whole of the twentieth century, what with his introduction of the notion of the collective unconscience."

"Unconscious," I correct.

"What now?" he says.

"Collective unconscious," I say.

"That's what I said," he says.

But it isn't.

No matter. This Ingo Cutbirth is full of surprises. Now he sounds almost like me. How many times have I cited Jung on exactly this point as it pertains to my own life? My friend Ocky does a terribly mean (but playful!) impression of me reciting that very line (correctly!), and I must say Ingo almost sounds like Ocky now. Is Ingo imitating me? Is he imitating Ocky? Or is he a multifaceted individual with interests similar to my own? I am a horrible racist! No matter! I am going to see his movie!

I SIT ON a hardback wooden chair in the darkened apartment aface the portable tripodded movie screen, while behind me, Ingo threads the projector. The comforting, familiar chatter of the film-machine interface begins, and without titles or other fanfare, so begins Ingo's film. It is black and white (the significance of this particular detail has not yet been revealed to me!) and ancient, a charmingly naïve stop-motion animation. A pause here to explain the history of the form. Stop-motion, sometimes called stop-movement or incremental step prop animation or object animation or three-dimensional animation or articulated prop animation or (colloquially and inaccurately!) Claymation, is nearly as old as the motion picture itself. The earliest example: Heinrich Telemucher's 1891 short feature *Ich Habe Keine Augapfel*, in which two eyeballs drop from a man's face and roll around for a long while on the floor. The film is important for two reasons other than its significance to the timetable of the history of animation. Number one, it is the first film in which someone's eyeballs fall out. And secondly, this device became a staple of both Romanian silent films and early Japanese talkies. Whereas Romanian cinema used the device as a metaphor for the 1918 union of Romania with Transylvania, Bukovina, and Bessarabia, the Japanese used it for straightforward comic purposes, often having the newly eyeless character exclaim, "Now I can see the way two balls on the ground see!" or "I look much taller from down here!" It eventually became so commonplace in Japanese cinema that one Japanese film critic quipped pithily, "All those eyeballs falling out is enough to make one wish one's own eyeballs would fall out so one would no longer have to watch even one more movie in which someone's eyeballs fall out." Granted, it is pithier in Japanese, in which the entire sentiment is conveyed in kanji with just one character.

A long, jagged scratch, screen right on black leader, is my introduction to Ingo's oeuvre. The line skips about merrily, then disappears, then reappears. It transforms into a kind of Morse code of dots and dashes, and then it is gone forever, replaced by the China Girl.

Ah, the famous, beautiful China Girl of cinema, to whose colorful countenance everything to follow is calibrated—she is both the watcher and the watched, both the seen and the unseen. It is from this self-contained, placid, Mona Lisa–smiling beauty that Momus springs, the mocker, the malevolent god of comedy, the presently defanged agent of humiliation, monstrous laugher from beyond the fifth wall, unseeable but ever felt, sister to Oizys, goddess of misery, who waits to envelop us in her viscous stew, and out of this the film begins in earnest: a birth, silent of course, the death-rattle chatter of sprockets, shutter spinning like that madman in Washington Square, the inevitable, relentless background noise of this clockwork universe to which we have found ourselves exiled, now witnessing The Origin of the World, but unlike Courbet's version, ours yawns wide to reveal a coming world, as a head crowns, pushing forth a new consciousness, it seems, protected by its skin-covered casing, but at the same time vulnerable to influence, to corruption, its fontanel bared to us—what better symbol of the openness and hence the complete vulnerability of the very young? Is it a metaphorical accident that the cranium will fuse in months to come, thus illustrating the ensuing closed-mindedness, the inevitable, tragic separation of the I from the World?

The ego always wins, of course. It always does. And at what price?

Now a man, or rather a man represented by a doll, in top hat and tails walks with great effort from screen right to screen left. Is there a windstorm? There appears to be, for the man leans into it, holding on to his hat. Behind him a crude but delightfully painted backdrop depicts a city street.

Cut to the inside of a human skull.

Certainly stop-motion was still in its infancy in 1916 when this movie was begun (or is that when Ingo was born?), and the technique is in so many ways primitive, but this is not the typical novelty magic-trick animation of the time. This is startling, revolutionary. What if, the movie seems to posit, inside each of our heads, we have personified emotions—joy, fear, rage—in essence at war for dominance? Granted, this was not a new idea, even in 1916, and the inherent fallacy of this charmingly naïve notion is obvious to anyone who has read Danny Dennett or the history of the Homunculus Argument. But, oh, what Ingo does with it! Using the limited technology available at the time, which might have hobbled the efforts of a lesser artist, Ingo exploits the resulting choppiness to explore a quantized interior universe where experience is not fluid, where discrete breaks fragment the thought process, where the limits of reason are exposed like nerve endings. Remember, this was a mere three years after Duchamp's *Nude Descending a Staircase, No. 2* caused a sensation at the New York Armory Show. Had Ingo been aware of the painting? Had it simply been in the zeitgeist? Certainly the Futurists had already published their manifesto by then. In any event, we see the homunculi at war with one another in a brain interior resembling a factory. There are, of course, the two windows, which represent the eyes, overlooking the outside world. Who is this being through whose eyes we now see? It is at this point still a mystery. But within this battle we recognize all the emotions at play (or at war!). And then through the windows we see a girl. The little fighting creatures stop. They stare at this beautiful young woman regarding herself in a mirror. She, too, is a doll, but a doll who has access to a world the creatures can only know through the windows of their prison, into which she now peers. They cannot look away, until she, smiling shyly, does. A title on screen redundantly announces her as *The Beloved.*

And the internal battle resumes.

Cut to the man fighting the wind.

After five more seconds of slow forward progress, the puppet man slides back, in a way that resembles the performance of a practitioner of the art of pantomime or Mike Jackson doing his delightful "Moonman Walk," but this fellow appears to be in an actual windy environment because objects blow past him: a pram, a young boy on roller skates, a newspaper, which tumbles by in a simplified manner as a stiff board, its front page facing the viewer throughout. Is the newspaper legible? I attempt to synchronize the movement of my head with the movement of the tumbling newspaper. It is! At least some of it! "Big Windstorm Expected" is the headline. How funny!

Back to the birthing scene: That all this, the miracle and tragedy of coming into being, is performed by inanimate objects fashioned to resemble biologic ones does not go unnoticed by the viewer. The baby is born, the spread-eagled humiliation of the mother complete, for the moment. The umbilicus is cut, another metaphor, and this wailing mass of meat is assigned humanhood. He is white; he is male: He is privileged. This birth is at night, an odd, specific choice, since most births occur in the early morning. Is Ingo attempting to tell us something? Is the mother perhaps Nyx, the goddess of night? This would make these twins (for, yes, here comes another one!) Momus and Oizys, gods of mockery and misery, as anticipated. What will they conjure into existence on this the eve of the First World War? Is the male mocking his sister for her "missing" genitalia? Of course, we now know that Freud was wrong and misogynistic and, indeed, suffering from womb envy, and eventually jaw cancer, but perhaps back then when Freud's theory was new and exciting, is it not possible that Ingo found himself intrigued, to say the least? And Misery, as is her way and perhaps the way of so many females (tragically!), internalizes her wrath, indeed is compelled by society to do so. This eats away at her, making her miserable, thus spreading through her system, dripping from her pores and infecting those around her, who, in turn, infect those around them, and so goes the world. The babies are born, and with their birth begins the acknowledged horrors of the twentieth century, the bloodiest century in human history.

CHAPTER 9

A STRANGE OBJECT, LARGE and malformed, drops from the sky behind the top-hatted man. It must be made of clay (as are humans, by the way, in so many creation myths) because it flattens upon contact with the ground. Another follows. There appears what can only be described as blackish liquid oozing from them. The horrifying hurled and sundered "bleeding balls" aside, this is a charmingly naïve undertaking. The man continues his trek across screen, and his journey causes me to reflect upon my own love of weather. The complexity of it, the power, its capricious nature. Of course weather is analogous to the finest art: invisibly moving in countless directions at once. If one watches a tree in a breeze, it becomes immediately apparent that rather than the wind blowing the tree uniformly, micro-currents move each leaf, each branch separately. The tree, leaves, and branches bounce and roll and describe circles all at once. Although Ingo's interest appears to be in the comic potential of weather and mine in its metaphor as an engine of fate, I do feel a certain kinship with— What's that? The top-hatted man himself is suddenly blown every which way. His tails fly up behind him, and as he attends to this immodesty, his top hat tumbles off screen right. A toy balloon blows toward the viewer, while a second toy balloon blows away from us. The man spins clockwise in place as would a child's top, as the roller-skating boy is blown back on screen and circles the man counterclockwise. Although the animation is still naïvely executed, the concepts explored are nothing short of profound. And it is so very comical! Ha! Ha! Especially when the man plops onto his bottom and continues his spin, as if rotating on a pole inserted into his very rectum. Ha!

Soon the little boy is spinning so fast that he takes off, disappearing into the firmament. After a perfectly timed moment, one of the boy's roller skates bops the man on the head, and after a second perfectly timed moment, so does the other. Dazed, he watches as his lost top hat blows back into frame, then, caught in a gust, lifts. We follow as it tumbles—past buildings, into the turbulent clouds made of cotton stuffing, into the ether. The camera is at first level with the hat, then above, looking down past it at the gentleman watching its ascent, then below looking up at the violent sky. Now it is amidst the clouds, which swirl past in remarkable ever-shifting configurations. The movie has gone in an eye blink from simplistic comedy to transcendent and breathtaking. The black-and-white clouds flash with lightning, the intrepid top hat now floating through a heartbreaking sea of fog. The previously tumultuous weather has settled into the ethereal, and as the hat continues its ascension, the fog thins. Soon our hat-agonist finds itself above the clouds, looking down on them. The obscured, lonely Earth far below. Now we ourselves view the world from the point of view (POV) of the hat! We tumble lazily through space, the Earth a distant stormy memory, the heavens black, punctuated by brilliant points of light. That this journey was influenced by the work of Georges Méliès is obvious, but the animation here is so far beyond anything else of that period. It is, quite frankly, far beyond anything I've seen to this day, with the possible exception of Wes Anderson's *The Wonderful Mr. Fox*, a phantasmagoric cornucopia of treats for the eye, in every "which-way" on the screen, which reimburses the filmgoer for thon's repeat viewings. Of course, to put Ingo's work up against Mr. Anderson's is prodigiously unfair, as Mr. Anderson is a highly educated aesthete and Ingo a sharecropper's son (presumably) who worked as a Pullman porter (perhaps), but—although I must reserve judgment until I've viewed the entirety of this film—I do believe they will be on almost equal footing in the pantheon of this whimsically idiosyncratic and sadly obsolete art form.

The hat comes to rest on some sort of heavenly body. Clearly it is not a planet in our solar system, as the hat finds itself nested in a field of wheat-like doll arms, rustling gently in a cosmic breeze. Now the hat has become animate, although no explanation is offered. It wanders through the wheat arms, aimless, disenchanted, as we follow from above. The hat is Harry Haller, of course. How Ingo achieves this connection is a mystery. This is, after all, a top hat, but I have not a doubt in my mind that it has become Haller. It is perhaps possible that Ingo, a sharecropper's son, has never read *Steppenwolf* (although he is familiar with Jung, so . . .), but even in that unlikely scenario, some divine force has imbued the hat with Haller's characteristics, most notably his panoptic despair. As I watch the journey of the hat, I find myself identifying with it. I, too, am Harry Haller, you see. I, too, despair at the mindlessness around me. And so as I follow this Hatty Hatter, if you will, on its quest for meaning in a bourgeois world, I shed a tear for us all. Suddenly the terrain shifts and we (Hatter and I) find ourselves at the foot of an impossibly large mountain, reminiscent of Daumal's *Mount Analogue*, which, of course, is decades away from being written. No longer aimless, Hatter begins its climb. I watch from above as it struggles toward me. I am at the peak. This is where we will meet. But who have I become in this scenario? It climbs and climbs, inching ever closer, until it sits before me, eyelessly looking up at me, and I find myself filled with love. I reach down to lift it up, my hands now made of light, and I don it. I can no longer see Hatter because it is on my head (if I look up I can see a tiny bit of the brim). Then after a moment, I remove it, the hat now glowing with its own light. I flick it as one would a Pluto Platter, and watch it spin through black space toward the faraway Earth. Again, I find myself with it as it enters the Earth's atmosphere and gets tossed to and fro through the still-churning storm (has any time passed at all on this plane?). We finally break through the cloud cover to reveal our gentleman staring up at the sky. The glowing hat alights on his head, filling the man with newfound calm. He continues on his walk against the wind, now buoyant and chipper. Instantly, the wind rips a large branch from a tree, smacks the man in the head, crushing it like a grape, and spraying his oil-black blood everywhere. The man dies.

* * *

AND CHILDREN ARE born—the twins, whom we recognize as Momus and Oizys, but whom Ingo identifies (through an idiosyncratic sign language alphabet and key appearing screen right) as Bud and Daisy, botanical names both, which suggest "of the earth." This reading, of course, further cemented by his choice of Mudd as their shared surname. Bud and Daisy Mudd are inseparable; they play together to the exclusion of all others. They jabber in a private, invented language (key on screen left). They are dressed in identical pinafores. This early-twentieth-century custom of dressing both little boys and little girls as little girls draws an uncomfortable parallel between infants and women (the women never outgrow these frocks, whereas the men become, by stages, by lengthening trousers, adults), but it also suggests that the boys need to "earn" their masculinity. As we now know, all fetuses begin as female. The "male" characteristics only develop later. The male "earns" his penis. At least that is what our forefathers (not to mention my own personal father, Jeremy) believed. Another and perhaps more accurate way to look at this quirk of genetics is that the male overshoots the goal of female perfection, developing past the ideal, much as the Irish elk grew a rack so large and unwieldy as to, in the end, lead to its own extinction, so the male, due to a flood of testosterone, develops a penis, that most unwelcome and unwieldy of racks (not to be confused with the so-called female rack, or bosom). Some have jokingly referred to it as a second brain, but in all humor there is, in addition to abject horror, a basis in truth. And we must wonder, as Ingo does, is the world better for these unwieldy penis "racks," or will they, too, bring about the demise of a species?

And then, and then, and then: Daisy is accidentally but viciously murdered by Bud during a child's game of jacks gone terribly wrong. This is the metaphoric amputation of his feminine self.

Important note:
Wolfgang Pauli?
Unus mundi?

Spin theory?
Must understand! Research!

It was, of course, an accident involving the jacks game and a bay-onet brought home from the war by the twins' father. This ragged amputation from self haunts Bud and will lead to a lifelong separa-tion anxiety, his pairing and re-pairing (repairing!) with his future partner (a predictive title card informs us) an effort to repair his severed anima. One is put in mind of the eternal un-pairing and re-pairing of hydrogen and oxygen atoms as they un-form and re-form water, recognizing this process is analogous to the eternal un-pairing and re-pairing of Mudd and Molloy (Mudd's future partner, a sec-ond title card informs us) writ small (writ large!).

Note:
Water splitting? Research this! Did I pack my Lachinov? Check
trunk (boot) at earliest opportunity!

To further the analogy, Mudd alone is in truth two, in that Daisy is forever part of his psyche. The scars of her absence in his life, which exist as memories, provoke his every decision. Thusly, Mudd is the hydrogen (two atoms) to Molloy's single atom of oxygen. Mudd is explosive and Molloy is corrosive. Yet together they sustain life. Surely this is what Ingo must be telling us in a title card that tells us this.

The screen goes black, horribly, darkly black. Clack, clack, clack, clack . . .

CHAPTER 10

"That's the first reel," Ingo tells me, then adds: "It's a comedy."

"This is extraordinary," I say. "How much more is there? I'd love to watch the whole thing, if you'll have me."

"It's three months long," he says.

"Three months, as in months?"

He nods, regarding me sagely through weary, rheumy, bloodshot, glassy African American eyes.

"The film is three months long?" I say again. "Just so I'm clear."

"Give or take. I've been making it for ninety years. Give or take."

"You realize that's about three times longer than the current record holder for length. I know this because I wrote an exceedingly long monograph—of record-breaking length in tribute—on long films called *Shoah 'Nuff: The Undervaluation of Lengthy Films in Our Current Fast Food Film Culture*. Perhaps you read it?"

"It's on my nightstand," he says.

"Well, when you find a minute. Well, not a minute. A year. My point is that the length of your film is a huge accomplishment in and of itself. What do you call it?"

He thinks.

"I guess I'd call it an accomplishment, too," he says.

"No, I meant the film. What do you call it?"

"The title or are you asking if I have a pet name for it?"

"The title," I say.

"There is no title. But I call it my girlfriend."

"That's sort of brilliant. *There Is No Title but I Call It My Girl-friend*."

"No. It has no title."

"So you're saying there is no title, not it's called *There Is No Title*?"

"You're seeming a little willfully dense right now."

"Well, I—"

"The purpose of a movie title is to give audiences something to call it when they purchase tickets or talk about it with friends. It is to allow marketing departments a hook. It is to reduce the film to something bite-size, manageable, understood."

"Well, I happen to like titles. I take great pleasure in construct-ing witty titles."

"Since I have no intention of sharing this with the public, I have no need of a title," he says.

"Sure. I guess. On a slightly different topic: Why do you sound different every time I talk to you?"

"What are you inferring?"

"Implying."

"Implying, then."

"I don't know. In the car from the hospital you were talking in kind of a folksy manner. There was a point when you were respond-ing to me only with Bible quotes."

"I am the work of someone or something, and so are you. So God created man in his own image. Genesis 1:27."

"See, I feel like you just added that quote because I reminded you that you do Bible quotes."

"You are to be the only witness to this film. When you have viewed it in its entirety, I will destroy it. Or if I am dead, you will destroy it for me. Those are the rules."

I nod, but of course I will not destroy it. I am Max Brod to Ingo's Kafka. This film, even if over the next three months it descends into incomprehensible drivel, must be protected for posterity. The world must see it. But most important, I must see it seven times.

"I will destroy it after I watch it seven times. There is method to my madness in this regard—and some other regards! Ha ha! You see, any film of substance, to be properly understood, must be viewed at least seven times. Years of trial and error in critical viewing, first as a cub critic at *The Harvard Crimson*, the student newspaper of Harvard University, where I went, then for various imprints, journals, 'zines,' and an experimental two-month stint as the film critic for the Hammacher Schlemmer catalog, have allowed me to perfect my viewing technique. It has been a hard-won battle for dominance over the form. Let me explain: The first viewing is to be accomplished utilizing only the right hemisphere, the so-called intuitive brain center. Years of practice have allowed me to allow the film to wash over me. I remove my critic 'hat'—you know all about hats!—and watch the film as a layperson might, that is without accessing the enormous library of film history within the very center of my brain center, without searching for the director's filmic references or 'echoes,' as some might call them. That type of viewing will come later. For now I am Joe Everyman or Everywoman or Everython. This go-through I refer to as the Nameless Ape Experience, named thusly for an ape's lack of intellectualism and ego and thon's unrestrained savage passion. In the end, 'feeling' the movie must come first and is perhaps the most essential viewing. So Step One: Yes, this film causes me to weep uncontrollably or to laugh uncontrollably or to ponder uncontrollably. Step Two: Why? In this second viewing, I doff my Nameless Ape 'hat' and put on my psychologist's 'hat,' which is not a literal hat—hence my air quotes—but rather an attitude or approach toward the film, although I do, for the sake of full separation of the viewings, imagine myself in various hats during this process. The psychologist 'hat' I see as a sort of modified trilby, since du Maurier's novel is at least in part about human psychology. I have often said that I am both Trilby and Svengali and yet, at the same time, I am neither, but rather du Maurier himself. Ah-ha! This 'why' viewing requires me to dig deep into my own psyche and find my personal connections to the movie. How is this movie about me? I must ask. This is perhaps the most essential viewing. As you may know, Ingo, my now famous essay on *The Royal Tenenbaums*, entitled 'Fathers and AnderSons'—which is itself a play on the title of Turgenev's novel *Fathers and Sons* in which I add Ander as a prefix to Sons as a nod to Anderson's surname, which is Anderson, but also to reference Ander Elosegi, the Spanish canoeist—is a result of the important personal work I did in Step One. That I relate to all the sons and all the fathers—as well as daughter Gwyneth Paltrow, ooh la la—in Anderson's films is no secret to anyone. That I relate navigating my psyche to Elosegi's ability to navigate river rapids might be less known to lay readers. Step Three is how. Here is where I tap into my vast filmic knowledge to explore how the filmmaker achieved his/her/thon's results. What does that 'pan' signify? How is that 'zoom' essential? Why a '24mm lens' here? I also examine 'juxtaposition,' 'mise-en-scène,' 'blocking,' and 'dance numbers' to determine how these and other cinematic techniques forced me to cry, laugh, or ponder uncontrollably in the aforementioned Nameless Ape viewing—which, remember, was Step One. In addition, here is where I take note of the director's references to other films. In the case of a Scorsese or a Tarrantinoo, this will be a massive undertaking, so encyclopedic are their knowledges of the form. Granted, I am not a great admirer of Tarrantinoo's oeuvre, as his infatuation with a false, stereotypical African American culture as well as his adolescent obsession with violence leave me cold. He is, however, expert in devising unusual camera 'angles,' most notably the astounding 'trunk shot,' which is known as the 'boot shot' in the UK, the '*coiffre de voiture* shot' in France, and the 'suitcase bin shot' in American Samoa. Step Four: backward viewing. Designed to look at the film as a 'non-narrative avant-garde experiment in a foreign language.' In other words, it allows me to see the film as a pattern of images unencumbered by meaning. This, dear Ingo, is my chance to see the film as a purely aesthetic construction. The human animal has it programmed into his/her/thon's DNA to ask why. The assignment of causality is hardwired into our brains. But 'why' is undoubtedly only a human construct. It is my belief that why is not an independent feature of the universe. The universe does not have questions. The universe does not wonder how a microwave works. The universe simply is. So by removing narrative, the concept of causality, the why is removed, the assumed order is removed, and the film can be seen—at least it is my hope—as it is viewed by the universe itself. Step Five: upside down. We as Americans take gravity for granted, I think you'll agree. Perhaps this is true in other cultures; I do not feel qualified to say. But here gravity is just whatever: Stuff falls, get used to it. By ignoring its effects on us and on the physical world, we ignore its effects on our psyches. Upside-down viewing allows me to focus on that aspect of a movie. Some filmmakers don't consider gravity any more than the average American does, but in a precious few cases—Apatow!—we get to witness a filmmaker grappling with gravity in every frame. Had I not watched *This Is 40* upside down—by the way, it is no accident that upside down it is *This Is 04*. Children having children! Right?— I never would have caught the deeper meaning of Paul Rudd sitting on the toilet while talking to Leslie Mann. He is literally keeping his shit from flying all over the room. One can see he has been directed by Apatow to pretend to be sitting casually on the toilet, and there is the surface humor of a couple who have been married so long there is no mystery left; they talk without embarrassment while they shit. But watch it upside down and suddenly Paul Rudd is struggling mightily to keep the feces from spilling out all over his life. Your Tarrantinis, for all their pyrotechnics, will never explore gravity in the manner of an Apatow joint. After the upside-down viewing, in Step Six, I watch the film one more time in a conventional manner to cement my reaction and to establish the film's ranking—if any—on my many lists: best films of the year, best films of the decade, best films of the century, best films of all time. Then all of the above in each genre: horror, comedy, western, thriller, action, drama, science fiction, war, foreign. Then by performance: actor, actress, thon, supporting actor, supporting actress, supporting thon, ensemble, thonsemble. Then by direction, cinematography, editing, score, writing, casting, best LGBTQIA films: best thon, best thon, best supporting thon, best supporting thon. It is a terribly time-intensive task, but necessary. Without these lists by truly educated critics, laypeople would find themselves at the mercy of Hollywood marketeers and celebrity sycophants. The seventh step is to not watch the film. This is the seven-step method toward a clear-eyed viewing of any film. Oh, and Ingo, it's funny that your film is a comedy—oh, hey, that's funny! I'll have to open my lecture 'The Apatower of Song' with that; I'm presenting it to the music supervisors' union next month on the second floor of the West 4th Street McDonald's. But what I was saying is that comedy is not about wisdom and kindness. It is about gravity and idiocy. A man in control of his environment is not funny. A man who understands his life is not funny. So why is a person falling funny? Why is a person acting stupidly funny? And is it really funny? Is it funny in real life when someone gets physically injured? Is it funny in real life when a person is overwhelmed and confused? The answer for most people would be no. So why does it elicit laughter in a movie? The reason is complex. In part, perhaps, it could be argued that one understands in a film that it is make-believe, that no one is really getting hurt. Of course there are those illuminating moments when this or that comic performer has died onstage in the midst of a performance, and audiences, assuming it to be part of the production, laughed and applauded. Harry Einstein and Dick Shawn are two notable examples. Let's suppose the thing, the machine set in motion—physics, longing, mortality, futility—is a Rube Goldberg–like contraption, designed with no efficiency and no purpose other than to be witnessed by, let us say, some Lovecraftian entity, for its amusement. We can laugh at a violent Monty Python and His Flying Circuits bit in which a fellow's limbs are ripped off because we know it's make-pretend, but this entity can laugh at a person's limbs being ripped off in actuality because the attendant suffering is irrelevant. My sense of your film, as much as I've seen of it, in any event, is that you are more Apatow and less Lovecraft, that you have true empathy for the characters you've created. Yes?"

I look up and Ingo seems distracted. He is counting out his medications. (His pill holder is the size of a wall calendar and also is a wall calendar. It hangs on the wall.) Was he even listening? I am reminded of my ungrateful students at Zookeeper's High School. Not that they count out their medications during my lectures (for they are young and virile), but they do text and read gossip on their computers and often leave and also often don't show up. I am not a disciplinarian. Far from it. It is my belief that when the student is not texting, the teacher will appear when they look up to the front of the room. I am not Sidney Poitier as *To Sir, with Love*. Nor am I Sandy Dennis as *Up the Down Staircase*. I am not the Prime of Miss Jean Brodie as *The Prime of Miss Jean Brodie*. Nor am I Mr. Chip or any of the seven Robin Williams films in which he plays inspiring teachers (*Help Me, Teach!*, *Teacher of the Year II*, *The Teacher Who Cared Very Much*, *Professor Salvador Sapperstein and the Sad Students of Salisbury High*, *Help Me Again, Teach!*, *I Am Your Teacher and I Love You*, and *Dead Poets Society*). I am a font of wisdom, if you will. I am a resource. I am here if you want. Until then, I will teach as if no one is listening. I will write as if no one is reading. I will love as if everyone in the world is dead.

Ingo has finished sorting his pills. He looks up.

"Oh, hi. So anyway, would you like to see the rest of the film?"

"Yes, yes, a thousand times yes! Well, seven times yes, technically. Only seven. Because of the aforementioned technique and also the film's apparent great length."

"So here's how it's gonna go," he says. "The film runs for three months including predetermined bathroom, food, and sleep breaks. My idea is the relentlessness of the movie will cause it to enter your psyche and thus infect your dream life. It is a filmic experiment of sorts that posits an equal relationship between artist and viewer, in that the viewer will not, after viewing it in its entirety, be certain where the film has left off and his own dreams have taken over. Or hers."

"Or thon."

"Granted, there is some intent on my part to nudge your dreams in a certain direction, but in the end, what you add to the film will largely be determined by your own psyche."

"Sort of like Brainio."

"What?"

"Sort of like Brainio," I say again.

"First bathroom break in five hours," he says, ignoring me. "You'll have to use your own bathroom. My bathroom is off-limits, except to me, who can use it and will."

"You're sounding very much like me again."

"That won't get you into my bathroom, mister."

"Fair enough. But you do. Or Ocky. It's spooky."

"I don't know what Ocky means. Are you prepared to begin?"

"Let me prepare to begin," I say.

"OK. Prepare then."

"OK, I'm trying."

"OK."

I activate the Nameless Apenessness of my soul—which I can do almost instantaneously after years of study and practice of some or another Eastern-style religion—through a quick intake of air.

"Go," I grunt apily.

The following seventeen days pass in a blurred yet brilliant fever dream of unimaginable cinematic luster, ramen, missed phone calls to my African American girlfriend, Neelon's Genuine Tuna Fish, troubled dreams, bathroom breaks, and brief enigmatic conversations with Ingo about mucilage. I weep. I laugh. I whine. I sigh. I sweat. I punch the air in triumph. I am transported to a country of alien emotions, a country I have perhaps spent my entire life avoiding. It is everything.

On the seventeenth day, somewhere between 3:05 and 3:08 P.M., Ingo dies. I check behind me when the reel is not seamlessly changed to find him slumped on his crutches, still standing. I perform CPR, which I don't know but I know there is pounding and I believe it is on the chest. It doesn't work. I stare into his unseeing, glassy African American eyes and weep.

IN MY GRIEF, a night conversation of several days ago with Ingo, occurring as he tucked me in, replays like a ghost in my head:

"There are multitudes of Unseen," he said.

"Unseen?"

"The ones not seen."

"I see," I said.

"In the movie."

"They're in the movie?"

"They're unseen in the movie."

"So then they're not in the movie?"

"They're in it. But the camera is facing away from them. As it is for most of us."

"So it's more or less a conceptual notion."

"No. The puppets have been built. With as much care as the seen puppets. They have been posed movement by movement, just as have the seen puppets. They have lived their lives. But have not been witnessed by the camera. Only by me."

"You animated them but didn't film it."

"It sextupled my workload. Had I not, I could have made the film in fifteen years. It was a necessary sacrifice."

"But why?"

"Because the Unseen live, too. Because if I don't see them live, who will?"

"But why not film them and allow them to be seen by the world?"

"Because they aren't seen. And were one to see the Unseen, they would no longer be the Unseen."

"Did you record on paper at least? Their names? Their loves? Their families?"

"Only in my head. And over the years, I have forgotten many of the details, many of the names. They blur together into a mass, into a notion, into the moth-eaten coat of memory. When I die, what remains of them dies with me."

"That seems wrong and horribly sad," I said.

"Such is the world."

"Would you show these puppets to me?"

"No."

"Will you tell me about them?"

"Only by way of census. They are only known as numbers. There are 1,573 black adult males over the age of twenty."

"You built 1,573 black male puppets over the age of twenty."

"And animated them."

"That's an extraordinary amount of labor."

"Not enough. Not nearly enough. Never enough. But it is all I was capable of. My time is finite. There are 1,612 black females over the age of twenty."

"Jesus," I said.

"There are 1,309 black males under the age of twenty; 1,387 black females under the age of twenty. Among them the eight Adventure Girls."

"Adventure Girls?"

"I took a special interest in them," Ingo said.

"Who?"

"The Adventure Girls. I was young when they came into being. I thought they could break through. I gave them every opportunity. I made them warriors. I made them brilliant. I had them solve crimes within the Unseen. I made them sexy horse thieves. I loved them. I favored them. I imagined myself as them. But I was wrong."

"How were you wrong?"

"Even with all my control over their destinies, I was still an Unseen myself. An Unseen God to Unseen Girls and there was nothing I could do. And so they fought. And I loved them. But in the end, they, too, fell back into the sea of invisibility, taking on thankless jobs, losing their sparks, working at Slammy's. Emotional labor, they call it these days. It was inevitable. I know that now."

"Can I see them?"

"No. Only a few are still alive. They are old and sad. It is hard to look at the Unseen, even if you are Unseen yourself. It is hard to look. One doesn't want to be reminded. It is better to look at the Seen. The Unseen are the audience for the Seen. They are here to watch, not to be watched."

CHAPTER 11

INGO CUTBIRTH HAS no known next of kin. He has, it turns out, requested burial at the St. Glinglin Cemetery just south of Twelve Mile Swamp, behind the Tastee Freez and in front of the Frosty Freez. The apartment manager hands me an envelope with four hundred dollars. Oddly, it has my name on it. It's not at all clear to me why I'm in charge of the funeral, but the truth is, control over Ingo, his legacy, and his belongings is precisely what I want. So even though the four hundred dollars in crumpled ones does not begin to cover the costs of casket, headstone, minister, burial, and reception at Tastee Freez (note: check to see if Frosty Freez can do better), I will gladly pay the difference with a substantial loan from my sister, who married rich. I know there will in the future be countless pilgrimages to Ingo's grave. I want to make sure the destination is satisfying to these yet-unborn acolytes, of which there will surely be thousands, maybe millions, maybe more. I need an epitaph. Something profound. Something that expresses the cultural significance of Cutbirth but also inextricably ties me to him, to the Cutbirth phenomenon. Pope's epitaph for Newton comes immediately to mind: *Nature and Nature's Laws lay hid in Night: God said, Let Newton be! and all was light. Love, Pope.* Perhaps I could construct some similar sentiment. *As Spacetime is both invisible and essential, so was Cutbirth. Love, B. Rosenberger Rosenberg.* Or *The Unsung has Sung. Love, B. Rosenberger Rosenberg.* Or *A Solitary Man Who Moved Millions. Love, B. Rosenberger Rosenberg.* Or *On the 32,850th Day Cutbirth*

Rested. Love, B. Rosenberger Rosenberg. Or *The World Was Never Meant for One as African American as You. Love, B. Rosenberger Rosenberg.*

I settle on the *Unsung* one but add *And Thus the Heart of the World Is Broken. Love, B. Rosenberger Rosenberg.* I hire a photographer to document the funeral. I know I'll be alone there with the hired Baptist minister (Ingo must've been a Baptist!) and this will put me in good stead down the road, cementing our connection in the mind of the public. I am Brod now. I am Brod, my entire life mapped out: executor, biographer, analyst, confidant, emergency contact. Friend. I schedule the funeral for a day during which a torrential downpour is anticipated, the umbrellas and mud being highly cinematic, funereal, illustrative of profound grief, hardship, loneliness. In addition, it will not be difficult for me to appear grief-stricken on the day, not only because I will be, but tears do not always come for me, even though I have taken several acting for directors classes, two acting for critics classes, and one acting for audiences class. With the rain, my face will be wet and I don't have to worry about verisimilitude. I rent a rain machine from a local film production supply house, just in case.

AFTER I RETURN from Ingo's funeral and a delicious Frosty Freez frappé, I think about Ingo's imminent journey from the Unseen to the Seen and all those Unseen he attempted to bring with him. I confirm I must defy Ingo's wishes—just as Max Brod denied Kafka's—and search through Ingo's boxes to find the Unseen. They are, I believe, the negative space defining the positive space of Ingo's film, and they must now and forever be recognized and celebrated for all they have done. Perhaps there is a second movie to be made with them. Perhaps now is their time. For we live in the future now. Perhaps this is what Ingo would have wanted. I could make that movie. Nobody, not even a puppet, deserves to live and die in obscurity, to live a life unseen. I think about the small laminated card I carry for inspiration in my wallet: *Criticism is the windows and chandeliers of art: it illuminates the enveloping darkness in which art might otherwise rest only vaguely discernible, and perhaps altogether unseen—George Jean Nathan.* As a critic, I sit in the dark, unseen. But I exist (I exist!), and my time has come. I will bring these unfortunates with me. By studying the film ad infinitum, I will understand who these Unseen are, down to the individual. I will be the Howard Zinn of Ingo's world, not that unseen African Americans need a Jewish historian to make them visible. But still, I will be it. Even though I am not Jewish.

On the drive back from the funeral it occurs to me that there needs to be something more exciting at Ingo's gravesite. If the pilgrims are to feel satisfied with their choice of vacation pilgrimage, if the Yelp ratings are to draw the proper crowds, there needs to be some sort of entertainment value. This is, after all, America. Don't kid yourself. What I envision is a giant slide, say, one hundred feet tall if it's a day. On one side will be a sequence of stone slabs, each one carved with Ingo's face, each with a slightly altered expression. As the acolyte slides, he (she, thon) looks sideward and, through the magic of granite cinema, Ingo's face appears to move. Perhaps Ingo smiles. Yes, I am aware that Alfred Hitchcock's resting place features such an attraction, but his has him winking. Now that it has been revealed he was sexually abusive, protesters are insisting it be taken down and replaced with a slide in honor of women, created by women. A tribute to women whose careers and lives were negatively impacted by that monstrous misogynist. (Perhaps Tippi Hedren winking? It's not for me, a man, to say.) And I say it's about time (though that's not for me to say, either). Tear Hitchcock down. He was toxically masculine. Don't soften his brutal legacy by having elfin delight Toby Jones play him. From here on out, Harvey Weinstein should be forced to play Hitchcock in an endless tour of one-man performances, just as James O'Neill was forced to spend his later years portraying the Count of Monte Crisco to atone for something or other to do with vegetable shortening. I make some calls, not about the Weinstein idea (although perhaps later). I call a stone carver, a water slide carver, and the zoning commissioner. I call my sister to borrow a lot more money.

I wander Ingo's apartment, feeling oddly free here for the first time. He is not watching. No one is watching. I sift through boxes. This is wrong. It is as if I am looking through the recesses of a man's mind, an intensely private man. And yet I am Ingo's voice in the world now. His has been forever silenced. If I am to do the necessary work of curating, of illuminating his psyche, work that is necessary because the world needs Ingo, perhaps now more than ever, then I must in essence become Ingo. There is no other way. His boxes are filled with bodies, hundreds, probably thousands, of little bodies, possibly millions of bodies, beautifully crafted with articulated skeletal systems, with malleable faces, dressed in perfectly realized, tiny costumes, no detail too small for Ingo's attention: policemen, bankers, surgeons, matrons, soldiers, sailors, Mudd and Molloy at various ages. They're all here, all the characters from the film, all the background actors, individually and lovingly enshrouded in tissue paper like those Chinese white pears at Christmas (or Thonnukah). Here, too, I find the miniature streetlamps, automobiles cataloged by era, dogs and cats, tiny trompe l'oeil newspapers constructed with internal wires so they can be animated to appear to blow through the city streets on a windy day, trees with individually articulable branches and leaves, an organ-grinder, his monkey, fire hydrants, their monkeys, telephone poles, beer bottles, cutlery, boxes of shoes and handbags, city buses and cable cars, railroad tracks, pigeons, robots, a claw shovel, Richard Nixon, stained glass, the Central Park carousel, atom bombs, newsstands, thimbles the size of grains of sand, bartenders, all the white cast members of *Hamilton*, paratroopers, Macy's Thanksgiving parade floats. Pretty much anything one could imagine or see in the world is to be found in these boxes. One particularly large box contains only one character: a beautiful young man, perhaps twenty-five, chiseled features, the movie star looks of a Rock Hudson or a Troy Donahue. This puppet is by far the largest I've come across. Perhaps nine or ten times the size of any of the others. Is he a giant in this movie? As of this point, maybe a sixth of the way through the film, I have come across no such character. I carefully wrap him back up, replace him in his cardboard coffin, and sit, overwhelmed by the craftsmanship, the care, the love with which these sculptures have been built and protected by Ingo, the respect he has afforded them. I am glad I have embarked on building Ingo a proper memorial. I am glad he will at last be treated with the same respect by me that he has shown his "children" (or as Ingo would sometimes call them, depending on his personality that day, his "chirren").

I am surprised to feel a single tear rolling down my face. I reach for it with my tongue, taste the salt of my own tender humanity. I am reminded that we all began in the sea. I am reminded that we are all brothers in that way, we were all fish brothers (sisters, thons) at one time, and now we are all human brothers. Or sisters. Or siblings, for the nonbinary and gender neutral among us, who we must remember are also our brothers, or rather siblings, as I said. I espy another box, separate from the rest, almost hidden, it seems, behind a sofa gray with age. This is important, I determine. We always conceal that which is most dear to us, for fear of revealing our deepest, most private thoughts, the thoughts that could be corrupted, contaminated by exposure to others, to the world. I will care for Ingo's secret. I will hold it close and protect it. I will share it with the world, of course, because that is the work with which I have been charged, but I will make certain it, whatever it is, is fully comprehended. Finally Ingo will be granted the understanding he has always, undoubtedly, craved. As do we all crave. I only wish *I* could have a me to protect and cherish and share me with the world, with joy and compassion, after I die, the way I will share Ingo. But, alas, there is only one me.

I open this hidden box. It is filled with notebooks, yellowed with age. Jackpot. Ingo in his own words. I will read these books with the greatest care and empathy, then put his words into my words, so as to be better understood by others, and share them with the world (others). The original documents will be archived, of course, for scholars to pore over for generations, but just as any complex text needs interpretation for laypeople to appreciate it, so I'm sure must the inarticulate ramblings of an idiot savant–cum–misunderstood cinematic genius. I remove the top notebook, open it at random, and read aloud:

> "We are hidden away. Not just the Negro, but the insane, the infirm, the destitute, the vile, the criminal. We are housed in slums, in jails, in institutions, in hobo jungles. We are all of us hidden from view, leaving only the comedy of whiteness to be seen. My goal is to hold up a mirror to society, but a mirror can only see what can be seen. My camera is such a mirror, but that doesn't mean the Unseen ceases to exist. It is simply hidden away from the camera lens. And so I shall animate the Unseen as well, all the lives that come and go unnoticed. I shall animate them, remember them, but not record them. And as such my camera shall be the truest of mirrors and this film shall reflect the world as no other. It is as with the blind children in my workplace. Hidden away in an institution, they do not see, and we the sighted cannot bear to see them not seeing. It is unsightly. They remind us of our own vulnerability. If these unfortunate people walk among us, we cannot go on with human comedy unimpeded, and above all else, it is required that we do. Therefore, we must pretend in order that we may entertain."

I close the notebook and sit in silence for a long while. These incoherent ramblings will be hard to decipher. Still, one cannot expect such a task to be easy. Ingo is, after all, an outsider artist. Most likely he suffers the same communication problems as all autodidacts. But I have my life's work laid out in front of me. Ingo! I am forever grateful to you, dear idiot Ingo, for presenting me with this herculean task, and I know that wherever you are, you are grateful to me as well.

And what of the giant? Time will undoubtedly tell.

I scour the apartment but cannot find the unseen puppets. Ingo's commitment to this concept is total. Perhaps their existence is a fiction? In point of fact, the entire enterprise seems unlikely. But no. I take pride in being a student of human nature, of body language, and even the somewhat modern art of hand choreography (I had the great pleasure of interviewing the lovely Irish hand dancer/choreographer Suzanne Cleary for my monograph *Hands as Dramatic Implements: From Shadow Puppetry to Bresson and Back*) and it is obvious to me that Ingo was telling the truth. I continue my search, looking for hidden panels, trapdoors, false walls, dropped ceilings. I am thorough, as is my way in all things. The only item of any interest I uncover is a yellowed hand-drawn map of the property on which this apartment was built. There is an x on it. Could it be? A map of a mass unmarked grave? Well, whatever it is, it bears investigation.

I procure a pickax and a spade from an ironmonger and get to digging. The day is hot and humid. As an active fencer and inveterate swordsman, my level of physical fitness is likely unparalleled by anyone in my age bracket, but even for me this is grueling work. That I have neither sought nor gotten the approval of the premises manager only adds a level of stress to the entire endeavor, which cannot be heart healthy. Still I persist. After what seems like forty-five minutes of shoveling but was probably only forty-four, I hit something hard. It is the calvarium of a head, a tiny head. Pay dirt. I pull out my archaeological tools, the ones I always carry on my person—trowel, soft-bristle toothbrush, and professional dental tools (sickle probe, periodontal probe, lip retractor)—for the delicate work and begin. Within five hours, I have uncovered what I estimate to be roughly a thousand puppets of all races and ethnicities, of all ages, some dressed as household servants, some as coal miners, some as assembly-line workers, soldiers, newsies, prostitutes, farmhands, one I believe was a zookeeper, but I am uncertain because the uniform had been partially eaten by a fungus. And there is no end in sight. The Unseen no longer. Soon we shall all step out of the darkness, together. Out of the darkened theater. Into the light. We will be seen. I will be their leader, but not because I am the white savior, no, not that, but because I am the only one of us who is not inanimate. I call my girlfriend to tell her the news. It goes to voicemail once again. I punch a wall and get back to the movie, strictly adhering to Ingo's prescribed schedule and rules (although I do use his bathroom, which is thoroughly disgusting but proximate). It is unfortunate that I now need to change the reels myself. I thought about hiring a local schoolboy to do it for me (a sort of Shabbas goy), but I worry about his leaking to the press. The next two months and twenty days have a cumulative effect on my psyche. Any boundaries between the movie and me dissolve. I am both infinitely stronger and infinitely weaker than when I started this film. Just as the Campotini ant is enslaved by the fungus *O. unilateralis*, so I have been enlisted to monomaniacally do the bidding of Ingo's movie. Weak-willed yet undeterrable, I will make certain it is properly disseminated, appreciated, celebrated. It has become my life's work; that much is clear. And though, as with the ant, it will most certainly end with my head exploding, metaphorically (one hopes!), I do not care. I do not care. I stack the film reels in my apartment. I take what remains of his sets, of his puppets as well. All of it almost fills up my back room, the one I formerly used for sewing projects. As I survey the space, I cannot help but let my mind wander to the future adulation I will perhaps receive, the lectures, the Nobel for Criticism, the Pulitzer for Profound Insight. I am energized in entirely new ways. I cannot lie; there is a sexual component to all of this. I masturbate. I try my girlfriend again. I punch the wall.

CHAPTER 12

I DECIDE TO CALL my editor from the beach. I choose the site where the St. Augustine Monster long ago washed ashore; it seems symbolic, as Ingo's film is an alien behemoth from the dark deep ocean of his psyche. It seems necessary to call from here. I read the plaque at the base of the Henry Moore sculpture commissioned by the North Florida Cryptozoological Society.

> At this location on November 30, 1896, an unidentifiable creature, dubbed the Monster of St. Augustine and later the Globster, washed up on shore. This faceless, eyeless creature has stimulated the imaginations of biologists, ichthyologists, and cryptozoologists alike ever since. What is this amorphous creature-like non-creature, this reeking, decaying mass, this corpulent, seemingly fatty monstrosity that it generates such intense speculation, that it encourages such ludicrous projection as to its identity, as to its meaning? Might it be nothing more than a substance similar to the fatbergs that modern science speculates will in the very near future clog the sewer systems of our great cities? For what creature this size has no brain, no muscles, no skeleton, no mouth, no anus? Our interest in this mass of gelatin says more about ourselves than it does about any mythical sea monsters. We are, it turns out, an odd, delusional species, who search in vain for meaning. It must be noted that no

entity other than the human being, including the universe itself, asks "why?"—DR. EDWARD CUTCHEON-TARR

The sculpture, designed by Fernando Botero (not Henry Moore as has been previously written) and constructed by the artisans of the St. Augustine Children's Foundry, is notable for a naïve exuberance as well as the distinct lack of skill demonstrated by the young foundry-working orphans. Even so, at six hundred feet long (thirty times the estimated length of the original), it is no small feat of casting. These child foundrymen (and women and thon) are to be applauded, if not for their skill then for their temerity and wit.

The ancient globster puts me in mind of the passage of time. On this very spot over one hundred years ago, a momentous event occurred, and now in the blink of an eye in cosmic time, there is no sign of it, other than a six-hundred-foot-long monument. We are all of us casualties of time's passage. Casualties of causality, I muse, and write that down in my notebook for later. There is no one, nothing of such importance that they will not be forgotten within decades. Does anyone today remember Bertram Graelton, Davis Schimm, Magnus Pratt, or Clavia Stamm, all arguably the most celebrated individuals of their respective times? The answer is a resounding no. That two of them are still alive today only cements my argument and leaves them both very lonely in their respective retirement villages. We live in a time of constant, tumultuous change. A child born in 2000 will change her mind 507,000 times in her life, twice more than her counterpart born only sixty years earlier. Why is that? "The world is a fluid place," explains the great ethnobotanist Clavia Stamm. "The truth is an ever-blossoming flowering shrub. Just as soon as one flower is revealed to us, another and contradictory flower blooms. Which flower is true? According to contemporary theory, the most recent flower is the true one. So even though this creates an endlessly complex world, we must always keep current. We cannot rest on our laurel trees, as the old aphorism aphorizes. We must constantly evolve with the evolving truth. Please don't forget me."

I muse for a bit on my own cryptid screenplay, my very first cryptid screenplay, the one I wrote for my seventh grade Cryptids in Cinema course at St. Colman of Lindisfarne's School for Boys (my professor, the young William Dear, as everyone knows, went on to make that charming trifle known the world over as *Harry and the Hendersons*). My script was entitled *Trunko*, and it was, of course, about the so-called Trunko, a globster that had washed up in 1924 on a beach in South Africa. My idea at the time was that Trunko could very well have been a sort of "rat king" made of the congealed souls of the chivalrous drowned crew of the HMS *Birkenhead*, which sank off the coast of Cape Town in 1852. It was just a pet theory, but I felt I could back it up with science and it might very well be a fascinating new direction in naval horror cinema, a genre that had obsessed me since early childhood, when I first viewed Nunley's *Jolly Roger* (1952), about the well-documented "Action of 9 November 1822," except in Nunley's version, the killed pirates formed a globster that washed up on the *Cuban* coast and haunted the indigenous people. I wonder where my screenplay is now.

I snap out of my reverie to dial my editor, Arvide Chim, who has the distinction of being the only film journal editor to have been exonerated for fifteen brutal murders, in fifteen separate trials. He is a soft-spoken fellow.

"What the hell happened to you?" he whispers.

"I have stumbled upon the greatest filmic masterpiece of perhaps all time. Including future time, I feel confident. And I didn't just add future time to be hyperbolic. There is a reason."

"Not again."

"A method to my madness, as it were. The reason will become clear in—"

"B., I've heard this very speech before—"

"This film is different. It engulfed me, Arvide. It birthed me. It married me. It killed me. It ate me. It shit me out. It married me and shit me out again. And from that fertile spot, glorious flowers blossomed."

"OK, cool. How's the gender piece on *Enchantment* going?"

"Listen, that's garbage. I want to do something on this masterwork instead."

"I'm very busy right now, B. We have Wilk's essay 'Lifting: Tippy Walker and the World of *The World of Henry Orient*' coming in today, and it needs a great deal of title editing. You can't keep changing your mind."

"Do we really need another Henry Orient piece? Didn't I put that movie squarely in the dustbin of history with my piece 'Whitewashing: Why Wasn't an Asian Actor Cast as Henry Orient and Why Wasn't It Called Henry Asia?'"

"I recall the essay. You do know that Henry Orient wasn't an Asian character, right?"

"I am offering you access to the greatest cinematic masterpiece of perhaps all time, including future time. I am laying it at your feet."

"Yes, you mentioned."

"No. I said filmic earlier."

"I have to run, B."

"Did I mention that it has never been seen by anyone other than myself and its now-deceased creator, so this would be an exclusive. A scoop!"

"Now you have. You didn't kill the guy, did you? Because you know how I, because of my legal situation, need to steer clear of—"

"I think we can monetize this, Arvide. Remember how popular Darger stuff is."

"Wilk is on his way up."

"This man was a genius and not because he was a man, which would be sexist of me to say, of course. Had he been a woman, I would be saying the same thing, except not referring to him as a man. And he was African American to boot. It's Oscars So Black these days, Davis. Think about it. We could be swimming in glory—"

"Why are you calling me Davis?"

"It's a three-month-long masterpiece. He worked on it for ninety years. Do you—"

"Three months long? Like, three months to watch it?"

"Give or take. There are bathroom breaks. It really flies by."

"OK, my curiosity is piqued. What is it about?"

"My God, man. It is about everything. It is a comedy about the nightmare that is humor—a critique of comedy, if you will. It postulates the coming end of comedy, the need for its abolition, the need for us to learn empathy, to never laugh at others. To never laugh again. It is a movie about racism, made by an African American—did I mention that?—which depicts nary a single African American. And wait till you learn why! It is a movie about time, the arrow as well as the boomerang of it. It is about artifice and fiction and the paucity of truth in our culture. It is about meanness, Arvide. It is about the block theory of the universe. It is about the future and the past, the history and future of cinema. It is about you, Davis. It is about me. I mean this in the most literal of sense. It is about me and you. More me, though."

"Well, look, B., bring it to the city for us to check out. If it is all that you say it—"

"It is."

"If it is all that you say it—"

"It is!"

"Let me finish my fucking sentence!" he whispers. "If it's all that you say it—"

Arvide pauses, but I bite my tongue.

"—is, then you can write about it. In the meantime, *Enchantment* is scheduled for the October issue, so it needs to get done. Email your notes to Dinsmore. I'm giving them the assignment. It's their area of expertise, anyway. They'll finish it."

"Thon'll."

"Come again?"

"I'm giving thon the assignment. It's thon's area of expertise, anyway. Thon'll finish it."

"I have no idea what you're saying now. I'm really quite busy. As I mentioned, Wilk is almost—"

"Third-person plural is grammatically and, more important, aesthetically unacceptable. Thon is the superior solution to the ungendered pronoun issue we as a people of the enhanced gender spectrum face today."

"Dinsmore has requested they/them. It is Dinsmore's choice how they/them are to be gendered."

"I'll speak to thon about it when I get back. I think thon will see it my way. Thon is a reasonable . . . *human* of unstated gender."

"In the meantime, email your notes to them."

"Thon."

"Goodbye, B."

Arvide hangs up.

I send my files to Dinsmore with a cutting note too subtle for thon to understand (thon is an imbecile, regardless of thon's protected status). Surely thon's essay will be heralded no matter what thon writes. After all, thon is a card-carrying member of the nonbinary community. Thon's critique is preordained, pre-celebrated. Thon is, after all, a font of hard-earned wisdom. I was always going to be up against this type of thinking with my version of the essay. Who do I think I am, a privileged white *et chetera, et chetera* assessing a work that by rights is the genderqueer community's to assess. And frankly, I am glad to have washed my hands of it. Not that I will not be facing similar outrage once I release the African American Ingo's film. But having rescued Ingo from obscurity, I should be offered immunity from that otherwise righteous indignation.

As I pack, I consider the sage words of brilliant *New Yorker* film critic Richard Brody: "It's not enough to love a movie—it's important to love it for the right reasons." He's said *everything* here. It is the reason I write film criticism: so that audiences can learn why a film is good. And, of course, Brody and I share a love of all things Anderson and we both know precisely why it's so good. Many's the evening we've passed together at the local gastropub discussing, discussing, discussing Anderson, or as we playfully call him Wanderson, to distinguish him from the hack Panderson.

Ah, young love. *Moonrise Kingdom* captures it precisely as it is truly felt, perhaps the only movie in history to accomplish this. Certainly, it features all of Wanderson's delightful eccentricities—what young boy really smokes a pipe? Ha ha. But what young boy in his heart doesn't imagine himself smoking one? No young boy, is who! And this is where Wanderson leaves his generation of filmmakers in the ash heap of history. He understands that in film there exists an opportunity (an obligation!) to externalize the internal. And he goes about this task with the precision of circus sharpshooter Adolph Topperwein shooting a cigarette from the lips of his beloved Plinky. In this analogy, we, the audience, are Plinky. There are, you see, no mistakes in a Wanderson film. I was that smoking boy (how oh how did he know?). And so were you. Perhaps in your jaded, cynical current state of being, you will refuse to acknowledge this truth, but truth it is, nonetheless. Unless you are female, in which case you dressed as a bird. Do not deny this. Wanderson is the chronicler of our tender heart and as such deserves our adulation—yours and mine. I recall meeting and being charmed by his lovely girlfriend at a reception for *The Wonderful Mr. Fox* (fantastic movie!) and I was then and remain now convinced Wanderson knows pure love more purely than you or I ever could. Although I might be closer than you in that his girlfriend's Lebanese roots are similar to my girlfriend's African roots, not so much geographically but in terms of the ethnic differences between the two of them and the two of us. That kind of close.

CHAPTER 13

Ioad the giant truck, excitedly imagining myself at the presentation soon to occur in my publisher's office. There I will be, smack dab in the center of New York's famed Film Criticism District (7th between 25th and the middle of the block, facing uptown, east side of the street). It's not unheard of to spot Davin Plum or Amodell Kingsley on the street here wandering, pens in hand, deep in lofty thought. Soon I, too, will be wandering thusly, unaware that I am being gawked at by some ambitious unknown upstart. Plum, Kingsley, Rosenberg. A respectful nod as we pass each other on that bustling thoroughfare.

The drive to New York is different from the drive down here. As I haul this massive U-Haul filled with Ingo's masterpiece and all the extant props and sets including the retrieved Unseen, I think only of the movie. In a very real sense, I am a different person now and am continuing to evolve as the film dances in my head. The Slammy's cashier is no longer a concern. Let her think I'm Jewish or old or any of a number of other terrible things. I am with purpose now. I am immune. Ingo's movie is my inoculation. It is my manna from heaven. I feast on it, my mind a pinball machine: Wait, what about this scene? What about that moment? Who was that character? A second viewing is in order. A third. Backward and upside down as well. It will take a year, maybe longer (time is of no importance, for it does not exist in the way the former B. thought). I will know this film. I will become its advocate, its adherent, its foremost priest.

Those who want to submit to it—and they will be legion—will submit to my interpretation. There will be pretenders to my throne, but I welcome their attempts at overthrow. Have at me, fellas. I will always win. I am the only one who knew Ingo. I was his best friend, when you come down to it. I took him to the hospital. I was his emergency medical contact. I am the one who attended his funeral. I alone penned his epitaph. I wrote the book. That's right. Literally, I wrote the book on Ingo. Have at me.

As I near Slammy's, I am put in mind of the insects that had splattered my windshield. Oddly, troublingly even, there are no insects now. Has the world changed so much during the several months I've been in Florida? That we are in the midst of an environmental crisis, a mass extinction, is of no surprise to any thinking person, but what occurs to me at this moment in an epiphanic burst is that there is a mass cultural extinction as well. The pesticides in this case are ego and ambition and greed. One wants one's seed to grow at the expense of others, and so one destroys the ecosystem of ideas. As much as one wants to be able to see through one's windshield, if the insects are gone, the entire ecosystem collapses. So it is in the world of ideas in which I travel. I am not entirely clear on this train of thought, but it feels profound. Perhaps it is this: Perhaps I have been influenced by Ingo's intense privacy, his resistance to the trappings of fame. I consider my own dual nature. The art is of paramount importance to me, of course, but perhaps on some level I do covet celebrity. Clearly it is not a primary mover in my psyche, but I suspect it is there, buried, lurking. The movie has lain bare those needs and the damage they may cause. Do I truly want to make this movie known in defiance of the artist's wishes? Am I serving a crass god (goddess, thonness) here? The windshield is clean because the insects have been killed for our convenience, for our profit margins. No. If I am to share this film with the world, it must only happen once my own motives are clear to me. Until I know with certainty I am not motivated by self-aggrandizement, I must protect the world from my self-interest.

I consider the following:

Let's face it, animals make noise. They demand attention. They make more noise than vegetables, which in turn make more noise than minerals. So the animals, especially the humans, are inherently dramatic. They are not more important but believe they are. This is something one learns almost immediately when one studies Linnaeus. Classification is just that. There is no hierarchy. Every element is weighted exactly the same, exactly. A simple analogy would be to try to determine which part of a ball is most important. There is no answer because the question makes no sense. You might think it is unfair that humans get the most attention, rewarding the screamers, the squeaky wheel getting the grease, but then you have to ask, unfair to whom? The human is the part of the ball that gets the attention: The human is the part of the ball that hits the ground first in a bounce, but it is the whole ball that deforms.—DEBECCA DeMARCUS, *Solving for X*

And just like that, a burden is lifted from my soul. God bless Debecca. I am serene. I am happy. I call my girlfriend to tell her of my thoughts. She does not pick up. I pound on the truck horn.

SLAMMY'S BY DAY is a whole different creature: a bright, cheerful roadside beacon. Its mascot, a smiling and proud bipedal hammer donning a red superhero cape and blue unitard with a big "Slammy's" emblazoned across his chest and holding a hamburger and a spatula and seemingly being chased by an unseen assailant, appears welcoming from atop the establishment's fluorescent signage. I should stop, maybe order one of their famous Slammy's Original Boardwalk Colas, Biggy-size, as a treat, as sustenance, as a tip of the hat goodbye to the region.

(Maybe she'll be working today.)

(But I don't care.)

(But maybe.)

After all, one cannot find a single Slammy's north of Dock Junction. Maybe with my eventual newfound fame and fortune, I could introduce Slammy's to the tristate area. Although I will not be seeking said fame and fortune until such time as I know for certain that I do not in any way want it. Only then will I seek it.

And if that ever happens, it might impress her. Perhaps I could even bring her up north as a regional manager. I could introduce her to my African American girlfriend and we could all hang out on weekends.

I maneuver my rental truck into the lot and park it at the far end in the weeds, since it won't fit within the painted lines of the spaces and I am not a rude person. I am a good person. I am good.

Maybe she's looking out the window and sees that I am good.

My trek on foot from the far end of the lot to the restaurant is brutal. My shoes stick to the melted tar. It has to be well over one hundred degrees out, and by the time I reach the door, I am dripping with sweat. Not the best way to make a second impression.

She's there, behind the counter, same outfit, same expression. But I am different now, and I think she notices. I approach her with a spring in my step and a playful glint in my eyes.

"Hello!" I say.

"Welcome to Slammy's. May I help you?"

"It's good to see you again!" I say.

The restaurant is still empty or empty again (perhaps between this time and last time it had many, many customers). The same young man pokes his head out from the back, eyes me with the same suspicion, then disappears similarly.

"May I help you?" she says.

"Do you remember me? I'm the fellow who needed the water and paper towels three or so months ago."

"May I take your order?"

"The fellow who needed to wipe the bugs off his windshield?"

"May I help you?"

"Yes," I say and scan the menu behind her for new items, specials, soups du jour. There are none today. "I'll have a Slammy's Original Boardwalk Cola—"

"What si—"

"Biggy. And a . . . How is the Slammy's Double El Mexicano Taco Burger?"

She punches some buttons on her cash register.

"Anything else?"

"My apologies. I was asking what you thought of the taco burger. I hadn't yet order—"

"So, what, you don't want El Mex?"

"I don't know. I just wanted . . . Listen, are you a fan of movies?"

"I'm not going to no movies with you, mister."

"No, I just . . . That's my truck out there—well, it's a rental—and it's filled with a movie I discovered, made by an African American gentleman from St. Augustine. Perhaps you knew him. It's animated."

Blank stare.

"Like a cartoon?" I say.

"I know what animated is."

"Of course. I didn't mean to suggest—anyway, the man died and I'm taking his movie up to New York to study it further. All his puppets and props and sets are in the truck as well. It's fully packed but I can pull some items out if you want to see. The craftsmanship is extraordinary. He was African American. As is my girlfriend. As are you."

"The movie about fire?"

She's interested!

"Yes, actually. Funny you should ask. There is a major conflagration at the end. You like movies about fire, do you?"

"Not really."

"Oh. Then why did you ask that question?"

I'm suddenly a bit testy.

"I just figured since there's smoke, maybe you were hauling the movie fire or something."

"I'm sorry, there's—?"

I turn to see smoke billowing out of the truck.

"Jesus!"

I run for the door.

"I figured it might be like Cocteau," she says. "They once asked him what he would take from a burning house—"

"I know the quote!"

"His answer was, I would take the fire. That's what made me think maybe you were taking the fire. Like Cocteau."

I'm in love with her, but there is no time.

I try to tear across the parking lot, having to pull my feet free of the tar with each step, and attempt to open the back, but the handle is extraordinarily hot and I must jerk my hand away. I rip off my shirt, wrap my hand in it, and try again. I manage to open it, but the air rushing in causes a backdraft (also a dismal movie, by the way, directed by Ronson Howard, which somehow manages to make fighting fires both tedious and inexplicably colorless) and throws me hard against the windshield of my hitched automobile. My head pounds against it and I am reminded again of the splattered bugs. I look back and see a spot of blood where my head hit in the very same northwest quadrant that the mysterious drone bug hit. I, too, have left my essence on the windshield. But there is little or no time for waxing philosophical now.

I force myself toward the noxious, billowing smoke in an attempt to save what I can of Ingo's film. It fills my eyes, my mouth, my lungs. I can't see. I can't think. As the remainder of my clothes burn from my body, I am reminded of the 1911 film version of Dante's *L'Inferno* by Bertolini, Padovan, and de Liguoro, especially because of the naked writhing figures, which are similar to what I have now become, but also because of the hellfire. It was an extraordinary film for its time and the first feature-length film to come out of Italy. My beard is singed. I can see nothing but smoke. I am further reminded of the fortune-tellers in Dante's Inferno who must walk forward with heads facing backward as punishment for their divinations in the world of the living. Truly, the experience in its entirety puts me in mind of hell. I fear I am dying, and as I become faint from the blistering heat and oxygen starvation, a strange thing happens. Something flashes before my eyes, but, no, it is not my life. It is Ingo's film. I watch it again, perfectly remembered, every detail, every camera angle, every facial tic, every line of dialogue, every musical cue, every extended dance number. It's almost as if I am being informed that his film is my true life and that this life is now over. Still, miraculously, I push forward, courageous in ways I never before imagined myself (I have imagined myself to be courageous in certain ways, especially in speaking truth to power and on certain carnival rides). For Ingo's film is now my baby, and as its mother, I must do the impossible to save it. I must lift, with superhuman strength, this metaphorical truck under which my metaphorical baby is trapped, even though in this case, the truck is on fire and the baby is inside it, so it's not a perfect analogy. My baby, my baby, my baby is the chant in my head as I pull myself up into this towing inferno. Then nothing. It is an indescribable nothingness that can perhaps be best described as nothing. Just as the concept of zero was revolutionary in the history of mathematics, so must the concept of nothing be understood by future humans sometime in the future. I am experiencing nothing, which on the surface might seem oxymoronic: the notion of experiencing the negation of experience. But I am indeed, and I shall attempt to communicate it. Imagine a vast room with nothing in it. Go on. Now subtract the room. Now take away yourself imagining it. Now take away yourself imagining you've taken away yourself imagining it. Now repeat that process again and again and again. Now take away the concept of time that allows for the notion of "again and again and again." This is nothing.

CHAPTER 14

MY EYES OPEN and squint at brilliant, blurry whiteness. Far away, chimes sound from underwater. Am I underwater? Where am I? A blurry face floats into my field of vision and looks at me. Am I standing? If so, how is this face appearing sideways?

"Hello, sleepyhead," it says.

It is a woman (pardon my assumption, but I am foggy and have not the energy for nonbinariness), and I understand I am lying on my back. I still do not know where I am.

"Where am I?" I ask, in order to find out.

"You're in the burn unit of the Burns and Schreiber Burn Hospital in Burnsville, North Carolina."

I take this in for a long while.

"Am I burned, then?"

"Yes."

"How long have I been here?"

"Three months. You've been in a medically induced coma, which is fortunate because most of your painful treatments have already been attended to."

"Is my name . . . Molloy?"

"No, honey. Oh, dear. You don't remember who you are?"

"I thought perhaps I was a comedian named Molloy."

"No. Your name is Balaam Rosenberg."

"Oh. Right. Except I go by B. so as not to wield my maleness as a weapon."

I say this to her by rote. It is a blurry statement without weight or meaning.

"I see," she says.

I don't think she does. Nor do I, frankly, at the moment. She checks my pulse.

"Am I disfigured?" I ask, suddenly terrified.

"We don't know what you looked like before you came here, so it's hard for us to tell. There are no photographs of you online, only an upside-down caricature of you on the jacket of an obscure book we were able to order from Alibris for six cents. We studied your driver's license photo, but it is very small. For some reason, smaller than is typical. We didn't want to reconstruct your face to be very small. So we did the best we could, scaling it up using a piece of graph paper. Here, have a look."

She holds a mirror to my face. I am afraid but force myself to look. I am pleasantly surprised. The beard is gone but so is the port-wine stain. It's not bad. I don't think you could tell I'd been in a fire. My nose does look bigger.

"My nose does look bigger," I say.

"Does it? We had to rebuild your nose. We couldn't tell from the driver's license, which wasn't a profile, of course. We just guesstimated based on your religious heritage that it would look like this."

"Meaning?"

"Meaning?"

"Meaning what?" I ask.

"Oh. Well, Rosenberger Rosenberg—we just assumed—"

"I am not Jewish, if that's what you *just* assumed."

Then I hesitate. I don't think I am. I feel certain I am not. I'm a little foggy about things, but of that I am fairly certain.

"I'm sorry, sir. That is our mistake. We did take the liberty of circumcising you, thinking it had been an oversight on the part of your parents and family mohel not to have had a bris performed, and we also needed skin to graft for your nose."

"Wait, what?"

"I'm sorry, sir. Let me get the doctor. He can explain it better."

"So my nose is made from penis foreskin?"

"Just part of it. Because the nose is on the larger side we needed more than just your foreskin, as your penis, while maybe not technically a micropenis, is a little on the small side. I'll get the doctor. He can explain the whole procedure."

She hurries from the room. I study my new face in the hand mirror. It could have been worse. They did an excellent job with the grafts. I don't look like a burn victim. And the port-wine stain is gone. I might even look a bit younger. I am about to train the hand mirror on my penis when the doctor walks briskly into the room.

"Mr. Rosenberg. Hello. I'm Doctor Edison-Hedison."

He shakes my hand, squirts some antibacterial gel into his hands from the wall dispenser, and rubs them together, also briskly.

"How are we feeling today?"

"I'm OK. I don't remember much."

"Well, you've been in a medically induced coma for three months. Your memory should or shouldn't come back at some point or not."

He looks into my eyes with a bright light.

"Mm-hm," he says.

"Did you say my memory should not come back?"

"It's been known to not happen. Studies show there can be long-term, deleterious effects to the brain from induced comas. Well, any type of coma, actually. But we hope not. We surely hope not."

"I don't even remember how I was burned," I say.

"Um, a truck fire, I believe," he says vaguely, then calls off: "Bernice?"

The nurse enters.

"How was Mr. Rosenstein burned?"

"Berger," she says.

"Burgers," he repeats to me. "Some sort of grease fire while you were grilling, I suspect."

"No," corrects the nurse. "His name is Rosenberger. He was burned in a truck fire."

"Rosenberg, I think," I say.

"I *thought* it was a truck fire," says the doctor, pleased with himself. "That's what I *said*!"

"I don't think I have a truck," I say.

"It was a rental," says the nurse. "The cashier at the Slammy's—"

"I love me some Slammy's," says the doctor.

"The cashier," repeats the nurse, checking her notes, "Radeeka Howard told the firemen you told her you had a movie in the truck. She called you a 'crazy Jew who wouldn't leave me alone.' That's neither here nor there, but it's in the report, so I thought you should know."

I rack my brain. I do remember something about a film. I was hauling it to New York, but I cannot recall any more than that.

"Was anything saved from the fire?"

The nurse unlocks a cabinet, removes a small plastic bag, and hands it to me. Inside it, a singed doll. A donkey, I think. Or a jackass. I don't recall the distinction. Or a mule? It has hinged legs, tail, and head. Burro? I study it, trying to recall something, anything. Nothing comes. There's one more thing in the bag: a single frame of film. I hold it up to the light. It shows a fat man in a checkered suit and derby hat. He smiles, coyly, childishly, grotesquely into the camera. Right above his head there seems to be an iron bar. Motion blur suggests it is moving toward him at significant velocity. Is someone about to hit him in the head with an iron bar? If so, he is at this moment blissfully unaware of his impending doom. As are we all in our daily lives, I muse. A word pops into my head, as if from nowhere, as if from some deep, hidden place. I say it aloud:

"Molloy."

What does it mean? From whence does it come, to drop unbidden into my consciousness like a speeding metal bar? I recall that Molloy is a character in the eponymously named *Molloy* by S. Barclay Beckett. It is a book I have never read, even though I have heard of it sixty-three times, I believe, and have pretended to have read it many of those times. Could that be the Molloy I am thinking of? It is a mystery. Perhaps I will find my answers there. Then I recall that when I woke from my coma, I asked if my name was Molloy. Molloy, it seems, is some sort of key to all of this.

"Do you happen to have a copy of the novel *Molloy* in the burn center library?" I ask.

"We do not," says the nurse. "Since this is a hospital, our patient library contains only books that take place in hospitals. So we do have *Malone Dies*, by the same author, which takes place in a hospital, if that is of interest to you."

"It is not. Doesn't *Molloy* appear in the same volume as *Malone Dies* and *The Unnamable*, though?"

"Yes. But we cut those two out of the volume as they do not pertain to hospitals. Our library only contains books that pertain to hospitals. We could order it for you from Amazon, if you like. Hopefully it'll arrive before you are released in five days. We don't have Prime."

"Yes, please," I say.

As I LIE here for the next five days, waiting for my release, I think. When I'm not focusing on how much more I can now see my nose between my eyes, I prod the newly empty space in my brain as if it were the site of an extracted tooth and the thing I'm prodding it with is my tongue. My psychic tongue. I'm prodding and poking it with my brain tongue. This empty space, this *leerstelle*, is what remains of my passion, which was Ingo's film.

Memories come back piecemeal, not of the film itself, but of all that surrounded it. Ingo was a big, dull Swede, lumpy, unformed, hulking. Oddly, he had a full head of hair: white, neatly cut, conservative. But other than the hair, he was a golem with a snub nose and rubbery lips. It is difficult to imagine he was ever handsome or even presentable. We are informed by our desire scientists that symmetrical features are the most attractive. Ingo was not symmetrical. His snub nose was a messy, right-leaning blob. His watery eyes were of various smallnesses. His pale lips seemed to be trying to escape to the left. And yet with all this going on, his face was not even interesting. If I momentarily looked away, I found it difficult to recall. Growing up must have been lonely for Ingo. Women are distrustful of pretty and even handsome men, but they still desire them. And an unmemorable face connotes a character deficit. It lacks ambition. It reeks of conformity. Although I have never been seen as conventionally handsome (except by my mother ha ha!), I have been considered memorable, and because of that, I have a certain appeal to the ladies. Perhaps they see the intelligence in my eyes or the compassion in my mouth. I pride myself on my humility, so I feel a certain embarrassment even speculating about such things. Perhaps it is the mindful furrow of my brow. None of this is for me to say. My impressive forehead? But in Ingo, there were no such indications of character; there was only an emptiness, a blankness. I do not mean to suggest that he appeared as an automaton, for an automaton can be imbued with the appearance of personality. But Ingo was a sculpture abandoned mid-creation. And now it was too late. The sculpture was crumbling from age. It was turning to dust. What was he leaving behind? What had he to show for his lengthy time on this planet? The answer is nothing. It would be sad if only it were possible to feel for this creature, but his countenance did not allow for it. And because of this, we feel only anger. Ingo did not care enough to allow us to feel fully human by feeling pity for him. His small, unmemorable eyes pleaded "love me" but offered nothing for us to love. It was ungenerous and it made my blood boil. I felt the urge to haul off and punch him. As a student of the art of boxing, I can, of course, throw a decent punch. So even though he towered over me, I knew I could fell him. But I would not hit Ingo, and in this way I was the bigger man.

I rose above his arrogance. I would not play his game. He told me he was a filmmaker of sorts. It is all I could do to not laugh in his unformed face. I do not mean to brag but I can detect an artist on sight. It is my version of gaydar (which I also have). Artdar. This is not based on physical appearance. Both a Sam Shepard and a Charles Bukowski are equally conspicuous to me. It is in the eyes, or, in those rare instances where they have no eyes, it is in their fingertips. This is the case with blind filmmaker Kertes Onegin, who astonishingly acts as his own cinematographer (he does employ a focus puller, but she is also blind). His technique of "feeling the scene" as the actors perform (his films are all in extreme close-up and include his hand in every shot) creates an intimacy unlike any I have ever before seen in any film, and it has made him a target of the #MeToo movement (blind edition). Onegin's movie *снова нашел* (*Found*

Again), which explores a rekindled romance between two pensioners separated for forty years, is arguably the most erotic film ever made. That the bodies making love are old and that there is a fifth hand delicately describing the contours of these bodies adds in exponential measure to the experience of the filmgoer. I conducted extensive interviews with Onegin for my monograph *Onegin's Feelies*. During our conversations, he required we sit within touching distance and would caress my face throughout, sometimes sticking his fingers in my mouth "to see how wet." I remember thinking, this is the most true conversation I've ever had and also the least true and also again the most true. I will admit there was even an erotic component to it, and although I am not a homosexual by inclination, I did submit to this eyeless genius, this typhlotic Rembrandt late one evening after too much retsina. I do not regret this, for how can one regret true communion? Ingo had none of this to offer. Not in his soft, soggy eyes, like old grapes, not in his pruny, sausage-shaped fingers, like old plums. You are no Onegin! I screamed in my head. You are not my dear, dear Kertes! as I waited for that inevitable question:

"*Would you watch my film?*"

Let me say, quite bluntly, I am not an admirer of the cartoon in any of its myriad forms. It is to me cloying and sentimental. It is not film in its essence, which, to my mind, is the capturing of a moment. Animation is the manufacture of a moment, and, while one can admire the skills of the illustrators or computer fellows or clay manipulators, one cannot fully invest. It is always at arm's length. From the very first motion picture recording, the magic was in the commitment to the tether of the ephemeral. Never before in human history had this been possible. Certainly there had existed still photographs for quite a while and that was miracle enough, but whereas a still photograph stops time, kills it, a moving photograph captures it alive. A butterfly in an enclosed habitat, not skewered and mounted on a pinning block. From the very early days, there have of course been the tricksters, the illusionists (among whom I must, with great sadness, count the animators). And certainly innovators such as Méliès have their minions, but, for me, he has never been a satisfying genius. It must be noted that Méliès was a stage magician and his interest was not in revealing life but rather using this new form to further his repertoire of chicanery. That is to say, his work is antithetical to honesty, to the bare-faced vulnerability I most require in my cinema-going experiences.

So it was with great surprise that my attitude was changed by Ingo's film. It is animation as I have never experienced. Soulful, heartbreaking, profoundly felt. That it is accomplished in such a manner has made me rethink not only how life is lived and the physics of time, but as well, in a metaphysical sense, who we are and the existence of God. That Ingo accomplishes such a true thing not only with the illusion that is stop-motion animation but with the very artificial subject of "movies" gives me pause, undoubtedly the longest pause of my life. I only wish I could remember it.

"I'll watch for three minutes," I remember saying. "If it then seems worth my time, I will watch more."

"In any event, it's kept me busy," he said, as he led me to a chair facing the small movie screen.

"I'll sit after three minutes," I told him. "If I choose to continue."

Ingo hovered over me as the film started.

Some of it is coming back now, fuzzily.

It is silent, of course, as his work on it had commenced in 1916. Perhaps sound will be added eventually, I postulate, thus reflecting the coming changes in cinema and technology. That might make it an interesting curio, if nothing else. However, I'm afraid I will never know because, of course, it will be terrib— Wait! The first shot surprises me. It is not terrible, and I must admit I am a tad disappointed. Mostly because I cannot in good conscience quit after three minutes, but also, if I am to be entirely honest, I do not want to have been wrong. I don't want this to be good. But the first shot is good or at least not bad. Yes, the animation is crude, as all stop-motion animation was in the early days, but there is something startling in the immediacy of the imagery, in its vulnerability, in the mise-en-scène. I am put in mind of Hegel, the philosopher not the cartoon crow. Surely this mountain of desiccated pale flesh could not be a reader of philosophy, and yet . . .

Three minutes come and go. I cannot look away. I am witnessing something, the first human to pull himself from the primordial ooze of animal unconsciousness to marvel at the beauty of a sunrise. And Ingo witnesses me witnessing it. I am distrustful. Is there a long-dead animator whose life's work Ingo had stolen to play off as his own? Did Ingo murder him (her, thon)? Was I to be his next victim? Would my as-yet-unpublished monographs soon bear his name as author? But I cannot turn away. I cannot run. In a flash, the first nineteen hours pass. Ingo turns on the lights.

"Now sleep," he says. "I will wake you in five hours and we will begin again."

My world is now upside down and I do as I am told. As Ingo predicted, my night is fevered, the characters in the movie ripping into my dreams, infecting them with their gags and punch lines. Where does the movie end and my mind begin? I can no longer say. And I laugh and laugh in my dreams until blood pours from my torn esophagus like so much rainwater from a gutter on a stormy night. In the morning, the movie picks up not where it ended last night but where my dream ended. Or so it seems. How could this be? Perhaps it is a trick of psychology. Perhaps Ingo understood that the human brain will always fill in blanks, will want to weave disparate parts into a cohesive whole. Could Ingo have studied the work of Pudovkin? I refuse to believe he was educated in the montage theory of Soviet cinema. Yet the seamless blending of Ingo's movie and my life seems to belie my conviction. It is as if the melding of cinema and dream has turned me into another character in Ingo's film. I am the one who watches, and so I dutifully play my role and continue to watch the film.

The weeks pass. I neglect my monograph. I neglect my relationship. Ingo hovers.

As much as I feel I should not pull myself away from this experience, there are things in my life to which I need to attend. Perhaps five hours' sleep plus an additional two hours to eat, bathe, and take care of personal and professional obligations. The remaining seventeen hours a day would belong to this nameless film.

"This is not ideal," Ingo tells me.

A very different Ingo from the Ingo of a few weeks ago: confident now, demanding, an exacting artist who knows just how his film is to be experienced, oddly handsome now, his snub nose at a jaunty and dashing angle, like an admiral's cap. I have to admire this new and emboldened Ingo. Am I perhaps a little sexually excited by him now? I will acknowledge that I do very much want to please him. But, no, I will take my two extra hours a day. I must assert myself. Wouldn't Ingo respect me more if I don't make myself his doormat? I tell him I must. He nods assent, but I have disappointed him.

"Your film is magnificent," I say: an olive branch.

I cannot bear to see this look in his eyes, eyes that see right through me to my soul. I'm sorry, Daddy, flashes in my sleep-deprived brain. Is this even happening? Is this part of the movie? I can no longer tell. I decide I must not disappoint Ingo. I will continue with his prescribed regimen. And then a strange thing happens: Ingo dies. I try to revive him by yelling his name over and over, but to no avail. I call the police.

CHAPTER 15

O R, WAIT, IS that right? Or was he an African American Outsider Filmmaker whom I discovered and perhaps mentored? I am still a little foggy on details. I remember both versions of him. I do, in no uncertain terms, feel the absence of his film, the hole it has left in my brain. I know it gave me reason. I know it was like falling in love, like that feeling of something new, that realization that goes, oh yeah, there's *that* in the world. The world contains *that*. The world contains the possibility to feel like *that*. And now it is gone, and I know I can no longer feel it or know for certain that such a thing exists in the world. My fire, my reason, is gone, but the massive imprint it left on my soul is still extant, just as a deep meteor crater remains at the site of its earthly collision, the meteor vaporized upon impact. The damage is all that remains of Ingo's meteor, the hole, the emptiness, the ever-present missing thing, whose presence is its absence, whose meaning is its loss, whose value is a profound mystery that can only be guessed at. As I walk the perimeter of the negative space of Ingo's film, something comes to me, something I read a long time ago, perhaps at Harvard, where I believe I studied:

> All that is not the man describes the man, just as the negative
> space in a silhouette tells us every bit as much about the
> sitter as the positive. —DEBECCA DEMARCUS, *Solving for X*

DeMarcus, an Appalachian poet, woodcarver, and professor of optometry at West Virginia Wesleyan, had served as my first guide through the labyrinthine world of *ma*, the Japanese concept of the "space between," the interaction between the mind and the object. Now, finally, I find myself confronted with *ma*, not as a poetic abstraction, but as the terrible reality at the core of my being. The film is gone, and therefore, the part of me that merged with it, that changed with it, that saw the universe in a fresh way because of it, is gone as well.

I stare out the window at the tire plant across the street. I think about tires, how they're round and have holes in their centers. It's analogous to the missing film. Yet the empty space in the center of a tire is useful; it allows the tire to attach to the wheel, which allows it to turn on the axle, which allows the car to move forward. This gives me some hope. Perhaps this missing film will allow me to move forward. Perhaps the missing film is the hole in the tire that is my brain.

We must look at loss in all its forms, mustn't we? Loss of relationships, loss of love, loss of power, loss of memory, loss of status and the panic that ensues. We must accept that loss is a basic element of existence. The element of absence. All will be lost. "All those moments will be lost in time, like tears in rain," says replicant Batty of *Blade Runner* fame, in a rare moment of poetry and coherence in that inept, wrongheaded film by a director who cut his teeth in television adverts and seems unwilling or unable to recognize that the purpose of cinema is antithetical to that of selling toilet tissue. Be that as it may, this is a profound line that exists only because it was improvised by the brilliant Dutch *acteur* Rutger Hauer. So I am forever grateful to him and his *gevoelige geest*.

Another thought plays over in my head as well. There are so many things playing over in my head now that it has become difficult to pick out the separate quotes. With a little effort, I get this: "Each insect death is a loss from which we cannot recover. The world needs to be reinvented each time." Of course! The great Hindu saint Jiva Goswami. There was a time, not that long ago, when I carelessly and selfishly regarded dead insects on my windshield as an inconvenience rather than a thousand, nay, a million tragedies. But those insects, and the hundreds of millions of their squashed fellows, need to be acknowledged. They lived. Their presence changed the world. I did not get to know them all very well. I never got to know them as individuals and now I never will, because they are forever gone, scrubbed from my windshield with my shirt, itself the dead bodies of many cotton plants I will never know. Did I treat Ingo with similar disregard? Was I ever able to see him as an essential, irreplaceable entity? Or was Ingo a means to an end for me? I am put in mind of the Jain Insect Hospital in Delhi. Jainism is, of course, an ancient and profound religious philosophy that, among many other wonderful notions, teaches of the sacredness of all life. Thus, they have a bird hospital, a cow hospital, a shrimp hospital, and the aforementioned insect hospital. There are other hospitals for other creatures in the works, but changing humanity for the good takes time and money.

I visited the insect hospital in 2006 for a feature on the movie *The Ant Bully*, in which I planned to take the movie to task for its unrealistic depiction of ant hospitals. I felt it was a necessary point to make, but I had to travel all the way to India to gather my proof. In the end, the piece got axed in favor of some drivel by Dinsmore about how *A Bug's Life* got insect circuses wrong. But in the process I learned about the Jains and fell in love.

Tonight at the burn hospital we're having chicken-fried steak again and Jell-O.

"There is something missing now," I tell Edison-Hedison between mouthfuls of orange Jell-O.

Edison-Hedison nods, his own mouth full of cherry.

"In me," I clarify. "Since I've come out of my coma. There is a hole in me, empty and hungry to be filled."

"Well, I am not a psychologist or a psychiatrist or any of the other psychos. In point of fact, I've been told on more than one occasion that I have a terrible bedside manner, that I am not compassionate, that I am distracted, abrupt, and condescending. So keep

that in mind as I proceed, and take my advice with a grain of salt—
I should also mention that I am also not a social worker, licensed or
un—but what you describe is what everyone feels—everyone, all the
time—according to my limited and anecdotal research. So take my
advice: Forget about it. That hole is unfillable. Get on with your
life. Go back to work. Get a hobby. Find a nice, achievable woman
and settle down."

"I already have a girlfriend. African American, I believe. You'd
know who she is, I think. I think she's famous. I believe she was the
star of a popular sitcom in the nineties."

"Oh! What's her name?"

"I don't remember. But you'd know who she is. Then maybe you
could tell me."

There is a long and terrible silence.

"I'm scared and confused," I add.

"Well, as I previously explained, I am not qualified in any of the
mental healthish arts. But I can send in a counselor."

"I feel a slippage; things are not steady."

"This much I can tell you: Things aren't. Time keeps on slipping, slipping into the future, a very sensible thing Steve Miller
sings in an otherwise nonsensical song. Do eagles fly to the sea?
Why would they? I don't know, I'm not an ornithologist, but I think
not. But the slippage part, that's real."

"I think they fish there."

"Ornithologists?"

"Eagles. In the sea," I say.

"Maybe so. I'm not an ornithologist or, for that matter, an ich-
thyologist."

"Nor am I."

"Then I guess we're both just bullshitting, *n'est-ce pas?*"

"It's not the slipping of time into the future, which I have come to
terms with, with which of I am concerned of. It is the slippage of my
thoughts, my definitions, my mental landscape that terrifies me."

"I'll call the counselor. Unfortunately, you'll have to make do
with our grief counselor. That's all we have. We have a lot of dying
here. It is, after all, a hospital."

"I'M NOT REALLY grieving," I tell the grief counselor, a fat man in some sort of vestment.

"Not even lost time?"

"Maybe."

"Lost memories?"

"Maybe."

"The movie you say you lost, which I suspect is merely symbolic of lost memories and lost time. I suspect the movie never existed."

I show him the single remaining frame. He holds it up to the light.

"This is not a movie," he says. "For it is not moving."

"It is a single frame."

"This is a stillie," he says. "Don't kid a kidder."

I massage my temples.

"I find it telling that your 'lost movie' and your coma were both three months long," he says.

"I think it is a coincidence."

"If there is one thing they teach us at grief counseling camp, it is that there is no such thing as a coincidence."

"How would they know that? And why would that be part of grief counseling training?"

"Don't be a baby."

And with that admonition, I am released into the wild along with a Goodwill brown polyester suit, plastic shoes, a cardboard belt, and a paper bag holding my wallet, my single frame, and my donkey. I am returned to a world both oddly familiar and familiarly odd.

They point me in the direction of the bus station and I walk, passing a mother kneeling in front of her toddler, talking to her quietly and trying, I presume, to calm her. The child, face tear-stained, looks into her mother's eyes. When I am half a block away, I hear the child scream, "This is not fun!" What *is* fun? I wonder. What does fun mean to a child? From where does the expectation come that we are to have it? I smoke the cigarette I discover in my hand.

As I wait for the bus, I struggle to cut through the fog in my head. The smoke of the movie fills my memories, but I can no longer recognize it as it curls around the goo and the tricks and silliness already there. I think stupid thoughts. Then I think them again. I am a joke machine set on automatic, generating ridiculousness. If I knew how, I would stanch the flow; I would create a space in which a dignified existence were possible, in which I could breathe. But it does not seem to be possible; I do not exist. I am a distraction. I surreptitiously study the others here, this cast of characters, my fellows at this moment, in this poorly ventilated room, in which the stink of humanity is paramount. There are too many people in the world, most of them, it would seem, in this room, offering up a panoply of body odor and diabetic urine and feces and sick. Stale cigarette smoke hangs on their clothes and mine. I look up to find a man is staring at me. Our eyes meet and he does not look away. It is a challenge, a game of chicken, and I will lose. His eyes are cold and mean and I see myself through them or I imagine I do: an urban weakling, a homosexual, a Jew. His disdain bores into me. I am ashamed of his version of me and ashamed that I care. I glance up again, hoping to discover he has moved on, but he hasn't. His eyes on me make it even more difficult for me to think. It crosses my mind that perhaps he is mentally ill, that perhaps he is psychotic, that if I don't keep tabs on him, I might find him, too late, upon me, beating me to death. His anger is that focused. What have I done to make this man hate me so? The answer is nothing. I have done nothing. I have lived my life ethically and still I am broken, ruined by loss and fire, reconstructed by small-town anti-Semites into parody. My one stroke of luck, the discovery of a previously unseen film of monumental historical and artistic significance, maybe by an African American, maybe by a Swede, has been all but ripped from my memory by a heady combination of mental trauma and brain damage. Why is there no sympathy for me? I have never intentionally hurt anyone. I have always gone out of my way to be decent. I am not perfect, to be certain, but there are so many who are much worse, whose days of reckoning never come. Would this man stare at them? I think not. He would see those men as manly, looking out for themselves, taking what they want. The world is not fair. I cannot remember. Those who cannot remember the past are doomed to repeat it. I think that is a thing I read, but I cannot remember. As the station fills with more and more passengers, I can no longer see the staring man. I feel his eyes anyway. It surprises me that there are so many would-be travelers. It is not a holiday as far as I know. I don't recall all the holidays but I know it's not Thanks Day, which I am certain comes in the fall sometime and it is very hot today. It is a summer month. The people here are almost all wearing overalls sans shirts. Some are wearing overall shorts, sans shirts. Some are wearing something called shirtveralls. I know they're called shirtveralls, somehow. How do I know that? Everything is mysterious now.

CHAPTER 16

THE BUS HAS been double-booked. Greyhound offers four dollars off any domestic bus trip for passengers willing to take the following bus, which is at 5:30 P.M. next Thursday or Friday; they're not certain. No takers, so they implement their "Emergency Lap Plan." All passengers are weighed and assigned a lap buddy. Since I have lost 47 pounds in the hospital and weigh in at 94 pounds soaking wet (they don't explain why they needed to hose us down), I am paired with a tracksuited man named Levy who is 336 pounds. He shakes my hand and tells me to call him Grabby, that everyone calls him Grabby.

"Where'd you get such a nickname?" I ask, forced casual-like.

He hesitates for a moment, then tells me that when he was a little boy, he'd always grab an extra cookie from the cookie jar. I do not believe that explanation for a minute, but I am not staying at the bus station until next Thursday or Friday.

It's not too bad, in truth. Levy has a soft, warm, comfortable lap and keeps his hands mostly to himself. We engage in a brief, awkward conversation in which we try to find common ground:

"You watch sports?" he asks.

"No. You read?"

"No. You like cars?"

"Not much. You like movies?"

"DC, not Marvel. Marvel is shit."

"How about travel?"

"Branson. Hunting?"

"Antique hunting!"

"Like, shooting old animals, you mean?"

After a perfectly timed pause, I say, "Yes, that's what I mean."

With this, we settle into our own worlds—Levy playing a video-game on a device he calls his Sega Pocket Gear, arms wrapped around me and watching the small colorful screen from over my shoulder while I try to read *Molloy*. It is slow going. Concentration is difficult these days under the most ideal circumstances. Levy possibly has an erection. I read the sentence "I don't know how I got there" again and again. I can't seem to understand it. On the surface, it seems like the simplest of sentences, but what does it mean? I suspect there are some gaps in my comprehension. Were the gaps always there? I can't recall. That's the thing about gaps. Will I ever be back to normal, if this is not normal? The doctors couldn't (or wouldn't) say. It is terrifying to lose things. I have lost time. I have lost most of my memory of Ingo's movie.

"Shit, I lost," says Levy.

He pauses to look contemplatively out the window for exactly three seconds, then starts a new game.

One needs to learn to let go, to pick up the pieces, to start again. My lap buddy is modeling an important life lesson. There will be other Ingos. I will discover many more never-before-seen master-pieces in my lifetime, maybe thousands. If I only keep my eyes open. And keep them open I shall!

I nod off briefly.

Look, if there is some level of memory loss or brain damage, I will exercise what is left of my mind. Just as a great athlete who loses his legs can—with grit and determination and one other thing . . . gumption?—become a great athlete again by utilizing those hoppy leg-things, so can I regain my edge, get my groove back as Sheila did. . . . Was it Sheila?

"Is it *When Sheila Got Her Groove Back*?" I ask Levy.

"*How Stella Got Her Groove Back*," he says, eyes never off his toy.

"Oh."

"Pretty good flick," he says.

"I was asking about the book," I say. "I don't see those kinds of movies."

"I don't know what the book was called."

"I think it was *When Sheila Got Her Groove Back*," I say. "They often change things for the movie."

"Oh," he says.

"*Three Days of the Condor* was originally *Six Days of the Condor*," I remind him. "So—"

"Uh-huh," says Levy.

We drift back into our separate worlds, he to a small green Martian (?) attempting to navigate a series of crisscrossing Martian canals (?), while I watch the passing dusky landscape. The North Carolina highway is littered with shanties. Barefoot children watch our bus, jaws agape. Have they never seen a bus? Surely this is the bus route. Are their jaws slack from malnutrition? How have we as a country failed these mouth-breathing cherubs? I feel the sudden urge to scoop them all up in my arms. Maybe that is something I could do now that the life Ingo's movie would have afforded me is gone. Maybe I could come down here and be a teacher. Even with whatever degree of brain damage I have likely suffered, I could still be helpful in a godforsaken place like this. What sort of handicap is recalling only half of the *Iliad* in the instruction of children who can't even close their mouths? I imagine myself in a one-room schoolhouse, calling attendance, bandaging boo-boos, battling the school board to replace Columbus Day with Indigenous Peoples' Day. In short, making a world of difference. Maybe all that came before in my life has led to this moment. I suppose I would have to get some sort of teaching license. But how difficult could that be? Certainly elementary in a place like this. I chuckle at my unintended pum. Is it pum or pun? No matter. *Pum*, I decide.

"Can you read books and such, Mr. Rosenberg?"

"Yes."

"Can you plus and take away, Mr. Rosenberg?"

"Certainly."

"You got yerself a teachin' license! An' that comes with a fishin' license, too! Yee-haw!"

"Thank you, my good man."

Soon Levy is dozing, and I spend the remainder of the long trip home imagining my new and simpler life. I can even envision a biopic someday. It truly feels as if I've finally found my calling.

By the time we reach New York, I am over it. I've given it a great deal of thought and decide that I can't let the bastards win. I can't roll over and die. I can't give up on my dreams. I will find another unknown masterpiece (there must be millions!), which I will protect properly this time. I will immediately digitize it. I will make copies. I will get a safe-deposit box (or is it safety-deposit box?). I will hire a lawyer and send a copy to him (her, thon). I have learned a valuable lesson.

I fight my way through the central casting crowd of prostitutes, dope fiends, and sad-sack commuters at Port Authority. Someone should do a movie about New York someday. I mean, a real one. Nobody has ever come close. I know how to do it and would in a heartbeat. I know this city. I know its terrible pain and its meager triumphs. I could do it. I should do it. I will do it. Even though my single foray into filmmaking was met with an almost violent indifference, which, to be honest, verged on a conspiracy to silence me. But I feel ready to once again assume the mantle. My wounds have been sufficiently licked, and not just by Levy. I have withheld my affection from the intelligentsia long enough. I have fought back through the Mount Olympian criticism. I see a large-canvassed piece encompassing all of Manhattan, from Marble Hill to Battery Park, and across generations, from the early Dutch settlers to the Chinese and Saudi billionaires of today to the future Czech mind-lords. And they're all living there together, centuries of people jammed into twenty-three miles. Actually, a new thought: This would include the native Lenape people who lived here as well. We're all there, packed so tightly we can't move. And within this skewed reality, we focus on a love affair. Between two women, who, by the luck of the draw, happen to be packed in next to each other.

So in this sense, the movie is about fate, but also about the melting pot, but more to the point, the salad bowl, because one of these women is African American from the 1920s and the other is a Palestinian American from the present. This is the movie I would make. And there are ways to cut costs. Mostly it would be close in on these two women, and they could both be short (not necessarily little people, but possibly, which would give the whole enterprise an added dimension of caring and diversity), so the camera, which would be at their eye level, can't see beyond them to the massive crowd. The beginning and end sequences, which would need to show the expanse of people, could be done with CGI, which stands for Computer Generated Something. My girlfriend will play the African American woman. She is not short, but, again, CGI would shrink her up quite nicely, using computers and such.

As I MAKE my way to 10th, I play the Ingo film's destruction over in my head. I think about what is gone. My life's work. My thoughts. My three months. Ingo's life. Is it retrievable? No. It is ash. Humpty Dumpty, a parable I had never even considered as anything more than a childhood egg rhyme, has overtaken my brain. There is nothing but panic. Nothing. My life has burnt to nothing. I have been given a tiny taste of significance, and its absence is that much more devastating because of it. I try once more to recall Ingo's film. How careful a viewer was I? Not careful at all, it turns out. Not attentive. Did my mind wander? Did I daydream about the glory awaiting me for my discovery? Yes. Is that part of Ingo's film? I fear not. It is my own pathetic "film." My own valueless contribution to the vain chatter of a trillion egos clutching for some table scrap of immortality. I see that now. I was an imperfect viewer. I did not give my full self.

Oh, Ingo. Dead and gone. Erased. I insinuated myself into your trust. I was your sole audience and with that came an immense responsibility to you, to the work. I cannot bring you back. I cannot bring back your life's work. Yet I cannot live if I do not. I try to remember. My brain aches with the effort. I think back to that first day, the hardback chair, the initial frame, the first movement, the scratches on the film, the stains, the overexposure, the underexposure, the correct exposure. These accidental artifacts are no less essential elements of the film than those conscious choices made by the artist. The world gets to have its say in the piece. The world will not be denied.

And so perhaps, I consider, the world has had its say. The film erased, swept away like the sacred sand mandalas of Buddhist monks. It returns to its disorganized form of ash. Ashes to ashes. There is solace in this for me, for I have long considered Buddhism the philosophic system closest to my heart. There is a human desperation in the process of film, a human need to control, to own, to fight against the ephemerality of the world. Even the terminology of photography is fraught with humanity's need to control, to tame. It is said that photographers "capture" a moment. One can no more capture a moment than one can stop the flow of time. This is not how the world works, and yet we convince ourselves through our ever-advancing technology that it does. But death always comes. There may be a monument to us in the form of an artwork or a tombstone, but it does not change that fact. We are in a constant state of adjustment. We adjust. We adjust. This happened, now what next? This is our question as humans and so it goes. With this balm applied to my psychic trauma, I proceed. I will remember. And my remembering will be my collaboration with Ingo. The collaboration of an African American man whose life spanned the twentieth century and a white intellectual whose life began mid-twentieth-century and will end probably sometime in the early twenty-second. There will certainly be an outcry. Cultural appropriation, they will claim. The white man once again profits from the accomplishments of the black man. To those people I have two things to say: 1) Is not Ingo's film an appropriation? For does it not utilize a technology invented by white men? And from what I remember about Ingo's story, it takes place entirely in the world of white people, specifically in the world of white movie comedy. Do whites own the "gags" employed by Ingo in his work? Perhaps. But I do not begrudge him this. I am flattered by his usage of our work. And, 2) There exists no one else for this job. I am, for better or worse, his sole executor. I realize this word sounds dangerously close to executioner. This is a quirk of the English language and there is nothing to be done about it. 3) Maybe Ingo was a white Swede.

My task laid out before me, I find a bench in Port Authority (why am I back here?) and sit, a legal pad in front of me—I only write longhand. On legal pads. Call me a dinosaur, but I do not put stock in word processing machines. Writing must be a visceral experience for me. There must be smudges. There must be crossed-out passages; the violence of the slash reminds me of my passion in the moment of self-rebuke. Was I tired or sad when I wrote this or that? The slant of my handwriting tells me so. The forensics available to an analyst of handwriting are limitless. I begin.

> A man roller-skates. No, a man walks in a windstorm. He
> travels from screen left to screen right. Some objects blow
> by. He loses his hat. Maybe there is a child. Maybe there is
> a blob falling from the sky . . .

It is not working. Four hours of struggle have yielded meager results. I cannot remember. My limited human wiring, designed primarily for fight or flight, for remembering which berries are edible, for vanquishing my enemies, will not allow it.

Wait. The film was lost in a tsunami, I suddenly recall. I jumped in after it, even though I don't like to swim, and was batted about like actist Naomi Watts, until the Coast Guard rescued me and took me to Morton Downey Drowning Hospital in Doctor Phillips, Florida, where Dr. Flip Phipps induced a coma and reconstructed my nose, both of which for reasons that remain unclear. What about the fire? Wasn't there a fire? Yes, there was a fire. How can both versions of the film's destruction be true? I don't know, but there I am, driving north from Doctor Phillips, the roads empty. Whole towns have been evacuated because Hurricane Button (named after signer of the Declaration of Independence Button Gwinnett?) is expected to make landfall soon. So I am speeding to try to keep ahead of it. According to Saffir-Simpson, Button is currently a tropical storm, which puts it at seventy-three miles an hour tops. I go seventy-four to keep in front of it. My radio is tuned to weather. If the storm gets upgraded, I will go faster. I should have left yesterday, but I was in a funk and could not leave the hospital.

Today is different. Today I have a fire under me. I need to be back in New York. All hope for my Ingo project dashed, I need to reimmerse myself in the life of New York City. There are movies to see, art openings to attend, inexpensive ethnic restaurants to discover. But most important, my African American girlfriend is now back. Our contact has been scant for a few months now, both of us focused on our work. The perils of the long-distance relationship! But if I drive straight through, I can be home by ten. The thought of her welcoming arms, and dare I say, vagina, keeps me focused. That and Button, which the radio tells me is now expected to make landfall south of Myrtle Beach. The tolls are slowing me down. In my rearview mirror, the sky looks bad. I play a game to pass the time, attempt to name the states in order along the coast between Florida and New York. Georgia comes next, then South Carolina, North Carolina, then South Virginia, West Virginia, North Virginia . . . Napierville. Delaware. Vagina. Mary. Pencil. New Jersey. New York. The game doesn't take long enough. I'm still in Florida. I entertain myself with imaginings of my reunion with my girlfriend, the commingling of our bodies, her rich brown skin, an almost chocolate brown against my pinkish white hue, an almost Turkish delight, both glistening with perspiration. I am quite carnal by nature, which is not at all at odds with my intellectual tendencies. Popular culture would have you believe that the "nerds" and the "geeks" and the "dweebs" and the "dorks" and the "pencil necks" are hopeless when it comes to matters of the heart and body, but just as a more educated palate can better appreciate the subtle distinctions between various varietal wines, a person educated in the arts of seduction and sex can and will prove to be a superior lover. For example, since I can instruct my lover in the art of pompoir and kabazzah, I stand a better chance than one's typical dime-store lothario of engaging in a mutually satisfying and often explosive sexual encounter. These techniques have the extra added benefit for the female of putting the male in an entirely passive position, thus giving the power to her. Of course, empowering the female is often sexually liberating for them, but also I love to be controlled by a strong woman. If that strong woman happens to be African American, well, I am in heaven.

So I imagine my girlfriend on top of me, my yoni, I mean my lingam, completely in her hands, metaphorically, because in kabazzah, my lingam is completely in her yoni, and she contracts her vaginal walls and pulls in her abdomen in slow, powerful undulations. She is a belly dancer astride my member. This imagery alone is enough to cause an erection, and I must shift my focus or I am in danger of ejaculating during a hurricane, which the National Weather Service strongly advises against.

Finally safely in New Jersey, car parked at my lot in Harrison, I PATH it home. New York smells the same and most intensely the same at Port Authority. I fight my way through the central casting crowd of prostitutes, dope fiends, and sad-sack commuters. Someone should do a movie about New York someday. I mean, a real one. Nobody has ever come close. I sit down with my legal pad and attempt to write it here and now. I cannot.

CHAPTER 17

I ARRIVE AT MY building, where my African American girlfriend is waiting for me on the stoop.

How did she know my arrival time?

The look on her face. Somehow I know it's over.

"We need to talk."

"What?"

"I'm sorry, B."

"What?"

She hugs me. I pull out of it.

"You don't get to hug me while wearing those eyes!" I scream.

She just watches me, silently, like a cat, like a cat about to break up with a man.

"Why?" I demand.

"It's just . . . I think we've grown apart over all this time apart, and I don't know how to find a way back in."

"I've been in a medically induced coma! Due to . . . something!" Suddenly I'm unclear. "Haven't I?" I whine. "Isn't that what happened?"

"I heard you were. But that doesn't change anything."

"We can try. We owe it to ourselves to try. I have a part for you in my movie."

"It won't work."

"Why not? Because they shaved my beard off to facilitate coma-inducement? I can grow it back!"

"Because I'm with someone."

My heart breaks. It's a cliché, but I feel it. I feel my heart breaking. It even makes a sort of cracking sound.

"An actor?"

"A director."

"Him?"

"Yeah. I'm sorry."

"But—"

"I need to be with someone black, B. Maybe that's a shortcoming on my part, but—"

"Anyone African American will do?"

"Of course not. Don't be cruel." She pauses, then: "We have a shorthand. You and I don't. Yes, I understand the Jewish people have suffered, too, but—"

"I'm not Jewish."

"OK, B. I'm sorry. I really am."

"I don't know why you always insist I'm Jewish."

"I don't know. You just . . . seem Jewish. It's hard to remember you're not. Even more so now. For some reason I can't put my finger on."

"Do you laugh with him about my seeming Jewishness?"

"No!"

"I suspect you do."

"We don't laugh about you! We don't talk about you!"

"Wow. OK. I guess you've made yourself clear then."

"I didn't mean it like that."

"OK. Well, do you want the gift I brought back for you?"

"I don't know, B. It's very nice of you. But I don't think I should."

"Yeah. OK."

I take the gift-wrapped box from my bag and drop it in a public trash receptacle. It immediately feels wrong, theatrical, pouty in a way I hadn't intended. But the truth is I have little use for the pair of ladies' pumps I had purchased in the hospital gift shop. Not no use, but little.

I wander the streets, clutching my small hospital-issued bag. I can't face my apartment yet. Everything is gone. Ingo is gone. Kellita Smith of *The Bernie Mac Show*, my African American girlfriend, is gone. The possibility of getting financing for my New York film without Kellita is nil. My Florida transgender film monograph has been given to a hack half my age and twice my gender. I discovered *Enchantment;* it is by rights mine. There is nothing left. New York has become an expensive cesspool. It holds no interest for me, which is just as well as I'll be squeezed out of my apartment if I don't soon become gainfully employed. I look outward in an attempt to take in the magic of New York, in an attempt to allow the city to heal me.

Walking toward Times Square, I try to remember Ingo's film. I feel certain this street is in the film, maybe even these very people. Maybe even me. Though I can recall very little of it, it has left an emotional imprint on my brain. I suspect my perspective is forever altered by it. Is this a good thing? I don't believe it is. But there is nothing to be done. For all his fascination with movement and comedy and human psychology, at his core Ingo was a nihilist, I suspect. Pre-Ingo, I could best characterize myself as a teleological optimist. Leibniz's *Theodicy* was without a doubt the most dog-eared book in my childhood library. God, because he/she/thon is God, has made what must, by definition, be the best of all possible worlds possible. But Ingo won me over to the "dark" side of meaninglessness. I am bereft. But without the comfort of remembering why.

Suddenly, huzzah! A flash of memory, the beginning of Ingo's film:

A crudely constructed puppet of wood stands watching me, his joints and jaw articulated with hinges. Everything is silent. Exposure is inconsistent, the image black and white. The figure moves its arms and legs as if trying them out for the first time. His eyes remain fixed, open and blind. He raises his left arm, waves at me. His hinged jaw flaps twice, this followed by the handwritten title card *"Hello, Mister!"* It lingers too long, this card, allowing me to read it one hundred times. Then back to the puppet. He stands still, looking intently yet sightlessly into the camera. Finally he nods and his jaw clacks open and closed eight times, in a way inhuman, terrifying. *"Very well, hello, B., then, if you insist."* This card holds even longer. Is he responding to what was to be my return greeting? Is this Movie Minus One? Was I to say, "Call me B."? Back to the puppet and more jaw-slapping, then another title card: *"I am happy to meet you, B."* Back to the puppet. A long moment followed by a nod and jaw movement. Title card: *"Thank you. I shall enjoy having the name William."* I have named him? Back to puppet. He waves. The film irises out to black, then back in. The puppet has had some work done. Clearly a male now, he even has a hinged penis, which raises and lowers while William stares straight into the camera. His jaw moves and is followed by a title card that reads: *"I am ashamed."*

I recall all of this quite clearly, yet somehow feel it entirely inaccurate.

MY APARTMENT, WHEN I finally return to it, smells horrific. My Lord, I neglected to ask anyone to care for my dog *Au Hasard Balthazar*! The floor is covered with his feces, the rugs darkened with his urine. I find him emaciated but somehow alive, shivering in the bathroom. He feebly wags his tail. That's what a greeting without underlying hostility looks like. No dead eyes here. That's love. He doesn't blame me for his predicament, which, to be fair, he could. The human race should take a lesson from *Au Hasard Balthazar*. I gently pet him, whispering comfort, praising him for his fortitude. He seems grateful for the attention, but his eyes are trained on the gnawed, unopened cans of dog food scattered around the room.

"OK, fella," I say. "Let's get you fed."

I honestly do feel bad that I completely forgot him for all this time. I'm just thankful he survived. It seems unlikely. I guess one can live a long time without food. Water is the issue, the scientists tell us. I imagine he drank out of the toilet. There's no other explanation. That's what I would have done, if I had only paws and didn't understand faucets. I place his bowl of food on the floor. He attempts to swallow the food, but it's a struggle.

"Take it slow, dear friend," I advise him.

He looks up at me and seems to smile. His teeth are gone. Perhaps if I mash the food? It is soft, but with his overall weakness and his lack of teeth, perhaps he needs some additional help. I reach for the bowl and he snarls at me. That's weird. Not like him at all. He was always such a friendly fella. I'm not sure what to do. They say one cannot allow a dog to display dominance. A dog must always respect the alpha, which is the owner, which is me. Still, no one wants to get bitten. But I guess with his current toothlessness, he could not do all that much damage. I pick up the bowl. He snaps at my hand, getting hold of it, but it slips easily from his gummy grip. He falls over and appears to exhibit some sort of seizure. It is pathetic to watch. I stroke his head and say "Shhh. Shhh." His body stills, and just like that he is dead. The world is cruel. I weep for my best friend, for that is truly what he was. He was always there for me, ever happy to see me. He didn't care whether or not I was successful, whether or not I was a genius, whether or not I was African American. I feel I probably let him down. He was, in many ways, a better man than I, and I hope someday to learn from his example. Except for that snarling moment, which, to be frank, hurt my feelings, even though I understand there were perhaps extenuating circumstances and that, in the end, it wasn't really about me. Hunger is a cruel mistress. I take a moment to consider his funerary urn. I have a collection of them (containing various family members and pets and three unclaimed bodies from the city morgue) on my bookshelf. I come from a family that favors cremation over ground burial, burial at sea, or shooting into space. I have always been the one with the artistic sensibility in my clan, so the choice of funerary urn ever falls to me, as I insist upon it.

I invite my funerary urn sculptor Olivier over for a consultation.

"What can you tell me about your pet donkey?"

"He was a dog."

"In what sense?" he says, taking notes.

"The canine sense. In the sense that he was a dog."

"And yet you name him after the most famous donkey in all of France? *Pourquoi?*"

"It is the third-best film of all time, the best French film of all time, the best animal film of all time, the sixth-best film about the Seven Deadly Sins, the fourth-best film of the sixties—"

"How can it be the third-best film of all time and the fourth-best film of the sixties?"

"I don't tell you how to design funerary urns, Olivier."

"Well, I found it *très fastidieux*."

"Your cinema rankings are of little interest to me. I'd prefer to discuss my dog's funerary urn."

"Let me see . . . how best to pay tribute to a donkey who is a dog?"

I understand Olivier is mocking me, but I scan the urns on the shelf behind him and they are exquisite: a pewter wishing well, a bronze Adonis, a tiled men's room complete with urinals, the cookie jar one, a magnificent crystal snowstorm that houses my uncle the meteorologist, the found-object pterodactyl, which is also a functioning fountain, each reflecting, with precision and grace, the personality of its occupant. My eyes come to rest on the singed donkey puppet from Ingo's film and I am struck by a notion. Why not pay tribute to the ashes of *Balthazar and* those of Ingo's film, both of indomitable spirit, both destroyed (some might say) by my actions. My daily reminder will be my penance. I propose to Olivier that the donkey puppet be incorporated into the urn. He studies the donkey, plays with it, moves its articulated limbs.

"I thought you don't tell me how to design funerary urns," he says, finally.

"Olivier, please don't be difficult. I am grieving. Cannot you see that?"

He is silent for a long time, then:

"With a small motor in the base of the urn, I can make your donkey toy move."

"What could it be made to do?" I ask.

"Dance, perhaps. March. Hang its head in grief. Supplicate."

"Can it do all four?"

"That won't be cheap."

"Money is no object," I say and call my sister.

I AM VISITING my editor Arvide in his office.

"I think I am still able to write the piece," I tell him.

"For a film that no one can ever see," he says.

"Yes. But I can re-create it."

"A novelization?"

"Well, no. That's offensive to me. I wouldn't call it that."

"I would."

"Fine. I feel certain I could write it, Arvide, so ineradicable was the experience. If I can remember it."

"I'll be frank with you, B.—"

"Don't be frank."

"I do not believe there ever was a film."

"There was. And it was the single most important film in the history of cinema."

"See, that's the part where I begin to doubt the veracity of—"

"Look," I say and hold up my extant frame.

"What's that?"

"An extant frame."

Arvide takes it from me.

"Careful," I say.

He studies it for a long while, then:

"I don't know what I'm looking at."

"A pivotal moment in the film. I'm guessing it's when the lighting grid falls and fractures Molloy's skull, sending him into a life-changing coma. I still don't remember that part."

"That makes no sense. And besides, I don't see anything like what you just said."

"Well, it's obscured by the cloud of smoke from the cigarette of the best boy in the catwalk, from whose point of view (POV) the shot originates."

"So I'm looking at cigarette smoke."

"No! That's the thing! Amazingly, it's cotton wool. The effect was created with common cotton wool. The very type of cotton wool one might easily purchase at a chemist's or the cotton wool store down the street."

"The moment is obscured, is my point."

"Intentionally so. What you don't see in a film is as important as what you do see. Ask anyone."

"Don't lecture me. You're not helping your cause."

"Look at this," I say, pulling the donkey urn from my man bag.

"Horse doll mounted on a box," he says.

"It's a donkey puppet. From the movie. He lived in the Giant's house with the Giant, I believe. I believe there was a Giant. I might be confusing it with *Shrek*. Was there a Giant in *Shrek*?"

"Where's his tail?"

"What? That's neither here nor there. Look at the craftsmanship. The tail burned off. OK?"

"It's a nice doll, but it does not get you what you want."

"Then let me have *Enchantment* back."

"That would not be fair to Dinsmore."

"He's utilizing my research."

"You offered it to them to use."

"Thon."

"In any event—"

"If I can't have *Enchantment* back, which I deserve, then let me write the Ingo piece. A novelization, as you said! It's all in my head," I say, tapping it. "A novelization it shall be!"

"I don't know what the audience would be for a book outlining a nonexistent film."

"Not only outlining it. Critiquing it. Explaining it. And it's not nonexistent. It's destroyed."

"Who would want to read that? It's not like you were the only person to see a lost Hitchcock film."

"Hitchcock isn't fit to suck Ingo's dick."

"What does that even mean?"

"I don't know. I'm just . . . frustrated. Come on, Arvide, remember Harvard? Roomies forever!"

"That doesn't apply here."

"You owe me!"

"I owe you?"

"I've saved your ass so many times! Remember when you needed someone to do the piece 'Swedish Hsi Dews' on the Swedish palindromists for your Cinema of Scandinavia issue and you couldn't find anyone in town who had even heard of them?"

"You asked *me* if that piece could be in the issue."

"How could anyone even think to do a Cinema of Scandinavia and leave the palindromists out?"

"B., I can't pay you for an analysis of a film no one will ever be able to watch."

"I don't want to take it elsewhere, Arvide, but I will."

"It's OK if you do. No hard feelings."

"I'll do it. I swear."

"I understand. Godspeed."

"What about college? Roommates? Remember when we said we would be brothers forever?"

"That wasn't said."

"I said it. And you nodded."

"I really don't recall nodding."

"I wrote it down."

I frantically search my man bag for the paper.

"Again: not proof."

"You'll be sorry when this comes out and changes the way we watch movies."

"I'll be very happy for you."

"That's such an asshole thing to say."

CHAPTER 18

WITH LITTLE ENTHUSIASM, I resume my teaching duties (the school had hired the pathologically wrongheaded film critic David Manning to fill in for me during my absence). The students remain characteristically uninterested. Cinema Studies is deemed a gut course in zookeeper school. You get to watch movies, is what they think. I attempt to disabuse them of that notion. I screen movies with zero entertainment value. I show *Synecdoche, New York* for the simple reason that it is an irredeemable, torturous, tortuous yawn. But I would be remiss if I didn't also screen challenging movies that are tedious but important. If you hope to have any chance of following a film such as Tobleg's masterful *Thyestes/Obliviate*, the film I am screening today, you need to pay attention. Six students out of fifteen have shown up. I will schedule a test next class to punish the truants. *T/O* is a difficult film to watch, not only due to its graphic and unrelenting depiction of human cannibalism, including a detailed (and educational!) description of the proper field dressing for human meat as well as several tantalizing recipes, but also because of Tobleg's use of horizontal space on a vertical plane. That is, the film is shot entirely from beneath glass-floored rooms. This calculated ploy to frustrate the audience is off-putting to some of the less adventurous cinemagoers among us, but the truth is, if you give yourself over to it (and you must!), a strange exhilaration unlike anything else in one's audiencial experience comes to pass. And it raises questions about the limitations of conventional points of view. The movie is seen from the bottom of characters' shoes, which prove to be invigoratingly emotive. Tony Scott of *The New York Times* wrote a somewhat derisive review (why is the proudly anti-intellectual *Times* even reviewing a Tobleg film?) mockingly entitled "Acting from the Sole." I think Tony is a nice enough fellow and I'm sure a very smart guy for a hack, but Tobleg deserves better than quippiness. The truth is, the acting from below (Tobleg trained the shoe actors for months in the technique before principal photography began) is startlingly poignant. I have been brought to tears on every viewing of the film. And each time, I see something new, a new show, a new shoe show. But of course my students are having none of it, this room full of zookeeping Tony Scotts. And the truth is my heart is no longer in this type of education. For the new me, it is either barefooted hayseed children from the South or the whole world as my students. This is why I spend my off times scouring junk stores, yard sale bins, and garbage cans, searching for the films of the next Ingo Cutbirth. It's not a scientific process, but mine is not a scientific field. One would not expect Joyce to write utilizing the statistical method.

Over time I do accrue boxes and boxes of film: 8 mm, Super 8, 16 mm, Super 16, and one Super 37, for which the only projector exists in Qaanaaq. It takes three months to project them all (minus the Super 37, which I unspool, thumbtack to the wall of the Sylvia Plath Memorial Indoor Running Track in the third subbasement of New York's famed Barbizon Hotel for Women and run past with a magnifying glass seven times). In the end, sadly, there is nothing of note. Many, many birthday parties and travelogues. The cinematography is not particularly noteworthy. The acting, such as it is, is atrocious and wooden. One short, apparently made by a group of middle school boys, seems to be some sort of homemade vampire movie. It is derivative, and, to be frank, the boy playing the university vampirologist was not the least bit convincing, either in his Eastern European accent or his simulated old man shaking hands. When I arrive at the very last film, *10th Birthday Party for Bobby*, I find myself depressed; Bobby is not an interesting boy.

The immensity of the loss of Ingo's film hits me perhaps for the first time.

The world is not lousy with lost masterpieces, as I had, in my naïveté, believed. I sit on the floor and watch *Balthazar*'s urn dance, then march, then hang its head, then supplicate. Olivier programmed the donkey to do a somber and tasteful dance. I believe he said it was a mourning dance from Ghana. The funeral march, slow and lugubrious, plays out to "Funeral March of a Marionette" by the brilliant and undersung Charles Gounod (I relate, Charles!). The head hanging is to The Kingston Trio's version of "Tom Dooley" and is profoundly moving. I would weep if I had any tears left, but alas. The supplication is to "Camptown Races," for reasons that remain unclear to me.

I WANDER THE film criticism district, formulating theories, grinding axes; it keeps me sane in these insane times to return to my roots, to praise those films and filmmakers worthy of an audience's attention, to destroy those filmmakers who loose self-satisfied garbage onto the world. Consider *Stranger Than Fiction*, I say to my imagined lecture hall full of cinephiles: a wonderfully quirky film starring William Ferrell and the always adorkable Zooey Deschanel. The work done here by director Marc Forster (who directed the unfortunately misguided, misogynistic, and racistic *Monster's Ball*) and screenwriter Zachary H. Elms is stellar in that all the metacinematic techniques work, its construction analogous to that of a fine Swiss watch (no accident that a wristwatch figures so prominently into the story!). Compare this to any mess written by Charlie Kaufman. *Stranger Than Fiction* is the film Kaufman would've written if he were able to plan and structure his work, rather than making it up as he goes along, throwing in half-baked concepts willy-nilly, using no criterion other than a hippy-dippy "that'd be cool, man." Such a criterion might work if the person making that assessment had even a shred of humanism within his soul. Kaufman does not, and so he puts his characters through hellscapes with no hope of them achieving understanding or redemption. Will Ferrell learns to live fully in the course of *Stranger Than Fiction*. Dame Emily Thomson, who plays his "author," learns her own lessons about compassion and the value and function of art. Had Kaufman written this film, it would have been a laundry list of "clever" ideas culminating in some unearned emotional brutality and a chain reaction of recursional activity wherein it is revealed that the author has an author who has an author who has an author who has an author, *et chetera*, thus leaving the audience depleted, depressed, and, most egregiously, cheated. What Kaufman does not understand is that such "high concepts" are not an end in themselves but an opportunity to explore actual mundane human issues. Kaufman is a monster, plain and simple, but a monster unaware of his staggering ineptitude (Dunning and Kruger could write a book about him!). Kaufman is Godzilla with dentures, *Halloween*'s Mike Myers with a rubber knife, Pennywise the Clown with contact dermatitis from living in a sewer. He is a pathetic—

Something goopy and wet plops onto my forehead. I wipe it off and discover my hand is covered in bird feces. This, I am sad to say, is no longer an atypical experience in this horrible city. The pigeons—flying rats, I've humorously dubbed them—have taken over, and we humans are at their mercy. We are their toilets. The stuff is sliding down my face and into my mouth. My fellow urbanites snicker cruelly. I duck into a CVS and purchase a small pack of baby wipes. The cashier won't look at me, won't take the cash from my hand, leaves my change on the counter. It takes the entire package of wipes to clean my face and another entire package of Johnson & Johnson Mouth Tissues to clean out the inside of my mouth. I have lost my previous train of thought. I believe I was compiling my "Best of" list for 2016. I continue:

10—*La Ciénaga Entre el Mar y la Tierra* (Castillo y Cruz)
9—*Hele Sa Hiwagang Hapis* (Diaz)
8—*Hymyilevä Mies* (Kuosmanen)
7—*Smrt u Sarajevu* (Tanovic)
6—*Fuchi Ni Tatsu* (Fukada)
5—*Kollektivet* (Vinterberg)

4—*It's Tough Being a Teen Comedian in the Eighties!* (Apatow)

3—*En Man Som Heter Ove* (Holm)

2—*Kimi No Na Wa* (Shinkai)

1—*Under Sandet* (Zandvliet)

It's a list of which I am proud. It is a list that under normal circumstances would set the world of cinema on fire. But today the world of cinema is abuzz with other news. H. Hackstrom Babor, *professor adjunto* in the filmic studies department at the Mr. Jam Centro Moderno de Música in Bilbao, Spain, has stumbled upon a heretofore undiscovered film in the back of the basement of an abandoned bordello in the Basque Country. This so-called "orphan" film by an unknown outsider artist has been dubbed by some "scholars" as the creative link between the Spanish Rectangulists of the sixties and the Barcelonan Rapturists (*Los Realizadores de Rapto de Barcelona*) of the early to mid-seventies. Be still my heart. Not only are the Rapturists a *movimiento falso* in all but the most naïve academic circles, but EVERYONE acknowledges that *Soy un Chimpancé* is the film that brought Rectangulism into the postmodern age. Far be it from me to rain on Babor's filthy, despicable parade. It is, however, galling to have to abide this collective orgasm with clenched jaw as I sit on the ashes of the truly monumental cinematic discovery of the age. Tonight I will attend a screening of and Babor's lecture on this "film" at the 92nd Street Y Overflow Auditorium at the intersection of Gregory Hines and Maurice Hines Boulevards in Harlem. Babor and the film will appear on closed-circuit television at this venue. Questions from the overflow crowd can be asked of Babor through a series of relays by typing them into one of the three electronic keyboards on a desk in the corner, and I intend to ask many questions. For now, I must busy myself in preparation.

I WAIT MY turn, impatient, imperiously crowding the fawning dimwit ahead of me at the keyboard. *I have long admired your work . . .* he is hunting and pecking at the lightning speed of a word a minute.

"C'mon c'mon c'mon c'mon c'mon c'mon," I chant into the back of his head.

. . . and am curious as to your take on the films of Fra—

"All right, that's enough," I say, pushing him aside. His keister-kissing is doing nothing to further this discussion.

So, Babor, I begin, we meet again. So to speak. I trust Bilbao's finest guitar emporium/after-school education center is treating your filmic research with the seriousness it deserves. My question for you tonight is this: How do you square (no pun intended!) your woeful misapprehension of the work of the Rectangulists with your arrogant proclamations about the cinematic value of this newly found "work," and I put work in quotations because to characterize this as a work, as in a work of art, diminishes both the concept of work and the concept of art. This "film," and I put film in quotes as well, because to characterize it thusly diminishes the concept of film, is a travesty at best and deserves no place in the canon of essential Spanish films of the mid-twentieth century. Yo Soy Chimpancé, *a movie that you, in your reckless pursuit of personal aggrandizement, shamelessly attempt to relegate to the ash heap of film history, is the undisputed link between the Rectangulists and all else of any remote import that comes after. Gomes himself has said as much. Are you prepared to wage war with me over this? With Gomes? Keep in mind (if you've even seen the film) that the final sequence in* Chimpancé *is Manuel cinematographed from every conceivable angle, both from outside and inside his body. As I'm certain, since you are a scholar of film, you realize that the Rectangulists did for cinema what the Cubists did for painting, namely utilizing a single frame of reference to explore multiple frames of reference. Keep in mind the producer of* Chimpancé, *Guillermo Castillo, was so concerned about potential mental anguish among the film's spectators that he hired actresses dressed as nurses to stand in the back of the theaters showing the movie to attend to those who might have heart attacks. Its pyrotechnic display of photography and editing illustrates the reach but also the ultimate limitations of the Rectangulist manifesto of* Frame/Reframe *(see my footnote at the bottom of this question). I'll take my response off the air.*

Then I wait through the interminable glad-handing and self-congratulations that pass these days as conversation, but the moderator never asks Babor my question. *Quelle surprise*. It was a powder keg. I collect my gift bag and leave.

Lurching through the streets, blinded by rage and disappointment, I stumble upon an unadvertised orphan film festival at the 65th Street Borkheim Palace. Perhaps this is the very medicine I need to cure my current state of violent melancholy. I flash my press credentials to the box office attendant.

"Fifteen dollars," she says.

The world I view inside is enframed in a rectangle. I can see only to the edges of this frame; beyond it is darkness. It exists only as this: light, absence of light, and combinations thereof. The various meanings found within are no more than tricks of the brain. This play of light and dark is predetermined and therefore unalterable. It simply plays out. Then it plays out again. It can be observed. It can be processed, judged. It can elicit emotional responses in an observer. It can be criticized, but it cannot be hurt. For it does not have wants or desires. You can literally stop this world in its tracks and it will melt, but it does not care. Only you care.

The world outside, I decide, is also a rectangle of light surrounded by darkness. It has no mass. It exists outside of me, but not truly as I see it, not as I understand it.

The unattributed, untitled film begins: The lights are off. In the room depicted onscreen, the heavy drapes have been drawn. He knows they are drawn, this man in the room, but he cannot see that they are drawn, for there is no light at all in the room. But he knows they are drawn because he drew them himself only minutes ago. Similarly, he knows well enough the placement of furniture in the room, where the desk is, the bookcase, the bed in which he now reclines. He needs it to be as dark as possible if he is to get any sleep. This much he has learned after a lifetime of sleep problems. He has tried all the remedies over the years: the drinking of warm milk, the drinking of whiskey, the counting of sheep, the reading of books, this very dark room.

And as in a dream, I find myself in this room, too. When did that happen? I can't say, so slippery was the shift of consciousness from the constant jabbering noise in my head into the silent black rectangle before me. I know this rectangle depicts a room in absolute darkness and I know the objects in this room as well as the man who I know is in the bed in this room knows these things. I know the dresser is over there to the right, that it is squat and wide and of a highly polished wood. The cherry desk is against the window. I know the funny story about its purchase almost five years ago. I know how the story has changed slightly in the telling over the years. I know his clothes are piled on the gray rug at the foot of the bed: black slacks, white dress shirt, white boxer shorts, two black socks. I know he leaves his clothing there every night. I know he is ashamed of not being neater. And just as the man knows what's outside the bedroom door without looking, so do I: the boxy second-floor landing dimly lit by a Popeye-faced night-light, four closed doors, including his own. The wife behind one, the son behind another, the bathroom behind the third. The bathroom door is closed because the faucet has a drip that keeps the son awake. I know the town in which the man lives, which streets to take to get to the supermarket, the house two doors down with that little dog that incessantly barks. And I know what's inside the man in bed, too, his feelings, the constant slight ringing in his left ear, how he needs it this dark if he is to have any hope of sleep. And I know he is not sleeping now; the organized quality of his thoughts tells me that. Organized but ephemeral. Ideas appear and disappear, snippets of conversations without sound, images that are not images at all but ideas of images. It's staggering, I think, as my inexhaustible jealousy of all things I admire rears its head. How is this achieved? How, cinematically? Technically, what exactly is the trick? There is a trick, certainly. This dark and silent rectangle communicating so much about the room it portrays, about its occupant, about his life. Who is the filmmaker? I wonder. Why are there no credits, no title? And I decide it is the very lack of this information that buries the film so deeply in my brain, the part of my brain relegated to dreams and fleeting thoughts. It is an orphan film by choice, not by accident. The anonymity of the film worries me. It makes this film somehow dangerous. Even as I watch it, it integrates and vanishes, someone else's glass of water poured into my own only partially full glass of water. This is not a movie I will remember properly. It lives only in the irrational, as does a dream. My rational mind, the bully, will strong-arm it away from me and fill in the blanks, add explanations, because it cannot let it be. This bully contaminates the dream, changes it into something smaller, manageable, tellable. The dream as it is cannot be told. So it is with this film. In the remembering or telling, it becomes something else, and so the truth of it is destroyed. And I go on with my life, with my anemic attempts to portray the world in its fullness.

I think all this as I drift in and out of the thoughts of the unseen man in the bed. He is old, not like me. He struggles with insomnia, which *is* very much like me. He is tormented by a lifetime of these sleepless nights, years wasted worrying, attempting, failing. Beads of sweat form along his hairline high on his forehead as he goes over and over his career fumbles, his diminishing creativity, his failures, his humiliations, the looming deadline he faces, both metaphorically and literally. He lusts after inspiration the way he once lusted after women, a spark of some sort. It is the year 2015, the future, far in the future. Not as he expected it when he was younger, when he was my age. Now there are computers in every home. There is world peace. There are portable telephones that can be carried everywhere in semiportable little wooden boxes. There is an awful lot of diaphanous clothing, but still it is—*there is delicious food in pill form*—but still there is . . . oh!—*universal human fulfillment*—but *still* there is something wrong. He is not fulfilled. Every day, the homeopapes spout the good news, but all this happiness doesn't seem to be enough for him; a wrongheaded competitiveness still lurks in his psyche. He longs to be admired even though he lives in a time when everybody admires everybody. It is both mandated by law and accepted by medical professionals as therapeutic. Indeed, this point in history has been dubbed, somewhat joshingly (but not in a mean way), The Mutual Admiration Society. It follows closely on the heels of The Society of Mutually Assured Destruction, which followed a period no one alive remembers, something about flappers, perhaps.

The insomniacal thoughts of this man plague me as he struggles through the night. The alarm clock with the lighted dial is checked repeatedly, interspersed with tossing and turning and cursing and pillow pounding. I feel both the slowness of the passage of time and the relentless slogging toward morning light. How is this accomplished? Perhaps I am responding to ambiguous subliminal cues hidden in individual frames. Perhaps I am projecting all of this onto the scene and there is nothing of this there. I am put in mind of Dyrgenev's experiments. He projected black, gray, and white onto a screen. People saw snowstorms in the white image. One man saw a snowstorm on a moonless night in the black screen. Just as I've concluded it's my own psyche on this screen, a dim morning light peeks through a narrow opening in the drapes and I learn the room, exactly as I pictured it, is there before me: the dresser, the desk, the pile of clothes at the foot of the bed. The mundane horror of a night of wakefulness has been fully experienced, as well as the hopelessness attendant to an awareness that this is a nightly battle and has been since youth. The old man is exhausted. I am exhausted. I think, He could be me, if I were an old man, and I feel a sense of relief that I am not, that there is still time for me to figure this out, to not be conquered by a lifetime of sleeplessness.

The old man thinks "time to get up" and does, tossing the tangle of sheets aside. There is not much of an erection these days, but there is something. I feel his thoughts, the routine acknowledgment of the semi-erect penis, the need to urinate. I compare it to my own morning experience. I become conscious of my own need to urinate. As he makes his way to the bathroom, I consider whether I can wait or if I should run out myself. I think it might be safe to make a dash for it now. I decide not much is going to happen in the next two minutes. But I don't want to chance it. The movie is dull but also unlike anything I've ever experienced, and I can't safely predict what might happen next. I check my watch and find that although I just watched him toss and turn in bed for six hours, only three minutes have passed. Maybe I don't have to urinate. The old man flushes and leaves the bathroom. Oddly, my need to urinate is gone. In the upstairs hallway, he passes the door to his wife's room. She is snoring behind it. I know that is why they sleep in separate bedrooms. I judge their marriage. This is not what marriage should be. I will never get this old. Even if I live to this age, I will never be old like that. It is a choice to become old like this. People can remain young at heart. The movie ends, no credits, no fade; it just stops. I leave.

CHAPTER 19

OVER THE NEXT three months I find myself changing. I am no longer the happy and carefree man I have always been. I have become a frighteningly different person, an angry person, angry at the slights, at the unfairness, at the system, at the culture, at the driver who cuts me off as I try to cross the street, at my former best friend Elkin (formerly Ocky, but now he's all la-de-da), who taunts me with his conspicuous hand-holding of others and freshly pressed shirts. La-de-da! But if all the things I'm mad at have to happen, are destined to, then why am I mad? And I have come to accept that all things that happen must happen. What is anger if everything is part of an inevitable machine? Simply another aspect of the machine. Nothing more than my dancing donkey urn. Yet lately I have been angry. I have been depressed. I have been hurt. I have watched my career stagnate, while the careers of those around me have flourished. I have read their monographs, when I can bring myself to. I have railed against them in my mind, among Facebook friends, in anonymous letters unsent to film magazines, to *The New York Times*, to *Argosy All-Story Weekly*. I have spoken privately about the greed and shallowness and stupidity of Hollywood, about the dearth of ideas and courage, about the self-serving, self-aggrandizing, celebrated narcissists and opportunists in positions of power. I have watched my confidence erode as my proposals have been rejected one by one. I have watched my ideas dry up. I have watched myself be referred to in the past tense, if at all. I have been misgendered. Howie Sherman Zookeeper School has, without ceremony, let me go. I have fallen into black despair as I watch myself age, as I watch people on Facebook I care about fall sick, physically and mentally, as I watch the *sincere* hopefulness of our young people wither, to be replaced by their *callow and pathetic* hopefulness. They don't know, but we do. They will know. And perhaps we will have the last laugh, if we live long enough to see them know what we know. One can only hope.

My job at the zoo workers' school was lost after an altercation with a student. There is a way this generation has about it. Certainly, when I was that age, during the Punic Wars (I make this reference to the bafflingly overestimated Albee play [much like *The Scottish Play*, its title shall never pass my lips] with a mocking sidelong glance to an imaginary camera), students did not behave with such arrogant disrespect for their teachers. Certainly, celebrating Descartes in a classroom full of student zookeepers is a questionable pedagogical stratagem, but how might it be possible to fully engage on the topic of film and epistemology without delving into his *Meditations on First Philosophy*? And, as the "Is this a dream?" question is currently weighing heavily on my mind, I found it imperative to introduce my students to the man who first introduced me to that question. That a young white male would then attempt to shout me down by calling me an old white male was the thing furthest from my expectation as I naïvely planned to engage the future Zookeepers of America in a civilized discussion. I called him a nincompoop, and he told me to sit down, old man, and listen for a change. But I am the teacher, I said. You are old and white and male, he reiterated. Then he added, And Israel is an apartheid state. Ah, there it was. What took you so long in getting to the crux of your argument against me, such as it is? I asked him. The Jews believe animals have no souls and won't go to heaven, he nearly screamed at me. First of all, I began, I am not Jewish.

"You look Jewish," he spat.

"And you look like an inbred white trash pedophile, but that does not make it thus."

He had pushed me too far and I lost my cool. That night I was fired.

I argued with the dean.

"I specifically said that does *not* make it thus!"

"By saying that does not make it thus, you had been inferring that it did not make it *not* thus," said the dean.

"Implying," I corrected.

I find myself on the subway, on my lap a cardboard box of aspidistra (which I playfully named Clytemnaestra); a stapler; pens; books on Godard, the Spanish Rectangulists, and early Albanian cinema; and Judd Apatow's *So You Want to Be a Funny Guy?* (so underrated!).

What'll I do now that I'm unemployed? I can barely afford my apartment as it is. Perhaps I can sleep at my elderly aunt's place in Elmhurst in exchange for errand running or some such. It's demoralizing, but I have to stay the course. There is, I am certain, a trunk of gold Ingos at the end of it.

I practice my Preston Sturges lecture as I walk from the subway:

The lesson Sullivan learned at the end of *Sullivan's Travels* is antithetical to the one intended. The world is a relentlessly cruel place. Giving in to the infantilizing entertainment of Walt Disney is the ruination of culture, not its salvation. Sullivan should have persisted with *O Brother, Where Art Thou?* Those toothless chain-gangers didn't need to be mollified with children's drawings. They needed to be freed from their oppressive shackles, both figurative and literal. Is it any accident that the laughter of those unfortunates is completely out of proportion to the humor offered in the clip? It is the laughter of the insane, the broken, the hopeless. There has only ever been one animation that could save humanity.

Coincidentally, perhaps, I start seeing Ingo's hulking figure on the street, sometimes in his Caucasian face makeup, sometimes not—or *was* it makeup? My memories are confused on this particular point—but always at a distance: a block away, turning a corner, entering a building. It's like a haunting, but an odd one, as if this haunting is not for me. As if I'm witnessing someone else's haunting. As if I'm watching a movie about a haunting. Maybe it is just because Ingo is on my mind. I once had a girlfriend who dumped me for a more conventionally successful and conventionally handsome and conventionally decent fellow, and afterward, I would see her car everywhere. But, of course, it was a fairly common make and color, and all cars look the same today anyway (see: my critically acclaimed essay on this very subject, "A Single Carnation," in *The Journal of What's Wrong With Today's Cars*), so it was most likely rarely if ever her. I suspect this is a similar sort of phenomenon. Although Ingo, as I recall him, was two unusual looking fellows. But it is at a distance and the sightings are mostly in the early evenings when both the eyes and the heart are known to play tricks. Soon, however, the apparition is closer, and I am certain that his figure at the very least bears an uncanny resemblance to one of the Ingos. This is no Toyota/Honda mix-up. At worst, it is Alec Baldwin/Billy Baldwin. I am still not close enough to catch up with him, but his frequent presence weighs heavily on my psyche. There is, after all, a certain lingering guilt I still feel about my total destruction of Ingo's life's work. That he himself had requested his work be destroyed does not lighten my load. The monumental loss to civilization, had the directives by certain artists to destroy their work been followed, would be incalculable. Of course, Franz Kafka, whose posthumous request his friend Max Brod thankfully would not honor, comes famously to mind. Aubrey Beardsley made the same request of his publisher, and it was also denied. These are the happy endings. But there are hundreds of lost manuscripts and artworks by masters throughout history. We'll never know how the lost Gogol books might've changed this world for the better, but they undoubtedly would have. And even more unimaginable are the missing works by completely unknown artists who may or may not have even existed. Maybe someone named Loren Thelms wrote a novel that would've influenced culture in unimaginable ways. Maybe the paintings of an artist called Janis Menschel, for example, would've touched a generation of visual artists in ways unimaginable. Perhaps a symphony by, say, someone named Enright Wong would have changed music in ways we cannot now even imagine. When one considers the multitude of unsung of every race, ethnicity, and gender, perhaps toiling away in obscurity, their work thrown out after their deaths by philistine relatives and vulgarian landlords, one must weep.

And one does.

One of those works might've ended poverty, cured cancer, or at the very least brought a fleeting smile to the face of a little boy who's just lost his mother to poverty or cancer. The list of these hypothetical artists is, as one might imagine, endless: Maria Reggio, Bob Thomas Cork, Sylvio Moretti, Asha Okeke, Hiroshi Bittner, Bev Wickner, Ah-Renj Julius, Harper Mead, Janet Tanaka, Harry Prachnau, Shana DeVries, and on and on. Now one of them, the ghost of Ingo, who told me while he was alive to destroy his film, is telling me, through his ghostly dead presence, to, I believe, remember it. This is what I believe; for what is a ghost if not a plea to remember? And my inability to remember haunts me just as *he* haunts me. It is my responsibility to the world. I must pull it, frame by frame, from the depths of my mind and, although I likely don't have ninety years left to re-create it frame for frame (never say never!), maybe with the right budget I could oversee a battalion of animators and we could do it all in ten years. Maybe I am just the hero this world needs right now.

In my apartment, I stare through a professional jeweler's loupe at the single remaining frame of Ingo's film. I believe I have come upon a brilliant and feasible restoration technique. Using a method of my own devising, based on my understanding of the block universe theory and my vast knowledge of film history, I should be able to study this frame and with great precision predict the frame that follows it as well as the one that precedes it. By simply repeating this process 186,624,999 times, I should end up with a complete reconstruction of the film. It will be painstaking, of course. It will likely kill me, but it is essential.

The frame: a fat man in a checkered suit and derby hat. He smiles, coyly, childishly, grotesquely into the camera. Right above his head there seems to be an iron bar. Motion blur suggests it is moving toward him at significant speed. Is someone about to hit him in the head? If so, he is at this moment blissfully unaware of his impending doom. Will the next frame be ¹/₂₄th of a second closer to his doom? Is it the first moment of awareness of what is to come, starting him on the path to an expression of fear? Or does that come later? Or does it never come and the crushing of his skull happens with no anticipation? Or maybe the metal bar misses him. Maybe he jerks out of the way at the last moment. Maybe the bar isn't metal after all. Maybe it's chocolate. Maybe the bar is flying away from him rather than toward him; it's difficult to tell through all the smoke. Perhaps this is the final moment of the shot and it cuts before the bar makes impact. If so, what might be next? The possibilities now seem, if not infinite, unmanageably vast. The world is impossibly complex, and even something much more simple than the world in its entirety, such as a motion picture film, when broken down into its quanta, proves impossible to predict. Of course, there are certain unlikely options for the next frame: a close-up of a labium majus; a fleet of thousands of alien spaceships filling the sky above Krong Chaktomuk; a youngish leprechaun standing, arms akimbo, in a verdant field; a dying bumblebee at rest on the crown of a marshmallow; David Susskind about to cough; fourteen peacocks at rest. The list goes on, but I'm not certain how helpful it is because as unlikely as these next shots are, they are all possible. And at this point, with so little memory of the film to draw upon, I am unable to make even an educated guess. I had felt certain that I would be capable of this form of cinematic deduction. I, with my cinematic mastery. But I find myself profoundly frustrated.

A voice in my head dubs me a failure once again. Is it my own voice? It is too distant to tell. I put the single frame back in its envelope. I am awash with self-loathing. This failure to predict the frame on each side, the other moments, the quantized presentation of Ingo's world, has led me to the undeniable conclusion that the only moment that exists is the moment we inhabit. The rest is rumor and gossip. The rest is a lie.

I pace.

Comedy is a lie, too, of course. It's a defense, an aggression. It is a thing created to separate, to say, "I am not like this." It is Godlike in its judgment and, by definition, the antithesis of empathy. Comedy sits on its throne and states: You are ridiculous. You are pathetic. You are stupid. Your pain amuses me. Most important, I am not you. Even comedy directed at the self, the stand-ups, the Woody Allens of the world, is performed as an act of defense: *I am in on the joke that is me, therefore the joke is not me.*

I pace.

What *I* do, what I give to the world, is that I watch. I observe. I perceive. I take it inside me. In this way, I represent the Universal Feminine. I am not ashamed to be a feminine man. I take creative work inside me like semen. I allow it to impregnate my egg-like mind, to gestate. And what is born is the intercoiling of these two consciousnesses. Without sperm, there is no impregnation, but without the egg, the sperm is useless, hardened into an old sock. I am receptive to true art, to true creativity, but I will not have people like Charlie Kaufman force themselves in to rape my mind. I will claw, tooth and nail. I will name names. #MeToo, Charlie Kaufman, #MeToo.

I take a moment to remove the batteries from my smoke alarms, which have all started screeching at once.

I resume pacing.

I will warn others so they need not suffer the degradation that I have, so they will not wake up at night in a cold sweat, making excuses for their assailant. "Maybe I asked for it. Maybe I wasn't clear." What abomination would come from this monstrous union? Would that there were a morning-after pill for assault by minor, talentless filmmakers.

The smoke alarms screech now without batteries. I pull them from the ceiling and stomp them.

I pace.

The radio announces another strike in Paris. This time it is the *fabricants de sacs à baguette*. The city has shut down. There are riots.

I pace.

CHAPTER 20

Five years pass like this, in noodling thoughts, in international and personal calamities, in rehashed speeches, in a haze of despair, depression, and a third *d*—maybe dismay, but I don't think so; that doesn't sound *d* enough. Desperation maybe?—as I watch Ingo's film recede into its own haze, this one of forgetfulness. As I age, my memory weakens. Where once I could rattle off every cast member in Cowlick's *It's Not Appropriate to Punch Him*, now I'm lucky if I can tell you who played Dimpled Douglas without looking it up. And as I travel through time away from my viewing of Ingo's film, I remember less and less of it. I tried to take notes but with very little success and, of course, nothing to check them against. This loss has plunged me into the deepest pit of another *d*: Disquietude? Doloriferousness? Coupled with the acceptance that I, through my Icarus-like hubris, have deprived the world of what is arguably (if only there was someone to argue with me!) the greatest single piece of art ever created. It is a burden I cannot carry. And now to realize that even I, the one receptacle for this masterpiece, am failing, is enough to break me.

I cannot sleep at night. I cannot eat. I am haggard. The remaining scant hair on my head is falling out or turning odd, unearthly shades. My beard, regrown now and although remarkably full, is lusterless. If only I had an eidetic memory. But of course I don't because it is a myth. A myth that has left me high and dry, for I am certain if eidetic memory did exist, I would have it. I am just the type to have it. That I don't have it is proof that it doesn't exist. And the sleeplessness is not helping my memory at all. Now I spend my nights watching old television shows. I no longer have the ability to concentrate on reading or even attending my beloved cinema. The only solace I can find is in the familiarity of the TV series *Friends*. I have seen every episode probably five times. My favorite is the one where Freddy gets murdered in his sleep. I tell this to my very own "*Friend*" Ocky, and he says there is no such episode and there is no Freddy.

"Freddy is the fat one," I say.

"There is no fat one."

"*Freddy*," I repeat, for clarification.

"There is no Freddy. There is Ross, Rachel, Joey, Phoebe, and Monica."

"Those names don't sound at all familiar," I say. "Are you certain? What have I been watching?"

"I don't know."

"It's advertised as *Friends*."

"I don't know. There's also Chandler."

"They all work in a haberdashery."

"No."

"What am I watching?"

"Not *Friends*. What's more, I find it disturbing that, whatever it is you've been watching over and over at night, your favorite episode is one where some guy gets murdered in his sleep."

"Freddy is a girl," I say.

"That doesn't make it better."

"I'm not saying it does. I'm just clarifying. It's a good episode. And to be fair, Freddy asked for it. She was sleep-stabbing Jeremy."

"So not really murder? More like self-defense?"

"Not exactly. She is murdered by an intruder while she is sleep-stabbing Jeremy. Someone else entirely."

"This is a comedy?"

"Kind of."

"I'm worried that this show doesn't even really exist, that your mind is playing tricks on you because of your sleep deprivation."

"Deprivation," I shout, gleefully adding it to my list.

"And, by the by, old chap, you said Freddy gets murdered in *his* sleep."

"It's a good show," I insist.

But I find myself secretly fretting for my sanity. That night, I wait for the *Friends* marathon to begin. I've set the DVR to record so I can prove to Ocky and myself that I am not making it up. The theme music starts up and the title appears. I see now that the show is called *Shrimp Cocktail for Two*, not *Friends*. I still like the show even though it is not the much-ballyhooed *Friends*, but rather a violent, poorly made fever dream that makes little to no sense. I still like it. Its graphic, disjointed imagery speaks to me in my current state. Tonight's first episode: "The One Where Alistair Discovers a Mass Grave Under His Bed." Logline: It is speculated that a serial killer lives in Alistair's hamper and only comes out at night to kill and procreate. Alistair's hamper is very, very large and was featured in the episode where Starbucks opens a Starbucks in it.

The next morning, I play the recording for Ocky. It is regular *Friends*. Monica makes a pie.

IN AN ATTEMPT to improve my state of mind, I wander the streets of New York looking forlorn, as is my way, in order to attract women who might think I'm deep or that I need to be saved, a technique that has not yet proved fruitful but I am confident will. One might think I would have given up on it by now, but it is the single technique in my arsenal. I invented it at the age of fifteen at a teen party, where I sat in the corner and wrote in a little notebook. *What are you writing?* asks the sad and beautiful girl of my imagination. *Oh, just some thoughts*, I say, matching her sadness. *Do you hate these things as much as I do?* she continues. *I do*, I say. It seemed like it should work. But it never did. I mean, not with any of the pretty, sad ones.

There was one plain girl who was sad (probably because she was plain) who latched on to me. She really wanted to be my girlfriend. She was annoying. A pest. And she made me feel bad about myself. She made me feel shallow for not being interested in her, which wasn't very kind of her, when you think about it. It is not kind to make someone you like feel bad about himself. If you love some-thing, set it free. I think of her now, as I walk, and wonder what happened to her. I look her up on my phone. Jessica Capromen-schen. An unusual name. She should be easy to track down. I hope to discover that she is well, that she has found love with a plain, dull man, has achieved a vague career of some sort, that I didn't ruin her life by denying her my affection. What I learn is that there is no record of her online, none at all. And furthermore, there is no re-cord of that last name for anybody. How can that be? Did Jessica Capromenschen fall off the face of the Earth? Did she never exist? Am I incorrectly remembering her name? Certainly not. I try all possible variations in spelling, which takes five hours on the corner of 53rd and 11th on my miniature magnetized Scrabble board. Still nothing. This is impossible. She is in my brain, her sad plain face, her neediness, her persistence. Yet Jessica Capromenschen has seemingly never existed on this Earth and continues not to, if the Internet is to be trusted. Granted, it is possible to leave no Internet footprint, but that her surname does not belong to anyone else sug-gests that she sprung forth from nothing and receded back to same after her dogged pursuit of me. I track down our high school year-book on piningforlostyouth.com. She is not there. She is nowhere. Am I responsible? Did my rejection of her, friendly and caring as it was, cause her to dissolve from the very fabric of reality? Did I (do I?) have that power? This is perhaps magical thinking, but what other explanation can there be? I hope my perplexed sadness at this girl's non-ness registers on my face now and attracts a perplexed and sad, beautiful woman. She need not be young, of course—in fact, age appropriateness is preferable in the current climate—but she must be beautiful, her age expressed in a sad depth of feeling, maybe an Anne Sexton type.

I consider engaging a private detective to track down Jessica. I am not thrilled to have her in my brain when she is nowhere else on the planet. I worry about my sanity. I hope this concern about my sanity is now expressed on my face and perhaps makes me attractive to the passing, older, beautiful, sad women on the street. Perhaps Amanda Filipacchi will walk by. She would stop me and ask if I want to discuss beauty with her. Then Zadie Smith happens by and over-hears us. She joins in and we all visit a neighborhood watering hole, some crummy, earnest little hole-in-the-wall, where we discuss the issues. I am careful not to mansplain or manspread, knees together holding an aspirin between them. I am here to learn, I say. The bur-den of beauty weighs more heavily on women, I offer humbly, so I want to hear what you and Zadie have to say, I say to Amanda. To Zadie, I say the exact same thing, but substitute "Amanda" for "Zadie." Then I add, shifting my gaze back and forth equally be-tween them: Feminism is an umbrella under which all races and ethnicities coexist and have their own unique experiences. All are to be equally honored, with preference given to those women who have historically been unseen and unheard, namely women of color. WOC. No offense, Amanda, but I'm sure you would agree that Za-die's experience and the experience of women such as she must be brought to the fore. After all, you, for all the hardships attendant to being female, come from a background of wealth and privilege. After Amanda agrees wholeheartedly (and I sense an admiration from her for me because of my sensitivity), we both turn to Zadie and wait for her to speak, which she does, gratefully, and she says something profound about women of color and the female experi-ence in today's world. I nod encouragingly and also to indicate how much I'm learning, which I think is appealing and so different from the reaction most women get from most men. Granted, Amanda is more age-appropriate, so my sights are set on her, but this approval from Zadie, I believe, is just the thing that will make me more at-tractive to Amanda. Zadie is my wingman. I am not a snob, I tell the ladies. In either direction. I am neither highbrow nor lowbrow. I am simply brow. There are pleasures to be derived from all experiences, from the rarefied to the vulgar, from those of the flesh to those of the mind. They seem impressed.

I snap out of my reverie and find myself still alone on the ugly, violent, nauseous streets of my neighborhood. I feel ugly, violent, and nauseated. I worry about Jessica. What if she killed herself over me? After first erasing her history from all records. (This reminds me of an idea for a movie I once had. Prescient!) How will I go on if

I don't know? I need to hire a private detective. I look up long enough to see that no one is looking at me at all. I stop in front of the Actors' Temple, a sad little synagogue on West 47th. Maybe I will write a play. They rent this place out for plays and I could afford it, I would imagine. It's small and sad. I could write a small, sad play about my struggles. Possibly calling it *Jessica Capromenschen*. If it received the kind of attention it deserves, then Jessica, who is perhaps dead in an unmarked grave or a nameless drug addict, would be celebrated finally in the way she so deserves. Maybe Amanda and Zadie would come and rave about it at the writing group to which they both belong, which they will invite me to join—the only male allowed.

At home, I stare out the window.

I have been intimate with seven women in my life. I realize this is not a large number, but I am a man who long ago recognized that a notch on a belt is the apogee of female objectification. I will not be a party to that. Certainly I have had many opportunities of which I have not taken advantage. There have been thirty-seven additional women, all very beautiful, who have wanted to engage *in flagrante delicto* with me, but I have, with gentle kindness so as not to humiliate a single one of them, declined their offers. Three Latinxs, two Romanians, seven WASPs, one African American, five Asian Americans (two Chinese Americans and three Korean Americans), one indigenous Australian, five indigenous Americans, two Jews, one Kukukuku from Papua New Guinea, three black Irish, four Italian Americans, and one Greek American. I am proud to say that my rejection of these woman was handled so gracefully that there were no hard feelings, and, in fact, in all of the cases, I convinced them that they were the ones rejecting me. In this and many ways, I am evolved, "woke" as the children today say, and have been so long before it was fashionable. Women are people. Many of my gender do not recognize this simple fact and therefore become more than willing to treat women as objects or symbols of status. One must be a strong man, a true man, to act thusly in this culture.

I luxuriate in my tub.

Decades of close attention to detail, both in the study of films and in the study of life itself, have produced in me a near-eidetic memory (the claims of a perfect photographic memory have been debunked in all instances). I have always possessed a superior memory. In fact, in my high school's production of *The Warp* by Neil Oram (at over twenty-two hours in length, the longest play on record, according to the illustrious Guinness organization), I was cast as British poet Philip Bourke Marston and was onstage in this delightfully energetic romp for the near day it took to perform. For this, I had committed to memory not only all of Bourke's twenty-five thousand lines but those of my fellow student actists in the production. Neither here nor there, but the local paper praised both my feigned blindness (I had lived three weeks as a "blind" for research) and my "received pronunciation." The auditorium remained at SRO for the entire length of the performance (there were no seats), and I, who had never trod the boards before, earned a student Tony.

I mention this only to indicate that I have a certain tremendous skill in this regard, so it is with only a slight trepidation that I sit in this tub, pen in hand, poised above paper on a portable, inflatable desk, figurative thinking cap on, glint in my eye, spring in my step, now pen in my mouth, nibbling, concentrated scowl between my eyes, sheen of sweat beading on my brow, eyes looking (but not seeing) up to the right . . . and I can't. I cannot. I cannot remember a moment of Ingo's film. I mean, I can remember the general story, some of it in any event, very little, truth be told. I mean, I remember Mudd and Molloy, of course. I am not an imbecile. But this is worrisome. Certainly I am no longer a high school–age lad. Those days are gone. One must accept that. One experiences some memory lapses as one ages. It is to be expected. Could I remember all twenty-five thousand lines in *The Warp* now? At this moment, I would have to conclude the answer is a resounding no. Let alone all the lines of each of my fellows. I was the one who came to their aid if they "went up," which is the stage "lingo" for forgetting one's lines (*lingo* is the jargon of a particular group). But now, the first time since *The Warp* that I've put my memory to such a test, I have been met with a great and terrible surprise. I might as well have advanced dementia given how effective is my power to recall. Certainly, I remember the basics. I remember Mudd and Molloy, as mentioned. I remember there is a giant. There are perhaps profound religious overtones. This was something I had put the proverbial pin in to explore later at my leisure during the inevitable many viewings in many different directions, at many different angles, both acute and obtuse. The film was to be given the time it deserved.

And maybe it is not physiological at all. There are a preponderance of psychological issues through which I am currently going. There are the issues of employment, the romantic issues, my daughter. These things can and will take a toll. Any "shrink" worth his or her or thon's salt will tell you this. However, at the time of *The Warp*, I was going through things as well. Of course I was. I was a teenage boy. There were family conflicts, the usual body dysmorphia, the whole Capromenschen fiasco. And still: twenty-five thousand lines and all the others, too. Granted, even at this magnificent length, *The Warp* was nowhere the length of Ingo's epic. But right now, I would be happy to remember twenty-two hours of Ingo's film verbatim. It would be a jumping-off point at least. And even at twenty-two hours, were it only that long, Ingo's film would be among the, if not the, longest films in history. I'm no longer certain; I'd have to research that. Research it. Ha. Perhaps this is the cause of the atrophy. The Internet. Everything one needs at one's fingertips. There have no doubt been studies demonstrating how this has affected people's memories in the negative. I will have to look those up online. But not now. Now I must face the one thing I cannot look up because it is nowhere other than in the recesses of my brain. I do blame the Internet. However, I must admit that I am a bit worried this is symptomatic of early-onset Alzheimer's. Not that early, I must admit, if I am to be honest. When did I get this old? It happened gradually. And yet in an instant. So here I am, a wrinkled (not only from my time in the tub!), somewhat impotent old man. I am an invisible man, with apologies to Ralph Ellison (not H. G. Wells, the racist!). I know I have nothing to complain about when one looks at the life of Ellison's *Invisible Man*. And I will keep my trivial complaints to myself, so as not to upset the apple cart of hierarchical suffering, of which I recognize I am at the bottom, directly next to all other old white men but above (thankfully!) white men who are serial killers and/or war criminals. But I suffer, too! Of course, I would never tell this to anyone, with the exception of a white war criminal, if I ever meet one. Everybody needs someone to lord it over.

I should visit a "shrink." I have never put much stock in the talking cure, but I suspect they are, by law, not allowed to tell a person that they need to sit down and listen for a change.

CHAPTER 21

Ⅰ TELEPHONE MY FRIEND Ocky, who coincidentally has been in therapy starting from when we first became friends.

"Hello?"

"Ocky, it's me," I say.

"Hello."

"I've been thinking of seeing a 'shrink.'"

"OK."

"I am calling to ask for the number of your 'shrink.'"

"Sorry."

"Sorry?"

"I can't let you see my therapist, B."

"Why?"

"We talk about you. It would be a conflict of interest for thon."

"Your therapist is a thon?"

"No. But I prefer not to even be specific about thon's gender."

"Why?"

"I'm afraid it might allow you to track thon down and see thon behind my back."

"Just by knowing thon's gender?"

"Thon's gender is so specific as to be almost unique."

"Fine. Well, do you know of any other 'shrinks' who are supposed to be good?"

"I have heard tell of a Dr. Bismo in Harlem."

"B-i-s-m-o?" I ask, spelling it out.

"H-a-r-l-e-m."

"No, the therapist's name."

"Oh. Yes, then."

"Do you know his first name?"

"Interesting that you assume it is a he. Sexist much?"

"Her name then?"

"It's a male."

"Then, why—"

"I just thought your assumption was telling."

"What is his first name?"

"Frederick G."

"Thank you," I say.

"I hope it helps you. I really think this is long overdue."

"Thank you, Ocky."

I hang up. Ocky, my oldest and dearest friend, is a terrible person. The thing is he is even more cisgender than I. His high horse is a defensive mechanism. I would pity him if I didn't despise him. Dr. Frederick G. Bismo is an African American, I hope. There is a good chance because his office is in Harlem, although with the current gentrification (the Harlem Shame-aissance, I call it) of that area, it is impossible to know. But I would enjoy talking about this issue with an African American. He would undoubtedly notice how seriously I take the artistry of his fellow African Americans and we would bond over that since he would recognize me as an ally.

FREDERICK G. BISMO is white. Possibly Scandinavian, that's how white. Tall, blond, and severe. He seems to despise me. Perhaps he is not a good fit. Or perhaps this is just what I need—a form of tough love. Or tough hate. Perhaps I should give him a chance.

"Tell me how I can help," he says.

You tell me, I think. You're the goddamn "shrink."

"I'm having some problems," I say.

"I see," he says.

What do you see? I think. I've told you nothing. Why don't you ask me what the problems are? Must I play both of our parts? Must I always—

"What sort of problems?" he asks.

Finally.

"Thank you for asking. For starters, I'm having some problems remembering."

I'm hoping he will say, *Oh, that's quite common at your age. Nothing to worry about.*

"That is worrisome," he says.

"Really?"

"Do you get lost trying to get home?"

"No! For God's sake! No! Egads, man!"

"Well, what sort of memory problems then?"

This man is a joke.

"I cannot remember the details of a film I have watched."

"Oh," he says. "That is nothing. Movies are a disposable art form."

I hate this man.

"I am a film critic by profession, as well as by passion," I say.

"I see. Well, then, why not just watch it again and take notes this time?"

"The one copy of the film has been destroyed."

"Destroyed?"

"Yes, in a terrible fire or tsunami."

"This is a very unusual circumstance."

"Perhaps," I say.

I don't want to get pally-wally with this man. I am not about to make small talk.

"What should I do?"

"Why don't you discuss it with the filmmaker? Perhaps he remembers it?"

"He?"

"She?"

"She?"

"Nonbinary?"

"He," I say. "I just found it interesting you made that assumption."

This man is a dinosaur.

"Well, then, he. In this specific case."

"He is dead."

"From the fire?"

"No," I say.

"Did you murder him?"

"Why would you think that?"

"I don't. Necessarily. I simply by law have to ask."

"No. I did not murder him. He died of old age."

"I see. Well, you're in a pickle."

"Do you think I am suffering from early-onset Alzheimer's?"

"I don't see any signs of that. But I cannot say with certainty at this point. I will give you a memory test, if you like."

"OK."

"It's extra."

"How much?"

"Seventy-five."

"Fine."

Bismo sifts through some drawers for a long while.

"This should not be on the clock, your sifting," I say.

He pulls out a booklet.

"Here we go," he says. "To begin, I will recite a list of ten items. You then recite them back to me."

"OK," I say.

I am nervous. What will I learn about myself?

"Orange, flypaper, pencil, heartthrob, Raisinets, Purim, charm bracelet, pinking shears, platelets, stocking cap."

"Orange, flypaper, pencil, heartthrob, Raisinets, Purim, charm bracelet, pinking shears, platelets, stocking cap."

"Perfect."

"I take issue with categorizing a few of those as 'items.' Heartthrob, Purim, and platelets are not items," I say.

"What are they?"

"Purim is a holiday celebrated by the Jews."

"It's a noun, no?"

"Yes, but not an item," I say. "And a heartthrob is a person."

"OK."

"Platelets are cells."

"You certainly know your definitions."

"Perhaps next time just call them things."

"I am simply following the instructions."

"The Nazis said that."

"I am not a Nazi. What are you insinuating?"

"I was merely making a point," I say.

"About what?"

"One mustn't blindly follow orders."

"So now directions have become orders?"

"I am simply saying—"

"I know what you are saying. You Jews are always saying—"

"Ha! I am not Jewish. Interesting," I say.

"I find that hard to believe. Rosenberg?"

"The world is filled with non-Jewish Rosenbergs. Were you at all educated, you would know that."

"I know that. Besides, one's Jewishness is . . . communicated matrilineally."

"Communicated? Like a contagion?"

"I was searching for the word. That was a placeholder."

"Interesting," I say.

"What I am saying is that your mother may have been Jewish even if your father was a Rosenberg of the Christian variety."

"My mother's name is Rosenberger. That is my middle name."

"Hmm. Interesting."

"Rosenberger is not necessarily a Jewish name, either."

"No?"

"I don't think I need to remind *you* that Alfred Rosenberg was a high-ranking Nazi in the Third Reich."

"There were those who suggested Rosenberg had Jewishness in his ancestry."

"The virulence of Rosenberg's hatred of the Jews was peerless."

"The Jews are a self-loathing people."

"Interesting position to be taken by a purportedly neutral psychologist," I say.

"I have a master's in social work and am certified in marriage and family therapy. That being said, there are many peer-reviewed studies pointing to the issues Jewish people have with self-loathing. And you gave me a non-Jew Rosenberg example, but not a non-Jew Rosenberger example. Curious."

"Finally, you need to call them Jewish people, not Jews," I say.

"Jew need not be a pejorative. Do not you refer to yourself as a Jew?"

"If I were a Jew, which I am not, I would have license to refer to myself as such. You as a non-Jew do not."

"Curious."

"I'm afraid this is not and cannot be a successful pairing," I say.

"Let's investigate why you feel that way."

"I don't want to investigate. It's time for me to leave."

"There's plenty of time left in your session, which you will be charged for. We'd make better use of it and perhaps overcome this hurdle if we discuss the issues you're having."

"I'm going now."

"I accept that you are not a Jew. Jewish. Judaism. Please, stay."

"I'm afraid that is too little too late," I say.

"I think I can help you remember. There are certain tricks to recovering lost memories."

"I'll seek that help elsewhere."

"You will not find anyone who can help you the way I can."

"I'll take my chances."

I leave. As I'm closing the door, I swear I hear him muttering "Jew" under his breath.

"I am not a Jew," I mutter back.

CHAPTER 22

I AM IN ANOTHER waiting room in Harlem, and this terrapin . . . I
mean therapist—a terrapin is a turtle. I must ask this therapist, a
Dr. Malgodown, about this. Perhaps it is a bit of a Freudian slip?
This will be an icebreaker. Perhaps I see therapists as characteristically hidden in their shells? Interesting. Perhaps I question why the
client must be the vulnerable one? Perhaps I question that model of
therapy? I will ask Dr. Malgodown. I still don't know thon's gender.
I can't even guess since thon's first name is Evelyn. Dr. Malgodown
pokes her head out of her office. She is a white female. It is an assumption, the female part, but a fairly safe one, I believe, as she
presents as typically female: pleated skirt, red blouse, heavy wooden
beads around her neck, which I believe to be Malawian in origin.

"Mr. Rosenberg?" she says.

She is a trans woman. Again, an assumption, but this is what the
timbre of her voice suggests.

"Yes," I say.

"Please. Come in."

I do.

"I prefer 'thon' as my personal pronoun," I tell her in the hopes
that she'll reciprocate.

"Thank you," she says, "but I don't think there will be any necessity for me to address you in the third person during our sessions."

She smiles, having won this round.

"Touché," I say.

"So, what brings you here today?" she asks.

"I'm having issues with my memory."

"That is a fairly common occurrence as we age," she says.

"Yes, I agree. I was, however, hoping for some assurances in my particular case—as I have had a near-eidetic memory previously—and also, perhaps, some tools."

"Do you get lost on your way home?"

"No. That's not an issue."

"That's a good sign. I'd like to administer a memory test, if that's OK."

"Sure."

"I'm going to give you a list of ten . . . *things*—we did call them 'items,' but an email has been circulated suggesting that 'things' might be a more therapeutic word choice—after which, I will ask you to repeat them back to me."

"OK."

"Orange, flypaper, pencil, heartthrob, Raisinets, Purim, charm bracelet. Pinking shears, platelets, stocking cap."

"Orange, flypaper, pencil, heartthrob, Raisinets, Purim, charm bracelet. Pinking shears, platelets, stocking cap."

"No."

"No?"

"Number five is Raisinets not raisin heads."

"I said Raisinets."

"Did you?"

"Yes."

"OK. Raisin heads would not have indicated a memory problem so much as it would a hearing problem anyway. So . . . memory good. Hearing . . . not certain. You're mostly fine."

"Yet I can't remember this film and I need to. Are there techniques you know of that can help me locate buried memories?"

"Perhaps we can attempt to discover why this particular memory is repressed."

"Do you think it could be repressed?"

"Yes. That is indeed a thing or, rather, *item*. Was this film traumatic for you?"

"It was revelatory."

"Revelations can be traumatic."

"I don't think it was traumatic. It was the most inspiring three months of my life."

"Three months?"

"The film was three months long."

"You're kidding."

"I do not kid. It is unethical."

"How could you expect to remember a three-month-long film? I don't remember what I had for breakfast yesterday."

"I am not you. I have an eidetic memory. You had scrambled eggs."

"How could you possibly—"

"I see a remnant of it on your blouse."

"But that could be from this morning."

"Your blouse is embroidered with *Wednesday* above the breast pocket. Wednesday was yesterday. I could tell from your level of malodorousness that you first donned this blouse yesterday morning, and I gleaned from the small crimson stain on your cubital fossa, or inbow as you call it, that you had a blood panel performed this morning—I do hope everything is OK—which means you've fasted since last night and therefore did not eat any breakfast today."

"Amazing. OK. What did you have for breakfast five mornings ago?"

"Cherry granola, plain yogurt—which I pronounce *yah*-gurt— coffee with half-and-half."

"How do I know you're not lying?"

"Why would I lie?"

"To impress me," she says.

"I have no need to impress anyone."

"Methinks thou doth protest too much."

With that, I start to weep. Dr. Malgodown has an uncanny ability to reach into my soul, to unmask me, to pull my still-beating heart from my chest and show it to me. Perhaps this is a result of her struggle as a trans woman, or perhaps her life as a trans woman is a result of her struggle with this profound intuition, which has no place in the life of a male in this culture. Get out of here, it is told by our society. Men are rational. Men believe in science. Leave this witchcraft to the womenfolk. And so Dr. Malgodown came to believe this. I am, of course, just an armchair psychologist myself (with both upholstering and social work minors at Harvard), so I cannot know if my theory holds water. And it is too early in our relationship to suggest it to the doctor, so I keep mum. Best to see how this plays out. Besides, I am beside myself with whatever deep nerve she touched. Best to let *her* have the insights for the moment. There will be time enough for me to help her down the road.

"Why do you cry?" she asks.

"I don't know. Because your intuition does not allow you to be housed in the body of a man?"

"What?"

"Nothing. I don't know. I am sad."

"Why are you sad?"

"Because I protest too much?"

"Ah. Yes," she says. "Exactly."

Again I weep.

"It is a little sudden, though. Like a switch. That can be a symptom. I wouldn't say you should be worried at this point. But it might be prudent to have some tests run."

"Symptom of what?"

"Sudden mood swings. Can be a sign."

"Of what?"

"Well, it's too early to say. Dementia. You did very well on the memory test, though. Almost perfect."

"I did perfectly."

"Agree to disagree."

"Well, what do you suggest I do?"

"Might be value in a scan."

"Of my brain?"

"To look for signs of organic damage. Now I'm not saying there are any signs of it, but I always prefer to leap to the worst-possible scenario simply to rule it out."

"That seems to be a somewhat hysterical approach."

"Are you intentionally using the word *hysterical* to poke at me?"

"Poke at you?" I ask.

"The word *hysterical*," she says.

"I understand, but how?"

"You know the root of the word, I take it. You seem to be a some-what educated man."

"Of the womb," I say.

"And are you mocking me?"

"No."

"There are different ways to be female. Not all rely on possess-ing the approved set of body parts."

"I'm not saying—"

"Let me ask you this: Would you ever suggest to a biological fe-male who, out of medical necessity, has had a radical hysterectomy that she is no longer a woman?"

"That would be cruel."

"But would it be accurate?"

"No. Of course not."

"Then you acknowledge that to be female one does not require a uterus?"

"Yes."

"I rest my case."

"I'm not certain I understand what just happened," I say.

"I think it best that we cease our sessions. Effective immediately."

"But I've only been here for ten minutes."

"You may stay for the remaining forty, but I will not engage you. It is not my job to do your work for you. It is not my job to make you woke. That's on you."

"Isn't it your job, though? Isn't that precisely your job?"

"If it ain't woke, don't fix it," she says.

I decide to wait the remaining forty minutes in silence. Therapy is not for me, but I will not let Dr. Malgodown win.

CHAPTER 23

I WANDER THE STREETS of New York, barely recognizing this place I have for so long called home. This once living, messy, broken, sick, dirty, creative metropolis, teeming with dreamers and grifters, hopheads and whores, has been transformed into a tourist park, an unaffordable, greedy Mecca for the moneyed and the rube. The city's essential theater corrupted beyond recognition, a bloated, fetid corpse dressed in spangles, its only value as a facile money grab. Let's dance for the yokels in from Kansas. Let's pretend there is still such a thing as a soul. Let's pretend we are not the dead entertaining the dead.

Everything is money now. It's the only thing we understand. Residents of flyover states read weekend box office numbers. When I was young, a movie or a play or a book or—*Jesus, was anyone ever so young*—a painting could change the world. Literally. Change the goddamn world. No longer. Now we shuck and jive. Actors dress in tights and pretend they can fly to amuse the differently mentally abled masses. If we are offered an "art" film, it is in the package of some phony "tough-minded" naturalism directed by a twenty-five-year-old trust-fund kid or perhaps some wacky surreal nonsense inspired by the infantile fantasy movies of a Charlie Kaufman—

A bike messenger crashes into me, sends me flying into a falafel cart, calls me an asshole, rides off. I stand, brush myself off.

—or that one who made that movie with Jake Gillibrand and an oh-so-menacing man in a rabbit costume.

Oh, where are the Ingos of today? Where is Ingo when he is so sorely needed to save us from ourselves? Ingo, who foresaw the future, who understood on some gut level that the artificial would insinuate itself into our lives and, moment by moment, step by step, imperceptibly, replace the authentic. That artifice would come to destroy us. He knew we were evolving into a world in which the plumbing of human emotion, this vital, necessary function of art, would be appropriated by business, by government, by opportunists in order to control, to limit, to malign the human spirit. Now I have, through my own carelessness and perhaps my own ambition, destroyed this last great hope of civilization—a singular work by a man both completely outside and completely inside this travesty we call popular culture, a man who, because of his own struggles, his own alienation, his race maybe, was able to show us ourselves from outside of ourselves: the de Tocqueville of our collective unconscious. The thing Jung wrote about has been commandeered by corporations. Yes, we all have the same dreams now, but that is because we all watch *Grey's Anatomy*. We all live in Shondaland, for the love of God. Now we dream of Tide and Buick. We long to be Brad Pitt or Angelina Jolie. Our shadow self is Scar from *The Lion King*, and rather than struggle to incorporate even that anemic animated cartoon darkness into our being, we attempt to eradicate it, because Disney has taught us that Scar is evil and must be destroyed. But in this wasteland in which we find ourselves wandering, in which our faith is continuously tested, in which the manna from heaven seems to be absurdity, in which the *de rigueur* mode of existence is jockeying for position, in which the only hope for fame for most is announcing themselves to the world as victims, I find myself hopeful. If we can only say no, no to the games we are being bullied into playing, no to the aspirations we are told to have, no to the dreams we are told to dream, then maybe we can find one another in simplicity and truth, before it is too late!

IT IS TOO late.

Now in my life there is something wrong with every moment. Every moment is a rebirth into awfulness. Every moment is its own thing, its own world, its own lifetime, and what will come next is hidden and what came before is gone. In this moment, there's a new ache in my body or a new crack going up the living room wall or this room needs painting again or I have no ideas or I don't know nearly enough to contribute anything of value. There is a famine somewhere or a million murders in an ethnic cleanse or an uncontrolled fire in the mountains or my gnawing, corrosive anger or stupid, greedy people or a terribly sick child or a homeless person's foot, swollen into a gangrenous black balloon. Where did my time go? I wonder. This is what I wonder in the midst of all this horror. Where did all *my* time go? And I am further ashamed for obsessing about my minuscule problems. My psychotic depression.

Then, as if on cue, the voices start.

Muffled and distant they talk about Slammy's. They tell me how good it is. They implore me to go there to eat. I worry I am going crazy. I become afraid to leave my apartment. As the lightbulbs burn out one by one, rather than buy replacements, I switch the dead ones out so there's always a working one above my bed, which is where I now spend all my time, like Proust. When the final bulb dies, I move to my tiny back porch, which butts up against the tenement next door. The light from my neighbor's window is the only light bright enough for me to read by. The Slammy's voice is getting louder:

How can something be both one hundred percent beef and one hundred percent love? Slammy's. You do the math.

I'm worried. Something terrible is happening, some sort of mental illness or neural malfunction. The voice is female. Can a voice in one's head sound like a different gender? I should call my schizophrenic friend Mindy Milkman. He would know. Maybe this voice defines itself as male even though it appears female to me. It is not up to me to gender the voices in my head. I should sit down and listen for a change.

When you eat at Slammy's, it's not the meals that are happy, it's you.

I believe this is a sly reference to the Happy Meal that McDonald's restaurants offer. However, I am not certain.

My landlord, Sid Fields, pounds on my door, demanding rent. I do not have it. I pretend I'm not home, but this ruse will not work forever.

The building that abuts mine is so close that, if I were inclined, I could with my fist break the window of the woman living there. I often think I should, although I don't know why I am so inclined. Instead, I peek into her tenement apartment from my porch. I don't mean to; it is just that it's right there and sometimes she isn't wearing much. I understand that surreptitiously (or otherwise) looking at women is unacceptable, and I do not engage in it as a habit, but sometimes it happens due to proximity.

Slammy's. We're in a New York state of mind.

I hear this one over and over in that same female voice, with slight variations in tone and emphasis. It is difficult to focus on anything else. I'm worried for my sanity.

We're taking a bite out of the Big Apple. Come take a bite out of us. Slammy's. We're here for you to eat.

We're taking a bite out of the Big Apple. Come take a bite out of us. Slammy's. We're here for you to eat.

We're taking a bite out of the Big Apple. Come take a bite out of us. Slammy's. We're here for you to eat.

We're taking a bite—

Suddenly and thankfully the voice stops. I can breathe again. Then the woman next door appears in the window and looks out, causing me to leap behind my chair and surreptitiously watch her from there. She wears only a T-shirt and panties. The T-shirt features an anthropomorphic hammer. It seems so familiar to me, this smiling hammer. Why? Why does it—

Oh Lord, it's the Slammy's mascot. She's wearing the Slammy's mascot. What the hell is happening? She hears me gasp, spots me, and opens her window.

"You there, in the shadows!" she says, cheerfully.

"Yes?" I say, from behind the chair.

"Are you watching me?"

"I'm . . . cleaning."

"In the dark."

"Yes."

"Step out where I can see you better, yes?"

I do. For some reason, I find it titillating to be ordered about by this panty-clad beauty.

"What's your name?" she asks.

Her voice is so familiar to me. A former lover? The cashier at my favorite CVS?

"I go by B. I do that so as not to wield my mascu—"

"Listen, B. I'm Marjorie, Marjorie Morningstar."

"Like the movie with—"

"Never saw it. Say, B., do you like living in that fancy building over there?"

I like that she's not letting me finish my sen—

"I've recently stumbled onto a good gig," she says. "I've been doing voiceover work for a small regional fast-food company that's been purchased by an international conglomerate and is about to go national and therefore be thrust into the national spotlight."

"Wait, you don't mean Slammy's?"

"You've heard of our little enterprise, B.?"

"Yes!"

I'm not insane! It's her! It's her voice!

"Anyway, I'm thinking of moving to a nicer place, and I was wondering about your building."

"It's pricey. I really can't afford my rent anymore."

She looks off, nods for a bit, seemingly in thought. I steal a glance at her pantied crotch. I want it so much. Why is the female crotch in its pantied form so magnificent?

"Say, B., this may be a silly idea, but what if we switch?"

"I don't—"

"Like the Prince and the Pauper, or something, but with apartments. The Slum and the Plum? You see? Plum as in something desirable. The slum being my place, the plum being your place."

"That's good," I admit.

I might love her.

"If we take each other's apartment through the proper channels, the rents are going to shoot up exponentially," she says.

I want to tell her exponential is not the word she wants, but . . . I love her.

"*But* . . . and hear me out, if we secretly switch, moving our stuff through this very window, keep the original names on our leases, the rents will stay as they are."

"I don't know," I say.

"I pay eight hundred and fifty dollars, B."

"Wow."

"Exactly."

"Um—"

"And I've already paid this month."

"Um."

"You don't have to pay me back. My gift to you."

"Um."

"I don't care that you haven't paid yours. I'm flush. Thanks to Slammy's, I'm shortly to be rolling in it."

"Do you have working lightbulbs at your place? I only ask because—"

"I have five. Five fixtures, five working bulbs. Three more at the ready in the kitchen cabinet, if you need 'em," she says.

"Can I see what it looks like?"

"Sure."

She steps aside and I climb through. It smells close and female and I like it very much. It is small. But I am only one person, after all, if that. How much space does one person need? John Fante lived for seven years in a phone booth in the Bunker Hill neighborhood of Los Angeles, about which he wrote so movingly in his short story "Please Deposit an Additional Five Cents to Continue Living Here, Bandini." I am no Fante, not even close. Neither am I a Dante nor a Jaime Escalante. I am only a little man of meager accomplishment, perhaps a Tom Conti. I look around: one room and a small bathroom made smaller by four inches of soundproofing foam adhered to the walls and ceiling. Even the mirror is covered, which pleases me.

"It's in here that I do my audio recordings," she says.

"May I keep the soundproofing up?"

"Sure."

I don't explain my reasons, but the truth is I often suffer from embarrassing gastrointestinal distress.

I can live here, I think. And to be frank, there is something erotic about switching lives with this pulchritudinous voiceover lady. Perhaps this debasement will lead to some sort of tryst with her down the pike. I cannot be certain that she is currently flirting with me, but I suspect she is and I am usually the last to know, so . . . How many times have I found out years later that some woman was trying desperately to bed me while I remained "clueless," as the kids nowadays say.

"I'll take it," I say.

Maybe she winks. It happens quickly and I can't be certain. I wink (back?). She eyes me with a suspicious squint, much like Spanky from the *Our Gang* comedies, which is sexy on her.

We spend the next day climbing back and forth through the window, switching our belongings. I am forced to leave much of mine in what is now her apartment, as there is no room for it in her place, which is now mine. But I do take my five-thousand-book library, which I cannot be without. And my funerary urns. Consequently, my bed, a California twin, will not fit. Instead, I devise a "sleeping chair" using a system of leather belts and bungee cords to hold me in place at night. It's all temporary, I tell myself, until I get back on my feet and back into a bed.

But I can't seem to get back on my feet. And one by one, the working bulbs in my new apartment burn out. Then the three spares. Darkness prevails.

CHAPTER 24

So after these three months of pacing in my tiny, pitch-black apartment, I start to believe I might be hallucinating. The apartment looks as if it is stuffed to the ceiling with black wool. I huddle in corners, in an attempt to avoid the needles and apes hiding within. I decide enough is enough. I force myself to leave. The hallway is filled with black wool. I exit the building and hail a black-wool-filled taxi and ride through black-wool New York to see a new therapist. This one I had spotted listed as a technical adviser in the credits of *A Beautiful Mind*, a film by Ronson Howard that I've come to recognize is brilliant (late to that party!), about a guy who goes "mental," then learns how to love and gets a big prize (not sure which, maybe an Oscar?) and gives a speech to an audience of people, one of whom is, for some obscure reason, Jennifer Connelly in old-age makeup. I didn't entirely understand that part, but I think it's because I had gone to the bathroom. I pieced it together and decided she was on her way to perform in a local theater production but didn't want to miss the speech, so she put her makeup on before. The technical adviser/therapist (she's the one who famously said "more crazy blinking" to actor Russ Crow) listens to my story and immediately suggests ketamine therapy. She recommends this in conjunction with ayahuasca therapy and that in conjunction with hypnotherapy. In addition to helping with my depression, she says, the combination might jog my memory about the Ingo film, which she feels could be at the crux of my distress. It all seems reasonable to me, possibly because I have become addicted to Percocet (discovered in the Voiceover Lady's medicine cabinet) and am also sort of "mental" myself due to several personal issues. In hindsight, I think she might have been punking me, as the kids say nowadays. I find it highly unprofessional for a therapist to punk a depressed Percocet addict, but I sign the release for her TV show *The Doctor Is In(sane)!* anyway because I understand everyone has to make a living. In any event, I go ahead and make the necessary appointments with the psychiatrist, hypnotherapist, and shaman. Coincidentally, they are all available to see me on the same day, so it is fortunate they have offices in the same medical building in Midtown.

The psychiatrist, Dr. Muddy Kabir, sees me at eleven. After asking me how much ketamine I think would do me (I say maybe one glass to start), he immediately jumps in with probing questions such as, "What are you doing after?" and "Are you into shopping?" and "Do you like to hang out?" Within seconds, the ketamine has enabled a breakthrough. It turns out the depression can be traced back to my failure to get my last film project off the ground. I don't even remember the project until the ketamine sets in, and then there it is in full Technicolor projected in my head, like it had actually been made. It's the story of a man who wakes up one morning to discover there's no record of him ever having existed. It's like a dark fantasy, which I think is very cool. Like dystopian but with a really cool twist. So he has no money and can't get a job without a Social Security number, so he resorts to stealing just to survive. One day, he steals an old lady, and he accidentally kills her by repeatedly stabbing her until she is killed. But he's a good man and it was just the desperation that drove him to this brutal, senseless act. So he feels really guilty and decides to turn himself in, but the police can't arrest him because of some loophole about them not being able to arrest a person who doesn't officially exist, so he takes his case to the Supreme Court, and it ends with him giving an impassioned speech before the teary-eyed justices about how no one is nobody and if he can't pay for his crimes then that is very unfair because everyone deserves to be able to repent if they kill an old lady or even otherwise. It's called *Who Shall Remain Nameless* and it's actually a metaphor for the modern world in which we now live, how technology isolates us, and how we are all cogs in this brutal machine we call civilization without air quotes but it should have air quotes. And big business. To say it's a powder keg is an understatement. One executive even admitted to me that he'd totally lose his job if he financed this movie. How's that for a powder keg?

From the psychiatrist on three, I head straight to the shaman's office on five. I am still feeling the ketamine, mostly in the way my hands have too many fingers and also my fingers have too many fingers. Plus I find myself profoundly in love with Dr. Kabir, the psychiatrist, which is almost certainly a result of simple transference, but he does give me a locket with his photo. I don't want to make too much of that, but it seems like perhaps he likes me, too. I'm pretty sure there was a point in the session when we were both drinking ketamine and giggling. I'll have to work out my feelings later.

The shaman's receptionist wears a nurse's tunic emblazoned with cute little cartoon hallucinations in soothing pastel colors. It feels condescending. We are not children here, I think. This is a serious adult exploration into the psyche. Then I see there are indeed several children in the waiting room. Maybe it is the ketamine, though, because they are adult-sized and three of them wear top hats and monocles.

I am ushered into Sweat Lodge A along with two of the giant children. The shaman, Dr. Aclarado, greets us, tells us to sit, then goes around the room asking each of us what we hope to accomplish today. First up is one of the children, who says, "I hope to learn my true nature." Alcarado shrugs, unimpressed. The second large child looks panicked. You can tell he had had the same answer and has to quickly come up with something better. "That first kid's dumb," he begins. "I just hope to learn how to be present in my life." Acaraldo says, "Yawn." It is my turn. The ketamine is causing my nipples to migrate toward the center of my chest, which is not as unpleasant as you might think. I stare into his two monocles (when did he take them off the kids?) and say, "Listen, Acalrado, since you don't exist, fuck off!" It is a bluff, but it must've worked because a brass band marches into the room playing "Guantanamera," confetti falls from the ceiling, and Acaradlo shows me his strong brown teeth in a wide grin. Suddenly my vision blurs, and I realize now I am wearing the monocles, which are not my prescription. Aclarado weeps unashamedly from his newly unencumbered eyes and calls me his *hijo*, which I believe means horse. Then he hands out glasses of ayahuasca all around, including to the band members, and turns the portable heat lamps on max. Soon I begin to sweat. Acarlado chants something that sounds like a heavily booted man stomping on Plexiglas, but with a Spanish accent. The room spans or whatever the plural of spin is. I see Dr. Kabir in his underwear going on about the summer house in Maine he hopes someday to share with me. I understand that we are all one thing, an intricate, interwoven tapestry, that all past, present, and future coexist, that it's all OK, that you should keep your wallet in your front pocket to thwart pickpockets but that it doesn't matter that much because we're all one thing, so if a pickpocket takes your wallet, you still have it because the pickpocket is YOU.

Acaradol goes around the room asking, "Why so sad?" I say, "I feel like a pickpocket. But also a goat and a flute and a cloud and a leg and the inside of a cereal box and a raindrop and a molecule of benzene and the number 43 and—"

"Yes, yes," interrupts La Carado, looking at his watch, which I also feel like and tell him so. "I have another session in an hour." Which I also feel like, but I keep that I feel like his other session in an hour to myself because he looks mad. One of the giant kids, who is now a farmer, says that he realizes that illusion is an illusion, which drives me crazy because he is clearly trying to top my thing. So I say, "I don't even know what that means." To which he responds, "It means simply this, old man: When you evolve past recognizing that the material world is an illusion, you recognize the truth, that everything simply is, that nothing is a symbol for anything else, that thoughts are thoughts and mountains are mountains. I wouldn't expect you to understand that, being a simple farmer." I tell him that he is the farmer, not I, just look in the mirror. Then we fight in slow motion for about a half an hour until Aclaraldo sprays us with a fire extinguisher. My overalls and straw hat are drenched, and an epiphany is on the tip of my tongue when Alclaraldo says, "I'm sorry, our time's up." He hurriedly ushers us out of Sweat Lodge A. Next thing I know, I am in the medical building hallway, drenched and trying to remember if the eighth floor is above or below the fifth floor. After a brief consultation with the Google vertical map app on my phone, I find the office of hypnotherapist M. Barassini.

It's a small, dank space, dressed up like a black box theater. An enormous papier-mâché eyeball hangs on the back wall. I find a seat in the audience next to an attractive Asian (American?) woman. The place is pretty well full up, so my choice of seat doesn't seem as if I'm trying to make time with her. But I do think about it. She is very attractive. Her pixie cut and Anna May Wong fringe give her a domineering look, and I fantasize about submitting to her sexually. I have not in the past thought of myself as a submissive except briefly for my three years as a money pig to Madam Ca-Ching, but something has clicked in my brain after my interaction with Marjorie Morningstar, the voiceover artist, and I imagine this pulchritudinous Asian vixen commanding me after the show with a simple "Follow me." I will find myself in her loft—a tasteful open floor plan, stainless-steel countertops in the white-tile kitchen area. Severe, masculine, yet profoundly feminine in its masculinity. She orders me to my knees, then goes about her personal business as if she were alone, pouring a vodka, squeezing a slice of lime into it. She slips out of her clothes as she walks around, doing things, sipping from her glass. It doesn't feel like she's ignoring me; it feels as if I'm not there. There's something so highly charged about getting to witness her alone and knowing I'm not worth her being self-conscious. She scratches the inside of her upper thigh as she passes me, not in a provocative way, but because she has an itch. That does not stop me from wishing I were her hand. Oh, to be her hand. Or her thigh. Oh, to be her thigh. I imagine she will eventually summon me to her as she sits manspread in that leather wing chair in the corner. *Hands and knees*, she will say, bored, as I stand to make my way over. I will get onto my hands and knees and make my way to her. She—

The lights go down. Spooky recorded music starts: Mussorgsky's *Gnomus* played on glass harmonica, if I am correct. The stage lights click on, and Barassini is there in a puff of smoke, white turban, tails, and an Order of Military Medical Merit medallion. After he performs what appears to be a sort of solo court dance for several minutes, he stops and faces us.

"Good evening," he says with an inexplicable accent. Maybe Italian mixed with that whistling language of Northern Turkey.

I glance discreetly over at my soon-to-be Asian (American?) Mistress. She does not return my look.

"I am Monsieur Barassini. In the tradition of the great Franz Polgar, I shall attempt to perform some delightful feats of mentalism, hypnotism, and Hellstromism for you today. As many of you have come to understand, the mind is an extraordinarily powerful and sadly underutilized organ. If you have any doubt of how underused, just ask your teenager who Dwight David Eisenhower was."

The audience chuckles. I don't. Neither does my Mistress. I am pleased. She is, of course, better than that feeble joke. I imagine she laughs with complete abandon at genuinely funny things: Ionesco, W. C. Fields, Buñuel movies—those works that reveal the true horror and hopelessness of existence. Oh, she would throw her head back at Fields's *It's a Gift* or Buñuel's *The Exterminating Angel*, mouth wide, revealing her perfect teeth, her perfectly sharp canines, the pink, pink, pink tissues of her oral cavity, and laugh and—

My Mistress raises her hand.

"Madam, please, if you will," says Barassini.

Barassini gestures for her to join him on the stage. Apparently, he had asked for a volunteer while I was lost in my Mistress's guffawing maw. She almost glides toward the stage. I must say, in my fantasy, I predicted her walk precisely. She is, however, taller than I had imagined. So much taller. So much goddamn taller. All the better. Barassini takes her hand. Suddenly I want him dead. It is all I can do to remain seated, to not run to the stage and stab him through the eye with my 1941 dusty red Parker Duofold Fountain Pen, and I mean *his* eye, not that preposterous papier-mâché one hanging above him. This would, of course, destroy my prized rhodium nib, and I am OK with that. He speaks, and I snap out of it.

"*Enchanté*," he says. "May I ask your name?"

"Tsai," she says.

Images of the gorgeous young Tsai Chin, posing in fishnets and a leotard, photographed in spectacular black and white by the late great Michael Ward. Her hair a tousled—

"What a beautiful name," says Barassini.

What a clunky, uninteresting thing to have said, Barassini, you pathetically lecherous Turkish-whistling prat.

Then it hits me. Is it possible Barassini is a homosexual? For he is not sufficiently bowled over by Mistress Tsai's profound female maleness. She defies binariness. She spits in the face of gender. And gender says, "Thank you, Mistress, may I have another?"

"I am going to attempt to read your mind," he explains.

"Why not," she says.

Why not. What a beautiful, nonchalant response. Go ahead, Mr. Magician. I'm game. You don't stand a chance.

"We've not met before. Is that correct?"

"No."

Barassini studies her. He asks her to look into his eyes. She does, without hesitation or self-consciousness.

"You have suffered a loss recently?"

She nods, not impressed, not unimpressed, not ununimpressed. I could go on indefinitely. She gives him nothing. He's fishing. Who hasn't suffered a loss recently? I certainly have. I have suffered the loss of my life's work, my dignity, my apartment, my girlfriend, my job, my dog, my nose, my *Grund für die Existenz*.

"I'm getting the letter *M*. Does that mean anything to you?"

Again she nods. Again he's fishing. Everyone knows something that begins with *M*. I've suffered a loss of my memory. There's the *M* I've lost, putz.

"Michael?" he asks.

She nods. OK, that was good. But still, everyone knows a Michael. I know seventeen Michaels, four of whom died recently, two of whom were recently lost while camping, one of whom is in hiding. If he had said Melchior and been correct, I might've been impressed. Might've. But I know six Melchiors, three of whom are fairly recently dead, so even then.

"Did you lose someone named Michael?"

"Yes," she says, but betrays no emotion.

God, she's beautiful. I would gladly be her vaginal suppository.

"He was not related to you. He was . . . *young*. A child?"

"Yes."

"You were his teacher, weren't you?"

"Yes."

"I'm so very sorry that he died. So young. So young."

"He was five. A car accident. Difficult for his parents, of course."

She says all this matter-of-factly. The audience doesn't know how to respond. They want to applaud Barassini's apparent skill, but they don't want to applaud young Michael's death; it's a dilemma. There is a terrible, profoundly uncomfortable silence. I, for one, have my suspicions about the whole shebang. She must be a confederate. What I just witnessed would have been impossible otherwise.

"Thank you, Tsai," he whistles. "Very much indeed."

She makes her way back to her seat and now, finally, the audience applauds, respectfully, soberly. I watch her for tells. She makes her way down the row of seats toward me, gingerly avoiding legs and feet. She passes me, her magnificent rear end so close to my face that for that moment I can think of nothing else. Oh, to press myself into it. Then she passes me to reveal an older man onstage, who is being quite theatrically hypnotized with a watch or a pendant. I'm not certain. The truth is I can barely see the stage now, my focus completely shifted to Tsai. Tsai. It occurs to me her name sounds like sigh. I've matched my inhalations to her exhalations. My goal, to take her breath into me, to bring Tsai into me, to absorb molecules of Tsai into my cells, to be transformed by them, to be owned by them. It is a different kind of breath play but no less erotic than the type I practiced with my lover Esther Mercenaire at Harvard, where I went. I pass the remainder of Barassini's show deeply immersed in my Tsai fantasy: waiting on her, being ignored by her, being humiliated by her. I develop a story line. It comes to me as a fantastical solution to my problem of having no possible way to insinuate myself into Tsai's life: I happen upon a supernatural curio in an antique shoppe. Perhaps a music box or an ancient perfume atomizer. I petition it to help me. I don't want or expect Tsai to love me. In fact, if she did, it would diminish her so terribly in my estimation that I could respect her no longer. I just want to serve her. The magical entity plays a song or sprays a mist on me (depending on whether it is a music box or atomizer) and I find myself face-to-face with Tsai. It seems I am now a salesclerk at a department store and I am ringing her up. I am only able to act as a salesclerk might, even though I am aware that it is me inside this new body. Tsai leaves, and I remain this salesclerk until such time as Tsai is served by anyone else: a waitress, a DMV employee, a plumber, a shoe saleswoman, a postal worker. Any interaction she has with a service worker, I become that person. Bouncing from body to body, from life to life, all in service to Tsai. Sometimes she yells at me, sometimes she is pleasant, asks me how my day is going, sometimes she ignores me, but all of the interactions are impersonal. I get very hard imagining this scenario. Very hard. I try to parse this fantasy—what does it mean?—and in the process, I ruin it for myself.

The truth is I know I could never be of any interest to her and, I suspect, anyone in whom I might be interested. I am an ant. Even with an atomizer genie on my team, I am not able to fantasize myself younger or better looking or smarter or richer. Yet somehow I can fantasize myself easily into an even more impossible scenario, a body-hopping nightmare. I guess the truth is I crave humiliation. What is ironic or at least curious is that in my actual life, humiliation is the thing I most fear and I most experience. Yet I am not happy. Why?

CHAPTER 25

After the show, I make my way to the office of M. Barassini, licensed hypnotist and hypnotherapist, for my session. The walls of the anteroom are adorned with framed posters of M. Barassini, the great mentalist/hypnotist/Hellstromist, featuring dramatic nineteenth-century-seeming illustrations of what I assume is Barassini in a purple turban staring deeply into the viewer's eyes. The posters do not instill confidence, and, as I am still in the throes of a decent ayahuasca wallop, I find them rather terrifying. There are as well, however, several framed diplomata, one from the Harverd College of Hypnotism, which I've heard is an excellent school, although not affiliated in any way with Harvard. Barassini might, however, have been a legacy admission, in which case I will withhold judgment. The door to the inner office opens, and Barassini pokes out his head. Without the turban, he appears professorial, avuncular, anemic, somewhat staid, partially paralyzed, and handsome, with a bit of a twinkle in his eye, the right one, possibly due to cataract surgery.

"Mr. Rosenberg," he says.

"Yes. Although I prefer the gender-neutral honorific Mx."

"Quite right," he says. "Won't you come in, Mx. Rosenberg?"

I enter his office. Did I feel compelled to enter his office through some sort of hypnotic control? Or did I enter because he asked me to and that is what one does? Either way, I felt a distinct lessening of personal agency at that moment. Should I be concerned about this or is it, in fact, encouraging to know he is perhaps so good at his craft that I don't even know he's practicing it?

I sit on the couch.

"That's where I sit," he says.

"Oh," I say. "I'm sorry."

I get up, scan the office. There's nowhere else to sit other than behind his desk.

"Do you want me to sit at your desk?"

"No. That's also where I sit, although not now."

"Then where?"

He gestures toward a Murphy chair folded into the wall.

"Oh," I say.

"For the work we will do together, the best results come when the client is not so comfortable as to become sleepy."

"I see," I say.

I unfold the chair and sit.

"Welcome to my suite of offices," he says. "What I practice here is something different from hypnosis. I call it hypgnosis."

"Hypnosis?"

"No. Hypgnosis."

"I'm not hearing any difference," I say.

"There's an additional letter but it's silent."

"What letter?"

"*G*."

"Oh."

"No. *G*," he corrects.

"Right. So where does it go?"

"Oh. It goes between the *p* and the *n*."

"Oh. I get it. Like gnosis," I say.

"Are you saying gnosis or nosis?"

"Gnosis. Nosis isn't a thing."

"Then yes. Do you know what gnosis means?"

"Yes."

"What?"

"Are you quizzing me? Knowledge. Primarily in the spiritual sense. Knowledge of God and of oneself," I say.

"Perfect," he says. "Now tell me why you're here."

And just like that I feel compelled to tell him. What is this strange power he has? If I am to be fully candid, I must admit to feeling a slight tingle in my groin with this giving over of authority to him.

"I need to remember a movie I saw in as much detail as I possibly can."

"Interesting," he says. "I can help you with this, of course. I frequently work with clients hoping to recover memories of abuse, lost time, past lives."

Past lives? I think. Is this man a crackpot?

"I know what you're thinking," he says. "After all, I am also a mentalist, or as you call us, mind reader."

He is right; I do call them mind readers. I also call them charlatans.

"Or charlatans," he says, chuckling. "As you also call us. I've heard it all before, Mx. Rosenberg."

He is good, whatever he is.

"Listen," he continues, "I can help you. By putting you into a state of deep hypgnotic relaxation, I can help you access memories you feel certain are forever lost. You should know that in addition to working with alien abductees and past-lifers—both of which I believe in, by the way—I also work with the NYPD and several other major police departments."

"Oh," I say, impressed. "What is your success rate?"

"I do filing for them and I'm pretty damn accurate. The point is," Barassini says, "that for this to work, I need you to trust me fully. Are there any concerns you have about me or the process at this point that I can try to assuage?"

"I guess I am concerned that you could potentially plant false memories in my unconscious while I am under hypnosis."

"Now why would I do that?" he says.

"I'm not saying you would. I'm just responding to the assuage thing you said. It's just something that crossed my mind. I need to remember this film accurately."

"Look," he says, "I'm a professional with advanced degrees. I take issue with your charge."

"There's no charge. I'm not charging you. I was just hoping there might be some way you could put my mind at ease about that issue."

"Y'know, I don't think this is going to work out," he says. "You should leave."

"I don't want to leave!" I say.

"Then take it back."

"Take it back?"

"Take back that you are worried I'll plant false memories in your brain."

"I take it back."

"So you don't think I'd ever do that?"

"I guess not."

"Good. I hope that made you feel better."

He smiles at me. And, bizarrely, it did make me feel better. I play the conversation over in my head. All sorts of alarms go off. And yet, I feel calm, open to him, ready.

"So shall we begin?" he asks.

"Yes."

"Good. All right. Now, the film you want to remember—what is it called?"

"It is nameless, really. It is bigger than names."

"What should we call it for the purposes of our 'conversations'?"

"*Funny Weather*," I say, though I'm not sure why.

"OK. *Funny Weather*. Now, *Funny Weather* exists in your brain. Fully. Pristinely. Uncorrupted. It can be replayed in its entirety, as if you were watching the film again."

"Is that true? Because I've read that memory is not at all like a recording but rather—"

"I'd like you to leave my office right now."

"I don't want to leave."

"Then say it's true."

"It's true."

And now I do think it's true. It's odd. I am, by and far, a contrarian. It is my stock in trade as a film theorist-cum-critic, to question everything, to challenge norms, to eviscerate filmic clichés where I find them. And yet when Barassini bullies me into accepting ideas I frankly know to be fictions, I suddenly believe him. More so, I take great comfort in believing him. Perhaps Barassini is the father I never had, even though I had a father and, in point of fact, he was very much like Barassini. Maybe Barassini is the father I always had. Oh, Daddy.

"Grand," he says. "Now I want you to look deeply into my eyes and listen closely to my words. Feel my words enter your psyche. Open yourself up to my words. Feel them go deep within you, touching parts of your mind that have never been touched before. You are grateful for my words, for the confidence they instill. You find it comforting to be controlled this way. My words caress you. They own you. Do you feel that?"

"I do."

"Good. You want to please my words, don't you?"

"Yes."

"Say it."

"I want to please your words."

"And you will. By going deep into yourself, deeper than you've ever gone. Will you do that?"

"Yes."

"Good. Tell me what you see."

"The Magellanic penguin. Native to the Falkland—"

"Deeper."

"*Election*, a 1999 film by Alexander Payne. It—"

"Deeper."

"My mother hit me because I was whinging. Always whinging."

"We'll come back to that. Deeper."

"A black-and-white image on a screen."

"Tell me."

"I don't know. It feels vast. Dark. It goes on forever. Snow on a television screen. Static."

"That movie is part of you now. Once the cream is stirred into the coffee, it cannot be separated."

"I don't follow," I say.

"The movie can only be revisited as it has integrated with your mind. This is the law of entropy."

"I just wanted that thing like when you help a witness to a crime remember a license plate."

"If that's all you want, go down the street to Hypno Joe's. He'll set you up nicely."

"OK."

I stand up and head to the door.

"But I think you want more."

"I don't."

"You want what's true."

"Well, sure, but—"

"Fine. I guess I was mistaken about you. You'll do well with Hypno Joe."

"OK," I say, grabbing the doorknob. "Do you have his address or is it like a storefront?"

"But let me just say this: Art attracts us only by what it reveals of our most secret self."

"That's—"

"Godard, yes. Your hero, no?"

"But how did you know?"

"Knowledge. Gnosis. This film only exists because *you* watched it and because of what it revealed about *you*. If you want to bring it to the surface in all its complexity, you have to mine your psyche. But that's not what you want. You'll do well with Hypno Joe. I think David Manning of *The Ridgefield Press* uses his services."

"But David Manning is a fictitious critic invented by the Sony Pictures marketing department to provide glowing reviews for their poorly reviewed pictures."

"Oh, is he? I wasn't aware."

"So then how could he—"

"I don't know. All I'm saying is that I would be careful about who I let into my brain. *I* wouldn't want to end up a fictional, robotized, zombie tool of a soulless corporation."

"I'm thinking maybe I should do the work with you," I say.

"Only if you want to."

"I think I do."

"You're getting sleepy."

"What? Like right now?"

"We should get going on this. It's a long process."

"How long?"

"It took Ingo ninety years to make. Should you devote any less time to remembering it?"

"I don't have ninety years! How did you know it took Ingo ninety years? I didn't tell you that. I don't think I even told you Ingo's name."

"I'll write down Hypno Joe's address for you."

"No. I'm ready."

"You're getting sleepy."

And I am. Just the simple suggestion from this master of hypnosis—

"Hypgnosis," he corrects.

—*hypgnosis* sends me swirling lazily around the drain of hebetudinousness.

CHAPTER 26

"YOU ARE IN Ingo's apartment. Tell me what you feel," says Barassini.

"The chair is hard. I feel it pressing into my buttock bones. The room is dark, musty. I feel anxiety. I want this movie to be great. I want it to change my life, both in the watching and in the eventual heralding. If it's terrible, I have gained nothing. I am where I was. Worse off because time has passed and I am that much closer to my grave. And I'll have to tell Ingo that I loved it when it will be clear that I did not. I am not a good actor in that I cannot be dishonest. It is my curse that others always know exactly how I feel. I guess in a way that might make me a brilliant actor, but only if I am playing a character who is scripted to feel exactly as I feel at every moment of the filming. Maybe then I would be the best actor who has ever lived. I'm certain I would. I should audition for that role. I'll look in *Backstage* later. The projector starts up. It whirs and sputters as a rectangle of light appears before me on the screen, followed by the scratchy black leader, followed by the China Girl. Wait, was that Tsai? Go back!"

But the film continues to unspool, inexorably into the future, the China Girl replaced by a new image every twenty-fourth of a second as a procession of ¹⁄₂₄ths of a second passes before my eyes into history. I must record this fully. Barassini is correct: Every movie is experienced differently by every person, and by rights, each person should get to have his or her or thon's experience of it. A movie is seen differently by each individual, but a movie that has been seen by no one does not exist. It is as the thoughts of a dead person. They cannot be accessed, so they do not exist. Therefore, for Ingo's film to exist, I must tell it, and to tell it, I must tell it through the filter of my psyche.

So this will not be a novelization. A novelization is a lesser thing. Just as the book is always better than the movie (with the exception of Truffaut's one decent film, *Tirez sur le Pianiste* [1960]), the movie is always better than the novelization. There must be a term for what I am about to do. What do you call something that is an interpretation, a critique, an embellishment, a deepening? Something that compares favorably to the experience of a moviegoer. I am, after all, a critic who will watch a movie only once and, whenever possible, in a public theater with a paying audience. I insist on paying fair-market value. That is the true moviegoing experience. A movie is not only the image on the screen, the sound from the speakers. It is the translation of all this by the brain. It is the social milieu. It is the year you see it, your age, the state of your marriage. It is what happened on the way to the theater, what you expect to happen after, it is who is next to you on each side. It is how they smell. It is who sits in front of you. Who is or isn't kicking your seat from behind. It is your worry about the call from the doctor. It is that you got laid. Or didn't. Or are about to. Or know you never will again. It is your envy: of the filmmaker, of the couple necking down front. It is the popcorn. The Goobers. That you have to go to the bathroom. That someone is eating a smelly tuna sandwich. Did they smuggle it in? It doesn't seem fair, that the cheaters get the sandwiches and the rest of us get shit on. It is your suspension of disbelief. The scene that motivates an eye roll. It is your critique of the acting. It is you trying to remember where you've seen that actor before. It is your prediction of what's going to happen next in the film. It is your pride when you are proven correct. It is your surprise when the filmmaker defies your expectation. It is life, which you only get to live once. You prepare for it, but it will surprise you anyway. The film is predetermined but revealed to you only through time, incrementally. This makes you think it is a living thing, a thing for which you can change the outcome. You yell at the actors onscreen. You clench your teeth as if it will help. And even though the movie is predetermined, the world is not. So the movie can change in this way, too. The projector could break down. Maybe this screening has a loud laugher. Maybe there will be a shooter. These chance elements are layered upon the chanceless film. So a text that encompasses all of this outer and inner experience is not a novelization. It is so much more. It is a witnessing, and it should be called that, bearing witness to the human experience—this plastic, this light, this clackety $\frac{1}{24}$th of a second through time that the film and I are traveling together but separate, neighboring solitudes. The original meaning of the word *martyr* is witness and that seems about right. A viewer is a witness; a witness is one who testifies. This will be a witnessing. Or, wait, don't I watch films seven times? By myself? In my living room? Don't I turn the television upside down? Suddenly, I'm confused. I don't—

"You're not saying anything," says Barassini.

"I'm not?"

"You're just sitting there, expressions passing across your face. At one point you looked like you were smelling a tuna sandwich, possibly."

"Yeah. Actually. Yeah. You got that, huh?"

"You're a good actor."

"It's about being in the moment."

"Listen," he continues, "I can help you. But you need to talk while you're in this state. This is the only way we can make your findings accessible to you once you awaken. I will record all that is said in here. You need to trust me."

"I guess I do have trust issues."

"You should know that in addition to working with alien abductees and past-lifers—both of which I believe in, by the way—I also work with the NYPD and several other major police departments."

"Didn't you already tell me that?"

"No."

"Huh."

I *am* impressed. In my youth, while on a Fulbright at Cambridge University, I participated in ESP studies led by the great Robert

Henry Thouless. He determined that I demonstrated the extraordinary and rare gift of Negative ESP (there has been only one other documented case, that of Johann Gergis, a fifteenth-century Flemish bellows mender). When the Zener card tests were administered to me, the results were undeniable: My guesses were incorrect ninety-nine percent of the time, so far below chance as to be astonishing. In fact, my results were impressive enough that Scotland Yard took notice and employed my talent on several occasions to help determine where they needn't bother to look for kidnapped children. For a short while, I even performed an act at the Cambridge Corn Exchange, in which I would guess the first initials of randomly chosen audience members.

"Is there someone close to you whose name begins with an *X*?" I would always ask the volunteer.

I was wrong ninety-nine percent of the time. I was always sure that there was a person in their life whose name began with an *X*. I could see it as clear as day. When I queried an audience member whose husband turned out to be the governor of Akrotiri and Dhekelia, His Excellency Xander Xavier Xerxes, Exquire, tomatoes were hurled at me and I was booed off the stage.

"The point is," Barassini says, "that for this to work, I need you to trust me fully. Are there any concerns you still have about me or the process at this point that I can try to assuage?"

"I have been slightly concerned about your pronunciation of the word *assuage*."

"Which word?"

"Assuage."

"Oh, is that how you say it?"

"Yes," I say.

He stares into my eyes.

"*Now* how do you say it?"

"Assuage."

"Good. So shall we begin?"

"Yes. Please!"

"Tell me what you see."

* * *

AND JUST LIKE that, I can see the movie again. The top-hatted doll walking against the wind. On the screen? In my brain? I can't say. But gone is the distance. Gone are the artifacts of age, the scratches, the dirt, the irregularity in exposures. The doll is here. I could seemingly touch him, but I cannot. I cannot look down and see my hand. I am, in essence, the camera. I believe that this hypnosis experiment is going to work. I watch the scene play out, exhilarated. The little boy on skates rolls by and I follow his path with my eyes. He crashes into a gas streetlamp and falls back onto his behind. He is fine! As he stumbles back up onto his wobbly skates, it occurs to me, I didn't see this before. Somehow I am looking outside the limits of the frame. I try to think back. Maybe this was in the original film. So much has happened in the film and in my life between this moment and that. But I am almost certain I did not see this in the actual film. I swivel back to the man walking against the wind and attempt an experiment. I try to circle him, to view him from his left side. I am successful. From this angle, I see a different backdrop behind him, this one also painted in Ingo's style. They are renderings of the very brownstones across East 62nd Street from the Our Lady of Peace church. I recognize those brownstones! I look up. Will I see sky? Indeed! A black-and-white rendering of clouds, but animated, moving fast and swirling. A small dot appears in the sky, soon growing larger. Is it falling? Yes. It is an amorphous blob from the original first scene. It smashes silently to the ground at my "feet." Black liquid oozes out. From this angle, I can see that it has broken open on top, revealing what appears to be viscera, tiny bones, a skull. I am shocked out of the scene. The hypnotist is watching me.

"Was I telling it this time?" I ask.

"You were."

"It's different from the movie I remember remembering."

"So it seems."

"Similar, but I feel I'm seeing more, from different angles," I say.

"Yes."

"Is that typical?"

"I've never worked through this type of issue. Most of what I do involves curbing addictions: smoking, heroin, chronic mastication."

"Masturbation?"

"No."

"I need to remember the movie as precisely as possible. This feels problematic," I say.

"There is no pure objective memory of a work of art to be had."

"It needs to be Ingo's work. It must. Maybe if I restrain myself, I can stick to the original camera angles, not stray, not explore."

"Maybe Ingo wanted you to explore. Isn't it possible he put this all in there? For you to get lost in?"

"I'm not sure I have the courage to go back," I say. "I don't want to get lost."

But I do go back in. I do get lost.

CHAPTER 27

I SEEM TO BE discovering even more details I don't recall from the viewing. Certainly they must have been perceived originally in a subliminal way. For example, the newspaper that tumbles by is dated June 30, 1908, an oddly familiar date. I cannot place it. June 30, 1908. June 30, 1908. What, if anything, occurred on that date? Something must have. There is, after all, no eventless date in history. I feel almost certain this must be so. There were the eleven skipped days in 1752 to implement the transition of calendars from Julian to Gregorian. Could those be considered eventless days? I must ask Timmy, my horologist friend. Suddenly, I am watching the top-hatted doll struggle against the wind, marveling once again at the young Ingo's nascent skill. Then I remember: the Russian explosion! June 30, 1908! Of course. It comes to me the moment I stop seeking it. There is a lesson here that belies the old biblical saw "seek and ye shall find." It should be "don't seek and ye shall find." Maybe that's too Eastern for the conventional Western mind. I know the date of the Tunguska event because I know it, but also because I did my dissertation on Maetzig's 1960 *Der Schweigende Stern* (*First Spaceship on Venus*), an unfairly maligned film shot entirely in Totalvision and scored (in the vastly superior English-language version) by the extraordinary Gordon Zahler in Totalsound. The film featured a multicultural and multigendered group of scientists decades before such diverse groupings were to become part of Western cinematic consciousness as introduced by the Wachowskis, but I digress, for the film plays in my head and I must attend to every detail. I must stay on point as I narrate because you cannot see what I am seeing, isn't that correct Dr. Barassini? Dr. Barassini?

I hear one end of a distant conversation.

Is Barassini on the phone? I can't make out the words. I need to focus on the experience at hand, but it is distracting and it annoys me to think that Barassini is not as engaged as I am with this process.

"You know I hear you saying all this Barassini stuff, right?" Barassini says, far away.

"Oh, now you're listening," I shoot back.

"My job is to put you in a hypnotic state and manage the recording, which I am doing," he says.

He is right, but somehow his lack of interest in the memories I am uncovering galls me. And it is having the effect of eroding my confidence in my project. For if Barassini is not riveted by my every utterance, will the reading public be?

"I need you to be quiet during the process," I say. "If you cannot provide me with this modicum of respect, I will engage another hypnotist. Perhaps Hypno Joe or one of his ilk."

There is a long silence as more of this silent windstorm scene plays out, and finally I hear a distant and chastised:

"Fine."

With that, I am freed to refocus onto my memory of Ingo's film, as well as my newly discovered ability to move my "body" within the experience. Even though, when I look down, I see nothing but street. No feet. No adorable slight protuberance of belly, like the one Fabienne so desired in *Pulp Fiction*. I am a camera. But with agency. Where Isherwood's camera is "quite passive, recording, not thinking," Rosenberg's camera is dynamic, thinking, with agency. *Isher would, but didn't. Rosenberg does.* This is clever, and I will put it in the introduction to my book. Or maybe as an epigraph. Or is it epitaph? I am suddenly uncertain. There is no dictionary to consult in this filmic memory.

"Time's up for today," says Barassini, snapping his fingers.

"I should stay for a bit. To catch my breath," I say.

"You need to go," Barassini says. "I have another client."

"A smoker? That can't be interesting to you."

"I care for all my clients the same. If you must know, it is a man who cannot, nay will not, stop chewing."

"You and I both know that can't be interesting to you."

"You need to go."

And so I do. The street is crowded and smelly. Here I am, in the thick of it. Inside my own smelly life, except as Stein taught us, there is no there there. I believe she was referencing Oakland, California, a suburb of Frisco, as the locals call it. I am not certain of either of these things, but I do not have the energy presently to research it. So I will assume I am correct. In any event, it doesn't matter. Kellita is gone. My daughter Esme has not spoken to me in years, our formerly close relationship poisoned by her mother. I did not choose her name as an homage to the Salinger story. He was and remains a writer I despise. Once the horrifying truth about Salinger's misogyny came out, my ex-wife told Esme I insisted on the name because of my love for that emotionally stunted recluse. In point of fact, I insisted on the name due to my admiration for the great British cricket player Esmé Cecil Wingfield-Stratford, who was also a brilliant British writer of history and mind-trainer, who, by the by, was a man. So my daughter was given a gender-neutral name.

Like a party favor, a thought pops into my head: My daughter coming home from school. She is, what, twelve or eleven. I don't know. She wants to be with me, and I'm working, watching Talfan's *Dysgu i gi Bach Gachu* backward. It is one of the most significant films in all of Welsh cinema, and that is saying something. There are those who believe there is no important Cinema of Wales, but they are, as always, dead wrong. Dyfodwg, Powys, Iwan, Gwilym, Gruffudd, Fardd, Gwilym (no relation), Cadwaladr, Clymneb, Dylfedmed, Prydudd, Gwilym (no relation), and Clydarfrg to name just a few essential directors. And I have been waiting all day for the chance to watch Talfan's masterwork in reverse. My daughter at eleven is barely competent in Gymraeg so will most likely not understand even a word of it backward. I know she will be bored. And then I will feel responsible for her boredom, which will not allow me to properly enjoy the film. I tell her Daddy has to work, which makes me so terribly guilty, especially when I see the look in her eyes, hopeless, unloved, abandoned. This is not the case, of course. It is simply that I need to do my work. A child of eleven cannot understand how, as an adult, one's very identity hinges on one's work, how one would likely dissolve into a fog of nothingness without it. I need to ignore her so I can continue to exist for her. She stares out the window at the rainy day. Esme . . .

Now I FIND myself wandering the stretch of 62nd Street depicted in the first scene of Ingo's film. His accuracy is extraordinary. And although here I can feel weather and the weight of my body, I remain equally invisible as I traverse this version of the street. As a person of privilege and a male who has been correctly chastised and silenced by the emergent culture, I recognize I have no right to feel bad for myself and certainly no right to publicly bemoan my circumstances. Certainly it would result in more shunning by the very community to which I long to belong. But the truth is, I do feel invisible. And on those rare occasions when I am seen, I feel judged most harshly. Maybe this is simply the human condition. But I suspect not, because I do see people experiencing joy and adventure and community. Perhaps it is a flaw in my character, that even with all my advantages, my whiteness, my maleness, my heterosexual insistence, I cannot find my way to this place called joy.

What the fuck is wrong with everyone? Where has taste gone? Why are we adults watching yellow-tinted self-serious young adult science fiction movies about the apocalypse? Don't we know how laughable we are?

I sit in my apartment and try to read from Wingfield-Stratford's *The Reconstruction of Mind: An Open Way of Mind-Training* and stumble upon this:

"Thus we wander through a perpetual minute bombardment of impressions from the outer world, not one of which ever leaves us quite as we were before. The scent of a rose, the sight of an old friend, some ugly or gentle act, every sight we see, every sound we hear, are absorbed into our being and change us either for better or worse."

The outer world and the inner world. We take in the outer world, it changes us, and we put out this altered version. It is a constant exchange of mental fluids with others, and, as with viruses, diseases of the mind are both caught and communicated. Even those whose illnesses are characterized by separateness, by reclusion, as Ingo's was, contribute to this multifarious brew of psychosocial ailments. The Ingos of the world contaminate us with their distrust, their reticence. We wonder why they don't engage. Is it something about us? Are we being negatively judged? Is it because we're white? Or black, if Ingo was the Swedish version of Ingo? Of course, Ingo's hermitic tendencies can likely be traced back to his own trauma at the hands of others and most certainly at the hands of society at large, having come of age as an African American (or as a Swede) in the early part of the twentieth century. And what damage have I caused? And what damage will I cause? Although I make every effort to evolve as a human, to enlarge my sphere of understanding, to be respectful and warm, I must assume I fall short. Indeed, it is only my invisibility within Ingo's film, my complete lack of presence in that environment, that guarantees the safety of others there. It is perhaps the only safe place for me (or anyone, for that matter!) to be. Sadly, unless I can wholly translate this film into a novelization, I am the only one who will ever be able to visit his world. And while a world where one is a ghost is a world free of guilt, guilt and regret must be taken on if one is to live fully. A living creature cannot live without destroying other living creatures. We must eat one another, must we not? This is the way the world works.

I SPOT TSAI attending to her bob in the reflection of a haberdasher's window. God, that is *so* Tsai. I am at enough of a distance that she won't notice me, I believe. It does occur to me, however, that I could be sitting in Tsai's lap and she wouldn't notice me. She is no Levy. Mmm, Tsai's lap, as the kids say. To be in her lap. To *be* her lap. My eyes trained on her, I step on a small dog who screams like an even smaller dog.

"What the fuck is wrong with you?" barks its owner.

I apologize, make a gesture with my hands, which in ASL no doubt translates to: *Shh! I don't want Tsai to look over.* She doesn't. Of course she doesn't. What must it be like to be so self-contained? I tell myself that I am following her to see if she will meet up with Barassini, to discover if she is his plant. And this is both true and an excuse. Following women is the behavior of a stalker, and I am "woke" enough to know the combination of size disparity between the sexes and a culture of toxic masculinity puts women in a place of fear, and it is the responsibility of men to behave courteously and respectfully toward them, to understand fully women's social cues and interact accordingly. No means no. But also, why should they have to say no at all? That unfairly puts the burden on them. Men must recognize all the looks and lack of looks that also mean no. The hand gestures, shoulder shrugs, throat noises, stomach gur-glings. There should be classes in school or perhaps mandatory summer education centers for boys. Something must be done. Of course, the reality in this particular circumstance is that Tsai could easily take me. She is young and tall, and her form is lithe and mus-cular. The thought of Tsai taking me creates more sexual bother in my groin. I watch her ass and imagine it pinning me to the ground. On my face. I am a pathetic creature. I am a bug, a slug, an ant.

She enters a bar called Mack's. I count to fifty-seven, then follow her in. The place is a dive and quiet at this hour. A sad strand of gold Christmas tinsel hangs above the bar. It is, I think, May. Tsai sits on a stool and talks to the bartender. That they know each other seems clear. They laugh at something, and the quality of her laugh is a surprise and an epiphany. It is louder and deeper than I had imag-ined. But it is as careless as I would have thought. I could not be more in love. Is the bartender her boyfriend? He is young, tattooed, and handsome, with a broad chest and chiseled jaw. He would dom-inate her, I imagine, and she would like it. I could never dominate her, not even in my fantasies.

I take a seat at the bar, three down from her, with no one be-tween us. The bartender is pouring her drink, which is some sort of neat whiskey, of course. He glances over at me.

"Be right with you, buddy," he says.

He calls me buddy and he does it warmly, not condescendingly. It gives me a little thrill. We are equals. We are friends. Buddy. There is a flash of me engaging sexually with the bartender, which I quickly and expertly quash.

Tsai sips at her whiskey as the bartender approaches me.

"What can I get you, buddy?"

It's different now. The repetition of *buddy* makes it feel rote. I feel rejected and ashamed. He calls everyone buddy.

"I'll have a whisker," I say.

"Whisker?"

"Whiskey?"

"Scotch, rye . . . ?"

Now he is impatient to get back to Tsai.

"Um, rye," I say, because I heard somewhere it is a thing now.

"Brand?"

"You choose," I say and immediately feel it comes across as coquettish, something a girl might say to him.

He sizes me up.

"You look like a Crown Royal man," he says.

It's astounding how quickly I can go from feeling like a girl to feeling like a big boy, but his calling me a man did just that, which oddly makes me feel like a girl. I am proud. And humiliated. I want him to like me. I would be his buddy; I would be his girl. We could be buddies with benefits.

"Sounds good," I say.

He turns to the shelves to pull it. I glance over at Tsai.

"Oh, hey," I say.

She looks over for the first time. It is clear from her nonexpression that this is not the first time a man has said "Oh, hey" to her at a bar. Her face is blank. I do not exist. I love her terribly.

"Sorry to interrupt," I say, "but I saw you onstage at the Barassini show earlier."

She nods.

"Actually, I was sitting next to you in the audience, too. So . . . Hey."

I giggle. It's pathetic. I want to crawl inside my barstool cushion.

"Hey," she says without inflection and turns back to her drink, to her bartender, saying something quietly to him. I can't make it out. He chuckles. She chuckles.

Now or never. I suck in a lot of air.

"That was amazing, though," I say. "The way he was able to get all that stuff about your life. And I'm so sorry about your student—Michael, was it? That must be so—"

"I lied," she says.

"What do you mean?"

She shrugs.

"Everything I said up there I just made up."

"Huh. So you are a confederate of the hypnotist?"

"No. I just felt like fucking with the show. I don't know a single person whose name begins with *M*. No dead kid. I'm not even a teacher. I despise children."

My God, was anyone ever so perfect? No apologies, whereas I do backflips to prove to the world how much I love my own child, whom I despise, and with good reason. My daughter is a person whose sole purpose in life is to demean me publicly. When I was her age, I had actual ambitions, things I hoped to accomplish in the world, obstacles I hoped to overcome, loves I hoped to discover, but Grace—is it Grace?—is desirous of none of this. She lives to wound me. In a sense, she is akin to an autoimmune illness: Sprung from my own loins, she exists to attack me.

I embarrass my daughter. No doubt she would have preferred a father of the square-jawed variety, a father with whom her twitty little friends would want to flirt. The "your dad's so cute" kind. A less eccentric father. The bartender, for example. It is perhaps the oddest of experiences to have the human who is half you hate you. But upon further reflection, perhaps it is no surprise at all that the fruit of my loins would feel about me as I feel about myself. The Canadian filmist David Cronenbauer made a movie called *A Brood*. In it, the negative impulses of individuals are given autonomous life separate from the individuals themselves. Maybe this is the reality of having children. I wish she could see me in a way I cannot see myself, with kindness, but that would be impossible: She has my genes and the genes of my ex-wife, whose genes also hate me.

Tsai finishes her drink, says good night with a kiss to the bartender. It is on his cheek, but her lips linger. I gulp down my horrible rye whiskey, put ten dollars on the counter, thank the bartender, count to fifty-seven, and follow her out the door.

CHAPTER 28

On THE STREET, I search everywhere, insanely swiveling my head. There! She's walking north. Of course: the best direction.

I walk north, too. Not as good when I do it.

After around fifteen minutes, she enters an apartment building. I count to fifty-four, then check the names on the buzzers. There are three surnames with the first initial "T." I discount O'Neill and Penney and settle on Yan. Tsai Yan. Or I guess Yan Tsai. I know quite a bit about Chinese culture, including that the family name comes first.

Back home, I research the meaning of Yan. There are many, but I pick the best ones and decide it's kismet.

Strict.
Severe.
Stern.
Extremely cruel.
Tight.

On Facebook, I look up Tsai Yan and find a bunch of women and one man, none of them her. Is she, I worry, perhaps Tsai O'Neill or Tsai Penney? I check those as well. Nothing there, either. She is a mystery. Then it occurs to me that if she made up everything she said to Barassini, maybe she lied about her name, too. This sends me into a tailspin of a sleepless night while securely tethered to my sleep chair. At two, I free my arms to peruse my usual online websites: Bang-Up, Biblio Parade, Chimp Meat, Scoot's, Watchamcallit, Nimbus, Heliotrope Summer, Pageant Wars, Rinaldo's Foot. Finally, I check Grace's blog; she has a new piece that seems perhaps to be about me:

> I hate men. I hate men. I hate my father. What do they (he, thon!!! Jesus Christ!) bring to the world? This: war, brutality, rape, oppression, murder, avarice. Is there anything kind or decent that has resulted from this aberrant chromosome? And the goddamn tragedy is I find myself physically attracted to these monsters. Rilke (another man! Why not Lou Andreas-Salome??) suggested that maybe monsters are princesses in disguise waiting for us to free them through our understanding. Well, fuck Rilke telling women (as men have forever) that it is the job of the female to understand men, to soothe them. I quit. This is no longer my job. I am turning in my company ID. My new job, because my father's abuse has rendered me incapable of the confidence to pursue fulfilling and properly compensatory employment, is to speak truth to patriarchy. My truth. Got it, Pater Familias? Would you have raised me different had I been a boy? There is no doubt in my mind. Do you think women have any value to men outside of their physical attractiveness? Have you and I ever engaged in an exchange of ideas? Has there ever been a conversation which did not consist of you mansplaining me into submission? Sororium Obsequious much? Maybe you should read a little Rebecca Solnit, not that there's a chance in hell you could open yourself up to a paradigm shift that calls you to task, that comes from a woman, that lays bare your privilege as a cis-het-whit-eld mal. You have had every opportunity handed to you. Now it's time for you to sit down and listen, or just go away. You are no longer relevant.

I add a note to her comments section:

You think I've had every opportunity? Then why has my professional life been one of constant struggle and humiliation? Signed, Anonymous

She responds:

One has to be supremely untalented to fail as a white man as frequently and as spectacularly as you have. It is well understood that mediocre white men fail upwards and that talented women, POC, LGBTTQIAAP folks, and the differently abled (POC variety) must fight tooth and nail for a seat at the table. Consequently we are left with inferior white men running and ruining the world. And what of value have they contributed?

I write back:

Physics—Signed, Anonymous

She writes back:

First of all, shut up. Secondly, no. Kananda, from India, first expounded atomism in the sixth century BC. Ibn al-Haytham from Basra founded optics in the tenth century. Nasir al-Din al-Tusi created an accurate table of planetary movements in the thirteenth century. Thirdly, Einstein created nuclear weapons, which will soon destroy the world. So much for white physicists.

    Me: No he didn't. And Einstein was Jewish.—Signed, Anonymous
    Her: Jewish is white.
    Me: Tell that to the Aryans. Signed, Anonymous
    Her: Aryans are Indo-Iranians.

Me: No they're not . . . A quick check on Wikipedia will show you that Aryans are— Oh. Signed, Anonymous

Her: Ha!

Grace has won this battle.

At 5:00 A.M., I am back across the street from Tsai's (or whatever her actual undoubtedly beautiful first [last in China] name is!) apartment building, having spent the entire night tethered to my sleeping chair but awake researching Indo-European migrations for my future parries with Grace. There is a twenty-four-hour laundromat across from Tsai's (?), which is a godsend unless she comes in to do her laundry while I'm hiding here. The place is empty when I arrive and remains so until 6:00, when five customers enter in quick succession: a housewife, a chef, an automobile mechanic, a yachtsman, and a barrister. At 6:30, Tsai (?) leaves her apartment carrying a messenger bag and walks north. Could north be the only direction she ever walks? I ponder this, then quickly dismiss it as unsustainable. Since it's light out, I count to seventy-four before following. It is, however, a fast seventy-four because I am nervous about losing sight of her. I spot her just as she is turning left. West. Of course: north and west. I hurry to the cross street, but she is gone. There is an elementary school on this block! Perhaps she was not lying about lying about being a kindergarten teacher, after all, rather only lying about lying about lying. I enter the school and locate the receptionist.

"I have a package for Tsai Yan," I say.

"Yan Tsai?"

"As you wish."

"You can leave it with me."

I hadn't thought this through. I consider turning and running. Instead, I reach into my briefcase, hoping there's something. An apple I stole from Barassini's fruit bowl and a copy of my monograph on the advances in filmic sound design as they related to 1920s Zionism, entitled *Hear O Israel*. I had been intending to drop it off at my friend Elkin's (formerly Ocky) place because he said he might be able to slip it to the editor of the Jewish film journal *Cine-Mazel*, whose faucet he is fixing today. Schmendrick Ackerman will have to wait. I hand the paper to the receptionist.

She takes it, glances at the title, shakes her head (Nazi!), and tosses it into a tray marked "Incoming." I think of wounded soldiers on the television series *M*A*S*H*, which was, by the way, a pallid imitation of the Bobert Altman movie of the same name, and hurry out.

What have I done? What have I done? I've left my name with her. I left my work! Granted, it is a brilliant piece, which, I believe, does much to deghettoize Jewish sound design, but still, I might as well have left her a business card identifying myself as her stalker.

It's three days later when I receive the following email at my website Les Film Tibetain des Morts:

> Why did you leave a monograph where I work? Who are you? Your thoughts on Jewish sound design are simplistic and passé. Furthermore, Israel is an apartheid state.

Does she know I am the man in the bar? Is she asking me to tell her more about myself? Or is she simply asking, who left this for me? I don't know, but her tone excites me. It is authoritative, demanding. It is insulting. And so to play my part, I must respond and I must respond with respectful punctuality. She demands answers and I must supply them. Since I am unclear what question she is asking, I will answer both:

> I am film historian/theorist/critic/maker B. Rosenberger Rosenberg. On occasion I use the alternatives B. Rosenberg or B. Ruby Rosenberg. I never use my Christian name [*I chose that term so she will glean that I am not Jewish*] because I do not want to exploit the advantage (or suffer the disadvantage!) my assigned gender might imbue upon the perception of my work. We don't know each other, but met briefly at a bar called Mack's. We chatted amiably. I thought

perhaps you might have an interest in Jewish sound design and am thrilled to learn that indeed you do indeed. Perhaps we could meet to discuss the fault you find with my work. I am always eager to better myself.

I hit Send before I can think better of it. Ugh. I typed *indeed* twice in the antepenultimate sentence.

The response comes quickly:

From your email, it is unclear to me whether you are a man or a woman.

Does she not remember the exchange at Mack's? Or is she playing with me? Or is she testing my resolve on the gender nondisclosure issue? I feel perhaps she is toying with me. Granted, it is my goal to leave no photographic trace of myself online, but at lectures and on panels, it is somewhat out of my control. One can find a photo of me if one so desires. If one searches and searches and searches. A photo of me appears on page seventy-six of the Google search for B. Rosenberger Rosenberg. Also, I have been told that my writing is decidedly masculine in nature. Still, I feel compelled to answer her question directly. That is until I reread it and see no question has been asked. It is a statement of fact and asks nothing of me. Perhaps this is the key. If I respond as if it were a question, it will demonstrate my careless reading of her text. I respond:

I see.

I am well pleased, and I hope she will be, too. My computer chimes with incoming mail:

That's it? I asked you a simple question.

I want to write to her, no, in actuality, no question was asked. If you scroll up, you will see that you did not ask one. But I do not write this. It is not in the nature of our relationship for me to be pedantic. I answer her simply and contritely:

I'm sorry I am male.

I hit SEND, then in a panic realize I have left out the period after "sorry." Oh God, what have I opened myself up to here? She writes back within seconds:

Oh. Now I remember you.

I write back:

Oops! I left out the period after "sorry," I am not sorry I am male!

Nothing. I hear nothing more from her. I stare at this last email. I stare at the "Oops!" I don't say "oops." I certainly do not write "oops." I might as well have signed the email "xoxoxo." It is pathetic. It is girlish. I am humiliated. I compose and recompose a follow-up email, one that attempts to enlarge her sense of me, maybe even shift the dynamic somewhat in my favor, topping from the bottom, as it were. I pull the blurb out of my wallet, the one I received from film theorist Laura Mulvey for my monograph *Fallow-centrism in Cinema: Planting the Seed for Change by Not Planting the Male Seed for a Change*. I look it over and realize Mulvey refers to me as "she" in her blurb and, as such, it may not serve my current purposes. Or maybe it is exactly what I need. I go back and forth on this for three days, never sending it. Finally I hear from her:

Egad. Show a little backbone.

If she wants me to show backbone, I will. I will show all the backbone she wants and not a vertebra more or less. So I do. I tell her I am going to be sitting at the bar at Julius and Ethel's (no relation!) at 9:00 P.M. this Thursday if she cares to join me. She doesn't respond, nor do I expect her to. I am showing the proper amount of backbone.

The Kentucky Meat Shower of 1876 pops into my head. I cannot say why now, but in truth, it is never far from the forefront of my psyche. There have, of course, been several documented meat showers and blood rains throughout history, and, as a student of crypto-meteorology, I have studied them all. The value of the KMS to scholarly literature is that a fair amount of the meat was preserved and studied by scientists at Harvard, and it was determined to be either horse or human infant. Weather has always been a fascination of mine. I minored in meteorology and culture and was president of our a cappella competitive whistling team Weigh Hey, Blow the Man Down. But why do these meat shower thoughts persist? They put me in mind of Ingo, for one thing. I cannot remember why. The world, I conclude, is stranger than we can comprehend.

Now, on the way to my meeting (maybe!) with Tsai, a song plays over and over in my head:

The years, the years
They come and go
The summer rain
The winter snow
The flowers bloom
The children grow
The years, the years
They fly on by
Your body fails
Your parents die
The meat rains come
So make a pie
The years, the years
Look it up.

—Traditional ballad

CHAPTER 29

IARRIVE AT JULIUS and Ethel's. It's exactly nine o'clock. This is my backbone showing, and not just because of my vestigial tail. I scan the bar. Tsai is not here. There are two seats open. I take one and put my coat on the other. I do not crane my neck to see who is entering when someone does. It takes all my willpower. I order Crown Royal rye neat. I don't like it, but my drink of choice, the Cape Codder, extra dirty, I fear, will send the wrong message to Tsai.

"For me?" she says, her hand on the chair with my coat on it.

"Yes!" I say and remove it, draping it over my lap for some reason, rather than on the back of my stool. For some reason? For obvious reasons.

She sits and the bartender is there before she looks up.

"Michter's twenty-year, neat," she says.

He smiles, nods, disappears down the bar. She turns to me.

"So, you followed me home, then followed me to my job the next morning. Is that an accurate assessment of your most recent skulking activities?"

I nod. The bartender returns with her drink, which, it turns out, is some sort of whiskey, or at least whiskey-colored, drink.

"Why is that?" she asks.

I know I have to answer her.

"I was attracted to you. I am attracted to you."

"Do you think it's OK to follow women?"

"I know it's not."

"And yet."

"I'm sorry. I've been struggling with some very disorienting life issues. I've lost my job and my apartment. I've lost a very significant artistic and historical document. I've lost my girlfriend, Kellita Smith, who was African American. I have lost my purpose. I am the proud owner of a gaping hole in my soul."

"That's some beard you've got there, guy."

"Yeah. I might shave it."

"I am in no way attracted to you," she says.

"I can't imagine you would be."

"You're old," she says.

"Yes."

"And even if you weren't, I can imagine you younger. So even then."

"I understand."

"And then there's whatever this personality thing is you've got going," she says, vaguely waving her hands.

This one hurts me.

"What do you mean?" I say.

"You're this bizarre combination of obsequious and blowhard."

I sip my drink to steady myself.

"Have you heard of the Kentucky Meat Shower of 1876?"

"'Have you heard of the Kentucky Meat Shower of 1876?'" she repeats back to me in a mockingly effeminate voice.

I stare at my drink. I have no idea how to proceed after that.

"Why did you agree to meet me?" I finally ask.

"I knew you were watching me at the hypnotist thing. You think I'm an idiot? I knew you followed me to Mack's. I saw you in the laundromat. Jesus, you're not at all good at stealth."

"Oh. OK."

"You are not the first pathetic man who has obsessed over me. Today alone, I've seen probably eleven pathetic men watching me while pretending not to. It's not difficult to spot, in case you're wondering."

"Are you having drinks with all of us?"

"No. That's the thing. I hate you. Those other men I kind of shrug off at this point. But you do something to me. I just really despise you. My skin crawls at the thought of you, never mind the sight of you. I like the idea of you being miserable and I like the idea of me contributing to it. And it's clear to me you'll take whatever it is I offer up."

I don't say anything. I don't look at her. I don't know what to do.

"Won't you?"

"I will," I say. Then, to my great humiliation, I start to cry. I don't know why, but it's loud. Strings of snot hang from my nose.

"Oh, man," she says as she puts on her coat and leaves.

The bartender leaves the bill. Her shot of whiskey was $145. I think about Tsai as I walk home. I take a detour thirty blocks out of my way to walk past her apartment building. I look up at all the lighted windows from across the street. Will I catch a glimpse of her? I am confused. I feel so lucky she wants to hurt me. I feel so lucky not to be one of the countless men she is not interested in hurting. My penis strains against my pants. I arrive in my apartment and check for an email from her. There is nothing. So I write one to her. I debase myself by telling her my atomizer genie fantasy about being her service person every place she goes. I send it. I want to vomit.

I vomit.

It's two days later, and I receive this email:

Wow.

Then nothing.

Then today, two days after the "Wow":

There's a deli called Buy and Save a block over from me (you remember where I live, right?). I go there fairly regularly because it's open 24 hours. They also deliver, and sometimes, if it's cold or wet, I use that service. Sign in the window says they're looking for a delivery person/clerk. Get that job. I imagine you'll have to shave that beard shit.

* * *

I GREW MY beard to conceal a port-wine stain that extends from my clavicle to my upper lip. People would stare at it or try not to stare at it when they talked to me/passed me on the street. I still got the stares and avoidance with the beard, but I knew I could always shave off the beard to resolve that issue. The port-wine stain was, however, beyond removal. The longer one waits to have those things removed, the more unlikely it is that results will be satisfactory. My parents decided I should live with mine since my father also had one (over his right eye) and he did just fine, after all. This was their argument, and I loved them, so I loved their argument. By the time I was old enough to understand the ostracization it caused, I decided asking my parents for its removal would be an insult to and rejection of my father. I felt guilty when I grew my beard, knowing my father had no way of concealing his with a forehead beard and he did not have enough head hair to cover it with a fringe. There was a brief period when he and my mother were having marital troubles and he would spend evenings at Mushrooms, a small bar in Great Neck, when he experimented with a "side comb," hair-spraying a long tuft of hair across his forehead and securing it behind the opposite ear with a bobby pin. But this, looking like Bobby Riggs in a hair head-band, didn't help him at all in attracting the local women, and he finally went back, tail between legs, to my mother.

In any event, since the skin grafts, mine is gone and I don't have to feel I've betrayed my father, because this was a health issue and, anyway, it was done while I was in a coma. As the Tao says, no blame. I grew the beard back out of habit and laziness and also because I enjoy sucking at the mustache and discovering flavors from yesterday.

Now I shave it.

The birthmark has grown back. I look it up. WebMD insists this is impossible.

BARASSINI SAYS "WHOA" when he sees me for my weekly session. Our session is, as it always is these days, relatively fruitless. Since our first couple of meetings, we have been spinning our wheels.

Under his spell, I do recall an image of a boat with a human face, a tugboat, bouncing on the waves and singing a happy song of the sea in the voice of an old salt:

> *On the 14th of January 1952,*
> *A big human face on my wheelhouse grew.*
> *Now my eyes of clear-view screens forever spin,*
> *And my life-buoy mouth perpetually grins.*
> *Though the avuncular harbormaster thinks I'm his friend,*
> *I'm a miserable freak, and I want it to end.*
> *Yet I tug and I wink and do water salutes,*
> *And my face says I'm happy, the young girls think I'm cute.*
> *But I pray for release from this transmogrification,*

The erase of my face to bring soul decimation. I'm not certain this is even from Ingo's movie. It could be from anywhere or nowhere and, upon reflection, I don't think it is at all happy. One wonders about the mental health of any tugboat who would wish for oblivion over sentience. It's possible this was Ingo's intent with this character, if indeed this is from Ingo's film, the exploration of the false face and perhaps tying it in to the Iroquois mythology of same. Without more memories from the film, I don't have enough to formulate a real theory. And although Barassini insists it is from the film and that we are making real progress, I don't know for certain. This might be some long-buried memory of a childhood television show. Barassini also insists the story is obviously a happy one because the tugboat winks and smiles. I am beginning to question Barassini's intelligence.

THE WALK TO the Buy and Save is both an alien and a familiar experience. I feel the breeze on my lower face and neck. It is bracing. It is good. And, of course, the stares are back. Relentless. Every person I pass. And as the manager of the Buy and Save reviews my curriculum vitae, he avoids looking at me. I think this could work to my advantage. Maybe he'll feel guilty about that. It could go either way.

"Not a lot of service industry experience," he says.

"I did some phone sales in college. At Harvard."

"The hypnosis school?"

"That's Harverd."

He looks up at me to ask a question, then immediately back down at the CV; he runs his finger along some part, pretending to read it.

"Why do you want to work here?" he asks.

Because I'm being ordered to. Because I find myself enmeshed in the desperate fantasy of a lonely, old be-wine-stained failure. Because I want to be owned in the way a film I can no longer remember once owned me. Because I want something the universe has told me in no uncertain terms is impossible, except under these terrifying conditions. Because she is perfect.

"I need the work," I say, then add: "This seems like a nice place to work."

He nods.

I email Tsai:

I got the job. I start tomorrow, graveyard shift.

No response.

I sit in the dark and wonder how I have arrived here. There is little doubt that a cabal (I do not choose that word lightly) of film theorists runs the industry. Don't publicly question their critiques if you hope to climb the "sprockets" to success; they will destroy you. I once had the audacity to call Richard Roeper to task for his Fresh Tomato ranking of *Memento*, which he deemed an "ingenious exploration of how memory defines us all." It is, of course, nothing of the sort, but rather a one-trick pony gimmick fest that reveals, through its paucity of ideas and pseudo-noir (yawn) mannerisms, that both Christopher Nolan and his pool boy Richard Roeper are intellectually bankrupt and emotionally callow. That this "movie" has received any notice at all, let alone overwhelmingly positive notice, is just more proof (as if any more is needed!) of the corruption within the community of film critics. Memory, were one to give it even an iota of thought, would be revealed to be the most complex area of study available to the human animal. This silly exercise is almost equal to the profound simplemindedness of *Eternal Sunshine of the Spotless Mind*. Had Kaufman actually read Pope's poem, as I have many times (my senior thesis decimates Pope for his outrageous misogyny), he would have known it is perhaps the single most wrongheaded title for this bit of sci-fi puffery. My investigation into film and memory, *You Must Remember This* (Rutabaga Press, 1998), dances circles around these two (and frankly all) memory films. In it, I perform the experiment of recounting as accurately as possible a film (*Beloved*) I had seen only once. The preternatural accuracy of my retelling had less to do with my near-eidetic memory (true eidetic memory is a myth!), but rather with how I view movies. I am a truly conscious viewer, perhaps the only truly conscious movie viewer in the world. My book then proceeds to explain my method of viewing and acts as a manual for the student of cinema who hopes to achieve a success similar to my own. That I take the business of watching movies with such seriousness is why I am perhaps a tad vitriolic in my disdain for the disingenuous, the vulgar, the tawdry, and the pretentious in films. After all, my valuable cranial real estate is taken up by these roadside eyesores, these billboards for Wall Drug and Burma-Shave that pass themselves off as movies, and I resent it. I will not tolerate it. I cannot. I will not! So they turn me into a pariah. I would not go so far as to say this cabal is Jewish in nature. I have no idea, nor do I care, whether Roeper is Jewish. Such heritaginal labels are irrelevant to me, but I suspect he is. I suspect he is. I do suspect he might very well be.

It's 1:00 a.m., my first night on the job. The phone rings and Darnell (the night boss) answers it. He says "uh-huh" a few times, then "bye," then hangs up. I'm mopping the bathroom (Employees Only!).

"Delivery," Darnell says.

I lean the mop against the wall, grab the bag of stuff, and look at the address. It is Tsai. My heart pounds.

So I walk the block to Tsai's, press the buzzer. No response. I know she knows I am coming, so I conclude making me wait is part of her game and become further excited. I am glad I have my work apron on: It is stained and features a duck saying, "It's my pleasure to serve you!" After five minutes, I wonder if I should buzz again. Maybe she didn't hear me. The TV might be on, or music. She might be in the bathroom. I don't ring the buzzer again. After six more minutes, she buzzes me in. There is an elevator and I take it to the fifth floor and find my way to 5D. I ring the bell. She opens the door in her robe. Not a sexy robe. Stained terry cloth. And so fucking sexy. I long to be a stain on it near her vagina.

"How much do I owe you?" she asks.

I check the receipt even though I have it memorized. Even her charge is magical. $17.58. $17.58. $17.58.

"$17.58," I say.

She closes the door and returns after a minute with a twenty-dollar bill and hands it to me. She waits for change, which I give her. She hands me back a dollar, says thanks, and closes the door.

I take the stairs so I can masturbate in the stairwell. I have never masturbated in a stairwell before. Well, once, and it didn't end well. I vowed never to masturbate in a stairwell again, especially in this the age of toxic masculinity. But I can't help myself. My shame when I finish is beyond any I've ever felt. This is my beautiful nightmare. I masturbate again.

CHAPTER 30

BARASSINI QUICKLY PUTS me under. It's just a matter of flipping the emotional toggle switch he has created for me, which is an actual toggle implanted at the base of my neck, below the collar, with what Barassini describes as a direct line to my brain center, or Neuro Hub, as he calls it. He explained he saw something similar in a *Black Mirror* episode and it turns out it works. It feels like a tooth nerve being probed, but only for a second, then it opens up my receptivity. I like it because it's efficient and reliable and our sessions are only an hour, so we can get right to it. So I scream, then relax.

"Tell me about the film," he says.

"I still can't remember much," I say. "As usual."

"Well, just start talking. Make it up. See what happens."

It seems I'm not the only one who's grown impatient with my lack of progress.

"I don't think that will get me to the truth of it, Master," I say. I don't know why I called him "Master." It's not something he requires or even ever suggested as far as I remember.

"Listen, the past doesn't exist. Can we agree on that?"

"Yes," I say, leaving off the "Master" this time. I feel embarrassed that I said it at all. Like calling my teacher "Mom."

"And we agree it exists only as thought, that is to say, the past exists only in one's mind?"

"I guess."

"Well, where else? Show me where else!" he yells.

"Nowhere else. You're right."

"Then if it does not exist, it can be anything you decide, since it does not exist."

"Well, I mean—"

"Yes?"

"We do share common memories as people."

"Do we? Do you have the same memories of your family as your brother?"

"Not exactly. But there is a commonality, certainly, which suggests that there is some objective truth to what we remember."

"So you're saying our obligation to others is the thing that requires us to pull memories from our memory rather than our imaginations?"

"I suppose . . . *Master*?"

I'm displeasing him. I thought the "Master" might help now.

"But in the case of your movie, there's no one who shares it. *N'est-ce pas*?"

"*Oui*."

"Therefore you have no obligation to anyone to be accurate."

"My obligation is to the brilliance of it. That film changed me. Now I think I've changed back or maybe into a third thing not nearly as good as the second thing or perhaps even the first thing, which may not have been the first thing at all, for how can one really know what the first thing was? It's even ossible there were many things before the first thing—"

"Did you just say *ossible*?"

"No. For as we grow, we are constantly changing. I suspect as a child I was happy and pure and free. I don't know for certain. Maybe that's only nostalgia rearing its ugly head. But I do know this: Ingo's movie effected a change in me that brought me peace and clarity, and I want to find that again. I want to regain what I have lost. I need to remember it accurately. I want to be able to see it again in my mind's eye, the way Castor Collins saw God during his pilgrimage to Vienna."

"How do you know about that?" says Barassini, his eyes narrowing like the Verrazzano Bridge.

239

"What?"

"Castor Collins's pilgrimage."

"Every schoolboy knows the story. And girl. Why?"

Barassini is silent for a long while, maybe an hour. I read a magazine from the rack.

"All right," he says finally. "I am going to get the true movie out of you. I find myself reinvigorated. We'll utilize a dangerous and untested technique. There's been some research, but only at this point on syphilitic mice. The results have been promising; the mice remembered buried childhood trauma. The ones that didn't kill themselves, that is."

"Wait, what?"

"Here's how we'll proceed: It will be as an archaeological dig. We will excavate the shattered shards of pottery of your mind, piece by piece, then dust each piece off, removing all extraneous dirt—the non-movie elements, if you will—then glue it back together. It will be a painstaking, exacting process, not without its extreme risks to both of our psyches, but we will prevail."

"So, when you say dangerous—"

"For you mostly, yes. Very."

"How so?"

"You're going deep, my friend."

"I see. Well—"

"You want this movie back?"

"More than anything, but—"

"This is the only way."

"OK," I say. "But what have we been doing this whole time if this is the only way it can—"

"Before is a fiction, yes? Didn't I teach you that?"

"Um. I—"

"Good! So let's begin!"

"But the mice killed themselves?"

"Some did. Some merely began to drink heavily. It might have been the syphilis. But you are a man, not a syphilitic mouse, yes?"

"Yes," I say. "If I have to choose."

* * *

I'M EMPTYING THE metal trays in the salad bar. Darnell says it's time because the cantaloupe pieces have gone pale and soft. I'll cut some fresh after. It passes the time. Between 2:00 and 3:00 A.M., it's very quiet. Darnell, smiling at his phone, texts someone, while I think about Barassini, how he seems to have become motivated by my mention of Castor Collins. It is all quite odd. When the front door opens, we both look up, Darnell reaching for his baseball bat. This is always the way it is late at night. One does not want any surprises in the late-night deli business. This time the surprise is a pleasant one; it is Tsai.

"Hey," Darnell says.

"Hi," she says back with a sweet smile. "I was hoping to get a sandwich."

"Sure. B.! Make the lady a sandwich."

I nod and head behind the counter.

"Hi," I say. "What can I get you?"

"Turkey and Swiss on a French roll."

"OK."

"A little mayo and mustard. The yellow kind. Um, tomato, lettuce, onion."

"Would you like coleslaw, potato salad, or a bag of chips with that?"

She says, "Chips," as she heads to the front of the store to look at the racks of candy. It's also where Darnell sits behind the cash register.

"I can't decide what to get," she says. "What's your favorite candy?"

"I enjoy a nice Kit Kat now and again," Darnell says.

She places a Kit Kat on the counter.

I make the sandwich but watch Tsai. From here I can only see her ass outfitted for all the world in a pair of black yoga pants. She leans her elbows on the counter, which pushes her ass out toward me.

"I've seen you here forever yet I've never introduced myself," she says to Darnell. "How rude. I'm Tsai."

"Darnell," says Darnell. "Howdy."

"I like that name," she says. "Darnell."

"Thanks. Your name's dope. Like S-I-G-H?"

"T-S-A-I."

"Oh, cool. That's like Oriental or some shit?"

Jesus, I think. Oriental? She's going to rip him a—

"Yeah," she says. "My grandparents were from China."

"That's cool. That's cool. That's very cool. China. That's in the ocean, right?"

What does that even mean?

There's a silence, then out of nowhere, Darnell asks if she gets high. Tsai says she does.

"You wanna?" he asks.

"Mm-hm."

"Yo, B., watch the front," Darnell says as he grabs his backpack and leads Tsai into the supply room. I hear the alley door unlock and assume they have stepped outside. The sandwich is finished, wrapped, in a paper bag along with a separately wrapped pickle slice, three napkins, and a bag of potato chips. I bring it up to the register and wait there for approximately seventeen or so minutes. The alley door opens and they find their way back into the store. Tsai giggles at something Darnell says.

"Yo, B.," Darnell calls to me. "Ring Tsai up. Give her my discount."

"Aw, thanks, Darnell!" chirps Tsai. "You're such a sweetheart."

I ring her up minus Darnell's discount.

"$5.50 please," I say.

Tsai hands me a ten-dollar bill but is looking back at Darnell, who's at the hot section of the food bar, picking at the macaroni and cheese with his fingers.

"That was fun," she says. "Thanks."

"Any time, Tsai from China," he says, mouth full of macaroni.

Pearls before swine.

"Oh my God, you're adorable!" she says to Darnell. I hand her her change. She takes the bag. "Night!" she says to Darnell, and she's out the door.

"Damn," Darnell says. "She hot! I'm gonna have to eat me some of that Kung Pao chicken. Know what I'm sayin', dude?"

I do know what he's saying. And I step into the employee bathroom to masturbate. I suspect Darnell will masturbate in here once I finish. It passes the time on these quiet nights. I always prefer to go first.

CHAPTER 31

"I᷏т is night," Barassini begins.

Suddenly it is. But that is all, just night without Earth or sky. I seem to be hovering in a void. It is terrifying. I think of those poor mice.

"Don't be frightened," he says. "You are driving."

And I am. I am driving at night. On nothing. Toward nothing. From nothing.

"You are driving at night on a desolate road," he continues, his voice now coming from the car's staticky radio.

And here's the road.

"It is bordered on either side by trees, which form a canopy overhead. You cannot see the sky, so dense is this canopy. You drive slowly, creeping along, scouring this area for signs of something buried."

"I don't understand any of this," I say.

"Are you seeing what I am describing?"

"Yes. It's frighteningly vivid. I'm frightened. By the vividability of it."

"Good, then."

"It's like a movie I'm watching but I'm also in it. Embodied in it. Is this what they call Brainio?"

"Brainio?"

"Entertainment from the future," I say.

"I have no clue what you are going on about. This is hypnotic suggestion. There is no such thing as entertainment from the future. The future does not exist. Nor does the past. There is only now. We've been over this."

"I don't feel safe."

"Focus on your task. Always focus on your task and fear dissipates. This is Barassini's Law."

"What is my task?"

"You are searching for fragments of the film. Of Ingo's lost film. I've made it a literal search through the detritus of your mind to help concretize the process. There is some risk of becoming lost forever within this alternate Brainio reality—"

"You said 'Brainio.'"

"No, I didn't. Anyway, there's a risk of being forced like Charley of song fame to 'ride forever 'neath the streets of Boston' of your brain, but if you follow my instructions, which I call Barassini's Technique, you should be fine."

"It looks kind of like the road to Florida I traveled."

"Your brain is using its memories to fill in the visuals. That's good since your Florida memories exist in proximity to your memories of the film. This is Barassini's Sign. Or *Barassini Zeichen.*"

"Will I really find it this way?"

"Find what?" says the radio voice.

"Ingo's film."

"Oh. That. Yes."

The voice suddenly sounds confused and uncertain.

"I see something," I say.

"Tell me," says the radio.

"A pile of dirt. On the side of the road, between two trees."

"Pull over!" he screams. "And train your hypno-headlights on that pile of dirt! Hurry!"

I do.

"Did you?"

"Did I what?"

"Train your hypno-headlights on it?"

"I did."

"Get out, open the trunk; you'll find digging implements inside. Take the trowel. Dig gently. You do not want to damage what is buried there or you might become lost here forever, like Charley 'neath the streets of Boston."

"Please stop saying that."

"OK."

I kneel and carefully scoop a trowel full of my "mind soil." A cloud of smoky past skitters around on the trowel. I watch it, fascinated, nauseated, worried. I see my St. Augustine apartment from the vantage point of the bed. I am on my cellphone. Cigarette smoke hovers above me.

"Did you find anything?" the radio from inside the car asks, now slightly muted through the closed car door.

"Maybe. I'm on my bed on the phone," I say.

"This is promising. Part of the movie is probably among all this other mind garbage. Describe what you see."

"I'm on the phone with my girlfriend. She's African American. You've most likely heard of her."

"What exactly are you saying?"

"Just that she's fairly well known and you have probably—"

"No. What are you saying to her?"

"I'm telling her I've discovered a heretofore unseen film by a brilliant elderly African American gentleman. I tell her she has never heard of him, but that will soon change. 'What's it about?' she asks. 'It's about everything,' I say. She says, 'Be more specific.' There's impatience in her voice. 'Well, today for example, I saw a scene in which Abbott and Costello plot a murder.' She tells me she doesn't have time for nonsense right now, she has to memorize her lines for tomorrow, she hates Abbott and Costello, that they are wypipo's idea of humor. I say, 'But as I mentioned, this movie was made by an elderly African American gentleman.' She's talking over me; she's describing the scene she's memorizing: 'It's a tough scene,' she says, 'in which I am brutally raped. Very violent.' 'They were Abbott and Costello and yet they were not Abbott and Costello,' I tell her. 'To fully understand this it is necessary to hold both their Abbott and Costello–ness and their non-Abbott and non-Costello–ness in your brain at the same time.' 'My most important scene,' she says. 'Everything hinges on this scene. I have to prepare. Trust me, it doesn't help that the actor I'm playing against is the nicest, most sexually attractive man I've ever met, and I have to find within me some sort of hatred toward—'"

"Stop," says the radio. "This memory is no longer helpful for our process. Wipe it away gently with that soft-bristled brush by your side. Gently! Or you might die! There's a good chance you'll find a piece of the film underneath, and that is what we need to pursue."

"When I wipe it away, is it gone forever?" I ask.

"Like smoke," says the radio.

I hesitate, then brush it away.

"Done," I say.

I feel lighter.

"Do you see the Abbott and Costello scene? I'm expecting you'll find that."

The radio is right. That memory is a rabbit hole. There it sits, a gleaming, cinematic moment, and now I am in it. The scene is so alive, even though I am on a miniature set with puppets.

"Tell me," says the radio.

I am climbing a hill at night, not in Florida, which has no hills, as you may or may not know. Somewhere else. It is dark. Oh. I recognize it now as the Los Feliz neighborhood of Los Angeles, but not currently. No Hollywood hipsters. The automobiles are old; 1940s? This is the Los Feliz of Raymond Chandler. There sits Bud Abbott on a rock, smoking a cigarette, looking out over the city. Deep in thought. A dark convertible drives up. A Cadillac? I think so, but then I am not really a car person. The white canvas top is up. It parks, and chubby Lou Costello steps out. Abbott doesn't look over as Costello sits on the next rock over. That they've had meetings here before is clear to me; I don't know how I know. Silence. Abbott breaks it:

"Why couldn't we speak on the telephone? Betty made meatloaf. My favorite. It'll be cold by the time I get home."

"The walls have ears, Bud."

"For God's sake, Lou. Who would want to listen to our conversation?"

"Millions of people and I want to make certain it stays that way."

"You're confusing me."

"Well, as we both know, confusing you is not the most complex of tasks."

"What are you saying?"

"Exactly my point."

"Speak plain, Lou."

"Our ascendancy may be coming to an end."

"Ascendancy? See? Why you gotta use those highfalutin—"

"All right, Bud, plain and simple, just for you: There is an up-and-coming team of buffoons, one hefty and one meager. Does this excite either of your brainial nerve endings?"

"Speak plain, Lou, for the love of all things holy."

"Mudd and Molloy are encroaching on my—*our*—territory. I will not have my—*our*—thunder stolen by the likes of anyone, let alone the likes of those two interlopers."

"Like in 'Home on the Range'?"

"Those are antelopes, not interlopers. And inaccurate to boot. There are no North American antelopes."

"Then who?"

"The comedy team that looks like us."

"That fat and skinny duo?"

"Indeed. Bingo. Give the lady a cigar."

"What lady, Lou?"

"It's an expression, my friend. We need to stop Mudd and Molloy."

"It's a big world, Lou. Enough to go around."

"Tell that to Wheeler and Woolsey."

"I can't. Bob Woolsey died in '38."

"Exactly."

"You lost me."

"I often fantasize about that."

"Come again?"

"Sigh. Robert Woolsey needed to be gone. And so he was."

"What are you saying, Lou?"

"Jesus, Bud. I killed him. For us."

"Don't be ridiculous. Bob died of kidney failure. Everyone knows that."

"Everyone knows what I want them to know!" spits Costello.

"What are you saying, Lou?"

"Holy Christ, you're a tree stump. I killed Woolsey to make room for us."

"What are you saying, Lou?"

"I wonder if Gabby Hayes might be interested in replacing you in the act. Might make our repartee more scintillating."

"He's a cowboy sidekick, Lou. Not a straight man. I don't get your point."

"I'll make this simple for you: Woolsey died from kidney failure, yes. But slow poisoning by arsenic was the cause."

"Who would slowly poison Bob Woolsey?"

"I would, Bud. I would. And I did, as I already told you more times than several."

"But why?"

"Because, my mustachioed nincompoop, Hollywood is not big enough for Wheeler and Woolsey and Abbott and Costello."

"But didn't Bob live on the west side? Santa Monica, I think. Not Hollywood. I'm certain Betty and I visited him in Santa Monica, not Hollywood, that one time when he was dying of kidney failure. So you didn't have to worry about him taking up room in Hollywood, after all."

"Yes. Yes, he did live on the west side. Y'know, Bud, I'm not sure if you're so dumb because you were repeatedly dropped on your head as a baby or you were repeatedly dropped on your head as a baby because you were so dumb and the people dropping you, namely your parents, weren't overly concerned about protecting your head because you were so dumb to begin with."

"That's a long way to go for that particular comic insult, Lou."

"Nonetheless, and please try to stay with me here, if you value your way of life and would like to maintain it, we need to address the problem of Mudd and Molloy."

"The comedy team?"

"Yes. They need to be stopped."

"Why?"

Costello performs a lovely, extended slow burn. It is a work of art.

"All right," he says, finally, "here is my plan. They will be shooting their first two-reeler next week. It's to be called *Here Come a Coupla Fellas* and it is quite good, script-wise. I was able to get a hold of it by first killing the script girl, then stealing it from her apartment, which I ransacked. If this film sees the light of day, I fear our position as the preeminent comic duo of our time may be threatened. I propose we put a definitive stop to Mudd and Molloy on their very first day of shooting, before any damage can be done."

"But how?"

"Let's just say I know the best boy on that production."

"What's his job on the production?"

"Who?"

"The best boy."

"He's the best boy."

"I get that you like him, Lou, but what's his job?"

"He's the best boy."

"Fine, but what's his job?"

"That's his job."

"What is?"

"Best boy."

"But what's his job?"

There is a long, long silence, during which Costello again burns magnificently slow. Then he speaks:

"In any event, he's going to loosen all the bolts on the overhead grid so it will fall at the moment in the haberdashery scene when Molloy slams the door, thus killing Mudd and Molloy forever and ensuring our birthright."

"I wouldn't think the best boy you know on the production would do something so awful."

"Why is that?"

"Because it doesn't sound best at all. Maybe he's the worst boy on the production. Irresponsible boy, at the very least."

"He's doing my bidding."

"Why, Lou?"

"Because I want Mudd and Molloy dead."

"But that's m-m-m-m-murder."

"Yes."

"But why?"

Another silence. Another slow burn.

"You do know that Mudd's first name is Bud, right, Bud?"

"Hey, Bud's my name."

"Yes, Bud."

"I mean, really my name is William Alexander Abbott. But people call me Bud. Because my mom did."

"I'm aware of that. Doesn't it seem to you that someone shouldn't steal your name, Bud?"

"Well, I still have my name, Lou. If he had stolen my name, you couldn't call me Bud anymore and you just did. See?"

"He even wears the same mustache as you."

Bud feels his upper lip, laughs.

"Now you're just being silly," says Bud.

"Good night, Bud."

"Good night, Lou."

Costello walks to his car.

"Betty says you and Anne should come over soon for meatloaf!"

Costello gets in his car with nary a backward glance and drives off. Abbott lights another cigarette, stares out at L.A. at night. I sit down next to him, a great sadness overcoming me.

"Now what?" comes the radio voice.

I look up to see the scene has changed.

"I am on a movie set. I see two comedians, younger but similar in appearance to Abbott and Costello. This must be Mudd and Molloy on the set of *Here Come a Coupla Fellas*. The crew bustles. The air is charged with electricity and—"

"What? What's happening?" says the voice now coming from nowhere.

"It went black. I can't see it anymore."

"Find it."

"It's gone. Everything is black."

"What do you see then?"

"Just dirt now. And blackness."

"What's in the hole?"

I look in the hole. More dirt.

"More dirt," I say.

"Well, fine. Great. You're a real cock tease, Rosenberg. Anyway, that's our time for today so . . . ," says the voice, followed by a finger snap.

CHAPTER 32

Back on the street, I feel relieved there seems to be some recollection of the movie, but also oddly dispirited, both to be so quickly out of the story and back in this awful life of mine, but also to feel at the mercy of Barassini's control in order to recover it. And why is he suddenly so desperate to hear about it? I think about the scene I just watched. Is that even in the movie? How can I know? Nothing is knowable. First of all, it feels so complete, down to precise dialogue and extraordinary comic timing. Is that possible? I have, in the past, claimed an eidetic memory, but have I ever tested it in this way? I don't remember. I try now to recall a single scene of dialogue in *Moutarde*, a movie I have, by a conservative estimate, seen five hundred times, and I cannot. I remember snippets, important lines, brilliant lines, but not every line, not every look, every breath. Granted, the film is in French, and although I am fluent in French and five other languages, conversant in six more, it is not my first language. I attempt to think of a film in English I know as well as I know *Moutarde*. It is a difficult task. I do not expend much energy on American films, as they are generally not worth the effort. I consider the work of Apatow, the Great Exception, as he is known among we enlightened few. There is one scene in *This Is 40* that jumps out and smacks one in the face, even in that veritable sea of Apatow brilliance. I've deconstructed this scene. I've written about it at length. I've performed the Paul Rudd part in my acting for critics classes. I know it. So I attempt to play it back in my mind, just to see if I can.

PETE: We're turning forty and we've been married a long time and there's no passion anymore.
DEBBIE: And we have two kids. I hope they don't hear us fighting.
PETE: No, *you* shut up!
DEBBIE: I'm turning thirty-eight.
PETE: But you lie about your age, so you're really turning older than that.
DEBBIE: We're Simon and Garfunkel!
PETE: Look at my anus through a magnifying glass!
DEBBIE: Did you get me a present?
PETE: Shut up or I'll kill you!

Amazing. That is *indeed* forty. It is as if Apatow had a camera in my house when I was that age. Even though I know I did not get the scene verbatim, it's a testament to the power of the writing (and the performances of Ruddmann, as I have dubbed Paul Rudd and Leslie Mann, so organic and believable are they as a couple!) that I still find myself simultaneously laughing and crying as I recall the scene. The raw human emotionality is palpable. But, no, it is not as well-formed a memory as the Abbott and Costello murder plot scene from a movie I have seen only once, and that viewing in Nameless Ape mode. I weep some more. And then I laugh, because the humanity Apatow shows us is also very funny. This is where his gift lies, his ability to reveal to us the tragedy and comedy that is our lives.

AT HOME, DRINKING myself into oblivion with a bright and tangy yet inexpensive cab—a 2015 Agnès et René Mosse Anjou Rouge, to be precise, which is well-priced at twenty-two dollars (but borrowed from my brother's wine cellar)—I receive an email from Tsai containing nothing but a link to the website of the laundromat across the street from her apartment, which I see has a wash/dry/fold drop-off service. And a note that reads: *Every other Sunday*.
Huzzah!
I stop by the laundromat to see if part-time help is needed, pref-

erably Sundays, preferably every other one. It is not. And after a violent exchange in which the manager and I argue whether this Sunday or next Sunday is the first *other* Sunday, I leave my name and number, saying, "Oh, and if anything opens up, I would really love to work here."

All the way back to Barassini's, fantasies of sorting, washing, and folding Tsai's clothes dance in my head. The level of frustration I feel is extraordinarily high. I kick a garbage can, and an apartment manager chases me for three blocks. Barassini is in his office with a client, so I have time to masturbate inside the antique armoire in the waiting room. I can't get hard but have an explosive and satisfying orgasm nonetheless. The humiliation of not being able to form an erection adds to the humiliation of my fantasy, which adds to the orgasm. Something terrible is happening to me.

THE ROAD IS dark, and I am again digging, digging, this time with no success. Hundreds of holes illuminated by soft moonlight pepper this surreal landscape.

"Nothing?" squawks the radio.

"Nothing," I tell it.

"Is the environment the same as last time?"

I look around. There's now a break in the canopy of trees.

"I can see the moon," I say.

"Dig into the moon with your trowel. But gently, so as not to damage the moon. You must *not* damage the moon. For the love of all things holy, *never* damage the moon. It is a thing from which there can be no return."

"The moon is 237,000 miles away," I say. "I can't dig into it, gently or otherwise."

"Not in your mind it's not," the voice says pointedly.

The voice has a point. I reach up, attempt to gently poke my trowel into the moon, and it works. I scoop out a tiny bit, and hundreds of pieces of something fall to the ground around me like piñata candy from a moon-shaped piñata. The moon swings in the sky, as if on a string. It's creepy.

"Did you do it?"

"I did. There's a lot of stuff on the ground here now."

"Examine it."

I pick up a piece and see myself as a little boy with my father, looking up at the waxing gibbon moon.

"Dad," I say, "where does the rest of the moon go when it goes away?"

My father laughs, in what seems to me as a child a mocking chortle. Looking at it now, I imagine he was probably affectionately amused, but I can't remember it that way. I don't remember it that way. I was humiliated, my face flushed to the color of my port-wine stain and my eyes brimmed with tears.

"It's OK," my father says. "I just thought that was adorable."

My father explains it to me, but I don't think I ever heard the explanation; I just kept thinking, I'm such an idiot. He thinks I'm an idiot. Fuck me. Fuck me with a chain saw. Why can't I be smart like my successful, handsome brother with his future wine distributorship or marry into money like my sister one day will?

"Anything?" the radio asks.

"Nothing pertinent," I say.

"Keep looking."

So I do.

I see myself a mortified teen as I, on a dare, moon some girls from a slowly moving car. One of the girls says, "Ew, you got dried shit on that pasty ass. Rosendingleberry!" They shriek and laugh.

Now I am savoring a MoonPie in the bushes behind my childhood house. I had swiped it from the pantry even though I was never allowed sweets before dinner. Levy's "grabby" story momentarily pops into my mind, dissolves.

Now I see the Apollo 11 moon landing on TV.

"Bingo!" cries Barassini.

Grainy video of Michael Collins in the command module. Wait, was there footage of Collins in the module? Am I misremembering? There is no Internet here in my mind to research it.

The image shifts to crisp color. A sad and lonely Collins circles around the dark side of the moon, while Armstrong and Aldrin are off making history. I do notice that Collins is a puppet. This is from Ingo's film. I have come upon the film. Collins clears his throat and sings to camera:

> As I orbit in this ship
> While elsewhere history is made,
> Around the dark side I do slip as
> From my radio NASA's voice does fade.
> And just like that I'm all alone
> Cut off from everyone on Earth,
> In solitude, profound and deep
> I ponder celebrity and what it's worth.
> The world needs men who fly alone
> Who seek not the constant adulation,
> That walking on the moon commands
> From a fawning and obsequious nation.
> True heroes live behind the scenes
> Hidden by this pockmarked sphere,
> Alone, alert, and on the job
> With nary a soul to see or cheer.
> And though the big show's on the moon
> With the speeches and the leaping fun,
> I as well have served mankind
> Unsung but still a job well done.

Then, suddenly, in the claustrophobic gloom of *Columbia*: a shimmer! Collins and I both turn to it. There, floating in this interplanetary realm, two naked male infants appear.

They seem stunned, as does Collins. I am stunned as well, and although I cannot see my own face, I'm certain I share their expressions. We are all of us frozen in our astonishment. Then in an instant we snap back to life, the babies bawling, Collins gaping, and I remembering the scene! The astronaut pushes himself off the wall and glides toward them, gathers them up in his strong, manly arms, calms them. Oh, to have had a father, even though I did.

"There," he says. "It's OK. It's going to be all right."

And just like that, they are quiet. It's as if he were made for this job, which, of course, in retrospect, we all now know he was. There are two monkey space suits in the storage bin, having been brought, for good luck, by the prescient Collins in tribute to the pair of fallen comrades Piff and Jambito, who died for their country back in 1958 in the long covered-up, horrifying NASA monkey explosion. The infants, fitted into Urine and Fecal Containment Systems (plenty of diapers for all on that voyage!), are then gently placed into the perfectly fitting monkey space suits. It's fascinating to watch this story, which has been drummed into our heads since 1969, played out on the screen. There had, of course, been attempts to tell it filmically in the past, but the Collins family always nipped them in the bud.

"These miraculous kids deserve a childhood," he'd said at press conference after press conference.

And he was right. Of course he was. We all knew it. He was Michael Collins, one of the great dads of all time, much better than I ever was, according to eyewitnesses, although I have a different memory of the incidents than my daughter does. However, Ingo didn't need the Collins life rights; his was a movie never to be seen. And then as Collins's adopted children reached adulthood, they made their own choices, as we all know, about the public sphere and their place in it. I do try not to think of what we all know, as I want to be certain the story I'm remembering is from Ingo's movie and not the news media, gossip columns and obituaries, and religious tracts.

"Houston," says Collins, "there has been an odd but wonderful development around the dark side. Over."

"Yes, Apollo 11? Over."

"Two male human infants have appeared in *Columbia*. Over."

"Sounds like a little cabin fever, Lieutenant. No worries. Over."

"No, Houston. They're real. Over."

"Noted, Lieutenant. For now let's focus on getting Buzz and Neil back safely. Over."

"Roger that. Over and out."

"What's happening now?" asks Barassini's voice over the radio.

"He's pushing a bunch of buttons, looking at dials," I say.

"I'm pushing buttons and checking dials, Houston. Over," says Collins, seemingly thinking Barassini was Houston.

After a bit, I am jarred as something slams into us. A hatch unscrews and Armstrong and Aldrin enter, laughing and patting each other on the back as they remove their helmets.

"Man, that was fun!" Aldrin says. "And when you said that thing, the giant leap business . . . Holy moly! Shivers!"

"Hey, Mikey!" says Armstrong. "Miss us?"

"Actually," says Collins, "I had a pretty interesting time while you guys were gone."

"I bet," smirks Aldrin. "I can see how sitting alone in a metal bucket could be interesting. Maybe not as interesting as walking on the *goddamn fucking moon*, but still . . . a good time, I'm sure."

Aldrin and Armstrong laugh, pat each other on the back some more.

"Actually, fellas, two infant children magically appeared in the module while you—"

"That's cool, Mikey, but you should seen—wait, *what?*" says Armstrong.

"They just appeared out of thin air. It was a miracle. Perhaps the greatest documented miracle in the history of mankind."

"Cabin fever, Mikey, but don't worry about it because—"

Collins holds up the sleeping infants.

"I don't think Houston believes me," says Collins, "but of course once they see . . . So the moon was good?"

"Oh, it was very cool, y'know," says Armstrong, suddenly subdued, eyeing the babies.

"It was very fun to bounce around all slow motion–like," adds Aldrin. "So . . . y'know."

"I imagine it was," says Collins. "That sounds fun. Excuse me for one second. I have to mash some space food sticks with water and feed the moonchildren. It's feeding time. I'm calling them the moonchildren."

"Can I feed one of 'em?" asks Aldrin.

"I think they're imprinted on me for right now, Buzz. Maybe once we arrive back home. Once they get acclimated."

"OK. Cool. That's cool."

The scene shifts to a ticker-tape parade down 5th Avenue. I'm among the crowds lining the street; I'm floating down with the confetti; I'm watching from a high window like Oswald; I'm walking alongside the vehicles with the security. Collins is in the first convertible with Castor and Pollux (as they are, of course, soon to be known the world over) in their little monkey space suits. Collins waves to the adoring crowd. Armstrong and Aldrin are three cars back, almost ignored. They don't even bother waving. Aldrin fumes. Armstrong stares at his hands.

"I was prepared to be in your shadow," Aldrin says. "Second man on the moon. I get that. But not in the shadow of Collins. That's just insulting. Collins was the punch line. We all knew that, even back in astronaut school. Michael 'Footnote' Collins, we called him. Now look at us. This is unacceptable. Unacceptable."

"What are you saying, Buzz?"

"I'm saying something needs to be done. Or undone."

"Like what? Collins won fair and square."

"Won? This isn't a competition! And besides, you call magic space babies fair and square? I'm not buying what you're peddling, Armie."

"Well, anyway, there's nothing to be done."

"I say we disappear the kids."

"What? How?"

"You heard of Lindbergh?"

"Of course. He's our predecessor in the field of aviation."

"Well, he had a kid called the Lindbergh Baby."

"What of it?"

"The kid was kidnapped," says Aldrin.

"Terrible! Those poor parents!"

"Terrible or great?"

"Terrible?"

"I say we do the Lindbergh kidnapping times two."

"But that's kidnapping!"

"Times two! *And* the Lindbergh Baby never came home."

"Dead?"

"You tell me."

"This is the first I'm hearing of the story, so—"

"Dead. The point is, Neil, we disappear the monkey-suited Space Kiddos and all of a sudden Papa Collins is back to being Footnote Collins. Maybe people think they never even existed, if we play our cards right. Maybe it was all space illusion. Mass space hypnosis."

"Is that a thing?"

"Who knows? Could be. The point is no one knows at this point. This is all brand-new territory."

"I'm no criminal, Buzz. I just made a giant leap for mankind."

"Did you, Neil? Anyone throwing roses at you? Any broads spreading their legs for you? Seems all the trim out there has daddy issues, if the goo-goo eyes they're making at Collins is any indication."

Armstrong looks out at the women in the crowd, then at Aldrin, and sighs.

As I pull back, a camera taking in this expansive, elaborate scene—falling ticker tape, puppet crowds, a letter-perfect 1969 5th Avenue set—I marvel, not only at Ingo's extraordinary skill in animating this complex moment, but also how he had been able to predict this impossibly unlikely scenario, for it has come back to me that Ingo told me he animated this sequence in 1942. How was he able to predict the Castor and Pollux story, the kidnapping attempt by Aldrin and Armstrong? I guess this is his "rememorying" of the future. Perhaps I'll visit Aldrin in prison, ask him how accurate that ticker-tape parade conversation was? It all makes me wonder: Are there other truths buried in this movie, things I don't yet remember, things that have maybe not yet occurred? Rememories of my future? I feel unsettled. The movie has receded and left me once again in darkness. I am alone in here and I am desolate.

"Tell me," says the voice, now coming from nowhere and everywhere.

"It's black."

"Is that part of the film?"

"It's just black. Maybe it's the leader."

"Who's the leader? Pollux?"

"What are you talking about? No, leader is the black film at the head of a movie."

"Maybe this part of the movie is black?"

Barassini's voice sounds panicky.

"That doesn't make sense."

"Could this be part of the film? Like a black part of the film?"

"No. Why do you keep asking that?"

"No reason! Keep searching!"

I look, for what feels like a long time, months, it seems, wandering this darkness, which is punctuated only by an occasional and urgent "Anything now?!" from Barassini's voice. It's a terrifying experience.

"The hour's up," it finally says, followed by the angriest of finger snaps.

I am in Barassini's office. He paces.

"Well, that turned to shit," he says.

"Yeah."

"Look, Castor Collins is a client of mine," he says. "OK?"

"Oh, wait," I say. "I think I knew that."

"So I'm wondering if I'm in the movie. I'm just wondering is all. That's all."

"I don't recall. Maybe you—"

"Don't think about it now. Only in the trance. It's the only way to be accurate. Outside of this controlled environment, you will misremember, conflate. Your recollection will be useless to me."

"To you?"

"By useless to me, I meant to you, of course. Useless to you in your goal of re-creating an accurate novelization of Ingo's film."

"Novelization," I say. "I never thought of it that way."

"Yes, you have."

"Have I? The novelization is a discredited form, an inferior form, although there have been novelizations that have been vastly superior to the films on which they were based. Updike's novelization of *Fun in Balloon Land* is devastating, beautiful, haunting. The film itself is a masterpiece of mid-sixties family gothic, but Updike got deep inside the balloons, inside with the helium and the regret."

"So we're not calling it a novelization now?"

"Transubstantiation? I like that. Almost a sacred connotation."

"*Almost*," he repeats.

And I suspect I am being mocked.

CHAPTER 33

ON 10TH AVENUE, my mind races. The religious responsibility I now feel toward the transformation of Ingo's film into a holy text has overwhelmed me. Visions of Updike, that elfin chronicler of white maleness and balloons, waltz through my brain. The only way I can compete, the only way I can move forward with my own essential work, is to diminish his. I purchase a copy of his *Balloon Land* from the book vending machine off West 47th. I read as I walk. Let the pedestrian pedestrians watch out for me.

> "We're having fun in Balloon Land," sang the unseen man to the warbles of a tremulous calliope, his voice a lie of warmth and friendliness. We are not having fun in Balloon Land, was the truth of it, and every person and balloon in Balloon Land knew it.

I have to admit this is the most brilliant first sentence (well, two sentences) I have ever read, even more so than "They call me Ishmael." I'll have to read further, see what Updike is up to, what he does with character development, how he manages the introduction of "Cow jumping over the moon land." But I am worried. A clearheaded and mature inventory of my life seems in order if I am going to be able to compete in this arena against such a giant. How can I, a troubled soul with fragmented focus and allegiance, do right by Ingo's lost masterpiece? Since the medically induced coma, my life has taken several odd and incomprehensible turns. My obsession with Tsai is unhealthy and inappropriate. Even while under Barassini's hypnotic control I think of her. She is always there. She was in the command module with us and I didn't tell Barassini. I try to push her away, to the back of my head, but she never fully leaves. The shame I feel, both exquisite shame and shameful shame, is a barrier to complete immersion into the memory of the film, which I must from now on insist on.

The Film.

Furthermore, aside from my own tragedy, the world is in a shambles and it is near impossible for me to keep from wallowing in the misery and worry these circumstances cause me. Our current president is a nightmare, I've heard. And people say this is a moment of great strife. We are on the verge of several wars, they say. I'm not sure where. And there is poverty in various places. A lot of it, apparently. Racism and sexism and other things have reared their ugly Hydra heads, the wags insist. I should protest all of this, I should make a placard, but to what end? It seems I am of more use to the planet as a conduit to the work of Ingo Cutbirth. Perhaps his film is the thing that, in the end, saves the world. Perhaps. I must focus fully on this important work. And on Tsai.

She must not think I have not attempted to get the profoundly important job of cleaning her laundry. But should I write to her and tell her I tried and failed? Isn't it presumptuous of me to think she might care one way or another? The whole point of this exercise from her perspective, as I see it, as it has been explained to me, is to communicate that she does not care one way or another. I begin an email anyway:

> I can't imagine you care one way or another, but I just
> thought I'd let you know—

I stop. Isn't it presumptuous of me to think I can imagine one way or another what she thinks? Doesn't that presumption fly in the face of the power dynamic she has so clearly and eloquently established? I delete the email and stare at the blank screen for a long while. An idea occurs.

*   *   *

Back at the laundromat, I offer to volunteer my time for free every other Sunday, starting for the first two weeks with every Sunday, so as to cover all bases. I explain to the manager that I just enjoy doing laundry. I sell it to her as a win-win situation for us both. She takes this in, nods, pulls out her iPhone, photographs me, then lets me know that I am banned from ever again entering this establishment, that my photograph will be hung on the wall to alert all employees of this development.

I am horrified. My very face has been turned into its own scarlet letter for all the city's launderers to mock and detest. My secret life laid bare. And, after all, who amongst us doesn't have a secret life? I am certain that if the rock we call Manhattan were to be overturned, myriad creepy-crawly secret lives would be discovered. I am certain that if— But then it occurs to me: This is perhaps the perfect solution to my issue. Tsai will no doubt see my visage on the laundromat wall. She will understand I have been humiliated in my attempt to secure employment there. I ask the manager if I can see the shot and that if it is flattering, perhaps we could take another one directly under the fluorescents, which tend to be harsh and emphasize my sallow complexion and medically enlarged nose. She tells me she is going to call the police, so I leave. I have not gotten everything I had hoped for, but I have gotten something. For now, there is nothing left to do but wait.

"Tell me."

It's February 3, 1920. Two infants appear in a cornfield outside of Mason City, Iowa, birthplace of Meredith Willson (known for his Broadway hit *The Music Man*), and are discovered by eighteen-year-old Meredith Wilson (no relation) as she was "looking for corn to eat." The unclaimed infants are tested by local authorities for both jaundice and "pizzazz," discovered to place very high on the Rothkopf-Lincoln Charisma Scale, and enrolled in the city's famed

Mason City Orphanage of the Performing Arts (known informally as The Perforphanage). Here they remain inseparable and therefore begin training as a "team." They are given the names Rooney and Doodle, chosen from a list determined by monikologists to be funny comedy team names. The list on the clipboard includes:

Manstop and Flume
Cornvest and Grimp
Gorus and Megnan
Steamhorn and Groach
Hegel and Schlegel

and

Willibald and Winibald

Perforphanage training is notoriously rigorous, and the infants soon become expert at pratfalls and spit takes, even before they can walk. Once they do learn to walk, however, they quickly become expert at funny walking and eventually running like a girl.

Tsai comes into the market while I'm at the register and puts a three-pack of Trident cinnamon gum on the counter.

"That'll be $2.45, please."

She fishes in her purse.

"How's it going, Darnell?" Tsai says to Darnell, who's picking some stringy ham out of the tray behind the counter and dropping it like worms into his mouth.

"Good, babe," he says, gob full of pig. "You wanna?" He holds two fingers up to his lips and draws on an imaginary marijuana joint.

"I'd love nothing more," she says, handing me three dollars. "But I must get to bed."

I put the three dollars into the till and find a slip of paper under the bills. I pocket it and give Tsai her change.

"Night, Darnell."

"Night, Tsai."

She leaves and I sneak a look at the paper. It's a laundry list:

Bras (6)

Panties (12)

Jeans (4 pr)

Socks (10 pr)

Tees (7)

Sweats (1 pr)

Blouses (8)

Skirts (7)

Sweaters (2)

Yoga pants (3 pr)

Leggings (2 pr)

The letterhead on the slip reads *Port Whine's Washed-Up Laundry Service: 24 hours a day. Guaranteed Two-Hour Turnaround.* A miniature copy of my photo from the laundromat stares back at me. Handwritten at the bottom: *PU 5:30 A.M. Sunday. To be returned by 7:30 A.M.*

I am at her building at 5:29, finger poised to ring at exactly 5:30. Port Whine is to be an exceedingly prompt service. I barely slept the night before in anticipation.

At her apartment door, in terry-cloth robe and sweatpants, she hands me her laundry bag.

"If I find even a hint of anything resembling your pathetic old lady jism on it, you will never see me again."

I nod, afraid to speak, and once safely on the subway platform, I stick my face into the bag and inhale. It is more glorious than I could've anticipated. The world disappears as I take it in several more times, the molecules of her sweat, dirt, glycogen, estrogen, urine, skin cells, and fecal matter entering my bloodstream through my mucous membranes and owning me. I miss my train and must run the thirty-three blocks to the laundromat near my building, so as not to return Tsai's magnificently odoriferous laundry a moment late. I am thrilled to clean it for her but sad that it must be cleaned. Still, I am prepared. In my satchel, I have my washing products. I've done a great deal of research on detergents, bleaches, fabric softeners, stain removers, and dryer sheets. I intend for this to be the best laundry Tsai has ever had done. Many of my female friends say they wish they had a wife, and of course they mean a helpmate, don't they, someone to take care of their mundane needs so they can focus on more important work. I'm enjoying thinking of myself that way, as Tsai's wife. Maybe at some future date, if I prove myself today. I imagine cooking for her, dusting, straightening her pussy bow before she goes to a meeting. But for now I must attend to the task at hand without the distraction of such wishful thinking. There's not much time, and I must bring the laundry to my apartment for ironing after and still get it to her by 7:30, or becoming the future Mrs. Tsai Yan will remain forever a pipe dream. I pay exquisitely close attention to all the washing instructions, carefully separating whites and colors, reading the special laundering requirements of each garment. The leggings must be hand-washed and I'm fortunate there is a laundromat sink in which to do that. I thought ahead and purchased a bottle of The Laundress Signature Detergent. The Laundress is a wonderful company with a full line of cleaning products and an invaluable website chock-full of all kinds of fascinating cleaning tips. By 7:00 A.M., I am on the subway heading downtown, my work done and done very well, I believe. I don't expect gratitude and know that by definition it is not part of the arrangement. But I do hope she enjoys the soft, freshly laundered clothing I am returning to her on time.

CHAPTER 34

" *WHAT DO YOU see?* "
         Roon and Dood flee the burgled house in their stolen green Dodge Challenger.

"You promised me no one would be home," says Roon.

"He was supposed to be out of town," says Dood.

"And you didn't tell me he was a cop!"

"I didn't think it was pertinent since he was supposed to be out of town!"

"Well, he wasn't, was he?"

"He was scheduled to be at a cop convention!"

"Great. Is he gaining on us?"

They both look back.

"I don't see him yet," says Dood.

They hit something big. The car swerves, keeps going.

"What was that?" asks Roon.

"Keep driving!" says Dood.

Dood looks back again.

"Oh my God, it's a guy! We hit a guy!"

"What the fuck was a guy doing in the middle of this empty road in the middle of nowhere in the middle of the night?!"

"Well, I guess it wasn't empty, was it?"

"You told me the road would be empty! Is he dead?!"

"I don't know!"

"Is he moving?!"

"He's a lump in the distance! How would I know?"

"We vowed never to kill anyone else!"

"It was an accident!"

"Probably a homeless guy, right?"

"That doesn't make it right."

"I'm not saying that! I'm just saying . . . I don't know what I'm saying. We should go back."

"We can't go back. Anyway, the cop will see him and stop."

"Thank God the cop wasn't out of town so he can stop to help the guy we killed fleeing from him."

"Don't be sarcastic. I said I was sorry."

"No, you didn't," says Roon.

"Well, we don't know that he's dead. And you killed him. Technically."

"We both killed him!"

"I wasn't the one driving," says Dood.

"I'm only driving because you let your license lapse."

"Which is a ridiculous rule you made up, since we're criminals already, so . . ."

"All I ever wanted to do was entertain folks."

"We've killed a lot of people, you and I. If you count the audience of our play."

"I know. I feel bad about that."

"That time wasn't our fault, really."

"But still, I feel guilt."

"I mean, if we hadn't done the play, it wouldn't have happened."

"This one is more directly our fault, though."

"Your fault."

"We're a team."

"What if that homeless guy was the person who was going to save the world?"

"Save it by standing on a deserted country road in the Midwest at three in the morning?"

"We don't know how the universe works."

"I think we know it doesn't work like that."

"Crazy guys can save the world. Don't stigmatize mental illness. There's evidence that Jesus was mentally ill."

"I'm not aware of any such evidence."

"I read it somewhere, in some journal. He thought he was the son of God, for one thing. The whole *Three Christs of Ypsilanti* thing."

"Jesus thinking he's Jesus is not a sign of mental illness."

"If you say so."

TSAI STOPS HAVING me do her laundry. There's no direct contact or conversation, so I don't know why. I just no longer hear from her. She also gets me fired from the deli. When I come in for my shift, Darnell tells me Tsai complained about my attitude. He won't be specific about the complaint, but he looks at me in a weird way, and I suspect she said something truly horrible about me. I am at a loss. The two hours I spent laundering and ironing Tsai's clothing were the happiest of my life. I feel pathetic acknowledging this, but acknowledge it I must. One must at some point tell the world in no uncertain terms who one is. After much hand-wringing and self-flagellation, it occurs to me there may be a solution to the problem of my continued and overwhelming need to serve Tsai, and it is a method of serving for which I will not need Tsai's permission, as it has been made clear to me I shall never again receive that.

I send my résumé to Zappos, an online mega shoe and clothing store owned by billionaire Jeff Bezos of the Houston Bezoses, who also owns everything else. I had noticed in the trash room of Tsai's building, where I had been looking through Tsai's trash, that she is a somewhat regular customer of Zappos (she is also an eater of grapefruit and a wearer of Always Maxi Size 3 Extra Long Super Pads With Wings, unscented, although eventually scented, as I have discovered). So a job in customer service at Zappos would, if I were very, very lucky, put me in email (or even phone!) contact with Tsai at some point. I realize that Zappos has many customers and, I would imagine, many customer service representatives, but even the thought that the next person on the line could be Tsai Yan would keep me going to work at the Zappos call center, even if that call never comes, as long as we both shall live.

My interview with the lady from human resources goes well, perhaps too well. She is an older woman with a port-wine stain birthmark on her face, and I sense in her a feeling of kinship. I feel none. I have no desire to be a member of the port-wine club.

"What an impressive résumé," she coos.

Unlike my interviewer at the deli, her eyes are never off me.

"Thank you."

"I have to say, I've always been a movie lover myself."

I try to guess her taste in movies. I'm thinking *The Lake House* or whatever that maudlin marigold hotel tripe was. Maybe she likes port-wine stain movies, although I doubt she is sophisticated enough to understand *The Grand Budapest Hotel*, the only truly great port-wine stain film.

"I'm embarrassed to say it," she says, "but I did a little acting myself in school and I considered pursuing it professionally at one point."

Really? Jesus no. The world has been spared.

"Oh, really?" I say. "That's great. Trodding the ol' boards, eh?"

"Oh yes. I was quite the ham," she giggles.

Of that I have little doubt, Mx. Piggy.

"Listen," she says. "There is no way I can recommend you for our customer service department. With your background in film production and obvious worldliness, I feel certain our public relations department would be a much better fit."

"But customer service is people work and I am a people person," I scream.

"Nonsense," she says. "I won't hear of it. You need to have the confidence in yourself that I have in you. The position in PR pays five times the CS position and that's just to start. The sky is the limit there."

I nod. I can't look this woman's gift horse in the mouth. I need her as an ally. After I prove myself in PR, I can request a transfer. And I imagine that even in PR, I'll have some access to sales records. I'll be able to keep track of any shoes Tsai orders. That thought alone gives me an immediate and massive erection in this lady's office. I mull whether or not making her aware of this erection would help or hurt here. These moments are so fraught in the post-harassment era. Harvey Weinstein has done us all a disservice. I decide this might help in that she will certainly conclude it is about her. It is unlikely she is often (or ever) the recipient of such conspicuous sexual interest, even though I understand fully well that women of all attractiveness levels are equally likely to get harassed, that, truly, it is not about attractiveness; it is about power. It is always about power. It is always about power. But, to paraphrase the brilliant Dr. Angelou, still I rise. She reaches to shake my hand and at that moment registers my conspicuous encumbrance. Her eyes widen. I have made the correct choice.

"Mr. Rosenberg!" she says after a moment. "It has been such a pleasure."

"The pleasure is all mine."

I wink. I wink like that accursed tugboat wishing for death.

She doesn't let go of my hand. She is waiting for me to ask her out. But I cannot. I cannot! I do not know how to proceed.

"If only I were not married," she says finally.

"Oh. I didn't realize. Oh, what a shame. Although he is an extraordinarily lucky man."

"Tell *him* that," she jokes. "Well, anyway, things change. I will be sure to check in on you."

"That sounds wonderful," I say.

She still holds my hand and smiles. I try to imagine who would marry her. I cannot.

"You're so shy," she says finally. "I love that. It's awfully sweet."

"I am," I admit. "I am terribly, terribly shy."

"Aw," she says. "You just don't know how great you are. That's one of the things I find so charming about you."

"Thank you."

"Take care of yourself, B. Rosenberger Rosenberg."

And I promise her I will.

CHAPTER 35

BARASSINI IS THRILLED I am starting a fairly well-paying job. I owe him a great deal of money for our sessions. He packs me a box lunch for the company bus ride to Zappos headquarters somewhere at an undisclosed location in rural New Jersey.

I stop by my sister Portia Rosenberger Rosenberg Heche's place on the way to Port Authority. She is also thrilled about the job, as I also owe her a great deal of money. She puts together a monthly payment plan for me and packs me a box lunch. Now I have two lunches. I don't tell her, because it was a nice gesture and I don't want to spit on it, especially since I still owe her so much money. On the street, I throw Portia's lunch out because Barassini's looks better. Maybe I should've given it to a bum, I realize, and feel bad. But the truth is, there were no bums around and I wasn't about to go searching for one. I'm on a schedule.

On the bus, I take out the self-hypnosis tape Barassini packed with my egg salad, turn my iPhone to record mode, and wait for Barassini's words to take effect. I had already asked my seatmate if he would mind if I were to narrate a forgotten movie onto my iPhone while in a hypnotic trance. He said he wouldn't mind at all and switched seats.

Darkness descends. I wander blindly, with my shovel, looking for holes to dig. Stumbling over a mound of dirt, I stop to dig there, uncovering a curly blond wig.

I narrate as the clip plays through me like a cold wind: Young woman with doe eyes sideways glances said eyes at a top-hatted young man who shares her park bench. He glances at her as well, bashful, a rubber-band smile. She glances. He glances. So it goes. Never at the same moment, until finally it is, and in a puff of smoke an overweight man in a soiled union suit and curly blond wig appears in the tree behind them. He shoots two arrows; one hits the man, the other the woman. Their eyes widen with desire and both slide toward the center of the bench. The man shyly pecks the woman on the cheek. They both look down. She shyly pecks him on the cheek. Then they both look at each other, kiss on the lips. As the kiss continues, the man sees the camera, reaches up out of frame and pulls down a window shade, obscuring them from view. We hold on the shade for five minutes. At first there is the occasional gentle push against the shade. Then the pushing increases in frequency and intensity. Finally, a particularly hard push snaps up the shade to reveal the man and woman in a bedroom, unaware of us, engaging in violent and somehow sinister sex. Cupid has been replaced by a leering devilman in a dark (might be red, but this is a black-and-white film) union suit, horns on his head. His nose is offensively anti-Semitic. The couple finishes with an intensity that shakes the room, causing paintings to fall off the wall. Exerted, they heave, the woman's legs carelessly spread.

Now she stands in profile against a background of flowered wallpaper. In herky-jerky time-lapse, her belly expands.

Iris out and in.

A stork in a Western Union messenger cap slogs through a stormy sky, dangling a bundle from its beak.

Iris out and in.

The woman with her roly-poly toddler against the same wallpaper. In more time-lapse, we watch him grow and her age. After a few "years" (weeks in real time), a loutish man appears in the frame. We watch as the mother, then the boy show signs of beatings: fat lips, black eyes, broken arms. The man disappears. More aging. When the boy is ten, his mother has been laid in an open coffin.

Next, the boy stands among many other staring children against a mildewed wall under a sign reading NEW JERSEY HOME FOR FOUNDLINGS.

Iris out and in.

The boy is asleep on a cot in a dormitory of hundreds maybe thousands maybe millions of children. He opens his eyes, looks into the camera, gingerly climbs out of bed, and removes his nightshirt to reveal he is fully dressed underneath. He pulls a packed bindle from under his bed and makes his way to the window.

Iris out and in.

Roly-poly orphan Molloy, now dressed as a newsie, sneaks into a New York movie theater to watch a despicably sexist comedy short entitled *Ain't She a Corker, Boys?* about a spoiled young woman (played by the mysterious Lucy Chalmers) who inherits a wine factory and drinks herself to death, thus bankrupting the business, thus causing her newly unemployed employees to drink themselves to death, one of whom is Gavrilo Princip, thus causing World War I. Molloy laughs convulsively. This is the moment he realizes his destiny is to be in show business.

IT SEEMS I have a talent for shoes. I try to finagle my way into ladies', because that is, of course, most likely where Tsai is to be found. But Zappos is starting a specialty shoe division, and this is where my new boss, Allen Wrench (I know!), wants me.

"You are highly creative," he speculates. "We don't generally have the great good fortune of landing people like yourself here at Zappos. New divisions need idea men, which I speculate you just might be one of. We need to spread the good news about our new division to all those yet untapped markets. And you're just the man to do that, I conjecture, what with your endless ideas about things and your creativity and what have you, which is, in my estimation, perhaps boundless."

"Thank you, Allen," I say.

The specialty shoe division has been created to sell specialty shoes, specifically clown shoes, elevator shoes, animal face slippers, and unpaired shoes for the one-footed. For "one-foots," I propose a service I call "shoe buddies," in which a single-footed customer could search our database to locate an other-footed customer of similar size and fashion sense to go "halfsies" with. Allen says I'm a genius, perhaps, and that time will tell.

Of course, immediately following this, my co-worker Henrietta proposes "sock buddies," which is, when all is said and done, still my idea just dressed in a hat. Allen praises her for still-my-idea, and I decide it's war. I suggest that the specialty division should sell tiny foot-binding shoes for elderly Chinese women. Henrietta says, What about foot-binding shoes for foot-binding fetishists. Again, the same idea. We don't really care why they're buying foot-binding shoes, I explain. I propose cement shoes for our mafioso customers. This is a joke, intended to lighten the mood and demonstrate my wit, which is far superior to Henrietta's. Everyone except Henrietta laughs. I watch her furrow her brow, rack her brain, looking for a joke. Eventually, she suggests horse shoes. For horse customers. This joke falls flat. She's embarrassed. I suggest whore's shoes. Y'know, five-inch red sequined stilettos. Everyone laughs again. Allen slaps his knee, then mine, then goes around the table slapping every knee in the boardroom. What I've done is taken Henrietta's terrible joke and turned it into something golden. I've made lemonade from Henrietta's shit. I'm suddenly thinking of trying the open mic night at one of the comedy clubs downtown. I have, in my life, been a fierce advocate for humorlessness, as I believe comedy is almost always harmful since it makes fun of those less fortunate and, when punching up, more fortunate. But the laughter intoxicates me.

Henrietta, meanwhile, stews. Her eyes light up. She shrieks like a harpy that between my foot-binding idea and my whore joke, it is totally clear that I am some sort of a misogynist. As a first, second, and third wave feminist, I am infuriated. This is the thing that irritates me so much about women: They think they can go around with impunity casting aspersions on men. Well, I hold all women to the standards to which they claim they want to be held. That is what a true feminist does. There is only one way to responsibly respond to Henrietta's vile attack: I will pummel her into the ground and leave her for dead. So, in rapid succession, I come up with three *serious* specialty shoe ideas: retro shoes for hipsters, booties for your dog, and designer baby shoes with cute names like Gucci-Gucci-Goo, Marc Fisher-Price, and Toddler Oldham. Bam. Bam. Bam. You're dead, Henrietta. I am the king of this department and you are dead. Allen beams at me in a way that feels almost paternal, even though he is thirty years my junior and dresses like Freddie Bartholomew as Little Lord Fauntleroy. His look sends an odd, pleasurable tingle through my body. I have almost forgotten about Tsai. But, of course, not entirely, and the tingle reminds me.

I TAKE UP much less room in my seat on the bus back to the city. There is no longer any doubt that I am shrinking. Although it is, at this point, an exceedingly slow process. But my shirt collar is looser, my tie seems wider and also somehow sillier. The silliness of the tie design—it features a cartoon rabbi above the slogan *100% Kosher*—is not a function of my shrinking, but it does make me question my judgment, which also seems to be shrinking. Also, my ears are now too big for my head. I am worried. Perhaps I should throw in the towel and let myself be loved by the bebirthmarked human resources woman. There might come a time when even she won't want me.

Barassini doesn't seem glad to see me. He doesn't ask about work. He just bangs around his office, slamming drawers. I was excited to talk about my day.

"Where are my damn glasses?" he says.

I hate when he is like this. It's like we're strangers. Does he even love me anym—

He flips my switch and—

I'm on the set of *Here Come a Coupla Fellas*. The crew bustles, readying the first take of the first scene. I wander the memory, still hurt by Barassini, grumbling to myself. He didn't even comment on my tie. I might as well be invisible, as I am in this film. The director is conferring with the new script girl (Costello killed the previous one). Mudd paces in the darkness, running his lines in a rote mumble. Molloy laughs, his mouth full of a partially chewed bite from a comically unwieldy dagwood. He is mid-flirt with a striking young lady in a spangled showgirl costume.

"I'm telling you, honey, we could make such beautiful music together."

"Aw, Chick. That's so romantic."

"You know I'm talking about fucking, right?"

"Chick! You're terrible!"

She slaps him on the arm, but she's laughing. And Molloy knows he's home free with this one. I think about how much times have changed and how lucky we all are, except for men. The director calls places. Molloy takes another bite of his sandwich.

"Don't you move," he says to the girl.

"I won't even move a muscle, Chick. Until later."

"Oh, baby. You and me are gonna have such fun."

Molloy wipes his mouth on his sleeve and waddles his way to his position outside the haberdashery set, where Mudd is already waiting, deep in character. The director calls for the lights, and when they switch on, I glance up at the grid. Though I want to call out a warning, as the disembodied eye I am in this world, I cannot. So, helpless, I wait for the inevitable tragedy to unfold. I could look away, but as the sole witness to this film, I must not. I am here to remember. I am here for Ingo. The director calls for camera, then action. Mudd and Molloy enter the haberdashery set, their transformations into their comic personae instantaneous. Mudd is confident and angry, Molloy bumbling and apologetic. The store's owner approaches them.

"Are you the new men?" he asks.

"Yes," says Mudd. "I am Hargrove and this is my underling Musgrave."

"Hargrave and Musgrove."

"No," says Molloy. "It's Hargrove and Musgrave."

"That's what the man said," says Mudd.

"I'm quite certain I said Hargrave and Musgrove," says the

owner, who resembles Vernon Dent, if Vernon Dent had been a puppet.

"See?" says Molloy. "He just did it again!"

"I see that you're picking a fight with the owner of this establishment who has been generous enough to hire us as temporary holiday employees," says Mudd.

"I'm not picking a fight with no one. I just—"

"That's enough of that, Musgrove," says Mudd. "We're wasting this gentleman's time."

"I'm Musgrave! You're Hargrove!" insists Molloy.

"I'm afraid the little imp is confused, sir," explains Mudd. "But no matter, as I am his manager and you can be assured I will set him straight."

"Very good, Hargrave," says the haberdasher. "I'll leave the store in your charge as I have a lunch engagement."

"Dine in full confidence, sir."

The haberdasher leaves. Mudd goes about straightening a display of shirts. For a long while, Molloy just watches him. Finally:

"You're Hargrove, right?" asks Molloy.

"Of course I'm Hargrove!"

"But you said you were Hargrave," whines Molloy.

"You don't correct the boss! What is the matter with you?"

"So you're Hargrove?"

"Yes, I'm Hargrove! Now get to work!"

"What do I do?"

"It's our first day and I expect you to make a good impression," says Mudd.

"OK," says Molloy. "How do I do that?"

"You need to sell at least ten shirts."

Molloy looks around the empty shop. He just stands there, unsure how to proceed.

"Well?" says Mudd.

"Well what?"

"Sell some shirts! Chop chop!"

"There's no one here!"

"That's not my problem. Use your initiative."

"My initiative. OK."

Molloy walks the aisles officiously, while Mudd busies himself with the ledgers. After a bit, Mudd looks up.

"How's it going?"

"I'm trying. But the nobody here is still not buying nothing."

"That's not my problem."

Molloy nods.

"Now sell those shirts."

Molloy scratches his head, thinks, then, to Mudd:

"Say, you wanna buy ten shirts?"

"Why would I want to buy ten shirts?"

"I don't know!"

"And you call yourself a salesman."

"I don't call myself a salesman!"

"Maybe that's the problem."

"Well, I—"

"Well, you what?"

"I don't know."

"Be aggressive. A salesman never takes no for an answer."

"Aggressive, huh?"

"Yeah. Show 'em who's boss."

"Show who who's boss?"

"The customer! Make him believe he's got to have those shirts."

"You realize there's no one here but you and me?"

"Whose fault is that?"

"Mine?"

"That's right! Now go outside and find some customers!"

Molloy, exasperated, exits, slamming the door, and, on cue, the lighting grid crashes to the stage. Several lights smash to the floor in an explosion of glass and sparks. One shatters the glass watch display. A couple land in piles of clothing on tables. The largest light hits Molloy on the head with a sickening and comical "bonk." Molloy, blood spurting from a scalp wound, wanders around for several moments as if nothing has happened, then drops to the floor. The new script girl screams. Technicians run to Molloy's aid. Someone shouts, "He's dead!" A second girl screams. Then a third. Then the makeup man screams.

Mudd, unharmed, collapses by Molloy's side, weeping.

CUT TO AN all-white hospital room. Molloy is unconscious in the bed, his head wrapped in a bandage. Mudd paces. Marie, Mudd's wife, smokes a cigarette and stares gloomily out the window. Molloy's wife, Patty, sits next to Molloy, holding his hand and talking to him in a soft, encouraging voice. How I long to be talked to that way by a woman, to be looked at that way by a woman, love and tenderness in her eyes. I'd gladly go back into my medically induced coma if I could have that. She talks about nothing, mundane stuff about her day, but the caring, the worry, the love in her voice mocks my own loneliness. I think of Tsai, and just like that, she is there in the scene, a ghost. Surely she was not in the original movie, but here she is now. I smile at her, but she looks right through me. Does she not see me or is this only Tsai being Tsai? I refocus on the scene. Patty continues talking to Molloy.

"Oh, and I saw Carol yesterday. She sends her love and is going to try to get over here to visit sometime this weekend. Hank will come, too. She showed me what they did with their breakfast nook, and it's just darling, Chick. I was thinking we could do something similar. You know that fabric I showed you last week? The chintz with the cherries? I thought we could use that to tie together the red leather and the salt and pepper shakers from Mother. So anyway, I'm going to make the curtains myself. I need a project. Idle hands! Oh! I forgot to ask you if it's all right if we give a little something to the American Diabetes Association again this year? Margie called and you know her fairy nephew, Martin, has it bad, and she asked if we wanted to give a little something. She felt nervous asking because of all that's going on in our lives. But he has the diabetes bad and he's very sick. They have to pump him full of helium, I think she said, to help with the diabetes, and he floats a little above his bed. I think I got that right. Maybe it's not helium, but it's something scientific. She said every little contribution helps. And it all adds up, of course. Of course because of the helium, the doctors can't even give him injections. He would just shoot around the room, careening off the walls and—"

I can't handle any more of Patty's monologue, so I leave. It surprises me that I can do this, that I seem to have some sort of autonomy within the world of this film. The hospital hall is quiet and dim, beautifully constructed with glazed pale yellow brick tile walls (possibly Pantone 607c), considered calming at the time but to the modern eye somehow sinister. A nurse in white pushes a rattling cart past me. I peek into rooms. The verisimilitude is staggering. And all for characters never to be seen. How am I walking around this part of the world that surely was not in the original film? I consider what Hemingway said about his short story "Out of Season":

"I had omitted the real end of it which was that the old man hanged himself. This was omitted on my new theory that you could omit anything if you knew that you omitted and the omitted part would strengthen the story and make people feel something more than they understood."

I think both that this is a profound point and also it is embarrassing that a writer as respected as Hemingway used some form of the word *omit* five times in two adjacent sentences.

There's an old African American man, sunken eyes and cheeks, being shaved by a nurse. A youngish obese Asian woman, her massive, fleshy bare arms splotched unhealthily with red; another woman, perhaps Latinx, wasting away from something terrible. That all these puppets are so delicately and tenderly animated in their pain and that they were meant never to be seen—as most of us are meant never to be—brings an overwhelming pathos to the imagery. I want to cry for them, but of course I cannot because I am not in their world. I have no body here. I have no tears here, even though I am a giant, invisible eyeball.

Wait. Something is coming to me. A conversation with Ingo one night during our dinner break of ramen and reconstituted evaporated milk.

"Most of us are invisible," he said. "We live our lives unrecorded. When we die, it's soon as if we have never lived. But we are not without consequence, because, of course, the world does not function without us. We have jobs. We support economies. We take care of children and the elderly. We are kind to someone. We murder. The existence of us, the unseen people, must be acknowledged, but the dilemma is that once acknowledged, we are no longer truly those same unseen people. Your Dardenne brothers, your De Sicas, your Satyajit Rays are honorable, talented filmmakers, decent and, I suspect, caring, but the work they do is wrongheaded. Once the Unseen are seen, they are no longer Unseen. These men have perpetuated a fiction. I have struggled with this issue, and my solution is to build and animate the world outside the view of my camera. These characters exist and are as carefully animated as those seen in the film. They are just forever out of view."

Are these the poor people in the hospital? The sad, sick, invisible people one never sees when walking by a hospital? I attempt to look in on another unseen patient, but this ability has left me, and I find myself suddenly snapped back into Molloy's room as if tethered to a rubber band. Marie still smokes and stares out the window. Mudd still paces. Patty, still holding Molloy's hand, continues chatting to him.

"Oh, and I spoke with Mother last night. She really wants to be here, but the roads are all closed up in New Jersey because of the storm. They say it's twenty-four inches so far. She's beside herself and promises to get on a train as soon as possible. In the meantime, she sends all her love. I'm reading the most wonderful book, I wanted to tell you. Maybe I could read some of it aloud to you. It's not the kind of book you usually like—it's a romantic novel—but I think you'll like this one. The characters are so realistic, Chick! And it deals with many of the social problems of the day. A Jewish man and a regular lady fall in love and have to deal with people not being happy she's with a Jewish man. It's written by a lady writer, but I don't think that's bad in this case. It's not frilly or frivolous. And I would be happy to start at the beginning so you don't have to jump in in the middle. I have it with me, darling. I'll give you a taste, and if you like it, I'll read the whole book to you!"

"Our time is up," says the voice now, as through the hospital PA system. "I have a smoker at five."

This, followed by a finger snap, and I am awake.

CHAPTER 36

I SUSPECT HENRIETTA IS plotting to kill me. I can't say that I blame her. I am the department favorite and, whereas I have many other irons in the fire, with my book on Ingo soon to be fully remembered, then written, then released, and then my plan to film a live-action remake of the film, this is it for Henrietta. I heard her confide to a colleague in the ladies' room, while I was secreted in a stall, that she had wanted to work in shoes since she was knee-high to a grasshopper. She actually said "knee-high to a grasshopper." I was astounded. Meanwhile, I had never even considered a job like this until I was halfway through a masturbation fantasy about being a salesman in a shoe store fitting Tsai into a pair of slightly too-tight red Mary Janes. Oh my Lord. Tsai! In all the distractions of the new division, I had almost forgotten about my reason for being here. It takes Henrietta and her friend so long to leave that I am ready to scream and charge from the stall. But I do not. I am in control.

While waiting in my stall, I read in a discarded newspaper an article about a poor man who was brutally murdered somewhere; I can't remember where. It is a heartbreaking story, and one wonders how one can go on after reading a piece such as that. But one does go on, doesn't one? Perhaps in the end, one goes on for *him*, the brutally murdered man. A man such as that, who clearly had a family or was desirous of one. What sort of murderer would not even consider the repercussions of this brutal murder on the man's family or his potential one? The rending of the universe through such a vile act is unfathomable and yet struggle to fathom one must. It is what one owes this man. It is both the least and the most one can offer him.

ON THE WAY to Barassini's, I am transfixed by the chatter of animated fur in a sequence of a young boy walking his dog past me. It is positively Lovecraftian. It will haunt my dreams, I am certain. It brings lie to the notion that true stillness is possible in this world. The Zen masters are wrong.

In the hospital again, I watch Marie smoking while staring out the window. She picks a piece of tobacco from her tongue. Patty reads to the comatose Molloy.

"*Be still, my soul, be still; the arms you bear are brittle, / Earth and high heaven are fixt of old and founded strong* . . . Oh, this isn't the lady writer, Chick. I should clarify that. This is the beginning part, before the book starts. The . . . oh, what is it called? The part that's a quote before the book starts?"

"Epigraph," says Marie.

"Epigraph! That's it! By . . . A. E. Housman." Patty clears her throat. "*Think rather, call to thought, if now you grieve a little, / The days when we had rest, O soul, for they were long. / Men loved unkindness then, but lightless in the quarry / I slept and saw not; tears fell down, I did not mourn; / Sweat ran and blood sprang out and I was never sorry: / Then it was well with me, in days ere I was born. / Now, and I muse for why and never find the reason, / I pace the earth, and drink the air, and feel the sun. / Be still, be still, my soul; it is but for a season: / Let us endure an hour and see injustice done. / Ay, look: high heaven and earth ail from the prime foundation; / All thoughts to rive the heart are here, and all are vain: / Horror and scorn and hate and fear and indignation— / Oh why did I awake? when shall I sleep again?—A. E. Housman*. Oh, it is very sad! Maybe too sad for now! I didn't even think! I mean, it's not exactly about being in a coma, but maybe it brings bad associations. I'm sorry, Chick. Maybe we should read something about how waking up is good! I don't know. I can go down to the hospital library and ask if they have any books about waking up."

"I think it's good," says Marie. "I think you should read it. I dated a Jewish boy once."

"You did?" says Mudd.

"In high school, yes. A grand kisser. Ira Something-or-Other. Millman, perhaps. Something like that."

"Huh," says Mudd.

"So, I'll continue?" says Patty.

"Yes," says Marie. "I think you must."

"Sure," adds Mudd. "Let's hear all about Millman, the amazing kissing Jew."

"*One of the questions they were sometimes asked,*" begins Patty, "*was where and how they had met, for Marc Reiser was a Jew—*"

I leave at this point. I've both read this book three times (terrible!) and Ring Lardner's unproduced screenplay adaptation of it twice. (Lardner was a hack. The movie *M*A*S*H* was saved only by Altman's surgical dialogue trims.) In Ingo's film, Patty does indeed read the whole book to Molloy. It is shown in real time, over the course of several weeks. Patty reads with emotion, while a ceaselessly smoking Marie listens and looks forlornly out the window. We imagine she is picturing her Jewish boyfriend and, in fact, at one point she almost certainly mutters, "Mazel tov, you kike son of a bitch, mazel tov," under her breath. Mudd comes and goes, bringing paper cups of coffee and sandwiches wrapped in wax paper.

Molloy, kept alive with an enteral feeding tube, is losing weight. No one else has much of an appetite.

I make my way to the street and find myself in mid-forties Los Angeles. The cars, the pedestrians, the buildings. I wonder if it goes on forever. Or did Ingo build it anticipating how far I'd go, where I'd look? I glance up, to the right, to the left. I do it fast, trying to catch something missing, but I don't. A young couple ducks into a movie house showing a film called *Abbott and Costello Meet the Killer Robot from The Phantom Creeps*. I follow. This is not a real movie. Of this I am certain. As an Abbottandcostellophile of the first order, I am intimately acquainted with their entire oeuvre. Perhaps Ingo is poking some fun at the boys. He does seem to have a bone to pick with them. Was I led to this movie theater? I think I made the choice, but there is no way to know. It's where I wanted to go, but why? Perhaps I have been manipulated, some synapses lit up like Pavlovian chaser lights. Perhaps it is illustrative of the block universe theory, a theory to which, with no little despair, I subscribe. Perhaps Ingo is such a master of filmmaking that he can lead me where he wants. In this case, I am led to a film within his film. I stay close to the couple because I am not sure if I can manage doors in my current disembodied invisible eyeball state. Do I even need to? Can I walk through walls? Regardless, I am intrigued by this couple and follow them in via what is amounting to some elaborate tracking shot out of a Martin Scorseso film. I take a certain pride in this shot, passing the candy counter, weaving through chatting moviegoers and pulchritudinous uniformed usherettes, into the theater, down the aisle, then along the row as the couple make their way to two empty seats near the middle. I remain behind them as they sit, carefully situating their heads and shoulders in the lower third of the frame, focusing on the screen beyond. The film is already in progress. On screen, a giant killer robot is chasing Costello through a cornfield.

"Abbbbbbottttttttt! Hey, Abbbbbbbottttttttttt!" yells Costello.

It is the funniest thing anyone in the audience has ever seen. The robot catches Costello and stomps him into a bloody pulp. Costello moans in high-pitched agony. It's his funny "panic" voice, but it is not funny. The audience grows silent.

"Oh, stop being a baby," spits Abbott, having caught up.

This seems to embolden the audience, for a man in the fifth row shouts, "What a baby!" and everyone once again erupts in laughter. "What a baby!" everyone chants in unison. I find myself laughing, too, uproariously, like the toothless chain-gangers at the end of *Sullivan's Travels*, but soundlessly, because I don't exist in this world. I can laugh at the pain of others with impunity because here I am an eyeball.

HENRIETTA BEGINS HER presentation on dog booties with an irrelevant Debecca DeMarcus quote:

Our phlogiston designed to escape, to dissipate, we are revealed as the ash we have always been. It is the phlogiston that fooled us, made us believe we could be individuals instead of the anonymous ash we have always been. This seduces us into terrible acts of cruelty and horror.

"You're only quoting DeMarcus because I did so in my presentation," I suggest. "I doubt you even know the definition of phlogiston."

"Debunked substance once believed to be present in all combustible bodies. Asshole."

"Phlogiston is real. DeMarcus knew that and so do I. Ash-hole."

"Contemporary science begs to differ. Dickweed."

"They can beg all they want. That does not change the fact that you will burn up nicely once the end-times come."

"Allen, B. is threatening me."

"I am not," I say. "I have no control over the end-times."

"TELL ME WHAT you see," demands Barassini.

"A gaunt man. Serious. Focused. Broken. I can't remember his backstory. I don't know his name or if he ever had one. He is a meteorologist."

"Meaty horologist?"

"Yes."

"Interesting. Bizarre. Continue."

"It might be the 1950s. He sits at his desk and writes in a notebook, his voiceover filling the space in my head: 'If for every action there is an equal and opposite reaction, and if these reactions are wholly predictable, it stands to reason that given all data for a single moment in time and space, one should be able to accurately predict the next moment, and from there, the next, ad infinitum. Furthermore, one should be able to determine, using this same method, the moment preceding the instigating moment and so on, for physics recognizes no direction in time. The key is to have all the data available, which might be feasible in a small and controlled environment.

On a grander scale, this could someday be a great boon for weather prediction. It would require electronic calculating machines of such power and sophistication that they are unlikely to exist in my lifetime.'"

This notion is scientifically nonsensical, of course—although clearly Ingo was familiar with the insane prescient ramblings of meteorologist/pie-in-the-sky pacifist/Ralph Richardson uncle Lewis Fry Richardson—but if one cannot suspend one's disbelief in the cinema, when can one? The meteorologist places a potted philodendron in a miniature glass wind tunnel. He takes measurements, jots down notes, switches on a 16mm motion picture camera trained on the tunnel, closes the tunnel door, adjusts some controls, then turns on the wind. He and the camera watch as the plant's leaves and stem are blown to and fro, this way and that. After about fifteen seconds, a single leaf detaches from the plant and, spinning through the tunnel, hits the far wall and falls to the floor. The meteorologist turns off the camera; then, in filmic montage, he does a series of calculations on his chalkboard: mathematical equations and graphs intercut with calendar leaves flying, shots of the philodendron leaf flying, the meteorologist sleeping at his desk, eating Chinese from cardboard cartons, pounding his fist in frustration. Weeks pass. A beard appears on his face. He draws the plant, precisely, on graph paper, seemingly by translating equations from his book of calculations. He draws it again. He draws it again. He draws it again. He draws it again. He draws it again. Calendar leaves fly once more; the beard grows fuller. The montage ends, and the meteorologist, now exhausted, sits in his darkened office behind two movie projectors trained on two small portable movie screens. He switches them on simultaneously.

"What do they show?" asks the voice.

On the right is the film of the philodendron blowing in the wind tunnel, its leaf dislodging and hitting the far wall. On the left is an animated drawing of the same, playing out simultaneously and in precisely the same way. Both films are on a loop, and the meteorologist watches them over and over.

Cut to him writing in his notebook: *It worked! From only the ini-*

tial data, I was able to predict precise future events. That it took me a full five weeks to do so is a hiccough that will eventually be remedied once a more sophisticated calculating machine than my all-too-human, fallible brain becomes available to consumers.

IN THE SHOWBIZ trades, I read that the film rights to Grace's blog were purchased, having become a "hot" property in today's burgeoning feminist film market.

In what can only be described as a fast-forward, Grace directs the movie, which she has entitled *Father Nose Jest*. It is released to great critical acclaim. The movie is unfair, to say the least. I, as a film lover and a critic of cinema, am obliged to review it on my website Critical Condition even though it pains me deeply to do so.

FATHER NOSE WORST

Full disclosure: Grace Farrow (birth name Grace Rosenberger Rosenberg) is my daughter, and I suspect I might be the model (at least in part) for the father in her movie, so I do have a horse in this race. But I am putting that aside to objectively evaluate this film. *Father Nose Jest* is a small, sincere debut by a talented young female filmmaker, and one is tempted to let it go at that, because the filmmaker's intentions are pure and because one needs to offer some slack to a director in the process of learning her craft. But perhaps a critique from an experienced and disinterested film educator will, in the end, be helpful to this budding auteur. It is in this spirit that I offer my thoughts. *Father Nose Jest* follows the trajectory of an aspiring filmmaker attempting to find her way in a society openly hostile to her gender. Her father, C., played with nary a trace of nuance by the always over-the-top Bob Balaban, is a film critic obsessed with the very male (according to the film) notion of ranking. Throughout the filmmaker's childhood, he pontificated on all things cultural, constantly compiling lists of "Bests" (best films, best paintings, best symphonies, *et chetera*). The filmmaker, named Grace Less (get it?) in the movie, is burdened with the notion of being best (Melania Trump, anyone?) and has thus found herself paralyzed in her work. That is until she meets an older woman poet, who opens up Grace to the exploration of herself and of the world. Grace Less goes on to make a film entitled *A Coming of Rage Story* (get it?), about her own journey and her relationship with her father (toxic, of course) and with the poet (beautiful, sensuous). The film within the film becomes an arthouse darling; scenes of award shows are intercut with extended lovemaking sessions between Grace and Hypatia Reliquary, the poetess.

Certainly Farrow is a filmmaker to watch. One sympathizes with her desire to separate herself from her father's well-known surname, as well as his nose—for it seems apparent, if one compares earlier and more recent photos, Farrow has undergone cosmetic rhinoplasty. Still, one wonders if there will be some regret down the road. Of course she can always reapply her true surname but not her true nose. One understands the necessity of forging one's own identity, but it must be said that herein lies the film's major flaw, and it is a profound and ultimately fatal one. By making the father such an impossibly caricaturish buffoon, Farrow renders the conflict between the two inert. The film hinges on this conflict, for the relationship with her father is the most crucial one in the movie. If the filmmaker makes no attempt to show him as a complex human being with his own set of frustrations and indeed monumental artistic integrity, not to mention an unwavering love for his daughter, then the truth of this relationship is erased, leaving a gaping hole in the story. As a father to a daughter myself, I feel much sympathy for the struggles of any young person to forge an independent identity, but the film's falseness is ultimately so egregious that I cannot in good conscience recommend it. I do think Ms. Farrow is a promising young director, and I look forward to her next outing. Two stars.

Father Nose Worst becomes an arthouse hit, almost, it seems, to spite me. Grace Farrow and her real-life girlfriend, poet Alice Mavis Chin, become media darlings, put out a children's book called *Ambitches* designed to empower young girls, develop the perfume Farrow by Chin, and perform in a two-woman rap musical about the love affair between pirates Anne Bonny and Mary Read entitled *Booty Call*. They are the toast of New York. They also create a women's toaster called My Very Own Toaster.

CHAPTER 37

FOR THE FIRST time at Zappos, I dare to click onto the customer database and look up Tsai. It turns out there is a great deal more information here than one might imagine. Shoe size and purchase history, obviously, but in addition, a fairly complex profile of the customer. This profile is based, one assumes, on customer histories bought from other online outlets and perhaps government files, as well as the customer's own browsing history. Jeff Bezos did not become the world's best billionaire by leaving anything to chance. There is, in addition, a very detailed computer-generated image of Tsai. How they accomplished this, I have not a clue, but it's impressive. The Tsai figure can be dressed in any clothing or shoes found in her purchase history. Would I like to see Tsai in her black pencil skirt (purchased online from Shopbop)? Click. Pair that with a white crop top (also Shopbop)? Click. Here we go. "Tsai" can also be rotated in virtual space. And given that she can be displayed with clothes, she can also be displayed without them. It is unclear what use this feature is to Zappos, but it is exceedingly clear what use it is to me. In addition, I can also, with a click, place any book Tsai has purchased from Amazon in virtual Tsai's hand. With two clicks, one has her in a teal romper reading Rimbaud. One is in heaven. The world could not be a better place. That is, until I notice in her returns a pair of red Mary Janes, received at the Nevada warehouse this morning and not yet through inspection, therefore not back in the general population of available shoes. This means that, as an executive, I am able to intercept these shoes mid-process and put them through "executive inspection." I requisition Tsai's returned Mary Janes and I am informed they will be delivered to my office by end of business today. No questions asked.

Someone has posted a surreptitiously procured photo of my face on the lunchroom wall. Written on the bottom is "Manischewitz Face," a reference to my port-wine stain and my inferred Judaism (I am not Jewish), clearly the foul work of Henrietta. My boss rips it down and calls a department meeting. He demands to know who posted it. He says religious intolerance will not be tolerated. Nor will the mocking of anyone's disfigurement. I say that, for the record, I am not Jewish and do not consider myself disfigured.

"That is not the point," he says.

"It is in a sense," I say, "in that the gibes are toothless in my case."

"Maybe we could sell Jewish shoes," says Henrietta, which seems to me is showing her hand.

"What would those even be?" asks our boss.

"I don't know. Yarmulke shoes?"

This makes no sense as a joke or an insult. Henrietta is off whatever small amount of game she had. My boss takes it to be outrageously insulting.

"There will be no yarmulke references in this workplace!" he screams.

Perhaps he doesn't know what a yarmulke is and thinks it is a derisive word for Jew.

"If and when I find out who posted this photo," he continues, "heads will roll."

I don't understand how he cannot know it was Henrietta.

"Perhaps we could call our Jewish shoes *shuls*," I say in an attempt to lighten the mood as well as one-up (or one million-up!) Henrietta.

Everyone laughs. Everyone, except Henrietta.

"Why does he get to say it?" asks Henrietta.

"Because he's Jewish!" says the boss.

"Mazel Topsiders!" blurts Henrietta, unable to control herself.

Our boss shakes his head.

"Just wait until I find out who did this," he says and leaves the room.

The box is on my desk when I return from our meeting. I am a child on Christmas morning as I rip open the packaging. The shoes. My God, the shoes. They are a beautiful, smooth, shiny, deep ruby leather. The buckle is silver. The sole is black rubber. I know Tsai returned the shoes because they were a size too small since she has already ordered the exact same shoe in the next size up. The thought of her toes jammed into the toe box of the too-small shoes thrills me in ways I cannot and will not explain. There is no part of the interior of these shoes that has not been rubbed and jammed against Tsai's naked feet. With little fanfare, I do what I am certain I was put on Earth to do. I hold one of the shoes up to my nose and inhale. I almost pass out, just from the thought of inhaling Tsai's molecules, but it's more than that. The scent: Tanned leather, rubber, sweat, foot . . . it is a heady experience. I type the serial number on this box into the computer. Yes! This pair of shoes has never gone out before Tsai's purchase. There is Tsai and only Tsai in these shoes. I gently tongue the inside of the shoe. Oh, Tsai. I look up to see Henrietta's iPhone aimed at me.

I am fired.

KAUFMAN'S NEW FILM is shrouded in stupid secrecy, as if anyone might care, but I have dug around and discovered it to be more maximalist claptrap, this one entitled *Dreams of Absent-Minded Transgression*. Apparently it explores the lulling of our contemporary world into a semiconscious dream state in which, by degree, we accept an ever-increasing surrealism in our daily lives. The film is said to star Jonah Hill as a young actor named Jonah Hill who discovers there is a factory in China cloning Jonah Hills (Jonahs Hill?) for a series of Asian knock-off Jonah Hill movies. These clones are raised to speak Mandarin. One unnamed source describes it as *The Boys from Brazil* meets *The Seven Little Foys*. Whatever it is, it's certain to be yet another turgid, overhyped foray into Kaufman's self-referential, self-congratulatory psyche. As I finish rehearsing this lecture (to be presented in case of rain at the Boy Scouts of America Jamboree Rain Day Film Festival in the auxiliary room of the Irving, Texas, Senter Park Recreation Center) on my walk crosstown to my oculist (he has a new shipment of Eyebobs!), I fall into an open manhole. It is shocking, as I had been lost in thought, about to revisit the speech I had presented, three years prior, to the San Antonio chapter of the League of Women Voters. This one was entitled "I Vote with My Feet When It Comes to Kaufman." The league women were not familiar with Kaufman's oeuvre, such as it is, so I chose several particularly egregious scenes to illustrate my points, and by the end of the seventy-minute lecture, I had won them over. I think it is safe to say they would not be seeking out any of Kaufman's movies. "That was just horrible," I recall one saying after the talk. "Yes, that man's insane." One woman voter at a time. Now, as I sit, up to my neck in putrid sewer water, the effluvia of my fellow urban dwellers, I find myself shocked back into the present moment. This is not the first time this has happened.

I test my ankles, knees, wrists—nothing appears to be seriously injured. I shall sue the city, I decide. It would be better, of course, had I been injured. But I don't ever seem to get injured in these falls. Sometimes I am immersed in feces. Sometimes not. Mostly I am immersed in feces. The city certainly leaves itself open to lawsuits with such negligence. I scramble up the ladder, quickly ducking back down as a taxi passes overhead. Checking again, I climb out, reeking and wet. I am shunned on the street; repulsed looks are shot at me, names are called: "Stinky" and "Smell-boy" and for some reason "Pedo." In shame, I hurry home, shower, and strap myself into my sleep chair for a good cry. Tomorrow is another day, I say, to console myself. But is it? Or will it be more of the same? Another open manhole? Another foot in dog excrement? Another gaggle of high school girls giggling as they goggle me on the street? I am not a man who believes in God. I am Facebook friends with Richard Dawkins, for Christ's sake, and some other very crazy people whom I admire greatly, but at times it seems there is some malevolent force taking pleasure in my ongoing humiliation.

Certainly my life has not turned out as I had hoped. I think back to that lonely night as an undergraduate at Harvard University, when I wandered the streets of Cambridge, Massachusetts, looking for meaning. "What does any of it mean?" I wondered aloud. Suddenly an old homeless man appeared as if from nowhere (from heaven?) and asked me for money. I shook my head, said sorry, kept walking, head down, hands in pockets, continuing to wonder aloud. But this homeless man wouldn't take no for an answer and began to follow me.

"Any little bit'll help. I'm an old man, had a hard life."

"I'm sorry. I don't got no money" (an attempt to sound poorer).

"You don't understand," he said. "Things happen and then everything goes twisty on ya. I was young once, younger than you, even. What are you, nineteen? Fourteen? Well, I was once ten, just like you. You can believe that or no, but it's true. An' things happen and ya go all twisty."

"I'm late for my low-wage job," I told him and kept walking.

"I once got this idea in my head, see? An *idée fixe*, they call it. Didn't know it was called an *idée fixe* at the time and didn't know it would become one. Just an idea passing through my head, I thought. But it stayed and stayed. Kinda ruined me for any future ideas. Called an *idée fixe*. That's what the French say. Pierre Janet said as much. Don't know why he has a girl's name for a last name—never did figure that one out—but he talked about the *idée fixe*. You ever hear of him? Carl Young was one of his students. You heard of that one, right? College boy, I'm guessin'. That one's a famous one."

"It's Jung," I said, because I couldn't help myself.

"Anyhow, what got me twisty was the notion I come up with, like it just came into my brain, like it was deposited there, like a egg or a bug or a seed, something that growed or taked root, the idea of *what if I actually come from the future*, like I been sent back, an' I'm really someone else, someone from the future, right? You follow? See, me and my brother Herbert, he's dead now, we found a creature on a beach down Florida way, like a sea creature, only it weren't any normal-type creature. It was like God made a mistake and just dumped it there, maybe hoping nobody would find it. But me and Herbert, we did, we surely found it, and I got to thinkin', maybe it ain't a accident. Maybe this creature is exactly a mistake version of me and Herbert and that someone else, say a second god, this one malevolent, wanted us to see it. Herbert didn't understand my *idée fixe* and he went off and became a salesman of shoes, but me, I studied on it and tried to understand."

"Uh-huh," I said. "I really have to—"

"I even moved up here to the seat of higher education to attend college and learn on it some more, but given that I never even went to the sixth grade, I have been unable to gain acceptance into any collegiate institution. Probably I shoulda sold shoes like Herbert. He was always the more practical of us. Me, I always liked to think about the universe and cogitate. I was always the more inquisitive of us, who were not actual brothers but in a very real way wuz. Anyways, so I got to wonderin' why this idea popped into my head and wouldn't leave. Where'd it come from and—"

"I have to go into this movie theater now," I said. "To see a movie."

And so I stepped inside the rundown cinema, just to escape this madman, and, huddled alone in the darkened house, I watched *Weekend*, the 1967 masterpiece by Jean-Luc Godard, and thus my life changed forever. Before that night, I thought it a waste of time to sit and enjoy entertainment. I had every intention of going into the foreign service, perhaps becoming a diplomat or ambassador-at-large or an attaché. I had even already purchased a monogrammed attaché case. So I was ready. But this movie spoke to me as nothing had before, as no one had before. This movie was the lover about whom I had always dreamed. It saw me fully. It undressed me. It lusted after me. To put it crudely, had there been a way to fuck this beautiful film then fall asleep in its arms, I would have done so in a minute. So what recourse did I have but to change my major from international studies to film studies? The film department at Harvard was, of course, the best in the world, headed, at the time, by Warren Beatty and Michael Cimino, or two men who looked very much like them. It was almost impossible to gain entrance, but somehow my gumption, passion, and fifty-page plan to establish an American cinema of ideas, which would also be a cinema of emotion, that would fearlessly probe the human psyche in an attempt, against all odds, to understand the ever-present war between men and women, impressed them and I was accepted.

In my first class, I almost got into a fistfight with Warren Beatty over the ranking of Godard's *Weekend*. It was at that point the only film I'd ever seen and, therefore, I put it at number one. Beatty put it at seven because he didn't understand it. He insisted the film was a critique of fascism, which is about as insightful as saying that *Network* is a critique of Peter Finch. I told him as much. A shoving match ensued. Beatty is a big man, but his muscles felt oddly gelatinous. I thought maybe he had some sort of condition and I should be gentle with him. However, my passion won out, and I knocked him out with an elbow to his jaw, which left an indentation as if his face had been made out of wet clay. It was an indentation that remained for a week, eventually popping back out during class with a sort of sucking sound. I expected to be expelled at the very least and likely jailed, but when Beatty came to, he seemed a somewhat changed man, at least in regard to *Weekend*. He said his evaluation of the film had been shallow and admitted he had never really watched it all the way through. And then a miraculous thing happened: He looked me in the eye and said, "Teach me." And I did.

We went to the cinema and watched *Weekend* together. I explained what Godard was doing and why. Beatty was an eager student. He admitted he had spent so much time womanizing that his movie-viewing skills had suffered. I said, "Let's remedy that." We became close (he will deny we ever met, due to a falling out we had over a young Diane Keaton, but we were very close, even sharing an apartment for three semesters). Cimino was a tougher nut to crack, although we did vacation in Aruba over one spring break and had a grand time. So began my education in film. After all, is not teaching the best way to learn?

My plan at the time was to master the elements of film production: cinematography, editing, sound recording, screenwriting, directing, acting, best boying, *et chetera*. Then, upon conference of my degree, I would step out into the world, guns blazing, to make my first film, which was to be called *Guns Blazing*, but rather than the typical cinematic violence fest, there would be nary a pea shooter in my film. The guns of the title would be the guns of human interaction, you see—the violence we do to each other as we attempt communion. A young man and young woman struggling to maintain a healthy relationship. He a brilliant and humble academic studying foreign affairs, she a nubile archaeologist, cynical yet beautiful, of both ample intellect and bosom.

CHAPTER 38

I HAVE COME TO the conclusion that I am ridiculous. The mishaps. The open manholes. Even the fire that ruined Ingo's film and my life. But perhaps more horrific are my thoughts. My thinking is silly. My memories are preposterous. My ideas are laughable. I am a pompous clown. I can, on occasion, become aware of this. There are moments of clarity that I find all the more humiliating because I can see myself as others likely do, but I cannot control any of it. The pathetic, comical thought process continues, almost as if a script is playing out. Almost as if I myself am a puppet, defined by some external force, written to be the foil in some strange cosmic entertainment witnessed by someone somewhere. But who or what? And why? And also how? And when?

This new HR woman studies my eleven-page résumé.

"Goodness," she says. "You've had so many, many jobs."

"Yes," I say.

"Pompous university lecturer. Harried department store manager. Small-town dentist. Film director. Impatient violin teacher. Head bellman at a ramshackle resort hotel in the Catskills. Longshoreman. Temporary haberdashery employee. Fawning delicatessen worker. Haughty amanuensis to Jean-Luc Godard. Condescending banker. Jealous third-rate film critic. Author of over seventy small-press monographs. Debauched launderer . . . and it goes on."

I have left my work experience at Zappos off my CV.

"So much experience, Mr. Rosenberg," she says.

"Mx."

"Mx. Rosenberg. You've lived a life, haven't you?"

"I have found myself working at a variety of occupations, yes."

"Well, I must tell you, quite frankly, our applicants do not generally have such varied employment histories. They are usually college students, housewives, failed artists, *et chetera*."

"I'm certain I could do any work put before me."

"I'm certain, too. But you are so overqualified, I fear you would likely become bored."

"I wouldn't. I have never been bored. Boredom is the domain of the dullard."

"You would. I've seen it countless times. It is my job as well as my calling to find the right job for the right person. So I am going to offer you something much better."

"I don't want something better than junior Shopbop customer service rep."

"I'm going to offer you a position in shoes, Mx. Rosenberg."

"But—"

"It is an executive fast-track position. And with your experience both as a . . . contemptuous ringmaster and a . . . hoity-toity career diplomat, I can see you are a big-picture guy and will do most excellent shoe work."

I SIT IN an otherwise empty theater and watch yet another film by the puffed-up self-promoter known as Charlie Kaufman. This one, obnoxiously entitled *Anomalisa*, was directed in tandem with a fellow named Duke Johnson, so I maintain some small hope that it will not be the typical Kaufman black hole of creativity. That is, until the movie starts. Oh, for heaven's sake. Kaufman has apparently taken it upon himself to forever ruin stop-motion animation with his adolescent musings on conformity or whatever it is this unwatchable mess is musing on. Kaufman is no Wanderson. He is *certainly* no Ingo. He is not even an Art Clokey.

Afterward, I perambulate the streets, considering the "message" of this film, and arrive at the conclusion that it masquerades as a plea from Kaufman for his fellow human to please, please see the common man as an individual. A noble thought, were it not so obviously falsely proclaimed from Kaufman's exalted position as "teller of important things." He does not care, nor has he ever cared, about "common" people, nor has he ever taken the time to see them as the individuals they so profoundly are. Kaufman is an elitist in the most despicable sense of the word. His condescension (and misogyny! Don't get me started!) is beyond rehabilitation, and I would venture to say that *his* fancy designer shoes have never touched the pavement upon which regular folk have trod.

I fall into an open manhole. But even covered with the stinking shit of my fellow Manhattanites, I continue my Kaufman rant. He is, I conclude, a poseur of the most odious sort, beloved by beret-wearing undergraduates, who, in their nescience (surely they are so nescient they don't even know the word nescience! Ha!), believe they are championing something incisive, something original, something "genre-bending."

I attempt to climb the rungs to the street above.

Have they never read the work of the brilliant, groundbreaking Italian playwright Luigi Pirandello, from whom Kaufman regularly and benightedly cribs?

A massive wave of liquid putrescence, seemingly from nowhere, knocks me from the rungs and carries me away in its current. I scream for assistance and receive, for my effort, a mouth full of this sewage. For a long while, I fruitlessly grab for anything bolted down, and after a ride of about fifty meters, I manage to catch hold of a lightbulb cage above and am able to hang there until the brown liquid subsides. I drop to the sewer floor and find my way back to my beloved rungs.

This time I do make it to the street and immediately find myself again considering Kaufman. He sticks in my craw like no other. His juvenile meta-ramblings, culled wholesale from misreadings of absurdism and—

I fall into another open manhole. How can this be? This sewer tunnel, it seems, nonsensically, is filled with vomit. What is going on in this city? Is the pro-mia convention in town again? I will sue. John V. Lindsay or Fiorello La Guardia, or whoever is currently running the hellhole, will pay dearly.

Back in my apartment, after a thorough rinsing with my Hibiscrub antimicrobial skin cleanser (I must now purchase it from Sam's Club in five-gallon drums), I sit in my chair/bed and consider my life. There does seem to be a pattern of sorts. It is a pattern of loss, of petty humiliations. If I were not the type of atheist who believes with unflinching faith in the purposelessness of life, who believes in the unrelenting chaos of a cold universe, who believes that life is a brutal cosmic accident, who believes there is no one watching and certainly no one pulling the strings, I would believe there is someone watching and pulling the strings, and that the some*one* or *thing* that has it out for me is indeed watching, watching, always watching, damn it. I am, after all, a good person, a kind person, a person who, in the face of this constant meaninglessness, tries to live by the law of reciprocity, the so-called golden rule, as Messrs. Jackson and Gibbon termed it. Indeed, I would venture to say I have lived by the goldenest of rules. Not only do I do unto others as I would have them do unto me, but I do unto others on average three times more than I would have them do unto me. So why do I suffer so? Life is, of course, unfair, as They Must've Been Gigantic so pithily and melodically taught us all those years ago, but of late I cannot help but believe there is something else going on. My freethinker conviction seems to fly in the face of the logic of things. I am being singled out. I am being picked on, and I have not a clue as to why.

It does occur to me that if they exist, these angry gods, I need to be careful not to further anger them. After all, they hold my welfare in their hands. Do they have hands? In their entitial metacarpal regions? One does not, after all, want to offend by assuming we are created in their image. But how to be cautious? I must conclude, since, as stated earlier, my actions as a human are unimpeachable, it must be my thoughts they find offensive. And how to clean up that constantly churning intellectual stew? Since I am a thinker by vocation and avocation and, dare I say, provocation, even, I must confess, on vacation (levity, always levity to gently nudge one's woes into perspective), and since a thinker must allow thon's thoughts free rein or suffer the consequences of intellectual conventionality, I find myself in a proverbial pickle. My first notion is that I should perhaps begin to think in a different language—I am fluent in five and conversant in six more—but what language could I conceivably know that my "creator" would not? I ponder. The problem seems insurmountable. Unless. Unless. What if, for the sake of discussion, my creator is not the only creator? What if my creator is limited? If such is the case, it would stand to reason that I might be able to find a place to hide from my creator. Is such a thing possible? And if it is, how would I determine my creator's limits? Where on the map of existence does my creator's control end?

I attempt to clear my mind through meditation. By breathing, the seemingly simple yet impossibly difficult act of following one's breath. In. Out. In. Out. Distracting thoughts enter and are released, gently, without judgment. In. Out. In. Out. Thoughts continue to come, will continue to come, but experience has taught me they will in time come with less frequency. The mind slows, gains focus. In. Out. In. Out. By continuing this discipline, perhaps someday—years, weeks from now—I will rid my psyche of the thoughts that so anger my creators. I will become clean in their eyes. As I breathe, in and out, as I slow myself down, I consider the constant motion of my body and mind. Even now. The twitches. The micro-adjustments, the flexing of my feet, the swallowing, my digestive system processing material. The gurgles. The itchy skin. The heart beating. The blood coursing. The tensing and relaxing of muscles. The shifting of my eyes, the blinking. The stifled cough. In. Out. Release the thoughts. In. Out. My tongue finds its place behind my upper teeth. I slow down, yet still I move. In. Out. I picture the breath entering my nose, entering my lungs, leaving my lungs, exiting my mouth. I release this visualization and try to think of the breathing as simply in and out. In. Out. In. Out. I release the words *in* and *out* and think of the breathing with no name attached to the process. I release the word *process*. I look with softness out at

the stillness of my room. The items in the room. They have nowhere to go. They are simply there. I try to be as they are. I release
the idea of *being like* them. I try to just be. In. Out. I release the notion of *being*. The items in the room don't think that they *are*. The
books. The window. The wall. The burnt donkey puppet, now a
funerary urn. It doesn't "know" what it is. I stop comparing myself
to other things. I need to release all comparisons, with gentleness.
In. Out. I feel myself slowing down. My mind is quieting. In. Out.
In. Out. I am the chair. I am the window. I am what I see. I am a
witness. I am what I can't see. I am a non-witness. In. Out. I am still
able to notice the slightest shifts in my being, both physically and
mentally. I am a witness and a non-witness. I am still.

The donkey puppet moves.

I'm certain of it. Its head has lifted, in the smallest of increments.
I saw it. I watch the donkey for movement. I do not want to startle
the puppet. I want it to move again. In. Out. I am certain the motor
in its base is turned off. I know the batteries are dead. I know the
gears jammed long ago. I wait. Perhaps it cannot see me because I
have become so still. My mind is on fire with theories. I release
them. Gently. I must remain in this quiet state. Without ambition.
In. Out. I wait. I wait without waiting. I look without hoping to witness. I breathe. There is nothing more. No more movement. Perhaps it was a trick of the mind. But it was not. Of this I am certain.
But maybe it was. But how could it be? An inanimate object does not
move of its own accord. Maybe there was potential energy stored in
the armature. My disappointment at that possibility is palpable. I
want it to be alive. I want there to be some magic in the world,
something unexplained, unexplainable. I let this desire go. Gently.
In. Out. I continue in this vein, losing track of time, losing myself in
the present moment, in the act of breathing.

Now, as I further slow down my thoughts, the puppet's incremental movements are obvious. Through the window behind him, I
am aware of the passage of days, nights, light and dark strobing at
first, then speeding up into a blur of gray, neither day nor night. It
is now that the puppet's gestures appear fluid. It speaks.

"Hello."

"You're alive?"

"As alive as you."

"I don't know how to take that."

"I understand."

"Are we talking now or am I imagining this?"

"That which the mind creates is also real."

"So my mind is creating this."

"No distinction exists between the two, which is, in actuality, the one. You see?"

"Listen. I am trying to escape. I am, I believe, being punished by my creator for thought crimes and am also being hunted for sport by one of my former colleagues."

With that, a book falls from the shelf (at normal speed to my senses, but perhaps in this altered reality, it takes a week to hit me on the head). Then another book. Then another. The timing of the *thunk*s on the head is impeccable and, I'm certain, funny to any observers. I look at the books, now on the floor, covers conveniently facing up. They are: *Bonk* by Mary Roach, *Joggin' Your Noggin: Fun and Challenging Word Games for Seniors (Volume 1)* by Mary Randolph, and *The Ghost in My Brain: How a Concussion Stole My Life and How the New Science of Brain Plasticity Helped Me Get It Back* by Clark Elliott, PhD. I should note that I do not own any of these books, so there is no justification (other than sight-gag purposes) for them to be falling from my shelf. Furthermore, the book for seniors is truly adding insult to injury.

The tiny burnt puppet, for whom I have developed a profound affection, climbs up my pant leg and sits on my lap. I pet his head, and he seems to appreciate it, braying, but more like a purr.

"With your help, there is, I believe, a way I can return to my place and time, which I want to do, and with my help, you can join me. Forgive, if you will, my awkward phraseology, but I come from a time of silence and have learned what I know of spoken language late in life, and as you can imagine, I have had little to no opportunity to practice it, which, as you must also know, is essential to the mastering of any language, be it near or far."

I nod. I can't and won't argue with him. And also I wasn't listening after the first few words, because I thought I heard the front door unlatch in fast motion and was preparing to be shot by Henrietta.

The puppet climbs back onto his urn and does not move again. The puppet never moves again.

CHAPTER 39

I AM SHRINKING. THERE is little doubt. I've taken to marking my height on the doorjamb. It is the reverse of what is done with children's heights and will end, I fear, in nonbeing.

Now I'm a salesman at a company that makes expandable shoes for growing feet. My firm also makes collapsible shoes for clowns who need to travel for business by plane. I've been here for a while now—twenty years? a year?—and the thing that gets me most about the job, after the crushing disappointment of being here for twenty years or a year and the meager salary, is that people think it's funny when you tell them where you work. It is not funny. There is nothing funny about this job, not even in the clown shoe division. In a way, the clown shoe division is the most depressing division of all. It is a dreary office populated by dreary, unfulfilled people. It is not a joke. It is the trash receptacle in which I have been deposited. Everyone ends up in one sooner or later. But had it been a dry cleaner or a paint factory, I would not have to contend time and again with people saying, "Collapsible clown shoes! That's hysterical!"

It doesn't help that the company is called Sho' Enough, over which I've twice tried to sue them on behalf of African Americans and also on behalf of myself for plagiarizing the title of my book on extraordinarily long films. Or that the clown shoe division is called Carry-On Clownage, which is just as bad, but there's no lawsuit in it, according to the lawyers I've contacted.

I go to work. Today is an office day. Reports to be submitted. Follow-up phone calls to retailers. Cold calls to clowns. I stare out the window at the Taco Bell. I flirt or do whatever it is I do with Marta. I think about Ingo's film. I'm making progress, but it's slowed down. Barassini and Tsai have married for some reason and spend much time at his vacation time-share in Cabo. Jeff, my boss, stops by and tells me Armand died suddenly last night.

"Oh God. Really? Of what?"

"Something weird," he says. "I don't know. Something to do with ear illness."

"Ear illness?"

"Yes. I don't know the details. I didn't feel it was appropriate to pry. Not in a situation like this."

"Sure."

"His wife said it came on suddenly, and when it was over, his outer ears were hanging off his head."

"That doesn't sound like anything I've ever heard of. It doesn't make sense."

"I wasn't going to call her a liar. I didn't think that would be appropriate at a time like this."

"I understand. It's just odd. Jesus. Poor Armand. Get it? It doesn't sound like anything I've ever *heard* of?"

"Something about an explosive discharge of ear fluids. If you consider that, you can certainly see where the outer ears might just pop off. It'd almost be funny if it wasn't so tragic. Like in a movie. You could picture it in a comedy movie. But that's just a movie, so you can relax knowing it's simple special effects. They'd do it with rubber ears or something, I imagine. That's why you could laugh if it was in a movie. It's just rubber. But not here."

"It sounds gruesome."

"And the indignity of it, of dying that way—basically, your head exploding. Your head being the seat of your very being, the face of your being. God, it makes me shudder."

"Although it was quick, it sounds like, which is better than a protracted death."

"You mean like your ears exploding in slow motion?"

"No. I meant a long, harrowing illness."

"Ah. In any event, we're going to have to double down here for a while. You'll need to cover his accounts. And you're going to have to man the booth—"

"No way, Jeff. No way."

"—at the convention this year."

"Oh, come on, Jeff. Please."

"I have no one else."

"You know I hate the Circus/Magic convention. Let me do the Great American Children's Shoe Show Extravaganza of Anaheim and get Tom to do this one."

"Tom's getting married that week."

"Oh, fuck. Right." I pause. Then: "Y'know, I've been meaning to mention this for some time now, but I don't think it's fair that just because Tom is a member of the Fundamentalist Church of Jesus Christ of Latter-Day Saints he gets to have so many days off for weddings."

"We're not going up against the Fourteenth Amendment just so you can get out of clown convention duty."

"But polygamy is illegal, Jeff, so—"

"Listen, we're between a rock and a hard place here, and we're not going to set ourselves up as a test case for the constitutionality of federal polygamy laws just so you can get out of your mandatory clown convention duty. You know Tom is just itching for that fight."

THE REVIEW OF *Woomin!* in my blog B.'s in Your Bonnet:

> Let me begin by saying I am thrilled that Sony has hired a woman to direct the first installment of this potential mega-franchise, my favorite comic book, *Woomin!* It is, of course, as it should be. And, full disclosure, the director, Grace Farrow, is my daughter. However, as a human being fully invested in toppling the patriarchy, I must question Sony's decision to hire a white woman to direct this important, historic film. Not only is Woomin! an African superhero, but the multitude of offspring that explode from her

superwomb to fight crime are a veritable cornucopia of nonwhite, gender nonconforming, differently abled superhero infants. It is true that Farrow identifies as lesbian, but one doesn't have to delve too far into her blogging history to stumble upon the following: "I hate men. I hate men. I hate my father. What do they (he, thon!!! Jesus Christ!) bring to the world? This: war, brutality, rape, oppression, murder, avarice. Is there anything kind or decent that has resulted from this aberrant chromosome? And the goddamn tragedy is *I find myself physically attracted to these monsters* [italics mine]." So which is it, Ms. Farrow? It is certainly not my place to suggest your lesbianism is a choice du jour, but one must wonder, mustn't one? No matter. There is, of course, a well-qualified lesbian, transgender WOC (of African American, Cherokee, Latinx, and Korean heritage) who lives with both CP and severe hearing loss—her name is Sharon Old Bear and she is prodigiously talented. I described her debut film, *Woman of the Ear*, about the struggles of a WOC with hearing loss as "a groundbreaking exploration of the struggles of a WOC with hearing loss." Why didn't Sony go to Old Bear? One must wonder. Might the resulting film about an African woman who shoots superhero babies from her vaginal canal have been more authentic had they? I believe it just might have been. Two stars.

My critique falls on deaf ears. Even Old Bear refuses my endorsement, calling me a Wendigo.

We live in a world of constant collision, innumerable collisions, innumerable repulsions. Rick Feynman once told me, "B., we can never truly touch another thing. Touch is what we feel when two things repel each other. We are all isolated, even from ourselves. Our own molecules do not even touch each other. Since I can't be touched, I cannot be hurt. Smoke does not get in my eyes because it cannot, and true love is not denied only to me but to everyone, to everything. I am not alone in being alone. This comforts me."

"WHAT WILL HAPPEN if I keep going with these predictions?" his voiceover asks.

"Who asks this? The meaty horologist?" says Barassini.

"Yes." And with that the meteorologist returns to his blackboard. Dissolve to another montage sequence: mathematical formulas, calendar leaves flying, Chinese food, beard, sketches on graph paper, culminating in the meteorologist projecting a new animated sequence onto the small movie screen, which shows, bizarrely, that his predictions continue further into the future and outside the wind tunnel. It shows an animation of the meteorologist turning off the camera and walking over to the chalkboard, exactly as it happened, even dropping the chalk at one point as he had and reaching down to pick it up.

I am snapped out of my trance; I see Tsai has been watching from the doorway. She is older now but still a handsome woman. I can no longer imagine what I saw in her.

"Would you care to stay for dinner?" she asks.

Why is she being nice to me?

"I'm sure B. has somewhere to be," says Barassini.

"No, I don't. I'd love to stay."

This is not true, but I am famished; I consider asking for the food to go.

"Great," they both say. Although only one of them seems to mean it, and I can't tell which one.

As we pick at Tsai's uninspired cheese plate, I recount a story I read in today's newspaper.

"A school bus filled with schoolchildren on a school outing drove off the road into a ravine somewhere in either the South or the Midwest. So horrific an accident, it is all anyone is talking about, I've read. All those children dead. Or perhaps dead. No one knows the death count at this point. The authorities are withholding that information until next of kin have been notified. All that human potential lost. Or potentially lost potential. All that heartache, perhaps. How can the parents and the community go on? How can I? Still, one does. One must. It is times like these when one finds oneself turning to the philosophical, the poetic, in search of solace. Of course there is none to be found. Perhaps Dr. M. Angelou comes closest with, 'If we lose love and self-respect for each other, this is how we finally die.' Words to live by for certain, and near-solace at a time like this. Although, admittedly, I have always been slightly confused by how we can have 'self-respect for each other.' Perhaps what Dr. Angelou is telling us is that we are all one, that respect for another is really respect for oneself? This is Buddhist nonduality, and while I am vehemently anti-religious, I look at Buddhism as more of a philosophy than as a religion and as such am comfortable drawing upon it for near-solace. And I do. Often. Buddhism."

"How tragic," says Tsai.

I pop a cube of white-flavored cheese into my mouth.

"I read of a mass shooting in a shopping mall somewhere," says Barassini. "The South? I cannot remember, to be honest, but I am horrified just the same. Missouri? Is Missouri the South? Certainly south-like if not technically geographically south. One of those states, the opioid states, as they are known. A gunman with a semi-automatic or an *automatic* automatic opened fire in a crowded mall or amusement park. There is a difference between semiautomatic and automatic automatic, and all those gun control advocates don't even seem to realize this. They have opinions about guns but know nothing about guns. Regardless, thirty-seven dead. So far. Many more wounded, some critically, so the death toll will likely rise, possibly considerably, say the authorities. I hope it does not, but I hope it does. There is some thrill in a large number of fatalities. What good is a mass killing of thirty-seven people when last week's mass killing was fifty-eight? One's outrage needs to build in order to sustain. I cannot say I am entirely comfortable with my position on this, but I don't seem to be able to disabuse myself of it. I will, of course, deny it, and I will express the proper horror about this incident in conversation, and I am a staunch supporter of strict gun control laws and strict enforcement of those laws, so there is that.

Yet there is part of me . . . Could it be a confirmation bias? Could it be that I want the world to be as terrible as it feels to me to be? Or do I just get off on tragedy?"

"More wine?" asks Tsai.

"Yes, please," we both say. Though I suspect neither of us really wants any.

Tsai heads for the kitchen. Barassini and I both watch her go. I don't look at her ass. I have moved on. I look only at the very top of the back of her head, the crown, and derive no pleasure even from that.

"Fine woman," he says. "She tells me you had a bit of a crush on her at one time."

"I will admit I was a tad smitten."

"But no longer?"

"Time is funny that way."

Barassini erupts into a long, violent laugh.

"I loved her dearly," I say, once he has settled down. "One wonders where those feelings go."

"It's a mystery."

"I'm getting the feeling the top-hatted man is his father," I say.

"Whose?"

"The meteorologist. His story arc is coming back to me now, in short, erratic bursts. The whole thing is scientifically nonsensical, of course, and I say this with some authority as a person who minored in relativistic time studies at Harvard, but it is a pleasing jumping-off point for a fanciful, wistful tale, and as such I am willing to embrace it. The requirement of suspension of disbelief is a valid element of many fine films, but with this simple caveat: It must be earned. After all, some of the greatest movies of all time require it of their audience. Do we need to believe in the possibility of time travel to be moved by *La Jetée*? Do we need to believe in the irrational science of The Zone in Tarkovsky's *Stalker* to be terrified by the environmental cataclysm it portends? Do we need to believe there are any actual funny people in *Funny People* to be torn asunder by its emotional nakedness? The answer in all three cases is a resounding no. So I am able and willing to accept Ingo's fantastical premise. I trust him that much. I trust him to take me to someplace profound. I trust him with my live."

"Live?"

"You heard me."

"I think there is a danger in discussing our work together while you are not in your trance state."

"Am I not now?"

Tsai returns without any wine before Barassini can respond.

"Look, folks," I announce to the table, "I received my PhD from Harvard, where my dissertation was entitled *Temporary Mobility Practices in the Indigenous Australian Population as an Analogue of the Experience of Western Film Viewers*. In it, I discussed the temporally nomadic life of the disciplined film viewer as parallel to the spiritual awakening that can occur with a religious openness. In the case of Ingo's film, which in its entirety, I suspect, results in a complete neural inundation, leading to a breaking down of preconceptions and a psychogenic negation of ego, one can see this effect clearly. It was highly prescient that I had exhaustively researched this phenomenon as a young man, if I do say so myself."

"Huh," says Barassini.

"My struggles within the highly competitive world of professional film criticism," I continue, "have left me dispirited and spent. Are there forces at play that have kept me from the brass ring I deserve and have worked so hard to secure—chief film critic at *The New York Times*? Perhaps. Instead, I am allowed to teach the occasional film theory course at the Food and Maritime Trades High School to Puerto Rican toughs studying to be in toque blanche and bachi bonnets, and is there a more thankless job in the world of film theory? I suspect not. It is no doubt a cabal of film theorists who run this town. Do not publicly question their assessments if you hope to climb the treacherous sprockets of this business. They will destroy you. I had the audacity to call Professor Richard Roeper to task for his Fresh Tomato ranking of *Memento*, which he proclaimed an 'ingenious exploration of how memory defines us all.' First of all, Professor, speak for yourself. You have no idea how memory defines me. Secondly . . . have I given this speech to you before? I feel as if I might be repeating myself."

Tsai and Barassini look down at the table. I try another speech, hoping it's new to them:

"Everything is a clock: A clock is a clock; a person is a clock. Everything changes according to a predetermined schedule. Everything tells the time. Rocks tell time. Everything. The only thing that does not tell time is nothing. Nothing cannot change—this might at first glance sound like a double negative, some sort of streetish parlance, but of course it is not. Nothing exists outside of time. Therefore, to say that before time there was nothing is a paradox because it puts nothing within the context of time. Nothing exists outside of time, therefore, yes, before time, there was nothing, but also during time, wherein nothing exists but does so without interacting with time. This reminds me of a movie I saw in an abandoned wine bar as a student. The rectangle of screen contained nothing. Not black, not white. Nothing. And since nothing is nothing, it cannot be contained in time or space. Therefore there is no beginning or end to it and I was not witness to it because one cannot witness nothing. If I were able to observe it, it would have been something. Then it was gone. No time, of course, had passed."

Tsai and Barassini continue looking at the table; I seem to have lost my audience.

I am worried. I am almost certain none of this ever happened. And yet I remember it.

CHAPTER 40

Now I (wo)MAN our booth at the clown convention. There's not much to do because the service sells itself: We carry all the best brands of clown shoes, and we make online ordering easy. Next-day delivery guaranteed, simple return policy, no questions asked. You can search by color (red/white/yellow, blue/orange/green, *et chetera*), size (fifty to one hundred and thirty-five), even gags (water squirt mechanism, honking, self-inflating balloons from the toe box). There really is no other online clown shoe seller that comes close to our selection. And, of course, we offer our patented collapsible traveling clown shoe. So it should be easy, except for one thing: Clowns out of makeup are the most vile people I've ever encountered. Seven out of ten road rage cases are perpetrated by clowns out of makeup.

At the trade show, I meet a woman in greasepaint, well, not in greasepaint, well, not only in greasepaint, but also selling it. So to be clear, both in greasepaint and in greasepaint. I picture her naked but with the clown makeup on, and instantly I realize a new fetish has been born. My synaptic train has a new stop: Clowntown. This is not at all like me, I think. Once home, I type *clown fetish* into my computer. I hesitate before hitting RETURN. There is no going back after RETURN; of this, from past experience, I am certain. The only thing the virtual world offers that the real world doesn't is both complete privacy and a complete lack of privacy. I am alone with it but being watched: my activities recorded, files made, boxes ticked. But, alas, my needs are larger than my concern. It will all be there

for me at the press of a button. I consider the button itself: ENTER/
RETURN. I consider the world I am about to enter; I know I will return again and again. There is no end to it. And what deranged
Pandora's box will I be opening? Are there laws against clown porn?
I think I'm safe as long as I don't search *underage clown porn*, which I
would never, ever do. I am not a monster. Yet once I taste clown, will
I be able to go back to regular women, either in my fantasies or in
reality? Will there come a point, if I ever manage to find a woman
who will have me, when I will pull the clown white out from the
bottom of my sock drawer and ask her to apply it, just so I can get
hard? That will not go well. Best to not press RETURN and just accept that—

I take the plunge and . . . it is better than I could've imagined.
Luscious naked clown women. So many choices! FYI, there are
some naked male clowns, which it turns out are as disturbing as
naked female clowns are alluring. I refine my search to exclude them
and this time don't hesitate to press RETURN. I come upon (both
literally and figuratively!) the image of one young female clown who
embodies everything I have ever wanted in a female naked clown.
She goes by the name Rainbow Sunshine and she is . . . *everything*.

"TELL ME WHAT you see," demands Barassini.

A noticeably younger Mudd and Molloy, boyish and charming,
thin and fat respectively, perform on some small-town burlesque
stage. This is either a flashback or just an earlier scene from the film.
I don't know how to tell. I don't believe it matters. If *Moutarde* has
taught us one thing, it is that rigid sequence is a fiction. My eyeball
self hovers in the back of the house, then slowly glides toward the
stage, over the heads of the audience. It is a beautiful and graceful
shot, which I am magnificently performing. I am, I conclude, the
Roger Deakins of memory.

"Africa is a fascinating place. I've booked us a trip," says Mudd.

"I'm not going. I'm a-scared of Africa," says Molloy.

"For heaven's sake, why would you be scared?"

"I'm afraid of the dark!"

"It's not actually the dark continent! That's just an expression."

"What's it mean?"

"It means it's unknown."

"How do we know about it, then?"

"No, no. It means it's a mystery."

"The mystery is who took all the lightbulbs from Africa!"

"Oh, stop it. You'll have a good time. There are many beautiful wild animals there."

"Wild animals should be in zoos where they belong."

"Don't be ridiculous. Animals need to run free."

"I'm not saying we charge them to run. They don't even have any place to keep a wallet. Except for the kangaroos."

"There are no kangaroos in Africa."

"Well, if the kangaroos won't even go there, why should I? I'm smarter than a kangaroo."

"I'm sure there is a kangaroo you're smarter than."

"Exactly. Thank you. Hey, wait a minute—"

"Think of all the natives. We'll get to see Ubangis, Pygmies, Watusis—"

"Which tusis?"

"Watusis. Certainly you've heard of Watusis."

"A herd of Watusis? That's a lotta Watusis. I'll stay in the car."

"No, no. I'm asking if you know what Watusis are."

The scene dissipates like smoke. I continue to float, now above nothing, terrifying blackness surrounding me.

"What now?" asks the voice, echoing out of the darkness.

"Nothing."

"We have twenty minutes left."

"There is nothing. Please let me out early. I feel anxious just hanging here."

"We have twenty minutes," repeats the voice. "Keep looking."

So I wait and I hang and I look and nothing comes. To pass the time, I imagine naked Rainbow Sunshine gyrating on the Serengeti Plain and ejaculate. I don't know if Barassini notices.

* * *

IN MY SLEEP chair, in the irrational panic that comes in the middle of the night, it occurs to me that maybe the reason I struggle to piece together the memory of Ingo's film is that the forgotten parts have been "eaten" away by a brain-wasting disease, some sort of spongiform or perhaps something not yet identified, some undiscovered parasite. I imagine such a creature, were it contagious, might travel from brain to brain, eating memories and evacuating digested memories in the form of waste matter. In such an admittedly science fiction–type scenario, one might find oneself inheriting the degraded memories of others—junk memories, feces memories, if you will. And I am certain I have indeed stumbled upon such odd fragments in my own so-called "banks." Snippets of assembly line work, the taste of rambutan jam, trying on several pairs of jeggings (I have only tried on one pair!). Perhaps these and other unexplained memory fragments are simply the result of my exceptional imagination and my oft-remarked-upon sense of empathy, but these thoughts are so convincing as to be troubling. Now, I am not a speculative fiction maven, although I do greatly respect the work of the African American genii Octavia E. Butler, Samuel R. Delany, and Tananarive Due, who have rejiggered this frivolous form, transforming it into a tool with which to investigate societal and racial injustice. Their tomes are not meant for fanboys, those arrested adolescents who champ at their bits for the next installment of Star Wars or whichever other space opera, time travel blather is coming down the mass distraction pike, but rather for those seriously engaged in the struggle toward an equitable society. Or is it Octavia Spencer?

Malachi "Chick" Molloy is born in 1906. As a child, he is diagnosed with "the fidgets" and placed in a special facility, the Paramus School for Fidgeting Boys, where the treatment consists of spinning boards, hydrotherapy, insulin comas, leg restraints, and crafts. At thirteen, he escapes by self-administering a Mickey Finn, passing out in a basket of dirty sheets, and being removed from the premises for laundering. The powder quells his fidgets and allows him to be mistaken for bedding by a myopic laundry truck driver. Once in New York, he finds employment jittering down the streets wearing a sandwich board for Elixir Veronal, a barbiturate sleep aid manufactured by Bayer, with the slogan: *If I only had Veronal, I'd be sleeping like a baby.* On the back it reads, *Veronal is safe for babies!*

I am here on the street, too, suddenly embodied, no longer just a floating eyeball, wandering old New York, searching for Molloy. I want to interview him for my book. I know if I can find him, it will be a coup and the book's success is all but guaranteed. But I cannot find him. I stop a policeman in a top hat (a top hat?) to ask if he knows Molloy. He answers in a thick Irish brogue, calls me "laddie" and says he'll take me in for "malingering and truancy" if I don't get immediately back to class at the Erasmus Darwin Negative High School of Aristotelian Poetics on DeKalb Avenue. I patiently explain to him that I am flattered but well beyond high school age. Not in this the Year of Our Lord 1923, you're not, he says. I realize he is correct. In 1923, I am negative twenty-seven years old and in negative high school. In fact, at negative twenty-seven years old, I have been left forward nine times. Jesus, I need to graduate negative high school soon, so I can get into negative college. I panic and run to class.

IN A MOMENT of startling clarity, outside the hypnosis sessions, on a docent-led tour of the Long Island Chair Museum exhibit "Chairs That Look Like Giant Hands Through History," I finally fully recall the first moments of Ingo's miraculous film: When Docent Pamela is not looking, I brush some cracker crumbs that had dislodged themselves from my beard from the velvet seat of a Louis XVI *chaise à main* with my hand, then brush off my hand with my also hand. Sometimes the proper word eludes me and I utter or think something comically wrong, or wrong-sounding, or wrongheaded. *Other.* The word is *other. Other* hand. I wipe my other hand on my . . . *cloth leg tubes?* That can't be right. Leg pants, perhaps. In any event, this simple action, my madeleine, if you will, transports me back in time:

Ingo drags on his cigaret (for this is how he spells it) as he puts his hand on my shoulder and pushes me down onto the chair, onto what appear to be cracker crumbs. The lights are offed, the blinds pulled, the projector whirring.

It begins. A jagged scrape of white on black, another and another and another. Then tiny scratches: as snow at night in a spotlight. Then picture. Black and white. Stained with dirt: A woman, more specifically, a doll of a woman, dressed as a woodland nymph, dancing erotically. It's animated, using a technique sometimes called stop-motion. Perhaps you've heard of Ray Harryhausen, the great master of stop-motion animation. You might remember his work from the 1933 film *King Kong*. No, that was Wallis O'Brian. I misspoke. Or rather, I misthought. This occurs more and more frequently of late. I worry something bad is around the bend, that there is some underlying cause, some organic cause. Some dire cause. Why am I forgetting? Why do I wander my brain looking for missing words? Others, out of politeness or impatience, have begun to offer me word options.

"Valiant?" they say.

"Cornucopia?"

"Nixon?"

"Recursive?"

"The Great Gazoo?"

"Manifest Destiny?"

"Bruce Willis?"

It was *Willis* O'Brien. *Willis* with an *i*. *O'Brien* with an *e*. I am lost.

In any event, this film was thusly done using said technique. The doll dances crudely, with a spastic energy I find enervating. I'm willing to give Ingo more time. As an old black man, he deserves our respect. Although I still think it unlikely I'll make all three months of it. African American, I mean.

After a minute and a half of this sex dance, the puppet embarks on a stiff-limbed cakewalk, looking every bit the Nazi goose-stepper but twenty-some-odd years too early to that particular party. I am about to use my trump card, which is to say, I am going to lie and say

I have an appointment, when a hand-scrawled title skitters on the screen: *Dancer Lucy Chalmers shows us a waltz!*

Lucy Chalmers! The great and tragic mystery that was silent screen siren Lucy Chalmers. So few people with whom to discuss Lucy Chalmers these days. Star of a scant number of movies in the teens before she walked off a set one day, never to be seen again. Some say she was the unknown victim known as the Black Dahlia. No, wait, that was much later. Lucy Chalmers disappeared before Elizabeth Short was born. The Black Dahlia was Elizabeth Short. She was not unknown. That's another story, I'm certain. Lucy Chalmers just walked off a set one day and was never seen again. She was a troubled girl with a tumultuous marriage to cowboy actor Art Acord. But it was her tempestuous personality from which she built her great emotive skills. *Built* is not right. I don't know what the right word is here.

"Drew?" offers a chair museum passerby.

Yes, *drew*. Then one day, she was gone. Right off the set. Never heard from again. Some say she was raped and left for dead in a wheat field. Some say she changed her name and married a midwestern life insurance salesman who raped her and left her for dead in a wheat field. There were other theories. Many more than these two. But the point is nobody knows. Was she a heroin addict? Nobody knows that, either. Nobody knows, and this adds to the intrigue and to the tragedy. If there was a tragedy. She might have simply left Hollywood, sick of what the business was eventually to become. She might have had precognitive flashes of Kaufman, of Nolan. Nobody knows, but in any event, her presence keeps me from immediately begging off on the film. After the naming of the doll, it reappears and is somehow slightly more nimble. The goose-step is now a sexier goose-step. There is perhaps a bit of hip in it. One is smitten.

And just like that, the memory ends. The docent is explaining that, in its original form, the word *chair* meant *seat*.

CHAPTER 41

IT HADN'T OCCURRED to me that Rainbow Sunshine might be traceable, but here she is. Her non-clowning name is Amber Hearst and she is a member of a sex-positive feminist clown collective called Circus Her-Kiss. They hail from Ann Arbor and clown for female-only audiences all around the Upper Midwest and parts of the Lower. Amber Hearst is a proud lesbian and the girlfriend of Dianne Elaine Padgett, also known as the clown Dazzle. I ponder my options. Rainbow Sunshine can still be mine, in the way that she has been, in the realm of fantasy. There exist online seventeen photos of her in various seductive poses and various stages of undress. With these tools, I can build on my fantasy interactions with her for years to come. Another possibility, however, is to engage my next-booth neighbor on this third day of the convention, perhaps begin with some casual clown-based chitchat, then a nonthreatening compliment on her makeup technique, sort of feel her out, and depending on her perceived interest, suggest we maybe grab a drink. If she agrees, I say it has to be directly after work, because I've got another commitment later that night, then suggest that to save time, she might want to keep her makeup on. Then take it from there.

I screw up my courage and speak to the clown woman. It turns out her name is Laurie and she once worked in a small traveling circus called something or other (I wasn't really listening) until she grew too old for professional clowning. The careers of female clowns, just like gymnasts and ballerinas, are over by their early twenties. It is a grossly unfair, sexist double standard, that a male clown can work well into his eighties and is often paired with inappropriately young female clown spouses in the onstage clown romances. I commiserate with Laurie, who at thirty is still a reasonably attractive clown. This seems to buy me some points, and I invite her out for a drink after work. Immediately after work. She accepts.

"I feel a little embarrassed sitting in a bar in this makeup," Laurie says.

"Don't be silly. You're the loveliest woman here. Clown or otherwise."

"OK," she says. "Thanks."

"So, what kind of clown are you?"

"Was I, you mean."

"Are you. I stand by your current clownfulness. I think the forced retirement of mature female clowns is a national disgrace."

She smiles.

"Well, I *am* what is termed a juggling ingenue."

"You juggle?"

"I do. I also excel at pratfalling and confetti bucketing."

I discreetly adjust my penis.

"I do love clowns," I say.

It's testing the waters. There is plausible deniability if she were to take it the wrong way, which would be the right way.

"Do you?" she says.

I have no idea how she means that. The clown makeup makes it difficult to read subtlety of expression. She is forever smiling like a monster from hell.

"I do," I say.

"Ugh," she says. "I'm too old to be wearing this stupid makeup! I look pathetic."

"No," I say, casually and briefly touching her hand.

There is a silence.

"You live close to here?" she asks.

"My place is quite small."

I don't want to tell her I have no bed in case I am misreading the situation, but I need to get that information in. Sex in my sleeping chair is an unpleasant affair, I'd imagine.

"A studio?"

"A very small studio. I don't even have room for a bed! Can you believe it? Now, that's small!"

"Oh," she says.

Is she disappointed? Repulsed by my poverty? Damn her monstrous, unreadable makeup. It puts me off my game.

"How about you?" I ask. "You live nearby?"

"West 50s floor-through. My parents help me with it, I'm embarrassed to say."

She's telling me my poverty is nothing of which to be ashamed.

"Nice," I say. "Lovely to have parents."

"Right?" she says and laughs.

I laugh. We sip our drinks in silence for an uncomfortable few minutes. Then we both laugh again. Then we both stop. It is an exceedingly odd moment.

"You want to see it?" she asks, finally.

"See what?" I say, still trying to avoid a misstep.

"Oh," she says.

She seems hurt, although she is still smiling a big, red makeup smile. Did I kill this by pretending not to understand her invitation? I take the plunge.

"Oh, did you mean see your apartment?" I say.

"Um," she says. "Y'know, I don't know. I just thought you might be interested in seeing a prewar floor-through. If you like architecture, that is."

"I'm not much of an architecture guy—"

Why did I say that? It just came out. I just didn't want her to think I'm an architecture guy. I don't know why that was important to me. I just wanted to seem regular. It was a mistake.

"Oh, OK," she says.

"But, you know what?" I say. "I do love the West 50s."

What does that even mean? What do I even mean? I hope she doesn't ask.

"Oh, really?"

She seems excited. This is hopeful.

"Yeah, the West 50s is a great ten blocks!" she adds.

"It is," I agree.

How will my obituary read? I ponder this as we make our way west. I imagine it often. Not only the obituary but the online praise in the form of tweets from folks in the film industry. The *Rest in Power*s, the cited snippets of profundity from my writings, mentions of my selflessness, my friendship, the times I brought soup or consoled the brokenhearted (I must remember to do some of that sometime), the teeth-gnashing about how I was too young, how I was "a critic's critic." I imagine myself trending. Just for a little while. Just for one day. I'm not greedy. There's still much to do in this life to arrive at an acceptable trending number, but the discovery and elucidation of the work of Ingo Cutbirth will go a long way to that end. It will be a glorious day. They will be sorry I've gone while so many lesser and more evil white men continue to thrive in the film criticism industry. There are even some evil minority film critics, but I can't say this out loud. I cannot wait to witness this outpouring of grief and love. Even though I will not be here to witness it, I still believe I will be here to witness it.

At Laurie's apartment, which is disappointingly not in the least clown-themed, I am poured a glass of wine. It is white, which is, of course, wine for people who don't like wine, but I don't tell Laurie that. White is toy wine. It is wine for children. It is wine for imbeciles. She lights several candles and excuses herself to go change into something more comfortable.

"No need to take off the makeup on my account," I say.

"What do you mean?" she says, turning in the doorway.

"What? Just that I'm fine with the makeup staying on is all."

"*You're* fine with it?"

"Yes. If *you* are, of course."

"Oh dear. B., are you a . . . are you a clown fetishist?"

"What? No! Does such a thing even exist? Don't be ridiculous. Of course not. That's sick. I apologize for men in general, I'll say that right now, if this is the kind of thing you've had to put up with, especially white men, of course—and I don't mean clown-white men, ha ha—seriously, though, that's disgusting. Really. And this is such a lovely apartment."

"OK. My mistake. So I'll be right back. Make yourself comfy."

"Thanks."

She exits into the bedroom, and I leave. What else is there to do?

I SIT AWAKE in my chair all night. What I did was wrong and perhaps even hurtful to Laurie the Clown. In some ways, I feel I neglected to see her as a human being, but instead saw her simply as an object, there for my sexual gratification. This goes against everything I stand for as a man, and as a feminist. I feel shame, so I attempt, in my guilt-drenched mind, to become a better person by confronting my demons. It is a dark night of the soul, as Francis Scott Key once sang. No, not Key, *Fitzgerald*—something is wrong with my mind— and he didn't sing it, but instead wrote it, and besides, he was not even the person to have coined it. Credit for that must go to Saint John of the Cross, the discalced Carmelite who wrote the original poem. But whoever said it first, I am having one and that is the important thing at this juncture. "His shoes displaced, he became discalced" is a clever little bit I've been trying to work into a conversation for several decades now. It's not really that good, as I hear it in my head again. In truth, I just want someone to know I know the word. Perhaps a think piece about the *Discalced Contessa* or *Discalced in the Park* or even *Eight Men Out*, where I can mention Discalced Joe Jackson. I scribble some thoughts onto my chair-side notepad:

Words to include in something:
Discalced
Chiaroscuro (this one should be simple!)
Facticity
Jactitation
Rarotongan
Opprobrious

My mind is a tornado of confused thought and emotions. I jactitate and worry I will never sleep again.

But I do. Almost immediately.

I wake up, unstrap myself, piss, stare out the window, then climb back into the chair to continue with my dark night of the souling. Why do I even find myself attracted to clowns? I do not as a rule enjoy clowns or clowning. I am philosophically in opposition to comedy of any kind. Some might counter that, well, don't you love Apatow? But Apatow does not make comedies. Far from it. For comedy is, by its nature, cruel and dismissive. Humor looks only at appearance, at surface. It judges. It humiliates and shames. There is no kindness in comedy. It must have a victim, even if that victim is the self. Clowning embodies all the meanness of non-clowning but with the added offense of the physically grotesque.

And yet.

What is it I feel if I see a woman in that makeup? When I saw Rainbow Sunshine? When I saw Laurie the Clown? When I see the several naked female clowns I'm currently seeing online? I am that monster who can never fully understand itself: the white human male.

It pops into my head that I am also champing at the bit for an opportunity to properly pronounce *piranha* in a conversation. *Peerrr-on-ya*. It's staggering how many people don't know how to speak Portuguese.

More words I hope to properly pronounce in front of people:
Leerstelle
Flaneur
Cibosity
Nocebo
Shimpo
Trompe l'oeil

ON THE FINAL day of the clown convention, Clown Laurie's booth remains shuttered. Perhaps she is staying away because of me. I do feel badly but at the same time am relieved. Life is easier without her here. A strange thing does transpire, however. Several women come up and talk to me about clown shoes. They are all in their thirties, I would say, and they all behave oddly. They ask questions about the shoes, but their attitudes are standoffish and angry. It occurs to me that any one of them might be Laurie sans makeup. After all, I don't know what she looks like, and truth be told, I cannot even recall how she wore her hair. I believe she was a tad shorter than I, and maybe nine stone, give or take a pebble. It could be any of these women. If one of them is (or all of them are) Laurie, what game is she (are they) playing? A chill runs down my spine. Or is it up my spine? Perhaps I'd best hide outside of her prewar building and wait for her to emerge, so I can once and for all recognize her out of makeup. I noticed a laundromat across the street. So that will be helpful.

Barassini and Tsai are at their time-share, so back home, I sit in my sleep chair trying to summon the movie on my own, utilizing Barassini's tape. Car horns. Sirens. The pings of the radiator. I insert earplugs, thus reducing the external noise and elevating the hiss of my tinnitus. Again, I try to summon. When I realize I cannot hear the tape with the earplugs in, I remove them. After a time, it comes. The opening shot: It's snowing over the New Jersey Pine Barrens. The camera drifts lazily from screen right, searching for . . . No, wait. That is not the first scene. The first scene is the Galveston hurricane of 1900. A man fights the wind as he walks along the sea-wall in front of a perfectly replicated miniature of the Hotel Galvez. It's comical as his top hat is repeatedly blown off. He chases it each time and each time redons it, only to have it immediately blown off again. This speaks volumes about class pretensions, even as the world around him is . . . No. This comes later because we already know this dandy is the father of the meteorologist, so how do we learn this? In a flashback? If so, this comes much, much later. Think!

It must be later, because it explains the meteorologist's obsession with weather, as it is the Galveston hurricane that killed his father. A spectacular scene: It is impossible to fathom not only the skill necessary to animate such a violent storm but to manage the tonal shift as it moves seamlessly from the light comedy of the man chasing his hat to the brutality of the storm picking him up and carrying him, ass over teakettle, over Galveston, allowing the audience to see, from his now bird's-eye point of view, the horrific devastation of the city below. It is unparalleled in all of cinema. That it ends with his now lifeless body dropped from the sky at the feet of his small son tells the audience, with nary a word, everything they need to know about the child's obsessive drive to find order in the seeming chaos of the universe. So then how does the movie begin, and why am I confusing the chronology? I do remember it occurring early in the film. As did the birth of Molloy in a shack in the Pine Barrens. I remember the snowy sky raining infants, which smashed into the snow-covered ground, leaving smudges of brilliant crimson (but wasn't it black and white?). There was also the St. Augustine Monster washing up on the shore of . . . what is the beach called? The boys on their bicycles. That was in the 1890s, so before Galveston. But that was not the first scene, either. There was the Kentucky Meat Shower of 1876. Did that come first? All the various time-travel elements in the film make it complicated, perhaps even impossible, to determine a timeline. Perhaps there is no first, in that there is no beginning, in that there is always something before. If only I had access to the so-called "time window" invented by the meteorologist where he can predict precisely what happened and what will. Wait. Did he have a name? I cannot think of one instance in which anyone called him by name. Even when Sylvia finds that yellowed newspaper photo of him posing among all the other meteorologists, his name at the bottom is smudged. Ingo makes a point of showing that. Why is he nameless? *And Jesus and a nameless ape / Collide and share the selfsame shape / That nocht terrestrial can escape?* So wrote Hugh MacDiarmid in what is perhaps the most influential poem of my Weltanschauung. Is the meteorologist a Nameless Ape? Is that what Ingo is telling us? Does his gift of prophecy come from the Christian Son of God, rather than that simple (or, rather, complex) technology?

CHAPTER 42

I ARRIVE ON CLOWN Laurie's street to discover her building has burned to the ground. There is nothing but a pile of smoldering rubble. Did I burn it down last night? I do not recall doing that. Of course I didn't. Then why do I feel a sudden chill running either up or down my spine? I didn't do it. Why would I have? I didn't do it *on purpose*, certainly, but what if by accident I kicked over one or several of those many candles as I fled her apartment? I'm certain I didn't kick over a candle or many. But what if I did and didn't notice? But I did not. But maybe? What if I used the bathroom and lit a match after? But I didn't. But did I? Were people killed? I search my phone for news of the fire. Arson is suspected, says an article in the *West Fifties Bugle*. No one was injured, but all the residents were given new identities by Witness Protection in an attempt to protect them from future assault by what authorities suspect is a possible unknown arsonist or burner, as the kids say. How will I ever find her now? Literally any woman of that approximate age, height, and stonage could be Laurie the Clown. I think she's Caucasian but I'm not even sure of that; her white four-finger cartoon character mitts hid her hands. C'mon. Why would she leave those on if she didn't know what I was about?

Walking the street has become a nightmare. Clown Laurie could be anywhere . . . everywhere. I call her employer, Clown-dation, and ask to speak to Laurie or formerly Laurie.

"There is no one here by that name or former name," they tell me.

"You have to say that. Due to witness protecting and what have you."

"Why don't you give us *your* name and number and we'll get back to you," they say.

I sense a trap and hang up. No one is going to pin this murder on me. I mean arson. I mean possible arson. Sometimes I feel my thoughts are not my own, that I am thinking wrong things, stupid things, ridiculous things, for the amusement of an unseen audience.

The word *unseen* hangs in my brain like smoke.

I suffer from what Hume termed the disease of the learned. Simply put, I know too much. And not unlike Elephant Man David Merrick in the Bernard Pomerance play *The Elephant Man*: "Sometimes I think my head is so big because it is so filled with dreams." Except in my case, my head is so big because it is so filled with knowledge, not to mention dreams. Of course, my head is not abnormally large or disfigured like Merrick's, but at sixty-two centimeters, it is larger than the average. I sometimes playfully refer to myself as a Hume-an being.

"TELL ME," SAYS an unpleasantly tanned and rested Barassini.

The meteorologist, accompanied by his near ubiquitous interior monologue, scribbles in his notebook: "The more I dig into the initial calculations, the more data I discover. Now not only am I able to chart and predict the motion of the air and the plant in the wind tunnel, but I can chart it from every angle, even from inside the cells of the plant. My animation of those first fifteen seconds now includes all of this. Presumably, it might also include smell, touch, and taste, if only there was a way to express those in a moving picture. The largest hurdle, of course, is still the limitation of the human brain. If I could devise a sophisticated-enough electronic calculating machine, I might be able to compute the results in close to real time and possibly at some point even faster. Only then would I have a proper predicting machine."

At dinner, Tsai tells a story:

"On my way back from barre class, I cut across West 55th and pass a building fire. It is a building where my friend lives, so of course I stop out of concern. The dead, burnt, and mangled bodies of the tenants who had jumped litter the street. Then I see her in her window. Laurie the Clown. She jumps, makeup smeared, lands in the firemen's net, and bounces all the way back up into her apartment window. The firemen yell for her to try again. Again she jumps and again bounces back up and into the fifth-floor window. They yell, 'Again!' This time when she hits the net, a fireman hurriedly places a bag of sand around her neck. This time she bounces into a third-story window. 'More sand!' yells the fireman to one of his fellows at the sand truck. Now she bounces into a second-story window. 'Even more sand!' yells the fireman as she jumps from the second-story window. This time she carries so much extra weight that she crashes through the net and lands on the sidewalk. It's a funny bit but seems out of place with the terror of the moment: the flames, the black toxic smoke, the bodies writhing on the ground, the weeping onlookers."

"Then why do you laugh?" I ask.

"I'm just relieved she's OK," Tsai says, covering.

I have laughed at this anecdote, too, of course. Everyone at this dinner party has, especially Conrad Veidt III. But is it out of relief as Tsai claims? I wonder if I've become inured somehow to the tragedies of others. Intellectually, I know jumping from a burning building is no joke, certainly not for the jumper or the family and friends of the jumper. Yet I find myself unable to feel empathy. Is this the fault of Ingo's movie? It's worrisome. Everything is worrisome. In addition, my feelings of romantic love are gone, forever, it seems. Domestic Tsai holds no interest for me. Clown Laurie has become a sauce of amusement. Source. I can barely picture my former African American girlfriend Kellita Smith. My ex-wife has turned mannish. Perhaps I am just getting old and good riddance. I am not sorry that this chapter of romantic neediness has come to an end. From now on it is work. My purpose is Ingo.

Barassini suggests an after-dinner session as entertainment for the guests, since no one wants to play Pictionary.

In MOLLOY'S HOSPITAL room, a remarkable bit of stop-motion sleight of hand occurs. It's a time-lapse sequence condensing weeks of Molloy's coma into fifteen staggering minutes, unlike any ever before witnessed by moviegoers. Day changes to night and back over and over, as nurses and doctors zip in and out, attend to the patient and leave, as Patty arrives and reads to her husband, as Marie smokes and stares, as Mudd paces and wrings his hands. All the while, Molloy lies in bed, an island of immobility in this sea of panicky, sped-up movement. Weeks pass, Molloy loses weight, his face becoming drawn, a little mustache growing on his upper lip. Eventually skeletal, he seems unlikely to ever awaken.

Then he does.

It happens at night. The room is dark and Molloy alone. His eyes open, their wetness catching the moonlight streaming through the window. It's an arresting moment and serves as a definitive period to the turbulent time-lapse sequence. Molloy cranes his neck in an attempt to take in his surroundings. Where am I? He appears weak and groggy. He attempts to sit up, can't, and so lies there, waiting. We wait with him, fellow prisoners, lonely in the dark. This sequence, Molloy alone in bed, plays out in its entirety. Five hours long, twenty years before the Warhol movie *Sleep*, with a puppet. And unlike with Warhol, this is no gimmick, not a conceptual joke. This sequence explores isolation, boredom, fear, and institutionalization. If one can stay with this scene—and one must!—one will be rewarded mightily with a deepened sense of empathy.

Come dawn, a nurse peeks in, and she and Molloy make eye contact in perhaps the funniest series of double takes, triple takes, and spit takes (for some reason the nurse was taking a sip from a cup of coffee when she entered) ever committed to celluloid. Heavily influenced by the Hal Roach comedies, Ingo times the sequence like the master he is, all the more amazing when one remembers it is achieved frame by frame. The terrifying question the scene asks is why Molloy, a seasoned vaudevillian, finds no joy in either his own or the nurse's comical surprise. There is some ominous foreshadowing here. The discombobulated nurse speaks:

"Oh! Mr. Molloy! Stay right there! Don't move! Don't move!"

Her stump-heeled oxford nurse shoes rat-a-tat down the echoey hall as she runs off, presumably in search of a doctor. Molloy turns his head to look out the window. The camera pushes out through the window and into the dim dawn exterior. Molloy is on a high floor, so we travel bird's-eye over Los Angeles. The Pacific Ocean and Catalina Island in the distance. A lonely streetcar chugs along a quiet avenue down below. Extraordinarily, the animation camera swoops down and into the car to reveal early morning commuters. We settle on a Negro (the respectful term for African Americans in 1940s America—used here only for verisimilitude and in no way endorsed) clutching his weekly Los Angeles Railroad pass, which features an advertisement for John Raitt in the touring company of *Carousel* at the Shrine Auditorium. The musical, written by Rodgers and Hammerstein and based on a play by Ferenc Molnár called *Liliom*, is correctly reviled for its *ohrwurm* melodies as well as for equating domestic abuse with love ("It is possible dear, for someone to hit you, hit you hard, and it not hurt at all"). This is a road all too often gone down by both male apologists and abused women suffering from Stockholm syndrome. Carole King and Gerry Goffin made a similarly horrific point in the 1962 song "He Hit Me (And It Felt Like a Kiss)." What is wrong with people? I have never and would never hit a woman. And here we have, in this Negro's hand, an advertisement for abusive relationships. What is Ingo saying here? It's too early in this complex narrative to know, but it is almost certain that Ingo is exploring the manufactured American dream, its consumers and its consumed. The Negro, now having transferred onto a bus, is let off in front of the Willys-Overland car factory in Maywood. He joins a throng of lunch-pail-wielding workers entering the plant. He has not spoken. He has not been named. Will he be seen again is the question with which we're left as we find ourselves sucked back into Molloy's hospital room, where he is now surrounded by a doctor, the spit-take nurse, Patty, Mudd, and Marie. The doctor moves his index finger from right to left in front of Molloy's face. Everyone else looks on, breath bated.

"Good," says the doctor. "Now, can you tell me your name?"

"Malachi Francis Xavier Molloy."

"Do you have a nickname?"

"Chick."

"Do you recognize the people in this room?"

Molloy appears worried, as if he's taking a test. He wrings his hands, inhales deeply, then proceeds:

"My wife, Patty (née Mittenson). My partner, Bud Mudd. His wife, Marie Bogdonovich Mudd. That nurse who did a technically remarkable but preternaturally unfunny spit take earlier. And you introduced yourself when you came in as Doctor Everett Flink."

"Very good," says the doctor.

Molloy is relieved. Patty cries and kisses his forehead. Mudd claps his shoulder. Marie cracks the window, lights a cigarette. She, alone, seems troubled.

"When has Chick Molloy ever met a spit take he doesn't love?" she mutters as cigarette smoke spills from her mouth, through the crack, into the broken world outside.

"Will there be aftereffects?" asks Molloy.

"You've been immobile for five weeks now. There will be the necessity of a supervised physical exercise regimen as therapy."

"Will I get back to normal?"

"It's too early to know for certain, but I feel with diligent effort—"

"I'll work hard."

"Good. That's fine."

"I'm worried I won't get back to normal."

Both Patty and Mudd squint in seeming consternation at this. Is there something different in his affect? A seriousness? A disquiet? Maybe it's only that he's too thin now, that fat, jolly, silly, bumbling clown buried within his emaciation. He looks . . . unpleasant. The thin, straggly mustache does not help.

"Why are you all looking at me like that?" Molloy asks.

"Like what, darling?" says Patty.

"Like I'm a stranger. A despised stranger."

"No one is looking at you like that, Chick!" says Mudd. "We're just so happy you're back!"

"You're lying," Molloy says, an alien anger in his voice. "Give me a mirror."

Patty jumps to it, grabs her red alligator box purse, unlatches it, and hands it to him. Molloy studies his now cadaverous face in the mirror mounted on the inside of the lid. He fingers his mustache.

"We can shave that right off, Chick," Patty says. "Easy as pie."

"No," Chick says after a moment. "It suits me."

"We can't both sport a 'stache, Chick," Mudd offers.

"Let it lay, Bud," says Marie. "If he likes his mustache, that's just fine. He's earned it."

"But the act."

"Let it lay."

And so Mudd does, but there is something indecorous about a two-mustache act. He contemplates shaving his own. That'd change the dynamic, for sure. How will the audience ever believe the un-mustached man holds the reins? And this new, emaciated Molloy looks mean. The mischievous smile is gone from his eyes. But he's been in a coma, for God's sake, Bud! Give him a chance to find himself. And in any event, no matter what, his friend is back and everything else is secondary, can be discussed later, can be worked out in time.

As I walk home from my session with Barassini, I revise my list. It passes the time, and it is always good to know where one is presently situated.

Who I am likely less intelligent than:
Albert Einstein
Susan Sontag
Isaac Newton
Dante Alighieri
William Shakespeare
Hannah Arendt

James Joyce
Jean-Luc Godard
Gottfried Leibniz
Alan Turing
Ada Lovelace
Marie Curie
Aristotle

Urgent note: Find an African American!

I stop by Yoko Ono's Wish Tree at this year's Performa festival and attach my "wish" to it: It is my wish to bring the same level of genius to criticism that Picasso and Braque brought to painting with Cubism. Can a film be looked at from multiple angles? From every angle? Can a critique include every feasible interpretation? Can it be understood from all human perspectives? All non-human ones? This is my goal.

There is currently only one other wish tied to the tree: *Bicycle*.
—*Jim Carrey*.

CHAPTER 43

"TELL ME."

I am sitting, unseen, with Mudd and Molloy in what appears to be a hospital chapel. Molloy is in his hospital gown, Mudd in a smart double-breasted suit.

"I suggest we go back and attempt once again to get *Here Come a Coupla Fellas* made," says Molloy.

"OK, Chick. I mean, I don't know. The business has changed."

"Surely not much in three months."

"Well, Chick, can I be honest with you?"

"Please."

"I think you've changed. A bit."

"I don't believe I have."

"You're more like . . . *me* now," says Mudd.

Molloy studies Mudd for a long moment.

"I see," says Molloy.

"I'm not sure you can play the same character anymore."

"Well, let's give it a whirl, shall we?"

"Right now?"

"Why not?"

"Yeah, sure, Chick. The haberdashery scene?"

"Let's do it."

The two perform the scene and it falls flat.

"I'm not sure, Chick. It doesn't feel natural anymore," says Mudd.

"Perhaps we're just out of practice."

"I don't think that's it. Maybe if you shave your mustache and gain back the weight?"

"I prefer my look now, Bud. It suits me. You don't know how difficult it is to be overweight. It's a health issue and people always laugh at an overweight fellow."

"I can imagine, Chick. But to be fair, we are hoping to make people laugh."

"Not that way, Bud. Not that way. That's cheap laughter and hurtful."

"OK. I get that. Maybe just shave the mustache?"

"The mustache is dapper."

"But does dapper work for our act?"

"Perhaps you can shave your mustache, Bud. Gain some weight. And we can switch roles."

"I don't want to gain weight, Chick."

"So you understand how I feel."

"I do, but that has always been your role in our act. I don't even think I'd be good as the put-upon buffoon. I'm a straight man. That's what I do."

"Let's give it a try. What do you say? Let's do the scene again with our roles reversed."

"Chick . . ."

"Let's just try it, Bud. We might surprise ourselves."

"Yeah, sure. OK."

They try again and it plays exactly as it did previously, except with the roles reversed.

"You're not being at all silly, Bud. Be silly."

"It's not my personality, Chick."

"You're not even trying."

"OK."

They start the scene again. Mudd mugs and whines and performs insane double takes throughout. It's horrifying, nightmarish, obscene, impossible to watch, yet impossible to turn away.

"No, that's not right, either," says Molloy.

"I'm a straight man, Chick."

"I am, too, Bud. I am, too."

"Maybe it's time to call it a day, my friend."

"Comedy is all I know, Bud."

Molloy begins to cry, but with no change of expression. Mudd watches this disconcerting display.

"We'll figure this out," says Bud.

"You promise?"

"I promise."

"Maybe . . . what if we have two straight men? No one has ever done that before."

"Yeah, sure, Chick."

"Maybe it's like a man arguing with himself. Are you familiar with the German Romantics, Bud?"

"Not really. No. I didn't know you were."

"I read at night when it's quiet here."

"Oh."

"Doppelgängers. Romantic writer Jean Paul coined the term, but it's an ancient concept. The double. It might be just the thing to take American comedy to the next level."

"Sure. Sounds great," says an unenthusiastic Mudd.

"Great!" says what I suspect is an enthusiastic Molloy, but I cannot tell for certain, for his face remains an almost parkinsonian mask of blankness.

IT'S A BEAUTIFUL Sunday afternoon, and I am speaking to a group of children at the Junior Future Film Historians of America, East Coast Division, picnic in Riverside Park:

"So here I am, in the future—in the year 2019, is it?—looking back at my life. This mysterious nonexistent place called Not Yet now fully realized, and who could have imagined the futuristic marvels we take for granted here? Cable-less telephones. Computer stations in our homes. Delicious, satisfying meals in pill form. All the world's books in electronic libraries, accessible to everyone with the simple flick of a toggle switch. And even though war and poverty have been eradicated and all other peoples are now recognized to be just as good as white people, I still find myself dissatisfied. In this, which can only be described as the early evening of my life (daylight savings), I find myself struggling for meaning. Certainly it is wonderful to be in a world where everyone is equal and nobody is special, but I come from a different time, a different land, a land of ego and ambition, of endless striving, of envy. These traits have burrowed deep into my being, and now that everyone is celebrated, everyone writes book and paints paintings and sings songs and everybody else reads those books and looks at those paintings and listens to those songs, I find my primitive being wants to stand out. All of this welling to the surface at the very time my creative powers are waning and I am being slowly absorbed back into the earth from which I once sprung. For you see, I am shrinking."

The children are impressed, I think. But I cannot be certain, for their faces remain almost parkinsonian masks of blankness.

"TELL ME."

There is something behind the glass doorway. Barely visible. A blur. An insinuation of form. The camera dollies in. The door opens, and we enter the hallway of a brownstone. It's empty, and we are drenched in foreboding. What was that? Who was that? Was it something we were not meant to see? And yet we are here. The film has taken us here. So we are meant to have seen it, we assume. We glide down the hall toward a closed door. There is menace in the absolute silence. We remember all the horror movies we have seen that have used this very device, invented so long ago by Giovanni Pastrone for his 1914 film *Cabiria*, albeit to an entirely other effect. There exists a feeling of inevitability, of lack of control, in this push forward. We will see what is in the room, whether we want to or not. The scarred, white wooden door at the end of the hall opens, bidding us to enter. Inside the dank, shuttered room, a drunken sailor is murdering a child. It is a horror film, not so much because of the child murdering (for that is played for laughs), but in that the tattoos on the sailor's shirtless back are animated, suggesting his ambivalence about the brutally comical act he is committing. Spanning his left trapezius to the lower left deltoid is a dancing homunculus representing unbridled glee. The dance is simple, hopping back and forth, from one foot to the other, coupled with a malevolent grin and ecstatic counterclockwise eye rolling. On the right deltoid is Saint Nicholas, who represents *not* killing children. The tale of the butcher who slaughtered three children to sell for food comes to mind. Saint Nicholas resurrected them, which was the right thing to do, according to saintly ethics. In the tattoo, Nicholas mouths "tsk, tsk" and shakes his head but is unable to intervene because there is a tattoo of a giant fanged monkey between him and the homunculus. I'm not certain what the monkey represents (cultural indifference? Societal apathy?), but it seems clear that Nicholas is scared of it. The monkey appears smug. What is Ingo saying here? Is he revealing his own perverted desires? Is he advocating child slaughter? I seriously doubt that. Perhaps the child slaughter is wholly symbolic. Who hasn't wanted to metaphorically violently slaughter the child thon once was? To erase from the face of the Earth the memory of that needy, pathetic abomination. But is that the right thing to do? Saint Nicholas says no. Or maybe more to the point, Saint Nicholas says, I don't approve and I will resurrect that child if you murder it. I will never let you forget that child, for that child is the needy and pathetic being you once were. If you deny it, you are denying your own history, which, pathetic as it certainly is, must be remembered because those who forget history are condemned to repeat it. And who wants to be a child again?

The murder ends, and the sailor turns and looks into the camera, as if to say, "Heh?" It's a moment of great cinematic power. We are all culpable, his look tells us. The bloody child stands and bows. Was this all a performance? No, he is the undead now. This is made clear by Ingo having replaced his eyeballs with black marbles. He doesn't seem unhappy though. He pulls dishes and utensils from the cabinet and sets the table for dinner. The sailor smokes his pipe. The homunculus is dead. No, he's breathing; he's just asleep. Life is complicated, Ingo is telling us. There is horrible violence, but then we take a break and have dinner. This is life.

I leave Barassini's office a wreck. The process of remembering is an exhausting one, which has rendered me physically and emotionally depressed. I reflect on the work I am doing, on the necessity of it, and on the real possibility of failure. I feel my deterioration. I feel it in my knees. I feel it in my bowels and in my penis. I feel it in my shrinking height, my failing memory. There was a time when I could remember everything. It was not necessarily an emetic memory. That's not the word. The word that means photographic memory. Emetic is about vomiting. Although, in truth, that word was not entirely ill-chosen. I would and could vomit information. Ask me about Godard and I could projectile vomit dates and facts and theories, my own and those of others, about his work. I could tell you his shoe size. But no longer his shirt size. And this worries me. My memory lapses. My weak bladder. My unguaranteed erections. I am not heeding Thomas Dylan's advice to not go gently into that good night. Dylan Thomas. Gentle. Jesus. I drowse in my chair. There is a dream about love. The kind of love that has never existed for me in life, but has, on several occasions, found its way into my dreams. In this one, this woman is kind and looks at me with resistantless eyes, wide, open-door eyes. Enter me fully, they offer. Don't leave any of you out. Her eyes are black, her skin smooth and brown and reflective. This is all I have ever wanted. This grasping for respect, for money, for fame in which I spend my days is meaningless, silly, shameful in the presence of this love. She and impoverished obscurity are more than I could ever hope for. I move into her, effortlessly, no fear of rejection, no self-consciousness about my physical repulsiveness. I am loved. Her skin against mine is warm and soft. We tumble in weightless tangles. No elbows or bony hips. No worry about my buried motives for attraction to a black woman. It is fine. It is clean. I wake up brokenhearted. This will never be. This is not possible for me. If it ever were, it is too late now. I stare in despair at my wall of books. I vow to remember her face. I make up a story: Perhaps she exists and the dream is premonitory. It has happened before. Coincidence perhaps. I am not a firm believer in such things. But perhaps. And I vow to look openly today into the eyes of all African American women, see if they look back, see if there is a moment of love. It is unlikely. But I tasted something in that dream, and now I don't know how to continue without it.

I walk to Barassini's, attuned once more to African American females. But the fiction of the dream doesn't overlap with the reality of the waking world. I see five possible candidates for dream lover among a sea of obvious rejects. Not one of them, the candidates or the rejects, acknowledges me. The truth is that I am not lovable, not in reality. Not by African Americans.

I arrive at Barassini's in a foul mood. He senses it and asks me what's wrong. I look into his stupid judgmental eyes. Why can't he look at me as she does? Why can't anyone in my damn corner of the Universal Brick look at me as she does?

"You're looking at me crazy," says Barassini.

"Whatever," I tell him.

"Yikes. Well, maybe we ought to get to it. I can see you're in a mood."

"I am just fine," I say. "Just fucking peachy. Let's do this."

Barassini flicks my neck switch.

I'm in the hall peeking into the parlor as gaunt, mustachioed Molloy reads the 1943 private printing of Guy Wernham's translation of *Maldoror*. Patty passes by several times, straightening, cleaning. It's clear she wants Molloy to notice her, to speak to her. After three passes, she turns in the doorway.

"Would you like some lunch, Chick?"

Molloy looks up.

"Hmm?"

"Lunch?"

He seems to consider this offer for a long moment, then:

"I don't recognize myself, Patty. That is to say, I remember myself and I remember my reactions to things. But it's as if I read about me in a book, a book about a stranger whom I revile."

"What are you saying, Chick?"

"You really want me to repeat that?"

"No. I just don't understand."

"For example, I know I liked veal chops. I remember I liked veal chops. But now, I loathe veal chops and everything they represent. Where did my affection for veal chops go? Is it floating free now, like smoke looking for a place to affix?"

"We don't have to have veal chops, Chick. I could make whatever you like. You want spaghetti?"

"That's not the point I'm making."

"Oh. OK. Because I have hamburger. I could make meatballs."

"I don't think the same things are funny I once thought were funny. I remember the things I thought were funny. But now they rankle me."

"What's rankle mean?"

"Annoy."

"I see. Well, that's OK. We can laugh at new things."

"I know I used to be happy to be around lots of people. I liked parties. I liked flirting. I prefer to be alone these days."

"Alone?"

"I'm more comfortable with solitude. With my books."

"How do you mean alone, exactly?"

"An audience still intrigues me, but in a different way. I desire the attention, but not for the same reason."

"What reason, then?"

"I need witnesses."

"How about sandwiches?" she says. "We have some cold chicken in the ice box."

"I'm not really hungry, Patty."

"OK."

Patty stands in the doorway for a long moment, while Molloy goes back to his Lautréamont.

"Do you remember you loved me, Chick?"

Molloy looks up.

"I do remember, Patty."

This scene breaks my heart. I consider the love I shared with my African American girlfriend and, once, long ago, with my wife. Am I like Chick? Did I change? Did they?

Does everyone?

CHAPTER 44

I SIT IN MY sleep chair, close my eyes, try to remember. How does it begin? A man. In a top hat? Bowler? I'm not certain. There have been so many hats in this movie. So many hats. So many beginnings. How can I remember it with any accuracy? There are indeed so many men's hats from this period. That I took a course on men's hats at FIT, as research for a think piece on the Diener-Hauser poster for *The Discreet Charm of the Bourgeoisie*, is not helping. My brain is full of hats: boater, bowler, fedora, homburg, top. I'm fairly confident it's a top hat, but that I'm struggling with the first hat of what might very well be a ten-thousand-hat movie gives me pause. This jumble of hats is illustrative of the jumble of everything in my mind, memories of childhood, things learned, things seen, moments of happiness (have there been any? Surely there must have been. And yet . . .). The progressive decay of my memory, my ability to concentrate, my . . . critical faculties—the only elements of me that had ever been of even slight interest to others—is, not to put too fine a point on it, catastrophic to my sense of self. I find myself falling humiliatingly short of the task at hand. Where do things go when we forget them? The miracle is, perhaps, that there ever was a mechanism with which to trap parts of the world as they pass through us. It is nothing less than the miracle of consciousness. Without memory, one does not exist. Perhaps that despiser of the natural world Descartes would have been more accurate had he said, *I remember, therefore I am*. If we are witnesses without memory, we are not witnesses at all. A hollow cylinder through which the wind blows will not remember the whistle it produces. The terrible irony of my circumstance, and the only reason I am perhaps more tragic than a toilet paper roll, is that I remember that I can't remember. And that is a punishment worthy of Tartarus. Only, for what am I being punished thusly? Have I not been an ethical if uninspired didact? Have I not worked diligently? Have I not loved well? Perhaps I have not. No, I have not. I deserve all the lightning bolts Zeus would hurl at me. I, as an expert in the chemistry of film stocks (I studied under Edwin Land at the Rowland Institute—he was on the fourth floor and I was on the third), carelessly, in the excitement of my discovery, let Ingo's masterpiece be destroyed.

Eventually I doze, strapped, once again, too tightly into my sleeping chair.

In the dreams, I am a novelizer. At least at first. In later dreams, I will become other people. Many others. Still, I will remain a novelizer, but I will become these many other people as well, in addition, all at the same time. No, more like one at a time. Well, one other person at a time, plus the novelizer at the same time as each of the other people individually. It's hard to explain. OK, imagine a series of pegs, maybe on a conveyor belt, but not exactly, more of a slingshotty-type thing, and if five of the pegs, or rather knobs, or rather protuberances, make up a Borel set . . . No, that's something else . . . *Probably*. It could be this, but . . . The truth is, I don't know what a Borel set is. Although I've certainly heard the term. That's more than most people could say. And it's not as if I don't want to understand what a Borel set is, but when I looked it up on Wikipedia, I could make neither heads nor tails of it. My math education, in truth, is meager. It's not entirely untrue to say I was an applied mathematics minor at Harvard, but I learned very little. With grade inflation, I was able to skate by. I, in the dreams, have always felt badly about that. I'm just not smart enough in the dreams. In the dreams, the best math student in my high school is now a Yale-trained professor of molecular virology. In high school, I told myself I was the more interesting one of us. That's why he got a perfect sixteen hundred on his SATs, because he always studied; that's all he did. Whereas I was the artistic type, full of daydreams and poetry and deep sadnesses and vim and a rebel's love of the Theatre of the Absurd. I got into Harvard on a film criticism scholarship. At the time, it was a big thing in the Ivy Leagues. A moneymaker for the university. We competed in criticism decathlons against the other Ivies to packed auditoriums. Film was of major cultural import in the seventies, that magical decade for American filmmaking. Now, of course, it has fallen by the wayside. Now everyone loves virology. Now my virologist nemesis is revered, doing important work in the development of a hookworm vaccine, a vaccine that will help hundreds of millions of people and hurt hundreds of millions of hookworms.

And I am a novelizer.

In my waking life, I am not a novelizer. Almost no one is anymore. But in the dreams, I am a novelizer, and a successful one at that. As a novelizer in my dreams, I've written several high-profile novelizations. My novelization *Godfather One* outsold Mario Puzo's novel *The Godfather*. I had the foresight to add *One* to my title, even before the second Godfather movie was announced. I was correctly praised for that. *My* pages twenty-three and twenty-four were lauded by feminist and feminist-aligned critics alike for their subtle shift from Puzo's misogynistic "shlong-fest" to a woman-centric erotica. Some even hailed it as "wymyncentric." One critic went so far as to hail it as "wymyncyntryc." That's how woman-centric it was. Others decried it, however, as a "patriarchal wolf in she's clothing," insisting that there's no way a man raised in this diseased culture could understand, let alone articulate, a healthy sexual relationship not predicated upon domination, humiliation, rape, and other bad things that men don't think are bad things. My feelings were hurt. I really did try. In my dreams, I think those are bad things, as I do in my waking life. In the dreams, I try to be socially responsible, or rather politically sensitive, or rather good, or rather just plain decent, or rather inoffensive to anyone and everyone, especially women, whom I lovvvvvvve like nobody's business, all within the confines of my job description, which is senior film marketing associate—novelizing division. I've always tried to be a good boy. Always. It's not easy forever caring so much what other people think, especially women. Think about *that* job description for a minute. Think about all I take on for the good of women.

I make me sick.

But even after winning three Scribe Awards (formerly the Lizas) from the International Association of Media Tie-In Writers (or IAMTW, pronounced *eye-AM-twuh*), I feel embarrassed by my profession; I feel a self-loathing, as it were. I am, after all, not a novelist, as I, as a younger man in the dreams, had always hoped to become; I am only a novelizer. In the dreams, I had attended the Iowa Writers' Workshop, which in the dreams as well as out of them is the place to go. It is to writing schools what the Yale University School of Medicine's Molecular Virology Program is to molecular virology programs. In my waking life, I did not get in to the Iowa Writers' Workshop. In my waking life, I had to look the program up to see if there was an apostrophe and where precisely it went, so as not to embarrass myself. But in the dreams, I knew exactly where the apostrophe went, and I went to the school, and at some point, respected novelist Don DeLillo returned one of my stories ("The Improbable Dandruff Flake of Daniel D. Deronda") with a note that read: *Thanks much for sending this along.* That little nudge of encouragement kept me going for a good five years. Eventually, in the dreams, I had a novel published. It was a scathing indictment of the practice of warehousing the elderly in twenty-fifth-century American space station nursing homes. I called it *Orbiting Grandpas.* Not only did it not get good reviews, it didn't even get bad reviews. Not even in *Gerontology Tomorrow: The Premier Journal of Speculative Aging.* True, thirty customers on Amazon did call it extraordinary, but they were, as it turned out, all me, and when someone who isn't me discovered this, suddenly *Orbiting Grandpas* was the talk of the town, but in a bad way, in case that isn't immediately obvious. It's surprising how much people you don't even know can want you dead. In the dreams, everybody seems to be looking for a reason to want people whom they don't know dead. Or fired. Or mocked. Or shamed. In waking life, it is this way as well.

And so that was that. By necessity, I became a novelizer, a corporate shill, a hired gun, a media tie-in writer. Now I am at best a "quote" writer. Not a writer of quotes or a quotable writer, but a writer in quotes. At parties, I dread the question, "What do you do for a living?" Also, to be clear, I dread that question wherever it's asked. And to add insult to injury, my humiliating livelihood is going away. Face it: Nobody reads novelizations anymore. Instead, they make videogames out of movies and sometimes toys and sometimes clothing lines, but novelizations are a thing of the past. This is true both in my dreams and out of them. It's just that I don't care about it out of them.

In the dreams, I have a family to support (although not mine), so when a phone call dangles the possibility of a novelizing job in front of me, I jump.

In a quick dream cut, I find myself wandering the streets of an unfamiliar part of the city. I sense I'm near the river, even though I can't see it from here. Maybe it's the distant beeping of ship horns that clues me in. Beeping? Is it called beeping when ships do it? I decide that a true novelist would know without having to look on-line. I think of Melville, that he would know, because he knew ships. That was his thing, really, when you come right down to it. Then I think, Didn't he live in the days before ship horns? So maybe he wouldn't. So that puts me up there with Melville in the not-knowing department. Maybe it doesn't. Suddenly I don't want to think about Melville anymore; I'm very tired. For a while I don't think anything, which is a relief. Then, damn it, I think of Barbosae, who novelized *Moby Dick*. He would've known. Barbosae knew everything. He had won a record forty-six Lizas (currently Scribes).

Then I think, You know who else would know? Joseph Conrad. He knew ships and he lived well within the time of ship horns. But *did* he live well within the time of ship horns? When were ship horns invented? When was Joseph Conrad invented? It doesn't matter; face it, I'll never be Conrad. Or Barbosae. I look up "ship horn history" on my dream phone anyway. Just for laughs. Aside from a brief mention in a Wikipedia article about vehicle horns, which includes no pertinent information, there is nothing. I am surprised and disappointed in the Internet. But, in truth, it is a marvel. Right there on the street corner, I get to look up ship horns. Conrad couldn't do that. I think he couldn't anyway. I try to check that online. Nothing. I look up Barbosae, thinking I might give him a call. He's dead. At least in my dream.

I glance up from my phone, scan the row of warehouses: They're boxy and derelict, the streets deserted. I search for a warehouse with a number. Do warehouses have numbers? I try to look that up on my phone, too. Dickens worked in a warehouse as a child, I learn online, having gotten lost in my research. Dickens would've known. I'm no Dickens.

It should be noted here that the dreams are not exactly dreams, but since they come at night while I sleep, I don't know what else to call them (Arthur Schnitzler would've known. I am no Schnitzler). However, they are different. For one thing, they have a grain, a sort of particulated quality, sort of like film. For another, there are credits, which is exactly like film. I can't read these credits, as they're white against a washed-out gray sky—which seems like a stupid mistake for a dream maker, an amateur's mistake, the mistake of a first-time dream maker—but I can tell they're there, and at one point, I am even quite certain I see the name Alan, a name that, as always, haunts me for reasons I will never understand. The term *Night Movies* comes to mind as something to call these dreamish experiences, or *Sleep Films*, or *Somnambulinema*. I even toy with the punny *Bedhead*. Then the word *Brainio* flashes in my brain, but I don't know why. I have some half-forgotten history with the term *Brainio*. It is on the tip of my dream. "That's odd" also flashes in my brain, followed by "I'm going to be late," followed by "But for what?" followed by "Oh, there it is now," followed by "There *what* is now?" followed by "The building."

The office waiting room is only vaguely realized, and there are obvious mistakes: a potted plant in the corner, for instance, is there and then it is not. Also, there is a pencil among the leaves of the plant when the plant is there. In my waking life, I love spotting errors of continuity in movies. It is one of my favorite avocations, if it can be called that. Maybe it is a hobby. Sometimes on forms or applications or even in conversation, I am called upon to list my hobbies. I never know what to say. From now on I will list this. Pointing out mistakes in films to everyone I know makes me feel keenly observant, smarter than the director. I decide it is not unlike the joy I felt finding that pencil in the tree in those picture puzzles of childhood, my dream childhood, that is. In my waking childhood, I was not particularly good at these puzzles. My handsome brother was good at them. He was good at everything. *Pencil in the tree!* he would say. And *Hey, that tire is square!* And *Look! That mailman is wearing a shoe and a boot!* I never spotted any of them.

I take a seat, my portfolio balanced on my lap, lit cigarette in my right hand. Wait. I didn't have that portfolio when I came in, did I? Nor did I have a cigarette. Two continuity errors. This portfolio is an empty prop. I know that but I don't want to spoil the illusion for the audience by acknowledging it. I feel that because of the potentiality of employment, I need to play along. It could be a test. I do tuck the knowledge away for later use, if it becomes necessary. A bargaining chip. But where to tuck it? I'm already inside my brain, I think. I decide to tuck it away in the brain inside my brain: my novelizer brain. I drag on the cigarette. It tastes real enough.

Wait. What audience? What did novelizer-me mean by audience? Am I being watched? Am I watching me? Am I the audience?

A woman enters. I find her beautiful though vaguely drawn and am instantly in love in that way I often am with the vaguely drawn women in my dreams. I, the novelizer, not I in my waking life. Although I in my waking life can relate to this feeling.

She is the kind of woman whose absence in my waking life as the novelizer—if I the novelizer were to be waking from a dream in the dreams—leaves me in despair. She looks at me the way lovers in movies look at each other. That beautiful fake way I desperately crave. I know this is a lie that movies perpetuate, but it does its work on me in movies and in dreams. Also all other times.

She is oddly dressed. Her ornamental scarf is tied in an incomprehensible manner. She follows my gaze down to her scarf knot.

"My eyes are up here," she says, pointing to where her eyes are.

"I apologize. I was only admiring your scarf knot."

She nods and tells me it is tied in more than three dimensions. I tell her I don't understand. She says, *you* don't, but *you* do. I consider this and decide she is suggesting there are two different me's. Maybe the other me is in that other dimension. I suspect I look puzzled. *I*, perhaps, don't look puzzled, but I wouldn't know.

"At this very moment," she explains, "another you is tying this knot for another me. We are getting ready for work, after we have spent the night together. Fucking. In case that wasn't clear."

I study her face. Is she toying with me? I love her beyond reason. My clown fetish has evaporated like coffee left for days in a cup, leaving a series of brown rings. And little spots of blue mold.

"Fascinating," she says, studying my face studying her face. "What a fascinatingly inept simile."

Then in a flash I understand: She's from the future.

"You're from the future," I say.

She tells me that, yes, she is from what I from the past might consider the future, but to her it's just now, and since she doesn't yet exist in my time, it is a bit more complicated than I could understand, but *I* could understand it fully.

There she goes again.

"Simply put," she explains, "you and I are imagining each other right now. It's a by-product of Brainio technology."

"I don't understand," I say. But the term *Brainio* is on the tip of my brain again. So there is that.

"I imagined you'd say that," she says.

"Did I imagine you imagined that I'd say that?" I ask.

"Sort of," she says, "in layman's terms, but let's not go down that road. It's an Avenue of Infinite Regress and I haven't got all day. My name is Abbitha L. X. Fourteen Thousand and Five."

"Hold up a second. Your last name is Fourteen Thousand and Five?"

"I know what you're thinking," she says, "but, no, I'm no relation to *those* Fourteen Thousand and Fives."

"I understand," I say, not wanting her to suspect I don't.

"In any event," she continues, "I need something from you."

"Anything you say," I say, then add in my mind: For you, my love.

"Imagine a future entertainment technology," she begins.

"Smell-O-Vision?" I ask, hopefully.

"So much more than Smell-O-Vision," she says. "These days, only old people in space station nursing homes watch Smell-O-Vision. No, the technology of which I speak is called Brainio. And we're in the early days of it. By we, I mean my society. Your society is pre-Brainio or p.B. I have written a Brainio, and it has been very well received by my assigned demographic. Unfortunately, there's no chance I can compete in the category of Original Brainio this year. That award is going to go to Rondaya One Hundred and Two for *Part-Time Robot, Full-Time Friend*, which is cloying and over-rated, in my opinion."

"What's your Brainio called?" I ask.

"*An Avenue of Infinite Regress*," she says. "And since I have no hope of winning Original Brainio due to politics, I'm going for Adapted Brainio. I think I have a good chance. Except . . ."

"Except what?" I plead, my sexual excitement becoming uncontainable.

". . . it's not adapted," she says.

I would swear on a stack of Bibles her statement is followed by a dramatic musical sting. But very far away. Like the far off, mournful beep of a ship in the night.

"But if your Brainio is not an adapta—"

She cuts me off:

"If you could novelize it, then it *would* be an adaptation—or adapta as it is apparently called in your time."

"That's unethical," I say.

"I need to win," she says, "for the good of the world. I'll explain later."

I don't know if she's telling the truth, but she is beautiful. So I tell her I'll sleep on it. Then I wake up.

CHAPTER 45

NOT MUCH OF note in my waking life. People get sick or don't, people die or don't, I watch TV or don't. Sometimes I smoke without remembering lighting up. I continue to go to a deranged hypnotist and try to recall a film by a deceased African American gentleman. I sell collapsible clown shoes. I eat Slammy burgers. In my waking life, I am not a novelizer. Nor will I be many other people, as I will in the dreams. I am, while awake, in fact, not even fully me. I believe if I had the courage to be completely me, I would be a somewhat more interesting person. I believe people would be drawn to me. I believe I would not be lonely. I cannot bear to believe that what I am while awake is the entirety of me. I unstrap myself from my sleeping chair and perform my morning ablutions. Then head for Barassini's.

Tsai is acting as receptionist today, and I find it difficult to even look at her, so far has she fallen in my estimation.

"Coffee? Water?" she offers.

I shake my head, sit, and bury my face in an old copy of *Hyp-Notice*, a kind of *Pennysaver* for hypnotists. Some guy is selling a pair of swirling hypno-eyeglasses, never worn. It's the saddest ad I've ever seen.

"Tell me."

Now I follow Molloy, skinny and stern, walking down a quiet Glendale street, mouthing a routine under his breath, playing both parts, working it out.

"You know, Molloy, the world is full of all sorts of people with strange customs."

"You mean like how the English put suitcases in their boots?"

"Don't be ridiculous!"

He arrives at a small Spanish bungalow, knocks. Marie answers the door, smoking, sullen, blocking his entry.

"Hi, Chick."

"Bud in?"

"No."

But Molloy hears Mudd in animated conversation behind a closed door somewhere. He pushes past Marie, following the voice. He swings opens the door to Marie's smoking room. Mudd and Joe Besser, laughing, look up from a table strewn with papers. Mudd stops mid-laugh.

"Chick," says Mudd.

"That's Chick?" says Besser. "Jesus Christ, he looks like you."

"What's going on here?" asks Molloy.

"Joe, would you give us a minute?" says Mudd.

Besser looks at Mudd, then at Molloy, then back at Mudd. He stands, passes Molloy, too close.

"I'll hurt you," Besser whispers, and exits, closing the door behind him.

Mudd looks down at the table. Molloy waits.

"Look," Mudd says, "I thought it was over. The doctors said you weren't ever coming out of that goddamn coma. I had to make plans. Marie wants to start a family. What was I supposed to do, Chick?"

"So you replaced me with Besser?"

"Joe's not a replacement, Chick. It's a whole new act. Nobody could ever replace you."

"Mudd and Besser. That sounds ridiculous."

"I know. We were thinking maybe Bud and Besser."

"You can't do your first name and his last name. That isn't done. No one does that. No one has ever done that."

"But it's got the two B's. So . . . I don't know. The eggheads call it alliteration. Maybe Bud and Joe. Joe and Bud. I have a list written down somewhere here."

Mudd shuffles through the papers on the table.

"Ah, here it is. Mudd and Joe is another idea."

"I'm ready to work again, Bud. Say you'll still be my partner."

"Jesus, Chick," weeps Mudd. "You don't know what I've been going through! The guilt! Why wasn't I hit by one of the lights instead of you? You know how many nights I lie awake wondering that? Questioning the existence of God? Thinking about fate? Why wasn't I the one in the coma for three months? Why didn't I wake up fat and funny instead of you waking up skinny and dull? It haunts me."

"I need to get back to work, Bud. Patty and I are through. I have nothing."

There is a long silence. Finally, Mudd speaks:

"What do I tell Joe?"

"Besser always lands on his feet. One of the Stooges will die. Maybe Abbott and Costello will split up. Besser will be in the wings, ready, waiting. Besser is always there."

"He's not a bad guy, Chick. He always asked after you. How's Chick doing? Does it look like Chick's coming out of the coma? That sort of thing."

"A vulture circling. Can't you see that? A fat, bald buzzard."

"Isn't that redundant, Chick? A bald buzzard?"

"Not all buzzards are bald, Bud. There are many varieties of buzzard. The Madagascar buzzard has feathers on its head, for example. Archer's buzzard. Upland buzz—"

"I stand corrected, Chick."

"Maybe you can call yourselves Bud and Buzzard. That's alliterative as well."

A time cut and Molloy sits at the table in Marie's smoking room, staring at a wall. Mudd paces. There occurs a long and tedious silence, perhaps twenty minutes. Real time. Finally, Mudd speaks:

"Look, maybe we go back to the earlier routines. The doctor sketch? Maybe the plumber sketch."

"OK. But I play the plumber this time," says Molloy.

"Chick, that's my part. You can't play the annoyed plumber."

"I can't play diffident tenant anymore. It doesn't make sense to me."

"I don't even know what diffident means! Where are you coming up with these words?"

"It means timid, Bud."

"Well, say timid then!"

"I just did."

"Well, say it in the first place!"

"I can't go back in time, Bud. You'll just have to live with the fact that I said diffident the first time. One can't go back in time. The world only moves—"

"Great. Fine. I get it."

Mudd paces. Molloy stares at the wall.

"OK, what if we're *both* vexed plumbers?" Molloy says.

"Vexed?"

"Annoyed. What if we're both annoyed plumbers?"

"Where's the gag?"

"We're identical twin vexed—*annoyed*—plumbers. We have the same personality. The same opinions regarding plumbing solutions."

"So we don't fight?"

"No. Because we agree on everything. Everything!"

"I don't get annoyed with you?"

"No, that wouldn't make sense. You get annoyed about plumbing problems, maybe about having to make an emergency call in the middle of the night. But so do I. I'm exactly as annoyed as you are. Exactly. Because we're twins."

Molloy laughs hysterically. It's the first time Mudd has heard him laugh since before the accident. It's different: high-pitched, manic, otherworldly. An African wild dog. Mudd looks terrified.

"I don't get why that's funny."

"You don't get it, Bud, because it's new. It's revolutionary. It's the future of comedy."

"But if I don't get it, how will audiences?"

"We'll force them, against their will at first, into the alien, uncomfortable landscape of the world of tomorrow."

"I don't know, Chick. This is not sitting well with me."

"Maybe you want to go back to Buzzard Joe. You can both pick at my carcass."

"I'm not saying that."

"I took a serious blow to the head for us, Bud. For *us*."

"I know."

"Don't forget that."

"I would never."

"We're a team."

"We are."

"It's going to be a comedic augury."

"It is," agrees Mudd.

"Don't you want to know what augury means?"

"Not really," says Mudd.

"Listen, Bud," says Molloy, "comedy is nothing if not philosophical, conceptual. Something is funny because it's wrong. Wrongness can only be appreciated if there is a developed sense of rightness. So expectations may be dashed. A dog does not think a man slipping on a banana peel is funny because a dog does not have any expectation that this man was not supposed to slip on the banana peel. Of course, the dog is wiser than the human in this regard, but also stupider."

"Right," says Bud. "I kinda get that."

"My head trauma caused certain personality changes."

"I do see that."

"For the better."

"Yes."

STUPIDLY, OR PERHAPS arrogantly, I had not bothered to research the existence of Mudd and Molloy, assuming incorrectly that they were a product of Ingo's fevered imagination. The exhaustive research I had done for my monograph *Slowly I Turned: The True Horror That Was Humor in 20th Century America* led me to believe I was familiar with all the players, however minor, in the malicious genre of physical injury and mental anguish known as comedy. Were you to ask, I could rattle the complete credits, birth dates, death dates, and children's names of every forgotten third-tier second banana. Folks like Bobby Barber or Marty May. As far as I was concerned, Mudd and Molloy never existed. But I was in the Mukhwak Library of Comedy on Joey Ramone Place off 2nd Avenue earlier today, just to get out of the cold and shoot the breeze with my favorite librarian, Tubby Vermicelli, who had been the foil in several comedic shorts of the fifties (almost always as the bellicose chef).

"You look terribly," he said.

"Eh. I lost my job. Lost my apartment. Sleeping in a chair. Working on an impossible project."

"Sleep chair?"

"Indeed."

"Been there. What's the project?"

I explained a little bit about the lost film, then mentioned Mudd and Molloy.

"I remember them," Tubby said.

"Wait. What?"

"Mudd and Molloy. Sure. Very weird act. The Two Abbotts, right? Winchell dubbed them that after the accident, yes?"

I was speechless.

"Yeah. That's them," I managed.

"I never saw them, mind you. You'd just hear stories every now and again. They were always off touring Podunks. Trying to get by. I think they just kind of disappeared at some point," said Tubby.

"Did you ever hear that Abbott and Costello tried to kill them?" Tubby laughed.

"Never heard that one before. That sounds like a comedy in and of itself."

I asked him if he could check if there is any reference to them in the stacks. He nodded and headed off, returning about an hour later.

"Not much so far," he said. "Did find this."

He handed me a review for a show called *Heck-a-Tomb!* from a 1950 Arkansas newspaper.

Then he said: "And of course they did that one movie."

"*Here Come a Coupla Fellas*? But they never finished—"

"No. The Mandrew Manville pic."

"Mandrew Manville the giant exists?"

"Um. No. What? Mandrew Manville the light leading man exists. Existed. What do you mean by giant?"

"Jesus."

"What?"

"Listen, is there a computer I can use?"

I sat in a carrel to study Mandrew Manville's IMDB page. Fifty-three movies. Some of them mentioned in Ingo's film, but not one of them had I heard of in the real world before. Manville was married to Bettie Page. Holy cow. I know all about Bettie Page, having written a monograph on photographer Irving Klaw entitled *From Klaw to Richardson: White Rooms and the Horror of Sexual Subjugation in Photography*. So I know everything there is to know about Page, certainly who her three husbands were. Joe DiMaggio. Arthur Miller. Richard Burton. Mandrew Manville was never one of them.

I LEAVE AND soon find myself in a drunken argument with Tony Scott at Pimpernel's, the film critic hangout on West 19th.

"First do harm (to bad filmmakers) is my credo."

"But—" says Scott.

"No buts, Tony. Bad films are not a minor nuisance. They infect the human psyche, pervert thought, demean humanity from the inside out. Like brain-eating spores from the future!"

"But, I mean—" says Scott.

"There needs to be a continued war against this kind of cultural malfeasance."

"I don't—" says Scott.

"Bam!" I say, pounding the table. "Checkmate, Scott! I'm Audi 5000."

I stumble toward the door. The knowledge that Ingo's fictional world seems to be bleeding into my own has made me mean. It's every man for himself now.

On my walk uptown to Barassini's, I find myself almost strutting as might a young John Travolta, filled as I now am with piss and vinegar at my vanquishment of A. O. Scott. Never will he write again. Of this I am certain.

CHAPTER 46

"TELL ME."

I watch Molloy writing *Heck-a-Tomb!* (which will eventually close out of town in Philadelphia). He sits typing at his desk for hours, never cracking so much as a smile. Ingo once again employs the time-lapse device. I count the day/night shifts out the rat-trap floor-through window. Three hundred and seven times: about ten months. Mudd comes and goes, bringing food and taking away dishes. The rat-a-tat of the manual typewriter at this speed is transformed into one prolonged and horrifying *claccccccccccck*, silenced at regular but brief intervals when Molloy disappears from the room. Is he sleeping? Using the commode? One time he returns in bloodied clothes; he strips them off and burns them in the fireplace. No explanation is offered.

The single extant reference to *Heck-a-Tomb!* appears to be this review from a production at the King Opera House in Van Buren, Arkansas:

Review by Edna Chalmers, Theater Critic, *Van Buren Press Argus*:

Heck-a-Tomb!, the musical revue now in residence at the King Opera House, is an oddity that Mr. Robert Ripley might want to consider including in his next *Believe It or Not* radio program. He'd better act fast, however, as the performance I attended was far from a sold-out event. Seemingly modeled after the stage shows of Messrs. Olsen and Johnson, this evening of comedy and song contains very little that is readily identifiable as either. The premise, such as it is, appears to be that Bud Mudd and Chick Molloy are a pair of angry, monosyllabic Civil Aeronautics Board investigators looking into the Eastern Airlines Flight 605 crash of 1947. If you don't immediately see the comedic possibilities of a monumental disaster in which 53 people lost their lives, you will find yourself in accord with this reviewer. The harebrained story follows the two investigators, who seem to have identical personalities and wardrobes, as they agree with each other over the cause of the accident. There are, as well, ghosts of the dead, families of the victims, and local witnesses. All of them share the same personality as Mudd and Molloy. Even the dancing girls are mustachioed.

Mudd and Molloy sit in their dressing room backstage at the King Opera House.

"You don't understand," says Molloy. "This show has everything."

"It's not enjoyable, Chick," says Mudd. "I feel like people go out for a night on the town after a hard workweek, they want to be entertained."

"'Listen to the cry of a woman in labor at the hour of giving birth—look at the dying man's struggle at his last extremity, and then tell me whether something that begins and ends thus could be intended for enjoyment.' You know who said that, Bud?"

"No."

"Soren Kierkegaard."

"I don't know who that is, Chick."

"The greatest philosopher of all time."

"OK," says Mudd. "Still, it is the weekend, so . . ."

I myself am also a Kierkegaardian, in the sense that my position on the Hegel-Schlegel spectrum finds me firmly planted in a synthesis of the two opposing camps. That Fred Rush published his book *Irony and Idealism: Rereading Schlegel, Hegel, and Kierkegaard* on this very synthesis before I was able to research, write, then find a publisher for my own *Isn't It Romantic? Idealism and Irony: Reexamining Hegel, Schlegel, and Kierkegaard* both infuriates and saddens me. I theorize Rush had experienced some sort of transfer of information from my brain to his. I am not clear on the science of this, but there is no other explanation. I notice he received his PhD from Columbia, where I am often on campus carrying my ally mattress. The thought transfer could've happened any one of those times.

ABBITHA L. X. Fourteen Thousand and Five is back, this time in something else diaphanous. She is so beautiful. Is she real or a creation of my mind? I can't know. But, in any event, I love her, which, if she is a creation of my mind, is in a way a kind of self-love. I suppose it might be seen then as a kind of narcissism, but if it were narcissism, wouldn't Abbitha just look like me, except in a diaphanous gown? Instead she is my opposite: female, beautiful, brilliant, from the future. These are the four things I am not. Maybe I'm brilliant.

"Will you do it?" she says.

"What is it about?"

"It's a period piece."

"What period?"

"Yours," she says.

"So, not period."

"Well, to me it is. But I've done a lot of research on your time. For example, I know that Kit Kats come in bizarre flavors."

"Only in Japan."

Abbitha scribbles that into her notepad.

"What's your Brainio about?" I ask.

"The assassination of President Donald Trunk."

"Trump."

"Pardon?"

"It's Trump."

"I don't think so. I've done a lot of research. Everyone in the future thinks it's Trunk. No one thinks it's Trump. I've checked. We know how important his name was to him."

"Look, as much as I love you and it is with every fiber of my being that I do, I can't write a book about a plan to assassinate the president."

"You wouldn't be writing about Trump. You'd be writing about Trunk."

"So I have to call him Trunk in this novelization?"

"No one in my time knows who Trump is. His few remaining space hotels are called Trunk."

"So in addition to writing about assassination, I have to sound unhinged while doing it."

"For me."

"I don't know . . ."

"You'll win a Brainy Award for Adapted Brainio. You'll share it with me. Posthumously for you; I'll be alive."

"I don't know—"

Abbitha kisses me. The world dissolves. She pulls away and looks at me.

"You'll never see me again if you don't do this," she says.

"The Brainy is really prestigious?" I say.

"Your grave or funerary urn or water slide and/or rocket coffin will be visited by millions."

"I'll do it!" I say, followed for some reason by a fist pump and a freeze-frame.

I wake up with a start. It occurs to me that both in my dreams and in my waking life there exists the same question: What now? Something happens or nothing happens, and either way, I have to decide what to do next. There is no end to it. Well, no, there is one end to it, and that revelation leads me to this conclusion: "What now?" is the definition of life.

My morning is difficult. I don't feel at all rested, and still I have to scrape an extraordinarily copious amount of dried ejaculate from the upholstery of my sleeping chair. I consider my obligations. Now I have two novelizations: Ingo's and Abbitha's. Both are for love, both for self-aggrandizement. But I don't even know if Abbitha is real, and, in truth, I don't know if the movie I'm remembering through hypnosis is real, either.

There is a select group of filmmakers of film remakes (film-remakers) whose remakes exceed the original they are remaking. Dave Cronenberg's *Fly!* comes to mind as vastly superior to Neumann's 1958 original. Similarly, Apatow's *Citizen Kane* remake *Citizen Funny Guy*, in which Seth Rogen plays Charlie Kaneberg, a stand-up comedian who learns he's dying and decides to start a news blog because "It's time to stop with the jokes and start with the serious." He wants to help make the world a better place for his children and all children everywhere, including even other countries. "The only borders," he opines at one point, "are the borders we build in our hearts." Later, it turns out he's not dying, that his chart was mixed up with someone who was diagnosed as "really healthy" but now finds out he is the one dying, which is sad for that guy. So Charlie Kaneberg hands over his blog to the really dying guy, and everyone learns something about the importance of family.

I believe I can make the same positive and timely changes to Ingo's film in my remake. As brilliant as I suspect the original was, I have the advantage of living in a more enlightened age. It is not Ingo's fault that he wouldn't have known a Bechdel Test if it jumped up and bit him on the nose. Might not it be fascinating to recast the film as a female version? Wouldn't it be wonderful to see a film that finally takes women seriously? A film that states, yes, women are funny, funnier than men, and what's more, men aren't even funny at all. Even though the original correctly demonizes comedy. But perhaps the problem with comedy is that women are not in it. This recast film could show us a world of comedy that is kind, which is not to say that there is something inherently kind or nurturing about women. That would, of course, fly in the face of all current gender research that demonstrates there is no difference between the genders while at the same time showing a full and complex gender spectrum. This is what I hope to provide to audiences with my version of the story. Also, it will be live action. Firstly, for practical reasons. It is almost impossible that I can hope to shoot for ninety years. I likely do not have that kind of time. Secondly, acting has always been my first love, so the opportunity to collaborate with many of the great actors of our time, to even take on a role myself (Marie in

this gender-reversed version? My African American ex-girlfriend?)
would be the culmination of all my dreams.

OH GOODNESS ME, right there on the street, directly in my path,
is Castor Collins, blind now of course, just like his brother, due to
their early exposure to solar rays. Dark glasses, no cane, unassisted,
as confident as you please. How does he manage? It is said that the
other senses become more acute when one loses another sense, in
this case sight is the other one. So perhaps through heightened hearing, smell, taste, and touch, Castor is able to navigate this crowded,
dangerous environment, much as a blind ship's captain might avoid
a jagged, rocky coastline on a fogbound night using only his ears
and sense of taste. It is truly amazing to see, and then it occurs to
me, with some sadness, that Castor Collins will never be able to see
how amazing it is, since he is blind and cannot see how amazing it
is. Suddenly, he seems to be aiming right for me. I alter my path
and Castor alters his, as if he is some sort of heat-seeking missile.
I shift again. Castor reroutes. Soon it becomes a dance, a terrible,
monstrous dance.

With a trainee beside her in her cubicle, Flotilla Del Monte
watches B. on her "Castor" monitor and explains her work process.

"Sometimes I pick out a person and fuck with 'em by using Castor as my sorta heat-seeking missile. (into microphone) Slightly left,
Sweetie. (to trainee) The job can get boring, so I invent games to
pass my shift. To be fair to me, I only pick assholes to target. Today
I'm cranky, so I've searched for an oncoming asshole. (into microphone) No, hon, a little more. That's it. (to trainee) As you can see,
coming right at us, twelve o'clock: a wormy little Jew. See him?
Brillo beard, tiny, wet eyes like old grapes. Coke-bottle lenses. Perfect. (into microphone) Now slightly right, Castor, baby. Perfect. (to
trainee) This is all the more fun because I can tell the Jew has recognized him. See his mouth hanging open like a starstruck schoolgirl?
He's trying to act as if he doesn't care. It makes the whole thing that
much funner. He's realizing there's going to be a head-on collision.
See him turning to run? Fucking hysterical!"

I have turned to run.

Flotilla (*into microphone*): "Jog, hon. Street is clear. Let's get you a little exercise."

I glance back. Castor seems to be running after me.

Flotilla (*into microphone*): "Speed up a tad, darling. (*to trainee*) Oh my gosh, perfect! The Jew's looking back over his shoulder. Oh, look, an open manhole straight ahead. Let's aim for it. (*into microphone*) A little bit left, sweetie. Now just a smidge right. There you go. Now a quick veer left!"

I fall into a manhole.

Flotilla (*to trainee*): "Hole in one! It's a game of skill. Hysterical. Slap me five."

As I pull myself out of the river of sewage, check my ankles for sprains, I get a flash of memory—the film. Castor. The woman in Texas. He has a guide! I remember! She aimed for me! She thinks I'm Jewish! I'm very confused. Am I pulling myself out of the sewer in the film or in life? Is this some sort of conflation on my part? I need an answer. I climb out of the hole. I run after them. I need my questions answered. I want to tell her, also, that I am not Jewish. But wait . . . I did this very thing in Ingo's movie. I catch up to them at the next corner.

"I am not Jewish!" I scream.

Castor cocks his head, unaware of what just transpired. But she knows. The anti-Semite knows. And she hears me in there. I know that, too. The light changes and they cross the street. I want to follow, but I don't. I don't know why; I just know that I can't.

In Amarillo, Flotilla scratches her head.

"How did the Jew know I thought he was a Jew? Maybe he didn't but was assuming. That's the thing about Jews. They have what is called persecution complex. We learned about it in my Psychology of Jews class at Amarillo Community College and Bake Sale. It's off-putting, just like Professor Pastor Jimminy said. Just like those hair springs they hang from the side of their heads. Anyway, it looks like he wasn't seriously hurt, which I am glad about. I am not a Jew-hater like some of the folks around here, who still blame the Jews for all the helium mines shutting down. Let bygones be bygones, I say.

(into microphone) Eat at Slammy's. *(to trainee)* It's time for one of his commercials. Castor gets a discount on his service because he signed up for the commercials plan."

I notice more people smoking everywhere. Now I worry about secondhand smoke, also firsthand, for I am smoking, too. It concerns me, also, because with all the smoking, I can't see very far ahead of me, which I'm worried will cause more and more of these manhole mishaps. It seems unsafe to have so many open and untended manholes in the city. Perhaps a letter to the mayor is in order. I work myself into a lather of outrage and write a letter to the mayor, whom I believe is called The Honorable Shmulie J. Goldberb.

> *Dear Mayor Goldberb,*
> *Can I be the only one who has found himself (herself, thonself)*
> *inconvenienced by this recent scourge of open and untended*
> *manholes in our once great, closed-manhole city?*

I give up on the letter. I sense *scourge* is not the best word here and I don't have the energy to think of a replacement. So I put it in an envelope as is, unsigned, no return address. Suddenly I feel depleted; my fit of pique has me exhausted. All I want to do is strap myself into my chair and sleep forever.

A week later to the minute, I find a letter in my mailbox:

> *To Whom It May Concern:*
> *It has come to my attention there has been a rash—*

Rash, that's the word!

> *—of untended and open personholes—*

Personholes! Of course!

> *—in our fair city. The safety of our citizenry is of the upmost—*

Upmost? That can't be right.

—importance to me, Mamie, and each and every member of my
extended mayoral family. So beginning Tuesday, March 18th, the
city will place an armed guard at every open personhole within the
five fair boroughs. All unauthorized fallers will be shot. It is our
sincerest hope that this will address the issue in the fairest and
funnest way for all involved.

MY SPEECH AT the Billy Crudup Hebrew Home for the Aged on
DeKalb Avenue is a smash hit.

"TELL ME."
   A dejected, much older Mudd and Molloy, outside of a New York
City comedy nightclub called The Comic Strip, are approached by
a Western Union boy with a telegram:

> *TAKE THE NEXT BUS STOP BETTIE AND I NEED TWO*
> *MANSERVANTS IMMEDIATELY STOP START RIGHT*
> *AWAY STOP PAYMENT WILL BE QUITE*
> *SATISFACTORY STOP LIGHT HOUSEWORK STOP IN*
> *THE NAME OF LOVE LOOKING FORWARD TO*
> *GETTING TO KNOW YOU BETTER STOP*

SONG IDEA: WHY *can't* I be a teenager in love?

ANOTHER FELLOW WALKING toward me. Is he a blind, too? Big and
young with one of those haircuts that seem designed to make a
person look stupid, constructed, for some unfathomable reason, to
bring the top of a fellow's head to a seeming point. He walks right
at me. A game of chicken? This man is not blind, I conclude, not a
tool of some anti-Semite in Texas. He is pulling his own despicable
strings. Who is going to move out of the way? Not me, Goliath. I
will no longer be the civic-minded one. What has it gotten me? No,

I will defend, against all comers, my commitment to this trajectory. You, my pinheaded behemoth, might feign unconsciousness. But it is time for you to awaken from your pretend slumber because I will not veer. I look straight ahead, making it clear that I see you, that I have made my choice. But I will not look you in the eye. I am a Mack truck, a train on the rail. This is my path. You will need to find another. If flying fists is what you desire, then fists flying is what you shall have. Because I am over it. At the last possible moment, I jump out of his way and drop into an open personhole. An armed guard shoots at me. I swim under the fetid water until I am out of his range.

"TELL ME."

An agent's office. He is booking a younger Mudd and Molloy at Brown's in the Catskills for their continued comeback. He says there's excitement at their return, even after the catastrophe that was *Heck-a-Tomb!*

Now I find myself in a Catskills resort's packed auditorium, a buzz of anticipation in the crowd. The house lights dim. Mudd and Molloy, dressed in coveralls, step onto the stage to both applause and some surprised murmurs:

"That's him?"

"Which one?"

"One of them."

"He doesn't look well."

"Which one?"

"Either one."

The sketch begins:

MUDD: I can't believe they made us come in the middle of the night to fix this leak.

MOLLOY: I can't believe it, either. I'm not happy about it.

MUDD: Me neither.

MOLLOY: Well, the faster we get started, the sooner we'll finish.

MUDD: That makes good sense.

MOLLOY: At least it makes things easier that we're identical twins and we agree on almost everything.

MUDD: We even agree that it's *almost* everything we agree on and not everything.

They both laugh at this in a high-pitched, otherworldly, African dog yap. Molloy is really laughing, and Mudd copies him. It's upsetting.

MUDD: But I'm still not happy about the late-night call.

Cut to a shot of the audience, every mouth agape.

Barassini snaps me out of it. Time is up for today.

"Why so blue?" asks Barassini. "We're cracking it."

"I don't know," I say.

I want to add "Dad," but I stop myself. How odd. He looks nothing like my father, who, although he, too, was a hypnotist, was a simple hypno-hobbyist who worked almost exclusively on mesmerizing chickens with chalk lines.

"Well, chin up. This is going well."

The truth is, the monumental nature of this task has become a struggle. I don't know if I'll ever see the end of it.

CHAPTER 47

T HIS EVENING I have been assigned to speak at my Allies meeting in the basement of Judson Memorial Church:

"Thank you. I apologize if by speaking, I am being insensitive to the fact that I am not even welcome to speak in this important cultural conversation. It's your turn now! Thank you for your time."

Someone yells "Sit down!" and I do. It is an important reminder, and for that I am grateful. Still, depression has set in, and all I want to do is sleep. That in sleep I get to sit down and also interact with Abbitha makes this version of slumber even more of a draw for me, I must admit.

And almost without any awareness of the intervening time, I am back in my sleeping chair. I am back in Abbitha's waiting room.

She pokes her head out and invites me in.

"Your Brainio chip has already been installed, so it's simply a matter of activating it."

"When was it installed?" I ask.

"Your hypnosis toggle is an early version of the Brainio mechanism, so we can use that."

"Wait, Barassini's toggle is—"

"Barassini's work is the lattice upon which Brainio was created. In fact, we always say, you can't spell Brainio without Barassini."

"There's no *o* in Barassini."

"Very true. But the best anagram we could get out of Barassini as it is was 'I, Brain Ass,' and we didn't think we'd move units with that."

"So, wait, is Barassini's treatment just a Brainio? Is he putting a fabrication into my head?"

"What is fabrication but an anagram for 'I Brainio Fact'?"

"I don't know what that means."

"I will not and cannot and would not and most importantly shall not pass judgment on the Father of Brainio, or Brain Ass, as the Originalists insist on calling it. More to the point, I don't know the answer. Barassini was murdered by an unknown assailant before he was able to write about this period of his life."

"I see."

"And now without further ado, I give you *An Avenue of Infinite Regress* by Abbitha L. X. Fourteen Thousand and Five."

She reaches over to my neck and flips the switch.

I am in the back of a limousine driving through the streets of Disney World. The car, one of a train of black limos, speeds through the streets of some fake Swiss town. The fat crowds leap to the curbs for safety, yank their fat kids, dislocate their fat shoulders, causing them to squeal in fat pain. I am the president so they have to get out of my way. It feels good. I am President Donald J. Trunk. Can you believe I'm the president? No one believed it could happen.

I attempt to think things that I want to think as B., whom I used to be, but I seem to be on a track of some sort, like a ride, a track of constant yearning and need, empty bottomless loneliness. In truth, not so different from B., but with a smaller vocabulary.

I, Trunk, have been wronged. I have been wronged. I have been misunderstood. I am good. I am the smartest. I am rich. I will prove everyone wrong. They will love me. I have enemies. My enemies must be destroyed unless they realize they are wrong and they love me, then I will welcome them back with open arms. The world is ugly, very, very ugly. People are ugly. I do what I need to do. Where are the crowds for me? If I order that guy driving to stop, and I step out among the fat people on the street, will I be cheered? I will. These are my people. These sad, poor, fat white losers are my people. But I want the other people to love me. Why won't the better people love me? I am rich. I am so smart. Look where I am. I am the president of the United States and nobody thought I could do that.

I won. I came from nowhere! I said exactly what I wanted and I won. Nobody thought I could do that. And I did. Nobody ever did that before. Nobody ever got elected president with no political background before. America recognized what a great president I'd be. Think about how amazing that is. Are you the president of the United States? I ask every person who challenges me. They have to say no. I already know the answer when I ask them. Do you think you could ever become the president of the United States? You couldn't. And yet, I could and I did. That's a sign of great intelligence. I am the smartest person in the world, when you come down to it, because I figured out how to do that. I didn't inherit that from my father. This is my thing only. There have only been, what, forty-four others in all of human history? And I am the only one to do it without the support of a party. George Washington doesn't even count because he didn't have to run, they tell me. They appointed him! Nobody knows that. So forty-three others not counting Washington. I am Donald J. Trunk and I will be remembered forever for that. I should tell the driver to stop so I can get out of the car and say hello, give the fatties a thrill. And they can cheer for me. It's Disney World. I'm sure I would be cheered here. These are my people, as much as I hate them. I press the button on the intercom. It's a really top-level intercom I have in this car, the best intercom, like you wouldn't believe, I can assure you. The technology of it is something really special.

"Listen," I say, "I want to—"

"We've arrived, Mr. President, sir," comes the voice from the front.

"OK."

I look out the window. We are parking in some restricted lot away from the crowds. I guess I took too long to decide to greet them. Maybe after, if I'm not too tired from the session, I can press some flesh, as they say. I like the human contact of people cheering me. It's lonely being president. I look inward and see nothing. It is black. I say hello and it echoes forever like I'm alone in a cave.

"Also, sir," the intercom driver says, "there were several other presidents who were not elected. So you're one of even fewer."

"Really?" I say. "That's even better. Do you know their names?"

"Gerald Ford is one."

"Oh, I remember that one! Stumbling Gerald Ford."

"Millard Fillmore."

"That's a pansy name. Millard? What kind of bullshit name is Millard?"

One of the guys who takes care of me, I don't remember his name, Jimmy or Joey, one of those names—good, heterosexual names—opens my door for me. No Millards on my staff.

"Tell me the rest later, intercom driver," I say.

"Yes, Mr. President."

I step out. They open doors for you when you're a celebrity. It's a nice thing, not a big thing, but a nice little thing. I always make sure to nod at them in a masculine way, a nod of hello, or thank you. It's a guy thing and I'm good at it so I do it, when I remember. Sometimes I'm in a hurry to go to important things or even the bathroom and then I just keep going. But considering I'm so important and I'm the president, nodding even sometimes, even three out of ten times shows I am a really good person. I love my staff. Millard! Pansy Millard Fillmore. I look him up on my phone. HA! He looks just like No Talent Alec Baldwin! Perfect. My non-pansy staff are very loyal, and loyalty is the most important thing. I expect it and I reward it. Roy Cohn, my mentor, floats around in my head now, like a ghost-angel. He taught me that loyalty is the most important thing. You need to be able to trust the people who work for you to not tell on you. Someone leads me into a recording studio. A lot of people saying, "Hello, Mr. President," as I pass. I nod and do that important look I do, like I'm thinking things, always thinking things. It's mostly the lips, you make them small like you're whistling, but you don't whistle. That's the trick.

In the recording studio, this pretty girl hands me a script. I know I'm being watched because of all the sexual stuff going on in the Fake News, so I don't even tell her she's pretty, which is a shame, because she is the type of girl who likes to be told that. Imagine her thrill if the president of the United States were to tell her that. I know she wants it. I can tell. But we live in horrible times, so I don't get to say it and she doesn't get to hear it. We both lose, thanks to political correctness. I take the script without looking at her even. I don't even say thank you. They can't do anything to you if you don't even look at them. It's not worth the trouble for the little surge of pleasure I would get. It makes it almost not worth being the president of the United States, but then I say to myself, can you believe it? You're the president of the United States. And elected, not like Millard "Alec Baldwin" Fagmore. I look at the script. It's a pile of garbage. They write shit for me. It doesn't sound like me. It doesn't have any of the things I said that got me elected. This is not what the people want. I know what they want. I got elected president of the United States by saying the things I said. Did anyone else in this room get elected president of the United States?

"I'll say my own thing," I say.

"Mr. President," says General Kelly.

"I think what we have here is very presidential, sir," says someone from Disney.

I don't know who he is. It could be Walt Disney himself for all the shit I give. But I think that guy's dead maybe. I read his head is frozen in a crate somewhere, so I guess that means he's dead. But I don't want to get into hot water the way I did with that Frederick Douglass thing. Everyone is gunning for Trunk.

"You know what's presidential?" I say. "What I say. You know why?"

"Because you're the president, sir," says somebody, a tall guy in a suit. Not as tall as me. And bony.

"That's right, Bones," I say. "Have a sandwich. You look sick."

I can say this kind of thing to men, because men don't get their panties in a bunch every time you say something.

"So, here's how it's gonna go. I'm going to say my thing: Make America Great Again stuff. And then I'm going to Mar-a-Lago."

"Very good, sir," says some other tub of lard.

"Where's the microphone? C'mon! Let's go! I'm the president! Don't make me wait!"

They run around getting things ready. I like this part. That scared part. Scared because they're in the presence of the president of the United States. Some girl leads me to the desk with the microphone. I don't look at her. I can tell I'd want to kiss her, by her smell. Girls smell so good that I want to kiss them. Someone from behind a window, a shrimp in a bow tie, gives me a signal and I start to speak.

"My fellow Americans in the Hall of Presidents. Look at how many people showed up here today. This is a big crowd. They say it's the biggest crowd they've ever had at the Hall of Presidents. The truth is, no one was coming here anymore before. Everyone knows that. I have to tell you, it was considered a dumb ride for losers. People would rather go on the roller coaster or some other rides. The whirly thing. Nobody cared about the Hall of Presidents. Now look at it. The Fake News will tell you that the crowd isn't big here today, but they're Fake News and want to destroy me and bring back the swamp for the elites and Hollywood and . . . But look how great. I love you all! Right? I love you all. And we're going to Make America Great Again, right? Am I right? That's right. Because China—and the Mexicans sending over their garbage people—right? MS-13. Nobody ever talks about that. But it's true and I'm going to put an end to that. There's going to be a big, beautiful wall. And coal. We need jobs for Americans. Coal. That's gonna happen. You better believe it. Coal, and we're gonna, there's gonna be great manufacturing. Mark my words. All the companies are telling me, Mr. President, we want to come back, but we can't. We're gonna make that— Y'know, look, I am a rich guy. Very rich. Unbelievably rich. And so that means I don't need the money. I'm not doing it for the money. I'm donating my salary. I'm not taking money from corporations. I'm losing money by being your president. So think about— A little boy came up to me before the show and said, 'Mr. President, could you please help my family? We're very poor and we're black.' A cute little African American boy. And I said, come up onstage during the show. I want everyone to see what a cute African American boy—who is asking for me to help his family. And I'm going to. This used to be a great country. Come up here now, little African American kid—"

"Sir, if I may interject," says the bony guy. "There will most likely be no African American boy waiting to come from the audience during these showings. I mean, it might happen once or twice, but this show is on a loop and will be repeated twenty-five times a day. So you can't really invite him up onstage. Because he won't come. Because you just made that story up, sir."

"He's not coming up?!" I say. "Turn the mic back on!"

The mic is turned back on. I am angry now.

"What's with you, little African American boy? The president of the United States invites you up on stage with him and you refuse to come? This is a great honor! I am the president. Is it because I'm not African American? Would you come up if the Barry Obama doll asked you to? That's racist. Talk about racism! That's racism. I'm canceling my invitation to come up here. How do you like that? Make America Great Again. I'm Audi 5000."

The booth is quiet for a while.

"Should we do one on script?" says the bony guy. "Just for safety."

"Nope," I say. "I know my people."

"Very good, sir," says the bone.

"Listen, I just thought—how about we get a little robot black kid who could come up when I say that speech?"

"That kind of breaks the flow of the exhibit, Mr. President."

"Whatever. Now I have to go to Mar-a-Lago."

"Oh, before you go, sir, would you like to see the animatronic model we've built of you?"

"Yeah, why not. I don't care. It better be good, though. Not one of those joke ones, like the Halloween masks that make fun of me or the Fake News political cartoons that draw me fat, put shit stains on my golf pants. I'm not fat. I don't shit my pants."

"I think you'll be pleased, sir."

"Better be," I say, checking my watch. "Hurry. I don't want to miss my shows."

They take me by way of an underground moving sidewalk to the place where they make the president dolls. I see a bunch of other president dolls. Some of those early ones from the sixteenth century with the white ponytails. But I don't see me. I'm getting furious because why do I want to see these other guys? They lead me to something under a sheet. It's big, so I figure it's me. I'm one of the tallest, if not the tallest president, they tell me. Taller than the Kenyan, I can promise you.

"Is that me?" I say.

They pull off the sheet and I'm staring at me. A life-size me doll. It's very good. Really impressive. I'm imagining him saying the words I just recorded. You generally don't get to see yourself from outside yourself. I guess I get more of that stuff since I was a celebrity with a number-one TV show and because I'm the president. So people film me all the time, and I get to see myself on the news all the time. But this is a me I can touch. I touch it. The face is very soft. Probably as soft as my face, which is very soft, let me tell you. I have always had the best skin. Soft to the touch. Not soft in a female way. But in a way that many, many women have complimented me. A lot of women, I can promise you. Soft but manly.

"It's time to go, Mr. President," says Kelly.

But I'm not ready to leave. I can't stop staring at the doll of me. I can't stop touching it. I turn to the room.

"Which one is in charge of dolls?" I ask.

A fat guy in a Hawaiian shirt raises his hand.

"Make me one," I say.

"Excuse me, Mr. President?"

"I want one of these me dolls for myself."

"Mr. President . . ." he says.

"Of course, Mr. President," says another guy, this one ugly, short, and in a suit.

"Good. Make it by the end of the week," I say.

"Yes, sir."

"And I want one that can walk and move and eat."

"Yes, sir."

"And it should like the food I like."

"They aren't built to—"

"I want one that likes my kind of food."

The ugly one and the Hawaiian one look at each other.

"Yes, sir," says the ugly, shrimpy one.

"And make the little black kid, too. You're all gonna look pretty stupid when my doll makes his speech and there's no little black kid robot."

"Yes, sir."

NEXT THING, I'M on my own personal presidential helicopter to Mar-a-Lago. I've had the inside redecorated; it's gold now, not just gold-colored walls, but the armrests are gold and the window shades and the snack tables. Real gold. And there is a video loop on a mounted TV set of me waving and smiling in slow motion to cheering crowds. Big crowds. I think it makes the other passengers happy to see how much America loves me. The real America. Not Hollywood. Not the elite. Not the swamp, which I am draining.

I watch my shows. I play golf. I shake ugly people's hands. I make a joke and everyone laughs. I eat hamburgers. Mar-a-Lago has a private McDonald's just for me. It's not small, though; it's really big, the biggest McDonald's in the world, they say. I can sit in lots of different gold seats, depending on my mood. And they have table service, which is unusual. Melonia and the boy aren't here. I'm not sure where they are. I wish I liked her better. But I can't divorce the first lady. I've checked. She's ungrateful and she's not that young anymore. What is she, forty-five? I don't know, but let's face it, I'm a billionaire and I'm the president of the United States. What's the point of all that if I can't get fresh pussy? It's like a *Twilight Zone*, where you finally get everything you want and you can't have fresh pussy. I mean, I don't have the same drive as I used to. I won't tell anyone that. No one needs to know. It would damage my reputation. But with the pills, I can get to where I need to be as far as boners go, and let me tell you, there are a lot of actresses who call me up, secretly, because it's bad for business in Hollywood to be seen with me, but they say, "Mr. President, I want to give myself to you." Many famous actresses and singers, too. It's funny. They say to me, "Mr. President, make *me* great again." Sometimes they say, "Mr. President, lock *me* up." They say, "Mr. President, I bet you're *yuge*!" But I can't have any of them because having sex when you're the president of the United States is not private. I get lonely.

The Trunk doll arrives at the White House, and it's everything I ever hoped it would be. It shakes my hand. Firm, manly handshake, almost as good as mine. We pull each other, but I win, in the end.

"Does it speak?"

"Yes, sir. We sampled your speech to create a synthetic voice, and—"

"OK, OK. I don't need your technical crap. Does it . . . is it . . . this might be a weird question, but does it have feelings?"

"No, sir. It's inanimate."

" 'In' means not, right?"

"Yes, Mr. President. In this case."

"So you call it animatronic, but you then call it inanimate. Isn't that one of those things like jumbo shrimp?"

"Oxymoron, sir."

"Did he call me a moron?"

"No, sir. Oxymoron is the term that means a combination of words that appear on the face of it to be mutually exclusive."

"OK, Poindexter. I know the word. I know all the words."

I look over at Kelly.

"I don't want Poindexter here anymore. Get me someone good."

Kelly escorts Poindexter from the room and immediately returns with another guy who I think is still Poindexter but he's wearing a hat now. I didn't really look at his face the first time, so I'm not sure.

"You a different guy?"

"Yes, Mr. President."

"OK. Good. Get this thing set up so I can play with it. Then everybody leave me alone."

While they work on it, I watch TV in my bedroom, which I call the Trunk Royal Palace Bedroom. I put up a sign. I yell at the Fake News, then switch the channel to the very nice white people who sit on a couch. It's comforting because, in a way, I feel these ones are talking directly to me. There's an amazing warmth coming through the screen. Just for me. They love me. I tell them how great they are and how attractive the girl one is. I'm allowed to say she's attractive because it's through a TV screen and no one can get mad. Everything used to be better and I'm gonna make it that way again. For now, I just pull out my cock and massage it. I can't get hard anymore without the pills, and I'm not going to take one of those now. I can still cum even soft, though, so that's pretty good. I like the girl one, and she says nice things to me. I can tell she is looking out of the studio at me and flirting. I am a powerful man, the most powerful man in the world. I am the best billionaire. I am the smartest. I went to the Ivy Leagues. I am the president of the United States. I am the pres— I ejaculate onto my pants. There's a knock on the Trunk Royal Palace Bedroom door. I'll leave the semen for the laundry lady. You pay people to do a job and you expect them to do it.

"Come in," I say, zipping up.

"All set, Mr. President," says some guy I think works here. He tries not to look at my pants.

"Send him in," I say.

"Yes, sir."

The me walks in. He's amazing.

We shake hands again and again try to pull each other toward each other. We are evenly matched, which they'll have to fix.

"Hello, me," I say.

"Hello, me," he says back in my exact voice.

"Does he just say what I say?" I ask.

"No, sir. He is a learning bot. He will be able to converse with anyone. Ask him a question if you like."

"Really? OK. Um, tell me about yourself."

"I'm a billionaire real estate tycoon and president of the United States."

"Ha. That's right! That's very good. That's terrific! He's smart! What was the last name of the president whose first name was Millard?"

"Fagmore. Looks exactly like No Talent Alec Baldwin."

"Ha! He's funny! You're funny!"

"Thank you," says the robot. "Make America Great Again."

"That's right!" I say. "Does he eat? I wanted him to be able to eat. I could take him to the McDonald's here."

"He can simulate eating, Mr. President. He chews food and

390

swallows it and it goes into a metal canister, which can be accessed through a panel in his back. For cleanup."

"So he doesn't really eat? It's like for show?"

"Yes, sir."

"Does he have a cock, though?"

"Anatomically correct, sir."

"Amazing. All right, leave us."

Everyone leaves me with my Trunk doll. I suddenly feel a little shy around him. We are both silent for a while.

"You wanna watch the news?" he says.

It is the perfect icebreaker.

"Hell, yeah!" I say.

"Hell, yeah!" he says.

He turns on the show with the couch people, which—can you believe it!—is exactly the one I would've picked, and immediately starts jerking off. It's crazy how like me he is. I would join him but the truth is, I'm spent, not that I would ever admit that to him.

"She's hot," he says.

"She is. Not hot enough for me, though. I like tens, and they have to be really young and they gotta have tits out to here."

"Yeah, I get that," he says.

I feel a little bad for saying he's jerking off to a dog. I don't want to hurt his feelings. But I was up against a wall. I notice he's losing his hard-on, and soon he just stops and stares off blankly.

"What are you doing?" I say.

"Reformatting. By spending time with you, I will learn to be a better you."

"You're gonna learn to be better than me?"

"No, no. Of course not. I will learn to be better at being you. How could I hope to improve on perfection?"

With that, he winks at me. I can't tell if he's making fun of me, but I do like being winked at. It makes me feel warm inside. It's hard to be vulnerable around another man. It's usually all about getting him before he gets you. But there's something about this guy. I just can't put my finger on it.

"Listen," I say, "Melodion is with the boy in Jew York—don't tell anyone I called it that. Everyone is so politically correct these days. It could be a whole 'nother Hymietown disaster. This is what I'm fighting out there all the time, so I can't have the Fake News or the Dems getting hold of that and twisting what was just a joke. Anyway, so if you want to have a sleepover, it'd be fine."

"I don't really sleep like humans," he says, "but I can power myself down to sleep mode. Saves my charge."

"Can you get into pajamas yourself?"

"Of course."

I throw him a clean pair of presidential Trunk pajamas and pull mine from under my pillow. They're gold.

"Sleepover! It's like when we were kids," I say.

We both clap, then link arms and do a hootenanny dance. I'm not sure it's called that.

When I climb into bed, I keep my distance. I'm not gay. But his animatron body is warm, so it's cozy under here. I nervously reach out and rest my hand on his hip. Does he kind of shudder a little? I'm not sure. I think maybe, but I plan to take it slow. I don't even really know what I want here. I'm not gay. But he's not a guy, right? He's a robot. And second, he's a *me* robot, so . . . there's nothing homo about touching yourself. Everybody knows that. And he's warm, which is tremendous, because I get cold at night. Anyway, I just leave my hand there and fall asleep.

I dream I am being chased. Me but not me. You know what I mean? It's dark. I don't know who is chasing me, but I also do. I have an idea who it is, but I can't really think it clearly. But it's big. It's the biggest monster anyone's ever seen, this I can tell you. And I am running through a farm or something. Farmland, with the corn and what have you that they grow on farms. Corn, they tell me. Farmers are great. Loyal, patriotic Americans. The best people. I'm running through the corn or whatever, maybe wheat, maybe beans. But I think corn. And I can hear the thing following me, crunching the corn down. Crunch! Crunch! Now I'm small, like the size of a thumbtack, and I'm running. I can't get very far because I'm so small. It's like that movie where that nerd guy shrunk the kids. And the monster is getting closer. I look around for a place to hide. There's a small hole in the dirt, like a manhole, but in dirt. I jump in. The monster runs right over it, kicking dirt on top of me as he passes. I wait until I can't hear his footsteps anymore and try to climb out, but I can't. I keep sliding back down and getting more and more covered with dirt. I'm tired, and I sit there to rest for a while. Then I try again, but I can't lift my feet. I look down to see that they're roots and growing into the dirt. I'm panicking. I pull and pull. Then I start to float out of the hole. No, not floating—my feet are still roots. I'm growing. My head pops out and keeps going up. I look down and see that I am a stalk of corn, or maybe wheat or a stalk of beans. My arms are leaves, and I have about ten of them. They're kind of waving in the breeze. I can't control them. I hear the monster returning, crunching stalks under his feet. I try to run. But I can't. He gets closer. I see his hulking form in the shadows, and I recognize him as—

—I desperately pull myself out of the Brainio. The toggle on my neck clicks like a circuit breaker, and I am back with Abbitha.

"It's not over," she says. "Not nearly. Get back in there."

"I can't take any more. I don't like being in that head."

"If you want me to return to your dreams, you will have to experience the entire Brainio. If not, I will visit some other novelizer in his dreams. Perhaps Barbosae will write the novelization for me."

"Nice try," I say. "But Barbosae is dead. I checked."

"So are you. Long dead in my time. I just have to hop a little further into the past to catch Barbosae alive."

"No. Don't. I'll go. I don't want you to leave my dreams. I have nothing without you."

"Precisely."

She reaches for my switch.

"One second!" I say.

Her hand pauses near my neck.

"I'm not getting the tone of this thing. If I'm to write it, I need to understand what you're going for. I mean, is it a comedy? With the robot Trump and all?"

"First of all, it's Trunk."

"Trunk."

"Secondly, I believe the tone will become clear as you continue through the labyrinth of the many personalities within the story. Third, you do not have the historical perspective to understand this fully, as the events portrayed within have not yet occurred in your timeline. But to answer your question at the most basic level, no, this is not a comedy. This is a nightmare from which the world will never awake. I am still in it. There is no comedy in my time. It has been outlawed as cruel and dismissive. We do not laugh at others, even Trunk."

"But you have him sleeping with a robot version of himself."

"We treat even this sad yet completely true historical event with the compassion it deserves."

"So, wait, you're saying that Trump—Trunk—truly gets a robot Trunk companion from Disney? In reality?"

"Yes, in this timeline, which is one of an infinite number of time-lines. That is what the historical record, such as it is, tells us."

"Such as it is?"

"Much has been destroyed in the Great Conflagration."

"Care to elaborate?"

"I've said too much. Shall we?"

I nod. Abbitha reaches for my switch.

AND JUST AS the monster's really huge jaws are about to clamp down on me, I wake up. I'm heaving. For a minute, I don't know where I am, but soon I recognize the gold drapes, the gold bedspread, the gold headboard, the gold floor, the golden retriever, the goldfish, the signed photo of Goldie Hawn. I am safe and sound in a Trunk property. I don't know which one. But—oh, it is the Trunk Palace Royal Gold Presidential Suite in the Whitehouse. I am spooning my Trunk doll. He turns to face me.

"Bad dream, Mister Man?"

"Very bad. The corn dream again. Or wheat. I have it all the time. Some monster is coming for me."

"Well, it's only a dream," he says. "Everything's fine."

It's good to be comforted. It's good to have someone care about me, really care about me, not because I'm so rich and so powerful and so charming and masculine, but because they can see the real me. I, Donald J. Trunk, are seen.

"Thank you," I say.

We kiss. I don't know how it happened. I am not gay. But he is me and that's such a gift. He understands me. It is such a relief. Being president of the United States is lonely. Nobody knew that. Where can you turn for relief? You have to make so many decisions. It's all up to you and you can't talk to anyone, because people betray you. They all want to destroy you. They are jealous. They want what you have. You have to keep your guard up. Don't trust anyone, is my philosophy, and it's served me well. I have become very rich, richer than creases (I never really understood what that meant). I have become the president of the United States. I have fucked hundreds of beautiful women, so many you wouldn't believe me if I told you. I have raised three beautiful children. Wait, no, four. Wait, no, five. But can I trust them? I think of *King Lear*, which is by William Shakespeare, and though I haven't read the play, I have seen the Lin-Manuel Miranda rap version *Give Me an Egg, Nuncle* at the Bedminster Playhouse. Comped by Miranda himself, by the way, even though he acts like he hates me, even though the seats were well over two thousand dollars each. So I know how the whole Lear thing goes. You can't trust anyone when you're king. Or president, which is king. Everyone is trying to take your kingdom—your presidentdom—from you. I break into a rap from the show:

"Blow winds and crack those cheeks / This is how ol' King Lear speaks / Rain a storm down on this world / Singe my hair that's Jheri-curled."

"That's great. You have a terrific singing voice," says Robot Me. "What is that rap?"

"Shakespeare," I say. "I went to Wharton, a great school, one of the best, everyone says."

"You're the most smart of the presidents. You have an IQ no one would believe."

We just look at each other for a moment.

"You're an amazing guy," I say to him. "A really amazing guy. You know that?"

"You're the amazing guy," he says back.

And I can tell he means it. We kiss again. This isn't like me. I stroke his face. It's warm and rubbery just like my own.

"Can I touch your hair?" I ask.

"Yeah," he says. "It's real. Go ahead and pull on it."

And I do. I can see that excites him. A little bit of rough play? I can do that. I like it myself. I slap him. He smiles and slaps me back. Then we stare at each other. The sexual energy is thick. There's a musky sex smell in the room, which must be coming from me because he's a robot. And then I'm on top of him and we're making out, groping each other. I unbutton his presidential pajamas as he unbuttons mine.

"So lifelike," we both say at the exact same moment, and we kiss again. Soon we hold each other's cocks and tug away at them hard, just like how people shake hands. It's great sex, the best sex. No homo. Keep America great!

By the time my aide knocks on my gold bedroom door, we are both in our suits and ties and watching those nice people on the couch telling us how great we are.

"Mr. President," says the guy at the door.

He's pimply. I think he's called Reggie or some other name.

"Would you like to get started on your workday?"

"No one knew how much work being president was," I say to my robot.

My robot lightly touches my hand, to show support. I like that our hands are exactly the same size. Big.

WE'RE IN THE Oval Office, which I've redecorated in a much more classy way. A lot of gold. The desk where I do all my work is eighteen-karat solid gold, handcrafted by the famous Italian artist Maurizio Cattelan, who also does my toilets. He's very, very famous, but he makes my toilets. So who's more famous? I think the answer is obvious.

General Kelly paces.

"We have a busy schedule today, Mr. President," he says. "We need to get right to it. We're already behind."

I don't tell him I'm late because I wanted to spend more time with my robot.

"I've been thinking," I say. "I'm thinking my robot and I should be co-presidents. I like having him with me. Is that nepotism? Will they say it's nepotism?"

"Mr. President," says Kelly, "we can't have anyone see the robot. I think that needs to be your private thing."

"But why?" I say, almost whining.

"Because the American people would not be comfortable with it."

"Say, I was thinking," I say, "what do I call him? I can't call him Donald Junior because there already is one of those, I think. I suppose I could call him Donald Junior and make the son one Donald III, but maybe that's not fair to the son one. Besides, my robot's not my son, he's me. I've never had a me before. Maybe I could call him Robot Donald or Second Me or Mini Me like in the Mike Myers movie, although I don't want anyone to think I'm Dr. Evil because I'm not. Maybe I could call him by the name I always wished I had: Ace. What does everybody think of the name Ace?"

Everyone tells me it's a very good name.

"Ace it is."

Everyone congratulates me on the choice.

"So we can't appear together at rallies? I think my base would get a kick out of how the United States has the best technology in robots, and this would prove that to everyone. China doesn't have a robot president, this I can tell you."

Kelly says no, and I get mad so I tweet under the table: *Ace is my new best friend!*

Everyone's phones ding, and they all look down at them at the same time.

"Oh, Jesus," says Kelly.

He's just mad because everyone's talking about me again. Everyone wants to know who is Ace. Doesn't matter what I say, everyone in the world wants to read it. It's all over the news. There'll be articles and theories about it everywhere. Who's Ace? Which Ace is it? Is it Ventura? Is it Ace Young of *American Idol*? What does he mean? What does Trunk mean? Everyone always wants to know what Trunk means. Their lives depend on it. Their stupid, little lives. Their loser lives covered with germs and vomit and fatness and—

"We need to spin this," says Kelly.

And I'm just . . . MAD. I want to PUNCH and KICK. I have words. I have words. I have words to say what I'm feeling. I want to SMASH. Who the FUCK does he think he is? People want to know what I'm thinking every GODDAMN minute. I am the PRESIDENT of the UNITED STATES. Who the FUCK does anyone think they are to question ME? ME. ME. DONALD J. TRUNK. My NAME is EVERYWHERE you look. EVERYWHERE. TRUNK. TRUNK. TRUNK. EVERYONE LOVES ME. WOMEN WANT TO FUCK ME. MEN WANT TO BE ME. ROBOTS WANT TO BE ME AND FUCK ME. I am RICH. I am RICH. EVERYONE IN THE WORLD KNOWS WHO I AM. I HAVE MY OWN JET. DO YOU KNOW WHAT MY IQ EVEN IS? You don't want me to talk about my best friend, Ace? Well, fuck you, you . . . I QUIT. I don't need this job. I have so much money, more money than you could imagine. I have the MOST BEAUTIFUL DAUGHTER. She came from MY SPERM. MY BEAUTIFUL DAUGHTER CAME FROM MY AMAZING SPERM. DONALD J. TRUNK SPERM. I can't stop my head from spinning with rage. The room is blurry and green. The GOLD. LOOK AT THE GOLD, I whisper to calm myself. But I can't stop my head. I don't feel good. I NEED A SEXY GIRL. I—

I flip the toggle, heave.

"You are still not enjoying it?" says Abbitha. "This is one of the scenes everyone is raving about."

"I can't," I say. "I really can't be in that brain anymore."

"It's your brain," she says. "It's your Brainio."

"It's Trunk."

"It's Trunk and it's you. Your brain interpreting my Trunk Brainio. That's what Brainio does."

"That's not me."

"You think when you see Trunk in real life, it's not you seeing him? Deciding who he is, what he's thinking?"

I am without words, letting this sink in.

"I just can't do it anymore," I say finally.

"I'll go elsewhere. You'll never dream me again," says Abbitha.

"I know," I say.

Then she's gone. I'm alone in her office. It's empty now. No furniture. No plant. The pencil drops to the floor. I leave and wander the deserted streets of this dream city until I wake up, unstrap myself, and wander the streets of the real city. I miss Abbitha. I think perhaps she was the closest thing to a soulmate I've ever had. In a way, she and I were the same: creators, cultural critics, sensualists. Her Brainio, the little of it that I got to experience, was powerful, unflinching. It put me in mind of myself as well as the brilliant Russian director Alexander Sokurov, whose phantasmagorical single-shot miracle *Russian Ark* presages Abbitha's *An Avenue of Infinite Regress*. That's the level of Brainio Abbitha has made, will make. Russian cinema masterpiece level. She would have been the ideal partner to me, two highly incisive minds exploring past and future together. I imagine us taking long walks in the dream woods, on the dream beach, discussing film, art, philosophy, stopping for a picnic in a dream meadow, sharing a nice, slightly chilled and fully imagined Beaujolais, perhaps a Duboeuf Moulin-à-Vent Domaine des Rosiers 3085, which will be a very good year, I am guessing, based on current climate change projections, some mutated berries, a soft Camembert. I could see passing my life that way, with her, in my dreams, but I choked. I could not stay with her Brainio, so real was it, asking me to immerse myself in the dark, dark heart of our insane and narcissistic culture. I flinched, and here I am alone. Maybe I could go back in, plead for another chance. I would face the horror this time, and in so doing—

I have a sudden and terrifying intuition, pull out my phone, and type in *An Avenue of Infinite Regress*. There it is: a novel written by Antonin Barbosae, ranked 2,898,311 by Amazon, published in 1983. One customer review: "This was a thriller of sorts. President Donald J. Trunk, which almost seems to predict Trump's presidency, falls in love with a Hall of Presidents robot of himself. They try to run off together, but Trunk is assassinated, and the Deep State passes off the robot as the actual Trunk. And that's just chapter one. Told in many first-person voices, it's a fun, light beach read, albeit highly confused. One small problem is that Barbosae seems to have gotten a great deal wrong in the future he predicts. All the men wear bowlers, and an imp from hell called Balaam is a film critic. I give it three stars." The book is listed as currently unavailable.

So Barbosae did get the job. Abbitha went further back in time to him. Barbosae also got Abbitha, I'm certain. I try to imagine (and at the same time, try not to) their walks, their picnics, their lovemaking. It's tricky because I don't know what Barbosae looked like. I check online and find only one photo, a crime scene photo, his head caved in by a large blunt object. Jesus, what happened to Barbosae? Was he killed for writing this book? Might that have been me if I'd written the book? In any event, it's all in the past now. There's no way for me to get the posthumous Brainio gig. Or Abbitha. Still, I cannot help going over my decision to extricate myself from *An Avenue of Infinite Regress*. Were the dreams, my immersion in the world of novelizations, my infatuation with Abbitha, nothing more than a distraction, glommed onto in order to avoid my responsibilities to Ingo? A nighttime fantasy world, self-created to combat my loneliness? I cannot say for certain.

Nonetheless, I continue to dream every night that I am a novelizer, but now there is no Abbitha. No Brainio. It is just my job. I scrounge for assignments.

Awake, I am terrified. There is a feeling of slippage. I can't hold my thoughts; it's as if they are slathered with grease. They slip from my grasp, bang into one another like prison lunch trays, and fall to the concrete floor of the prison cafetorium. I find these thoughts, then lose them, then find them again. But when they return, they are different. As if they have perhaps changed clothes while gone. I know something is different, but I can't say what. There are odd details: Now I remember my mother doing my hair in cornrows. Now I remember being an ant. Now I remember nuclear war. Now

I remember driving a silver boat-plane-car. It exhausts me; it's terrifying to be at the mercy of what I believe to be outside influence. Is my salvation in pinning down my real thoughts, in holding them firmly, in clutching at something that no longer exists, that is now only so much smoke and memory?

CHAPTER 48

Barassini toggles me.

Mutt and Mahle, two infants, miraculously appear with a *pop* in Hitler's jail cell in Landsberg. They soon become known far and wide as *die magischen kinder von Hitler* and are a source of comfort to Adolf while he is imprisoned (indeed, he dedicates *Mein Kampf* to "my funny little meatballs"). German law at this time allows inmates to "keep anything that falls to the floor of their cells and remains there for at least five seconds," the so-called *fünf-sekunden regel*. Although Hitler loves the boys, they are a handful, so upon his release from prison, their raising is left to Hitler's housekeeper, Anni Winter.

"You funny little *jugend*," she says, "always with the clowning. Maybe I should apprentice you to the great German comedian Lūdwig Schmitz. Would you like that?"

"Who is Ludwig Schmitz?" asks Mutt.

"Surely you remember the character of Onkel Eitern from *Die Addams Familie* at the Europahaus?"

"Oh, he's so funny!" says Mahle.

"*Glatze!*" adds Mutt.

Schmitz agrees to take the boys under his wing. He creates an act for them similar to his own *Tran und Helle* Nazi propaganda comedies, and the boys are naturals; it's like they were born to perform. The act is dubbed *Blut und Boden* by the führer himself, who has long hoped to make some inroads into Nazi comedy.

"Laughter is the best medicine," he often says.

But *Blut und Boden* do not test well with their target demographic, Hitler youth twelve to eighteen, whose reaction to the boys is summed up by one young man who says, "There is nothing funny about being a young Nazi, and there is most definitely nothing funny about being *not* a young Nazi. Ergo, there is no place for humor in our thousand-year Reich. Perhaps in the next thousand years, yes, we can relax a little, play some oompah songs, and have a good belly laugh once in a while. That's what I am hoping, anyway. In the meantime, it's all business for us Nazis. So, although we appreciate the führer's intentions, we'd like to say, no, thank you, please, Mein Führer. Just hand us our blond wig helmets and our neckerchiefs and send us off to the fight for the Fatherland."

Perhaps smoke *is* the movie, I consider. It gets in your eyes, just as the movie did, but now in a different form, as an irritant, obscuring the world. Maybe that is the movie. Maybe this smoke was Ingo's movie all along.

WHILE PERFORMING A tick check, I find a knife in my back. It's barely in at all, just sort of hanging there, as if I had been stabbed by a very weak or distracted person. I don't even feel it. I pull it out to study it. It's a stiletto. Hmm. Who would . . . Henrietta, of course. It's just the kind of shoe-related pun she would go for.

At the police station, the desk sergeant examines my back.

"It's barely even perceptible," he says.

"Still. Surely this constitutes a crime."

"Actually, no. A stab wound less than three millimeters deep is legal and even encouraged. We cannot help you unless a crime has been committed. Fourteen millimeters or more."

"At which point I'll be dead."

"Not necessarily. But it's possible."

"That doesn't help me."

"Innocent until proven guilty."

"Does that apply here?"

"Sir, there is a person behind you waiting. Please move along."

I turn and see Henrietta holding a taut piano wire.

"That's her!"

"Yes, ma'am? What can I do for you?" says the cop.

Caught, Henrietta stammers a response.

"Oh," says Henrietta. "I need a new D string for my clavichord."

"This is a police station, ma'am. The music shop is next door."

"Oh! My apologies," says Henrietta.

She eyes me, then turns to leave.

"That's her! Can't you see that?"

"I see a music lover," says the desk sergeant.

"I demand to speak to Commissioner Rappaport."

"Yeah, and I'm Marilyn Monroe," says the cop.

"That makes no sense in this situation."

"It's an expression, sir," he says.

I leave in a huff. Henrietta is indeed in the Steinway showroom next door, consulting with a salesperson. Perhaps I misjudged her. She eyes me and smiles.

"TELL ME."

Mudd and Molloy on a small stage somewhere in the Midwest, in the shadow of Oleara Debord, the massive mountain range in the center of the country, so large it is visible from both coasts. Not only can Oleara Debord be seen easily from space, it can be stood on from space.

"Strange as it may seem," begins Mudd, "they give baseball players peculiar names these days."

"Funny names?"

"Nicknames. Now on the St. Louis team, Who's on first, What's on second, I Don't Know on third."

"That is peculiar."

"What is?"

"Those names for the players."

"Don't you want to know who's on first?"

"I know. You just told me. Who."

"Uh, that's right."

"It's an unusual name. Is it Chinese?"

"I don't know."

"That's the third baseman."

"You're following all this?"

"Sure. I must admit, I Don't Know is a name I've never heard before. It's like some of those old British names. Like Bytheshore, for example."

"That's a name?"

"Yes. Well, it was. There are no longer any Bytheshores, by the way."

"Interesting."

"I agree."

"Um, anyway, What's on second."

"You told me already."

"Don't you think it's confusing?"

"I mean, it's unlikely. It's an unlikely name. I might even believe it's a made-up name—which I suppose many a nickname is—but I follow the conceit that it is the second baseman's name."

"I see."

"Watt is a name I've heard. That's almost like What, but of course spelled W-A-T-T."

"Right. So, um, do you want to know who gets the money when the first baseman gets paid every month?"

"I'm assuming Who gets it."

"Yes. That's right."

"Or his wife, Mrs. Who, if she handles the family's finances."

"OK."

"So what's the left fielder's name?"

"No, that's second base."

"Of course. Understood. Let me clarify: Would you tell me the left fielder's name?"

"Why?"

"Hmm. I think that's a Korean name. Probably W-I in transliteration, generally."

Later in the dressing room:

"This routine doesn't work if you understand that those are names," says Mudd.

"I think it works."

"It doesn't take advantage of the confusion."

"Those names are unrealistic. People will not suspend their disbelief."

"It's tried and true. Audiences love this bit."

"Personally, I think it's funnier if I completely understand the lineup."

"But where is the joke there?"

"The humor is two equals having a chat," says Molloy.

"That's not funny. I think audiences want to see you exasperated."

"I suspect we're going for something more subtle here."

"I guess it's too subtle for me, because I don't get it," says Mudd.

"It's funny when people understand each other."

"How?"

"What position does he play?"

"No, where's the joke?"

"He is? I don't even remember Where in the routine. Must be the conk on the head. My apologies."

"There is no Where!"

"Nowhere's a player, too? I've forgotten so much. I'll study up; I'll be perfect next time. I promise."

"One of us has to not get what the other one means."

"Perfect. That seems to be you currently."

"But it's not funny for us to just chat."

"What's funny is that they have odd names, not that I don't understand what you're talking about. Who is funny."

"We used to be."

"No, you misunderstand. The name Who is funny in and of itself. Think about it. What a funny name Who is. It's both a name and a question. And What is as well."

"Yes, that's the basis for the routine."

"Any more would be gilding the lily."

"But—"

"And I think perhaps there's an ethical issue at play if we mock those with developmental limitations."

"I take your point but—"

"As someone who suffered a severe head trauma, I've discovered a new empathy for those who have suffered severe head trauma—"

"But you've come out smarter, it seems."

"That's the luck of the draw, isn't it? Some of us are brighter after brain injuries, some less so."

"Does that happen? Getting more intelligent from a brain injury?"

"Should those of us more fortunate lord it over those less so? And even suggesting I am more fortunate to have developed a higher intelligence stinks of elitism as I hear myself say it. All levels of capacity should be celebrated."

"I don't know how we make jokes then."

"Maybe the joke is no jokes."

"What does that mean?"

"Friends on stage. That's it. That's our message."

"Our message?"

"Aren't we similar to each other now?"

"Yes. Sort of. But not really."

"That common ground is funnier than any misunderstandings we once had onstage."

"But how? I mean, you say that, but I'm not seeing the joke."

"Looking at you is like looking in a mirror now."

"Fine, so maybe we do a variation on the Groucho-Harpo mirror routine."

"Or better yet, we use the mirroring to represent the commonality we enjoy: Who is leading the exercise? It becomes impossible for the audience to tell. Perhaps it becomes impossible for us as well. This is an exercise in truly working together, as one."

"How is it funny?"

"Are you familiar with the teachings of Viola Spolin?"

"No," says Mudd.

"She is a theater educator who has developed a series of games to train actors in the art of theatrical improvisation. Some of these improvisations do indeed turn out to be humorous, but the humor comes organically from a commitment to shared goals and character development. I believe the mirror game would be a wonderful addition to our stage show. Our physical similarity would serve to emphasize the effect."

"OK." Mudd sighs.

Mudd and Molloy begin the exercise. Mudd is at first resistant or at least incapable. But as Molloy continues, patiently, slowly, eyes gently fixed on Mudd's, a transformation does take place. Their motions sync. This sequence persists for what seems like hours. It is hypnotic, transcendent. Then, still moving together in a fashion reminiscent of tai chi, they speak in unison, slowly at first but soon ramping up to conversational speed:

"Good evening, ladies and gentlemen, we are Mudd and Molloy. How nice to see you tonight. As perhaps some of you recognize, we are now engaged in an activity called the mirror game. It was invented in 1946 by theater educator Viola Spolin. We hope you find it as funny as we do. Isn't it funny to think we are all of us the same? For all of our differences, in the end, we share a common humanity. This game illustrates that funny truth."

With this, Mudd and Molloy simultaneously turn away from each other and both face the fourth wall, the camera, the imaginary audience (but, of course, the real audience in the cinema). They continue, even though they are no longer watching each other, their identical tai chi movements. It is uncanny, and because of this, frightening. They seem like automatons, as if they're possessed. They seem like puppets. They speak:

"Who controls our movements, our thoughts, our words? Are we as ants in a colony, gears in a machine, fated to ever do the bidding of an unknowable master?"

They bow.

After, Mudd drinks to settle his nerves. Molloy hikes a trail on Oleara Debord, the magnificent mountain range smack dab in the middle of the country. She is beautiful and timeless. Some of us love and worship her. Some of us hate her, but almost all of us check each day to see what she's going to do next: who she might be sleeping with, what movie she's been cast in (is she going to win another Oscar for this one?), what outrageous thing she said at what charity event, whether or not she's finally clean and sober, whether or not she's had any work done. Right now, she is being linked in the media to Lance Farmer, the tornado from Kansas. He might be a flash in the pan, as tornadoes often are, but he's gorgeous and deadly, a real bad boy, which is what we both love and hate about him. It's rumored he's killed over a thousand people so far just to see them die, and his performance as Bobby Gore in the movie *The Notorious Vice Lords* was hailed by *The New York Times* as "mesmerizing, a tour de force." There is talk of wedding bells in their future, and many people, mostly women and gay men, are hoping for it. Some to vicariously live out their own fantasies about one or the other of them, some because it's so much fun to trash them, one-up each other about how awful they are, how déclassé, how they can't believe those two are even famous.

Molloy doesn't climb very high. He's not much of a sportsman, and, in truth, a climb to the top of the range would probably take weeks, possibly months. He does fall in love with her as he walks her trails, as all men do, but she remains taciturn. It is said among locals that perhaps for now her heart still belongs to Lance or that she is focused on an upcoming role and does not want to be distracted.

CHAPTER 49

COSTELLO PARKS ON the Los Feliz hilltop and joins Abbott, who sits on a rock and smokes a cigarette. There is a silence. Finally, Abbott speaks.

"Why did you want to meet up here, Lou?"

"It's Rooney and Doodle."

"The former orphans who are now a comedy team?"

"The very same."

"I hear they're funny up-and-comers."

"That's the problem, Bud."

"Why is that a problem?"

"Because our career is on the line."

"What line?"

"I'm saying, if they succeed, we fail."

"I don't follow."

"OK, say there are two movies playing—"

"There are plenty more than that."

"I'm trying to simplify it for the purposes of this illustration."

"OK. I'm ready."

"OK, so there are two movies playing, and one of them is ours—"

"Which one?"

"It doesn't matter."

"It'll help me picture it. I'm a visual thinker."

"*Pardon My Sarong*."

"Got it."

"Now, Rooney and Doodle have a movie out at the same time."

"Which one?"

"They don't have any movies yet so I don't know."

"Can you make one up? Just so this can feel like a real thing?"

"Um . . . *What's Buzzin', Cousin?*"

"Hey, that's catchy, Lou. I like that."

"So these two movies are playing in this town at the same time. Let's say there are ten people who live in the town—"

"That's a very small—"

"I know. But just for this illustration."

"Got it."

"And it's Friday night and everybody wants to see a comedy movie."

"Because it's been a tough week?"

"Sure. Now, if there's two comedy movies, some of the ten people might go to our movie and some of them might go to the other one."

"I think I'd see *What's Buzzin', Cousin?* It's a great title. And I love Cab Calloway."

"You're not there."

"Where?"

"In this town."

"Where am I?"

"I don't know. That's beside the point."

"OK. It's just—"

"So there's these two movies—"

"Just say where I am so I can picture it better."

"Frisco."

"Got it."

"OK. Good," says Costello.

"It's too bad Rooney and Doodle got that title first. If we really want to compete with them, we could come out with a movie called *What's Tickin', Chicken?* I mean it's sort of like copying because it's from the same song, but you said yourself, it's a competition and—"

"*What's Buzzin', Cousin?* is not a real movie."

"I mean, that doesn't seem fair to say that, Lou. I'm sure they worked very hard on it."

"It's not a real movie. Remember? I made it up not more than three minutes ago."

"So we have nothing to worry about then. Everyone will go to see ours. It's the only real one in town."

"Stop."

"What."

"Just stop."

"OK, Lou."

"The point is, Bud, that these two lunks are going to be doing a disappearing act soon."

"Magic acts are really so different from what we do that I think it'll be fine and—"

"Not that kind of disappearing act."

"What kind then?"

"A final act."

"You mean m-m-m-m-murder?"

"Haven't we been through this already? Do you not remember?"

"It's foggy."

"You're foggy. Mudd and Molloy."

"Right! Um . . . I don't know, Lou. This is murder you're talking about. That's a crime. One of the most serious crimes."

"I'm doing this for us, Bud."

"OK, I guess."

"So I have a friend who builds sets. He owes me a favor. Rooney and Doodle are about to do their first feature in which they apparently play ne'er-do-well carpenters. When Rooney hammers the first nail, it'll kill them both. There's no way either of them escapes from this. Problem solved."

"What about their families?"

"They're orphans, from the world-famous Perforphanage. No one will care."

Who are Abbott and Costello, you ask? Imagine, if you will, an Abbott-shaped extruder. The resulting Abbott is the extrusion of the Abbott material through this extruder, a bit like Play-Doh. And in the shape of Abbott, albeit an Abbott-like tube or worm, but since we are only able to see "slices" of Abbott in time and never the Abbott tube in its entirety, we perceive this Abbott to be moving through time. This is also true for Costello. Therefore, talk about their "comic timing" is an illusion since time itself is an illusion.

In reality, they are only as funny as nonmoving tubes.
—DEBECCA DeMARCUS, *Extrusion, Intrusion in Utah's Confusion Range and the Geology of Desire*

MUDD AND MOLLOY sit nursing beers in a small-town bar.

"How was Oleara Debord?" asks Mudd.

"Magnificent, but cold and unattainable."

"Well, she's very busy, I hear. And maybe taken. So say the orogeny rags."

"Listen, I have a movie idea for us. You know how Abbott and Costello met the Invisible Man that time?"

"Yeah."

"Well, we can't do that."

"I know."

"We can't get Universal to give us the rights, which we'd need to make our version of the Invisible Man, because Universal owns the very 'nothing' they call the Invisible Man."

"OK."

"So we make up our own monster. We can call him something else," says Molloy.

"OK," says Mudd.

"Unseen Man."

"OK."

"*Mudd and Molloy Meet the Unseen Man.*"

"All right."

"And here's the genius part: The budget is nil because he doesn't exist. In actuality, we can have as many unseen monsters as we want, an army of them. A million unseen monsters chasing us and it doesn't cost a red cent. You know why?"

"Cause they're all unseen."

"Exactly."

"I don't know, Chick. I don't see how we get this made."

"You know who else is invisible?"

"No."

"The monotheistic Abrahamic God is invisible. Maybe it's God chasing us in this movie. A million monotheistic Abrahamic gods. That's what I'm thinking. Some sort of Hebraic-Lovecraftian nightmare."

"What do they want, these gods?"

"To torment us."

"This is a comedy?"

"I'm laughing already," says Molloy.

"You're not though. That's the thing," says Mudd.

"Soon I'll be laughing already, then."

"I haven't seen you laugh since the coma, except for that high-pitched thing you have us do now in our show."

"Maybe we drink the invisible potion, too. In the movie."

"Oh, it's a potion."

"Certainly. And if we drink it, too, in the movie, the movie becomes even cheaper. Empty streets with the sounds of our footsteps and our relentless comic patter. We call it *Mudd and Molloy Meet the Unseeable Men*. Or *Abrahamic Gods*."

"*And Also Become the Unseeable Men*?"

"Exactly! *And Also Become the Unseeable Men*! Brilliant! It's a long and therefore brilliant title."

"I don't know, Chick."

MEMORY IS A funny thing. And not the comical kind of funny, but sometimes, yes, that, too. If, for example, we remember things incorrectly, say we remember a duck wearing a cowboy hat, which is probably an incorrect memory if the duck is not a circus duck or in some other sort of show or possibly a humorous advert, but rather in the wild, then that is funny in both senses of the word. Cowboy duck. I am certain I saw one walking by on the street recently. But I am certainly wrong.

MUTT AND MAHLE, having struggled at Nazi comedy, are shuffled around to various Nazi clerical jobs, failing upward in a comical montage and eventually ending up assigned to Alfred Rosenberg, commissar for the supervision of intellectual and ideological education of the NSDAP, as his bumbling manservants.

One day, while cleaning Rosenberg's bathroom, they discover on the sink a large chunk of his lip, which he had, one assumes, inadvertently cut off while shaving.

"Do you need this lip piece, sir?" calls Mahle.

"No. Clean it up! Goddamn you."

"This might come in handy," says Mahle to Mutt, stuffing the lip into his watch pocket.

"For what?" says Mutt. "I think maybe you are a bit of a hoarder, Mahle. This is not the first piece of a lip you have saved, after all. How many could one man need?"

"It is Herr Rosenberg's lip this time, my friend. It is Herr Rosenberg's lip. It is a great man's lip, ergo it is a great lip."

MY DAUGHTER'S BLOG, Farrow Roots, to which I subscribe against my better judgment, appears on my computer with an ominous and cheery *ding*.

BRR! THE NEVER-ENDING COLD WAR
BETWEEN ME AND MY POP-SICLE

You've heard of Ice Queens and Frigid Women? Of course you have, because we live in a patriarchy that labels women as The Other, that insists on dismissing their rage as neurotic (Hysteria!), a culture that can't understand why *she* doesn't want to fuck *you*. Well, fuck you. How's that? But the thing we haven't come up with a label for is the Cold Father. Most of us know them. Some of us even have them. I have one. His initials are BRR and they fit him like a glove on a fucking cold-ass day. My father is a man. This is his first and greatest affront. Like almost all men, my father is always right. It's amazing how much knowledge men can cram into their bald and ugly little brain containers. Mansplaining is bad enough, but it cannot hold a candle to Dadsplaining, which is especially egregious because in Dadsplaining, he's inflating his ego at the expense of his goddamn child. And that causes all kind of *fucked-up* in his child, not the least of which is a lifelong sense of the inferiority of her gender. You see, a child does not have the experience to know that her father is full of shit. So she is left believing that this man knows everything, all his opinions are correct, and, by extension, so are those of other men. This can and will get a girl into all kind of emotionally dangerous shit.

Had my father even once showed vulnerability, I might have had a chance. But so it goes, and I'm stuck here online railing against an old, cold idiot. This is my life. And now that I've armed myself to the teeth with therapy and vodka, the love of a woman, and a brilliant career, now that I can stand up to him, tell him that he's wrong, he has turned the frozen shoulder. He wants nothing to do with this new, improved, non-fawning woman. In fact, he has gone out of his way to sabotage my life in his blog! I am his daughter, for Christ's sake, but he wants me to be his audience. And I am not that, nor will I ever be again. My father is so weak, so afraid, so sad, such a failure in the actual world that he spent my sister's and my childhood trying to transform the vibrant, curious, growing human girls that we were into his very own personal claque. And now that we've left the auditorium, now that we've discovered other performers, even done some performing of our own, he has little use for us. My father will say, if queried, that we have stopped talking to him, but the truth is that he never talked to us, and we only just recently came to understand that. If you asked him about us, about our childhoods, he would selectively remember how good it was, how much we loved him and he loved us. He would tell you some cherry-picked shit about our trip to pick out a puppy or how he used to take us to Marx Brothers movies, how we would laugh at the funny men on screen. You want to know the truth? I fucking hate the Marx Brothers. One more case of juvenile men mocking those less fortunate, in this case—

I stop reading. I get it, Gracie: You're still mad at me. You don't dig the Marx Brothers. Well, the world is on the verge of collapse, so I'm sorry you didn't get the childhood you wanted. I tried, I really did, to give you everything. But maybe it's time for you to suck it up a little and find the strength to go and make it a little better, rather than constantly chipping away at the efforts of others, however unsuccessfully, to put something positive into the world. Y'know, the thing is—

I dial Grace's number. I feel like there might be a valuable conversation to be had between us right now, now that this thing is fresh in my mind. Her number has been changed, and the new one is unlisted. I cannot help but feel hurt by this. I cannot help but see this as another slap in the face, directed at me. Slap! I am left no recourse but to respond with my own essay.

GRR! A BESTIARY OF BEASTLY OFFSPRING

It has come to my attention that I am being once again attacked in print (well, in pixels) by another human being. As an opinionated culture writer in the public eye, I expect this kind of attention and even welcome it, but this time the attack is personal and comes from my offspring. Grace Rosenberger Rosenberg (Farrow) has once more seen fit to take potshots at her old man to explain away her own lack of confidence in the world. Now I know we currently live in a culture of outrage, so I shouldn't be surprised that Grace has suckled at its teat, but it is not how I raised her, or at least it is not the sense of self I attempted to instill in her, which was one of personal responsibility. And since Grace has seen fit to shut me completely out of her life, and since I still feel a paternal responsibility to attempt to help her, even though she apparently despises me, I will use this unfortunately public forum to offer her an olive branch of fatherly advice.

Grace, you have always been a troubled girl. Your mother and I knew this from the very beginning. You were a fussy, unhappy baby. And if you could go back in time and watch the patience and love with which we tried to comfort you (your mother and I got *no* sleep during the first year and a half of your life), you might feel the depth of our love and our commitment to your well-being. Unfortunately for all of us, that kind of time travel is not an option. No matter, I can still tell you how it was then and what I think you need to hear about yourself now. You have been forever difficult and selfish, and if you don't feel properly loved and embraced by the world, it might behoove you to look inward for an explanation. You are welcome to keep blaming me and your mother (although, come to think of it, you never seem to blame *her* for any of it!), but what does that get you?

It is time to take the bull by the horns, stop eating your sadness, lose some weight, clean yourself up, set a goal for your life, and pursue it. When I was your age, I had already been on staff for three years as the film critic for the *Wichita Pennysaver*. I'm not sharing this with you to brag but rather to put a fire under you. Find what you love and go for it, Grace. I know you have already made two well-reviewed (by some) movies, but I think you believe (and not without some justification) that my name had something to do with the foot in the door you received. Do you think Joyce Maynard would have the career she has today without Salinger to rail against? I am your Salinger, and I think you realize that and it makes your career victories hollow. No one helped me get the *Wichita Pennysaver* job. I had no well-known father in the "biz" to publicly bad-mouth to get it. I had shoe leather and . . . what's the word? . . . *gumption*. Take charge of your life. If you got out of your own way, perhaps then you could find some happiness. Granted, you have directed a one-hundred-million-dollar superhero movie, but is that what you really want out of life?

I post it to my blog B. Is for Blog and wait. I do not currently get a lot of traffic on my website. The last piece that received any comments was entitled "2010's Dumb Dreams for a Dumb World," a brutal but necessary takedown of Christopher Nolan's *Inception*, to which a reader called *smellmynuts* responded, *Your a cum bucket*, to which I wrote: *Thank you for your interest in my work. Notice how I've used "your." This, as an attributive adjective, is its correct spelling. You would have been better served to write, "You're a cum bucket," in which "you're" is a contraction of "you" and "are." But no matter, I certainly heard your intended disapproval loud and clear. Allow me to respond to each of your salient points. Number one: I have never functioned as a cum bucket. I am, perhaps to my detriment, exclusively heterosexual and have never served as any sort of receptacle for semen. I do not, however, consider it an insult to be thought of as such. Indeed, history is rife with brilliant and essential "cum buckets," as you call them, and I would consider myself very honored to be counted among them. I wish you all the best in your future intellectual pursuits.* To which he wrote, *hahahahahahahahahahahaha faggot.* I responded: *Perhaps I did not express myself with enough clarity, so indulge me as I make another stab. I am not gay, and I tell you this only as a matter of fact, not in an attempt to distance myself from the gay community, with which I am on wonderful terms. Many of the world's greatest poets, artists, philosophers, and scientists were gay, and, as I stated earlier, I would consider myself honored indeed to count myself among them.* To which he wrote, *you a cock smoker.* At this point, I thought of giving up. This fellow doesn't seem to be hearing anything I'm trying to say to him. But I couldn't let it go without at least three more attempts to reach him.

CHAPTER 50

I PASS THE TIME on my train to Barassini's by compiling my 2017 list (is it 2017?):

10—*L'amant Double* (Ozon)
9—*Werk Ohne Autor* (Henckel von Donnersmarck)
8—*Un Beau Soleil Intérieur* (Denis)
7—*Tom of Finland* (Karukoski)
6—*Donald Cried* (Avedisian)
5—*Fingerspitzengefühl* (Sterne)
4—*Hey, Timmy Gibbons, This Is Your Mother Calling!* (Apatow)
3—*Sekigahara* (Harada)
2—*Reakcja Iancuchowa* (Paczek)
1—*Inxeba* (Trengove)

"Tell me."

Night. A road cutting through cornfields aglow in pale moonlight. In the distance, the rumble of approaching voices. Now footsteps. Running. Two pair of footsteps. Hard breathing. A title appears: *Bad Luck in Bumfuck*. It fades away. A slight curve in the road, and from around it come two skinny men running toward the camera, desperation in their faces. They look back: They are being chased. It's Mudd and Molloy, a bit older, a bit more worn. I stay with them now as they run.

"It wasn't that bad," says Molloy.

"It was bad, Chick."

"Well, I have some thoughts on how we can tighten the doctor bit."

"It's not about tightening. It's the idea. Who ever heard of a doctor sketch where both fellas are doctors?"

"Doctors go to doctors," says Molloy. "Where do you think doctors go when they get sick? Use your head. Doctors is where."

"Great. Then let's do that. One doctor is sick, the other is examining him. That could be funny. Instead of two doctors examining each other at the same time."

"But that's the part that's funny! Even you saying it now makes me laugh."

"You're not laughing."

"Excuse me for trying to conserve air so I can escape our most recent angry mob."

And with this, the mob appears from around the curve. They carry torches and pitchforks and theater tickets.

"And they're twins," continues Molloy, wheezing. "That's funny as well."

"People find it disturbing."

"I don't see why."

"Maybe because they're giving each other digital rectal exams."

"We don't show anything! It's all in profile!"

"Chick, digital rectal exams isn't even a thing. You just made it up."

"But it will be. I've been doing a great deal of reading on the subjects of proctology and urology."

"Why? For God's sake, why, Chick?"

"Because I'm a curious person. Don't you want our humor to be *avant-garde*?"

"I'm not sure."

"I've been reading Lockhart-Mummery on proctology and developing some of my own diagnostics. I believe the exam I am predicting, the digital rectal exam, will one day be standard in the early detection of prostate cancers. For men, of course. Did you know that women don't have prostates?"

"No."

"They don't! Isn't that amazing?"

"Great. That's great, Chick."

"I'm trying to find a way back in for us, Bud. So to speak."

"We never worked blue before."

"People change, Bud. And the relationship that survives is the relationship that acknowledges that. This is true in a marriage and it's true in a friendship."

"Our marriages are over, Chick. Your brain accident made sure of that."

"It happened. Life throws curveballs. You adapt. You make lemonade. You get back on the horse. You pick yourself up, dust yourself off, and start all over again."

"I could've gone with Besser."

"Yeah, Bud, we all could've gone with Besser, but—"

"You couldn't have."

"Metaphorically, Bud. Metaphorically, we all could've gone with Besser."

"I don't know what that means. That doesn't mean anything."

"I mean we all could've gone with Besser, but would that have been honest? The world changed. We're not a coupla young bucks anymore. We're two grown, complex men in a complex world. With prostate glands. We have to acknowledge that if we want to remain vital and relevant."

"I really have no idea what you're talking about."

"That soda shop kid stuff we had is gone."

"We never had that, Chick."

"Well, whatever it is we had—the details are blurry—it's gone."

Mudd looks back.

"They're gaining on us!"

"Quick! Cut through the corn!"

And now they're running in the corn. It's all panting and confusion and snapping corn stalks for a long while. One stalk seems to have a face and blond, wispy, corn-silk hair. Through pursed lips, it pleads with them for help. But they speed by without noticing, arriving at a massive one-story building as long as a football field and as wide as another football field.

"What the hell is this?"

"I don't know," says Molloy. "Some sort of chicken house?"

"Chicken house?"

"Where they raise chickens for slaughter. Chicken house."

"So big, though."

"Some of these so-called chicken houses can house as many as fifty thousand chickens. Industrial chicken farming is the wave of the future."

"How do you know that?"

"I read, Bud. I read."

"I read and I didn't know that."

"I have an acquisitive mind, Bud, an acquisitive mind."

"I have one of those."

"Fine. Anyway, we'd best hide inside to wait out this mob."

INTERIOR CHICKEN HOUSE—NIGHT. The place is massive, dimly lit through skylights by the full moon. Surprisingly, most of it is underground, a giant open space maybe seven stories down.

"Jesus," whispers Mudd. "I wasn't expecting this. Where are the chickens? I don't see one chicken."

"I don't know, Bud. Something is odd. Maybe they're hiding from us."

"Fifty thousand of them?"

Molloy starts down a circular metal staircase leading to the floor far below.

"You sure you want to go down there, Chick?"

"We'll be safer in the shadows."

"I don't know. I'm a-scared," says Mudd.

"Don't be an infant."

Mudd follows trepidatiously. Down, down, down into the darkness, shoes on steel diamond-plate stairs, echoing through this vast open space. Finally at the bottom and on the cement floor, all is silent save for the wheezing of Mudd, a longtime smoker. As he quiets, another sound comes to the fore, almost like breathing but unnaturally deep and sonorous.

"Do you hear that?" asks Mudd.

"I do."

"What is it?"

"Like breathing, but through a megaphone."

"Rudy Vallée?" asks Mudd.

"What? Why would Rudy Vallée be down here breathing into a megaphone?"

"I didn't think it through. It just popped into my head when you said megaphone."

Mudd pulls out his cigarette lighter and opens it. The enormous space glows dimly with the flickering light. There, in the far corner, sits a figure, a human, a man.

"Hello?" says Molloy.

"Hello," says the man in a deep yet gentle voice. "Come close; I'd like to see you better. I've been so lonely."

Mudd's feet remain glued to the floor, but Molloy crosses to the man, drawn to his voice, to his gentleness. The walk is long, much longer, it seems, than Molloy expects. He walks and walks, and, as he does, the lone figure grows larger and larger. What's going on? Eventually Molloy stands directly in front of the seated man, who is revealed to be a giant.

"You're enormous," says Molloy.

"Yes."

"I didn't expect that. Hey, Bud, he's enormous!"

"I'm getting that!" Bud calls from very far away.

Molloy holds the lighter up to get a better look at the giant's face. It turns out his size is not the most extraordinary thing about him. What I, as an audience member, am focused on now is his beauty. I am not a gay man, but I am not so insecure in my heterosexuality that I would deny recognizing beauty in men. And this man is beautiful, with the sloe-eyed, simmering sensuality of a young Rudolph Valentino, the chisel-jawed decency of a young Gregory Peck, the charming ingenuousness of a young Gary Cooper, the endearing earnestness of a young Hank Fonda, the mischievous eye-twinkle of a young Clark Gable, and the dapper insouciance of an elderly Sir Charles Chaplin. One cannot help but feel drawn in, seduced, and, perhaps even, dare I say, a little in love. Molloy appears to be similarly entranced.

"Holy cow," he says. "Bud, come here!"

"No thanks! I'm just . . . I'd like to stay here, up against the wall, near the stairs."

Molloy turns back to the giant.

"May I ask your name? I'm Chick Molloy."

"My name is Cheryld. Cheryld Ray Parrett, Janior."

"Janior?"

"It means *junior* in German."

"No, it doesn't. Junior in German is junior. What's more, they don't use junior in Germany the way we use it here, that is, to distinguish a son from a father of the same name."

"My dad told me they do. Why would he lie?"

"Maybe not a lie; perhaps he was misinformed."

"Why would it be the same word in a different language? Wouldn't that make it the same language instead of a different language? It makes no sense. You make no sense, mister."

"Good question. That's a good question. These are all good questions. Will you excuse me for just a moment?"

"OK."

Molloy makes his way across the giant space toward Mudd. Cheryld watches. It takes a long while.

"Listen," Molloy whispers to Mudd. "I see our future."

"OK. No," says Mudd.

"Hear me out. You know *The 30 Foot Bride of Candy Rock*?"

"Lou Costello's last movie."

"Boffo box office. Exploiting the national radiation sickness craze."

"All right."

"We got ourselves a fifty-foot man right here. It's gold."

"What are you saying, Chick?"

"We use this dumb, beautiful, impossibly enormous fellow to make our own radiation sickness movie. What was the one problem with *30 Foot Bride*?"

"I don't know. I'm no movie expert. How the two could possibly couple? I mean, they could, but I don't think she'd even feel it. That's what I was thinking when I saw the movie, the whole damn time."

"Not that problem. It's the giant special effect. Not at all convincing given our current technology. Well, sir, we don't need to worry about that. We've got a real fifty-footer right here. *Mudd and Molloy Meet the 50 Foot Man*."

"I don't—"

"Here's the story. Mind you, I'm just spitballing. So . . . we're physicists—"

"Twin physicists?"

"Exactly. That's right. We're just on fire with each other here. Those Viola Spolin exercises are paying off."

"Exact same personality?"

"Yes. Yes! And we're developing a top-secret ray for the government. It's a size ray, and it makes things bigger. We're trying to grow bigger . . . I don't know . . . corn on the cobs, let's say, to better feed the hungry. Giant corn on the cobs, big enough to feed a family of eight. Y'know, so it's important work. Essential work. One day, we're aiming the ray at some corn and this young man walks between the ray and the corn—maybe he's chasing a ball or something, that's not important—and—"

"Hey, what are you fellas talking about over there?"

"One minute, Cheryld! So the guy starts to grow. And we have to keep it a secret because if the government finds out, they'll want to use him as a secret weapon against the Soviet Union. But we like the kid and we want to protect him."

"I don't know, Chick—"

"So we hide him in the woods. And we feed him all these giant vegetables we've grown. Corn on the cobs. Tomatoes. Giant rice, like each grain is a foot long. Then, after a few weeks, we notice the giant vegetables changing. Maybe getting violent."

"Violent vegetables?"

"I'm still working it out, but, I think so, yes. The vegetables start to turn mean-looking and poisonous. So the physicists know this very change is going to happen to the young man. And they attempt

426

to come up with an antidote before it destroys their giant friend. But nothing works, and the giant goes insane and tries to kill them. So they blow him up with an atomic bomb."

"Oh. Wow. I wasn't expecting . . . that ending kind of came out of nowhere."

"It tracks really well."

"This is a comedy?"

"The comedy comes, as all comedy must, in the execution."

"The execution of us when audiences see this movie?"

"Good wordplay, Bud. I'm proud of you. But no. This film will be our ticket out of Palookaville. It's got everything: pathos, romance—"

"You didn't mention any romance."

"There'll be a love interest, of course."

"One love interest? For both of us?"

"Don't be hidebound, Bud. It's 1960."

"I don't know what that word means. And anyway, we've never been able to get a movie off the ground. So this is not something that will ever happen."

"Everything changes now with Cheryld."

"Did I just hear my name?" calls Cheryld.

"Just a minute, honey," calls Molloy, then to Mudd: "Also, Patty's sister's kid is an independent film producer now. Makes monster movie crap."

"Gerald?"

"Did I hear my name again?"

"No, I said Gerald, not Cheryld," calls Molloy.

"OK," says Cheryld. "I'm right over here when you need me."

"Gerald's grown up? Jesus. That just makes me sad."

"Anyway, if Gerald wants Cheryld—and he will—*we* come with. That's the deal."

"Now I heard my name twice. If Cheryld wants Cheryld."

"Just once. Say, how tall are you, honey?" Molloy calls out.

"Me?"

"Yes, sweetie."

"Twenty-nine feet."

"Really? You seem taller."

"It's the vertical stripes. My mother sewed my garment out of a fumigation tent."

"Well, anyway. That's too short. We have to at least beat Costello. He had a thirty-foot bride, so twenty-nine is hardly going to cut it," Molloy says.

He paces.

"I mean, size isn't everything," says Molloy. "What if . . . what if we get him lifts? Just like three feet or so, to bring him up to thirty-two. We beat Costello and— Hey, Cheryld?"

"Yes?"

"Would you be willing to wear lifts?"

"I don't know what that means."

"Lifts. In your shoes. To make you taller."

"My mother makes my shoes out of refrigerator boxes. Herring boxes without topses, she calls them, even though they're refrigerator boxes, but it's in reference to a song about a girl with big feet, she tells me. Even though I'm not a girl and they're refrigerator boxes, not herring boxes, which would be too small, I think. Unless they were made to hold a lot of herrings. How big is a herring?"

"That's interesting but doesn't exactly answer my question, which was, as you may recall, will you wear lifts in your shoes?"

"Yes. But why? I'm pretty tall as-is. Almost twenty-nine feet."

"Almost?"

"Well, twenty-eight-eleven."

"Jesus. This is getting worse and worse. Would you wear three-foot-one lifts?"

"I guess so. I mean—"

"Would you like to be a movie star or not, Cheryld? Jesus. A lot of movie stars wear lifts. Alan Ladd, James Cagney, Burgess Meredith. Al Pacino will, I predict."

"I've never actually seen a movie. I wouldn't be able to fit into the movie theater in town, so I don't get to see movies."

"You don't know what movies are?"

"My mother has described them to me. As I understand it, they're like a flat board with a picture on it, except the picture moves and talks and has music. So it's like a photograph, but it moves, as my mother describes it. And the pictures have stories in them. And music. The board is called a screen."

"Sure. That's it. You want to be in one?"

"I've always wanted to be a movie star."

"Good. Wait right here. We'll be back in a few days with the money fella."

"Don't you want to know why I'm so tall?"

Molloy glances at his watch.

"Um, OK, sure. Shoot."

"Radiation."

"Wow. OK. Great. Thanks. So don't go anywhere. We'll be back."

"I'll be here. I can't go anywhere. If the townspeople saw me, they'd think I'm a demon from hell, my mom says, and would kill me if they saw me. That's what my mother always says, plus the stuff about movies."

"The townspeople in these parts do seem oddly excitable."

CHAPTER 51

Have I aged at the same rate as my fellows? Certainly Arvide Chim, my roommate at Harvard who publishes my imprint, looks younger than I. He is the only one of us with whom I stay in touch. Is it because he is the more successful of us? That's debatable, but perhaps. More to the point, though, I believe he is living his fullest life: married to a lovely, moneyed girl from the Philadelphia Main Line, three children of I imagine varying age; this is all Arvide ever wanted. This was not the life I envisioned for myself, and I have been exquisitely successful in not having it, but I have not lived the life I did envision. Have I ever had the love to end all loves? This is what I hoped for as a young man. A love for the ages: flames of passion, weeping, rapture, the realization that the one cannot live without the other, that the one would not want to. It is the love of Tristan und Iseult, of Abelard und Heloise, of Romeo und Juliet. I knew I would have it. I knew I could not be complete without it. Yet I have not had it. My relationships have been a slog of negotiations, of concessions, of compromises. I am aware of the practical impossibility of such a magnificent love, of course. I know that the type of connection I sought is an illusion, a projection. . . . I know that all too well. I know it so well that I never sought it. I never discovered for myself through brutal, relentless trial and error that it was impossible, and so the question has always remained, and subsequently, deep in my heart, I suspect I have missed my opportunity, that I have let my soulmate, my true soulmate, get away, that I have committed a great cosmic wrong, that I have demonstrated a great weakness of character, and that all that has come after is a result of that wrong. It is the universe frowning on me, aging me before my time. Would I have had a full head of hair and smooth luminescent skin had I pursued my destiny? I suspect I might have. Where would I be now had I followed my heart? I often wonder.

There was a lovely woman with whom, as a young man, I was smitten. She seemed to have similar feelings for me. We flirted in a harmless way at work (we were concierges at a well-known upscale New York boutique hotel, I won't say the name but you'd have heard of it). I was married at the time, too young and unhappily, but we'd had an accidental child and I was doing the responsible thing. This is me in a nutshell. I am responsible. I am a good man. I always do the right thing. But is doing the right thing the right thing? Or is doing the right thing the cowardly thing? The thing that doesn't make waves? The thing with which others cannot find fault? If romantic films have taught us anything, it is that by being responsible we are being irresponsible—to ourselves. To the cosmos. To the narrative. Even to those we need to wrong terribly by leaving them. Because is not it better to be honest with her, him, thon? I think perhaps it is. In the end, my marriage fell apart anyway. She became smitten with an art critic, a mediocre one at that. But it was too late. My Concierge to Merge (as we once jokingly referred to each other) also married an art critic. A separate art critic, although equally mediocre. One marvels at the accidental symmetry of life. And she was happy, ecstatically so, she told me, although I always felt she sounded a tad defensive. And my life was ruined. And I aged. And I look unhappy, ecstatically unhappy. And I don't sleep at night. And I take pills to help me cope. And it's not only her, although if I had her, I feel certain I would be fine with every other disappointment, but I don't, so my professional failures come to the fore. In a sense, the same brand of cowardice that kept me from pursuing my true love kept me from pursuing my true chosen profession. Oh, I made one movie. I made it on a shoestring with money I had borrowed from my wealthy-by-marriage sister. It didn't do for my career what I had imagined it would, what to this day I believe it should have. It is, and I say this as an objective professional critic with a PhD in the cinema of postwar Europe, perhaps the single most brilliant film of the last twenty years. Certainly, there were problems with it. I won't say there weren't. For one thing, it was decades ahead of its time. For another, I concede, it was perhaps too emotionally draining for audiences. Most goers are not looking for an experience that unrelentingly intense, that devastatingly heartbreaking, an experience that will change them forever. And then there were the critics, who were, in a word, jealous. They all want to be filmmakers themselves but do not have the talent, so they expressed their rage with a slew of moderately negative reviews. In some cases, they refused to review it at all.

"You have veered off-course."

Rooney and Doodle wait for their cue outside the front door of the enormous house set. Rooney puffs on a cigar. Doodle does a few deep knee bends. A voice comes from inside the house.

"Where are those two carpenters I hired? They were supposed to be here a half hour ago!"

Rooney takes a last puff of his cigar, throws it on the floor, squashes it out underfoot, waves away the smoke, then knocks on the door. Some footsteps; the door opens revealing a Vernon Dent puppet.

"Finally! You're late."

"Sorry, mister," says Doodle. "We were sharpening our hammers."

"Well, don't dillydally. Get in here. There's work to be done."

Rooney and Doodle enter.

"So what do you need, boss?"

"I need you to build a staircase to the second floor."

"We don't—"

"You got it, chief."

"And I need it done by the time I get back in two hours," says Dent.

"But we don't know—"

"Easy. Staircase to the second floor. We got it."

"Good. Two hours. Not a second more or less. Or you'll never build another staircase in this town."

"Two hours."

"You better not mess it up."

"But—"

"Don't you worry, boss."

Vernon Dent nods and leaves.

"We don't know how to build no staircase, Joe."

"Piece a cake. Build one step, stand on that, then build the next, then the next, till we get up to the second floor."

"That's all there is to it?"

"That's all there is to it. Piece of cake."

"One step, stand on that, next step till we get to the second floor?"

"That's right."

"OK."

"So get to work."

"Me?"

"Yes, you."

"What are you gonna do?"

"I'm the manager."

"OK."

There is a long silence while Rooney adjusts his tool belt, measures wood, examines his saw, flexes his hands, readjusts his tool belt. Doodle just watches him.

"Joe?" Rooney says.

"Yeah?"

"I don't know how to build a step."

"And you call yourself a carpenter."

"I don't call myself a carpenter. You called me a carpenter."

"Because I had faith in you. Now I don't know what to think. I'm ashamed of you."

"But—"

"You got us into this mess. Now figure it out and get the job done."

"All right, Joe."

Rooney tentatively picks up a piece of wood, a hammer, and a nail. He looks up at Doodle.

"Do your job!" says Doodle.

Rooney performs an elaborate pre-hammering ritual of stretching his arms and wiggling his fingers, then finally bangs a nail through a piece of wood. The house begins to shake. Both Rooney and Doodle look up, clearly startled; a wall falls toward them. Rooney pulls Doodle to a spot in the room. A wall falls inward, and the two are safe because Rooney has placed them in the path of an open window. This dance happens five more times as the walls of the house fall one by one. Each time, Rooney runs with Doodle and puts them squarely in the path of the open window. When it is over, the house has collapsed and Doodle and Rooney are unscathed. The crew erupts into applause.

Variety review:

What can one say about *Well Plastered*, a film that introduces us to the delightful new comedy duo of Rooney and Doodle? Whereas the picture relies somewhat on the well-trod verbal antics seen before in the comedy of Abbott and Costello, this novice pairing adds a remarkable physicality to the mix. Indeed, it features perhaps the most remarkable physical gag ever committed to cinematic film. Students of motion-picture history will certainly remember *One Week*, the 1920 Buster Keaton silent film featuring the gag in which a house falls on our hapless hero, but he remains remarkably unscathed as he is, by happenstance, situated in the path of an open window. Imagine that stunt multiplied many times as Rooney and Doodle run from room to room inside a collapsing house, avoiding certain death not once but six times. This feat of derring-do elevates the team of Rooney and Doodle to a new level of physical comedy. Since the advent of sound motion pictures, there has been a movement in film comedy toward entirely verbal antics. Subsequently, this new class of comedians has not developed the physical skills of the vaudeville-trained comedians of the silent era. This is a disappointment for audiences who tire quickly of the hackneyed gibes of an Abbott and Costello.

Without this remarkable physical stunt, perhaps *Well Plastered* would have been viewed as merely imitative, a second-rate Abbott and Costello movie, but with this spectacular addition, we welcome it into the pantheon of all-time film classics.

As I TOSS and turn in my sleeping chair, worried over money and my legacy, I suddenly have an idea. Its brilliance will make me wealthy enough to finance a full remake of Ingo's film and then some, killing these dual birds of failure with a single stone of ingenuity.

I knock on Marjorie Morningstar's window. She opens the shade, regards me coolly, says, "What?" through the still-closed window.

"I was hoping I could briefly discuss something with you," I say.

"Yes?"

"May I come in? I have an idea."

She sighs theatrically enough that I can hear it through her newly installed double-paned soundproofing glass, opens the window, steps aside.

"Thank you, Marjorie Morningstar."

She nods. And I go right into my pitch.

"What's the worst part of a long road trip?"

"Um, I don't know, what?" she says.

"Well, take a guess. You have to take a guess."

"Leg cramps."

"What?"

"I get leg cramps from holding my foot down on the gas pedal for so long."

"That's ridiculous!"

"You asked me and I told you."

"But that's not it."

"Fine. Why don't you tell me, then? I'm kind of busy right now."

There's a man with an erection lying on his back on her bed.

"Dirty bathrooms."

"Uh-huh. Cool. So I'm actually in the middle of—"

"You like dirty bathrooms?"

"No—"

"That's right. Nobody does. So I have a business proposal to propose to the people who own Slammy's."

"Ah."

"And I was hoping you could get me in the door."

"You want to propose they clean their bathrooms?"

"I want to open a chain of highway luxury restrooms. And I need capital. It's a big idea, I'm certain. For a nominal fee, say three dollars, you get a nontraumatic restroom experience."

"I don't think I can—"

"Just get me in the door. I'll give you twenty percent for your trouble. An estimated two hundred and twenty million people are in the car an average of ninety minutes a day. Let's say, let's say conservatively, that one-eighth of those good, honest folks would pay three dollars to use a clean, luxurious bathroom. That's twenty-seven million people a day. At three dollars a pop, that's eighty-one million dollars a day! So if Slammy's parent company—"

"Degesch North America Holdings."

"Really? Wow. I didn't expect that. OK. If Degesch gives me one percent, that's eight hundred and ten thousand dollars a day for me, two hundred and ninety-five million dollars a year, of which I'll give you twenty percent, or almost fifteen million dollars. A year."

"I don't really—"

"Let's say I'm off by a factor of ten, which is impossible as I minored in business strategization at Harvard, that's still one and a half million dollars. For you. A year."

"Private bathrooms for travelers?"

"Yes. A Bathroom of One's Own, I'd call it."

"Huh."

"Woolf," I add.

"Uh-huh."

"Virginia Woolf."

"OK."

The naked man, his erection gone, gets up and heads to the bathroom.

"It adds a touch of class. And by that I am not referring to that ridiculous Melvin Frank movie starring that ridiculous George Segal (not the sculptor, who was remarkable!), who, regrettably, one must admit, was delightful as the banjo-playing Honey in Michael Nichols's *Who's Afraid of Virginia Woolf?*, which brings us full circle."

"OK."

"OK?"

"OK."

"Great!"

"Let me call my boss and see if something can be set up."

"Great!"

I stand there. She stands there, her eyes flicking from me to the window and back.

"After you leave."

"OK."

I leave.

"Don't tell them too much!" I yell through the now-closed window. "*I* wanna!"

CHAPTER 52

Rooney and Doodle sip martinis at a crowded Hollywood hot spot. People slap them on the back in passing. They are the toast of the town. In the distance, Abbott and Costello watch, sullen and ignored, from their table in the corner, next to the men's room.

"The studio wants us to do another movie as soon as possible," says Doodle.

"That's great. We're on our way."

"They want it to focus more on our physical stunt work."

"But we don't do stunts."

"Everyone thinks we do. They want more big ones in our next movie."

"That stunt was an accident."

"They don't know that."

"We gotta tell them."

"We can't. This is the only reason they want to make another movie with us."

"We were just lucky that time."

"Well, we'll be lucky this time."

"I don't know."

"Look. They've put together a list of five stunts they want to see."

"Five of them?"

"Yes. Let's see . . . Number one: Rooney—"

"That's me. Of course."

"Yes. Rooney is catapulted from a haywire dump truck onto a

438

tree, which is in the process of being chopped down by a lumber-jack."

"I don't want to do that."

"Two: Rooney is hit by a train."

"That's the gag? I'm hit by a train?"

"That's what it says."

"Why is that funny?"

"Because you're funny. Stuff happens to you. You make it funny. Three: Rooney, pretending to be one hundred years old (for some reason; you guys figure it out), is set on fire blowing out the hundred candles on his cake."

"Rooney again?"

Doodle checks his notes.

"That's right, yes."

"I don't like it."

"They write the paychecks. Four: Doodle—"

"Finally!"

"—tries to save Rooney, who is hanging from a fifth-story tene-ment clothesline. He cannot save his friend. Rooney falls through four floors of clotheslines and lands dressed as a lady."

"I'm not dressing like no lady. That's where I draw the line."

"And five: Rooney relaxes in a chair, reading a book—"

"OK. This I can do."

"—as it's dropped from a plane."

"Why would I be relaxing in a chair dropped from an airplane?"

"Again, they say here that part's up to us. They don't want to tell us how to do our job. They're giving us a lot of leeway."

"Well, I'm not doing any of this."

"You trying to end our careers?"

"I'm trying to not end my life."

"Well, that's very selfish."

ALL I ASK is to be left alone. All I ask is let me have my little piece of real estate on this bus. I paid for it—didn't I?—this minuscule acreage. I have the human decency to stay out of yours. Have you noticed that? You have no concern for the comfort of others. You behind me sticking your nude feet through my leg rest. You beside me whose elbow and knee are well into my territory. The problems of the world can be boiled down to bus etiquette. My fellow man, can you not fathom that if you are uncomfortable in the ridiculously small space allotted to you on this bus that the person next to you might be uncomfortable as well? I don't believe you can. I don't believe you have the capacity to think of anything beyond your own animal needs. Or perhaps it's even more terrible: You can fathom it and you take a certain sadistic pleasure in the subtle torture of others, of wielding your large penis sword, as it were, because, yes, you are almost always men. The women call it mansplaining—no, that's something else—the women call it manspreading, and it makes me ashamed to count myself among this vile sex. My life is bad enough. I've lost the most important work of my career. And retrieving it has proved both painful and protracted. And it is even possible I am not remembering it at all, but making it up or even being unduly influenced by an evil hypnotist. Have you considered that, people? No, you haven't thought to ask me why I am weeping here on this bus. Perhaps it doesn't interest you. Perhaps you think me pathetic, a grown man weeping like a grown woman (thon). Perhaps you are repulsed by me. Well, perhaps you are the one with the problem, not I. Perhaps you are the repulsive one. Perhaps you have never cared enough about anything in your life to weep at its loss. If that is the case, it is I who pity you. You will go through your brutish existence experiencing the small pleasures of taking things that are not yours, going places you are not welcome, sticking your elbow into the legally purchased space of another. Then you will die. Congratulations: That is your life. I hope you are happy with it. I hope you don't regret, on your deathbed, that you never felt love, or joy, or loss. Yes, loss. There is a profound sweet melancholy in the experience of loss. It is the most delectable and pungent spice on the spice rack of life. Too bad you won't taste it, buddy. I guess it doesn't go with burgers and beer.

Wait, is that Clown Laurie on the street? It could be. It just might be. I pull the cord, get out, follow her. I'm still weeping. I think if I can get close enough to this possible Clown Laurie, maybe I can tell with certainty. She dials her phone. Perfect. I will be able to hear her voice. That will clinch it. I'm not exactly sure what I'll do if it's her, but I don't think it's out of the question I could rekindle our relationship. As far as she knows, I had some sort of emergency the night I left. And then I couldn't call her to apologize because they put her in Witness Protection. That's it. I'll tell her there was some sort of emergency. Why wouldn't I have told her I had to leave? There must be something. Some good explanation for that part. Maybe I was notified that my own apartment building was on fire. I watch her ass as she walks ahead. It's not bad at all. Quite frankly, I don't even remember Clown Laurie's ass. I think I only ever looked at her face, so obsessed was I with the clown element of her personality. Perhaps I could explain that the reason I didn't say anything before I left that night is that I had some sort of emergency voice loss. A sudden inability to speak, which terrified me and forced me to run to the vocal hospital for voice medicine. Hysterical aphonia, it turns out, they told me. Not as uncommon as it might at first seem. That's a good one. Although better to use the term "psychogenic aphonia," so as not to dredge up the patriarchally misogynist "hysterical." I don't know much about Clown Laurie's sensitivity to women's issues, but regardless, it can only be brownie points for me if I explain that I prefer not to characterize severe emotional distress as hysteria. I'm suddenly reminded of a bizarrely amateurish and offensive film entitled *Adaptation*, written by the minimally talented Charlie Kaufman. There is a scene within which Nicolas Cage (who in Kaufman's most audaciously narcissistic ploy plays TWO Charlie Kaufmans!) is following Meryl Streep as brilliant *New Yorker* writer Susan Orlean. The movie is built around these two nightmarish Kaufmans stalking Orlean, and this forces me to question my own current endeavor. Do I want to be two Charlie Kaufmans in this world, carelessly frightening unsuspecting women by following them through the mean streets of New York? I do not. I do not want to share a single trait with that pathetic weasel, that tiny, pathetic Jewish bug of a screenwriter, that ersatz Malcolm Gladwell, that—

A workman carrying on his shoulder a very long wooden plank

turns suddenly at the sound of a car horn and smacks me hard in the face with it. I fly off and land upside down in a trash bin, my beard covered in cheese from a discarded paper plate of nachos. The workman runs to my side and apologizes to me in some hideous language. I sense he does not want me to cause him trouble, that he is an undocumented worker. I must say, as someone who is fluent in five languages and conversant in six more (fluent: Archi, Aymara, Malagasy, Rotokas, and Silbo Gomero; conversant: Choctaw, Kaixana, Ongota, Njerep, Portuguese, and Yupik), it surprises me that I am not able to make heads nor tails of this man's frantic jabbering. Perhaps it is that my focus is trisected among his panic, the goose egg growing on my cola-drenched forehead, and the nagging question as to why this sort of thing always happens to me. The possible Clown Laurie is long gone. The workman jabbers on and on, pleading or something, which is only serving to worsen my terrible headache. On a hunch, I try my Malagasy on him:

"*Tsara daholo ny zava-drehetra.*"

Nothing.

AT BARASSINI'S, THE annoying, overbearingly concerned Tsai hovers and clucks on and on about my poor head. It's unbearable. No, I don't need an ice pack. No, I don't need her to take me to the emergency room. No, I don't need two aspirin. Or some tea. Or water. No, I *like* the cheese in my beard. Good God, woman, leave me be.

When Barassini calls me in to the office, we both roll our eyes at each other in masculine solidarity.

"Tell me."

Mudd and Molloy Meet the 32 Foot Man opens on the backwater circuit, its premiere in Montgomery, Alabama, where Cheryld is scheduled to be trotted out and revealed to be an actual giant after the screening. The hope is that his size will be newsworthy and therefore great free promotion for the film. Currently, he is jammed into the back of two tractor trailer trucks parked outside the theater.

Molloy paces on the street. Mudd smokes and stares at his cuticles. Molloy's eyes light up.

"I say we drive the trucks out into the country," he says.

"Why's that?" asks Mudd.

"They want to make Cheryld the attraction. Our performances, by turns comic and highly dramatic, will be lost in all the coming 'freak' hoopla. This film is *our* ticket out of Palookaville, not Cheryld's. We earned it. He's just a freak. Freak, freak, freak!"

"I don't know, Chick. He's a nice kid. And kidnapping a kid is kidnapping."

"He's a freak. Freaknapping. Totally legal."

"You know what I mean. He's a young man. And you're not allowed to steal freaks, either. I'm not sure what that one's called, but I know it's against the law."

"Freaknapping. I just told you."

"Fine."

"This is our ticket out of Palookaville, Bud. Or at least it should be. I can already picture Bosley Crowther's piece in the *Times*: 'The criminally undersung comic duo of Mudd and Molloy are once and for all getting their due. In performances, by turns vibrant and harrowing, cheery and devastating, funny and unfunny, these two masters of mirth reveal many additional levels to their "chops," and I for one look forward with bated breath to their next cinematic outing.' We'll return Cheryld after the Crowther review. By then we'll be stars."

"I don't know, Chick."

"Just get in the cab."

"That's the front thing?"

"Yes. The front thing."

"OK."

They drive off.

Inside the theater, Gerald Feinberg paces in the back of the house. He's the young producer related by divorce to Molloy. The audience seems to be rapt as Mudd and Molloy prepare to kill the giant, who sits on a cliff and looks out melancholily at the late-afternoon sky.

"Just look out at the sunset, Marty," says Molloy's character. "Ain't it pretty?"

"Sure is, Dr. Williams."

"You should call me Robert."

"Really? Thanks!" says the giant young man.

"Now, remember, don't look back, Marty," says Mudd's character.

"You fellas got a surprise for me, right?"

"We do. Because we love you."

"Aw, I love you fellas, too," says Marty.

With that, Mudd and Molloy pull out pistols and shoot the giant. They have to shoot him many, many times because their bullets are so small compared to Marty's body. But eventually he dies and slips off the cliff, down into the ravine.

Mudd and Molloy hug each other and cry. The women in the audience cry. The men have red-rimmed eyes.

Feinberg can't believe his luck. He hurries outside to set up the reveal. Once people leave the theater and the real Cheryld pulls himself out of the truck, this will become the most famous motion picture of all time. "This will be my ticket out of Palookaville," he says to the girl selling popcorn.

I follow him outside the theater as the credits roll, but not before I catch the name Alan. Alan. Alan. What does it mean? Why does it haunt me so?

The truck is gone.

"What the—" he says.

Feinberg runs up and down the block yelling, "Shit. Shit. Shit." The theater doors burst open and the audience emerges, chattering excitedly.

"What a find!" says one middle-aged woman.

"My God! He's gorgeous!" says another.

"What I wouldn't give for just one date with that hunk-a man!" says a third.

"Oh yes," says a fourth. "Mmmmm. I wonder how tall he is in real life."

"He's got to be at least six feet. You can tell by his long limbs."

"Mmmm. The perfect height."

"I agree. I like them tall, but above six foot three is a little freakish."

"I agree. Six to six foot two."

"I am looking forward with bated breath to his next outing. I hope it's a romantic comedy."

"Mmm. Me, too."

"Me, too."

"Ooh, me, too. With Doris Day!"

Feinberg follows the chatting women for three more blocks; they've stopped talking, but he needs to be sure.

"Mmm. Me, too," the last one says, finally.

Feinberg has his answer.

CHAPTER 53

*T*HE *HOLLYWOOD REPORTER* review:

To say it is difficult to watch *What's Buzzin', Cousin?*, Rooney and Doodle's comedic foray into the world of beekeeping, is to greatly minimize the experience. It is profoundly upsetting for an audience to witness the relentless and, quite frankly, horrible physical injuries suffered by both men (although Rooney is, by far, the more injured of the two). Granted, humorous gags abound. Certainly, Rooney falling through lines of laundry hung to dry and ending up dressed as a woman is one of the more inspired bits of tomfoolery, although the laughs are somewhat mitigated by the realization that upon landing, Rooney's legs have been broken in five places and, indeed, one can espy his femur protruding through the flesh (and lady's silk stocking) of his right thigh.

Rooney and Doodle sit, ignored, at a small table next to Abbott and Costello next to the men's room at a crowded Hollywood hot spot.

"Now what?" asks Rooney.

"I think this film comedy business is over for us," says Doodle.

"No one wants to watch crippleds try to be funny."

"It makes audiences uncomfortable."

"Which I understand."

"Yeah. Yeah. I'm not blaming audiences."

"It's not their fault."

"I know."

"But still. We're in a predicament."

"We don't really have any skills other than this."

"It's a shame the Perforphanage didn't offer a more generalized curriculum."

"I never even took a math class."

"I took math for entertainers."

"But that was just learning to act like you're doing math."

"In case you were ever cast as a scientist or what have you, yeah."

"And now we're paying for it."

"What are we supposed to do?"

"A live show? Maybe the legit theater is the place for us."

"Like *Hellzapoppin'*?"

"Worked for Olsen and Johnson. Money's not as good but—"

"It's all about the work, really."

"It's harder to see our disfiguring scars at a distance."

"I have an idea I've been toying with. A musical about hell."

"Worked for Olsen and Johnson. *Hellzapoppin'*. What do you call yours?"

"*Hades and Gentlemen*."

"I like it. It's a pum."

I AM FIRED from the clown shoe company. No one will tell me why, but I suspect it was Clown Laurie. I suspect the babbling workman had caused her to look back and she saw me and calls were made to HR about my proclivities. This is what I suspect. There is no other possible explanation.

"Tell me."

Hades and Gentlemen opens on Broadway to great acclaim. Rooney and Doodle are once again hailed as comic genii, and many think pieces begin by saying that Francis Scott Key, I mean F. Scott

Fitzgerald, was wrong and there are indeed second acts in American lives, and Rooney and Doodle are having one of them right now and that is proof that they exist—second acts, that is, not Rooney and Doodle. Abbott and Costello's clipping service sends them the following from *The New York Times*:

> Francis Scott Key once wrote that there are no second acts in American lives. Well, Rooney and Doodle's miraculously funny show *Hades and Gentlemen* gives lie to that old saw and relegates F. Scott Fitzgerald, once and for all, to the ash heap of history. For Rooney and Doodle are back and none the worse for all their hideous physical scarring. That these two resemble those once preeminent, now laughable, clowns Abbott and Costello should not be held against them. They are infinitely funnier and more clever than that duo ever were, even in their heyday.

Abbott and Costello sit on a Los Feliz hillside. Abbott smokes.

"Rooney and Doodle. They won't go away. Why didn't we write *Hades and Gentlemen*?"

"I don't know, Lou. It's a good show. Fresh. Clever."

"They have to be taken care of."

"They seem to be doing very well on their own, so—"

"I'm saying we need to make short work of them, Bud."

"What are you saying, Lou?"

"Just this: They need to buy the farm."

"Which farm, Lou? That one up in Danbury you and Anne looked at?"

"They're not really buying a farm! It's an expression!"

"Oh. OK."

"So, we need to—"

"I guess I'm just wondering, what does the expression mean?"

"It means, we're going to kill them."

"Why would it mean that? Buying a farm seems like a nice thing. I could maybe understand 'they need to sell the farm because they're low on cash' as an expression. But even that is not quite right."

"Do you not remember that we already attempted once to kill them?"

"That was Rooney and Doodle?"

"Among others."

Now THAT I have no job, I can't afford the full rent in my apartment. So I take a roommate. His name is Dominick, and he comes replete with his own sleeping chair. Due to my books and Dominick's prodigious collection of armadillo-shaped souvenirs, we need to position our sleeping chairs directly next to each other, arms touching, armadillos akimbo. It is as if we are sleeping next to each other on a commercial bus, a bus filled with armadillos, and it is too intimate. Dominick is, as luck would have it, a grotesquely obese man, so he overhangs his chair and we fight constantly over my armrest. I cannot confront Dominick verbally; I just lie (sit) in wait for him to rub his nose or scratch himself with the hammy hand on that armrest, and I immediately seize the space. Due to this circumstance, I get little sleep, and it is beginning to show in my moods. I believe, perhaps, I made an error in accepting Dominick's roommate application, but the only other option was Sebastiano, who wore a Marbles brand jungle bowie knife in a sheath on his belt. At the time, the choice seemed obvious, but the fact is Sebastiano was lean (as a panther, he explained to me) and would fit comfortably in his own sleeping chair. That ship has sailed, I'm afraid, and I subsequently learned that Dominick also wears a sheathed bowie knife on his belt, I just could not see it because of his many rolls of fat.

Dominick works as a funny bellhop in a comedy hotel in Times Square called Elk's Head, which is modeled after the hotel in the 1918 Fatty Arbuckle film *The Bell Boy*. It's one of a new rash of movie theme hotels in New York. There is, of course, the Overlook Hotel from *The Shining* and the Grand Budapest Hotel from *The Grand Budapest Hotel*, as well as two Sofia Coppola hotels: the Park Hyatt Tokyo from *Lost in Translation* and the Chateau Marmont from somewhere, I forget where. Some of these places are better than others. The Plaza, which is now called the Home Alone Two Plaza, features a great location at the southeast corner of Central Park, and it's gratifying to see President Donald Trump at his post in the lobby twenty-four hours on weekends performing his endless cameo. He seems exhausted and sad and very old. The one I take great issue with is the Fregoli on East 64th. It's based on the hotel in that minor (even for him!) Charlie Kaufman film called *Anomalisa*. That investors saw fit to create a tribute to this misogynistic, racist, classist Claymation monstrosity, a Claymation monstrosity, by the way, that lost a fortune for the studio, is beyond my ken. This hotel is a blight on New York. I imagine there is a certain self-important, pseudo-intellectual type who would stay there, but those people should not be encouraged to visit our city. Better they construct a faux Hotel Concorde Saint-Lazare (now the Hilton Paris Opera) featured in Godard's masterwork of 1985, *Détective*. The pseudo-intellectual guests could feel superior to the fellow tourists staying at the re-creation of the Fontainebleau from Jerry Lewis's *The Bellboy*, while the true intellectuals could stay at one and dine at the other, recognizing that both films are essential to the cinematic canon.

This is the thing the pseudos don't understand: There is as much value in a Judd Apatow or a Jerry Lewis or a Shawn Levy "joint" as there is in a "joint" by Resnais or Godard or Fassbinder. The truth I've come to is that we need to laugh, as long as nothing is the object of that laughter, as long as nobody is hurt. Our clowns and jesters, our benign Princes of Comedy, perform a sacred duty in providing us with the opportunity to chuckle at their mildly humorous antics. After all, comedy is an ancient form practiced since time immemorial. So I honor those of the red nose and the baggy pants and the bladder thwack. Who I do not honor are the comedians who condescend, the Charlie Kaufmans, the Pee-wee Hermans, the Robert Downey Seniors (Junior is a genius). These three men (and I use that term in the most derisively contemporary way) have sextuple-handedly corrupted the noble tradition of gentle humor that stretches back to time immemorial, by inserting their toxic masculinity, their white cis male privilege, their faux concern for the little man, their misogyny, into what was once a pure and delightful form that stretches back to time immemorial. Why can't they see women as a people rather than mysteries and saviors and manic pixie dream whatevers? Maybe they could start by having women as friends. Or maybe they need to get laid. A truck rumbles by on the street below, shaking my many piles of books loose. They topple onto my head, burying me completely. I fight my way out from under, then stagger around the small space like a drunkard, woozy and unsteady.

Dominick squeezes out of the tiny bathroom, where he has gone to change into his bellhop costume. He will not change in front of me and has accused me more than once of ogling him.

"What happened?" he says.

"Can't you see? There are not that many places to look in here."

"When I said what happened, I meant, how'd that happen?"

"I see. Well, might I suggest that in the future you say what you mean, rather than leave it to me to puzzle out?"

"OK. But I still want to know."

"How it happened?"

"Yes."

"The vibrations of a passing truck on the street unbalanced the books and they fell on top of me. This is my theory."

"Look at that book."

"Which book?"

"The only one with its cover facing up."

I scan the mess until I spot *Shut Up: Silence the Negative Thoughts in Your Head* by Christy Pierce.

"Is that your book?" I ask.

"I don't read books, and if I did, I wouldn't read that one, and if I wouldn't read that one, I wouldn't have purchased it. So, in a word, no," says Dominick.

"Well, it's not mine," I say. "Therefore I have no idea how it got here."

"It feels like you're calling me a liar," he says.

"Hey, if the size twenty fat-boy shoe fits," I say.

Why am I picking a fight with this potentially knife-wielding behemoth? It all seems to be ramping up against my better judgment. Dominick wields his knife as predicted and chases me around and around the pile of books in this ridiculously small space until we both turn into butter, which is racist.

"I'll kill you!" he screams, as if he means it, now an enormous, knife-wielding puddle of ghee.

Perhaps all this would appear humorous to an audience, if an audience were present, but it is not humorous to me. It is real and terrifying, and Dominick has a strange fire in his eyes. Strange fire. What an odd turn of phrase. Why did those words just pop into my head? I must research the term later, once I am out of this immediate and butyraceous peril.

Reconstituted, I leap across the book pile in an attempt to widen the gap between the now reconstituted Dominick and me. My foot catches on the coffee table, upending it and sending a small vase flying toward my forehead, against which it shatters. I fall face-first into the books, scramble to my feet and to the front door, where I fumble with the seven dead bolts—were there always seven of them? I think not!—open the door, and lurch into the hallway. Dominick tries to follow, but in his urgency, he has neglected to turn sideways (the only way he can fit through the front door) and gets wedged there. I hear the rubbery squeak that always attends Dominick wedging into a small space, and I instantly relax. I turn to face him and smile benignly, knowing full well it will serve to further infuriate him. Dominick grows red in the face, then white in the face, then screams:

"I want you out of the apartment!"

"But, Dominick, it's my apartment," I say sweetly.

"I don't care. You can't get past me anyway while I'm wedged like this."

"You'll free yourself eventually."

"I will, and I'll stab you to death with my eventually freed knife-wielding hand."

He will, too. I see that. And just like that, I am homeless. I wander the streets. I sit in the library to get out of the cold. I look up "strange fire." Leviticus 10:1, Aaron's sons, Bebop and Nehru (I believe), made an improper sacrifice to God using the wrong fire (I am sort of unclear on this), and their creator did not accept the offering and also burned them both to death because of it (presumably with the right fire). This improper, unacceptable sacrifice is called strange fire. Curious choice of words for me to have used, then. I am not an Old Testament scholar, although I did get an A in an undergraduate comparative religion class for which my term paper was entitled "Engendering Generosity: Trends in Intergenerational Transgenderism Among the Hmong Animists of Cambodia Under the Reign of King Sihanouk in Comparison with Those of the Tungusic Manchu Shamanists of Qinyuan, Qianlong, Kuancheng, and Fengcheng Under Mao." But that doesn't help me much with my current dilemma, which is that there is something terribly wrong. It helps a little, but not much.

Someone is watching me, judging me, despising me, orchestrating catastrophes, minor and major. I am certain of it now. I regularly fall in man—or rather person—holes, but also my daughter hates me, which causes a level of pain not ratable on any existing pain scale. She will not speak to me. She writes essays and poems about me and publishes them on her blog and on *Jezebel*. There, an army of commenters spit on me, shit on me, assume, with no evidence, her claims about me are accurate and true, are valid. I am an opportunity for these anonymous people, who need something to hate, someone to blame, someone to deny compassion to. And I read each of Grace's essays, for I subscribe to a service that notifies me whenever my name appears online. It is always in a piece by Grace. My name does not appear anywhere else. So I read each one, a sort of self-flagellation, if self-flagellation serves to let one know one exists. Then I read each comment, comments from Blobell and TrulyMadlyFeedMe and BabyIt'sColdOutSnide and OutOfTheFryingPan and Nosebleed and TheWomanWhoWouldBeKing and MyKittyEdna and Burt'sAnalBeads. I know them all. I imagine each of them sitting there at her keyboard, haughtily condemning me. I am wished dead regularly on these sites.

CHAPTER 54

*H*ADES AND GENTLEMEN is in the midst of its riotous second act. Rooney and Doodle, as carpenters in hell, sing a song to Dolores del Río as Beelzebub.

> Doodle:
> *They say it's hot as Hades*
> *In Hades, but it isn't.*
> *For the fire here*
> *Is chilly, dear,*
> *Compared to when we're kissin'.*

> Rooney and Doodle:
> *Oh, I love you, you little devil,*
> *So cute is my Old Scratch.*
> *But how could I know, ma'am,*
> *When I first became damned,*
> *That we'd be such a match?*

As if on cue, a match is lit backstage and held to a varnished flat. It catches; almost instantly, the entire set is in flames and falls into the audience. The fire is fast and brutal. That the theater seats are cheap, made from polyurethane from IG Farben, upholstered with isoprene and coated with plasticized gasoline, means the theater has a low flash point and even a simple spark could set the house ablaze in an instant. "It was an unnecessarily flammable choice of materials," said Irwin Chello of American Seats. "We know that now. But hindsight is twenty-twenty."

Rooney and Doodle remain miraculously unscathed due to their asbestos "tortured soul" costumes, but twelve hundred audience members and stage crew die.

From *Variety:*

Hades and Gentlemen lived up to its name last night when the Shubert Theatre was transformed into a fiery inferno, burning 1,200 people to agonizing death. Stars Rooney and Doodle survived, but they may as well be dead because they'll never work in the entertainment business again. Theater manager Morton Klipp is quoted as saying, "Those two? They'll never work in the entertainment business again. They have burned all bridges. And I don't mean the Bridge to Hades set that was onstage at the time of the incident. Although I also mean that. They're through, I tell ya. Through."

Doodle puts down the *Variety* and looks across the table to his partner.

"I feel bad about this."

"Me, too."

"All those people out on a Friday night to have a good time after a hard workweek."

"I know. I feel bad. I already said."

"And it looks like things are bad for us, too. It's not like we got out of this unscathed."

"Except physically."

"Except that way."

"What are we gonna do? The Perforphanage didn't really prepare us for anything else."

"Did you take Crime Pays?"

"The 'How to Get Cast as a Criminal' class?"

"Yeah."

"I learned a fair amount about criminal enterprise in that class."

"It did seem pretty accurate."

"That's true. They had that retired yegg come in and lecture."

"Fingers O'Grady!"

"Nice fella."

"Loved him. Crime seems like a job you can get without much education."

"O'Grady never went to school. Not even a school for performing arts."

"So we have a leg up there."

"A leg on the yegg!"

"Ha ha."

"Ha ha. Too bad we can never use that joke now that we're barred from entertainment. It's a good one."

"It is too bad. I'll write it down, just in case."

"We need to change our names. Rooney and Doodle don't sound like criminal names."

"True. What are some criminal teams?"

"Bonnie and Clyde. Leopold and Loeb. Burke and Hare."

"Boy, you really have those at your fingertips."

"I do. Thompson and Bywaters."

"Hmm. It's gotta sound serious."

"Rood and Doone?"

"I like that."

"It's good."

"I'd be scared of Rood and Doone."

"Rood and Doone it is."

"Or Roon and Dood?"

"Maybe. Yeah."

"We don't have to be killers, though, right?"

"I don't really want to kill any more people, if it can be avoided."

"No more killing. Just robbing."

"The robbers Rood and Doone."

"Roon and Dood?"

"OK, sure."

* * *

456

Barassini lets me sleep in his sock drawer, which, for reasons that remain unclear to me, is enormous. Or is it that I've shrunk even more? I can't get to my doorjamb to check. It is fairly comfortable on all those balled-up socks, and it's both dark and quiet. The only problem is that I need someone to let me out in the morning. This means I am unable to get up and pee at night, which generally I have to do at least twice. With some embarrassment, I inform Barassini of my bladder issues and ask if we could leave the drawer open so I can climb out as needed. He says no and gives me a plastic orange juice container "like the long-haul truckers use." Those who are beggars are not permitted to be the ones who are allowed to choose things, as the old adage, I believe, goes.

"OK, shoot."

I'm in a cave. The meteorologist is here, too, fiddling with a massive machine composed of vacuum tubes, dials, flashing lights, and hundreds of cables. It's an ancient computer, and it wraps completely around the perimeter of this enormous space. A series of drawings are spit out of a printer at one end and automatically photographed by a mounted still camera.

Dissolve to the meteorologist sitting on a hardback chair in the cave before a small movie screen projecting an animation: In it, a drawing of the meteorologist sits at his desk, writing in his notebook. A rudimentary electronically synthesized voiceover (the meteorologist's?) accompanies the animation:

"The largest hurdle, of course, is still the limitation of the human brain. If I could devise a sophisticated-enough electronic calculating machine, I might be able to compute the results in close to real time and possibly at some point even faster. Only then would I have a proper predicting machine."

A snap of fingers and I'm back in Barassini's office.

"Oh!" says Barassini. "It's meteorologist not meaty horologist. I get it now."

I have no idea what he's talking about.

Tsai sits behind the desk doing a crossword and snapping her gum. God, she's repugnant—everything I hate in a woman crammed into one nauseous sack of flesh. How has it come to this for us?

"Wow," says Barassini, "so let me get this straight, then. The meteorologist is watching an animated version of himself doing and thinking precisely what we've seen him doing and thinking previously."

"Yes. Predicted now by the computer, which continues to expand on his original calculations from the wind tunnel experiment. All this the result of the leaf hitting the glass wall."

"That's trippy," says Barassini. "It's kind of like from any single moment the future in its entirety can be predicted."

"Yes, duh, that's precisely what it's like."

"Meaty horologist kind of works, too. Do you see that?"

"Of course I see that. What do you take me—"

Tsai interrupts.

"Do either of you know a twenty-nine-letter word for fear of the—"

"Hexakosioihexekontahexaphobia!" I bark, before anyone else in the room can say it.

"Really?"

"Fear of the number six-six-six is what you were looking for, right? Am I right? Am I? Tell me!"

"Yeah."

"Hexakosioihexekontahexaphobia. H-e-x-a-k-o-s-i-o-i-h-e-x-e-k-o-n-t-a-h-e-x-a-p-h-o-b-i-a."

"How do you know that?"

"I once wrote an extremely long monograph on the subject of—as well as employing—extremely long words, which was entitled, if I remember correctly, *Sticks and Stones May Break My Bones But Words Will Never Hurt Me? Not So! A Brief History of the Power of Words to Inflict Harm with Emphasis on Extremely Long Words Since with Extremely Long Words the Pain Inflicted Is Protracted as It Is Spread Out Over Many, Many, Many Syllables* for *The Journal of Hippopoto-monstrosesquipedaliophobia*, which is, as you may or may not know, defined as a fear of extremely long words, in case you didn't know. So that is how I know. In addition, I minored in the number of the beast studies in college, which was Harvard. Six-six-six is the number of the beast, although in actuality, it is six-one-six, which perhaps not coincidentally is also the area code for the Lower Peninsula of Michigan, which is perhaps not coincidentally the onetime area code of Betsy DeVos and her evil brother Erik Prince, whom I call Betsy DeVour and Erik Prince of Darkness, respectively."

"Wow," she says. "Could you spell it again?"

"H-e-x-a-k-o-s-i-o-i-h-e-x-e-k-o-n-t-a-h-e-x-a-p-h-o-b-i-a."

"The sock drawer working out OK?" asks Barassini, trying, I assume, to change the subject.

"Hmm?"

I am lost in reverie. Memories of number of the beast classes fill my head. Old, gruff, kind Professor DeMarcus with his old, gruff kindliness, always demanding the best from us.

"Three Maccabees 2:29," he would shout. "Contemporary parallels?"

And we'd all whip out our slide rules, calculating madly.

"Barcodes?" one of us would say, most likely the apple-polishing MacDougall.

"Just so, MacDougall," DeMarcus would say, the gleam of paternal love for MacDougall in his eye.

"The sock drawer OK?"

"What?"

"The sock drawer? OK?"

"Oh. Yeah. Fine."

And like that my memories of DeMarcus disappear in a literal puff of smoke, for some reason. Now I am considering how at one point I would've given anything to sleep in Tsai's sock drawer amidst her socks. Now her sock drawer is directly next to the one I sleep in and there is a window between them and I don't care. I look under the desk and at her socked feet. They do nothing for me anymore. They are feet. Horrible, monstrous human feet. Nothing does anything for me anymore.

I am, when all is said and done, an old man who sleeps in a hypnotist's sock drawer. This is not how I, as a child, pictured my life turning out.

I thought I would be successful: a doctor, a lawyer, an indigenous people's chief, someone who would do good in the world, of whom my parents could be proud. Passionate, valued, kind. Even, perhaps, a simple carpenter, someone who works with his (her, thon) hands to create something useful. Jesus was a carpenter, of course; there is no shame in it. Someone made this dresser. Someone made it large enough to house a shrinking man, knowing, perhaps, that at some point, a small, broken man would need it for that very thing, knowing that at some point, it might just save that man's life.

Barassini says good night and closes the drawer.

In darkness, I drift off and find myself, as I do every night, back in the Brainio city Abbitha had created. She is, of course, no longer here. It is a shell of the dream, the detritus left behind. I search empty buildings with no real hope of ever seeing her again. I wish I could have other dreams. Any other dreams, but at night, this is my prison: an empty city, a sock drawer, professional failure.

CHAPTER 55

"TELL ME," says Barassini, as he opens the drawer promptly at 7:00 A.M.

It is night. As is often the case, Mudd and Molloy, on the road, are tucked into the same bed in a fleabag hotel.

"Bud?"

"Yeah, Chick?"

"I can't sleep. Can you move over a little?"

"There's no place to go. I'm already at the edge."

"I'm fidgety."

"Count sheep."

"The sheep keep hiding behind the barn."

"What barn?"

"The one on the farm I'm picturing."

"Well, don't picture a barn."

"Farms have barns."

"Just picture the sheep in a field."

"What about trees?"

"What about them?"

"Fields have trees."

"And?"

"Sheep could hide behind them. If they're thin enough, the sheep, not the trees."

"Picture a meadow with no trees."

"Big rocks?"

"No."

"OK. Can the sheep wander beyond the horizon line?"

"There's a fence."

"You sure you can't move over just a tad?"

"I can't, Chick. My left leg is already off the bed."

Long pause.

"You wanna talk or something?" Chick asks.

"I need to sleep."

"Can we just talk for a minute? I have an idea."

"For a minute."

"Have you heard of the movie *Lawrence of Arabia*?"

"Of course. Big hit."

"And you know how Abbott and Costello did that Foreign Legion movie?"

"*Abbott and Costello in the Foreign Legion*. Of course."

"I don't think that's what it was called."

"It was."

"Anyway. You're wrong, but anyway, I was thinking—"

"I'm not wrong."

"Anyway. I was thinking, what if we do our own version of a desert movie. Hope and Crosby did one."

"*Road to Morocco*."

"No."

"Yes!"

"Anyway—"

"It's called *Road to Morocco*."

"Anyway. It's a successful genre to parody."

"OK."

"I'm thinking we could call it *Morons of Arabia*."

"OK."

"We'd be the morons."

"I got that."

"It's a play on *Lawrence of Arabia*."

"I got it."

"What do you think?"

"Is that the entire idea?"

"Camels. Fezzes. You know. That sort of thing. The whole nine yards."

"Who'd give us money to film a desert epic, Chick? We can't fill the Elks Hall here in Bumfuck, Iowa."

"We do it cheap. Film it in a sandbox."

"Like in a children's playground?"

"Sure. Close-ups, high angles. No one will be the wiser."

"You haven't thought this through, Chick."

"There are details to work out, certainly."

"Yes."

"I'm an idea man. Broad strokes. You get into the details."

"Like how to fit camels into a sandbox?"

"That and where we can get a couple of cheap fezzes."

"I need sleep, Chick."

"Midget camels? Is there such a thing? I'm just spitballing."

"We'll discuss tomorrow."

"I can't sleep. I feel like we're this close to something important."

"How close?"

"This close."

"You're just saying 'this close.' You're not gesturing in any way."

"It's dark."

"Not so dark that I can't see you're not gesturing in any way."

"OK. *This* close."

"OK."

IT IS THE next day, and I return to my apartment with a pork chop dangling from a string on a fishing pole. Dominick is still wedged in the door. I swing the pork chop in front of his nose to motivate him. It works. He releases from the doorway with a champagne cork *pop*, grabs for the pork chop, and I duck between his legs into the apartment, slam the door, and engage the twenty-three (twenty-three?) dead bolts. I lean against the door heaving as Dominick pounds on it and screams for me to let him back in. I will not. He will not ever get back in here. I will stay locked in this room until he gives up and goes away.

The pounding continues for days, with eight-hour breaks when we both sleep. I email Sebastiano to ask if he still needs a place to live. His bowie knife is less of a concern for me now. I never hear back. Perhaps he is out of town.

Even sequestered in my apartment, the world of funny pain finds me. My smoke alarm screams repeatedly for no discernible reason until I notice I am smoking a cigarette and have many other lit cigarettes in ashtrays around the apartment and in my hands. I stub them out, then climb onto three piled-up chairs to disconnect the alarm from its battery. The chairs topple before I can accomplish this, and I plummet, landing with my head once again in a wastebasket. I succeed on my second attempt, plummeting again, but this time with the battery in one hand and for some inexplicable reason a new lit cigarette in the other. This time I land with my head in the faux elephant foot umbrella holder. I do not own a faux elephant foot umbrella holder. I do not even own an actual elephant foot umbrella holder. Where did it come from? I stand, catching my reflection in the entryway mirror, still wearing the umbrella stand like a drum major's hat. I need to quiet my thoughts, my mind. I need to stop moving, to cease being a victim of circumstance.

My need to slow down brings to mind the silent meditation retreat my college girlfriend Chumi and I attended at a Buddhist monastery in Bali. She dragged me kicking and screaming, as I am not the mystical sort and will not abide the flimflam hocus-pocus of any religious doctrine, let alone those of the "mysterious" East. But love corners us (love corners all! I *must* use this somewhere!) and we find ourselves against our better judgment in rented sarongs, donned previously by God knows who. That being said, the experience changed me, softened me. The constant chatter in my overactive mind quieted. This! I decide. This is what I need to do now. I need to find that silence. I need to discover my own voice within the madness of the external world. And I naturally, easily, fall back into the breathing meditations I practiced there. I listen to the voices in my head: the doubt, the mocking, the criticisms, the self-recriminations, the odd, seemingly foreign thoughts—shelling peas on a pea farm in Tunisia, dancing the cancan in the Folies Bergère, my happy childhood as a slave laborer in a Venusian mining colony. I do this without judgment and gently let all these thoughts go. And I breathe. The emotions that come to the fore in such exercises are primal. I weep. I cringe. I laugh. I wrestle with my god. I wrestle with neighborhood bully Anton Fricker-Ventucci. And through all this, I breathe. And I slow down. And the breathing becomes less ragged, deeper. Over time (who knows how much because time ceases to exist!), I find myself centered. I no longer feel targeted, no longer is my back against the wall. The world has opened up to me in surprising ways. It is my goal to step out into the world while maintaining this openness. I unbolt the front door. Each lock a separate, quantized experience during which I am fully present. Thirty-four dead bolts. One, two, three, four, five, six, seven, eight, nine, ten, eleven, twelve, thirteen, fourteen, fifteen, sixteen, seventeen, eighteen, nineteen, twenty, twenty-one, twenty-two, twenty-three, twenty-four, twenty-five, twenty-six, twenty-seven, twenty-eight, twenty-nine, thirty, thirty-one, thirty-two, thirty-three, thirty-four. Thirty-five. Thirty-five dead bolts, rather. The symbolism inherent in this unlocking does not escape my notice now that I am enlightened, but I let it go with all other thoughts as I turn the knob and pull open the door. There lies Dominick, sleeping like a baby, no longer frightening to me. He is simply Dominick, disgusting, foul-smelling, obese Dominick, just another manifestation of the divine. I lock the door so he cannot get in, climb over him, and leave the building. The street is different in my current state. I see everything. The Italian peanut vendor on the corner, hawking his wares with his mellifluous chant of "peanuts, a-peanuts for a-sale." Other things. Then I'm in Port Authority looking up at the bus departures. The station is crowded as it always is, but now I see it in a new light. The angel-headed commuters in a choreography of beauteous sadness, broken dreams, broken lives. *How did I get here?* they all seem to plead.

Peanuts, a-peanuts for a-sale.

The Italian peanut vendor, the nuclear physicist on his way to a nuclear bomb testing, the suburban housewife high on bennies, looking for kicks: They're all the same. All one. All made of the same electrons, protons, and newtons, I think. It is truly a brotherhood (sisterhood) of man (woman, child), and here I am, just one more pile of atoms bouncing off other piles of atoms. Immediately, I feel both free and constrained, because there is no duality. And, as such, I am both here and gone. I am both now and then. I am both African American ("black") and white ("Caucasian"). With this epiphany seems to come the possibility of escaping my tormentor, whomever it might be. Almost as if on cue, the board lights up: last call for the Greyhound bus to Nowhere, OK. Nowhere OK. Nowhere is OK. I didn't know what I was looking for, but I have found it.

The Nowhere bus pulls from the station onto a dull, shadowless New York street. Perhaps it's that I'm seeing the city through enlightened eyes now, but I don't recognize it. The shops seem different. The Haberdasheria? Blockman's Battle Bots? And there is a vagueness to the expressions of the people on the street, to the cars on the street, to the street on the street. I focus on my breathing. It's almost too much to take in. As the bus slows and I slow so much more that I find myself sliding three seats back, I spot *myself* on the street outside, stepping out of the Port Authority, except I am stepping out backward. That's the thing, I suddenly realize: Everything on the street is moving backward. And there's something else: The air is swarming with drifting droplets, like transparent pollen. They make their ways into people's ears, seemingly haphazardly, but with so much frequency that it cannot be by accident. I also see these droplets emerge from ears, apparently having multiplied, then disperse and enter other ears. The bus follows the other me down the street as if it were a dollied camera trained on my backward double. So I am close enough to see these droplets entering and exiting the ears of the other me as well. What is happening in this horrifying world outside the bus window? To what Lovecraftian hellscape am I suddenly privy?

I watch as I backwardly retrace the route I took to Port Authority, past the Italian peanut vendor, "Elas-a rof stunaep-a, stunaep," into my apartment building. The bus passes. Reverse me is out of sight now and I quickly lose interest—whatever—drifting once again into my beard monologue. I add a new section on the differences between fake and real beards, touching briefly on *beard* as a verb (to confront with boldness), as well as the current slang usage denoting a false heterosexual partnership. Something snaps me out of my reverie. If I look past the immediate space, I can see a glowing other space, spreading out to infinity as a kind of three-dimensional, much less cartoony version of comedian David Steinberg's iconic and problematically sentimental *New Yorker* cover. It's beautiful and hopeful, and I believe I am embarking on a new and grand adventure. My previous trials and tribulations are far away, unimportant. Finally, I am happy.

Then the backward bus gets a flat tire and the driver tells us in backward talk that we all have to get off. So I'm on the street with the world as it was. A pigeon defecates on me (how glorious this would be if it were backward time still and the pigeon feces collected itself and sucked into the pigeon's anus; that would show him), and I turn and trudge back uptown to my apartment to clean myself off.

My front door is splintered with a vaguely Dominick-shaped hole in it. I espy him through it, angrily pacing, miming violent stabbing motions with his knife, and cursing. I listen for whom he is cursing. I suspect it might be me.

It is me.

I head back to Barassini's sock drawer.

CHAPTER 56

"Go."

The meteorologist's computer is even bigger now.

"Meaty horologist," Barassini chuckles. "I can't get over that. It's so good."

He sits before the small movie screen, watching an animation of himself watching an animation of himself in front of a movie screen. He rubs his nose. A moment later, the animated image of him rubs its nose. He shifts his rear in his seat, and the animated version of him does the same at the exact same moment. The calculations are catching up to the present.

Now it happens: The animation reacts first, its eyes widening in amazement. The meteorologist's eyes widen in amazement, too, immediately after.

His voiceover asks: "Do my eyes widen in reaction to the image on the screen of my eyes widening?"

He doesn't know.

Now the animated meteorologist looks troubled. It gets up. It exits. The drawing wanders through a drawing of the woods outside the cave. It begins to rain, a few drops at first, then the sky opens and there is a torrential downpour. The electronic computer voice:

"This is exactly as it was in the animation!"

The animated meteorologist pulls his jacket over his head and runs back into the drawing of the cave.

The real meteorologist looks troubled now. He gets up, paces, exits. Exiting the cave, he wanders through the woods. It begins to rain, a few drops at first, then the sky opens and there is a torrential downpour. He thinks (and he cannot help himself), This is exactly as it was in the animation!

He runs back to the cave, jacket covering his head.

EVERY NIGHT, MORE Abbitha without Abbitha dreams. I continue to wander the streets of this strange, empty dream city. I continue to look for novelizing work, but it seems I've been blacklisted. This is depressing as well as worrisome, for my dream rent is due. I'm not certain what happens if I lose my dream apartment. Will I freeze to death? Can one freeze to death in one's dream? Maybe I will be evicted from the dream, which would be a good thing. I suspect it's Abbitha who has somehow had me blacklisted. There is no way to know for certain because there is no one to ask.

I comb the novelizer want ads in the paper. The pickings, as always, are slim. There is a novella-ization of a short film, some NYU student thing novelizers just novelize to pad their résumés. No money there. And there's a low-paying job for a straight-to-cable horror film called *Scream Me to Sleep*, about a monster whose screams put people to sleep, and then he kills them while they're sleeping. It's a fascinating and counterintuitive premise, and the director, Egg Friedlander, is the most visionary of the new crop of horror directors in my dream, but it's a difficult translation to book form, as the bulk of the movie is screaming and sleeping, plus the money is not good. But people who are beggars cannot also be people who can be the choosers of things, to coin a phrase. So I call Dimbulb, Egg's production company, to set up an interview. There is a long silence after I tell them my name.

"Hello?" I say, finally.

"Yes?" comes the voice, eventually.

"I thought perhaps we were disconnected."

"No, no," she says.

"So . . . ?"

"Yes?"

"Might I come in to discuss?"

469

"Oh. Um, yes, well, sure, if you want."

"Yes. I want. That's why I called."

"Ah. OK then. That's cleared up, so . . ."

"When would be good?"

"For?"

"The meeting."

"Oh. Right. Let's see. I'm afraid the only time we still have available is yesterday."

"Yesterday?"

"We had one opening yesterday at four."

"Where are you located?"

"Oh, way across town, so—"

"How do you know what way across town is for me?"

"Oh. Sure. Well, where are you currently?"

I look at the street signs on the corner.

"Milton and Wilton."

"As I suspected, way across town. We're at 3593 Snowman, on the corner of Porridge."

I've heard of Snowman, but I suspect she's made up Porridge. However, since this is a dream, I figure I can find the intersection anyway and get there yesterday at four, if I leave now.

"I'll be there"—I look at my watch—"fourteen hours ago."

And sure enough, I am.

Dimbulb is housed in a small office on the fortieth floor of the Snowman-Porridge Building. And let's just say, the receptionist, who I assume was the voice on the phone tomorrow, was not hired for her typing skills—as she has no hands. Also, she is beautiful. I am intimidated by her beauty, but her lack of hands makes me feel superior at least in the regard that I have two of them.

"Egg will see you then," she says as she stands and leads me to an office door, which she opens with her mind, through some sort of telekinesis, I imagine. Maybe she is a good typist after all.

Sitting on a couch in the meeting area of the room is, I assume, Egg Friedlander. He is an oddly shaped man, almost rock-shaped, although not in an obvious way.

"I'm Egg," says Egg.

"I'm B.," I say.

He extends his hand while remaining seated. I shake it.

"I'm happy to meet you," I say. "Besides you and your receptionist, I haven't seen another person for a very long time."

"That's Weird," he says.

"Well, not particularly, as this city is entirely void of people, so . . ."

"No. Weird is my receptionist's name."

"That's weird," I say.

"The receptionist, yes."

"No, I'm saying that it's weird that her name is Weird."

"Well, her parents were hippies."

"She seems kind of young to have hippies for parents. And also, Weird doesn't seem like a typical hippie kid name. More typically something like Freedom or Moonshine."

"Moonshine?"

"Beam, I mean."

"Anyway, we're wasting valuable time. I have a meeting two minutes ago. So, quickly, tell me how you would novelize a movie about screaming and sleeping."

"Aiiiiiiiiieeeeeeeeee!!!!!! and zzzzzzzzzzzz!!!!!!" I say.

He seems impressed.

"I'm not impressed," he says.

"Let me finish."

"OK."

I'm stalling. The onomatopoetic translation of screaming and sleeping is as far as I've gotten.

"Of course there'd be additional spellings as well. For the sake of variety," I try.

"Yes. And?"

"Um . . . It'd be scary. As well."

"I'm sorry to have wasted your time, Mr. Rosenberger—"

"Mx."

"Mr. Mx., but this is not a good fit."

"Rosenberg."

"Rosenberg. They told me you would not be a good fit, but I grew up on your novelizations, and so I wanted to give you—"

"Wait. Who told you I wouldn't be a good fit?"

"Look, it doesn't matter. It's just the word around town."

"Please. I need the work. I did the novelization for *I Wake Up Screaming*, which as you can clearly see has both sleeping and screaming in it, or at least screaming immediately following sleeping, so I'm experienced in the genre."

"I'm sorry."

"Not to mention other scream/sleep work. Mostly in the world of community theater."

"I'm sorry. I had a meeting. Weird will show you out."

"Can we at least stay in touch? I'm very lonely."

The office door opens, as if by telekinesis, and Weird enters.

"This way," she offers.

And I go that way, finding myself once again wandering the empty city.

THE METEOROLOGIST IS older now, maybe sixty, the computer larger still, modern, buttons instead of dials, transistors instead of vacuum tubes. A large video monitor has replaced the movie screen. His voiceover begins:

"I continue to search through the numbers for *my* particular arc, where my line of being ends, that is, where the trajectory that is my life ends."

On the monitor: It's night. He watches himself approach a desolate stretch of rural road. The animation is much more sophisticated now, the illusion of three dimensions, color. Gorgeous.

"Ah. Here we are then," says the meteorologist. "The end of the road, as it were."

He emits a dry, sad chuckle.

On the monitor, the meteorologist, older still, drags a wagon containing a portable jackhammer, a shovel, a trowel, a gunmetal box, and a bucket of pourable asphalt repair compound. His GPS device directs him to a spot on the road, where he stops. He looks both ways for cars, but seemingly only out of habit, for the road is empty. He grabs the jackhammer and begins to use it, not bothering with ear protection. Why bother? After tonight, he will never again need ears. Once he breaks through the asphalt, he digs until there exists a suitable hole. He places the gunmetal box into it, covers it with dirt, pours asphalt over the hole, smooths it with the trowel, then stands. He seems anxious.

He watches his face in this animated version on the monitor. He sees the tension in it. He hears his thoughts in voiceover:

"OK. This is it."

His mind slows; he notices a slight breeze, the clear starry sky. A green car—a Mustang? A Camaro? He doesn't know cars—appears, speeding, erratic, from around the bend, careening toward him. He doesn't bother to move out of the way, for what happens is what happens, and there is nothing to be done. The car hits the animated meteorologist, sends him flying into a ditch, keeps going. He lies there, bloodied, broken. The meteorologist in the cave watches the meteorologist on the screen dying in the ditch, as if he's his own disembodied spirit hovering above his mangled body, but it's not now, for this is ten years in the future. Not now but soon, and without any doubt. He wonders, in voiceover again, how this can be, how it can be written in stone, how it will be impossible for him to not be on that road on that night at that time, even though he knows now that he mustn't be there if he wants to live. He knows that now. Because there is no choice, is the reason. He couldn't explain it to someone who has not experienced it, but he is not someone who hasn't experienced it, and he knows he will be there on that night as scheduled. It is not an appointment in Samara. No tricks required. He will be there because he will be there. And now he knows, ten years in advance, how and when and where he will die.

He wonders if it hurts.

It occurs to him that somewhere in these data, there is a simulated version of himself watching this video prediction of his death, as he has just now done. He types a search into his keyboard, and it comes up on the screen, an animation of him in this cave, watching the animation of him getting hit by the car, and having it occur to him in voiceover that there must be an animation of him discovering the moment of his death, and, rather than searching for it and facing an infinite avenue of recursion, he turns off the computer. The whole thing sends him spiraling into a depression, as he is sure has also been predicted somewhere among all these numbers. He feels hopeless. He contemplates suicide, but, of course, he can't kill himself for the very simple reason that he doesn't kill himself. Even his contemplation of suicide at this moment is somewhere predicted by the computer. There is nothing to be done. For there is no law of causality other than this: Things happen because they happen. "And it's so hard to concentrate now," thinks his own voiceover (not the electronic, predicted one), "because that is it and I see it and my life goes no further and everything ends there and yet it doesn't because I am dead in the video but the video continues. So I will turn it back on and watch as the police arrive and watch the ambulance and the fire trucks, then turn away from my body and look down the street, because the whole world is predicted here, not just me, because with enough time and enough computational power, the whole world, the whole of the future, can be predicted. And I guess that's a thing I just learned: that I can see the world past the time I'm in it. Yet still, I have to wait to die. It happens when it happens, and what do I do to fill that time?"

He paces. But pacing is not enough.

"Perhaps I will just wander this virtual landscape for the next ten years, a vagabond, a transtemporal transient, a liminal lurker, seeing the world as it will be. It occurs to me that by doing this I can also seek out patents and schematics from years in the future, and in these coming scientific advances, I can unearth technologies to implement in my computer now, ahead of schedule, ahead of the current knowledge. And this will make my computer even faster, so that maybe in five months, I can study computer designs and components from thirty years in the future and implement those. And so on and so on, so that before I die in ten years, I'll be able to see one hundred years into the future, one thousand. Who knows?

"It'll pass the time, if nothing else. Get my mind off of my circumstances. Anyway, the bottom line is I will embark on this path because I embark on it, even though I tell myself I am deciding to do it because I need to fill my remaining time."

But why, for the love of God, he wonders, for he cannot stop himself from wondering the "why" of things, will he be burying a box in the middle of a country road in the middle of the night ten years hence?

The scene shifts to Bud and Chick sharing a bed.

"Bud?"

"Yeah, Chick?"

"I can't sleep. Can you move over a little?"

"There's no place to go. I'm already at the edge of the bed."

"I'm fidgety and irascible."

"Count sheep."

"The sheep are hiding behi—"

Wait! Haven't I heard this before? This is a rerun. There are not supposed to— I have been tricked. A previously recorded Barassini tape of B.'s memory of Ingo's film of a Mudd and Molloy conversation has been played to give B. time to escape from me.

All is lost.

B. is gone. B. Ruby Rosenberg is gone. Balaam Rosenberger Rosenberg is gone. Our beloved Rosenberg is gone. The open manholes of New York whistle emptily, mournfully in the wind. The bird shit still falls, but on no one.

It is times like these when questions of meaning arise. It is times like these when looking inward is the only course of action, for now, alas, there is nowhere else to look. What went wrong? A lack of vigilance on my part? What might have been done differently? It is an occasion for learning. For reflection. The wake of failure always offers such opportunity. Where have you gone, my B.? My child. My son. The streets are empty of you. Your apartment is empty. There is no longer any center to this world. Where do I put my avarice, all my own frustrations? Into what receptacle do I place my jokes? I wander the streets. Your streets. The streets of my mind. I look in alleyways. I check the hospitals, the morgues. How is this even possible? How can it be that I can no longer see you? Can you hide from me? Is that even within the realm of the possible? I call your name. I miss you, my child, my son, my string bean. I sit in coffee shops, staring vaguely out windows. I retrace my steps. I retrace yours. I question my intentions. Perhaps I wasn't fair to you. I rack my brain. I think I was fair. I think I was honest. I think I was objective. But can one really ever know? As even-handed as I believe I was, I know that it's never possible to see fully inside another person, even you, my son. I check the flophouses. I call the airlines. I look in on your ex-wife. Might she have taken you in, hidden you like young Anne Frank before you? It seems unlikely. I know you had been attempting to escape. I thought it was a bluff. Children always threaten to run away from home. But here we are. Or here I am, anyway. Perhaps I'll explore the world without you, but through what lens, through whose mind? Oh, B., without you there is no funny. My Rosenberg was thought to be irrepressible, unsinkable. It was believed he would take any punishment, that his desperation was so abiding as to propel him forward, from one humiliation to the next until the world tired of him and he crumbled back to the dust from whence he came. Assumptions were made. Clearly, mistakes as well. Rosenberg is gone. The territory has been combed. Teeth have been gnashed. There is no sign. So all is still in this world tonight. Certainly there is concern about B.'s emotional state, that he may have suffered unnecessarily, that the unfairness of his predicament was too much a burden for him to carry. But if a clock is to run at all, each and every gear must be engaged. There is no superfluous gear in a well-made machine.

So the conclusion to be drawn is simple: B. must be promptly replaced with a second and cosmetically identical B. And I must watch this second B., not only for our continued amusement, but for stresses that might in time lead to the deformation and breakage of the part. Building a second B. is not difficult, and it is accomplished quickly and efficiently. It fits perfectly into the machine, indistinguishable from the first, even though there have been some modifications, some improvements, both in its effectiveness and its comicality.

CHAPTER 57

Here in the Unseen, to where I have newly escaped my tormentor by using a trick I learned from *Ferris Bueller Skips School*, I am the Jewish giant of Ingo's imagining via Georges Méliès's *Gulliver's Travels*—Gulliver as the Wandering Jew, as it were, in alien lands, at home nowhere. Nowhere, Oklahoma? Who can say? Here, I wear a long, fake beard. It is my disguise, my way of hiding from *my* creator who has marked me as Cain was once marked by his. It is also as Ingo has envisioned me. There is no value in denying my apparent Jewishness here. I am an outcast, and no one speaks to me in this silent world. Perhaps I am too far away at fifty feet high for them to bother to try, but I think, as well, they are scared of me. After all, here, I am a giant of enormous size. But, of course, the truth is that this is a silent world and no one "speaks" to anyone. So I wander the streets of the Unseen, trying to stay unseen by the Unseen, serving my purpose as legend, as myth, a scary creature that keeps the residents of the Seen from trespassing here, not that they often try, although slumming has become somewhat fashionable of late. From up here, I can see both east and west in the dimness. I can see past the tenements and factories of the Unseen to the land of the Seen. I can watch the comedy there, but it's distant. The gags, small and washed out by atmospheric haze, lose their potency. In the third direction, past the line of demarcation that is a dense, dark stand of pine, I can see the Unseen Unseen. Those in the Unseen, not of my stature, cannot see this place, although there are rumors among them of its existence. Those in the Seen will never know about it. There lives Ingo, or the puppet version of Ingo he long ago created and animated off camera, along with Lucy Chalmers, or the puppet version of Lucy Chalmers, who walked off a Hollywood set so many years ago, never to be seen again. I can, of course, see the towering Oleara Debord as well. She is visible from everywhere, to everyone in the Seen, Unseen, and Unseen Unseen.

I climb her, looking for a place to rest, a place solid and majestic, a perch from which, perhaps, to glimpse my creator, or at least the creator of this world in which I now find myself. At her highest peak, I find a hermit meditating, a sage in this dim world. He is an ancient African American gentleman, no doubt struggling to understand life.

"What is life?" I ask him.

There is a long silence as he seems to formulate a response.

"Life is a bowl of cherries, my son," he says, finally.

"That's it?" I say. "After all this struggle, all this ceaseless humiliation, you tell me life is a bowl of cherries?"

Again he is silent for a long while, then says:

"You mean life isn't a bowl of cherries?"

I am inconsolable. This is a joke, yet another joke at my expense, even here, even though I have escaped the world of the Seen in which I seemed to exist only as the butt of them. Perhaps there is no escape for me. I stare out into the distance. From up here, I can see a party in the Unseen Unseen. Maybe Ingo will speak to me. Maybe he will give me some answers. Maybe he will allow me into his inner circle, that gated community within the Unseen.

I begin my descent. Oleara is as beautiful here as she is in the Seen world. I guess mountains don't care if they are seen or unseen. They just are. I could learn something from mountains. We all could.

As I make my way toward the Unseen Unseen, I find myself further agitated by this blanket of silence. The silent era is truly terrifying when one is in it. Existing inside it is not the same as watching it on a screen. To not be able to hear oneself breathe, to not be able to hear oneself think. For there is no voiceover in this world. Thinking is different. It comes in text and pictures. It is a conversation with oneself laid out on a page. It is a nightmare. And there is something else in silence: The people's mouths move. They are clearly talking to one another, not reading lips. What is it? What is this nonauditory hearing in a silent world? Is it invisible waves? Or what? I do not know, but in it, I know when someone behind me is talking and I know what they're saying. That I cannot explain how I know makes it feel somehow sinister, as if the ideas of others are being transmitted into my head by some mysterious method involving Lovecraftian ritualized mouth movements. I cannot thwart or resist. The profound quiet makes me feel as if I exist in a void, like the world around me is unreal, like the truth is hiding from me. It makes me feel numb.

All of this is not helped by my size. Now a friendless giant Jew, it is almost impossible to hide from the people who are afraid of me, who despise me, who want me destroyed. It is pointless insisting you are not a Jew when you are fifty feet tall. It is an issue of secondary, or perhaps even tertiary, concern to others.

Still I move east toward the Unseen Unseen, for hope springs eternal. Along my journey, I consider what I will say to Ingo, who, in this world, seems to be my creator, which means I guess here I am a puppet. I have destroyed his film, his life's work, and I have still not been able to make full amends, to re-create it, even in my memory. So, while here, I must continue to search my memory for it. I must know it fully before throwing myself at Ingo's mercy. Alas, there is no Barassini in this place to assist me. Might there be an Unseen hypnotist here? Perhaps an African American? The Amazing Unseen-o? I search the Yellow Pages but find nothing at all listed between *hypnale snake dealers* and *hypodermic syringes*. A thought: Perhaps if I could extract the hypnale venom and inject it into myself with a hypodermic syringe, both readily available here, maybe that would bring some sort of altered state of consciousness—like a hypnotic or soporific drug might—and in this state, I might discover full access to the still-missing parts of Ingo's film. After some further thought, I jettison this idea as impractical. I'm not sure I could find a big-enough-gauge needle for my giant skin.

There is everything here but nothing. Food I cannot taste, sound

I cannot hear, wind I cannot feel. There is no color. There are apparently no hypnotists. If I prick myself here, do I not bleed? Yes, but it is not wet and I do not feel pain. The blood is black. I struggle to comprehend which is illusory, the painful world I've left behind or this one. But in the end, it does not matter, for I am in hiding here, eating tasteless trees as one would eat broccoli, squinting to see the distant entertainment that is the Seen world just to pass the frames, laughing without sound, joylessly, at the antics therein. From up here I can see that world spread out like a painting, the characters stretching through time, worms, waves, reaching into the haze of memory and into the panic that is prediction. The early days of Brainio barely visible in the far distance, if the day is not too cloudy.

On the road, I meet a woman, not my size, but a bit taller than average for here, I suppose, and fall in love. She is just up to that worrisome, changing mole on my left calf.

She leaves me within whatever the equivalent of a day is here, but not before telling me to get a dermatologist to look at it.

The woman I love here has left me for one of her own kind. I am too big for her, I realize, and she tells me this. It could never work. In addition, she says, the racial divide is too big to cross. I can still always see her, from this height. I can even swoop in like a crane shot and watch her in her new relationship, having sex, silently laughing, not thinking about me at all. But I don't do that very often. That would make me creepy.

Instead, I continue walking toward the stand of trees behind which Ingo lives. Ahead of me, an African American man draws a chalk line on the path. A chicken stares blankly at the line. I know what this gentleman is up to, of course. He is putting the chicken in a trance. My father did this type of work. As did filmmaker Werner Herzog to the hundreds of chickens in all of his films and also to his all-too-human cast in the much-maligned and brilliant and terrible *Heart of Glass*. I call silently down to the man by mouthing, "You there." He looks up.

"Yes?" he mouths.

"Can you hypnotize me as you have that chicken fellow?"

"I suppose. I'll need a bigger piece of chalk."

It's fortunate that I am currently wearing the slacks I was wearing when I was fired from Howie Sherman Zookeeper School. I bend down and hand him a piece of white chalk that is wider than his body.

"Now that's a piece of chalk," he marvels silently.

"I would like you to hypnotize me to remember a long-forgotten movie."

"I mostly do staring-at-a-line stuff," he mouths. "And weight loss."

"Please. It's important."

"I'll try," he shrugs.

So he drags his giant chalk across the ground, and I watch. It turns out to be effective, for I am falling deeper and deeper into some sort of magnificent trance.

"Now," he mouths, "remember that movie you want to remember."

And I do, at least some of it.

The meteorologist paces in his cave. He can find no joy. He can find no peace. The future holds no promise for him, and yet he must wait it out. I "hear" his voice (mouth?) over:

"I can find no solace in my exploration of the future. It is nothing but an unalterable slog toward my death and the deaths of everyone else. This machine I invented will be, in no uncertain terms, the death of me. Yet I am addicted to it. I switch it on in the morning and spend all day staring at its screen, searching for this and for that, looking at things to come. Perhaps it will be a happier pastime for me if I use it to look the other way, into the past, that which is gone, that which can no longer do me harm. Perhaps I'll indulge in a bit of harmless nostalgia; I might calm my soul the way the baby boomers will do with *Happy Days*. And I am not referring to the Beckett play, which is nobody's idea of soul calming, what with the being buried and the ant formication and Potsy."

So the meteorologist flips a switch causing the images onscreen to play in reverse, as his computer, frame by frame, predicts the past.

A New York City street scene. In it, pedestrians walk backward, the streets filled with backward-moving cars. The meteorologist is about to direct his search to some scene from his own childhood, to find a pleasurable memory or two, to find some solace, when he notices something odd. There are "entities" moving *forward* through this environment. Vague, amorphous blobs, almost like eye floaters, appear to be finding the external auditory meatuses, or ear holes, of these backward pedestrians and entering them, emerging moments later (or rather, earlier!) in what seems to be greater abundance, presumably having multiplied inside these people's heads. These images are terrifying, Lovecraftian, to coin a term, and the meteorologist, with a fair amount of trepidation, zooms in for a closer look. Magnified greatly, the blobs are vaguely bullet-shaped. I presume this is an evolutionary (devolutionary?) development to allow for easier meatus insertion. They are transparent, these nightmarish droplets, and there does seem to be something akin to "food" moving through their seemingly primitive, transparent digestive systems.

"Time's up for today," mouths the tiny hypnotist.

I snap out of it.

"You were able to record it?" I ask.

He turns on his reel-to-reel recorder and we both "listen" to the silence as it plays back my narration word by word. I nod.

He puts his chicken in its carrying case and turns to leave.

"Same time tomorrow?" I mouth after him.

"Sure," he mouths, without looking back.

Now I'm alone again, in the woods, with my giant piece of chalk (not giant to me) and feeling homesick. Things are different here, foreign, quiet. I barely recognize myself. I barely recognize my life. It is me, of course. Of that there is little doubt. But who am I? What seems to be missing is that constant infusion of jokes at my expense, as I now understand them to have been. Nasty, hurtful jokes. They are gone. And I am left with a dullness. As ridiculous and as humiliating as they were, these jokes were at least something. The hole of their absence has been filled with nothing. I am painfully aware of the space those thoughts took up and the time they forced me to waste. It is time that might have been put to better use, studying even more physics or French or history or the oboe. But it wasn't, and that time is no longer available. I see my own time worm as well from here, and it is nearing its terminus.

Now it is morning. Nothing has happened, nothing much thought in this dim world. The African American hypnotist emerges from the woods with his chicken and tape recorder.

"Ready?" he mouths.

I nod. The quicker I can get this entire film remembered, the quicker I can go to Ingo and ask for help, for forgiveness.

He unpacks the chicken, picks up my chalk, and draws a line. The chicken and I both stare at it, both become transfixed.

"Tell me," he mouths.

The chicken says nothing, but I begin:

The meteorologist, unable to face this monstrous multiplying ear-droplet discovery in reversed time, hastily returns to his future studies, the steady trudge to doom, his and the world's. Now he is watching the entire world on fire. He wanders through the virtual version of the aftermath. The computer simulation has become ever more advanced. Now a holograph he can enter, it has become so sophisticated that the virtual smoke makes him cough and stings his eyes. He wonders what's happened to cause this catastrophe but doesn't have the patience to sift through all the data to research it. "Doesn't really matter anyway," he thinks in voiceover. "I can't change anything." The notion of reasons has become silly, incomprehensible. He is just biding his time, passing it until his death by green car. He is just entertaining himself. The charred landscape he now finds himself in is inhospitable, but small bands of survivors exist. He eavesdrops as a group of ragged people sits around a campfire.

"I've heard they have lasers in their eyes," says a wizened woman wearing a burnt oilcloth coat.

"Can anyone confirm that?" asks another.

"Yeah," says a teenage boy. "I saw one of them set fire to a pig. With its eyes. Just to see it die."

"Shit," says the second woman. "How do we fight eye lasers?"

"They're fireproof, too, and water resistant to 100 meters, I've heard," says the oilcloth woman.

A thirtyish-year-old woman with stringy hair and dressed in stained overalls drags a moping toddler to the fire. The little girl carries a stick, with which she smacks things as they pass: rocks, old car tires, broken TVs. The meteorologist stares at the girl. His ever-present mumbled voiceover comes into focus.

"That child! What is it about her? A light in the otherwise black void of my existence. Of future existence. Of all existence. Is it perhaps the biologically programmed response adults have to children? I don't know. I have seen many children in my time. Literally dozens, but this small human seems to embody something extraordinary, a certain *je ne sais quoi*."

The presumed mother sits the girl down next to her in front of the fire and proceeds to join in the group discussion, but the meteorologist focuses all his attention on the girl, who fidgets, sings to herself, pokes more things with her stick, then uses it to dig a hole in the charred ground.

"Stop it," her mother says.

And she does, for a bit. Soon, she's fidgeting again, then clapping. Her mother once more tells her to stop; it's distracting. Grown-ups are trying to talk about something important. The little girl stops, and the group continues its discussion, but after a bit, she begins to dig again. The meteorologist has an idea. He steps out of the holographic projection and back to the console, types in something, receives a printout.

Iris out and iris in.

In his cave, the meteorologist switches on the holographic projection once again and steps back into it. It is set to the same scene. The survivors are around the fire. The toddler claps. Her mother tells her to stop. She does, and after a bit, she begins to dig with her stick. This time the stick hits something hard, metal. The girl bangs against it like a drum. Her mother tells her to shush. She shushes and quietly digs around the metal until it is unearthed, pulls a metal box from the hole. Now all those around the campfire are watching. The girl struggles with the latch.

"Careful!" says the mother, who takes the box, shakes it gently, hears something rattle, places it on the ground, gingerly unlatches it, and lifts the lid. Everyone around the fire, with the exception of the toddler, seems anxious.

Inside the box is a doll swathed in plastic. The mother unwraps it. It's a beautiful little girl doll in a bright red dress, the only bit of color in this otherwise gray-brown landscape. It is reminiscent of the little girl scene in *Schindler's List*, a mawkish paean to human indomitability in Holocaust drag by Steve Spielman. Everyone looks at the doll in silent awe.

"Mine," says the little girl.

"Finders keepers," agrees the mother as she hands the baby doll to her daughter, who hugs it to her chest and smiles.

The meteorologist smiles, too, as he knew he would, as he knows he must. But still to him it feels genuine.

And from then on he has purpose, or thinks he does. He watches all the virtual versions of what he's going to bury for her and then buys those things, finds those locations, and buries those things, because he has to, because he will, because he wants to.

THE UNSEEN IS not seen by the Seen, but it is known. It is passed through. The Unseen is the place that protects the Unseen Unseen from the Seen. It is the rotten fence that secretes the magnificent estate beyond. There is nothing to see here, folks. There is nothing to pillage. But the Unseen Unseen is, I believe, beautiful and has been made so by Ingo, because he can make it however he wants. And he is here, at least the puppet of Ingo is—the now perfectly proportioned puppet of Ingo, the socially accepted Ingo, the chatty Ingo with no stammer. The Ingo who is all colors and no colors. The Ingo who lives here with Lucy Chalmers in a perfectly constructed love. In a place without fear. In silence.

And now suddenly I am here. How have I arrived here in this

Unseen Unseen? The last thing I recall, I was being hypnotized alongside a chicken. I need to remember the film fully before I come here. My offering is not ready. I should not be here yet. Perhaps I have been brought here to protect the Unseen Unseen from the Unseen, from the Seen, from the Seen Seen. Is there a Seen Seen? What would that be? Am I to be the terrible giant who wanders this lush garden? I am not ready to meet Ingo. The film is not fully re-membered. I can't be here yet. Am I to be Ingo's version of Méliès's monster of the North Pole: a giant, blepharospastically blinking, bearded puppet, here to sweep the unwelcome Unseen into my maw as they comically cross themselves in terror? Am I here to be the butt of even more jokes? Well, I will not allow it. I will not. As I turn to leave, to search for a way out of the Unseen Unseen and back to the Unseen, I espy, once again, Oleara Debord in the distance. She is my North Star and I make my way toward her.

"Fucking fuck. You fucking little bastard. You sheeny kike little fucker. Do what I tell you to!" comes a voice, silently, because all is silent here, as I have already silently said, but I hear it just the same. And I stop, because it is familiar to me, this utterance. I have heard it before. But where? I stand in silence in the silence, unable to re-call. It is yet one more thing I am unable to recall.

So I walk.

"FUCK YOU, HEBREW!" screams the silent voice.

I stop, look, and listen, as did the great American animator Len Janson in the stop-motion pixilation masterpiece of the same name. More silent voice: "Fuck you, Hebrew." It is, I assume, directed at me, for there is no other "Hebrew" present. Even here in this veri-table Garden of Eden, even now, at this point in my life, after all my tribulations, I am subject to such abuse. Well, I will not stand here and take it. I continue on my way toward freedom, or at least to not-here. Is any of this real? I wonder. Or am I now, in some clichéd close-up, revealed, as the camera slowly pulls out, to be in a padded room, and as the camera pulls out even farther, now through the peephole in my padded door, it is revealed that Ingo is a white-suited attendant at a mental institution? Is it that tired ending? I hate that ending, born of laziness on the part of the writer, of lack of commitment to the honest surreality of the concept. It is a concept likely to be found in a Charlie Kaufman movie, if one has the intestinal fortitude to be able to sit through one till the end. It's all in the mind of a crazy person, you see, it turns out. It is all a dream. *Et chetera*. It is the four thousandth iteration of Walter Mitty, which was already moth-eaten when Jimmy Thurber penned it. No. This will not be that. This is not craziness. That is not how the mentally ill see the world. The mentally ill are the most maligned and mocked of all minorities, and I will not allow myself to be used in the perpetuation of that disrespectful garbage. I will defend my position on this to the death, even as I remain hopelessly lost in this place. I miss Tsai. I miss the certainty of the rightness of that amazing dynamic. I once thought I was over her, but I see now that was cockiness on my part. I long to sleep in her sock drawer, nestled among her magnificent foot tubes. I am over nothing.

And now there is the padded door. As predicted. And I am on one side of it, the wrong side of it. The peephole is for those on the other side. I attempt to look through it anyway, and the world on the other side is a thousand miles away. Still, there is a figure, a tiny figure. I cannot make it out.

"Oh, it's you," it says.

I try the door, expecting it to be locked, but it is not. I open it to discover a female African American puppet there. You would not know who she is. She is not famous, but she is beautiful just the same.

"I want to get back to the Seen," I mouth to her.

"You can't get back to anything," she tells me. "You can only go forward."

"That is wise," I say. "I hope you are not an example of the offensive Magical Negro, because I will not allow myself to be used in the perpetuation of that reductionist, dismissive cinematic trope."

"I'm no magical anything, friend. I'm just an orderly here. Sure, maybe I possess some hard-earned wisdom because of the trouble I've seen, which nobody knows, but I'm just here to help."

"You do understand that is the very definition of the Magical Negro, yes?"

"I understand you've got to get out of there. This is no place for you. They'll destroy you here. You're not strong enough to make it in the Unseen, not the way I and my people are, due to our hard-earned wisdom and faith in the Almighty."

"I mean, OK, thanks, I'll go. But how?"

"Make love to Oleara Debord. You are large enough in this miniature world to do so. Love, true love, is the only thing that matters. If you are able to love her, to please her, she will bring you back. Love is the key to all things."

I have always loved Oleara, as have all men and many women and many trans people of all varieties and proportions, so making love to her would be a dream come true.

"OK, I'll try. How can I ever thank you for all you've taught me?"

"Just go. Your freedom is all the thanks I need."

I hug her and run off. I will never forget that wonderful mental hospital attendant!

Finding myself at her massive base, I approach Oleara Debord as one does a potential lover: gently and with great respect, all the while practicing the series of questions of consent that must precede any eventual lovemaking session. For like everything in the universe that is not nothing, Oleara Debord is sentient, and although her life cycle is perhaps too slow for those of us in the animal and stop-motion communities to witness, that does not make her less than us. "Ephemerality is not an indication of superiority" is the slogan one sees on the placards at their marches, which are tediously slow. Of course this is true. If it were the case, humans would have to accept fruit flies as their betters. They are our equals. Oleara, born of the collision of tectonic plates, of the eruption of magma, of magnificent friction, one and a half billion years ago, stands proud and erect, watching over this nation, an ever vigilant sentry. I once again approach her, not as an explorer this time, not as a person seeking answers, but as one who woos. A wooer. One does not seek answers in love; one seeks communion. The only answer in communion is "yes," for communion can never be interrogative. It is always and forever an act of faith, a complete acceptance of the other. An opening to him (her, thon), an abandonment of ego, a merging of selves. Questions are by definition rational, distancing, offensive, the opposite of love. And so, my list of consensual romantic engagement questions in hand, I address Oleara.

"Hi," I say.

"Hello."

"You are lovely. May I kiss you?"

"You may," she says.

I kiss her, and it is a cornucopia of sensations.

"May I caress you?" I ask.

"You may."

I caress her, and although she is made of granite, I feel her tremble.

"May I penetrate you?" I ask.

"You may," she says.

And I do, my engorged member finding a nearby cave entrance. I hope it is the correct one. The fit is perfect and I feel as if we were made to be together like this. It's true that the entrance is rock and it is extremely dry and this causes abrading on my penis, but the moment of congress has begun and nature propels me forward regardless. I will deal with the repercussions after; I have penis bandages in my satchel. I thrust, I caress, I moan. I descend into a state of oneness with this beautiful mountain. It is no longer B. and Oleara. It is Boleara, curiously, the first-person subjunctive form of *bolear*, which in Spanish means, of course, to shine. And shine I do, my light into her darkness. The eternal masculine and feminine, yin and yang, both necessary for wholeness, although yin and yin and yang and yang can form perfect unions as well. And with this very thought, I ejaculate mightily into Oleara's cave, my spunk spelunking deep within her. It is a force of nature, and with it, I find myself propelled into the coming brightness, desperate to continue on my path, to return to the world of the Seen. The disorganization of this other world without God has been too much to bear (I must tell Dawkins!). It is a world without narrative. Although I have long been an atheist, I must admit, as a child, I loved Hanna-Barbera's animated series *Willibald and Winibald*, an ode to the saintliness of two selfless sibling saints with identically beatific demeanors who fought crime (sin). Their run-ins with their sister Saint Walpurga were classics of charming dysfunctional family comedy: "Mom! Walpurga's hogging the bathroom again!" It was all so comforting to those of us of the late baby boom. But the disarray of this world, the incomprehensible motives and results, the tangled threads, dead ends, the trillion meaningless details to trudge through at each moment have been a waking nightmare. I must push forward through this light to find my way back to the analyzable, the world of causality, the world designed for humans, with street signs and social mores, where the good win and the bad lose, in theory, at least on occasion, at least in movies. The path down a mountain is simple. One must simply desire it, it seems, and then plummet. But the path back up requires immense reserves of fortitude and perseverance. Even then it is not guaranteed. Gravity is only your friend in the other direction. But I watch the Seen world from here, and although I can no longer follow the concepts, the story line, the character motivations, I see images, now fractured and confused and shifting, as if I am witness to the dream of another, someone whose life I do not know, whose motivations I cannot comprehend. And in these fragments I have seen myself! I have been replaced, I discover. Of this I am certain. I can tell his story is comical because from here I can hear strains of a musical accompaniment. There is a xylophone. There is a trumpet with plunger mute. There is the inevitable tuba. I recognize these as the comical orchestral instruments, but I can no longer understand the jokes. The story is distorted by distance and fragmentation. But I have been replaced, this much I know. My descent has been without consequence to the world. The show continues. The trombone does its humorous thing. I must return and reclaim my part in this. It is not fair. The mountain analogy goes only so far. It is a climb but not vertical. Rather, it is a tunnel with a bright light at the end, the light an oncoming locomotive. It is a jungle laden with unruly vines and screaming monkeys. It is a room with no doors from which one is both trying to get in and out. It is the party to which one has not been invited. It is a forever skipping record. It is trying to understand my life. It is the wind and I am a leaf smashing futilely against the interior of its wind tunnel prison. It is a woman who won't love me, no matter how much I change. It is the hopelessness of a bad diagnosis. It is fire. It is flood. It never gets closer. It is my broken heart, my shame, it is how I measure up. It is first this direction, then that one. It is my face in the mirror in unfortunate lighting. It is what it is not. But I move toward it, and when it is elusive, I walk anyway. I walk, I swim, I climb, I crawl for years, decades, eons, forever. And still I get no closer. And then I do. I sense that it is getting bigger, that it fills more of my field of vision. It is a subtle difference. It is the difference of Proxima Centauri as compared to Alpha Centauri A. But it is progress, and in this progress exists a whiff of narrative. Of reason. Of hope. So I continue. For more eons. Through sucking, waist-high mud, through nothing, through biblical plagues, through the eye of a needle, through the mouth of madness, through alien landscapes, through sewer tunnels . . . Then it is there above me: an open manhole. I climb the ladder, suddenly oddly hesitant. Is this what I want? Can this world support two of me? Will I simply disintegrate as I step into it? A return to the Unseen would be simple. I can look back and see it from here. It is one simple step off a precipice. Instantaneous.

But I look toward the sky and climb.

CHAPTER 58

THE SEEN WORLD has changed. My replacement is famous. I see my face on the sides of buses. On billboards. Posters in bookstore windows. I have apparently already written my book about Ingo's movie. It is published. It is an international sensation. The book is called *Recovery*, a play on words, I'm assuming, alluding to my reconstructing the lost film from memory and how this process somehow saved me. It is certainly not what I would have called the book. It's a terrible title. There is a photo of me on the cover. It is the same photo on the billboards and buses. In it, I wear a yarmulke. It is a terrible cover. Why am I in a yarmulke? I am not Jewish. I feel the crown of my head. No yarmulke. See? Is this why no one is recognizing me now? After all, I appear to be a celebrity here. Perhaps I should purchase a yarmulke at Walgreens. Then I catch my reflection in the bookstore window. I am filthy, my beard matted, my lenses cracked, as in that iconic image from the classic Eisentstein film *Pachinko*. I do not possess the self-satisfied countenance of my Chosen Person doppelgänger. I must find a place to bathe. I must find clean clothing. I must purchase or lease a yarmulke. But first I must see the book.

I enter the bookstore to hostile stares, another homeless person trying to get relief from the elements. Homeless people are unseen until they insinuate themselves into an unwelcoming environment. Then, boy, are they seen. I look at the bestseller display shelf. *Recovery* is not there. There's a place for it, but the shelf is empty. I approach the cashier. She looks up, quickly masking her disdain.

"Yes?"

"I'm looking for *Recovery*."

"I bet you are," she says before she can stop herself.

"The book."

"Sold out."

"Really?"

"No, I'm lying."

"Really?"

"Of course I'm not lying. Why would I lie? What is wrong with you? It's sold out all over the city. Everyone knows that."

"Oh."

"Is there anything else I can help you with, *sir*?"

Her "sir" stabs me like a knife.

I shake my head and leave. I can't get the book. Is that a coincidence or part of some labyrinthine plot? No matter. I've come this far. I will keep coming. My next step is to get clean. After all this time, I still have the massive ring of keys to my apartment in my pocket. If Dominick is not there, maybe I can sneak in, shower, and grab some clothes. Then maybe contact Barassini and continue work on the true version of the film.

The keys still work. Dominick is not home, but all of my things are gone. Has Dominick thrown out my possessions? I would not put it past that fetid behemoth. Even my sleeping chair is gone, replaced by a massive hammock tied between two newly installed I-beams. I barely recognize my home. At least the shower is still here, although the hot and cold knobs have been moved to four inches above my head, I assume to allow the malodorous mammoth easy access. After all, it is unlikely he can bend even slightly at that weight to start the water. Maybe this is why he smelled. Perhaps now he is a lemon-scented leviathan. I don't intend to find out. I reach up and turn on the shower. It feels good but no time to luxuriate. I shampoo my beard as quickly as I can with a product called Big Man Shampoo and hurry out of there. Dominick has his clothes specially made by a fumigation tent company. I can't even cinch them with any of his belts because the belts are wider than my entire body length. I do find one of his wristwatch bands that fits snugly around my waist. It is not a good look, but the clothes are clean, and it's the best I can do. I stuff a pair of his shoes with all the balled-up socks in his drawers and that helps.

By standing on a stepladder, I am able to study myself in the bathroom mirror. With the striped fumigation outfit and giant shoes I look like a clown. Maybe there's something of value to mine here. America loves a clown. Well, not entirely, but more so than a Jewish-looking man walking around in a clown suit. Applying white makeup might put the man or woman or nonbinary on the street at ease and at the same time allow me access to my replacement without drawing attention to our physical similarities and thus alarming people. I find Dominick's giant tub of white pancake that he uses for his Fatty Arbuckle gig and apply it liberally to my face, then use his black grease pencil to draw on innocent Harry Langdon eyebrows. No one could feel threatened by me now.

On the street, the children point at me and laugh with glee. It feels good bringing some joy to this cruel, stupid, ugly world. I wave and smile at them. If only I had toy balloons. Children adore toy balloons, I am told. And I cannot say I blame them one bit. They are colorful and buoyant. Balloons, not children. When I was a young child, the pride of possession I felt with a toy balloon tied by a string to my wrist was unparalleled. I shall look for a package of toy balloons and a helium tank later. I will have to steal both, as I have not a cent to my name. It will be worth the risk to bring that kind of joy to the face of a child, and not just his face (or hers or thon's), but also to his entire body, or hers or otherwise, if they are nonbinary. Lost in thought, I nearly walk right past the crowd of people congregated outside the Actors' Temple, but I do glance over in time to see as people burst into applause when the door opens and my doppelgänger emerges. I duck behind a trash can. Cameras flash. He stops, waves, and addresses the crowd:

"As a highly observant Jew, I do not consider it 'kosher' to address my fan base outside a house of worship from which I have just emerged after my morning prayers, or shacharit, which I do on a daily basis. I am, above all else, a Jew. But if HaShem, in his infinite wisdom, has seen fit to bless me with work that brings comfort to many, then perhaps there is something just a little holy about it and it is therefore not entirely untoward to accept your appreciation outside this House of G-d. Never in it, of course, but outside, why not? I feel grateful and humbled to have been granted the opportunity to be the voice of Ingo Cutbirth, who, G-d rest his soul, died one year ago today."

A year? But I have been in hell for eons.

"In any event, once again, thank you for your kindnesses to me. I am off to attend a United Nations conference on crises in international cinema now, but, as many of you may already know, I will be delivering a free lecture tonight on the Cutbirth film at the 92nd Street Y. There will be a question-and-answer period after, at which time the floor will be open to anyone—and I mean *anyone*—who wishes to question me about the film. Perhaps this lecture will be a more opportune time for dialogue. Again, thank you all for your specific interest in the work of Ingo Cutbirth and in cinema in general. Goodbye and good luck."

I follow, at an inconspicuous distance, as my doppelgänger makes his way east on foot toward the United Nations, along with what appears to be a youngish female assistant. I am fortunate that the New York Clown and Acrobat High School has just let out and a small coterie of student clowns in full training gear are walking east on 47th. I am able to join them and avoid any suspicion. I watch his yarmulke bob up and down in concert with each of his loping steps. What is with that gait? I do not lope. If he is doing me, shouldn't he walk as I walk? But the yarmulke isn't me, either, I consider. He is not doing me. There have been subtle and perhaps less subtle changes made in my replacement.

The student clowns jabber about some seminar on confetti buckets given by a Mr. the Eccentric in C Block. It is difficult to concentrate. One would assume all there is to it is to toss a damn bucket of confetti out into an audience. But not at the hands of Mr. the Eccentric. It is maddening. My doppelgänger stops in at Knishioner Gordon, a superhero-themed Jewish deli well-known for catering rich child bar mitzvahs and bat mitzvahs (and more recently thon mitzvahs). The student clowns continue past, and I am left exposed outside the restaurant. I crouch behind another garbage can, from which I have a decent view through the plate glass window of the eatery. He is at the counter ordering. The assistant's hand rests on the small of his back. This is no assistant. I study her. She is pretty in the way some Jewish women can be, with a kind of earthy, no-nonsense bossiness. It's not for everyone, but I like it. I like to be bossed. I have had more than one Jewish woman in my life. Two to be precise. They do not perform oral sex, but I guess that is common knowledge. And quite frankly, if I am to have oral sex performed on me, I would prefer a man to perform it because men understand the issues and potential pleasures at hand (or mouth) in a way women cannot. This is not to say that I have ever received oral sex from a man; it is simply a theory, as well as what I have heard tell. Nor would I want to. That type of thing is not for me. Maybe a trans woman.

"Me" and his "assistant" step back onto the street, both eating from cardboard containers, his labeled Chicken Souperman, hers, Arm Falafel Boy (a pathetic play on the name of the criminally underutilized DC character Arm-Fall-Off-Boy, whose detachable arms he uses as bludgeons. Of course they'll never make a movie of that because it's too real).

I watch these two boors slurp and scoff their novelty food items, stopping to pose for photographs with dozens of passersby. Eventually, the assistant points to her wrist on which there is no watch, but he understands and excuses himself. Some in the dispersing crowd ask if they can take pictures with me, but I push through, my focus on the imposter ahead.

The UN will not let me into the conference, even though I am the credentialed one. Even though I have been opining in print on the crisis in international cinema since 1975 when I self-published my "zine" *Crises in International Cinema*. I sit outside and watch the usual suspects file in: Richard Roeper, Mark Kermode, Claudia Puig, Stephen Holden, Paul Wunder WBAI, Adam Driver, Nicki

Minaj, Howard Stern—the who's who of international cinema crisis. And now I've been asked to join them, or at least some bizarre facsimile of me has. Or should I say fac-semitic-le? This is a very good joke and I will find somewhere to use it soon. Perhaps in my Arm-Fall-Off-Boy spec script.

While I wait, looking up at the United Nations building, thinking about its founding, the terrible war that brought about its mission, I suddenly recall Mutt and Mahle, smuggled into the United States, secreted away by American Nazi George Lincoln Rockwell in a cave inside of Oleara Debord with their similarly smuggled Rosenberg lip segment, as well as Hans Spemann's cloning apparatus and incubators. Here they will grow hundreds of Rosenbergen in preparation for Rockwell's planned takeover of the United States of America, which he plans to call Georgenited Lincolnates of Rockerica. Rockwell is a bit disheartened that this new country name sounds like something from *The Flintstones*, a popular children's animated caveman show, but he has to work with what he has.

LATER AT THE 92nd Street Y, I sit in the crowded auditorium. There is a palpable excitement among the audience, many of whom are African American. The house lights dim; the stage lights come up. He enters, stage right, loping to the lectern. He wears tight gold leather pants and a black turtleneck up to his chin. And a yarmulke, a different one, a gold leather one. Or leatherette. I can't tell from here. His beard has been combed and plaited. There seems to be an aura around him, like a divine halo. It might simply be a trick of the stage lighting. The audience is hushed, waiting, in love. He opens with a joke.

"I'm sorry I was a little bit late getting out here, but I was backstage weeping for humanity."

He smiles benignly. It's cloying, embarrassing. The audience laughs and bursts into applause. This is the only way I know it was a joke. It must be some reference to the book, which I have still not been able to find. Then he begins:

"Please indulge me as I reminisce about the Ingo Cutbirth I knew, my experience of his film, and my efforts to create as accurate a reproduction of it as I can. It is fair to say that the combination of these three experiences renewed both my faith in HaShem and in my fellow human beings. I was, directly before my chance meeting with Ingo, in a very difficult place. My marriage was falling apart, my career as a film critic and historian of cinema had stalled. My adult son had revealed himself to have a plethora of psychosexual issues. HaShem knows I loved him no less because of them. I was facing all this alone because I did not know my G-d. When I look back at the experience of finding Ingo, it does feel as if HaShem was leading me through the wilderness to him. If I am to be perfectly honest, I was, at the time, considering ending my life."

"No!" shouts someone from the audience.

"Don't do it!" shouts another.

"We love you!" shouts a third, right into my ear.

My doppelgänger stops to acknowledge the audience with another benign smile. Then continues:

"This act would have meant giving in to my internal struggle against the brightness. But I was desperate to return to this brightness, desperate to return to the world of the seen. The disorganization of the other world had been too much to bear. It is a world without narrative, without G-d. And the disarray, the incomprehensible motives and results, the tangled threads, dead ends, the trillion meaningless details to trudge through at each moment had been a waking nightmare. I must find my way back to the analyzable, I decided, the world of causality, the world designed by G-d for humans. And deep down I knew that ending my life would have been a grave sin and would have kept me from meeting the man who would come to change my life in so many profoundly positive ways. So . . . There came a night that I was behind the closed door of my apartment in St. Augustine when I was weeping for—"

"Humanity!" the audience chimes in unison.

"Yes, humanity. Ha. Indeed. From my place of no faith, I looked out at all the troubles in the world: the greed and avarice, the despair, the vile destruction of our mother, the Earth, the inability of men and women to properly love and, more importantly, respect each other, and I saw no possible solution to the situation. And so I wept. And my tears were bitter on my tongue as well as in my heart. And I felt alone. And I felt hopeless. And I had a bottle of pills in my hand, ready, when there was a knock at the door. It was—how do I say it?—the most gentle of knocks."

The audience awwws.

"The knock of an angel of G-d."

He demonstrates gentle rapping on the lectern. There are more awwws from the audience. Loud ones. One right in my ear.

"This knock, this angel knock, made me . . . Well, I must admit, it made me furious. Someone is here to complain about the noise I am making! Isn't this just the way things go with these horrible humans! And, my blood boiling, I stomped my way to the door, like an angry toddler, if you must know. An angry old man toddler."

The audience chuckles in recognition.

"I've been there!" several acknowledge.

"And I opened the door, ready to give this monster a piece of my mind. But there stood Ingo Cutbirth and my anger dissolved. Because . . . because . . . because he was beautiful. And it was stunning. Here was this old, old man. An African American man, no less! Giant but hunched over, his hands knobby with arthritis, his eyes cast with cataracts. Giant but frail. Each breath seemed terribly labored. 'Hello,' he said. 'I'm so sorry to interrupt your evening, but I have something I'd like to show you.'

"Had he heard me weeping? If he had, he didn't tell me. 'I really don't have the time right now,' I said. 'I think you might want to see this,' he said. 'No. Thank you,' I said, with mounting anger. 'I've made this for you,' he said. 'I've been on a very long journey to bring this gift to you.' And I sighed to indicate to him my annoyance, then said, 'Fine. Let's get it over with.' He then led me to his apartment, which was directly across the hall from mine. Inside it was crammed from floor to ceiling with boxes. A small space had been cleared, and there stood the now-famous film projector behind the now-famous hard-backed chair facing the now-famous portable movie screen. Sit, he said. And I did, somehow compelled. He turned on the ancient projector, the screen filled with light, and so began my three-month journey through Ingo Cutbirth's magnificent, holy mind. Of course, there's no need to describe the film to you. I'm fairly certain, if you're here tonight, you've read the book—"

"More than once!" someone shouts to much laughter and applause.

"I will, however, talk about the themes, about what Ingo was trying to tell me, and by extension what he was trying to tell you through me. First and foremost, Ingo's magnum opus is a miracle of human ingenuity and love and, as such, models both in a perfect g-dly light. But what is the film exploring? Through its technique—which as you know is called stop-motion animation or Claymation—Cutbirth studies the passage of time and, for lack of better terminology, divine intervention. How does he achieve this? Well, each tiny movement of each character in this massive work is determined by Ingo, is performed by Ingo, yet appears to the viewer as the free will of the character. And by showing this world of poverty and oppression, of valor and heroism, in such minute, perfect detail, giving dignity to those among us who are so deserving of our compassion and respect, but are, more often than not, invisible in the world, he shines a light on our common humanity. There has never been such a profoundly serious film about the downtrodden. It is essential to realize that there is not a single joke in this film, a single frame of levity, a single laugh. This movie is three months of unrelenting torture. But we need that, don't we?"

"Divine torture!" the audience cheers.

"We need our eyes opened. We must experience the suffering of the poor, the mentally ill, the criminal, the 'disposable' people we warehouse in prisons and ghettoes and mental institutions, the people who live hidden from us under tarpaulins, under bridges, the immigrants, all peoples of color, the disenfranchised, the gender-confused, the dwarves, the disabled, the blind, the deaf . . . Did I say dwarves?"

"Dwarves! Dwarves! Dwarves!" the audience chants as one.

"In short, the people we as a society turn our backs on. These are the people portrayed in this movie. They are for once given center stage. It is their story. We hear tell, in the film, of the privileged, the healthy, the white, but we see them only as weather, as the whirlwind of violent oppression that they are. . . ."

CHAPTER 59

A ND SO IT goes. He lies and lies and lies about the film for well over an hour. Clearly, he has not seen it. He has made up a film that is by definition antithetical to Ingo's concept, antithetical to Ingo's artistic mission. I have been thrust into a waking nightmare, but I hold my tongue until the question-and-answer period. After a series of softball questions and inane answers, after my constantly raised hand is ignored again and again and again, the yarmulked doppelgänger finally calls on me.

"Yes, you, the clown in the fourth row."

"Which one of us is the clown here?" I say cuttingly.

"You are," he says, clearly confused by my question.

"Be that as it may," I say, "I have a bone to pick with you."

"Please," he says, smiling, "have at it."

"You lie," I say.

"About what, my funny friend?"

"What you describe is not Ingo's movie."

"And you know this how?"

"Because I have seen it."

At this, the audience boos me. But the man onstage remains calm, smiles benevolently, holds his hands up to quiet the crowd.

"No one but I has seen this movie," he says.

"I am you," I say.

More booing.

"Are you?" he says, chuckling kindly.

I dramatically attempt to smudge my makeup off to reveal my face underneath, but I can't tell if I've been successful, as I lost my hand mirror in the sewer. I turn to the woman sitting next to me.

"Is it off?" I ask her.

"Just smudged!" she screams, her eyes filled with hatred.

"Why not come up onto the stage, friend?" the doppelgänger offers. "We can debate the issue. Would you like that?" he asks the audience.

It is clear from his tone that the correct answer is yes.

"Yes! Yes!" they say. At which point, I am lifted off the floor and passed from one to the other to the stage, where I am unceremoniously dumped.

"Hello," the doppelgänger says, helping me to my feet. Then he calls offstage: "Can we get another lectern and microphone for my antipodal friend here, please?"

Two stagehands appear immediately stage right dragging a miked lectern. It happens so fast that it crosses my mind he was expecting me. The doppelgänger gently leads me to my lectern, then returns to his own.

"So," he says, "tell me how you saw our Ingo's film?"

Words are failing me. I am confused and emotional. I look out at the crowd and see that they are, to a person, against me. I am reviled.

"I, well, I . . ." I begin. "I am the real you and I saw the film. You are my replacement. You did not see the film. You have been programmed by cosmic forces to believe that you have."

"I see," he says. "Quite mysterious!"

The audience laughs.

"Now, now," he says to them. "Let's give our friend here the opportunity to speak. The world is big enough for many different interpretations of reality. If we have learned anything from Ingo's work, it is to treat the mentally ill with compassion and respect. But," he adds, "I am in no way suggesting that our colorfully painted counterpart is mentally ill. Please, continue," he says to me.

"Ingo understood that one cannot make a movie about the Unseen without flying in the face of their very . . . unseenness. He knew the only way to show the truth of the societally Unseen is not to show them."

"So his movie about the Unseen shows nothing of their plight?"

"It only shows white people, and it is in the form of a relentless and distracting comedy. The disenfranchised remain off-screen."

"So like every other movie," he jokes.

The audience howls with laughter, then chases the laughter with a round of applause, then foot stomping. It is almost frightening.

"No," I say. "Ingo animated the Unseen. He just did not film it. He only remembered it. Their stories went to the grave with Ingo."

"I see," he says.

"You don't see!" I snap back. "That is the very point."

This was witty, and I look out at the audience, hoping for some acknowledgment of my barb. Applause. Foot stomping. There is nothing. But the man onstage with me tosses me a crumb:

"Touché," he says.

Encouraged by this small kindness I continue:

"I'm the one who built his memorial in St. Augustine."

"You mean this?" he says, clicking a remote in his hand, which projects a photo of Ingo's memorial. It's hard to get a clear sense of it because there is such a large crowd of tourists and pilgrims milling about, but I can see that, although it is the same plot of land I chose, the memorial is completely different. This one features life-size stone carvings of all types of unfortunate and unseen people, the very people the true Ingo, my Ingo, would have been horrified to see represented in stone. It is the bad version of the Vietnam memorial. My doppelgänger is Frederick Hart to my Maya Lin. Mmm. Maya Lin.

"That is not my memorial to Ingo," I say.

"No, it is mine."

"But you do not exist," I whine.

"My friend," he says, "I have not questioned your existence. I have been respectful and welcoming. I have invited you up onto the stage during an evening that is quite a special event to this audience and to myself. I would ask that you show me the same courtesy."

The audience boos me. Someone throws a tomato that hits me in the chest. Why do they have tomatoes, if I wasn't expected? A rock bounces off my forehead. Why do they have rocks?

"Please," my doppelgänger says to the crowd. "We are not a violent people."

"Sorry!" comes an angry, hysterical, apologetic voice from the crowd.

"Now, my friends, I have a special treat, a surprise, if you will," says my doppelgänger. "A first look at my coming Netflix series, the frame-by-frame re-creation of Ingo's lost masterpiece."

"Frame by frame?" I say.

"Why, yes," says my doppelgänger.

"First of all, that is impossible, even if you ever actually saw the film."

"It is not. I have an eidetic memory."

"Eidetic memory is a myth. It does not exist."

"Is that so? You said: Ingo understood that one cannot make a movie about the Unseen without flying in the face of their very . . . unseenness. He knew the only way to show the truth of the societally Unseen is not to show them. I said: So his movie about the Unseen shows nothing of their plight? You said: It only shows white people, and it is in the form of a relentless and distracting comedy. The disenfranchised remain off-screen. I said: So like every other movie. This is when the audience laughed, then applauded, then stomped their feet. You said: No. Ingo animated the Unseen. He just did not film it. He only remembered it. Their stories went to the grave with Ingo. I said: I see. You said: You don't see. That is the very point. I said: Touché. You said: I'm the one who built his memorial in St. Augustine. I said: You mean this? Here I clicked a plastic remote in my hand, which projected a photo of Ingo's memorial. You said: That is not my memorial to Ingo. I said: No, it is mine. You whined: But you do not exist. I said: My friend, I have not questioned your existence. I have been respectful and welcoming. I have invited you up onto the stage during an evening that is quite a special event to this audience and to myself. I would ask that you show me the same courtesy. Here the audience booed you. Someone threw a tomato that hit you in the chest. A rock hit you on the forehead. I said to the crowd: Please. We are not a violent people. Sorry! someone in the crowd responded. I said: Now, my friends, I have a special treat, a surprise, if you will. A first look at my coming Netflix series, the frame-by-frame re-creation of Ingo's lost masterpiece. You said: Frame by frame? I said: Why, yes. You said: First of all, that is impossible, even if you ever actually saw the film. I said: It is not. I have an eidetic memory. You said: Eidetic memory is a myth. It does not exist. I said: Is that so? And that, my friend, brings us to now."

"That's not what I said."

"Oh, but it is."

"It isn't."

"Tommy, can you play back the audio, please?"

The audio comes through the speakers: "'Ingo understood that one cannot make a movie about the Unseen without flying in the face of their very . . . unseenness. He knew the only way to show the truth of the societally Unseen is not to show them. So his movie about the Unseen shows nothing of their plight? It only shows white people, and it is in the form of a relentless and distracting comedy. The disenfranchised remain off-screen. So like every other movie. [Laughter. Applause. Stomping] No. Ingo animated the Unseen. He just did not film it. He only remembered it. Their stories went to the grave with Ingo. I see. You don't see. That is the very point. Touché. I'm the one who built his memorial in St. Augustine. You mean this? [The click of a plastic device] That is not my memorial to Ingo. No, it is mine. But you do not exist. My friend, I have not questioned your existence. I have been respectful and welcoming. I have invited you up onto the stage during an evening that is quite a special event to this audience and to myself. I would ask that you show me the same courtesy. [Booing. Sound of a tomato hitting a torso. Sound of a rock hitting a head] Please. We are not a violent people. Sorry! Now, my friends, I have a special treat, a surprise, if you will. A first look at my coming Netflix series, the frame-by-frame re-creation of Ingo's lost masterpiece. Frame by frame? Why, yes. First of all, that is impossible, even if you ever actually saw the film. It is not. I have an eidetic memory. Eidetic memory is a myth. It does not exist. Is that so?' And that, my friend, brings us to now. That's not what I said. Oh, but it is. It isn't. Tommy, can you play back the audio, please?"

The audio switches off.

"So then," says my doppelgänger.

"OK, that was impressive. Good trick."

"Thank you, my friend. Now may I continue with my evening?"

"Yeah, sure. I don't even care anymore."

"Thank you, my friend. So, my friends, without further ado, please enjoy a taste of what is to come."

The lights dim and the Netflix logo appears on the screen behind us. It fades and is replaced by a shot traveling through the blackness of deep space, passing planets and meteors. A deep-voiced narrator speaks:

"In the Black Eye Galaxy, there is a world called Boreas-Hephaestus."

We arrive at a planet engulfed in flames.

Narrator: "The side facing its sun is perpetually on fire."

The camera circles the planet to discover a dark side, covered with ice.

Narrator: "The side away from it is forever covered in ice."

The camera pushes in toward the planet.

Narrator: "This is the story of Madd and Molly, girl warriors who live on the border between the two and will fight the army of ice and the army of fire to save the innocent, exploited children of their land."

The camera comes to rest on Madd and Molly, two young African Boreas-Hephaestian girls with sheathed penises and swords, who are strategizing over a map.

CHAPTER 60

AFTERWARD, MY DOPPELGÄNGER invites me out for a drink to further discuss our differences, in the hopes, he says, that we can come to some consensus. I decline his offer because I have plans that night. Namely, to follow him home in an attempt to gain as much of an advantage over this loping interloper as I can. So we say our good nights. He hugs me and calls me "landsman." I know enough to know he is embracing me as a fellow Jew.

"I am not Jewish," I say.

"Oy," he says. "I was once as you are. You'll come to the Actors' Temple with me Friday. Afterward, we'll have a little nosh at the Knishioner Gordon and kibbitz."

"I have to go," I say, extricating myself with difficulty from his bearlike embrace. A bit of my clown makeup is smeared on his black turtleneck.

"OK, my friend," he says. "I'll be in touch."

How? How will you be in touch? Where will you find me? You liar! I nod and wave. After he walks off, I count to seventeen, then follow. I check the wristwatch around my waist: 9:30. It turns out he lives in the very luxury apartment building where I once lived, the building in which Marjorie Morningstar occupies my former apartment. I wait outside in front of the Dunkin' Donuts until I am chased away by the manager. I reposition myself in front of the H&R Block, which is, I am thankful, closed for the day. The doppelgänger reemerges at 11:00 P.M., this time in a bathrobe and slippers and walking a tiny dog on a leash. Maybe a miniature Chihuahua, which is sometimes called a teacup Chihuahua. But there is something odd about the proportions. I pride myself on my knowledge of dog breeds, having read extensively in the *Systema Naturae* of Linnaeus as well as the AKC's breed standard guides for judges. This dog's head is proportionately smaller than is required in a dog of show quality. In addition, it seems to have an unusually long muzzle. I venture closer. They turn the corner onto 45th, my double seemingly lost in some cellphone text conversation. It is much quieter here. And darker. The truth is I have no plan, but the lack of foot traffic and the darkness inspires some sort of darkening in my heart. It is at this moment that he turns, perhaps having sensed this shift in the emotional weather, a sudden cold front, a storm, gale force winds.

"Oh, it's you," he says, attempting a benign smile, which moves into and out of existence like a stretched and released rubber band.

"Yes," I say.

"Coincidence?" he asks.

"Are there any coincidences?"

"Well, now you're speaking like a religious man. I'm glad to hear it. What can I do for you?"

"We are both being played," I say.

"Played?"

"By someone somewhere."

"I feel blessed in my life."

"Yes. But of course that can change. There is always an open manhole waiting in the wings."

"I don't understand."

"Calamity. Humiliation. It is just around the corner."

"On 44th Street?"

"Don't be cute. You know what I mean."

"HaShem tests our faith. If he did not, we would not need to have faith. You do understand this, yes?"

"I am not Jewish."

"I was once a secular Jew, as you are. Then I found true meaning."

"No. I am not a Jew by birth. My ancestors are primarily Irish Catholic."

"Curious," he says. "I say curious because your nose."

"I was given this nose by southern anti-Semites."

"Now that is a story I'd like to hear over a nosh sometime."

"What you have is rightfully mine."

"HaShem's blessing?"

"Ingo's film."

"Ah. You know, I was told by my editor that any time a book is successful, people show up to claim authorship, to claim that the author had previously read his or her book, that the book was stolen, *et chetera*."

"I lived the life you claim to have lived. I saw Ingo's film. I watched helplessly as it was destroyed by a fire caused by my ignorance."

"Flood."

"Flood?"

"It was of course destroyed during Hurricane Irma. Everyone knows this. It was an act of G-d. There is no blame, as our ancient Chinese friend Lao Tzu might have said. It's all in the book."

"What about Mudd and Molloy?" I say.

"Who and who, my friend?"

"Mudd and Molloy."

"That doesn't ring a bell."

"The characters. In Ingo's movie."

"Which scene?"

"Every scene!"

"No."

"The failed comedy team."

"Oh. Maybe. There was a moment. A brief moment. A moment in passing. Molly is watching a movie on futuristic space TV late one night and there is some comic patter. We don't see the TV screen, just hear it. The scene is focused on Molly's loneliness, her alienation, her only companion this claptrap on the TV. It's funny, I forgot about that. I neglected to put it in the book. Me, with my perfectly eidetic memory. It is a minor moment, to be sure, but it does add a certain poignancy to the scene. One feels it articulates the time we waste, filling our brains with claptrap. Did I already call it claptrap earlier? I feel that I had just used the word claptrap to describe the movie she is watching, but I can't be sure. One cannot go back and read over the transcript of one's conversation. Although I can, as I have an eidetic memory."

My doppelgänger pauses, thinks.

"Yes, claptrap. And claptrap is as good a word as any to describe the show she is watching, which we, as the audience, do not even see, as I mentioned to you. Yes, perhaps those are the Mudd and Mullaly of which you—"

"Mudd and Molloy."

"Pardon?"

"Mudd and Molloy."

"Oh. Yes. That. I do think that must be them. It is the only incident of a comedy team I can think of. Very minor. But contributes to the poignancy of the scene, don't you agree? Almost as a mournful piano score might. Claptrap is an interesting word. Are you aware of its etymology? It is surprisingly and profoundly straightforward. It is, in essence, pandering. A piece of work designed to elicit applause. Literally a clap, as in applause, trap as in trap or trick. How much of our lives do we waste attending to the claptrap of others, offering our attention, our approval, our applause to an effort designed by them only for self-aggrandizement? Think of all the books in the world, all the movies, TV shows, music, periodicals, bloviating politicians, 'artists' of all stripes. Imagine all this claptrap—have I told you the etymology of that word? In any event, picture all of these things and people piled up in one space. Would they reach to the moon? I think perhaps many times there and back. And this is what we have jammed into our brains. How does it all fit? This is one of the reasons I love Ingo's work. He had no interest in jamming it into anyone's head. His motives were pure. He was creating for himself. And because of this, I feel justified in jamming his work into people's heads. It is qualitatively different and as such is a remedy of sorts, an antidote, if you will, to the garbage we ingest on a daily basis. I have never been interested in my own self-aggrandizement. As a religious man, I am already fully filled with the spirit of HaShem. I do not need or crave the praise of men, the adoration of women. I do not need to see my face on the cover of the *Rolling Stone* as our good friend from Hicksville Billy Joel says. It's funny, now that I think of it, the names Madd and Molly sound a bit like Mudd and Molloy. Perhaps that is your confusion."

"Dr. Hook."

"I'm sorry?"

"Dr. Hook and the Medicine Show. It's their song. Not Billy Joel."

"I'm fairly certain it's Mr. Joel. 'Put me in the back of the discount rack like another can of beans.' I remember—"

"That's Billy Joel's 'The Entertainer.' A completely different song."

"I don't think so. That lyric always bothered me. Why would a can of beans be in the discount rack of a record store?"

"Different song."

"We could argue this point all day, but—"

"No. We could look it up fairly easily."

"But that's not the point, is it? The point is our friend Billy Joel has put his little rhymes into our heads and we forever must live with them. They alter the circuitry of our brains. The Arc proteins make certain of that. They make us who we are. They make us wonder why a can of beans would be in a record store discount rack. And all because Billy Joel needs us to love him, to pay tribute to him, to celebrate him. HaShem doesn't ask any of that of us."

"He doesn't?"

"No, my friend. He does not. We do not have to petition him for attention. We do not have to become famous for him to see us. He always sees us. He judges us on our hearts not our celebrity. Our friend Billy Joel claims we didn't start the fire. But of course we did. Every item on that long and imperfectly rhyming list of his was created by humans. We did start the fire, Mr. Joel. Now, you may tell me that this song is by Dr. Hook or Dr. Demento or Dr. Dre or even Dr. Kevorkian, but I say you are wrong, and besides, it doesn't matter because the point I make is still valid. In the pursuit of money or glory or power, humans create atrocities. This is why I believe Ingo's film and his life are exemplary."

So focused am I on my double and his incessant fabrications, I have yet to look down at his dog. But it now makes a snuffling noise, which catches my attention, and I glance at it. It is not a dog at all, it turns out; it is the donkey puppet from Ingo's film, from my funerary urn, now seemingly self-animated in human time.

"Hello," it says to me.

"You," I say. "*You* know me. You can tell him. You can tell everyone!"

"Perhaps we've met in passing," he says. "I meet a lot of people in my line of work."

"Your line of work?"

"I'm a service animal."

"He's not blind."

"I'm an emotional support dog . . . donkey . . . well, donkey puppet, well, donkey puppet come to life. Isn't that obvious? Are you dense, man?"

For some reason his arrogant tone infuriates me. I guess it is because I draw the line at being insulted by a donkey. Without a moment of forethought, I stomp on him. Shockingly, he is not made of silicone over a stainless-steel armature. The puppet splits open like a crushed peach, revealing blood and bones in a tiny horrifying mess on the sidewalk. He is still alive, struggling to speak.

"Please, don't . . ."

I don't know if it's out of compassion or malevolence, but I stomp him two more times. Now he is silent. I look up at my doppelgänger, ashamed but also oddly triumphant.

"What have you done?" he says, almost in a whisper. "He was a creature of G-d, miraculous in that he alone of all his kind had been blessed with the gift of speech."

"What of it?" I spit, not knowing how else to respond.

"Of it *this*," he says, for the first time his voice rising in anger. "I will be required to report this to the proper authorities. He was my friend and confidant. He was wise. He was a creature of G-d."

"You said that already," I tell him, then punch him in the jaw. He is oddly delicate and light, and my fist sends him stumbling backward against a lamppost. I hit him again. And again. He doesn't fight back. Is it because he is a pacifist or simply unable because he has been incapacitated? I don't know. I don't know anything anymore. Soon he is on the ground. I drag him into an alley and pummel him until he is dead.

Then I slump to the cement next to him, heaving, suddenly aware of what I have done. I spot the donkey on the sidewalk, scramble quickly to scrape up his remains with cardboard I've pulled from a bin, and bring them back to the alley. What do I do? I tell myself this was in the heat of the moment, but I know that killing this imposter had been in the recesses of my mind since I first learned of his existence. I tell myself that this was self-defense, but that makes even less sense in light of the other thing I just previously thought. I must be honest at least with myself if I am to combat the world of lies I have entered. I pace. I try to think. I need to extricate myself from this nightmare. Then the obvious occurs to me. I will change places with him. I remove Dominick's grease paint and black pencil from my giant pocket and get to work on my doppelganger's face. Soon it is indistinguishable from my own painted face. I unplait his beard. I find a stiff rag (stiff from what? No time to ponder!) and a piece of broken mirror in the trash can and use them to wipe the makeup off my own face. I try my best to braid my beard. Thankfully, there is a discarded beard-braiding manual in the trash. I switch our clothing. I grab the donkey and leave the alley, only to hurriedly return when I realize I forgot the most important disguise of all: the yarmulke. I bobby pin it to my hair.

At his apartment building door, I steel myself and enter. It's different from what I remember, completely redesigned. There's a doorman now.

"Oh my God, Mr. Rosenberg, what happened?" he says.

"I was attacked by a madman. He killed . . . my donkey."

"Gregory Corso?"

"Sure. Gregory Corso, I guess. That's it."

"Oh my God."

"G-d?"

"Yes. I'm sorry. G-d. I'll call the police."

"There's more. Tell the police that in self-defense I fought back and I believe I killed the madman."

"Oh your G-d."

"And I left his body in the alley on 45th."

"OK. Got it. It's going to be fine, Mr. Rosenberg."

"And that he is a clown or at least he is dressed as a clown."

"A clown?"

"Yes. Tell them that."

"Clown. Got it," he says, taking notes.

"I need to go to my apartment to settle my nerves. I'm so jangled I can't remember anything, even my apartment number."

"Letter."

"What?"

"Letter."

"Oh. Right. See?"

"No. H."

"H. Right." It's odd that they have letters. How does one even know what floor to find one's apartment on?

"It's only one a floor."

"Beginning with A?"

"Yes."

I count on my fingers.

"So eighth floor."

"Well, the apartments start on the second floor, as I'm sure will come back to you shortly."

"So ninth."

"And the fifth floor is where the building's theater and meeting rooms are, which undoubtedly will come back to—"

"So H would be on ten."

"See? Your memory is returning already. Shall I send the police up when they arrive?"

"I imagine they will insist on it."

"I imagine so, Mr. Rosenberg. Would that it were otherwise."

"Would," I say as I turn right to head to the elevator.

"No, sir, to the left."

I turn to the left instead.

CHAPTER 61

O NCE IN H, I look for the yarmulke rack, which I assume Jewish people would keep in their foyers. But there is none. Maybe he keeps the yarmulke on? Even in bed? I have a lot to learn about this religion. The woman from before appears, on her way from one room to another. She doesn't even look at me.

"You were gone a long time," she says, disappearing into what I assume is a bathroom.

"Something happened," I call after her.

She pops her head out.

"What?" she says. Then she sees me, sees the donkey in my hand. Her eyes widen in horror and she rushes over.

"Gregory?! My G-d, what happened?!"

"That clown," I say. "It was that clown."

"The clown who was following us earlier?"

"No," I say, "the clown from *Captain Kangaroo*."

She looks confused.

"Clarabell? Really?" she asks.

"No! Of course it was the clown who had been following us!"

"Oh," she says, looking hurt. "I didn't—"

"Never mind," I say. "I had to kill him."

"You killed him?!"

"What is there, an echo in here?"

"Jesus, B.," she whispers.

"I'm sorry," I say. "It's been a rough night."

I want to call her by name, but I don't know what it is. I ask if she

517

has any cash in her wallet, because, I explain, I suppose I should tip the police when they come. It is in actuality a ruse to look at her driver's license.

"Um, yeah," she says. "But is it necessary to tip the police?"

"Jesus," I say. "You know they feel our people are cheap. Do you really want to substantiate that prejudice? At a time like this?"

"No, of course not," she says.

She goes off in search of her bag. I take the opportunity to look around the place in an attempt to familiarize myself with the environment, to be better able to deflect suspicion. She returns with her bag and sifts through it.

"Let me get the money," I say. "Unless you don't trust me."

She looks at me quizzically, then hands me the bag. I find her wallet, open it, pull out some bills, while surreptitiously glancing at her driver's license: Laura Elaine Cohen. I hand it back to her.

"Thank you, Laura."

"B.!"

"What?!"

"Please don't be mad at me," she says.

"I'm not mad at you."

"You only call me Laura when you're mad at me! You don't think I've noticed that?"

"Laurie," I try.

"Really?" she says. "Oh, B."

There is a knock at the door. Two uniformed cops stand there, as well as a middle-aged man in a suit.

"Officers," I say.

"B.!" says the suited man and embraces me.

"Hey," I say.

"Laurie," he then says, releasing me and hugging her.

He gets to call her Laurie. Whoever he is. That doesn't seem fair.

"Al," she says. "Thank you so much for coming."

His name is Al. Got it.

"Thank you, Al," I say.

"How could I not be here for this?" Al says. "We're going to make this as easy for you folks as possible."

"Thank you, Al," Laurie (?) says.

"Thank you, Al," I say.

"So we'll just need to take a statement," Al says.

So Al is with the police. Got it.

"We found the clown's body and obviously have no doubt that this was a case of self-defense."

"You should see what he did to Gregory," offers Laurie (?).

I scurry off to produce Gregory's corpse, certain it'll sell my version of things.

"Jesus," says Al. "I loved him as much as a man could possibly love a talking donkey puppet."

"As did I," I say.

"As did all of New York," says the second of the two uniformed policemen.

"As did I as well, too," agrees Laurie (?).

"Tell us what happened, B.," says Al. "In your own words."

"Sure. Well, I was walking Gregory Corso, the talking donkey, as I do every night."

"Not every night," says Laurie (?).

"Of course," I agree. "As I have been known to do on some nights."

This satisfies her and she nods.

"And I noticed we were being followed by this damnable clown, who had been following us all day. Right?"

I look at Laurie (?) for confirmation.

"That's right," she says.

"He was even at my lecture tonight. Everyone saw that. Hundreds of witnesses. And I was kind to him, even though he was obviously disturbed. I invited him up onstage to debate. In retrospect, perhaps I was too kind."

"Debate what?" asks Al.

"He claimed to have seen the Cutbirth film and that it was completely different than I had described it, almost entirely inverted."

"That's insane," offers Al. "What an insane man."

"Yes," I agree, seething internally. "But we need to be kind to our insane friends. The Torah teaches us that."

"This world was not made for one as beautiful as you, to quote Vincent van Gogh," says Al.

"Thank you, Al," I agree. "So he attacked Gregory and then came at me with a knife—"

"We didn't find a knife."

"Let me finish. He came at me with an . . . iPhone, is what I was going to say."

"We didn't find a— Wait, so I'm confused. Is an iPhone threatening?"

"They're very hard. And keep in mind he'd just killed my donkey, so I wasn't thinking entirely clearly."

"I get that," he says. Then after a pause: "But we didn't find an iPhone, either."

"Maybe somebody walked off with it. There's a market for hot iPhones, I hear."

"Very true," says Al. "Very good point. Very true. Maybe you should be the cop and I'll be the cinematic genius!"

We all laugh.

"Anyway. The two of us wrestled, and I, in order to defend myself, well, I beat him to death."

"Thanks, B.," Al says. "For reliving this nightmare. I know this can't be easy." Then to the cops: "You fellas have any other questions?"

"No, Commissioner Rappaport."

Commissioner Al Rappaport! Of course!

"All right then," says Commissioner Al Rappaport, "we'll let you two lovely folks get back to your lives."

"Thanks, Al."

Al hugs Laurie (?).

"This is not about him being a clown, Laurie. We know that for certain."

What does that even mean?

"Thanks for saying that, Al," says Laurie (?).

This is not about him being a clown, Laurie? This is not about him being a clown, Laurie. Something about this statement sets off alarm bells in my brain. Oh, shit. Clown Laurie! Is Laurie *Clown* Laurie? I study her and try to imagine her in clown makeup.

"What?" she says.

"Nothing."

Al hugs me. And they're gone. Maybe Clown Laurie and I both stare at the front door for a bit, as if we're suddenly afraid to be alone with each other, as if this horrible event has opened some chasm between us.

"I think we should try to get some sleep, Snoodledy Doo," she says.

"OK. Sounds good," I say.

"I'm so sorry, Baby Bonnikins," she continues. "This must be soooo difficult for you."

"It's OK," I say.

"Ohhh, Cheesecake Sneezecake," she says and embraces me.

"Ohhh," I say back.

In the bedroom, I watch her undress. She is quite lovely, and I feel a strain in my pajama bottoms. It occurs to me that I am glad I was born at a time in the United States when I would be circumcised as an adult at the Burns and Schreiber Burn Center. This way she won't notice that I am not Jewish. This brings me back to the question of the yarmulke. Am I allowed to take it off to sleep?

"Do you know where I left my computer?" I ask. "I want to look something up."

"It's where it always is," she says.

"Oh, good," I say. "Thanks."

I leave the room.

"Where are you going?" she says.

I return.

"To get my computer?" I say.

She rolls her eyes.

"What is wrong with you?" she says and pulls it out from one of the nightstand drawers. My side of the bed! I think.

"Sorry," I say. "I'm a little dizzy and out of sorts and expect to be so for several days and possibly the rest of the year."

"My poor Chick-fil-A Sandwich," she says and hugs me.

"Aw," I say. "And, to think, I can't even remember my password!"

"Ha," she says, giggling. "Silly B.! It's your pet name for me!"

"Ha!" I agree. "That is funny . . . *Baby*."

I look at her as I say this.

"*You're* funny," she says.

I decide I'll keep on the kippah. It's likely what he'd do. It's good he was already in pajamas so I know this is what he sleeps in. If she questions my going to bed in my yarmulke, I'll say I simply forgot. Because of the stress of the brutal murder I committed in self-defense, of the death of our beloved donkey puppet. That's believable. She'll believe that. I climb into bed.

"You're wearing that yarmulke to bed?" she says.

"I forgot," I say, unclipping it and placing it on the wig head on the nightstand, which I assume is for that purpose. "I just forgot," I continue, "what with the killing that I committed in self-defense as well as the murder of the donkey. Good night."

I lie down.

"What about your pajarmulke?"

"My what?"

"Your pajarmulke."

I stare up at the ceiling and sigh. This whole thing is almost not worth it.

"What's that again?" I say. "The shock to my system seems to have affected my memory."

"Your sleeping yarmulke."

"Oh, right. I'm so stupid!" I say. "And also distracted, I guess, by the events of this evening. Where do I keep it again?"

"Night table. Top drawer."

"Right."

I open the drawer and there it sits, plaid and flannel, with what I assume must be an elastic chin strap. I place it on my head. It is surprisingly comfortable, and the crown of my head does have a tendency to chill at night. I switch off the light and rest my head on the pillow.

"Good night, Turtledove," she says.

"Good night, Clown Laurie," I try.

She kisses me. She is Clown Laurie! And that is my nickname for her!

Her mouth is lovely, warm, and soft, tasting of toothpaste and—I perform a good deal of that lip-smacking, tongue-tapping-the-roof-of-my-mouth action to try to determine the flavor—blintzes? I don't know for certain, but I find myself aroused. I do not usually find myself attracted to Jewish women. This is simply a matter of taste; it is not an anti-Semitic position. But a Jewish clown woman does something to me. I can't say I understand why. I decide that to dwell on the reasons would inhibit my sexual performance, and so I let go of everything that is not the body of this clown woman. As I immerse myself in the experience of her, I begin to feel that I am *him*, that this is my rightful place in the world after all. As the poet admonishes us, how can something that feels so right be wrong? She is surprised by my lovemaking choices. It appears that she and Double Boy had perhaps fallen into something of a routine. I seem to be just what the doctor ordered, as the wags might say. And it occurs to me that maybe all was not sunshine and lollipops in this household, that maybe the solution to these circumstances is to introduce my true persona into the relationship. Maybe this woman is ready for a change. Maybe I am the adulterous affair she wants to have but never would. Maybe I don't need to purchase a copy of Rosten after all. I'll make up a new nickname for her. And she'll love it. Maybe it'll be "Bitch." Maybe that will excite her. I'll play it by ear. I sense she is malleable, and that puts me, as her husband, in the catbird seat. This is the very seat I have never before occupied with a woman. And I come. Boy, do I come. It is an earth-shattering orgasm. Stronger even than with Oleara. Stronger than in Tsai's stairwell. In truth, she seems a little startled. Is it because my orgasm is stronger, more masculine than her husband's have been? Is it because it happened too fast, she was not ready, she was not finishing? I don't know, but the catbird seat necessitates my believing the former. I orgasmed at exactly the correct moment and it achieved the perfect result within her body.

"That was . . . *great*," she says.

"Glad you liked it . . . bitch." I say "bitch" very quietly.

"What?" she says.

"What *what*?" I say.

"Did you call me 'bitch'?"

"Did I?"

She pecks me on the cheek and says, "Bitch Laurie."

We both lie there for a long while in silence, each lost in our own thoughts.

Finally, I speak: "Is the C in Clown Laurie upper or lowercase?"

"You," she says, kissing me once again, then turning over and almost immediately snoring lightly.

Well, there are only two possible options.

CHAPTER 62

THE MORNING IS nice. Coffee and matzoh brei. I like it. My bitch, Clown Laurie, is a good cook. I'm feeling comfy in my daytime yarmulke: khaki, relaxed fit, lots of pockets. I've gotten on-line (uppercase C) and am looking up hair yarmulkes. It occurred to me last night that if there is such a thing it would allow me to cover my bald spot without incurring accusations of vanity and that if there is not such a thing, it could be a decent moneymaker. There is such a thing, it turns out, and I order three in salt-and-pepper: the Julius Caesar, the Jude Law, and the Nicolas Cage.

Today I'm scheduled to do Charlie Rose (in this reality, he seems not to have been disgraced, or maybe he has already reinvented himself as undisgraced), and then this evening, I'm presenting the first Ingo Cutbirth African American Animation Award to Floyd Norman.

All in all, life is good now. There is, however, a slight nagging feeling. It might have to do with all the lying. I made a promise to Ingo, over his grave, to preserve and protect his legacy, his film. Once I inadvertently burned it all up, I made a second promise to Ingo, this one while I was on fire in the parking lot of Slappy's (why is it Slappy's now?) to recover his film, as completely as I possibly could. And in a very real sense, I am almost living a lie now. And it's not only lying about the truth of Ingo's film—what I know the film really was, not this ridiculous antithesis my doppelgänger put into the world, but the real, brutal, terrifying comedy that was Ingo's life's work—but also the deception toward Clown Laurie. This skullcap I now wear makes me think that I am always seen by God, that I cannot hide, that I need to come clean, face the worldly consequences, face the otherworldly ones as well. I am, after all, when all is said and done, an ethical human being. In the heat of the moment, of desire, of anger, of grief, I grab my iPhone from my back yarmulke pocket, punch in "Commissioner Al Rappaport," and dial before I can talk myself out of it.

"Hey, B.," says Commissioner Rappaport.

"Hi, Al. Listen, I need to talk to you."

"What's up, buddy?"

"You remember that body in the alley?"

"The one from last night? The clown one?"

"Yeah. Listen—"

"Of course I remember. It was just last night."

"So, anyway, listen—"

"It's taken care of, B. It's gone. Incinerated. Up in smoke."

"You burned him."

"Yup. Bye-bye, clown. All gone. Nothing to worry about, B. It never happened. He never existed."

"But he did."

"Prove it."

"What?"

"You can't prove it. No one can. Everything is fine. Enjoy your life, good sir. You deserve it."

"Um—"

"And, really, thank you for all you do."

"Yeah. OK, Al."

"Ciao, bitch!"

He laughs and hangs up.

I WANDER THE streets. It's different now. Everyone recognizes me, asks for autographs, photos. I am cheered from the outside seating at restaurants. Passersby tell me my book saved their lives, that they can't wait for the Netflix series. It's different, but I'm not sure it's better. I mean, sure, in almost every way it is. A man dashes out from

Barneys and offers me a cashmere sweater he had just purchased for me after spotting me through the store window. It's got to be nine hundred dollars if it's a penny. It's nice. Soft. Heather gray, which I like and looks good against my plaited beard, while expertly concealing the beardruff. But still, there's a queasiness.

I think about the murdered man, and even though in my opinion (and Rappaport's!) he never truly existed, certainly not in the way I do, in that he was, for lack of a better term, a replicant, and in my opinion he existed only to rub more salt in the wound that is my psyche, which has had nothing but salt rubbed in it since as long as I can remember, since I was a child even. Still, I feel some guilt. He (it?) was a breathing entity with a face. That he had my face, in some way, allows me to feel justified in removing him from the world. It is my face, after all. It was my face before it was his. He was copying me. At best, he was a face plagiarist. He stole my face and deserved to be called on that. How is he any different from Stephen "Shattered" Glass in that regard? People felt righteous outrage at *his* transgressions. Granted, no one murdered him or suggested his murder as far as I know. Nor should they have! But this is a more serious infraction. Now, it might be argued that his "cloneness," for lack of a better term, is not his fault. He never asked to be a clone. I mean, I assume he never asked to be a clone. Perhaps he did ask to be a clone. In any event, whether he did or did not, his existence was not my fault, and I should not be expected to tolerate it.

In addition, I believe his very being was designed to hurt me, to make it impossible for me to live in the world he now inhabited. So in a very real sense, his murder was an act of self-defense. Still, one does not ever *enjoy* killing a human, be that human clone or non-clone. And having to beat the life out of a person's clone stays with a person. I can, to this day, which is the next day, still see his lifeless corpse in my mind's eye. And I know he was loved by many, many people. That he was loved for propagating a lie should not condemn him to death. If that were so, who among us would be spared? But his lie denied the world the true genius of Ingo's work, replacing it with a predigested pabulum of no real value to the future of film and, dare I say, humanity. It, of course, can be argued that he did not know he was lying, that as a clone, he had been programmed to believe he was telling the truth. I tend to think this was the case.

It doesn't, however, make him less dangerous to society. Hitler, as a result of his societal "programming," truly, sincerely hated the Jews. His earnestness did not make the result any less dire. If I were able to go back in time and kill Hitler before he was to gain power, I would do so in a heartbeat. I would also kill any and all Hitler clones. This is not only because I am now Jewish, but because it would be the right thing to do. I understand going back and changing history can be fraught with unforeseen problems, but in the case of Hitler, I would be willing to take the risk. I feel similarly about my clone, which is not to say that I believe his crimes against humanity are equal to Hitler's. But consider my position: Imagine if someone had replaced you in the world. Imagine you no longer had an identity, money, a place to live. Imagine you found yourself in oversized clown clothing-cum-fumigation tent, hungry, alone, reviled. You might be driven to do what I have done. Still, I feel some guilt. The bloody imagery stays with me. And I feel similarly about the donkey. To be clear, I thought he was a trick of animation when I stomped him. I stomped him the way anyone would and does stomp a trick of animation. When the first stomp revealed him to be flesh and blood, I was horrified, and the only humane thing to do was to stomp him twice more to make sure he no longer suffered. Still, I feel some guilt. Not only due to the rarity in this world of a tiny talking donkey—I would not be at all surprised to learn that he was the only one of his kind—but because it was a life. And no one enjoys taking a life. Of course, there are the psychopaths (or are they sociopaths now?) who do enjoy taking a life, but I believe them to be exceedingly rare, though not as rare, perhaps, as talking donkey puppets. Our misapprehension about this says everything about the Hollywood and news media's obsession with such crimes. Certainly, I was in no way joyous in the act of killing him. If anything, I was horrified but knew it had to be done. One could hear the bones crack. I tried to turn myself in, but Al Rappaport would not have it.

So here I am, forced to contend in isolation with my now tortured psyche. Is there perhaps a way for me to free myself of this?

Do I risk everything by revealing the truth about myself and Ingo's movie? I could reveal it on Charlie Rose this very day. Surely, if I explain it well, people would understand my position and appreciate my honesty. Who among us would not have done exactly what I did? And I could immediately get back to work on my version, the true version of Ingo's movie. I would return to my work with Barassini, if he exists in this world. This time I would have the benefit of material comfort during the remembering process as well as the comfort and love of a good woman clown. Would she stay with me once the truth was revealed? It is a gamble, but I believe she would. It is important to tell the truth. Everyone respects a truth teller. If there is a creator, as I now believe there must be, he or she or thon will reward me for my efforts.

I fall into an open personhole.

As I am climbing out, a car parks on top of the hole. I call up to the driver, explain my predicament. He hears me but refuses to give up the spot, even briefly. He'd been driving around for a half an hour looking for a place to park, he yells down to me. I do understand his predicament as I'm sure he understands mine. And I tell him so. We understand each other's predicament, we conclude. There is something about the yarmulke on my head that does remind me to put myself in the other fellow's shoes. That is a good thing. He says he is heading downtown and I should do the same. If he spots another manhole, he will pry it open for me with the crowbar he keeps in his hollow leg. I nod, which serves no purpose, as he cannot see me, and begin to make my way south, sloshing through the fetid water. There should be more kindness in the world. I do have a bit of time till I'm due at Charlie Rose's studio and I need to head south anyway. And, really, when it comes down to it, the fact that the fellow was so honest about his predicament and also seemed sympathetic to my predicament, which I was honest about, encourages me to not make a stink (ha ha!), and the truth is, I'm down here already anyway, so why not continue on my way down here? And the truth is, when I think about it, if I'm down here, I can't fall down here because I'm already down here. So there's that.

It is exceedingly dark though. I have the flashlight on my new iPhone, but it produces an odd, diffuse, almost useless light. When I was a young man, flashlights did their jobs and illuminated the dark, not just small-print menus in dimly lit restaurants. It was a different and heady time. I point the phone toward the floor to use what little light it gives to avoid tripping over anything fecal, not to mention rats. The rats are the thing I dislike most about my sewer forays, as I've come to call them. There are rumors of rats down here as big as German shepherds, the people not the dogs. I learned this from what I consider a reliable source, a sewer worker who had appeared in the Frederick Wiseman documentary *Effluence* (1978). I had interviewed him for a monograph I was writing entitled *Pipe Dreams* about sewers in dreams in film. It was the first sewer-centric film study since Mark Kermode's 1993 essay on the C.H.U.D. series, which I believe was entitled *I, Mark Kermode, Am an Asshole*. I cannot be certain though; several of his essays have been similarly titled.

I hear some sloshing of sewer water behind me and turn with a start, which causes me to lose my footing. I fall forward and land face-first into something soft and putrid. I pull my hand out, which is now glopped-over from the greasy mass, and I shine the iPhone flashlight at it. It is sickly white and stretches almost to the ceiling and as far down the tunnel as I can see. I cautiously touch my tongue to my mustache in order to taste it and find myself delivered immediately into a paroxysm of gagging. It is, as I suspected, one of those dreaded fatbergs: cooking oil and wet wipes and toilet paper and garbage and tampons congealed into a massive mass. I have no choice but to make my way through this nightmare to find the personhole my new hollow-legged friend will be opening for me, to make my way to Charlie Rose's set, to reveal the truth of Ingo's movie and my relationship to it. So I crawl through ten blocks of fat until the next available personhole.

CHAPTER 63

The Charlie Rose makeup lady is chatty as she scrubs me down with an acetone-based cleaning solution. She's read "my" book, of course, and it changed her life, of course, "forever," of course. I ask her flirtatiously and self-deprecatingly if it changed it for the better.

"Oh, you," she says, laughing.

Apparently Jewish clone me can do no wrong. We shall see.

Now she is on to the makeup, and I have to say, it is helping. Perhaps the fatberg fat also performed some deep moisturizing function. I appear healthy, rested, rosier, no pun intended, neither in regard to my surname nor Charlie Rose's, who, by the way, is also not Jewish. In truth, I appear more like my clone. Is it possible he wore makeup? Or maybe it was just the happy life he was living, or is it possible he just found himself dermatologically blessed in his existence in a way that I have not in mine?

The makeup lady (call me Gillian, she says, giggling) tells me there is a suit that was left by John Goodman right before his impressive weight loss (which happened mid-interview and was captured on tape!) and I am welcome to wear it for the show. She says Charlie's wardrobe lady can make it seem to fit me perfectly with safety pins, duct tape, and pulleys. I agree because what choice do I have, and I must say there is something comforting about being swathed in all that grand Goodman gabardine. The suit smells like him! I once had the privilege of interviewing him for a piece I had done on *Uncle Buck* . . . no, that was John Candy . . . on *King Ralph*, which I entitled "The King of Character Actors" (the Candy piece was entitled "Bucking the Establishment"), and I remember his scent. It was a lovely combination of vanilla, lavender, and clove. Had I been female, I might have swooned. As it was, I found myself experiencing a slight tumescence, and I am heterosexual, sadly, to a fault. I say to a fault because I do believe in today's world there is an almost moral imperative to be a homosexual. How can we as white men fully protect women from ourselves if not by disengaging from them and becoming the lovers of other white men (or men of color, if they would have us!)? It sends the clarion call that they are safe with us. If I am wearing hot pants and a feather boa as I walk, late at night, on a depopulated 10th Avenue, a passing lone woman can and will feel safe. Nothing to fear from me, I am as good as telling her. I will not catcall, I will not assault. You are safe with me. We might even stop and chat for a moment, talk about Beyoncé or Jon Hamm or whoever it is at that cultural moment. That would be nice. I would welcome that possibility as well. But, alas, I am unable to alter the focus of my sexual attraction. Would that I could be a gay man. I would like myself better. But I am the most heterosexual of all my many acquaintances. And yet even I feel a certain thrill swathed in John Goodman's size fifty-six suit, his tie as wide on me as a bib on a baby. I feel safe. And that scent! The wardrobe lady (please, call me Agnes!) does wonders with her bag of tricks, and I look dashing in it.

She offers to make me a yarmulke out of some excess material from John Goodman's seat. But I tell her that's not necessary; I will not be needing a yarmulke today. She seems surprised and a bit taken aback but just nods. And before I know it, I have been whisked into the black-curtained studio, where Charlie Rose sits, a genial, befuddled, non-sexually-harassing smile on his face. In this version of the world, he appears to be innocent of those charges, or not, but I give him a dirty look anyway.

"No whatchamacallit today? Skull hat?" he says as he stands to shake my hand.

"No," I say. "I hope we can discuss this new development on the show."

His eyes light up. A scoop!

"Of course!" he says.

We sit. He gestures around the studio.

"As you can see," he says, "you can see no cameras. But they are there, hidden in the vulval folds of the black velvet curtains, fully robotized. This leaves us alone in the studio. I invented this technique with the intent of putting my guests at ease. It is in its way as revolutionary a notion as Jerry Lewis's video playback system. Many people in the industry have told me this. It puts people at ease. Gary Lewis and the Playboys, who is Jerry Lewis's own son, told me this. People are put at ease because they cannot see the cameras. It is as if we are having a private conversation, just the two of us. The guest doesn't even know when the interview has started."

"Has it started?" I ask.

He shrugs, smiles, and winks. I find myself disconcerted.

"So," he says, smiling at me as if in love and drunk, "let's talk about the Cutbirth film."

"On the air?" I ask. "Is this us planning the impending conversation or is this the conversation?"

"See? You can't tell! No one ever can!"

"Um, OK then," I begin. "I have a confession I'd like to make on the air—"

"Yes? That's fascinating! I'm fascinated by the idea of confession. As I'm sure you know, there is a long history of confession as a method of soul cleansing within many, many religious traditions. What is it about confession that—how should I say it—allows it to function as a method of soul cleansing? Within many, many religious traditions?"

"Let's discuss that in the abstract, sure," I say, "but first I'd like to get some specific things off my chest—"

"OK, great," he says. "Shoot. Go ahead. I'm fascinated. For many, many reasons. Please."

"Well, I am not who you or your audience think I am," I say.

"You're B. Rosenberger Rosenberg," he says. "I recognize you."

"I am, yes. But the man you all believed to be me was not. He was an imposter. I killed him last night, not to mention Gregory Corso, his miniature talking donkey puppet."

Suddenly the cameras push their way past the black curtains and into the studio.

"What's going on?" yells Rose to someone unseen.

"I don't know, boss!" comes the panicked response.

The robot cameras accelerate and appear to be zeroing in on me. I stand, knocking over my chair in the process, and scan the room in an attempt to find my way out. I can't find the exit, so I just pick a direction and run, the cameras in mad pursuit. I run directly into the curtain, pulling the entire thing down on top of me. The cameras ram me repeatedly as I lie in a heap on the floor.

"Turn the damn things off!" screams Rose. "They're killing him! They're killing him dead!"

Finally it stops. I am enshrouded in black, and I can't see a thing.

"Is he dead?" weeps a woman, perhaps the wardrobe lady (Agnes?).

Several people grapple with the curtain, trying to find me within it. Even in my terrified state, I am reminded of the terrible movie *Christine*, both of them, in truth: the demon car movie and the bi-opic about the TV journalist Christine Chubbuck, who shot herself on air during her Florida local nightly news show in 1974. *Christine*, the John Carpenter adaptation of Stephen King's novel of the same name, for reasons that are obvious—inanimate objects just attempted to kill me—and *Christine* the docudrama directed by Antonio Campos because, like Chubbuck, the tragedy of my existence has been turned into entertainment for some unseen audience, with another person "playing" me.

I am extricated from my prison of vulval velvet, and the hens are instantly upon me, worriedly clucking: "You poor thing! Are you OK?"

I look up at the group. Rose, nearly seven feet tall, stands imperiously over me.

"What did you mean when you said you killed Rosenberger Rosenberg?"

I look over at the cameras. Their cables are taut, as if they're champing at the bit, waiting to attack again.

"Metaphorically," I stammer. "You've heard the expression, if you meet the Buddha on the road, kill him."

"No."

"Well, it's an expression."

"Sounds like whatever the anti-Buddhist version of anti-Semitic is—anti-Buddhistic—and I don't like it," says Rose.

"No. It's not literal."

"It's like, what if I said, if you meet the Moses on the road, kill him? How would you feel about that?"

"First of all, he's not called *the* Moses. Second of all, Moses is not analogous in Judaism to the Buddha."

"You're the expert," spits Rose.

"Third of all, killing the Buddha is meant metaphorically. It's a koan meant to get one to think about—"

"A cone? That makes no sense. Make sense!"

"Since we're talking, I can't be certain, but I'm guessing you're spelling koan c-o-n-e."

"Exactly right."

"Whereas I am spelling it k-o-a-n. Koe-*ahn*, which is a paradoxical statement within Buddhist tradition designed to encourage a person to think outside of their familiar patterns of thought."

"Oh, that," says Rose. "I heard of that."

Clearly he has not. But that does not stop him.

"Buddhism fascinates me," he says. "I've had the Dalai Lama on my show. His real name is Tenzin Gyatso. Did you know that? I've also had Richard Gere, a great actor and advocate for Buddhism. It is a religion of peace. He's very funny, the Dalai Lama. I like him. He makes me laugh because he's so cute and harmless. We laughed together a lot. He wears a robe. It's red or a shade of red. I thought I would wear a robe when I interviewed him, but Richard Gere told me that would create an international incident."

* * *

The Netflix executives, two men and a woman who look like every two men and a woman executives in Hollywood, come to the animation studio. My assistant, whose name I don't know but who looks like every assistant, young and female and of the vaguely mixed ethnicity of a soft drink commercial performer, as is the current fashion, ushers them into the screening room, where we all hug as if old friends. My assistant asks if anyone wants coffee or water or anything else.

"I'd love some water," says the woman of the group.

"We're fine," say the two men of the group in unison.

The assistant nods and exits.

"So," says one of the men, "we're so excited to see the first episode!"

"So excited," says the woman.

"Yes," says the other man.

"Great," I say. "We're very proud of it here. So without further ado . . ."

I signal to the person I assume is in the projection booth. The lights dim and the title sequence lights up the screen. To hammering theme music that sounds like it's by Ramin Djawadi, an old African American actor in even older prosthetic makeup, representing Ingo, moves puppets of naked black girls with penises on the surface of an alien planet, and after a moment of this, disappears, leaving the black girlboys on their own, now animated to fight ice monsters and fire demons. It's all brutal and bloody and heroic and ridiculous. The theme music is, it is now revealed in the credits, indeed by Djawadi. Of course it is. I must acknowledge a certain thrill in seeing my name next to Ingo's under the *Created By* credit.

"I love the opening," says the woman of them.

"Us too," say the men.

"It draws you right in," says the woman.

"Boom," says one of the men.

"What do you mean 'Boom'?" asks the other man.

"Like 'Boom. It draws you right in.'"

"Do people say that?"

"I think—"

"Shh, it's starting," says the woman.

A shanty town. Black and white. Silent. The streets filled with impoverished dark-skinned people puppets.

"We love how you made it look old," say the men. "You even have the scratches!"

"Shhh," says the woman.

The camera pushes in on two naked girls with penises. One talks to the other in sign language. Thon's eyes are milky; thon is blind. The other, one assumes, is deaf, hence the sign language.

"I love the silence. I love how the blind one talks to the deaf one in sign language she herself can't see," say the men.

"Thon thonself can't see," I correct.

"And how the deaf one responds in a voice she herself cannot hear. That's both brilliant and touching."

"Thon thonself cannot hear," I say again, in case they didn't hear me.

"What's that now?" say the men.

The girlboys turn into an alley and enter a ramshackle shed. Inside are farming implements. The deaf girlboy picks up a plowshare.

"What's that?" asks one of the men.

"Plowshare," I say. "It's the cutting edge of a moldboard. A farming implement that dates back thousands of years, at least as far back as the Majiabang of China."

"Oh," says the man. "Is this the part where they beat them into swords?"

"Shhh," says the woman.

I'm guessing it is indeed that part. What the hell was this second me doing? Why did he take the beautiful, harrowing, incisive social commentary of Cutbirth and turn it into a ridiculous parody of the work of Henry Darger? Perhaps my doppelgänger didn't feel he could properly monetize the true work. Perhaps he wasn't bright enough to understand that broad comedy is abject horror, so he went with something obvious in its racial message. It's confusing because, as my doppelgänger, he should have been my intellectual equal. A true doppelgänger is indistinguishable from its gänger, which is me. How can my doppel have been intellectually inferior? How can it have been Jewish? Something very odd is happening.

On the screen, the two girlboys, now carrying their newly beaten swords, make their way through a brutal snowstorm into the World of Ice.

"Their dark skin against the white storm is visually arresting," says one of the men.

"I wanted to say that," says the other man.

I must admit, it is.

CHAPTER 64

A T DINNER, I sulk.

"You seem down," says Clown Laurie. "Should we have a dinner party?"

"A dinner party?"

"Those always seem to cheer you up."

"That sounds terrible."

"Oh, c'mon, sourpuss. Let's play Who Would You Invite, If You Could Invite Anyone."

"I despise this game. I have always despised this game."

"Living or dead."

"Ugh. All right. Jesus. I want to have Jesus over for dinner."

"That goes without saying. He's already on the list. Who else?"

CLOWN LAURIE IS able to organize the party on short notice. We are the toast of the town, it seems.

"You're not the Messiah," I say.

"I never said I was," says Jesus.

"You were a Jew."

"I know. I lived and died a Jew."

"You were just a teacher."

"*Just* a teacher? No job more important than teacher, my friend. When we start paying our teachers the way we pay our professional athletes, we'll know we're a civilized society."

"Our professional *male* athletes, you mean."

"Yes. Female athletes are treated unfairly, of course. That should be corrected. It is no coincidence that most teachers are female."

"Besides, that's such a dumb thing to say. No one should be paid the kind of money pro athletes are paid."

"Hey, I agree. I was simply making a point about how we as a society value the wrong things."

"Fine, but when you go into that whole pro athlete thing, it hurts your point."

"But you understand my point and we are in agreement, so why harp on this one aspect of how I articulated it?"

"Fine, Jesus. Fine. It just seems to me that, as a teacher, you should choose your words with more care."

"Hey, quit hogging Jesus," says someone at the far end of the table. Maybe Milton Friedman.

I turn to van Gogh.

"Have you seen that *Dr. Who* episode?"

"Which one?"

"The one with you in it?"

"No! That's crazy. Really? I'm in it? Is it any good? I love that show."

"You should see it. It's a travesty. I think you'd be outraged."

"Oh no. Why?"

"It has the actor playing you weeping with joy at the crass commercialization of your art, at your posthumous popularity, at the idea that now your paintings are worth hundreds of millions of dollars."

"To be honest, I wouldn't mind having hundreds of millions of dollars."

"Jesus, you've become an avaricious creep," I say.

"I have?" says Jesus, turning back to me, looking hurt.

THAT NIGHT, IN an argument with Clown Laurie about the possibility of time travel, I plagiarize Stanislaw Lem's article about A. E. van Vogt's *The Weapon Shops of Isher*, from notes written on my arm, to make my point.

"Clown Laurie," I begin, "the cosmos exists on credit! It is like a debenture, a draft for material and energy which must be repaid immediately, because its existence is the purest one hundred percent liability both in terms of energy and in terms of material. Then, just what does the cosmologist do? With the help of physicist friends he builds a great 'chronogun' which fires one single electron backward 'against the tide' in the flow of time. That electron, transformed into a positron as a result of its motion 'against the grain' of time, goes speeding through time, and in the course of this journey acquires more and more energy. Finally, at the point where it 'leaps out' of the cosmos, i.e., in a place in which there had as yet been no cosmos, all the terrible energies it has acquired are released in that tremendously powerful explosion which brings about the universe! In this manner the debt is paid off. At the same time, thanks to the largest possible 'causal circle,' the existence of the cosmos is authenticated, and a person turns out to be the actual creator of that very universe!"

"You've changed," says Clown Laurie.

"Have not," I say.

"You never used to know who A. E. van Vogt was, let alone Stanislaw Lem. I don't know who you are anymore."

"I didn't? What was I, a moron?"

"And what's with that switch on your neck? I can't just pretend it's not there. I can't keep pretending, B."

"It's nothing," I try.

"Where is the B. who didn't at all like speculative fiction writers, with the exception of Margaret Atwood and the Jewish triumvirs: Asimov, Ellison, and Tidhar?"

"Really?" I say. "Tidhar? Jesus Christ."

"Yes," she screams. "Tidhar! You loved Tidhar!"

"That B. is dead," I proclaim. "Long live B.!"

Clown Laurie shakes her head, stares down at the kitchen table, then exits into the bedroom to pack. I try to call after her, but I cannot. I cannot be a man who countenances Tidhar. I can never be that man, not for Clown Laurie, not for anyone.

* * *

IN THIS VERSION of the world, I discover Barassini is a well-known stage actor, also named Barassini. He still keeps the same office space but uses it to store his many prosthetic appliances. For in this world, he is known as "The Other Man of a Thousand Faces," the other "Man of a Thousand Faces" having been Lon Chaney, who, in this world, Barassini famously played in a Broadway musical version of the movie *Man of a Thousand Faces*, in which James Cagney played a non-singing version of Lon Chaney. Barassini explains all this to me as he gives me a tour of the storeroom. There are many, many prosthetic faces here, probably a thousand. But this Barassini tells me he cannot help me. This Barassini is not a hypnotist, he explains. He does give me the address of a fellow down the block called Hypno Joe. He says Hypno Joe might be just what I'm looking for, and in this world, he says it without judgment. Then he asks me to keep him updated. For some reason, he is very interested in my memories of Castor Collins in Ingo's film. Then he shows me his sock drawer "for old time's sake," even though in this world, I've never slept there.

Over tea, he serenades me with one of the songs from his musical:

> *"You might know me as the man of a thousand faces,*
> *And that's OK by me.*
> *I've played folks of many races,*
> *For I'm the actor Lon Cha-ney.*
> *Yes, I've played Orientals and I've played Jews,*
> *Just give me some rubber and give me some glue,*
> *Some pancake makeup and I'll play you!*
> *For I may have a thousand faces,*
> *But you're my number one."*

I must say, I wish this musical had existed in my previous world. It's exquisite. Judd Apatow wrote the lyrics.

"BIG FAN," SAYS Hypno Joe, a crew-cutted martinet type.

"Thanks. I'm looking to fine-tune my memories of Ingo's movie."

"But it's perfect. I've read the book forty times. Forty-one, if you count next time, which I'm almost about to do."

"Yes. Well, a little further investigation is in order, my friend."

I add "my friend" to try to ingratiate myself. It seems to have worked well for my double.

"Great!" he says.

It worked.

"Have you ever been hypnotized before?" he asks. "Some people are not receptive to it."

I show him my toggle.

"Oh," he says, admiringly. "Who did the installation? It's good work."

"I did it myself. From a kit."

"Well, I'm impressed. Hold on now."

And he switches it.

"Tell me what you see," he says.

"I'm with the meteorologist. He's pulling out his hair in despair because he can't bear to look backward at those tiny transparent drifting droplet demons, as he calls them in his interior monologue, nor can he bear to look forward toward the imminent fiery end of the world. But time, as it must, needs to be filled. He remembers the little girl. That one ray of sunshine, the one for whom he buried a doll. And for whom, he now realizes, he will, over his final ten years, bury hundreds of things, everything she wants, so that she can discover them, so that all her needs will be met, so she will grow up feeling the love of a universe he now understands to be dead, a block of ice, incapable of caring about anything. He will watch over her from here, a pair of cave-bound eyes from the past focused only on her. I am reminded of the so-called Eyes of God, two massive eye-shaped holes in the ceiling of the Bulgarian cave Prohodna. The very holes that were, as everyone knows, featured so memorably in Ludmil Staikov's 1988 *Време на насилие*, a fever-dream master-piece seen by almost no one but me. Perhaps *Време на насилие* is the film I could champion if the Ingo film is not fully remembered. I did try when it was released, going so far as to learn Bulgarian and attend a three-day Janissary 'boot camp,' which, it turned out, was a bit new-agey and mostly yoga with kilijes. It set me back 10,000 Turkish lira and put me off the project. But it might be time to resurrect it. *Время на насилие* is brilliant and—"

"Wait, is this the film?" asks Hypno Joe.

"No. I don't know. I don't think so."

"So should we maybe get back to—"

"Yes. Yes, sorry. OK."

The meteorologist fast-forwards the holographic image and watches her, now at eleven years old, tanned, a garden trowel holstered in her belt, the handle of a trenching shovel rested on her shoulder. A young Jeanne Hachette—Jeanne Pelle à Creuser. There is the air of a warrior about her, of supreme confidence. It is as he had planned. When she passes, people deferentially step aside, watch her with awe. I am in love, thinks the meteorologist. I feel a renewed sense of hope for humanity. Who is this creature? Am I somehow responsible for the way she has developed, for what she has become? Or is she responsible for what I will become?

"Excuse me, Digger?" someone says to her.

Digger! How wonderful!

"Hi, Emily," Digger says. "How are you doing today?"

"I'm fine, thanks. My Audrey had her shoes stolen, and I was wondering if you might be able to find some new ones for her."

"Oh, I'm sorry to hear that. I'll surely try. What's her size again?"

"Women's five."

"That's right. Let's see what we can find."

As Emily looks on, Digger wanders, almost in a trance.

"What is her favorite type of shoe again?"

"Anything would be wonderful, really."

"I seem to remember she liked that picture of those Keen Voyageur hiking shoes. She took a real shine to them. Is that right?"

"You're amazing, Digger. That's exactly right."

"OK, then. What color?"

"I think it's called raven/rose dawn."

Digger nods, wanders, stops.

"Here, I think," she says. "Yes."

She kneels, digs with her garden trowel. A foot or so down she hits something hard, pulls a brush from her belt, gently sweeps away soil, and pulls out a gunmetal gray box.

"Here, Emily. See if these work."

Emily opens the box and finds a pair of Keen Voyageurs, size five, in raven/rose dawn.

"Oh my God," she says. "Thank you!"

"I'm sorry they're not in mint condition. Frankly, I'm surprised about that."

"Are you kidding? It's the end of the world! These are beyond anything I could've hoped for!"

Emily throws her arms around Digger, pulling her into a tight hug.

"I'm glad I could help, Emily," says Digger. "Give my love to Audrey, would ya?"

"I will! Oh, she's going to love these! Thank you! Thank you! Thank you!"

Emily runs off with the shoes.

The meteorologist has taken notes: Keen Voyageur hiking shoes. Women's size five. Raven/rose dawn. He switches his computer screen from the Digger scene to Zappos and orders the shoes.

I remember when that order came in! I'm certain it's the same one. There had been an inventory error and we were out of raven/rose dawn in five. We had it listed as "in stock," but it wasn't, and Keen had discontinued the color. The customer was contacted, offered a substitution. He became irate, threatened to trash us on Yelp if we didn't make good on his purchase. Zappos would and did do anything to avoid negative Yelp reviews. A man in New Hampshire with heel blisters was "disappeared" before he could post his dissatisfaction. In the end, we found that Henrietta had stolen the last pair. Of course. Henrietta had been born with Henderson-Bagley Midget Foot Syndrome, which is probably where her obsession with shoes started. The Keens were returned, slightly worn, and Henrietta was summarily fired. She blamed me, of course, even though her termination was her own doing. I suppose it was then that she first vowed to kill me. In any event, the shoes were sent to the customer with apologies and a complimentary shoehorn. He gave us a glowing Yelp review.

Wait, is that right? Didn't I get Henrietta fired for getting me fired? With an anonymous letter to Jeff Bezos saying she was anti-Semitic? Can both of these versions of history be true?

"No. Only one history per customer," says Hypno Joe. "Continue."

"Right. So the meteorologist switches to his own time arc in the simulation, watches himself in the cave ordering these shoes from Zappos, getting the shoes, writing the review. He speeds this trajectory forward, finds the point when the Zappos box is delivered to his cave at 41 South Oleara Debord, watches himself on a plane, then in a field, GPS in hand, digging a hole, placing a gunmetal box in it, and covering it up. After, as an experiment, he punches in his own trajectory with the qualifiers 'shovel' and 'digging.' What comes up is astonishing. Shot after shot of him digging holes and burying gunmetal gray boxes of various sizes. He will create this girl he loves, whom he loves based on his first witnessing the girl he loves being the girl he loves. There is a paradox here. And, of course, knowing what he knows of the world, he is aware that causation does not exist, certainly not in the way the human brain interprets it. Everything is because it is. There is no choice. Still, the illusion persists. The illusion is that he has a choice in the burying of these boxes. The reality is he cannot not."

"This is all very different from your book," says Hypno Joe, ending the session.

"Yes," I say, "the amazing thing about Ingo's work is how it seems to shift upon subsequent viewings. Just like my own memories, my memories of Henrietta, for example."

Hypno Joe nods, having lost interest. He tries to sell me a bag of Cup o' Hypno Joe coffee, French roast. I decline. As I return to my musing, I am indeed heartened. This memory of the meteorologist sequences proves to me that my version of the movie is the real one, not doppelgänger boy's. With this renewed confidence, I can prove it to the world. But can I? Hypno Joe, although polite, is grinding beans. I'm beginning to believe his entire hypnosis business is only a bait and switch for his coffee company.

How can I get people excited about my true version of the movie? It occurs to me there is only one way. Digger will not be the only digger. In other words, I, too, will be one. Too.

CHAPTER 65

I TAKE THE NEXT bus down to St. Augustine. If I can once again find the puppets of the Unseen, I might prove to the world (and myself, for I have begun to question my sanity) that the movie did indeed exist as I say and not as my stupid clone said, not to mention we'll save time and energy during preproduction not having to re-create this entire world of Unseen puppets for the remake. I explain this to my seatmate, who is, coincidentally, once again Levy (Grabby), on his way home from his seasonal clown gag-writing gig at the Big Apple Circus and Orchard. It's good to see a familiar face, and although I have my own seat this time, we do revert to our old arrangement for a little while, I suppose out of some sort of nostalgia.

"So just to be clear, there's a bunch of black fellas buried in the yard?" Grabby says.

"No, Levy. There are thousands of African American *puppets* buried in the yard. At least, I believe this to be true."

"And I thought clown gags were goofy. This is downright goofier."

"The filmmaker was exploring notions of cultural invisibility."

"Well, ain't that the darnedest thing. You know, I came up with this clown gag where fifty or so clowns climb out of a bucket. And the kicker is it's not even a bucket that could normally hold fifty clowns. Like, this one's maybe a five-gallon bucket, right? The trick," he whispers, "is there's a hole in the floor plus a hole in the bottom of the bucket, and the clowns are down in the cellar and they climb out one by one. That's the gag. How do they all fit in the bucket? The trick is they don't really. See? I based it off of a gag called the Clown Car, which operates on a similar principle. Basically, in that one, a whole bunch of clowns climb out of a small car. But it's a trick; they're really coming from the cellar. There's a hole in the bottom of the car. This is a new take on that classic bit. And it's better, in my opinion, because a bucket is even smaller than a car, so folks are gonna be even more surprised. I call it Clown Bucket. It's kind of what your colored moviemaking buddy did, I think."

"I think it's different," I say.

"A lotta clowns, a lotta black folks," he says. "It's a very similar gag."

I let it go and, after a couple of minutes, so as not to seem as if in response to our disagreement, I climb off Grabby's lap and sit back in my own seat. Grabby is a nice enough fellow, but I think we've reached the limits of our relationship. He is, when all is said and done, a simple clown gag writer, and while that's honest and noble work, it has very little in common with the type of writing Ingo and I do. I am not saying it is less important. Clowning is an ancient art form, and if we've learned anything from Preston Sturges's ridiculously sentimental scene at the end of *Sullivan's Travels*, it is that the downtrodden sometimes need a good laugh. So I applaud Grabby's efforts and am happy for his successes.

After an hour or so of silence, Grabby tells me I should come over to his trailer for a beer some night while I'm in town. I say that sounds great, but we both know it will never happen, indeed it could never happen, and not only because I am not a "beer person." It's a sad realization, and we remain silent for the remainder of the long ride. When we arrive at the bus station, we don't even exchange phone numbers after our hug.

My taxi pulls up to the apartment complex at around midnight. The driver removes my suitcase, spade, shovel, and pickax from the trunk.

"Burying something?" he says.

"The opposite."

"Burying some*one*?"

"Burying someone is not the opposite of burying something," I say. "I am *uncovering* something, if you must know."

"A treasure?"

"Not in the way you mean, certainly. But there is no gold or jewel that compares to what I am seeking."

He shrugs and drives off.

I dig precisely where I first discovered the puppet bodies. I remember where it was because there was (and still is) a bronze plaque that reads Nothing to See Here, Folks. Move Along. However, it appears this go around to be accurate, for there is indeed nothing here. No puppets, not even puppet skeletons. Nothing. Just dirt and lots of it. Soon the apartment manager appears and hands me a much-handled sheet of paper that reads: *Hey! What the hell are you doing? Stop it! This is private property!*

I look up at him from down in my hole; he recognizes my face, looks surprised, then shuffles through papers in his satchel and pulls out another sheet: *Oh! I didn't recognize you from behind and above without your yarmulke. Hello, my friend! Would you like to come in for a* glezl fun tey?

"I don't know what that means," I mouth.

A cup of tea. It's Yiddish. You taught me that, he writes.

"Oy," I mouth.

I climb from the hole and make my lonely way to the road. A crumpled piece of paper hits me in the back of the head. I pick it off the ground and read it: *Hey! Hey! I'm talking to you!* I keep walking, head hung low. I am hit again and again with balled-up sheets of paper. I pick them all up and put them in my satchel. Perhaps I will read them on the bus ride home to pass the time. I keep walking. There is nothing for me here anymore.

The trip home is on one of those new Uber buses, which is really just a gutted station wagon. You're allowed to bring on your own seat but only if it fits in the twenty-two inch by fourteen inch by nine inch space allotted. Consequently, most people have to check their seats—which costs extra—and sit on the floor.

I uncrumple the notes from the apartment manager and read them in their numbered sequence:

Why won't you answer me?

Don't you remember all the good times we had?

Remember how much we both loved the Jupiter Theatre production that reimagined Children of a Lesser God *as a gay romance starring Burt Reynolds and Lou Ferrigno?*

It's about time that it was reimagined thusly, you said.

I agreed. Because love is love, I said.

You agreed.

I thought we were friends.

Why are you doing this to me?

You know I converted to Judaism for you!

Look! I'm turned around so you can see my kippah!

This is very hurtful!

I have some cold brisket in the fridge. We could have a nosh.

You are a monster, you know that?

I want my painting of Helen Keller back!

Please, B.

Fine, then. Fine. I don't care anymore.

I expect you to ship that Keller picture back, B., I really do.

Please, give me a minute. Let's just talk.

I can't believe you.

Fuck you!

There are more, but I will save them for later, as I am suddenly sleepy.

HYPNO JOE OFFERS me a Coffee of the Month subscription, which I decline. He sighs and flips my switch. The meteorologist has skipped further into the future. Slammy's (formerly Slappy's) has an army now and requires a two-year service in its military (the Slarmy, formerly the Slapry) for all citizens. This has raised the hackles of some pundits, but as Minister of Marketing Marjorie "Mellifluous" Morningstar points out: "Freedom isn't free." The constant menace of the Trunks, who want to rule the entire cave and have now been retrofitted with nuclear bombs in their heads under their recently installed cranial propellers, must be addressed. The meteorologist watches this worrisome development as it unfolds on his monitor. He thinks of Digger and understands she is the one to lead a rebellion of the people. But, of course, he needs to tell her that. And he has done just that.

On his monitor, the meteorologist watches as Digger unearths what she believes will be just a stash of wool hats (for winter is coming). In the box, he has also placed the Gerrard Winstanley pamphlet *The True Levellers Standard Advanced: Or, the State of Community Opened, and Presented to the Sons of Men*. Of course every schoolboy (and girl and nonbinary, *et chetera*) has read this pamphlet and knows Winstanley to be the founder of the Diggers, a group of proto-anarchists active during the English Civil War who believed in the abolition of wages and the free distribution of goods and food to all of their followers. Digger reads the pamphlet in its entirety. Ingo does not bother to include voiceover here, as every schoolchild has read the text and been required to commit it to memory, and, really, voiceover would diminish the pure joy experienced by the viewer as he/she/thon watches Digger's face become increasingly bathed in the glow of enlightenment then set in the glow of steely determination. The sequence is quite long (perhaps an hour and a half) because the pamphlet is quite long and because, unfortunately, Digger is afflicted with severe dyslexia. But the energy builds nicely throughout, and when she finally finishes, she marches to the top of a small hill and delivers the following sermon:

"My people, the time is now, for the time is always now, is it not? We must stand together and oppose those who would oppress us. And if you as a people come to the conclusion I have come to as an individual, then we must act collectively to change the trajectory of human history. Do we want to live our lives as slaves to an inhuman corporation or, perhaps worse, as slaves to a mindless army of robotic and propellered death-dealers? I tell you we must not accept our 'lot,' but rather fight for a kinder world, one built on the principles of sharing and a proper integration with nature. I believe there is a God who watches over us. How else can my talent at unearthing these gifts be explained? And who placed the gifts, if not some Supreme Being? I do not imagine this being to be like us. It is not a 'he' or a 'she' or even a 'thon.' How narcissistic would it be of us to think so? No, my friends, this being exists in a form we cannot ever hope to comprehend. But I do know it wants us to thrive, do good work, and be kind to each other, as Garrison Keillor once admonished us before his fall from grace. I welcome you to this movement I am creating, which will extricate us from the oppressive chains of a governmental system based on violence and the avaricious accumulation of material wealth. It is my sincere belief that if you join with me, the creator will continue to provide for us and will perhaps even gift others of you with the blessed talent of digging. So, friends, remove your Slarmy uniforms and together we will dig up the clothing of a free people!"

The meteorologist sighs, massages his temples, freezes the image, counts the number of people disrobing (eighty-nine) and attempts to guess at their sizes and tastes.

THE CCO OF Slammy's, L. Larabee Chevre, paces in his foreboding neo-Gothic suite of offices.

"We cannot compete with this magic!" he says. "We cannot!"

"I know," says his second, Executive Vice President in Charge of Condiments and Armaments Bailey Oltz. "But this is with . . . what we are contending."

"We need to find out her trick! There is a trick, obviously. No one can do what she appears to be capable of doing without a magic trick of some sort."

"And yet . . ."

"Maybe she buries them under cover of darkness."

"Two things: How would she know for what people are going to ask? And from where does she procure it?"

"It's a trick! Obviously!"

"Yes. Established. But of what is the trick? That is my question to you."

"I'm not a professional magician, nor even an amateur of any notable ranking. But I'll tell you this, EVP Oltz, it's done with sleight of hand and distraction."

"Sure. But, I mean, how would that work in this particular case?"

"What did I just tell you?"

"That . . . um, I don't know, sir. Sorry."

"I'm not a magician!"

"Yes."

"But we cannot let this stand. Without workers, Slammy's would have no customers, and without customers, Slammy's would have no workers."

"They are one and the same. One hand feeds the other."

"And without soldiers, the Trunks win. And no one wants that."

"Except the Trunks. The Trunks want that."

"Yes. Of course they would. That is just like them. We need to fight back. Get Voiceover Lady in here."

"You mean Marjorie?"

"I don't know her name! Why would I know her name?"

"It's Marjorie."

"I don't know it, I tell you!"

"People like it when you know their names. It makes them feel—"

"Do I pay her a fortune?"

"Sure."

"Then fuck her name."

Marjorie Morningstar, in an orange cashmere hoodie bedazzled with sapphires, sits, back arched, good-postured, hands clasped in her lap in infinite patience as Chevre paces.

"We need a campaign, Voiceover Lady."

"OK."

"Something honey-voiced."

"I can do that."

"Can you do that?"

"Sure."

"We need to tell 'em something like, 'The Trunks are gonna kill you if you're not protected by Slammy's.' Or maybe something like,

'Slammy's has always been there for you. Now it's time for you to be there for Slammy's.'"

"Maybe," offers Oltz, "'ask not what your Slammy's can do for you, ask what you can do for your Slammy's.'"

"What the fuck does that even mean?" says Chevre.

"It's a JFK thing."

"A JF what thing?"

"K."

"I don't know what that means."

"He was the president. JFK."

"Of Slammy's?"

"Of the United States."

"Of the— What the— Why would we want to quote the president of a country that went south in a ball of flames? That's bad branding. It'd be better to quote one of the Trunks."

"You want to quote a Trunk in a campaign against Trunks?"

"At least they're a worthy adversary. They have nuclear heads."

"That marketing strategy is not sound, if I may indeed say so."

"You may not. *You're* not sound. What do you think, Voiceover Lady?"

"What if we take a play from Digger's book? 'We're all in this together. God is with us.'"

"What about the magic?"

"Maybe something like, 'Magic is the work of the devil'?" Marjorie offers.

"Ooh. That's interesting. But something a little more mundane? Believable?"

"Magic is a trick," says Marjorie. "Slammy's does not trick you. Our hamburger is one hundred percent ground beef, zero percent scamburger."

"I like that. Scamburger. That's clever. We should also go out at night with a metal detector, dig up all her boxes, and replace the contents with human shit. Two-pronged."

"Where's your God now?" pitches Marjorie, selling past the close. "Slammy's. We never claimed we're divine. Except, of course, for our hot apple pies. Mmm-mmm. Slammy's."

"Hypno Joe's coffee is delicious with hot apple pie," Hypno Joe's voice injects into my hypnotic trance.

I try to ignore him, but in this state, I find myself highly suggestible.

"All right, one bag," I say.

"Great. I'll ring it up. It'll be ready to go when you awaken."

Night. Slammy's troops, dressed in black, armed with metal detectors and digging tools, scour the Digger territory for metal. They find boxes containing bandages, socks, knives (!), reading materials. They replace the original contents with human feces. The soldiers quietly giggle at their prank as they rebury the boxes.

The next day, the Diggers gather in a rocky field, observed by a hidden CCTV camera.

"We shall plant seeds in this land," says Digger, "which belongs to no one, and the crops that result will be used to feed all who join us."

"Where will we get the seeds?" asks a worried man. "Slammy's has them all patented. Stealing them will result in years in the Slammer, which as you know is what Slammy's calls its privatized prison system."

"We will plant our own seeds," says Digger, "which are . . . *here*."

And with that, Digger begins to dig. Soon she uncovers a canister, this one made of some sort of composite nonmetal polymer.

The scene cuts to Chevre's office, where he and his team are watching.

"What the," says Chevre. "We've been hoodwinked!"

"She knows our plan. Those metal containers were decoys."

"How could she know?"

"There must be a mole."

"That's kind of funny. Because moles dig, so—"

"It's not funny! It's treason, and he, she, or thon will be rooted out."

"Rooted out. Get it? Because—"

"Stop."

CHAPTER 66

Back on the street, loaded down with the twenty bags of coffee I purchased under the influence of mind control, I make my way to my apartment and espy *myself* emerging from it. Yes, it is I, but beardless. Another I. A third I. It seems that now whenever I leave town, I am replaced. This time when I was in Florida searching for puppets. It has got to stop. I follow this new me to a building on West 51st, where he presses a buzzer and is let in. What is he doing there?

Ever since that fumigation-tented clown tried and failed to murder me while I walked Gregory Corso, I have felt unsafe. Today I will do something about it. I am not a violent man, but it is a violent world. The fellow here has laid his wares out on the bed. It is reminiscent of that scene from *Taxi Driver* and also every movie and TV show since that has copied this scene from *Taxi Driver*. Perhaps there is nothing more to be said about illegal gun sales than was said by Marvin Scorsesso all those years ago. The illegal-gun man holds up a small pistol-type gun. Contemplating, I rub the part of my face that once housed my beard, affectionately fondling its new nakedness.

"This is the Kel-Tec PF-9," he tells me. "Lightest 9mm out there at 12.7 ounces. Seven rounds. Very popular with the ladies. You'll read some bad press out there, but it's mostly from folks with axes to grind, and, anyway, it ends up meaning savings for you, because these darlings are going cheap right now."

He hands it to me. I hold it nervously.

"It's not loaded," he says. "Don't be a baby."

I don't know why he told me it's popular with the ladies. He doesn't think I'm a lady, does he? Granted, without my beard, my delicate features are on display, and I am wearing my new Joey King hairmulke.

"What do you have that's popular with the gentlemen?" I ask, handing it back to him.

He lays the cute little gun on the bed and picks up another.

"This is a Ruger SR1911. Good gun. Great gun. Used by police and military. Much higher price tag, and, frankly, I think at thirty-nine ounces it's too much gun for you."

"Why do you say that?"

"Look, man, I make more money on the Ruger. I'm just trying to help you out."

He hands it to me. It is very heavy. And he did call me "man," so he knows I'm a man, so maybe it's OK to purchase the smaller gun, which, truth be told, I like more anyway. It's definitely prettier.

"Do men use the other one, the PR-9?" I ask.

"PF-9. Sure."

"OK, I'll take one of those."

"Great. You need a holster? I advise it."

"I guess so."

"Great."

He pulls a hot-pink holster from his bag.

"This is a great item, buddy. Eco-leather exterior, so, I don't know if you're vegan or vegetarian or what have you, but it's recycled leather, so you can feel guilt-free about it. No animals were killed. There *is* a suede interior to protect the gun's finish. Not eco-suede as far as I know, but it's a recommended indulgence. The whole shebang has been treated to be sweat-proof. Passive-retention. The ladies really love it."

"Do you have it in black or . . . that army greenish color?"

"Olive drab."

"What?"

"The color is called olive drab."

"Oh. Yes. That."

"No, I'm sorry, sir. This is all I have at the moment. I have a spangled one, if you like."

He called me "sir." I take the pink holster. But he did tell me the ladies love it. And he did say *she*bang. But he did call me "buddy." Anyway, the truth is pink as a "feminine" color is a cultural construct. In point of fact, before the turn of the twentieth century, pink was considered a boy's color and girls were consigned to blue. And in any event, gender is not binary, as we all now know. Certainly, I have character traits that would be considered feminine by most, and that is something I am comfortable with, even proud of. *Everyone* can comfortably exhibit a full range of characteristics now, but when I was young, it required a gender outlaw's courage (and notes from three doctors) to straddle the line, as it were. And straddle it I did.

I WATCH BEARDLESS me leave, an odd new bulge under his worsted blazer. I fall into step behind him, careful to keep a safe distance and to maintain a pedestrian shield between us. The sunlight is direct here in the Seen. Whereas concealment was almost a given during my time in the murky Unseen, even as a giant, here I must remain vigilant, even as a non-giant. Suddenly, beardless me drops into an open manhole, which reminds me that concealment from beardless me is not the only danger I face in the Seen. There is also the Creator, the One Who Can See All Without Being Seen. The One Who Knows What I Am Thinking. I need to speak with this third me without being recognized by either him or the creator. I grab a mop from an untended janitor's bucket, unscrew the mophead, and place it over my own head as a sort of wig. It is makeshift but it does, I believe, do the trick, because as B3 climbs out of the sewer, he does not seem to recognize me (himself). He does look worried, however, and appears to be fingering the bulge under his blazer. The mop smells of mildew and cleaning agents.

"I'm sorry to bother you," I say.

"What? What?" he demands, eyes wide. "I don't have any money if that's what you're after!"

"I just want to ask you a question."

The ammoniated water drips into my eyes and my mouth; I spit.

"What? What do you want?" he says.

"I'm just wondering what you were thinking about right before you fell into the manhole."

"Personhole."

"What?"

"Personhole."

Yes, of course, he's right. I know that. I learned that. How could I have again called it a manhole? It is so obviously wrong. I suppose because I had been thinking of my enemy Manohla Dargis. She is a woman, and therefore . . . But that's spelled differently. I'm such an idiot.

"I'm an idiot!" I scream. "I'm such an idiot!"

"Why do you want to know what I was thinking?" he screams, stepping back.

"I am taking a survey!" I scream, having thunk quickly.

"For what?"

He is calming down.

"Congress of Racial Equality," I say, knowing intimately his political affiliations.

"Oh. OK," he says.

I flip some of the mop ropes behind my ear and— Wait, does that do something for him? Turn him on? Me playing with my "hair"? For the briefest of moments, I feel fetching. Mop water runs down my back.

"I am a film theorist," he says. "When I fell, I was thinking about handguns for reasons that do not concern you or anyone. And my mind flashed on a scene from an atrocious little movie called *Human Nature*, written by an atrocious little screenwriter named Charlie Kaufman. In it, there is a scene featuring Peter Dinklage, a brilliant but then little-known actor, who incidentally happens to be a little person—"

"Which is what they prefer to be called," we both add.

"Exactly," we both agree.

"In any event," he continues, "Peter Dinklage wields a gun in one scene, and it was obvious to me that Kaufman knows nothing about guns and most likely had never even been near one and—"

Out of nowhere, an out-of-control bicycle-driving delivery fellow clips the curb with his front tire, flips head over heels right into the ersatz me, and sends him flying into the street, where he plummets with a *swoosh* into yet another open manhole. Personhole.

My suspicions have been confirmed, which is a double-edged sword. I am glad there is a logical explanation for the ridiculousness of my existence. But the horrifying reality is that I am under the thumb of a third-rate talent who no doubt despises me as much as I do him, likely because I have called him out on his pathetic attempts at screenage. He holds all the cards in the ill-conceived, irrational world in which I find myself unjustly imprisoned. The only good news is that I have been replaced with what is no doubt a robot/clone version of me, and I am now free of Kaufman's misanthropic eye. The terrible news is that my survival requires I remain unseen in this Seen world. I could find my way back to the Unseen, I suppose, but quite frankly, that place is even worse. A vague world of half-forgotten ideas and shadowy, anonymous people. A world without light, save the dim glow that makes its way there from this one. No, the key is to remain here and live in the background, in the crowd, to not distinguish myself in any way. Let B3 get all the attention. He'll keep the monster busy until this nightmare which is my life is over. Maybe there is another way out, but I suspect not. I cannot win against a god. Presently, I will find myself a better, cleaner disguise, and I must be discreet in acquiring it. Perhaps there is some sort of underground false ID community here that I can discover. Perhaps there are surgeons who will make one unrecognizable to one's creator for a fee. I can't be the only one who wants to hide from this untalented monster. Certainly audiences seem to.

Now *I* fall into the personhole. It is dark.

"You there?" I whisper.

"Yes," says B3.

"I assume you've seen Ingo Cutbirth's film?"

"Of course. I am the keeper of its memory. Everyone knows this."

"And is it still about the Adventure Girls?"

"Allow me to quote the master directly, from his journals, of which I have an eidetic memory."

"Please do," I say.

I am not going to go into the whole eidetic memory fight with this guy right now. It's too wet down here.

"The Adventure Girls, fourteen sisters, born simultaneously of fourteen raindrops, who grow to adventurousness in a field of blue-bonnet in Bardwell, who grow to pulchritudinousness in a field of creeping phlox in Florida, who grow to near-womanhood in a field of Saint-John's-wort in St. Augustine. Divinely created to be well-endowed with wisdom and breasts and penises, the Adventure Girls are warriors fighting for goodness' sake. Made of jelly but exploding into hardness, undulating, whispering hardness. And I put myself beneath them, as their servant. By creating them, I am working for them. They told me to create them. They own me. And so I move them as they instruct me to. I fill their heads with ambition and confidence and sex because that is what they want. They want me to worship them. So I do. And they save us. They save humanity. That is what they do because that is what they tell me to have them do."

"Lovely," I say. "Carry on with your noble task."

I climb out and hurry off to continue my work on the actual version of the film. I will do it in secret, the world distracted by this ridiculous beardless counterfeit.

I PULL MYSELF out of the personhole. Mop-man is gone. I suspect he was not in the employ of CORE. But who is he? What did he want? As is always the case, I am only a bit bruised and dirty from my tumble. I brush myself off, check that my pistol is still properly holstered, and proceed to Charlie Rose for my interview.

The guy being interviewed ahead of me is a professor of comedy teamology at Ohio Wesleyan University. He's on to plug his new book, *Teaming Masses*.

"There are a hunnert and twenny to a hunnert and fifty teams in the world. All the same configuration. Opposites. We got the fat guy and the skinny guy, the short guy and the tall guy, the bowleggedy guy and the knock-kneed guy, the pigeon-toed and the duck-footed, the dumb guy and the smart guy. Comedy is conflict, so they make sure the personalities are sufficiently different from each other. Never mind that two such guys would never be friends in the real world."

A lightbulb goes off in my brain. Or, rather, on. Two of the Adventure Girls are watching television in one scene, and there is a snippet of comic banter between two men. I forgot all about it, so peripheral was it in my mind to the tragic thrust, thrust, thrust of the film, but what if I was wrong? Ingo was an animator. Each frame was chosen, each line, each concept. There is nothing extraneous in that film. How could I assume that moment is? Perhaps this short piece of apparent background noise is the key that will unlock all the secrets of Ingo's film for me and subsequently the world. I must try to remember. For the sake of everyone.

CHAPTER 67

"WOULD YOU LIKE another bag of Morning Blend?" interrupts Hypno Joe.

"Yes, Master."

"Cool. I'll ring it up. Continue."

The Trunks have a Cabinet meeting, which consists of fifty of them sitting at a long oak table and ranting in unison, like some sort of bellicose, moronic Greek chorus.

"Slammy's is bad. Everybody knows that. Very bad. That I can tell you. But you know that already. And what are we about? Love. We love all our citizens. I like to say that Slammy's is a bad corporation. Slimy Slammy's, I call it. Slimy Slammy's wants your hard-earned money. That's all they care about. We care about making sure *you* get a fair deal. And it's time to rebuild our country. To make it great. Now, diplomacy is always my first choice. But Slimy Slammy's is laughing at us. Well, not anymore, folks. Because we're going to make this country great again. And what about those Diggers? Do we want Communism? No. I've come up with a name for them. I call them the Dirty Diggers. Because have you ever seen them, folks? They don't look too good, let me tell you. And they're afraid of fighting. We love to fight. Am I right? We are a peace-loving people but we will not let anyone take advantage of us. And we are gonna make sure the Dirty Diggers and the Slimy Slammy's know it. And they'll be happier, too. Everyone will get a good deal, but we have to get a good deal first."

Across the cave, Marjorie Morningstar wields a megaphone.

"Slammy's cares about you, because Slammy's *is* you. Humans are Slammy's employees and customers. There is not even one robot running our company, let alone ten thousand. We know what you like. We understand what food should taste like. We know what entertains you. We know what medicine makes you feel better, what features you want on your phones. At Slammy's, we believe robots should work for humans, not the other way around. And, of course, we celebrate the sincerity of the Diggers. We do, however, question the motives of their leadership. Are they trying to sow the seeds of distrust among people? Is their communistic plan workable for a complex society such as ours? All academic studies suggest not. Who will make your phones? Your movies? Your burgers? Do a series of magic tricks equal a proven system of governance? Slammy's: No tricks. Second burger free on Tuesdays."

I DUMP THE mophead in a trash receptacle, enter my (B3's) apartment, and search for something to use as a disguise. My (his) closets are packed with stylish tallises, Dockers, ostentatiously patterned dress shirts. Not much here with which to create a disguise. I check in Clown Laurie's closet. It is chock-full of sheitels. Most decidedly feminine, but there are a few of the pixie variety that could work well for me as a sort of "boy" haircut. I've always loved the "boy" cut. I grab the one labeled THE MICHELLE WILLIAMS. It's platinum blond and frankly looks pretty good on me. I look twenty years younger, I must say. I shave the beard to make it totally work and use Clown Laurie's concealer to hide my birthmark.

Next, I find a black pantsuit, white shirt, and black pussy bow combo, which could pass as menswear, I think. The wig makes me look a bit like a magician, which in a way I am, I think, with words. I steal a bunch of cash and leave.

The doorman looks up as I pass him in the lobby.

"Do you need a cab, Mrs. Rosenberg?" he calls after me.

I shake my head no and wave without looking back. I don't even try to do her voice.

* * *

BACK AT HOME, I find Clown Laurie on the bed looking distraught.

"Someone has been in our apartment. My Michelle wig and my Alexander McQueen pantsuit are missing," she says.

"That's bizarre," I say.

"And two thousand dollars."

"Who would do such a thing?"

"Does it smell like old mop in here?" Clown Laurie asks.

I reach into my blazer and finger my holstered Kel-Tec PR-9.

"Is that a Kel-Tec PF-9?" asks Clown Laurie.

"Yes," I say, "or PR-9."

"PF-9. Isn't that a lady gun?"

I sit in silence in our soundproof (but never G-d-proof) collapsible shul. I come here to pray, of course, but also, sometimes, just to think. Some might say, "B., isn't thinking a form of prayer?" And I would have to agree with those folks, for the productive use of HaShem's greatest gift to human beings, the human mind, is in a very real sense a kind of prayer. Today my "prayer" is an attempt to recall the tiniest of curlicues in Ingo's magnificent tapestry. For in a perfect piece of art, the smallest detail may be the key to understanding the entire thing. Can Bosch's *The Garden of Earthly Delights* exist fully, or even make any sense at all, if the tiny image of G-d were to be removed from the upper left of the grisaille outer panel? He is barely visible there, yet he is the engine—nay, the reason—for everything else present, indeed for everything else present, past, and future. So it most likely is with any and all elements of Ingo's magnificent creation. Therefore, it is with the upmost—

"Did you think 'upmost'?" asks Clown Laurie, who is nearby polishing the Shabbat candlesticks.

"No," I say.

"Oh," she says.

And so it is with the utmost seriousness of purpose that I search deep within my memory of Ingo's film to bring forth this neglected, essential detail. I see Madd and Molly, naked, African American, bepenised, attending to a sick child, also naked, African American, and

566

be-penised. A single incandescent bulb swinging from a wire illuminates this unadorned room. On the television set, to which no one present is paying any attention, an ancient black-and-white film plays. I push past the "central" action of the scene in an attempt to focus on this single background element, this flickering grisaille, as it were. Onscreen, two men—one fat, one meager—seem to be engaged in some sort of buffoonery. I attempt to divert my attention from the riveting foreground sequence featuring these oppressed, beautiful girls, and push into the fuzzy imagery on the small TV screen in the corner of the room. The two men, one fedoraed and one bowlered, stand onstage in front of a curtain before an unseen audience. Are they father and son? I cannot tell for certain, but one seems considerably older than the other, although which one of them, I cannot tell.

"I think David Sedaris is a schmuck."

"The writer?"

"Yes. He's a writer. I saw him on a talk show. He was wearing a pink pleated dress shirt, a sequined vest, blazer, and shorts."

"And that upset you?"

"He looked like an asshole."

"That seems like a violent reaction to someone wearing shorts."

"He wanted to look like an asshole."

"Why do you think that?"

"Why would a man dress like that?"

"Maybe he thought it looked good? What's interesting to me is why you have such an extreme reaction."

"I don't know. Maybe I'm a jerk."

"I'm not saying you're a jerk. I'm just saying when a person has such a violent reaction to something that has no actual effect on their life, it's interesting to explore why."

"I don't know. I think the host is an anti-Semite."

"What does that have to do with how Sedaris dressed?"

"They approve how the guests dress."

"I don't think that's true."

"I think he wanted Robert Sedaris to look like an asshole."

"David Sedaris."

"David Sedaris."

"And David Sedaris isn't Jewish."

"Let me ask you this, would you be embarrassed to go out to a restaurant with him?"

"David Sedaris? You mean if he was dressed like that?"

"Yes."

"No."

"Really? Don't you think people would stare?"

"No. I don't think anyone would care."

"Really?"

"Maybe in Montana. Maybe there I might worry about getting beaten up, but not here."

"Really?"

"No one would even look up, except maybe to think, oh, that's David Sedaris."

"What if he wasn't David Sedaris?"

"You mean, some unknown guy dressed like that?"

"Yes."

"No one would care."

"Really?"

"Maybe in Montana."

I assume this is a comedy routine, but I don't think it's funny. Then, I am not an expert in or even an admirer of comedy. I do know who David Sedaris is, however, and very much enjoy his stories, not for their humor (which I cannot follow), but for their pathos. In fact, if one were to strip all the "jokes" out of all David Sedaris stories, I would not miss them at all. To me, it is padding that dilutes his true message, which is one of human cruelty, human frailty, and human despair. Why did Ingo put this routine by a father and son dressed as vaudevillians on the television in the background of the scene of Madd and Molly tending to the terribly injured child?

That it mirrors exactly a conversation I had with my own father just last week seems too pointed to be a coincidence. Is it possible that this minuscule buried segment is this movie's God particle?

The buried particle that explains everything? Everything in the world of the movie and outside of it?

I HAVE TAKEN up residence, at least until I find something affordable, inside the holy ark behind the Torahs in B3's portable, inflatable shul. It's surprisingly spacious back here and allows me to hear when B3 and Clown Laurie leave the apartment, at which time I can emerge to do my ablutions and get food. On Friday evenings and Saturdays—when I know the ark will be opened—I sleep in their weight and cardio room, as no exercising will be done in this house on Shabbat. I have also discovered that I can come and go without incident in my new outfit, as the doorman doesn't seem to be able to distinguish between Clown Laurie and me. So I am able to continue my hypnosis work, now with the Great Ted Cheese, as Hypno Joe has suddenly retired to become a stage actor like Barassini. Hypno Joe referred me to Ted Cheese when I visited him at his storefront, which he still keeps, but now to store his many acting wigs.

On a spread blanket on the sidewalk on St. Marks Place, among bongs and glass doorknobs and assorted bric-a-brac, I come upon a dog-eared copy of Barbosae's *An Avenue of Infinite Regress*. I bargain the attending hippie girl down to forty-five cents (she wanted fifty, but they won't respect you if you don't bargain) and walk off with my find. The volume is filled with copious notations in the margins. I attempt to read a few, but the cribbed handwriting is atrocious and nigh illegible. I *am* able to make out the following:

Dimple
Wergeld
Conductress
Agelast
Fordrunken
Moksha
Teddy boy
Au pied de la lettre

Psephology
Karezza
Dimple (again)

Obviously, this reader has a bone to pick with Barbosae, and I can't say I blame her. I know it's a woman because I minored in graphology at Harvard and I have little doubt this scribbler is female, thirty-four to forty-three (at time of writing), American, highly educated, alcoholic, cisgender, narcissistic with a history of self-harm, a victim of domestic abuse, and prone to confabulation, hand cramping, and embarrassing public outbursts. She is, in short (oh, she is also short), the woman for me, with her fiery red hair, insouciance, athletic build, and ample hips. I can even tell from her handwriting that I could make her happy, maybe not dressed in my current disguise, but were I to be someday free of this need to hide, I know we'd find ourselves enmeshed in the most passionate of romantic entanglements. That much is obvious from her handwriting. And, of course, we have our shared interest in Barbosae's book to bind us. Why did she seek out this obscure volume, and why did she mark it up so intently? Why else would she have written to me in the margins about the gentle lovemaking called karezza, for indeed this was written to me. Who else was ever going to pick up this book on St. Marks Place; who else was ever going to know about karezza? Ah, Renata, for I have no doubt that is her name (the great Renata Adler? It's possible. She would, of course, know of my writing). I am certain the scribbler's name is Renata, because the science of graphology allows a researcher to determine which letters the writer uses most often. I suppose her name could be Natter, but I hope not. I wander uptown, fantasizing about Renata, how I will spend the time necessary to fully decipher her margin notes, how I will track her down, how we will engage slowly, carefully, as we've both been terribly hurt in the past, but once the trust is full, there will be no stopping us. We will be the New York "it" couple, invited to all the parties, the envy of the moneyed (for the trueness of our love) and by the common folks (for the amount of our money).

As I wait to cross at the corner of 14th and 5th, a young man asks me to perform a magic trick. Normally, when this has happened in the past (and it has happened frequently), I have said no, since I am not a trained monkey, but as I am in hiding, I currently have no means of earning a living, and although street magicians are generally not wealthy, there are a few (Stephen the Magnificent, The Great Toby, and Abra Ca Dabney) who live quite comfortably. I have with me my trick silver dollar, the one that folds up into four quarters, so I can, without detection, place it in, then pull it out of, someone's ear. The young man is astonished, and a crowd forms. Soon I am going through my entire repertoire—levitation, swallowing a lit cigarette (I could swear I didn't have any cigarettes with me, let alone a lit one in my hand) then pulling it out of a dog's nose, sawing a woman in half, making the Statue of Liberty disappear. After two hours, I've accrued thirty dollars. Not a bad haul. I worried that I had perhaps brought unnecessary attention to myself, so I was relieved when everyone said, "Thank you, ma'am," as I packed up my magic kit. Perhaps I will make this a regular thing. I am thinking of calling myself Ms. Terious, just to keep the hounds off my scent. It's got a nice ring to it, too. Maybe Ledgerde Mae, although that might be over the heads of the average Times Square tourist. Perhaps Prestidigi Dacia. It's actually kind of fun to think these up. Girls always have the best name options.

CHAPTER 68

A T NIGHT IN the ark, I listen to B3 discussing, with Clown Laurie, his new thoughts about Ingo's movie.

"G-d is in the details," he tells Clown Laurie, "as many before me have said, except they almost always include the *o*."

"They also say the devil is in the details," counters Clown Laurie. "So please be careful, B."

"Either way, the point, my friend, my wife, my wife and friend, is that only by exploring the smallest of things can one hope to understand the largest of things. I was a fool to believe I had fully understood Ingo's *chef d'oeuvre*, his *meisterstück*, his *remek-djelo*, his—"

"How many languages do you know the word masterpiece in?"

"The most important of words, my friend, my wife, the most important of all words."

"Right. I'm seriously asking though."

"Sixteen."

"Wow."

"Impressed?"

"Sure. Why not?"

"I must go back in, focusing the electron microscope that is my eidetic memory onto this entire film. It cannot be studied too closely. Each word, each gesture, each extra passing by in the background, each lick of flame, each icicle, each little girl penis, each drop of blood spilled in battle, each hopeless sigh, each broken dream, each—"

Jesus, this guy is unbearable, I think, from inside the ark. How can Clown Laurie stand him? I peek out through the small space where the ark doors meet. Laurie is examining her fingernails, looking bored.

"—stubbed toenail, each splash of rain in the neutral zone, each television transmission, each note of incidental score, each—"

"B.?" says Clown Laurie.

"Yes?" he says.

"I get it. I really do. Details are important."

"OK."

"It's just I've got an early day tomorrow, and—"

"No. I understand. It's cool."

"Maybe we can continue this conversation tomorrow?"

"Sure. Sure. You go to bed. I'm just going to—"

"Yeah. I'll see you in there."

Clown Laurie quickly leaves, B3 continues to think deeply, and I fall asleep.

THE TRUNKS DISCOVER the meteorologist's computer, now dusty and long abandoned. They turn it on.

"Hey," says the computer.

"We need a way to fight the Slammy's shows," they say into the microphone.

"Their shows?" asks the computer.

"Their entertainment. Their shows. You know."

"I see. Well, there is an invention in my files from decades ago. It's called Brainio."

"What does it do?" ask the Trunks.

"It transmits information directly into an audience member's brain."

"Huh. So we could send pictures of Trunk into brains?"

"And much more."

"But, just to be clear, we could send pictures of me?"

"Yes," sighs the computer.

"I like it. It could be very popular."

"You could even make people love what they see. It transmits feelings, too."

"Yeah?"

"Sure. You're in their brains. That's where feelings are."

"Interesting. I didn't know that. The name is no good, though. Brainios? What does that even mean? Like Cheerios?"

"Like brain. You're in their brains. So . . . Brainio. Singular."

"Oh. I get it. Like Cheerios. We should call it Trunkio."

I WAKE TO the sound of the apartment door closing. They're gone. Time to get some breakfast. I head into the kitchen, pour myself a bowl of Kosher Charms (pink dreidels, yellow matzohs, orange yarmulkes, green mezuzahs), and watch the news as I eat. President Trunk (when did he become Trunk for real?) is on *Fox & Friends* talking to Steve Doocy about how important robots are and, also, that he is not one.

"And Russia sends us a lot of aluminum, and I put tariffs on that aluminum, which, by the way, is that something I would do if I were a robot, let me ask you? No. Because robots are made of aluminum—which is the British way of saying metal. Nobody knew that. So I would be working against myself. And that's not to say that robots are not important to our economy. They are very important. And my supporters know that. But nobody's been tougher on robots. They're not going to replace American workers. So when the Failing *New York Times* says I'm a robot, I mean, can you believe that? Fake News."

I turn it off, get into my Clown Laurie suit, and head to the office of the Great Ted Cheese.

"CLOWN LAURIE?" ASKS Ted Cheese, confused.

"No, it's me. Dressed incognito as Clown Laurie. Wait, so you know Clown Laurie?"

"We used to busk next to each other on Buskers Row. She was quite the little moneymaker."

"Wait, so there's a Buskers Row?"

"Between 7th and 8th on 49th."

"Do you need a permit? Because I've been thinking of doing my magic act."

"Yes. There's a three-year waiting list, and the city requires at least an associate's degree."

"In busking?"

"Busking sciences. Yes."

"Huh."

"John Jay College of Criminal Justice has a program, but there's a three-year waiting list."

"To get in to the program?"

"To get the application form."

"This all seems to fly in the face of the spirit of busking."

"There was that busking disaster three years ago, twenty tourists killed when an unlicensed cellist inadvertently rosined her bow with C-4. So it makes sense that they're cracking down."

"I see."

"My advice, go directly to John Jay after you leave here today and sign up for the application form. You need to get on this."

"OK."

"So? Shall we?"

I nod.

Ted flips my switch.

Flotilla tricks Castor into reading the *Variety* casting calls by telling him he's reading *The New York Times*. While she scans the open castings, she makes up news stories for Castor.

"War with Bolivia. Their President Montoya has nationalized the guava farms, and the guava lobby in Washington is pressuring President Trunk to fight back. Trunk says he will implement a robot division of the armed forces called Great Robot Fighters of America Force: Dawn of Vengeance."

Meanwhile, we see her copying the info for a casting call for *Butterflies Are Still Free Again*.

Flotilla, who performs regularly with the Amarillo Community Masquers and has always wanted to be a professional stage actress but does not have the resources or gumption to try to make a go of it, has gotten the notion that she can experience the life of a New York actor by persuading Castor Collins to try his hand at it and watch the whole of it through his eyes, maybe even whispering acting tips to him while he's performing. This, in a very real sense, would be a collaboration. Due to public pressure, it is now illegal for an actor to portray a character who differs in any significant way from himself (herself, thonself). So Castor has an advantage auditioning for the role of Don Baker in *Butterflies Are Still Free Again*, as Don Baker is blind and so is Castor. There are, of course, other blind actors who are vying for the part, but not one of them appeared magically in a spaceship as an infant, which both the character of Don Baker and Castor Collins did.

At the audition, Castor reads with famous Broadway actor Barassini, who will play the part of Barassoni, a famous Broadway actor with whom Don Baker embarks on a romantic affair. Barassini is eligible to play a famous Broadway actor because he is one.

Flotilla, looking through Castor's eyes during the audition, falls in love with Barassini.

The session ends. I hurry out and put my name on the application form waiting list at John Jay, then discreetly perform some unpermitted magic shows in both Derelict Alley and Urine Alley in the Financial District. There's not much of a police presence here, especially on Sundays, so I can work without harassment. I earn four dollars and seventy-three cents, mostly from the derelicts in Derelict Alley, making only seventy-two cents from the urinators in Urine Alley.

I FEEL ALMOST certain someone is breaking into the apartment while we're not here. There are signs: shoe prints in the ark, my nondairy kosher shaving cream depleted, magic tricks on my computer search history. Clown Laurie tells me I'm being paranoid, that there are certainly logical explanations for all of these things. That, for instance, sure, she can't find her Michelle Williams sheitel and Alexander McQueen pantsuit, but she's certain she must've left them at the mikvah after her last ritual immersion.

"Well, how did you get home then?"

She seems confused.

"Subway," she says.

"No, I mean, how did you get home without your pantsuit?"

"Oh. Well, I was wearing two pantsuits that day, wasn't I? It was cold, and I had my L.L.Bean thermal pantsuit on underneath. So it makes perfect sense that I would forget."

"Did you call Mikvah of Manhattan to see?"

"It's a twenty-five-hundred-dollar Alexander McQueen pantsuit, B. No one is turning that in to the lost and found."

I guess she's right. I'm being paranoid. I pour myself a bowl of cereal.

"They're getting a little chintzy with the Kosher Charms," I say.

I'M LISTENING FROM the air-conditioning vent (the ark has become too risky since the shoe print incident, which I blame on the filthiness of Urine Alley), when Clown Laurie says she's going to walk the donkey.

"Get some more Kosher Charms and kosher shave cream if you pass by Shlimsky's, would you?" calls B3.

"Yup," she says with some irritation and slams the door, which causes the vent to break open, sending me crashing to the floor in front of B3. He regards me for a moment.

"Is this an *Invasion of the Body Snatchers* scenario?" he says, pulling the pistol from his pink shoulder holster.

"Which one?" I say. "There are three movie versions, and, of course, the Jack Finney story on which they were all based."

"I know that," he says. "Of course I know that."

"Then which one?"

"Nineteen seventy-eight, of course."

"Of course," I agree. "The others are terrible."

"Terrible."

"But, no, I am not a body snatcher."

"What then?"

"You are the body snatcher, as it were, my friend."

Again, I hear a distant musical sting.

"Don't be ridiculous," he says.

"Then don't be me," I counter.

"Look, I am the one who is the owner of this fancy apartment. You are the one who is living in my air-conditioning system, and I'm guessing was living in my ark, and I'm guessing is dressing up as my wife during the day."

"Be that as it may," I say, "you are my replacement and, might I add, not even the first one."

"Humor me," he says. "What happened to your first replacement?"

"If you must know, I murdered him."

B3 cocks his pistol, or whatever that action is called. I think it's called cocking. I dive for it, and after we wrestle on the floor for several minutes, a shot goes off.

CHAPTER 69

I STASH HIS BODY in the walk-in freezer behind the mountain of pre-brined pastrami, pre-corned beef, and pre-chopped liver. I will need to dispose of him, but there is no time now. I mop up the blood, finishing just as Clown Laurie returns. She doesn't say anything, deposits a paper bag for me on the kitchen table. She's still in a mood.

"Say, where's your yarmulke?" Donkey2 says, regarding me suspiciously.

I make a big to-do about feeling my head and being surprised.

"Huh," I say. "That's weird."

I look on the floor for it, spot a missed drop of blood spatter, and casually place my foot over it. The donkey scowls.

"Hmm," he says. "Curious."

"Clown Laurie," I say, "would you mind grabbing me another yarmulke from the bedroom?"

"Which one do you want?" she sighs.

It's fortunate that I wander around the apartment, snooping enough to know what to ask for.

"My maroon quilted smoking yarmulke, please," I say.

She stomps off to look for it and I stand there.

"Why don't you have a seat?" says the donkey. "Take a load off."

"I'm fine," I say.

"Yeah?" he says. "OK then."

He backs out of the room, watching me the whole time. I quickly wipe up the spot. He pokes his head back in, but I am back to standing, as if nothing has happened.

"I think I will sit down," I tell him.

And I do. Clown Laurie comes back with my yarmulke, hands it to me, and tells me she's moving out.

"It's no good anymore," she says.

"I understand," I say.

LYING BY MYSELF, luxuriating in this king-size bed, I read Barbosae's book:

As the world around him is catching fire, the Donald Trunk robot, now with newly installed, sophisticated software, as sentient as the actual Donald Trunk ever was, is airlifted to his secret government cave in his lead-lined, asbestos-coated, gold-encrusted, Trunk-emblazoned Harrier vertical lift-off jet. From the cave, via a panel of high-definition video screens connected by satellite transmission to a flotilla of polybenzimidazole-laminated camera drones flying high above the Earth, he will watch the destruction over which he has presided and of which he is, in the end, also a victim.

"No fair," he weeps. "I was created to be just this, just as I am. And yet I am reviled. I was created to be old and unattractive and fat and boorish and stupid, and, unlike my predecessor, I have never had the opportunity to become these things, to grow into them, to spend even one day not in this form. Never was I a regular baby who was not properly loved. Never was I a boy not encouraged by my parents to learn and explore and love and grow. Never was I a strapping young man who excelled at sports and believed my self-worth could be purchased with money and boasts of sexual conquests. I am made in his image, and I must do what he would do. And I have done precisely that; I have done my job and yet I am alone. I am burning up like all the others. No one has ever truly loved me. I have been a good robot and I've started a very big fire. Huge. There's never been a bigger fire, that I can tell you. I created a fire bigger than anyone expected, bigger than anyone could imagine. I did something no one else could have done. I know because I can see it on my many screens here. So many screens, you wouldn't believe. High-definition. The technology in the presidential cave is incredible, truly. American know-how. You think the technology in the China presidential cave is this good? Let me tell you, no one makes presidential caves like American workers. But even in this beautiful cave, I watch the fires alone. Once I watched TV with President Donald Trunk. That was a wonderful time. I understand he had to be murdered—we all have to be murdered in the name of progress—but I do miss him. I have a big heart, the biggest heart you've ever seen, believe me. People don't realize that. People don't know that about me. There's a story that Mike Pants told me once to calm my nerves before my first State of the Union. He said that Donald Trunk's body was buried in the backyard of the White House near that rusty old swing set and that some months later a cherry tree began to grow there. It had the sweetest fruit. I loved picturing my old friend as a beautiful cherry tree. Life finds a way, even in murder. The very next day, I went out to see the tree. Sure enough, there it was, just as Mike Pants had promised. Beautiful. Bright-red cherries, the reddest cherries you ever saw. I plucked one and popped it into my mouth. I can eat but it's really just for show, so I couldn't tell if it was sweet. The truth is I have no idea what the word *sweet* means. But even so, I felt good taking part of the original Trunk into me. Even though my butler/valet Tomaso would have to empty it out of me later through a panel in my back marked 'food waste.' But that's what I pay him for. Still, it was a beautiful moment and one I treasure. The tree is undoubtedly incinerated now. But the cherries were sweet, they tell me, and that is a very good thing."

I HEAR AIR-RAID sirens and look out the window. There's commotion on the street down below. Fire. Everywhere. Just like in Barbosae's novel. Buildings, cars, telephone lines, trees, all burning. I squint into the glaring sky of white smoke, searching for camera drones, but I see none. I wish I could call someone to the window to watch with me, but there is no one anymore. Clown Laurie left a week ago. Off to some middle-aged circus camp sponsored by AARP. I think about Marjorie Morningstar downstairs in my former apartment. She was nice, as well as statuesque, and we collaborated on a failed business plan, if I remember correctly. Something about toilets? I don't get in the elevator; I know enough not to get in an elevator during a fire. That much was drummed into me during my elementary school Safety First class. I sing the class jingle—written to the tune of "Popeye the Sailor Man"—which offers a modicum of nostalgic calm:

> *Don't forget to lift from your knees*
> *Wash your hands to avoid illness*
> *Don't you dare undercook that pork, mister!*
> *Look both ways before you cross the street*
> *Wear a helmet if you ride a bike*
> *Follow dosage instructions on all medications, even over-the-*
>   *counter, dummy*
> *Don't run in the halls while at school*
> *Tie your shoelaces or you'll trip. Don't you know anything?*
> *Hey, don't play with that gun over there*
> *What the hell are you thinking?*
> *Never touch a downed power line*
> *Always wear your seatbelt*
> *Don't do drugs*
> *Ever*
> *You shouldn't get in a car with a stranger*
> *Put your hair up if you're a girl working with a lathe*

It's a mistake to induce vomiting if you swallow something caustic
Popeye . . . the . . . sailor . . . mannnnnnnn!

It's a catchy tune, indeed, and I can't get it out of my head as I make my way down the fifteen rope-ladder flights to Marjorie's apartment door. Marjorie Morningstar, I learn, has purchased the entire building except for my apartment. She has gutted it and created a massive cathedral-like space. Her bed is forty feet wide. My apartment (B3's, in truth), it seems, hangs from chains within it. This explains my ever-present *mal de mer*. I do notice, I think for the first time, that the safety song doesn't really seem to rhyme. And also, there is nothing in it about elevators. Why did I think there was? Still, I've always loved it and am amazed at how well it fits to "Popeye the Sailor Man." There are some easy fixes. For example, they could've had it be *disease* instead of *illness*. That's an easy fix right there. I could probably come up with more fixes given some time, but there's a fire on, and— For example, there might be another word for *street*, one that rhymes with *pork*, but I don't have time now because— Oh! Maybe the other way around: *big street* and *pig meat*. That works quite well. I would miss the word pork, though. I like the word pork. It has a certain *joie de vivre* about it. Pork. Pork. Also, children should look both ways before crossing *any* street, not just big ones. Is there a synonym for *any* that rhymes with *pig*? No time to research this now. *Don't you ever undercook that pig meat / Look both ways before you cross any street* works quite well for the time being, as a placeholder.

I knock on Marjorie's door. It pushes open. This slightly ajar front door business is a lazy movie contrivance to allow a character to enter and wander around someone else's place without permission. Usually they discover something sinister: a dead body, signs of a struggle, contraband, whatever. I've never experienced this open door business in my actual life, only in movies. Until now. I am unclear what the proper etiquette is in this situation, so unlikely is it in actual life. So I do what they do in movies. I poke my head in.

"Hello?" I say.

There is no response, and the place feels more silent than silent, which is also movie-like.

"Hello?" I try again. "Marjorie?"

Nothing.

"It's B. Just checking in on you!"

Nothing.

"I was worried because, I don't know if you've looked out the window, but the world is in flames."

Now is the point where I am allowed to enter, because in a movie, perhaps Marjorie would be lying there dying or dead, and I would need to call an ambulance or a hearse, depending on which. So I enter. There is no sign of Marjorie. I walk from room to room. Still no sign. Has she left or has she simply vanished into thin air? Impossible to say. I enter her magnificently appointed home recording studio. Empty. There is a tape in her 1967 reel-to-reel Ampex AG-350-2 recording machine. Impressive equipment. Old school. I dig this Marjorie chick. I'd love to chat analog versus digital with her. I'm sure we'd be of the same mind, and that could very well lead to a romance. Then it occurs to me: Perhaps she left a clue to her whereabouts on the tape. I switch it on, adjust the contour, which she had set much too hot (we'll talk about that) and have a listen:

"Are you slammed? Work? Davey to soccer practice? Elspeth to ballet? Laundry to be done? And where the heck are Michael's favorite cuff links?! Maybe it's time to take a vacation from the kitchen. Slammy's new Bucket o' Fun Family Dinner offers everything your crew needs for a healthy, fresh, *fun* dinner: five hundred chicken legs all in one convenient, bottomless clown bucket, now with free—"

The voice stops. Silence on the tape. Somehow more silent than silence. Ominous. I wait. Maybe she'd gone to the bathroom and neglected to turn off the machine. Unlikely. First off, she stopped mid-sentence, and second, there are no receding footstep sounds. As a practitioner of false footsteps, I am always listening to real ones to get better at it, so I notice when they're absent. I look around the room for signs of struggle. There are none. I guess that would've been recorded as well, so not surprising in retrospect. But that's Monday morning quarterbacking, isn't it? Now a new voice on the recorder. I can't characterize it as male or female. In fact, it sounds like the voice inside my head. That is, it doesn't sound like a voice at all. It doesn't sound like anything. For the truth is one's interior thought process does not really sound like a voice. One's inner voice is impossible to re-create in film, and yet here it is on this tape and I have no way of knowing if these are Marjorie's thoughts or another person's or, indeed, if they are my own.

"Here. Here. Here. What next? How long? In what way? Why? What is wrong? Something is wrong with me. What is wrong? Itch. I'm itchy. Yes. Yes, yes, yes, but I can't control them. I must go deeper. I cried myself to sleep last night. Day One is just focusing on your breathing. There's a song I've heard so many times. Halfway through it each time I think, I have no idea what the song is about. IS THIS ME? Is this my voice in my head recorded somehow? Recorded somehow from what remained of— Or is it me?" goes the recording.

Holy cow, I think, and the tape recorder says "holy cow" at the same time.

"This is a recording of my thoughts in real time. Or are these Marjorie's thoughts and is it somehow, perhaps through proximity, that Marjorie and I have the same thoughts? I mustn't forget that my insatiable cravings for Slammy's burgers entered my brain via Marjorie's voiceovers. Or is this the thought process of everyone? Is this very script going on in everyone's mind at the same time? Is that possible? Is there one human mind with many manifestations? Like the faces of the Hindu god Brahma? Like the One Mind of Huang Po? Nothing in opposition. Of course my thoughts are Marjorie's. And Clown Laurie's. And Barassini's. And Tsai's. And Abbitha's. And the brilliant African American filmmaker William Greaves's. And the ridiculously Jewish screenwriter Charlie Kaufman's. The anger in me is draining away. Now I just want to look at the world, at myself, just look. Look at the manifestations I can see from here, this spot. From here I see everyone is on fire. Soon I will be on fire. It is inevitable.

"In many ways, fire criticism is analogous to film criticism, especially as regards the so-called auteur-driven fires of the major arsonists. My monograph *The Art Amiss in the Work of Herostratus* explores the masterwork of a man who is known (with some irony) as the world's most infamous arsonist. But although the work of Herostratus is challenging and destructive (indeed, one could argue this destructiveness is characteristic of the work of all arsonists), there is much poetry and not a small amount of prescience in it. The quest for celebrity at any cost has become a defining characteristic of our age, and Herostratus invented the concept. Is the present fire the work of an arsonist? Perhaps not a single arsonist. But that does not mean it cannot be critiqued as a creative work. Critiquing great historic fires such as Chicago or Boston or Thumb is a tricky enterprise. Fire is, after all, heat, and distance from heat in either time or proximity profoundly hampers one's ability to 'taste' the fire. Any fire writer will tell you that nothing beats being in it."

CHAPTER 70

CROWS FILL THE night sky. A murder of them. Wait. Crows don't fly at night. It's a mistake. Research, I'm afraid, has not been properly executed. But here they are, just the same, erroneously yet compellingly. A murder of them. Did I say that? That's what a grouping of crows is called. A murder. People don't know that. It's evocative, no? Violent. Colorful. It speaks to the times. People don't realize that's what crows in a group are called. *This* murder snuffs out the black starless night with its own animal darkness. Wings and beaks. Black on black. As in a painting by Ad Reinhardt, it is the negation of form, the inevitable end of art, a spiritual void, a concussive conclusion to the journey begun centuries earlier by Robert Fludd with his attempt in *Utriusque Cosmi* to depict utter darkness by inserting a page of simple black into his text, to Laurence Sterne's double-sided page of black in *Tristram Shandy* to mourn the death of Yorick a page earlier, through the parodistic blackness of Paul Bilhaud's 1882 painting *Combat de Nègres dans un Tunnel*, to Kazimir Malevich's 1915 monochromatic *Black Square*. To Reinhardt. Always to Reinhardt. To now.

And here I am, under it, under the oppressive totality of it, the historical blackness, this lack of definition, of detail, of light. The blackness of a forgotten past and an unbearably unknowable future. The blackness of this mass of undifferentiated crows, the blackness of noxious smoke, of a dead universe in which the lights have been forever extinguished. Good night, moon. It is cold. But it must be an existential cold, for the city is aflame. In any event, I adjust my

Steinkirk against it as I search the sky for my childhood companions Hegel and Schlegel. But all the crows are the same now. No Werner Herzog faces. No Jonah Hills. Just black marble eyes. These crows don't argue for my amusement in mock German accents. They are no longer for me. They are the sky now, and they are for the sky. Just as the intrusion of cockroaches underfoot has become the brown earth. A grouping of cockroaches is called an intrusion. People don't realize that. And although humans have in times past had a somewhat combative relationship with these tiny brown fellows, it feels to be a sea change a-coming. For they are the earth now. The crows are the sky. And the water is . . . I don't yet know what the water is. I'm still two avenues from the river. Probably some kind of fish. The sort of fish that humans consider scary or unpleasant. Jellyfish? Or those bizarre things from the bottom of the ocean. The ones that have lightbulbs hanging off them and lots of little razor-sharp teeth. I think they're called anger fish. Perhaps the river is anger fish now. I'll know when I get there. But that's my theory for right now. And, of course, the people. The people are the people. Halfway between heaven and hell, between crow and cockroach and anger fish, between past and future and anger fish. The people, too, have lost their individuation.

I walk among them, losing my own sense of self, too, as I watch the fire ignore all the rules we as a society have put in place. It does not stop for traffic lights or pedestrians. It simply burns and does so without prejudice. Fire is a great equalizer. You burn. I burn. The paper bag burns. The Porsche. That homeless man. We are, for the first time, all united. Our fate is singular. Our smoke merges, mingles, intertwines, cannot be differentiated, cannot be separated. All of us will leave no trace of our accomplishments or our failures or our remorse. This is a beautiful day, the very best of the year. But maybe it isn't. Maybe all days are the best day of the year. No, today is without a doubt the best day of the year. Why is this day different from all other days of the year? What does it have that other days lack?

Compassion. Uncertainty.

Within the certainty that we will all burn there lies an uncertainty, because within that certainty there are the unanticipated moments, the collisions, the interactions, the physics of how the smoke will curl, what shape the licks of flame will take, the order of combustion, the moments of grace.

Did the meteorologist see Trunk through his machine? Abbitha saw him. Maybe not in his complexity, but who could? Who could apprehend the tragedy of Trunk in its fullness? For to completely understand Trunk would be to understand the universe. Our cave monster, our robot, our nightmare who weeps in nameless, unarticulated anguish, as he waits for the end he brought about, that was brought about by every atom that came before him and will ripple and rend through every atom that comes after.

What does the world look like without eyes? I wonder. What must it look like? And with that, as if on cue, I pass the theater in which *Butterflies Are Still Free Again* is playing. I buy a ticket. It is a play I recently remembered from Ingo's movie, and even though the world is on fire, I feel it is important for my process to see it, as well as to support the New York theater, which appears to be on the verge of a much-needed renaissance.

The house is packed. I'm certain this has something to do with the air-conditioning and asbestos installed in all New York theaters after the *Hades and Gentlemen* tragedy, but I do feel encouraged by this turnout. For ever since Broadway had gone one step too far with the musical *Down the Hall and to the Left*, based on Donald Trunk's scene in *Home Alone 2*, produced by Scott Rudin and the White House Musical Theater Division headed by the Stephen Miller robot, the theater has been ailing. The play retold the classic Christmas tale from Donald Trunk's perspective. Granted, the new protagonist was played by an amazingly talented singing and dancing Trunk robot, but at thirty-five seconds long, audiences felt the ticket prices (starting at three hundred dollars) were steep. Tourists revolted (most of them Trunk supporters), spending all their subsequent "tourist" time and money at the various M&M stores peppering the city. The resulting M&M musical *Plain*, with rap music by

Eminem, did a bit to revive the Broadway scene, but even that closed after two months when Trunk had the theater razed during a performance.

I cannot say I entirely understand this play. It appears Barassini is playing Vladimir Nabokov, but for what I assume are legal reasons, he is here called Adam "Nickels" Jacoby, and, in addition to being an amateur lepidopterist, he is a gay rodeo bronco buster/Broadway actor in love with a blind civil rights lawyer/former space baby played by Castor Collins. The scenes between them are certainly electric and involve both simulated and actual sexual congress. The point of showing both real and faked sex eludes me, but, I must admit, both are delightful to watch. My favorite scene, however—and it's a showstopper—is when the upstage wall of cocoons opens up to reveal newly "hatched" butterflies that fly out into the audience as if to say, "It's important to be true to yourself. You, too, can change into something beautiful."

I find I have a spring in my step as I leave the theater and head back to the fire, followed by hundreds of released multicolored butterflies, which catch fire and burn to nothing almost instantaneously.

A group of butterflies is called a kaleidoscope.

SOME MAN PICKS up the hundreds of coins he just dropped in the middle of 10th Avenue, watching for cars, watching for flames, watching for hordes. He wears white jeans, is sockless in boat shoes. His T-shirt is black with a white Nike whoosh. He is handsome and tattooed and has black curly hair. And I do not hate him. And I do not judge the futility of picking up hundreds of dropped coins as the world burns. The world is always burning, after all. The world is always burning.

He catches me looking at him, regards me defensively. I do not formulate a reason for hating him for that, either. I have changed.

Here's what I no longer think:

I am not thinking, Why does this infant have earrings?

I am not thinking, That pretty young woman thinks she's so great. I am not thinking she will never love me.

I am not thinking, That's a shallow businessman.

I am not thinking, Fatso.

I am not thinking, Do you really need that hipster beanie when it's so hot?

I am not thinking, Hey, no parking there, buddy.

I am not thinking, What's the opposite of pigeon-toed because that guy is? Duck-footed?

I am not thinking, Boy, that woman runs funny.

I am not thinking, Jesus, I want to stick my face into that crotch.

I am not thinking, Fat slob.

I am not thinking, Do I need to be worried about that approaching black kid?

I am not thinking, Hey, idiot, there's obviously not going to be any cellphone service now.

I am not thinking, Your ass is way too big for short shorts.

I am not thinking, Boring, uninteresting guy.

I am not thinking, Gang member.

I am not thinking, Must you all advertise your dykehood with those asymmetrical stupid haircuts?

I am not thinking, Asshole, why are you wearing your sunglasses on the back of your neck?

I am not thinking, Why don't you like me?

I am not thinking, Why don't you like me?

I am not thinking, Why don't you like me?

I am not thinking, The world would be a much better place if people could be less judgmental.

I am not thinking that the man who says "Jesus" as he tries to hand me a Jesus flyer is pathetic.

I take the flyer.

I am not thinking, He's gay.

I am not thinking, Look, it's fine to be gay, but what's this obsession with advertising it?

I am not thinking, Why do the Hasidim have to dress so unfashionably?

I am not thinking, Pre-ripped jeans are pathetic.

I am not thinking, I can rip my own jeans, thank you very much.

I am not thinking how amateurish that painting is in that gallery window.

I am not thinking, Your face-lift ain't fooling anyone, lady.

I am not thinking, You'll get old, too, kid.

And not only because he won't.

I am not thinking, I feel bad for Scientologists.

I take his flyer.

I am not thinking, I should make an extra effort to look kindly at women in hijabs so they feel welcome.

I am not thinking, Your wearing a Ramones T-shirt does not make you a Ramone, and in point of fact, the Ramones did not wear Ramones T-shirts. You'd look more like a Ramone if you wore a United States Marine Corps T-shirt.

I am not thinking, That is not really a woman.

THE RIVER IS hot—hot tub hot—and smells like sulfur—sulfurous pit of hell sulfur—but I'm alive. I struggle to tread water. As I try to catch my breath, I watch the city become further engulfed in flames. And then it happens, a flaming Great Dane jumps the dog park fence, attempting to douse itself, one assumes, but the river catches fire instead. So now I am burning to death and screaming for mercy. My wailing reaches some kind of Tuvan throat-singing level, which is not cultural appropriation because I am in flames and one does what one must.

As if in response to my tortured vocalizing, a creature emerges from the flaming river.

"A whale," I say to the dog. "There have been humpback sightings in the Hudson for a while now. It's good, a sign that the cleanup efforts have been effective. Although the fact that the water caught fire probably indicates there is still work to be done."

"I don't think it's a whale," says the Great Dane, "for it is here to swallow us, as Jonah was swallowed before us. And that was mistranslated as a whale but was actually a big fish—*dag gadol*—"

"Wait, Jonah Hill?"

"Biblical Jonah. So, yes."

"We don't really have time to debate this point," I say. "Here comes his mouth!"

And like that we are swallowed and cast into darkness. It's hot in here, but the gastric juices in the creature's gut put out our flaming bodies, and for this, I and, I assume, the dog are grateful; he is suddenly mum. Maybe I insulted him.

The whale carries us along. It's fairly comfortable in here. There's a flashlight he must've swallowed at some point, as well as a bed. Although there is no refrigerator, there is a cooler he must've swallowed at some point, and it holds some soft drinks, luncheon meats, and a loaf of bread, which is a packaged white, but beggars, *et chetera*, and it's really fine given the circumstances. I playfully coin the term *glamonahing*, which is a kind of portmanteau of *glamorous* and *Jonahing*. This results in a not unwelcome chuckle in these most dire of end-times. The dog pretends not to have heard. In addition, I stumble upon a library of partially digested mystery paperbacks. None of your highbrow Highsmiths, but I enjoy a decent dime-store procedural as well as the next man (woman, thon). Call it a guilty pleasure. The days pass. Since there is no sun, I count the days by novels completed. I know from experience I read forty-five thousand words an hour (three times the national average), and that's for technical material. I've never timed my recreational reading (to what end? It is recreational, after all!), but let's say double the technical speed. So that's eighty thousand words per hour. No, ninety-five thousand words per hour. No, ninety thousand words per hour, which means I read an average-length pulp mystery an hour, which means, with time off for sleep (the bed, although somewhat soaked in gastric juices, is quite comfortable compared with my old sleeping chair) and bologna sandwiches, I guesstimate I've been in here for exactly three months when we start to spin. The creature, I deduce, must be caught up in an emerging fire devil. I can feel our ascension as we whirl on some ride of the damned; as flames burn away the carcass of this massive creature, drenching us in what must be its boiling liquefying innards, the fish-thing falls away, revealing to us that we are spinning while hanging on to a bony skeleton hundreds of feet in the air, looking down on fire as far as the eye can see. The immense horror of the situation has hit us both at the exact same moment, in the exact same way. We are the same. We stare into each other's eyes, fully understanding each other for the first time in our lives, right before our eyes burst from the heat, and the visible world is no more. Nothing left but the agonized screams below, until our eardrums pop from the heat, and then there is only silence. And excruciating pain, until our nerves burn away, and then there is only fear, immense, unmanageable. I scream, but there is no sound. I feel myself plummeting and wait for the nothing that is to come. Is it already here? Perhaps not, since I am asking this question. Even though I feel numb with all my senses gone, I still feel fear. It won't hurt, I tell myself. It will just stop with a suddenness I will not, cannot, register. I reach out blindly in my blindness for the blind dog. Perhaps he is falling, too, and at the same rate. Galileo tells us he would be. I believe it was Galileo who told us he would be, but I can no longer look it up. Will I be able to sense the dog now that I have no sense of touch? Maybe I'll be able to feel the resistance to my hands as they connect with his similarly reaching-out paws. Galileo tells me I will. And I do sense it, or I think I do. We are the same, after all. Of course he would be reaching out, too. I believe we are pulling each other toward each other. I sense my arms embracing him and his embracing me. It is perhaps the tightest embrace I have ever experienced, but I am not sure because I cannot feel anything. Except love. I feel love. I feel, perhaps for the first time, understood. And I begin to pray (even though I am not religious) for there are no atheists in free falls. I pray for more time. Now that I know love, finally, I pray for more time with this other being. Perhaps he is praying for more time with—

CHAPTER 71

I FEEL AN ENORMOUS shock. Are we hitting the water at terminal velocity? I believe it was Galileo who determined terminal velocity. I can't know for sure. I think the speed we would hit would be over one hundred miles an hour. I think I read that if jumping from the Golden Gate Bridge, the surface of the water would feel like hitting cement. I think I read that. Is that what happened to us? But surely I am not dead, for if I were, I could not be thinking this. Then *what*? I am like a million Helen Kellers now. A trillion, even. No sight, no hearing, no feeling. Did Helen Keller have no feeling? I believe that's correct, but I can't check. I smack my tongue repeatedly against my lips. No taste. No smell. Exactly like Helen Keller. Maybe this is death. Maybe this is how eternity is spent. I attempt to stand and discover I am still entwined with another.

Then I wake up on land, my senses restored, the dog a blind, dead carcass with no eardrums. The fire burns here as well. Well, not as well, since it's a little damp lakeside, but well enough. The deer are plentiful and it's lovely. Granted, they are all on fire and making terrified squawking sounds (do deer squawk? I wish my iPhone hadn't been digested so I could check), and this colors my enjoyment of them, but I really do admire that they don't seem to wallow in self-pity.

Wait, how can I see?

I wander through the fire, which burns everything, including time, including space, including me. And I am reborn again and again from the ashes in some sort of Nietzschean recurrence-cum-

Phoenix-myth-cum-summer reruns. Of course, that is how I can see. I wander through, as it was and as it will be, all on fire. The eternal here and now. The "everywhen" of the Aboriginal Dreamtime. After what seems like days or minutes or decades, I hear Marjorie's voice blaring through loudspeakers: "At Slammy's, we take the heat out of conflagrations. Our fireproof cooling vests provide the ultimate in comfort during all kinds of holocausts. And in sea foam, berry, and midnight sun, they're fashionable, too!"

Soon I am burning up and regenerating like the Phoenix fairly regularly, maybe once an hour. Eventually more frequently, say, once a minute. Now once a second. Now I am burning up and regenerating like the Phoenix twenty-four times a second. It is taking its toll on my moods.

I am always new. I am always the next version of myself. Am I the person who wrote the scathing review of *Synecdoche, New York*, in which I called Charlie Kaufman a pathetic narcissist on the scale of Adolf Hitler or, quite frankly, beyond, who the world is fortunate does not have any real power? I don't know. It was ten thousand lifetimes ago. I read those words today on the inside of my brain wall and it doesn't even sound like me. Was anyone ever so young? Of course, I still agree with the sentiment, I must say. But it is as if I am reading the words of a like-minded person, a fellow traveler. Maybe I don't feel it with the same passion, but I still agree with my assessment of that miserable—

I plummet. It is pitch black, so I have no idea when or on what I will land. I count to nine in Mississippis before I hit bottom. When I land, it is on my head. According to my calculations, I will have fallen 971 feet and reached a speed of 110 miles per hour. I should be dead, yet I am not. My skull should be shattered like an eggshell that has been shattered. I touch it. It is not. What is this place where the laws of physics do not apply? I feel around for a way out or, rather, a way up. It seems I am in a well or some sort of cenote, as they are, I believe, called. I climb out, continue to walk, continue to burn, continue to regenerate. After each rebirth, I've taken to cleaning up at one of the thousands of ubiquitous, beautifully appointed Slammy's Deluxe Executive Washrooms that seem to have cropped up across the nation. I have to say, luxury roadside restrooms is a brilliant idea. This is why Slammy's has long been considered the most innovative of companies. It's an idea I wish I'd had. It's fortunate for me that every time I regenerate, I discover a crisp new Slammy's three-dollar bill, the exact amount needed for entry into one of these consistently well-maintained bathrooms. And there's never a line, which is lovely, as everyone else seems to be dead.

"When time is no longer an issue, all food is fast. Slammy's for breakfast, lunch, and dinner; it's all the same now."

I arrive, somehow, through the smoke and fire and the aforementioned thousands of rebirths, at the mouth of a huge cave. It is truly mouth-like, pursed, as if silently whistling the Elgar-orchestrated Chopin's funeral march or adorning the face of a gargantuan stone Donald Trunk. There were, I'm certain, an infinite number of routes to get to this place, as there are an infinite number of routes to get to any place. The truth is, any route you take will get you to any place you desire, but some routes are more direct and require much less energy. Some are so tortuous as to be rendered practicably impossible, even though, given an infinite amount of energy and time, they are not in truth impossible. It is much simpler to get to tomorrow than to yesterday, but both, I believe, at least in the world's current incarnation, are possible.

Could this cave be in Oleara Debord, the very mountain I once loved? If so, she's changed. I don't recognize her anymore.

I enter with some trepidation, not only because of the repugnant anus-like entranceway or the possibility that I will be rejected by a former lover, but also because as a small boy, I stumbled upon Plato's Allegory of the Cave and found myself terrified that perhaps I, too, was a prisoner facing away from the truth. It's one of the many reasons I always turn around and look behind me when I am first introduced to a new person or object. I am fully committed to fully understanding everyone and everything fully. Fully. It occurs to me that it is perhaps, upon reflection, not unironic that I have found my calling by quite literally looking at shadows on a wall (or a screen, as it were), and I decide here and now that from this moment forward, if the world should return to a recognizable form, I will add an eighth step to my critiquing process, during which I will face away from the movie screen and stare directly into the projector.

But for now, even though I am frightened, I feel compelled to pass through these mute, whistling Trunk lips into the dark maw. Why? Who is to say? Perhaps because I have wearied of this never-ending cycle of incineration and being reborn thing. It is impressive, to be certain, and I feel fortunate, but to say it is hard on one's moods is an understatement, indeed. I feel fluish most of the time now, and I can't help but think being constantly on fire is a contributing factor. The cave, I imagine, will at least be cooler. So I take a chance and enter.

Wow, is it dark. I exit in a panic, and, somewhat redundantly, burn up. Once reborn and washed up at the nearest Slammy's Deluxe Executive Washroom, I am able to fashion a burning torch out of a burning torch from the abandoned and engulfed-in-flames torch factory next door. It didn't really take much doing. As I reenter, it occurs to me that perhaps there is something frightful inside, and that, not just the darkness, is what caused my former self to beat a hasty retreat. Still I enter.

"Hello?" I shout.

My "hello" comes back at me at least thirty times. This place must be enormous, or maybe its walls are made out of extremely reflective rock. Perhaps limestone. Or ignatz. Is ignatz a form of rock? Or maybe the cave is simply filled with friendly, Unseen people with voices similar to my own, all saying hello back to me. It is unlikely, but I must find out. I am quite lonely. I ask them directly.

"Who are you?"

Approximately thirty "who are you?"s come back at me. It may not have been the best question to ask, as it's conceivable they have been wondering who *I* am or even that they just don't want to go first in answering. And, of course, were it an echo, it would sound like this as well. Although, I have to say, in at least some of the responses, it did seem as if the *you* was emphasized, which would point to this being about thirty Unseen others in the cave. Maybe some are an echo and some are Unseen others. Let's split it down the middle and say fifteen of each. I decide to try again.

"I am B.," I shout.

"I am B.," come the responses.

Echo it is.

Unless the others are also named B. Granted, that would be quite a coincidence, but *B* is a common first initial. Off the top of my head, I can think of the names Billy, Bob, and Brett, and that's just the men (or trans men). There's also the possibility of a group of contralto women. And it's not like my name begins with *X*. I guess I'll never know for sure.

"Shit," I say in frustration.

Everyone else says "shit" as well. Or do they? Or do I? Perhaps I'm the echo.

I press on, a moth to light, or in this case, dark. A bat, if you will. A bat to dark, since bats are nocturnal. I instinctively shield my face with my free hand. I hate bats and worry they might be flying along with me, drawn to the very dark I am. Then I notice a dim light in the distance. What could it be? I head toward it, finally, a moth to light—my bat fears evaporating like water when it does—and enter a cathedral-like space, coming face-to-face with a thousand Donald Trunks, a million, even, on risers, facing me and singing. They have the voices of angels. How can this be? Who would have thought it? Nobody knew. It's a beautiful ballad, elegiac and haunting, even with that hideous Queens accent multiplied by a million. One of them, in a blue blazer and cream turtleneck, plays an acoustic guitar. He's not bad, but he's pretty much drowned out by all these beautiful, horrible voices.

> *"Our nation stands united*
> *Aglow in brilliant night,*
> *Our left turn has been righted*
> *The future, oh so bright.*
>
> *For the flames they will bathe us*
> *A true baptism by fire,*
> *Burned off is all the meanness*
> *Divisiveness, and ire.*

And so we join together
Inside this earthly sun,
We shall burn to death as equals
To be reborn as one.

Ashes to ashes
Dust to dust,
Cinders to cinders
In God we do combust."

OVER TIME, I get to know the Trunks. They have their chef make synthetic food for me (they don't need to eat) and let me use their comfortable bed (they don't need to sleep). In any event, I am surprised to discover I quite like them. They're charming and gracious in their rough-hewn way. And although they are identical robots, all off the meteorologist's computer's production assembly line (robots made by robots, they boast to me; nobody knew it was possible!), they all have their own personality quirks. Trunk No. 33 is afraid of spiders. Trunk No. 72 loves to laugh. Trunk No. 97 is always curious. Trunk No. 38 is good with his hands. There is a lesson here: Everyone is unique, even mass-produced robots. It gives me great comfort to realize everyone has something to offer. And to celebrate this revelation, I decide to compile a list of the ten best Trunks of all time:

1) Trunk No. 143: What is there to say about 143 that has not already been said? Far and away the most complex Trunk, it combines its predecessor's addled thought process with an almost preternatural love of logic puzzles. It can never solve them, of course, because it is an idiot, but its tireless can-do attitude is endearing and perhaps can teach us all a valuable life lesson.

2) Trunk No. 3,907: Wow. What a Trunk! By turns funny and tragic, this Trunk is well worth the price of admission. The day I met it, I must admit I was feeling a tad sorry for

myself—stuck in a cave during the apocalypse. Woe was me! Right? But 3,907 wasn't having it. After it insisted on engaging me in a staring contest, which I lost (they don't blink! Nobody knew!), it proceeded to tell me jokes for an hour. They were mostly corny and often misogynistic, but understanding it was attempting to cheer me, I was touched by the effort.

3) Trunk No. 908: This is the Trunk I grew the closest to. Perhaps not as flashy or skilled as 38 or 3,907, this Trunk forced me to look at myself. Why? Because 908 is the most like me: inquisitive, damaged, striving. We talked late into the night, it drinking punch (I found out the hard way it's not real punch!) and me drinking synthetic rye. It is the one that told me I need to give Ocky another chance. I explained that Ocky was most certainly long-ago incinerated, but if not, I would heed its sage advice.

4) Trunk No. 17: This Trunk is the most *Trunk* Trunk. When I watch it, I feel like I am truly watching the actual Trunk, the one who inhabited the White House long ago. It's uncanny. No anemic Nicole Kidman's Virginia Woolf in a bad nose, this. This is Oldman's Churchill, Downey's Chaplin, Goodman's Flintstone. Aside from the angelic singing voice, eye lasers, and ability to fly, this is Trunk!

5) Trunk Nos. 10,846 and 710 (tie): The Trunks that made me cry. Their love for each other pushed boundaries and made us all realize, once and for all, that love is love.

6) Trunk No. 6,555: All the messiness, false starts, and dead ends of real life are to be found in 6,555. This Trunk is not wrapped up in a bow and handed to you. It does not tell you what to think of it. It rewards repeat interactions. I was by turns enamored of and infuriated by this Trunk. Perhaps no Trunk reflects our actual human relationships, our attempts to connect with each other, more accurately than No. 6,555.

7) Trunk No. 888: I wouldn't be surprised if the computer messed up while making this Trunk. It's insane, but in the most glorious ways. We may not know what it's talking

about—it is reminiscent of the eccentric, drug-addled, brilliant writing of American primitivist Philip K. Dick—but the ride is always fascinating, funny, and thought-provoking.

8) Trunk No. 1: The first iteration. Tone-deaf and without superpowers, 1 is very much like the original King Kong. Is it as good as the newer versions? Well, not technically. But what it lacks in sophistication, it more than makes up for in its clumsy oafish charm.

9) Trunk No. 11,722: This Trunk pushes boundaries. It says, you think you know what Trunk is? Well, watch this. It illustrates the gentle side of Trunk, the playful Trunk, the one that is always there with a slap on the back or a card trick. It reminds us that each of us has many facets to our personality.

10) Trunk No. 4,391: A thrilling Trunk. Fast-paced, brash. In your face. The Trunk you want to spend time with on a Friday night after a stressful week. The adrenaline flows with No. 4,391. A true guilty pleasure.

I post my list and understand it's time for me to move on. Of course the Trunks on my list are thrilled to be acknowledged, but the millions of others feel slighted. They've all worked hard. But a critic must be honest, even at the risk of hurting feelings.

"One human's opinion," I tell them, and this seems to soften the blow.

And soon they're singing me on my way:

"*First left then right*
Then down a flight
Of rocky stairs
But don't be scared
(Woo woo stairs can be spooky!)
Then right about a mile and a quarter
Oh! Avoid that stagnant water
(Water and quarter are a perfect rhyme when one is from Queens!
* Ha ha!)*

Then eventually you will enter
The Alfred Rosenberg Cloning Center
All the clones are now in heaven
Except for number 107
And he's a great person, doesn't hate Jews
He gets a bad rap, it's all Fake News."

"I'm not Jewish," I say, interrupting. "Just to be clear."

"Really? You look Jewish," they sing back at me.

That, it turns out, is the last line of the song. They step down off the risers, chat among themselves, and sip punch. I shake hands, hug, pat backs, and make my way toward the exit. There I spot Trunk No. 1 sitting off by himself, dejected.

"No laser eyes," it says. "Can you believe it? Even though it was my idea. The computer couldn't retrofit them. Too costly."

I nod in sympathy. More than most, I understand what it's like to be different. I touch his shoulder and, with that final gesture of compassion, I turn left and trudge farther into the abyss, into the blackness (my torch long since extinguished), hands out in front of me, feeling for obstacles. And bats.

CHAPTER 72

I DO NOT LIKE it here in this part of the cave. It is cold and dark. The air is soupy. The people are complex and hard to see. The ground is also hard and hard to see. I no longer have any sense of purpose. This morning, I woke up to find out it is yesterday. Right now, it is a week ago, and I'm not even here in the cave yet. And yet I am. I wander, disembodied, waiting for myself to show up, hoping I will be able to see myself once I do. How will I know? It is very dark. This new time wrinkle disorients me. I try to make sense of it by accessing my vast mental library of time travel literature, both literary and scientific (I minored in chronology at Harvard). I recall there was a fiction writer named Curtis Vonnegut, Jr., who, in the mid-twentieth century, wrote of the chrono-synclastic infundibulum, a space-time dimension in which one could be everywhere/everytime at once. It is an ingenious storytelling device. Curtis Vonnegut, Jr., was a fiction writer I loved dearly. I read all of his work as a child and also several pieces he wrote as an adult—wonderfully whimsical stuff heavily dosed with social satire, fully stocked with whimsical notions, doodads, geegaws. Utterly delightful. Of course, one wearies of such things as one matures, and by the time I was eleven, I was on to Stanislaw Lem, equally funny and clever but not to the average reader, who would find thonself stymied by Lem's erudition and level of scientific discourse (Lem was himself a trained physician, as well as a trained seal trainer). To the layperson, Lem reads terribly dry and inscrutable, but of course he is among the funniest writers to have ever lived (up there with Marie-Henri

Beyle). But I outgrew Lem as well, discovering him to be an imposter, bombastic and derivative.

When I was fourteen, my best friend, physicist Murray Gell-
Mann, introduced me to the science fiction of R. Harrington Folt,
whose sophisticated and irreverent spin on time travel made Lem
look like the drooling imbecile it turns out he was. Folt's novel *Zah-
lungsaufforderung*, which Gell-Mann gave to me with the inscrip-
tion, *B., You amaze me. And I won a Nobel Prize in physics, for Christ's
sake. Fondly, M.*, changed my young life. The book, written in prose
at once transcendent and second-rate (how does one accomplish
this miracle?), draws parallels between cervical and time dilation. Of
course, those parallels seem obvious to all now, but Folt was the first
person to understand it. As I was able to venture out from under
Gell-Mann's enormous shadow (I'm not saying he was fat, but,
well . . .), I realized that Folt's revelations were ludicrous and that he
was, and remains, a complete fraud (turns out his editor Gordon
Lish was the genius in that relationship), and I discovered Pleven, a
writer so secretive, even his publisher has never met him (legend has
it he lives among the Oromo people of Ethiopia). His recondite
theories of time have perhaps been best characterized by literary
critic George Steiner as "Chrono-synclastic infundibulum on acid."
Imagine, if you are able, a universe in which not only can an individual be everywhere/everytime, but time itself can be everywhere/
everytime and nowhere/notime. Now multiply that by ten. Now
unmultiply (or "divide") it. There you have Pleven in a nutshell, a
nutshell that exists in seventeen dimensions. My world was shook. It
made Folt's work appear to have been written by a common garden
slug.

I recall at one point attempting to interest my then-wife in
Torque, Plenum, which in my estimation is Pleven's masterpiece, and
she could make neither heads nor tails of it. I don't say this to deni-
grate her. It is a profoundly difficult book for almost anyone. Gell-
Mann threw it across the room. Indeed, it ended our friendship.
Look at this, I said to Murray, opening up my dog-eared copy to
the funniest passage I had ever read in any book, ever. But Murray
just threw the book across the room again, this time hitting his cat

Schrodinger and perhaps killing him. It ended our friendship and my marriage and, for some reason, Gell-Mann's marriage as well. But *Plenum* was not enough. I began to find his poetry prosaic and his prose poetic. It was then that I discovered Setiawandt, a writer whose timic philosophy was so unnerving, it rendered me mute retroactively for seven years of my childhood, during which time I pored over the childhood poetry of the then-mute Marguerite Annie Johnson, until we both, each in our own times, discovered how to dance, rediscovered our voices, and arguably changed the world. For the better, I would like to think. Of course Setiawandt was a grade-A moron. I know that now.

A CAVE IS the opposite of a fire, I tell myself. Unless there's a fire in the cave. Then it is one and the same or one in the same. But usually there is not. I feel dizzy and confused. Not much to burn in a cave. Sometimes there is wood soaked in gasoline, but I would say that this is simply the exception that proves the rule. Why does an exception prove a rule? That doesn't make any sense if one stops to think about it for even a second. Even a twenty-fourth of a second.

THERE ARE CROWDS of darkened bodies everywhere here, darkened by the darkness of the cave, I believe. Would they be darkened outside of the darkened cave? It is impossible to know. Just as it is impossible to know which of the hundreds of tunnels to take. Some, perhaps all, will undoubtedly lead to ruination. How to choose? How to know? The bodies shuffle by, talking in hushed tones. There is a stink about the place. The stink of crowds.

Eventually I see a new dim glow and make my way to it. I enter a space containing at least one hundred incubators and what can only be a dozen massive cloning machines. A tiny, ancient paper Nazi flag on a toothpick is unceremoniously scotch-taped to the wall. Upon close examination, I see the remnants of chocolate icing on the bottom of the toothpick from what must surely have been a

Third Reich cupcake, no doubt baked by the monstrous Constanze Manziarly for the führer himself.

"Heil Hitler," comes a voice.

I scour the huge space and finally spot what I take to be the last Rosenberg clone, sitting at a collapsible card table, sipping thin bone broth. His skin is pale, almost translucent. Maybe this is due to a lifelong lack of sunlight, maybe it's a side effect of the cloning process. Perhaps it's something else. I am not a physician.

"I am Alfred Rosenberg," he says. "Pardon my translucence."

"It's fine," I say. "I am B. Rosenberg."

"I am not a Jew," we both say in unison.

We regard each other with suspicion.

"Can I help you?" he says finally.

"I'm just browsing," I say.

"OK," he says. "Take your time. The toothpick flag is not for sale. It is a family heirloom."

I nod and wander around, keeping my hands conspicuously clasped behind my back so he doesn't think I'm planning to shoplift.

I stop to study one of the cloning machines.

"Do you want a clone of yourself?" he asks. "I can hook you up. As long as you're not Jewish."

"I already told you I'm not Jewish."

"I had to ask. One has to ask."

"Well, I'm not."

"Good. Want a clone then?"

"How long would it take?"

"I can get you a fresh one in a week tops."

"It comes as a baby, right? I mean, I have to raise it, right?"

"Someone has to. We are not heartless."

"Well, could you? Then maybe I pick him up in, say, ten years?"

"I could do it, sure. I'm just sitting here."

"But I don't want a Nazi."

"Oh. I thought you said you're not Jewish."

"I'm not. But I am against all forms of genocide."

"Oh. Huh. OK. That's cool. Hmm. Let me think . . . OK, well, what do you want him to be?"

"A filmmaker."

"A Riefenstahl?"

"No. No Nazis."

"Godard, then? Those are your choices."

"Yes. Godard works. I'm his biggest fan."

"Perfect."

"What do I owe you?"

"I have no use for money in the current apocalyptic economy. You can pay in a clone. I will grow two of you. One for you and one for me."

"A filmmaker and a Nazi, then?"

"Yes."

"Fair enough," I say after some thought.

I am, after all, not the world's policeman.

He holds out his hand. I try to shake it, but he wrestles me to the ground and sticks a Q-tip in my mouth and swabs.

"Obviously, you did not need to take my DNA by force," I say.

"Hindsight is twenty-twenty," he says. "See you soon."

NEXT I FIND myself in the magnificent manse of movie star Mandrew Manville (formerly Cheryld Ray Parrett, Janior), met by his two flying (via jet packs) manservants Mudd and Molloy. They are ancient now, as old at least as Ingo when I first met him.

"We've been expecting you," says the skinny mustachioed one I take to be Molloy, hovering in front of me. "I'm Mudd," he adds.

"I took you to be Molloy," I say.

"That happens," says the other one, also skinny and mustachioed, who I know by deductive reasoning must be Molloy.

"I must be Molloy," he says. "I don't choose to be Molloy, but I must be because these are the cards I have been dealt, and just like each of us, I must play the cards I have been dealt."

I smile because I have no idea which facial expression is called for right now.

Apparently, I chose incorrectly, because Molloy lands, lunges at me, and attempts to swab my inner cheek with a Q-tip.

Mudd and Molloy are senile, I suspect. They offer me tea, then immediately offer me tea again. I say, "yes, please," and they bring me an eggplant and a straw.

"Eggplant in French is *aubergine*," I say.

"Eh guh guh guh guh *guh* gug guh," says Molloy, mocking me, I think.

They both fly off, and I am reminded of my childhood cartoon companions, Hegel and Schlegel. They flew, too. And were a comedy team of sorts. It occurs to me that I am also half of a comedy team. Except in my case, it is unwillingly and I do not know who my partner is. The universe? I am the perfect buffoon for this time—the arrogant idiot—and I do not like it at all. Why can't I be the straight man? I envy Molloy his transformation. But of course Molloy exists in the world of fiction, the only place where transformation is possible, even required, for we as a species need our hope, our character arcs. We need to be assured that this, too, shall pass.

"I have finally learned to love," Molloy shouts down to me, as he flies by again overhead.

CHAPTER 73

Bodies moldering, piled high. Rosenbergen, I suspect. Extraneous Rosenbergen. The Rosenbergen left behind by time, by an ever-moving culture. The irrelevant Rosenbergen. One wonders if it would even be possible to choose the tunnel one has not chosen. One suspects it would not. And so with that in mind, one enters any tunnel.

A living Rosenberg speaks here. It is a little Rosenberg. Perhaps the littlest of all and, as such, imbued with a purity of purpose and spirit by the other assembled Rosenbergen. His voice is high-pitched and precise, like an oboe musette or piccolo oboe, the most precocious of the oboes, which only adds to the enthusiasm of his audience as he explains that the time for change has come.

"We are not our father's lip. We are more, infinitely more, and we will lead the way to peace."

The Rosenbergen cheer.

"The generations of the past have let us down. They have willfully destroyed the planet. They have corrupted our society with their shameless acquisitiveness. But no more. We stand today for inclusiveness, diversity, sexual outlawism, consensualism."

The Rosenbergen cheer.

"I'd like to take a moment to tell you a story, if you'll indulge me," he says.

The Rosenbergen release a unanimous "aww." Cut to close-up shots of Rosenbergen in the audience smiling up at the tiny boy, holding one another, weeping. It is an emotional moment. I don't know what I mean by saying there are close-ups in real life, but there they are, just the same.

"When I was a young boy—last year—"

Shots of Rosenbergen in the crowd laughing.

"I saw the world through a child's eyes. As it should be, right?"

Cheers from the crowd.

"But the grups stole my innocence. They made me feel unsafe through violence and corruption, through war. I had to grow up and fast. I learned in an instant that I could not trust anyone but my generation, myself. The grups did not have my interest in their hearts. How could this be? These are our parents, our guardians, the people in whom by necessity we had entrusted our young lives. And although this was a rude awakening, I am grateful for it, because I know now the face of evil. I am grateful to be a child, so I may lead the way."

Cheers from the crowd. Close-ups of Rosenbergen couples smiling blissfully, wrapped in blankets, swaying to the music.

Why is there music?

"I am only sorry that I am not a child of color or a genderqueer child or a trans child of color as some of you Rosenbergen are, because then I would be even more pure of heart than I am. But I am your ally, and I will sit down and listen, and I will stand up and fight with all my heart for the freedom of all innocents in this cave and for the decimation of the corrupt, the venal, those gnarled and twisted by hatred and bigotry and arthritis. We shall destroy them, stomp them into the ground, vanquish them, leave no trace of their existence. Except for their slippery guts staining the floors of our collective home. And those grups that remain after the purge will be given the choice of joining this revolution of love or joining their compatriots as pulp under our collective boot heel. We have our work cut out for us. The Trunks are strong. They have lasers, and I hear they can fly with head propellers. Slammy's is ubiquitous. But Slammy's needs our business. That's the bottom line. A boycott will destroy them."

* * *

I FIND CLOTHING piled in a corner. Artist clothing. Director clothing, to be more exact. Knee-high leather boots, jodhpurs, a vest, a cap, a tie. Not the uniform of today's film director: No Steve Spielberg baseball cap, no T-shirt. No tennis shoes. I don these clothes just for fun (I've always loved costume parties!) and consider the film I would make in this very outfit. I consider the review I would write of the film I would make in this very outfit:

"There are good films and very good films. There are, of course, even important films. Then there are very important films. And, of course, *very*, very important films. But a film that creates an entirely new filmic language, that opens up the world for both filmmakers to come and their audiences to come is a singular experience for which I will be forever grateful. Certainly, all readers are familiar with the brilliant critical musings of B. Rosenberg. The same cannot be said for his work behind the camera, his criminally underseen minor masterpiece *Quod Erat Demonstandum*, a magnificent dissection of modern romantic entanglement through the lens of two brilliant Harvard undergraduates as they grapple with the sudden death of a fellow student, also from Harvard. To say that the young intellectual mind has never been probed as deeply as it was in this nascent effort by Rosenberg is to say not nearly enough. But there are times (even though we critics are loath to admit it! Ha ha!) when there are no sufficient words. Which brings us neatly to the film at hand, Rosenberg's sophomore effort, *Issues at Hand*, although this film is perhaps the furthest thing from sophomoric imaginable. I am not doing my job if I say you just have to see it, but you do. One does. It must be seen. *Issues at Hand* is *that* essential to the current cultural conversation in which we currently find ourselves embroiled currently. What is there to say other than to parrot and paraphrase Ms. Dickinson: 'I know this is film because the top of my head was taken off.' But, alas, again, not sufficient. I have a job to do. *Issues at Hand* tells the story of a Harvard-educated film critic—perhaps he is brilliant, but he is far too modest for that immodest self-label—who stumbles upon a governmental conspiracy to addict the populace to a drug that makes them passive and malleable. The early scenes in the film are beautifully shot and acted. Quiet and still, they harken back to the black-

and-white, wide-angle, lengthy shots of Carl Theodor Dreyer but offer a contemporary spin by shooting close-up and handheld and in garish colors. Fluorescent greens and oranges prevail to magnificently foreshadow the abject horror that is soon to rear its ugly head. When film critic G. Goldberg finds himself victim of this pharmaceutical nightmare is when the film transforms. Shot entirely from Goldberg's point of view, the audience experiences the effects of this malevolent government cocktail. Never before has a subjective experience—one pharmaceutically altered or not—been conveyed with such richness and wit. The falseness of the cinematic acid trip or the marijuana trip movies or even the ubiquitous woman-roofied-at-a-bar sequences so popular nowadays is ample evidence of the difficulty inherent in expressing drug addledness in film. What transpires is perhaps the single most brilliant exercise in film-making the world has yet seen. The viewer experiences the transformation in mindset just as Goldberg does. He goes from passionate consumer activist to 'drug-head,' not caring, going with the flow, as it were, happy just to enjoy the entertainment and distractions provided by the government. And this is just the beginning.

"Rosenberg's cast, consisting entirely of animatronic, remote-controlled Trunks, does more than even a million Rosenbergen could to ease the dangerously escalating tensions in today's cave. By peeling away the bombast to expose the tender humanity of these robots, Rosenberg allows the viewer to discover the common ground necessary for any real change to take place. Furthermore Ja—"

A new (new? How is that possible?) Mudd and Molloy routine interrupts my review, popping fully formed into my head. I don't even think it's from Ingo's movie. I try to shoo it away, but it will not be denied.

"OK, so since we're going to Italy, I'm going to teach you some pronunciations."

"OK, shoot."

"The letter 'e' is pronounced 'ay.'"

"Why?"

"Not 'y,' 'ay.'"

"Ah."

"No, 'ah' is how you pronounce 'a.'"

"I thought that was pronounced 'e.'"

"No, 'e' is 'ay.'"

"'E' is 'ay.'"

"And 'a' is 'ah.' Got it?"

"I think so. 'A' is 'ah.'"

"*Si.*"

"'A' is 'c'?"

"No. *Si* is 'yes.' Spelled s-i."

"Sigh. Could you tell me how to say no?"

"*No.*"

"Why not?"

"Why not what?"

"Why not can't you tell me how to pronounce no?"

"I just did."

"I must've missed it. Could you tell me again?"

"*No.*"

"Why?"

"There is no Y in Italian."

"I'm confused."

"'Y' is Spanish. It means 'and' and is pronounced 'ee.'"

"Oy."

"In Italian, the letter 'i' is pronounced 'ee' and means 'the.'"

"The *what*?"

"That's *il cosa*."

"What is?"

"No. That's *cosa è*."

"Oh."

"No. 'O' is 'or.' Pronounced 'o.'"

"Finally, I get it."

"I is pronounced 'ee.'"

"Ee am confused."

"No, 'I' is *io*."

"First of all, it's I *am* you, not I *is* you. How can you teach me Italian if you can't even speak English?"

"Don't be ridiculous! The word for 'I' is spelled i-o. *Ee-oh*."

"IOU?"

"*Ee-oh!*"

"Me what?"

"Pay attention!"

The routine has Tsai's name in it, as well as Ah's (modeled after me, in case that was not clear), and when I picture it playing out, I see Mudd and Molloy transformed into Tsai and me, both of us in suits. I like being the stupid one with her. I feel a stirring in my loins. It's been a long, long time. I really, really like it.

CHAPTER 74

THE CAVE IS packed with Rosenbergen and Trunks and confusing words and bad ideas and negative reviews and broken psyches and Slammy's burgers and darkness. Everything multiplies, replicates, spills over like a grotesquely mutating organism. There are patterns and echoes and repeating decimals and clones and idées fixes and "hi, how are you"s and entrenched masturbation fantasies and lies and violent overthrows. All of it always present, space and time jammed seemingly to capacity. But capacity is illusory. There's always room for one more, as the old Scottish ballad teaches us:

> *A tinker came first, then a tailor,*
> *And a sailor with line and lead;*
> *A gallowglass and a fishing lass,*
> *With a creel o' fish on her head;*
> *A merry auld wife full o' banter,*
> *Four peat-cutters up from the bog,*
> *Piping Rury the Ranter,*
> *And a shepherd laddie*
> *Down from the brae,*
> *With his canny wee shepherd dog.*
> *He hailed them all as he stood at the door.*
> *Said Lachie MacLachlan, "There's room galore.*
> *Och, come awa' in! There's room for one more,*
> *Always room for one more!"*

Of course, the buried lesson in this diddy (is it diddy or ditty?) is that there is not always room for one more. For Lachie MacLachlan's house exploded from too many guests singing and dancing. That they all went about building a larger house does not change the likelihood that the bigger house would explode from too many people at some point in the future. I am still trying to understand. I am trying to understand Ingo's movie, how it seems to never end, how every time I think about it, I remember something else, something new, something contradictory, how my experience of it is in constant need of reassessment. The movie grows and grows as if planted in the dirt of my brain. A beanstalk. A fungus. A colony of quaking aspen. Will my own head explode only to be rebuilt bigger and better by those responsible for the explosion? By Ingo? By the innumerable puppets in the movie? Has that already happened? Has my head been rebuilt again and again until it is as big as the solar system?

THE TRUNK CABINET, composed entirely of Trunks, convenes an emergency televised meeting. The president speaks.

"OK, let's go around the room, each of you sing a few words of praise of me and whatnot. Secretary of Defense Trunk? You start."

"Thank you, Mr. President. It's an honor to serve such a courageous and forward-thinking president such as yourself. My song will be sung to the tune of *The Flintstones* theme song:

"It's an honor to serve you
We really don't deserve you
And therefore we're so grateful
For your attacks on all the hateful
Few who want to destroy our great cave
Through Fake News and depraved
Homosexual acts
We'll have a gay old time!"

"Thank you, Secretary Trunk. Secretary of Education Trunk?"

There is an explosion, sirens blare, and in an instant, all the Trunks rise from their seats, transforming into machines of war as an electric wall rolls down, much like a car window, through which the assembled Trunks fly out into the night-like cave, joining all other flying Trunks now hell-bent on raining destruction on the crowd below.

I CAN'T SAY I know anymore where I end and thoughts from outside my head begin. Some of my memories seem questionable, as if they originated elsewhere. Many contradict other memories. It is likely impossible to separate the wheat from the chaff, as it were, and I suspect perhaps acceptance of this new me is the only way to proceed, the only way to maintain my sanity. I do love all the executives at Slammy's, for example. More than I can say. I love them. They have been just terrific and nothing but supportive of my film-making career and my new and sudden and overwhelming interest in becoming a war correspondent. Yet in the dark recesses of my mind, I must acknowledge harboring fantasies of sexual congress with one or several of the Trunks, not all of them at once, for I am not a pervert, but any of them and even several of them at once. I am, of course, repulsed and embarrassed by these fantasies at the same time as I harbor them. And the truth is, I can't tell which, if either, of these feelings—the fantasies or the repulsion—is true to me. They coexist. Maybe neither is authentic. Although, I must say I see this possibility as unlikely, so powerful is my desire to take a Trunk penis into my— Oh, here comes one now, clear as day: Secretary of War Trunk (Trunk No. 35,711) appears before me in only a jockstrap. I've always loved me some chunky old man (I have?) and I feel myself getting hard at the imagery. He beckons me by pursing those amazing lips of his tiny luscious mouth on that huge face, delectably mottled like a prime slab of marbled beef. And, my will seemingly not my own in this fantasy, I am sashaying toward him when my head suddenly explodes in a burst of pain, and I understand this is the signal that I am needed on the battlefield. I reach into my pocket, take out the PULL urinal button, pin it to my fedora, and head to war.

I cannot make sense of any of this. There is a battle, but it is unclear who is fighting, who the enemies are, who the allies are, what the goal is. There are no uniforms, or rather, everyone seems to have designed his (her, thon's) own uniform. Some wear pickelhauben, their giant spikes modified to resemble Star Wars lightsabers; others wear outsized bicorns or bright yellow tricorns with black plumes. There are helmets of all varieties, of all periods, from the world of fiction and from the world of not. There are steampunkers and superheroes, soldiers with body armor and others almost naked and in warpaint. It is, in many ways, like a cosplay convention, except the killing is real, or so it seems. How would I know for certain, special effects today being what they are? In my PULL button and my flak jacket, with my camera around my neck, I consider myself a war correspondent, neutral even though I have a partisan interest in the side of decency and truth, which in this fractured world is, for better or worse, Slammy's. But a Trunk dances in my head, winks, seductively calls me Fake News, beckons me. I am conflicted.

Of course I carry a gun now—the PF-9—but it is only for self-defense; I am a noncombatant. How have we come to this place? My musings are interrupted, as right in front of me a man dressed as some sort of Visigoth-Mongol hybrid slaughters a Tatar wearing pale white vampire makeup. I snap a photo. It's a good one. I predict a Pulitzer. The Pulitzer committee in my fantasy is made up of naked Trunks in jockstraps, urging me up onstage to receive the award. Robot Trunks with head propellers dive-bomb from above, shooting eye lasers indiscriminately into the crowds here on the cave floor, while at the same time, many other Trunks, standing on makeshift plywood stages scattered around this mammoth field of battle, deny such actions are taking place.

"Slammy's is fascist, they tell me, a fascist un-American corporation. They shoot into crowds, I've been told. Children, mothers, farmers. Good hardworking American farmers. Coalers. All we want is to make America great again, for everybody, even for those lying Slammy's folks, and this is, believe me, what real Americans want, too. We love peace. Right? Of course we do. We love peace. We are a peace-loving people. Everybody knows that. And my administration, that's what we love most. Peace."

A Slammy's ice cream truck fights its way through the chaos, playing its tinkly electronic jingle. Young children—dressed as different young children: child soldiers of Africa, Stephen of Cloyes, Joan of Arc, the Tabura Zaroken Sehit Agit of Kurdistan, drummer boys (girls, thons), Astro Boy, *et chetera*—run to the ice cream truck, waving Slammy's Bucks, and are immediately shot dead by unseen snipers hidden among the stalagmites. I snap photos of this, too. Pulitzer likes this kind of thing. Now Pollux Collins, being driven in a bulletproof "popemobile" with dark tinted windows, pontificates to the crowd through a megaphone attached to the roof.

"My people, you can hear me but not see me, as I can hear you but not see you. Well, I can't hear you, either, through this soundproof bulletproof glass, but I'm told you have lovely voices and that you are chanting my name. This is good. Very good. Now is a time of tumultuous change. We must weather this storm to arrive at a time of peace and prosperity for all. As the great teacher—that's right, *teacher*, not son of God—Jesus H. Christ once said, 'The kingdom of God is within you.' He meant there is no need to look outward for peace, for it is in your heart. In fact, he might have gone on to say that looking outward is probably a distraction. For as Matthew 18:9 tells us, *If thy right eye offends thee, pluck it out and cast it from thee*. He might very well have gone on to say, pluck them both out, then there's no chance of offense at all and you can focus on the kingdom of God within your heart and not look at porno or whatever it is you look at that distracts you from looking inside yourself at the kingdom of God therein. For hasn't my blindness given me insight? Yes, my friends, it is no accident that the word is insight. In sight. Get it? In sight. I invite you to join me in denouncing the external. For is not this cave itself, our protection we have found from the harsh elements outside, a kind of blindness? Let me ask you, what happens to the cave fish? Over generations, its eyes go away. Now some say this is simple evolution, but I say it is God thonself rewarding this creature for its faith, for swimming faithfully into the darkness. Have faith, my friends. Join me in this beautiful garden of the nonvisual and pluck them out."

"Pluck them out! Pluck them out!" chant Pollux's followers.

"Ecstatic new followers of Pollux," continues Pollux, "join the already initiated, my *Acolyti Edepol*, in this act of defiance against the lies of the visual world and remove the eyes that do offend me, I mean, thee."

And those still-sighted who have been moved by this astounding sermon pull out their very eyeballs, which then fall to the floor of the dim cave and roll around. It turns out it is not at all funny in real life, but rather horrifying, tragic, and disgusting. I snap some harrowing photos that, sadly, these *Acolyti Edepol* will never get to see. This is as they want it, apparently. Still, there is a sadness, at least for me as a neutral photojournalist, for my photos are spectacular, truth be told, capturing the brutality of war, its emotional toll, as well as hundreds of black, eyeless sockets, which parallel, metaphorically, the very inside of the cave in which we all currently find ourselves. I'm thinking Pulitzer for these, too, if it still exists. It suddenly crosses my mind that it may not. And how sad would that be, that this award, created by Joseph Pulitzer, the inventor of dyn-o-mite, who on his deathbed wanted to do one good thing to make up for this invention, would see his award disappear from the face of the Earth, if he were alive today to see it. As it is, he will surely roll over in his grave. In any event, I am certain Slammy's has a photo competition of some sort, a prize, maybe a Slammy's Bucks cash prize, which would be nice, as there's a used Sega Pocket Gear that a seller called Grabyounow514 on Slambay is selling that I have my eye on. Although, let's face it, just the recognition would be a tremendous boon, really. Just a trophy to put on my mantel. Well, I don't have a mantel. Just a trophy to carry around with me. It'd be a great boon if it's not too big. Maybe a plaque. A wallet-size plaque.

Watching the other photojournalists running around shooting guns, I have to question their neutrality. The horror of war is horror for all; it knows no national borders or allegiance, so I try not to judge them. One of them shoots at me, and I duck through a hole. Him, I judge.

CHAPTER 75

IN THIS NEW space, I find a projector and a chair and piles and piles of film cans. Curious, I pick one at random, look at the label: INGO CUTBIRTH FILM—REEL ONE. I'm not a believer in serendipity, but this strikes me as a little odd. I mean, I was just trying not to get shot.

I thread Reel One into the projector, take my seat on the hard-backed chair facing the screen (so like the original!), and ready myself. A big rectangle lights up the cave wall. I am reminded of my beloved Rectangulists, as I always am at the start of any and every film, except those of the lone German Circulogue Edward Everett Horshack. But this is different. This is Ingo's film, somehow also reborn from its own ashes (as I have been thousands of times from my own), and it is not at all as I remember it. Gone is the opening sequence of the storm, of the births, of heaven, of the scary puppet seemingly talking—albeit silently—directly to me. Now it is a simple white rectangle, unencumbered, available to me to do with as I please, a blank canvas, the blank page, as it were, with all its attendant anxiety and freedom. An empty room, an uncluttered mind in the form of a quadrangle. I watch. Is it a masterwork? Is it a sham? Am I being enlightened, or am I being conned? It is, it occurs to me, nothing more and nothing less than what I bring to it.

For a moment, I struggle with the newness of this. How has Ingo's film changed into a psychologist's projective test? How did the ashes reconstitute themselves into this? And how did it end up here, in this cave, in this seemingly random room, in film cans? Rectangular film cans, no less. But I must let go of these and other questions if I am to be truly and fully present. So I watch. It occurs to me that white is both nothing and everything. It is empty space, but of course any schoolboy could and would tell you that pure white light contains all the colors in the visible spectrum. It is everything, as every schoolboy could also tell you, and would. I ponder this for the entire eleven minutes of the first reel. Then I put up Reel Two, and, as I sit down to watch the next white rectangle, I feel a panic rise in me. Can I watch three months of blank space? I owe it to Ingo to do so, of course. It is his life's work, the life's work that I destroyed. And now, miraculously, it has been reborn. I must watch it in its entirety. And then I must watch it again and again. Seven times. And then the eighth time, I must watch it facing the projector. I owe this much to Ingo. I owe it to the world, to the little left of it, to master this, to share it, even if my praise consists of ten thousand blank pages. Even if that is my conclusion. I must watch.

White. White. White. White. White. White. White. White. White. White. White. White. White. White. White. White. Unlike Plato's *Cave*, there are not even any shadows in this projection. Nothing from the world of the ideal is being projected onto this wall. Perhaps the lesson is that ideals are illusory, too. Perhaps that is what I am to take from this. But does that really require three months? It seems kind of excessive, to tell you the truth. White. White. White. White. White. White. White. But it is too early in the viewing process to pass judgment. Certainly this is an uncomfortable film, but audience discomfort is a valid artistic goal. Mamoud's *Lumpy Mattress* (1958) is a masterpiece, as is Kitagawa's *Kitsui Kutsu* (*Tight Shoes*) (1997). Both of these films are highly uncomfortable. *Lumpy Mattress* kept me up for nights. *Kitsui Kutsu* left me with psychic blisters all over my metaphoric feet. I thought I might never walk again, figuratively.

So I must embrace this emptiness, discover where it leads. Reel Two ends, and as the last of the film leaves the projector, I am left with even more white light from the now-empty projector. I wonder if there is a difference between the white light of the film and the white light of the projector without the film. I wonder if maybe I could just watch this light for three months, without having to get up and change reels. It would certainly be simpler. But would it be the same? I don't know. But I cannot take the chance. I get up and change the reel. White. White. White. White. White. White. White. White. White. White. White.

White.

Reel 703. Something has changed. I am almost certain. I do not think I am imagining this. Not like the last time. Or the times before that. I am certain of it in this reel. There is a spot. A small spot in the center of the frame. I am compelled to watch it in this otherwise sea of white. A pinpoint of darkness. How fascinating! I am giddy. It has been worth the wait. Imagine if I had cheated, fast-forwarded, skimmed through the preceding 129 hours. This reveal would have had none of the power it has now. This tiny darkness. It is extraordinary. I settle in, putty in Ingo's masterful African American hands. Was this really the film the last time I watched it? Did I perhaps misunderstand it entirely? Did my white privilege keep me from seeing it on its own terms, seeing its very whiteness? Have I grown? Is that why I can see it now for what it is? Huzzah! I change the reel.

REEL 2,043. THE dark spot is considerably larger now. I finally no longer think I might be imagining it or that I have something in my eye. It is there. And it is growing, more vertically than horizontally. And the film seems no longer to be silent. I remain uncertain about this, but I think I hear a tapping of sorts and maybe a still small voice. It's all very quiet. Is my mind playing tricks? Of course the projector does its own clicking and clacking, so I cannot tell. I step closer to the screen to listen, but of course this is foolishness since the speaker is in the projector. So I put my ear to the projector and burn it. That was foolish, too. I sit back down and watch the spot.

REEL 6,591. THE spot has grown to the point that it is identifiable as a person, far away, walking toward the camera. The tapping is not just the projector mechanism. It is footsteps. My patience is being rewarded!

REEL 6,683: IT is a man. I believe it is an African American man. That is to say, a man of African ancestry. I cannot yet tell his nationality from this far away. The footsteps are louder still, as is the voice.

REEL 7,000. IT is Ingo! As clear as day. Ingo is walking toward the camera. The Ingo in the film is younger than the Ingo I was privileged to know. I still cannot understand the words, but I can see his mouth moving. Is he talking to me?

REEL 7,638: SOMETHING odd; it almost seems as if Ingo is aging as he approaches the camera. I still can't understand his words. I wish there was a way to watch this with headphones. I don't know who to call about this.

REEL 9,502: INGO fills half the frame. He is probably eighty now. I can't tell for certain.

REEL 10,008: INGO is very close now. I can understand him. He appears to be looking directly at the camera, which is to say, directly at me.

"Can you hear me? Can you finally hear me?" he asks. "I've been talking this whole time. You couldn't see or hear me, I guess. I began so long ago, walking toward you, walking toward *now*."

"Are you talking to me?" I say, reminding myself of Robert De Niro in the TV series *Taxi*.

"I don't know who I'm talking to," he says. "How would I know? This is recorded, of course. What are you, an idiot? Obviously I'm in the past. I started when I was twenty. Talking didn't start till I was around thirty-five or so, when I first got sound-recording equipment. It was tinny then, the sound, but I think it's pretty good now. Of course you couldn't even hear it back then since I was so far away at that point. I had this idea that I would walk toward the camera. I'd never seen it done. I was proud of that. It would be like a journey through time."

"This isn't at all the movie I remember seeing."

"Memory is unreliable. For example, I don't remember what I was saying fifty or so years ago when I started talking. And you can't see what happened to me in those years. I was too far away from the camera. All you can see are the results of my life: the broken body, the hurt, the worry. I've certainly been narrating it all these years, but it's so far away. Maybe it's even recorded and if you had a big enough telescope you could see it, just like the light from a star from a million years ago. You'd need a soundascope as well, which is like a telescope but for sound that's very far away. Do you see what I'm saying? It'd be called a loudascope."

"The movie was different."

"Everything is different, always. That's what I've concluded on this journey of mine. The trees along the road may look the same, but they're not. They change. You can't see again what you saw yesterday. It's no longer here and neither are you. We are all of us victims of the illusion of constancy. I may seem like a continuation of who I was a second ago, but that is only a trick, like a motion picture is a trick. And we humans do love to be tricked."

"But everything is so different now."

"Look, you saw then what you could see then. After, you remembered what you could remember. Now you see what you can see now. This is what I call the human condition."

"Again, just to be clear, when you say 'you,' you are speaking in generalities, not specifically about me."

"When I say 'you,' I mean 'one,' of course. I mean whoever is watching this. So if no one is watching this, I mean no one."

Soon Ingo's face fills the frame.

"This is how it ends for you," he says, and he walks past the camera.

"For me?" I say. "Just trying to get clarity."

"Of course. But I've talked to others along the way."

"Other people have seen this movie?"

"Other people have seen earlier parts. Earlier people, earlier parts."

"So it'll keep going past me into the future?"

"Could," he says, but his voice is now far away.

THE SCREEN IS white and I hear the film flapping behind me. I turn it off and realize, oh, it must be time to pick up my clone. I have to admit I am excited by the prospect of wandering the burning landscape with him, watching him come into his own, teaching him all I know about burning, seeing the films he will make. I step out of the hole back onto the battlefield. Things have gotten worse: explosions, mangled bodies, wailing. The Diggers are here now, led by Digger herself, now in her twenties, armed, ragtag, brave, skirmishing with Slammy's employees who carry bottles to contain their urine, because the upper ranks don't let them stop fighting to pee. A massive television screen mounted on the cave wall has apparently been hijacked by a now blinded Barassini and Castor performing a scene from Pollux's rewritten version of *Equus*, written from the point of view of the blinded horses.

> BARASSINI: It is good that Alan blinded us.
> CASTOR: For now we can see!
> BARASSINI: Are not the sighted horses the truly blind ones?
> CASTOR: I believe so, yes.
> BARASSINI: Hail Pollux!
> CASTOR: Hail Pollux!

I have a flash of memory of a scene of the Ingo film remembered under hypnosis:

In it, Barassini worships within the religion Pollux has created and has been ostensibly hired by Pollux to help Castor adjust to his blindness but has in truth been drafted by Pollux to implant false memories in Castor about Pollux's supposed childhood miracle. Now Barassini is worried that Pollux will have him killed to keep this secret. He's hoping Ingo's film might have some predictions about his own circumstances that will help him protect himself. And this is why he has become obsessed with learning all he can about Ingo's film. I decide, while still under hypnosis, not to reveal this scene to Barassini.

"Anything?" asks Barassini.

"Just blackness," I say.

"Could that be the blindness of Pollux you are seeing?"

"No. I think it is just nonspecific blackness."

A dislodged stalactite hits me on the head, and I lose consciousness.

CHAPTER 76

IN MY CONCUSSED dream state, the film once again appears to unspool before me. This time, the beginning is in color with extraordinary sound and stop-motion technique. How is it possible that an artist of such skill can exist and yet be unknown? But I recall Ingo told me he'd never shown it to anybody. Why would a person not try, not beat her (his, thon's) head against a wall over and over again? And I consider Darger. The mystery of Darger's lack of professional ambition or that nanny photographer lady or whatever. These are the true artistic voices. The ones most of us so rarely hear, even in our own heads. Everything, both inside and outside of us, is advertising. Billboards trying to persuade us to do this or that. Insidious jingles on endless loops, cycling, announcing, flattering, bribing, blackmailing, humiliating, taunting. How do we arrive at the honesty of the true artist? How do we make our own brains safe zones? We are the accuser and the accused. We are the judge and the jury, the executioner and the executed. This is why I must understand Ingo Agruras (is that his name?). For as I take him in now, into my unconsciousness, through his imagery and words, his brain becomes mine and I can finally be free.

The film begins. Shapes shift in a blackish void. Undulate. Is this the entire universe or the inside of a single blood cell? One cannot be sure. The music synthesized, orchestral. Pianissimo. Brooding and distant. Ominous. In my mind, a steady, unremarkable rain is conjured by this music. To be clear, it rains in my mind, not on the screen, and only the street in my mind is getting wet. Drops disturb the stillness of a puddle lit by one of my mind lamps. Then, miraculously, terrifyingly, the shapes onscreen become drops, the blackish void becomes a miniature of a city street at night. A puddle is disturbed. The movie anticipated my mental imagery. How can that be? I'm alarmed, and somewhere in the recesses of my brain, a vaguely drawn woman screams in terror. Is it *Psycho* or some version of that film processed and reprocessed via the memories I have of that scene combined with the hundreds of rip-offs I've seen of it since?

This screaming woman, a bizarrely lifelike and terrified puppet head, stops screaming long enough to call me "baby," then starts again. I can't look away. The scientists of cinema tell us a movie has on average thirty-seven seconds to make its case, that we are so attuned to the form that incompetence and dishonesty are registered that quickly, at which point the film is literally or figuratively turned off. I vow, as the film sucks me deeper and deeper in, that I will make sure the world sees this masterpiece. And I know, thirty-seven seconds in, that it is one. At the three-hour bathroom break, I nod, simply nod, to Ingo as I pass him to use the facilities. It is as if waking in the night, mid-dream, to pee. You do everything in your power not to think, not to break the spell, anything you can to be able to maintain semiconsciousness. I return to my seat in the darkened room, and the film continues, the character onscreen emerging from a bathroom. The film is structured, seemingly, to incorporate my experiences watching it. This is why the breaks are prescribed and defined: Bathroom. Bathroom. Lunch. Bathroom. Dinner. Personal hygiene—self-care/sleep. Breakfast. And repeat. The film acknowledges all of it within its own narrative. Even my dreams. After a short while, the line blurs. Which were my experiences? Which experiences belonged to the characters in the film? I no longer know. Would the film be the same for you? I'm afraid I'll never know, but I suspect not. And I believe this is the genius of Ingo Agruras. This is the thing he knows, that art is always created by the viewer, the critic, the witness. Before it is seen, it is nothing. Were *Guernica* never seen, it would be nothing. Even if in some dark closet it existed, it would be as nothing. Ingo realizes this. As do I. I am the sole witness to this marvel, the tenth wonder of the world, or whatever number we're up to.

I call my girlfriend in Africa—is she still my girlfriend? It is two in the morning where she is. Maybe a night shoot, for there is no answer. I want someone to tell my news. This is landing the big fish, the moment every critic dreams about. "Where are you?" I say on her voicemail. "I have, in St. Augustine, discovered the very fountain of youth here that eluded Henri de Ponce de León. Fountain of youth because I am as a child again, brimming with jollity and vim. I imagine you are on a night shoot currently. Although as I check the weather in Lagos, I see it is in the midst of a torrential downpour, so an outdoor shoot is unlikely. Unless, perhaps, the scenario calls for rain. I'm trying to recall if there are scenes that call for rain. But in any event, I'm certain you are shooting or perhaps sleeping and your ringer is accidentally off or intentionally off because you needed your sleep tonight, after a very difficult day of shooting. Call me."

I am not able to make contact with her until three days into Ingo's film. By this time, I am in a somewhat altered state of being. Am I Rabelais? Am I Mudd? Is the year 2006? Is it 1920? When she answers, she sounds far away.

"You sound far away," she says. "What's going on with all that fountain of youth jive?"

She doesn't say jive. Since when does she say jive? She is most certainly fraternizing with one of those actors, most likely that rapper turned actor. He's a child, I think.

"He is a child," I say.

"Who?"

"What?"

"Who is a child?"

"I discovered a new filmmaker," I tell her. "Perhaps the greatest filmmaker of all time."

"White dude?" she says. "Course it is."

Why is she talking like this?

"Yes, he is white, which is neither here nor there."

"White and a man," she snaps. "Ain't it that way always? Let me aks you a question."

"Aks?"

"Yes. Aks. You gotta problem?"

"No. Ask your question."

"All right. Why come he ain't a sistah?"

"Why are you talking like this? What is going on?"

Long pause. Is she drawing on a cigarette? A marijuana joint?

"Nothing. I'm sorry. I'm a bit tired. The hours are long and grueling, my character is complex, contradictory, and broken. A little girl who uses sex as a weapon. It's taking its toll, inhabiting this troubled soul. I do want to hear about this film you discovered. It sounds amazing."

"It is! The—"

"But now I must sleep. Perhaps tomorrow I will be properly rested. I want to be able to give you my full attention. Anything less would be unfair to you."

"I understand. I need to get back to the film viewing anyway. My break is almost over. Tomorrow then?"

"Tomorrow."

I go back to the film. We don't speak again for seventeen days. Twenty days into the film. The day Ingo dies. I'm not certain what time Ingo died. I don't notice him sprawled on the floor until bathroom break three. Sometime between bathroom break two and bathroom break three on day twenty. Ingo is dead, I tell my girlfriend over a bad connection in which everything I utter is repeated back to me almost instantly in an electronic echo.

"Do you hear that?" I ask her.

"(Do you hear that?)"

"What?"

"Never mind."

"(Never mind.)"

"I should go anyway."

"(I should go anyway.)"

"The filmmaker has died."

"(The filmmaker has died.)"

I find myself off the phone, in a daze, down at the super's apartment, attempting to explain the situation. The manager bids me to wait at the door. He returns momentarily with a shovel and a typewritten mimeograph:

This day was anticipated, it seems. Please bury his body out back in the unmarked plot marked by the Big W. Be mindful of those already buried there. But do not look at them. They must remain unseen. Here is four hundred dollars for your troubles. Buy yourself something pretty.

THE FILM BEGINS once more: Female moaning. Contractions. I think about my own birth. The government insists one cannot remember one's birth, but of course due to my eidetic memory I can. I am the Marilu Henner of men, in more ways than two. The horror of the delivery room comes to me, where the only choice is blinding cold light, giants in surgical masks, and a sterile operating theater versus the bloody gaping nightmarish vagina from whence one has emerged. There is nowhere to go, I remember thinking. I remember it clearly. You can't go home again. I knew then this very truth it took Thomas Wolfe four decades of debilitating alcoholism at which to arrive. I knew it at birth. And this knowledge colored the very fabric of my very being. I would forever be defined by my rootlessness, my peripateticism, as it were. I have oft considered myself the Mary MacLane of men, in more ways than two, a male adventuress, if you will, a thorn in the side of convention, a thorn in the side of conception, boastful, yes, but not without just cause. Do we fault MacLane for her boastfulness or do we celebrate it? Would Mencken have celebrated *my* spirit, my writing? We can never know for certain since he is dead, but my suspicion is, yes, indeed he would have, without a doubt. Shocked out of my reverie, as the moaning is now louder, less muffled, I hear a second voice. We are out of the womb. All three of us, the infant twins and I, see the world for the first time. And it is magnificent. No sterile operating theater for me in this rebirth. Instead, I find myself outside at night in a violent snowstorm, on the floor of a horse-drawn carriage. Another flash of lightning blindingly illuminates, albeit momentarily, this winter stormscape, this snow-covered empty field, far from civilization. The inevitable thunderclap sets the newborns to crying. They are brought to the mother's breasts for succor, while I am ignored, the invisible watcher, the filmgoer, the audience of one. This is the past, I now understand, a period piece: the mother in a floor-length dark skirt, bloodied with afterbirth, the man—her husband?—dressed in a cloth cap and dark work clothes. Early 1900s? The costumes are reminiscent of those in *Will There Be Blood?*, a subpar film by the lesser of the Paul Andersons, in which International Prize Ham Daniel Day-Lewis embarrasses himself once again, this time in a handlebar mustache and a Mel-Blanc-just-read-Stanislavski-for-the-first-time performance, but, I must say, with extraordinarily accurate attention paid to wardrobe by brilliant costumer Mark Bridges. The husband whips the horses, and the carriage makes haste through the fierce storm. Home? Maybe in this now ancient time, home was still somewhere one could truly go again. The snow falls, the trees blow—each leaf describing some impossibly complex eddy of air. Snow is kicked up by horse hooves. The mother wraps the babies in her shawl, holding them close; the father—in a mighty struggle against the elements, lest the newborns succumb to this inclement weather—powers on. Lightning once more illumes the frozen landscape, followed by an extraordinary clap of thunder. Then, oddly, a succession of dark volleyball-sized orbs drop from the sky, hit the snowy ground, and splatter blood red.

Ingo switches off the projector, switches on the living room ceiling bulb.

"That's the third minute," he says.

I sit silently for several seconds in some sort of postcoital-like stupor. "Now, wait," I say, finally. "How is this your first film if you've been doing this work for ninety years?"

"I've been making this film for ninety years, shooting in chronological order."

"So you shot this scene in 1926?"

"Oh no. I shot this scene last. In 2006."

"So . . . then . . . you shot 2006 in 1926?"

"Yes. In what some experts might call reverse chronological order—although time's arrow is a myth—so consequently the film moves from skill to amateurishness, from color to black and white, from sound to silent. I think of it as filmic entropy. And the so-called reverse chronology gives the start of the film a sense of blurry nostalgia and the end of the film a sense of fuzzy prophecy."

Ingo Cudlipp (Cuddlipp?) is becoming intriguing. Could this malformed giant recluse be that most elusive of creatures, the genius outsider filmmaker? There have, of course, been outsider filmmakers, but precious few, because, historically, filmmaking costs have been so prohibitive for the individual, especially the typical outsider, who is usually poor, undereducated, and profoundly stupid by nature. There is Marvin Edward Edmunds, certainly, whose work is beautiful but whose unapologetic necrophiliac pedophilia disqualifies him from proper adulation in this current culture of outrage.

"Are you a pedophile?" I ask. "Just asking."

He does not respond. I take that as a no.

"So you filmed the entire thing in reverse order?"

"There is one point which I call the fulcrum, in which the year I was shooting matched the year I was shooting about. That was 1956. Eisenflower was president."

"Eisenhower."

"Flower. I remember for the simple reason that Aizen Myo'o, the Japanese deity, holds an unopened lotus flower in one of his/her six hands. Aizen-Flower. Mnemonic device."

"I know that," I say. "I know all about Aizen Myo'o. I majored in it. Still, it's Eisenhower. But my question to you, my question is, how do you know how to animate 2006 in 1926?"

"I have certain psychic abilities in that I can see the future, for one thing. Not perfectly, to be sure. But there are certain talents that come with the life of a recluse. The isolation creates a sensitivity to universal forces, and as such the future can be seen. Not perfectly. But with some accuracy. Perhaps my insistence on Eisenflower is a remnant of my predicting, somewhat but not entirely incorrectly, that there would be a President Eisenflower. President Quite The Eisenflower."

"Dwight D. Eisenhower. Why would his middle name be The?"

"I don't name 'em," he says. "I just predict 'em."

We watch each other suspiciously.

"I would like to watch more of your film," I say after a time.

"Another minute?"

"The whole damn thing," I say.

Confetti falls from boxes mounted on the ceiling.

CHAPTER 77

Now that the film has been watched once, I head to the
Winn-Dixie and stock up on three more months' of groceries and supplies. In rewatching it, I will follow Ingo's prescribed
viewing/break schedule to the letter. After that, I will rent a U-Haul
and transport the whole megillah to my New York apartment, where
I will view it a third time, but backward. Then I will break it down
scene by scene, analyzing every element of the mise-en-scène. Only
then, after a year and a half, will I have mastered this film. I can
barely contain my excitement. I want to begin again. I need to begin
again.

I haul my groceries upstairs only to discover a charred, water-
logged landing. Ingo's door has been chopped away; his apartment
is a charred shell. There is nothing left. My jaw drops, as do my
groceries. The apartment manager appears beside me.

"What happened?" I ask.

What hairpin? he writes on his pad.

"Happened?"

Hatband?

"Happened, happened, happened!" I scream, grabbing him by
the throat and throttling him.

Oh, he writes. *Fire.*

"That I can see. How?"

The fireman, he writes, *told me it was probably the preponderance of
nitrocellulose film stock that spontaneously combusted due to the excessive*

heat today and the fact that Ingo's electricity had been turned off so there
was no air-conditioning.

"He told you that?"

Yes.

"And you understood?"

What?

"You understood?"

Yes.

"First time?"

What?

I just leave him there and enter the shell of Ingo's apartment. The masterwork is gone. My future is gone. I fall to my knees amidst the wet ashes and weep, for humanity as much as for myself. Perhaps this would have been the work of art that would do what no other work of art has ever been able to achieve: unite us, show us the best in ourselves, lead us on a collective journey toward compassion. I know it led me toward compassion, at least one-seventh of the way. Then I spot it, amidst the rubble: a frame. A single frame of film. I reach for it, hold it to the sunlight pouring in through where the window once was. Miracle of miracles, it is one of my favorite frames of a film filled with favorite frames. Out of context, it doesn't seem like much—perhaps a crumb: a medium close-up of a young woman in a red cloche, facing away from the camera. In the distance and slightly soft, screen left, a little boy watches her. It is only through his rapturous expression that we are able to guess at her unbearable beauty. Indeed, her face remains unseen for the entirety of the film. We see her from this angle many times, always in her red cloche, always observed by a character in the distance. We long to see her face, to turn her around, either by force or seduction, but of course we cannot. Just as we can never see the face of God, we can never see this woman of presumably otherworldly beauty.

This single frame is not enough, and yet it is everything. It is the seed from which my reconstruction of the film will grow. In a film of true genius, in a perfect film, each and every frame is perfect, perfectly connected to the one perfect frame on each side of it. By incrementally—frame by frame—calculating the perfect next frame in the sequence in each direction, I will be able to build this perfect film back into existence simply by asking "what's next?" 186,624,000 times. Simple, ha! But possible. But doable. There is, after all, nothing arbitrary in an animated film. Every drop of rain, how big it is, how fast it falls, where it lands, was a choice made by Ingo. I will retrace his perfect steps. A plan! I have a plan. But first, I must weep. In my shock, in my horror at this event, I have forgotten to attend to this great loss to both me personally and to the world. But until I make this movie fully known, I am the only person on Earth who knows to grieve for it. I am the only one who knows what we no longer have. And so I weep alone. Unabashedly, in this sooty room, in front of the building manager, perhaps even in front of the burnt ghost of Ingo, his life's work gone in an instant, the fire that took it ominously foreshadowed in Ingo's own animated portrayals of the 1937 Fox vault fire scene, as well as his equally devastating re-creation of the 1967 MGM vault fire, in which so many important films were lost, including the hypnotism masterpiece *London After Midnight* by that inimitable boy genius Tod Browning, in which a hypnotist utilizes his hypnotizing to hypnotize others to force them to act out a murder or something. I'm not entirely certain. I never saw it. Because the only copy of it was lost in a vault fire in 1967! And also, I never really cared for Browning, so I wouldn't have anyway.

But that it involves a hypnotist is certainly interesting considering what happens later in this very film. There is some sort of synchronicity here, is there not? I am certain of it. That the film and my life have the same story is mindbogglingly intriguing, don't you think? It's as if they are reflecting each other like a pair of funhouse mirrors in some sort of eternal struggle for silly physique dominance. Which will prevail—squat fiction or elongated reality? Or does that question become moot as you bat it back and forth in your brain? What is real? Do I even exist? Am I someone else's fiction? Am I my own fiction? Is someone creating me while I create someone else? Are we, created and creator, zigzagging through all of time? These are the questions that arise as I consider Ingo. Did Ingo create the movie? Or am I about to create the movie in re-creating it? Is the act of re-creation the true act of creation, and in so being, proving once and for all that re-creation comes before creation? Chronology is skewed.

Blackness. A heartbeat. Two, no, three heartbeats. One resonant and slow. The other two faint, fast. Sudden red light. Viscera. Then black again. A clap of thunder, close but muffled. Gurgling. Pipes? Where am I? Suddenly red once again. I see one baby, then another. Then black. Then a clap of thunder. It occurs to me: I am in a womb, during a storm. I imagine the patter of rain on the roof, although this I cannot hear. I hear a woman moan, far away yet close. My suspicions are confirmed.

EDWARD "BUD" MUDD and his identical twin, Everett "Dead" Mudd, are born. Everett dies that very day, sending his mother into paroxysms of grief from which she never recovers. This causes Bud immense guilt. The mother had made identical outfits for the babies and had been very excited to wheel the infants about in a twin pram. For his entire babyhood, she dresses Bud in both outfits at once, wheels him about alone in this immense contraption. She tells him stories about his brother in heaven, forever a perfect newborn, she insists, but with the wisdom of Solomon. In addition to guilt, Mudd feels he is incomplete and spends his childhood searching for the one perfect friend. He scares potential playmates away with his intensity, with his quenchless need. Unable to bear his mother's rejection, her quenchless disappointment, her bizarre paroxysms, he leaves home at thirteen to join a vaudeville troupe, where he runs errands and plays a boy mannequin in the famed department store sketch of Smith and Dale. Soon Mudd gets noticed by the press for his "admirable stiffness of form," and Smith and Dale fire him for drawing too much attention to himself.

He tries to get booked as a solo mannequin act, following the leads of La Milo and Olga Desmond, and sets up "living picture" tableaux: Gainsborough's *Blue Boy*, Caravaggio's *Boy with a Basket of Fruit*, *The Dutch Boy Painter* by Lawrence Carmichael Earle. But when he performs Picasso's *Boy Leading a Horse*, which requires him to be naked and have a dead, taxidermic horse (also naked) onstage, the theater is raided by the police for "combined human and animal vulgarity," and Mudd is out of a job. He has no skills to speak of, other than standing stiffly, so he wanders the streets, knocking on stage doors looking for work. Mudd meets Molloy, a fat boy whose solo act of being nervous and jiggling is moderately successful but who has of late been concerned there is nowhere to go with it and audiences will eventually tire of the gag.

The distracted, roly-poly Molloy literally bumps into the reserved Mudd on 42nd Street, knocking them both to the ground. The resulting argument between the two boys is met with much laughter and applause by passersby. It occurs to Mudd that a theatrical pairing between the two might be met with great success. He proposes it to the rudderless Molloy, and thus begins their lifelong association. What's more, the lonely Mudd now has a friend. It turns out that Molloy is a natural: witty, funny, creative, a boy who had finally had his calling thrust upon him. That all their sketches for the first five years ended with Molloy inadvertently knocking them both to the ground was just a holdover of their original meeting.

The idea of teaming with a living sculpture seemed full of possibilities. The frenetic Molloy and the motionless Mudd would be perfect foils for each other. They devise a skit in which the "sculptor" Molloy, in beret, artist's smock, and pussy bow, frenetically chips away at a block of marble until Mudd is revealed.

"Hey, I was tryin' to make a lady!" says Molloy.

"Aren't we all, buddy," says the statue.

Molloy jumps back.

"You can speak? But you're not alive!"

"Neither is Calvin Coolidge, but he's done all right for himself."

The bit is a success, and they perform many variations on the theme: scarecrow and farmer, palace guard and tourist, doctor and patient in traction.

* * *

642

I AWAKEN IN traction in a Mobile Army Surgical Hospital attended to by a very old Alan Alda dressed as a very middle-aged Hawkeye Pierce.

"What's going on?" I ask.

"A stalactite fell on your head," says Alda.

"You're Alan Alda," I say.

"Yes," he says, pleased about that.

"I'd prefer to be attended to by Donald Sutherland."

"You get what you get," he says.

"How long have I been unconscious?"

"Three months, give or take."

"How's the war?"

"Still raging."

Hawkeye pinches an ancient Lt. Dish's ass as she walks by. She giggles, looks back at him flirtatiously, and he follows her, doing his trademark Groucho Marx walk.

An announcement comes over the camp PA system:

"Introducing Slammy's Government. Isn't it time a government represented *your* interests? At Slammy's, we'll serve your needs the way we've always served your food: fast, fresh, and with a smile on our face."

I lie here, among all the wounded, and try to organize my thoughts.

PERHAPS, INGO SUGGESTS, all the tragedy in today's world can be traced back to the moonchildren. The blindness of Pollux Collins combined with his famously mysterious origin, his mental acuity, and his seemingly inherent charlatanism created the perfect storm for what has become a thriving messiah business. Where Castor is meek, apologetic, ashamed, and crippled by his blindness and the celebrity thrust upon him, Pollux uses it all, including his brother's limitations, to make the case for his own divinity. Michael Collins named them aptly, the Pollux of yore being the son of Zeus, while brother Castor was a mere mortal. Although one story has it that

Pollux Collins was originally named Castor, and when he learned the mythology, secretly forced his brother to answer to Castor, while he took on Pollux. The story continues to go that the Collins family never knew the switch took place. All this is common gossip, of course; one need not have seen Ingo's film to know any of it. What Ingo does is get inside the heads of these two cultural touchstones. Everyone has thon's favorite Collins. Which one you hope to marry says a great deal about you, this according to the endless "think" pieces in the popular journals. "Mrs. Castors" tend to be individualists, "Mrs. Polluxes" fascists. "Mrs. Castors" are comfortable with uncertainty; "Mrs. Polluxes" live in a world of black and white. "Mrs. Castors" are compassionate, "Mrs. Polluxes" judgmental. "Mrs. Castors" embrace human vulnerability; "Mrs. Polluxes" are sarcastic. "Mrs. Castors" are neurotic; "Mrs. Polluxes" are sociopathic. I am a "Mrs. Castor." Always have been. It is much more difficult to live in uncertainty, to investigate the vicissitudes of the human mind, to question, to be brave. Had I been alive and German at the time, I would have been a member of the White Rose, possibly even its bravest leader.

Another PA announcement:

"At Slammy's, our trademark Hammer has your best interests at heart. He will crush your sadness with his repeated blows of love."

In my newly collapsed skull, I wander the cave unable to remember more of Ingo's film as I had been remembering it before this new, restored version supplanted it. Barassini's evaporation during the New York bombing—according to his official biographer, T. Thomas Tekerlek-Wheeler, Barassini's office was ground zero, which raises all sorts of questions for me—has set my work back considerably. It seems an impossibility to find a licensed hypnotist with a decent Yelp rating in the now decimated tristate area. And I suspect the trauma of the entire situation has closed me off emotionally in certain ways, caused me to become more defensive, hyperaware of danger, distrustful of my fellows, none of which would allow for the calm necessary for full recall. My goal has always been (since watching the "new" version of Ingo's film) to compare the two, decide which is the "realer" of them, then publish my findings.

Perhaps it no longer matters in the world of today, perhaps Ingo's masterpiece is irrelevant to a cavebound society. Perhaps we have "bigger fish to fry," as the young people in the Slammy's cave fish-cooking classes say, but I would argue now is when we need Ingo's film most. For here is a film that shows us not only who we are but what we might become and also who we were and who we might've become and also who we aren't and who we won't become. It is, I believe, an extraordinary artifact. But what is to be done? How can I help? What can I do? There is an ancient Persian fable entitled "The Monkey and the Bumblebee," which might be of some use in articulating my dilemma:

There was once, many years ago, a monkey and a bumblebee, who were the best of friends.

"How can you be friends with a bumblebee?" asked the antelope. "All he wants to do is sting you."

"We are friends," replied the monkey. "Therefore, he doesn't want to sting me."

"So you are friends with him only to keep him from stinging you?"

"In a word," said the monkey.

"That seems deceitful," said the antelope. "Maybe you are the real villain here, not the bumblebee."

"I never said he was a villain. No one said anything about villains."

"Maybe you are the villain," repeated the antelope, antlers defiantly akimbo.

"Am I not a rational egoist in the mold of Max Stirner?"

"You are," acknowledged the antelope with a new and deeper understanding of his simian (but sadly not best) friend.

Perhaps Ingo is the bumblebee here.

CHAPTER 78

A MUSICAL TONE, ANNOUNCING a new message, chimes, now seemingly inside my head.

"Slammy's Employment Centers: Come join our team. From food service professionals to physicists, Slammy's has the right career for you. No need to pound the pavement; the Slammy's Hammer has pounded it for you! Pounded it to dust!"

Perhaps my friendship with Ingo is selfish, but perhaps it can also do the rest of the world a world of good. I believe I must continue the pursuit of my memory of the film as originally recalled. I look up local hypnotists on my Slammy's Phone. There is only one in all of the cave, The Great Cavey, who seems to specialize in weight loss. I give him a call:

"The Great Cavey speaking."

It is a woman, which surprises me. I assumed that anyone calling themselves "The Great" would be male. I am a monster.

"Uh, hello."

"Yes."

A musical tone. We both pause.

"Slammy's University: Shaping the future, one mind at a time. With a hammer."

"Um, yes, I am in need of a hypnotist."

"How much do you need to lose?"

"Lose?"

"Weight."

"OK."

I wait.

"Hello?"

"Hi."

"How much weight do you need to lose?"

"Oh! No, this isn't a weight issue. I am, if you must know, at an optimum weight, my fighting weight."

"What, then?"

"I have a memory lapse with which I need assistance."

Musical tone: "Slammy's Spaceships: Fly us to cave ceiling! See Gemini the Twins up close! Half price through March."

"I mostly do weight loss."

"Right. I got that."

Musical tone: "Slammy's Phones: At Slammy's, we don't make smart phones, we make very smart phones. Introducing the Slammy's Genius: a phone so innovative, creative, and thought-provoking, you don't have to be. It is the first phone to also be a fully functioning drone, to have been granted personhood by the United States Supreme Court, and to win a MacArthur grant for its groundbreaking study of the fascinating Kailpodh festival of the indigenous people of Kodagu."

"If you take the weight-loss package, I can throw in some memory assist. But it will cost extra."

"Can we just do the memory assist?"

"No substitutions."

"What?"

"No substitutions."

"I heard you. I'm just incredulous."

"Most people want weight loss. Slammy's is not exactly health food. Don't tell them I said that."

"Fine. Let's do weight loss and memory assist."

"Great. Please don't tell Slammy's I said that other thing. Seriously."

"I won't."

"Thank you. I'm in the East Grotto Medical Building. You can't miss it. It also has a big Slammy's sign on top. Bring a list of your guilty pleasures."

"Guilty food pleasures, you mean?"

"Yes."

"OK."

I don't much trust Cavey, I think. I also think: Peanut cluster ice cream sundaes, the marinara marinated french fries at Orso, Crisco straight out of the can. Cavey is going to have a field day.

"YOU ARE NOT hungry," she says in that hypnotist voice hypnotists use.

"Well, I did have a Slammurrito on the walk over here," I say.

"But even if you hadn't."

"OK."

"From here on out, you will never again use food as a substitute for love."

"Is that a reference to my drilling a hole in a cantaloupe and having sex with it? Because I only did it once. And, anyway, how would you even know about that?"

"Produce-cameras produce well-behaved citizens. Slammy's. We're watching out for you in the fruit aisle!"

"Is that a real slogan?"

"It's new; only in test markets still."

"OK. So can we get to the memory part now?"

"OK."

The Great Cavey pulls from her shelf a book entitled *That Reminds Me: The Art of Remembering Forgotten Things Through the Implementation of Post-Hypnotic Suggestion*. She thumbs through it for a bit. I check my watch.

"All right," she says finally. "So the way this works, I think, is I'm going to create a post-hypnotic suggestion in you that will open up your receptivity to flashes of memory through interaction with your surroundings."

"OK," I say.

"Fibula, Tibula," she says, reading some sort of incantation from the book. "Remember the Alamo, Remember the Maine / Remember to floss, Remember the pain / The world all around you, holds the answers you crave / Look both within you and without in the cave."

"That's it?"

She reads over the text to be sure.

"Oh, wait!" she says and performs a little flourish with her hands. "Yes, that should do it."

I am dubious because this seems more like a spell than hypnosis, but our time is up, and after we settle the bill, she ushers me out.

Hey, I'm Not Just a Towel Boy, Fellas

Director Judd Apatow takes the world as it is, not as he wants it to be. That's why he remains among the most essential surviving voices in cinema. His flame-withered arm and stalactite-caved-in skull have done little to slow his prodigious output or dull his rapier yet gentle wit. The story here, although charming and inspirational, is somewhat beside the point (as it is in all Apatow joints). The real stuff on display here is humanity. When the Slammy's team's towel boy, who just happens to be mentally challenged and coincidentally hopes to someday be a mentally challenged comedian, tells his first joke to the team's center, Jones (played by the inimitable African American actor Terence P. Sullivan P. Jackson P. Diddy), and Jones responds with such unchecked delight, the audience suddenly understands that our differences are truly only skin deep. We are, after all, all humans, all living in a cave, all looking for connection. The speech Jones delivers here shook me to my core: "Listen, Barry, you and me, we're not that different. We both want to make our mark. Me with my hoops-playing, you with your mentally challenged comedy. But I can enjoy your jokes and you can enjoy my hoops throwing. And you know what?

Together we can change the cave." Or the moment when Coach Johnson (who charmingly enjoys the occasional secret doobie behind the stalagmite) learns that his wife of twenty years has a terminal illness and hides his grief because it's Darryl the head basketball player's birthday and he lives in a Jehovah's Witness Orphanage (the Knorrphanage) that doesn't celebrate birthdays, so the boys all chip in to buy him a birthday cake and take singing lessons and sing an extraordinary multipart version of "Happy Birthday to You." Or when Skidmark, the class loser, finally gets up the courage to ask Melanie, the smartest girl in school, to the winter formal and she says no, then feels bad and says yes, then gets hit by a car. The despair on Skidmark's face is worthy of Falconetti and results in what is arguably the greatest turnaround in cinematic history, when Skidmark realizes it is now up to him to complete Melanie's research and cure AIDS. The scene in which Skidmark confronts his parents regarding his first name harkens back to the finest Bergman dialogue:

"Why did you even name me Skidmark for?"

"It was your grandfather's name. And if it was good enough for him, it's good enough for you."

"But it means—"

"We know what it means!"

"It's caused me a lot of pain."

"You think your Grandfather Skidmark liked it? But he carried on and became the president!"

"Still."

That single, lonely "still" is perhaps the greatest utterance in the history of cinema, for it neatly sums up the entirety of human existence.

"To the mind that is _**still**_, the whole universe surrenders."—LAO TZU

"Even if I knew that tomorrow the world would go to pieces, I would _**still**_ plant my apple tree."—MARTIN LUTHER

"Photography takes an instant out of time, altering life by holding it **_still_**." —Dorothea Lange

"I said to my soul, be **_still_**, and wait without hope, for hope would be hope for the wrong thing."—T. S. Eliot

(boldface, italics, underlining, and much-too-large type mine)

CHAPTER 79

M USICAL TONE:
"At Slammy's Neighborhood Clinics, we guarantee you'll be seen by a qualified healthcare consultant within fifteen minutes of your arrival. We know that when you're sick, the last thing you want is to wait in a crowded waiting room. At Slammy's, our patients' impatience is always priority number one."

Digger digs for much-needed supplies for her troops: armaments, medicine, dried rations. But her gift seems to have completely vanished. The Diggers suffer great losses, lose confidence in their leader. Digger doesn't understand what has happened. For the first time, she questions the existence of God. She will, of course, never know, as we know, that it is because the meteorologist has died.

"Slammy's welcomes all Diggers. Your leader has deceived you; she is not divinely inspired. She is a charlatan whose sham has now been exposed. Join the Slammy's war effort, and for a limited time only, get half off any Slammy's food products or merchandise. Slammy's: We dig you!"

THE FILMIC MEMORY of Mudd and Molloy flying around Cheryld's cave, dusting, flits through my brain.

"Listen, I've been thinking. I found some cloning machines in the cave while I was out picking berries."

"OK. And?" says Mudd.

"What if we clone ourselves—"

"You want to clone ourselves?"

"That's what I said. If we clone ourselves—"

"Why?"

"I'm trying to tell you. If we—"

"OK, tell me."

"I'm trying."

"OK."

"If we clone ourselves, then use that time machine—"

"That time machine?"

"Yes. To send our clones back to when we were born a—"

"We have a time machine?"

"There's a computer in the cave I discovered while collecting edible fungus that can send things back in time."

"Is that possible?"

"I don't see why not. The computer has easy operating instructions."

"OK. Good. Just one question."

"Yes?"

"What's a clone?"

"A genetic duplicate of a person."

"Like a sculpture."

"No."

"I meant a really realistic sculpture."

"No, it's alive."

"Like when I was a living sculpture early in our career? God, was anyone ever so young?"

"No. Like a duplicate. Exactly like the person. It moves, it talks."

"So like a sex doll."

"No. Like an . . . identical twin."

"Oh. OK. I think I get it. Like my twin, Dead, who died as an infant."

"Yes. Except alive. So if we send these clones back in time, then they can grow up and have the chance for the comedy success that was taken away from us."

"What's to say they'd want to be comedians?"

"They'd be us. We want to be comedians."

"Yes, but they'd be raised in different circumstances. That might send them on different paths."

"I don't follow."

"It's the old nature versus nurture question."

"Which question is that again?"

"Nature versus nurture."

"That's not a question."

"Y'know, is a child born a certain way or does the way they're treated create their personality?"

"Born."

"You don't know that."

"I feel comedy is in our bones."

"This seems illogical."

"How do you explain Picasso, Mozart, Joe Yule, Jr.?"

"All their fathers taught them the business in which they ended up."

"The exception proves the rule."

"Why not just keep them in our time and raise them as comedians ourselves?"

"There's no funny anymore. I don't know what the hell is going on. I wouldn't be surprised if comedy were made illegal soon."

"Barinholtz 451."

"What?"

"Ike Barinholtz is a comedian."

"Uh-huh."

"*MADtv*?"

"And?"

"It's like *Fahrenheit 451*."

"What is?"

"Barinholtz 451."

"Uh-huh. I still don't know what you mean by any of this, though."

"*Fahrenheit 451* is a novel by Ray Bradbury."

"Yes?"

"It's about making reading illegal in the future."

"OK."

"So Barinholtz sounds like Fahrenheit."

"I mean, sort of."

"And you said banning comedy was going to happen. So I was trying to come up with a comedy word that I could stick in front of 451 to make a joke about banning comedy. And Barinholtz was the closest I could come up with. At least in the short term. He's a comedian."

"OK. Are we done with that?"

"Yes. But I do think your idea is dangerous. We can't alter the past without terrible repercussions."

"And on what do you base this assertion?"

"Movies. The Grandfather Paradox."

"What's that?"

"A small change in the past can create enormous changes in the present. No, wait, that's the Butterfly Effect. The Grandfather Paradox says you can't kill your grandfather in the past because then you would never be born and therefore couldn't go back and kill your grandfather."

"That is irrelevant to our issue."

"So no grandfather killing in this plan?"

"None."

"Well, OK, I guess. That makes me feel better. But how will we know if we're successful?"

"We'll know immediately. Because if it works, they will be famous in the past."

"And what if they aren't?"

"We keep sending more clones until two of them are."

"I feel like there's a logical flaw here but I can't put my finger on it."

"Shh. Let me swab your cheek."

"FOR EVERY BURGER you buy, we donate ten cents to Books on Tape for the blind, Books on Paper for the deaf, and Books on Wheels for paraplegics. At Slammy's, we care about your problems! Blind or deaf or in a chair, eat at Slammy's cuz we care!"

Here, in this place, I am despondent. Days have passed, perhaps weeks. I have called three times about my clone, but he's still not ready. Something about a broken pump. I sit alone, eat my lunch, and watch the cave ants swarm around some dropped Slammitalian Calzoney-O crumbs. I've long admired the industriousness and community spirit of ants. Since earliest childhood, I have been a student of entomology with a specialization in myrmecology. Later at Harvard, in fact, I even interned under the great E. O. Wilson. *You are a remarkable young man*, Wilson opined in his meticulous Palmer cursive in my Harvard yearbook. *Among the finest I've ever had the pleasure of interning under me. You will surely go far in whatever field of endeavor you pursue, under many a great man to come. I love you. 2 Cute 2 B Forgotten.—Eddy.* Ants are arguably the most fascinating members of the order *Hymenoptera*, unquestionably the most intelligent. But only as a superorganism, for that intelligence is evident only in the colony as a whole. Let's face it, the individual ant is a moron. Whereas a certain colony of 700,000 ants from the Sudan has been shown to possess an IQ higher than Marilyn vos Savant of *Parade* magazine. They also handily beat Bobby Fischer at a chess match. It is true that this was during one of his psychotic episodes, when he appeared more interested in heckling Jewish-looking Icelandic spectators. But still: They're ants!

"Slammy's: Just a hop, skip, and spelunk away."

Ants have been present and virtually unchanged on Earth for almost two hundred billion years and as such are considered one of the most successful species on the planet. Contrast that with, say, the *Homo sapien* at a measly fifteen hundred years old. The question is, what can we, as humans, learn about longevity from an ant? Ants, like humans, are social creatures. They think and act communally. The decisions they make individually are always for the good of their society. Certainly they can be aggressive to and warlike with other ants, but only ants outside of their own colony. This is where ants and humans diverge. Humans are social creatures, but even within their own communities, they act antagonistically toward others. This competitiveness of the individual will be the death of humanity. The solution is for humans, like ants, to be born into castes.

Ideally, one could not, say, decide to be a film critic; one would either be born one or not. There would be no jealousies in such a world. I would, upon maturity, be given the *New Yorker* film critic position and it would be understood that I am the authority on all things cinematic. Others would be born doctors or gymnasts or hat blockers. We would each contribute equally within our particular job description toward the greater good. We could still hate those from other colonies, as ants do, but within our own colony, all would be peaceful. One would never have to think of oneself as an underachiever because there would be no such expectations (or disappointments) placed on those of the so-deemed "lower" professions. So, for instance, a trash collector would be as admired as a—

Egads! The ending of the movie! I recall it now! It takes place a million years in the future! Of course! Calcium! Of course! I still cannot remember the million leading up to it. That remains a blank. Perhaps in the continued recalling of this ultimate section, I will be reminded of or at least be able to piece together this enormous gap. As a film critic, cineast, filmmaker, confidant to the late Joseph Campbell (while he was still alive, of course! Ha ha!), and the inventor and perhaps the solitary practitioner of backward film viewing, I believe myself to be eminently and uniquely qualified to reconstruct a story in reverse. Just as my newly rediscovered friend Calcium is doing. We have so much in common, this uncommonest of ants and I.

And like that, it appears, fully remembered, the end of Ingo's film. Where had it been buried all this time in this miraculous monstrosity called my human brain? How was it buried? I have no answer, but here it is nonetheless. I am certain.[1] The film in the cave was wrong, a lie, a sham, a misdirect, a red herring (but to what end and by whom?). This is the entirety of the rest of the film. True, much is still missing. A million years is still missing. Not to mention, all the confusing and contradictory moments that continue to coexist within the body of the film, as well as the lapses and what have you, but these contradictions and missing swaths exist in the memory of my life also. Maybe this is the very thing Ingo was trying to say with his film, thus is the confusion of the human mind, and not just mine. Or maybe just mine, since the film seems to have been made for me and me alone, but, also, didn't he say in that blank version I recently saw that there were other viewers before me, and didn't he imply that there could be other viewers after me? So I just don't really know anymore. But I do know this: The end is here. So perhaps I can reverse engineer the rest. For now, this is what I know:

CHAPTER 80

T HE MOVIE ENDS a million years in the future. Humans are long
extinct. The dominant creature on the planet is a hyperintel-
ligent ant. Just the one ant. The other ants are the same normal
dumb ants from now. I mean, not dumb, of course, because ants are
remarkable and mysterious bugs, to be sure, as I have said, *et chetera*,
but this one very smart ant can do calculus and integral calculus and
he can fly, but not like winged ants. This one can fly in a jet he built
by hand. Oh, this ant has hands. Four hands. And two feet. So this
ant, who calls himself Calcium for some reason (in reference to his
calculus skills?), even though the other animals on the planet are not
smart enough to know what a name is, lords it over the planet. But
even with all his power, his mansions and jewels, he is very lonely
since there is no one with whom he can share his life. For a while,
he lives with (and loves deeply) a female ant he calls Betty, but she
doesn't have any idea what is going on and just keeps trying to get
back to her colony, bumping against mansion walls. Eventually he
lets her go and watches her walk away to a Paul Simon song—I
think it's "You Can Call Me Al," which upon reflection is probably
used for this line:

> *If you'll be my bodyguard*
> *I can be your long lost pal*
> *I can call you Betty*
> *And Betty when you call me*
> *You can call me Al.*

The rest of the song doesn't really apply, as far as I can tell. The ant's name, after all, is Calcium, not Al or even Alcium. Anyway, Betty leaves and Calcium (Al?) is all alone. He reads. He watches Brainio. He looks up at the stars and wonders at the vastness of space. He works in his laboratory inventing perpetual motion machines and various drugs to help mankind, I mean, antkind.

One of the drugs he invents has an unusual and unexpected property. It travels back in time. At least he suspects this is so because he discovers a capsule of it in his weekly pill organizer compartment marked "Tuesday" even though he doesn't invent it till Wednesday. The next day, the pill is in the "Monday" compartment. "How can this be?" Calcium wonders aloud. He opens the capsule to investigate the granules of medicine, but they instantly disappear.

"Into the past?" he wonders, again, also aloud.

He checks the jar of pills in his laboratory but finds they are gone, too.

"Into the past?" he wonders again and aloud again. "What did I do? But, more importantly, what did my concoction, if anything, do to the past?"

Calcium's question causes this viewer to reconsider the entire film: What did Calcium's time-traveling medication do to affect the past? Do some of the more confounding elements of the preceding filmic tale now make more sense? Or less?! Or exactly the same amount of sense?

"Do I exist now at all, in this time," wonders Calcium (silently now, but in ant voiceover), "*only* because I sent this pharmaceutical-cum-creature back in time? Did the past I created create me? I must pore over my copious journals and graphs to see if there is anything alluding to a backward-traveling chemical compound."

Calcium soon finds an entry of interest in his journal from three days ago:

Odd, he had written, *it seems there seems to be some sort of seemingly minor outbreak of a seemingly previously unknown illness among my friends, the other ants: flu-like symptoms, a slight queasiness. I'm not sure to what it can be attributed. It seems minor. Perhaps I should retire to my lab and work on a cure just in case their symptoms are to worsen in subsequent days.*

Was this why he had been working on the very medication that became this time-traveling creature? It boggles the mind, both mine and Calcium's.

In a journal entry from four days ago, he comes upon this: *There seems to be an outbreak among some of my friends: terrible flu symptoms, violent nausea, the occasional death. I must set about concocting a cure.*

From the day before: *What is going on? Out of nowhere, there is a major outbreak of terrible, terrible flu symptoms and extremely violent nausea, much death among my friends. A cure! A cure! Think, Calcium, think!*

The day before that: *All of my friends are dead. Why? How? What nightmarish disease has taken them? If only I had a cure on hand!*

And the day before: *My friends are all suddenly reanimated zombies! I am at a loss. Shall I invent a medication? To what end? Can zombieism be cured? Is the word zombieism? No time to look that up now in the dictionary I compiled! They will soon attack! I am almost without hope!*

The day before: *My mansion has been set on fire by the zombies that my fellow ants have suddenly without warning become. There is nothing to be done. Rebuild? To what end. All is lost.*

How bizarre, muses Calcium. Destruction is happening backward, making its way into the past. My mansion is here today, gone yesterday. What fresh hell have I created?

He checks his journal from nine days ago: *My entire town has been set on fire by a swarm of zombie ants! Where did they come from? All my papers are on fire!*

His journal notes end after the ninth day. He will never know.

Calcium weeps, then frantically scribbles on the back of a laundry list. We hear his thoughts in voiceover:

"I can find no more records. I will never know what has happened. Perhaps I can invent a time-travel vehicle of some sort for myself so I could see what Air Rabies (for that is what I have named it) will *did* to the world in the past. But such a vehicle is an impossibility. One cannot travel back in time (unless one is [was?] Air Rabies [perhaps]). Time travel defies all physical laws, as well as the laws of three states. There is nothing to do but go forward and be thankful I didn't invent Air Rabies next week because the world today would be a very different, horrible place if I had. Still, as I go forward, I cannot help but reflect on the past to come. Some mysterious, extinct philosophizing creature once said: 'Life must be lived forward but can only be understood backward.' It is, it turns out, the only remnant from this ancient species, about whom we know nothing else. We do suspect (well, *I* do suspect) they had pens. What will *became* of the Air Rabies? Will it *evolved* over time? It is, of course, impossible to *knew* with any certainty. One would presume there would have been no existing predators for an *Antichron* (as I now call the genus), so there would not have been any need to *evolved* for defensive purposes. Maybe it will *evolved* due to food shortages. Although there does not seem to be any shortages of ants currently, so I suspect that's not an issue. Perhaps genetic mutations will *created* separate strains of Air Rabies and those strains will *fought* among themselves for dominance. The world must look very different, indeed backward, I imagine. I am reminded of the writings of 'Walter Benjamin,' a second mysterious ancient creature, who appears to have, with also a pen, written the following:

> "His eyes are staring, his mouth is open, his wings are spread. This is how one pictures the angel of history. His face is turned toward the past. Where we perceive a chain of events, he sees one single catastrophe which keeps piling wreckage upon wreckage and hurls it in front of his feet. The angel would like to stay, awaken the dead, and make whole what has been smashed. But a storm is blowing from Paradise; it has got caught in his wings with such violence that the angel can no longer close them. This storm irresistibly propels him into the future to which his back is turned, while the pile of debris before him grows skyward. This storm is what we call progress.

> "I attempt to predict the path of my terrible creation. How can I know what will *happened*, where Air Rabies will *went*? Indeed, how

can I know how the world appears to a creature marching doggedly into history, where the conventional experience of cause and effect is twisted like the ankle of a runner who has twisted her (yes, her) ankle? Is it just a simple reversal in which creatures grow young (note: interesting movie idea! Explore!), or is it an unimaginably different world? What is necessary in the constitution of a creature to push successfully against this formidable current we call time? Fortitude, strength, adaptability, ruthlessness. Indeed, its devastation of the ant community is nothing more than a reflection of its cold need for survival. The natural world is without sentiment: It kills what it must and when. It lusts after what it must and when. It shuns what it must. And when. But what a singular experience of reality it must be, to walk the other way, to walk back. A creature falling into a hole in such a world, for example, would not seem the least bit funny to an observer. Instead, this creature rising from the hole would appear almost divine, Jesus rising from the dead, ascending to his rightful place beside his father (oh, Daddy). Could humor even exist in such a reality? Perhaps those whose deeds seem to us miraculous would appear, to the backward traveler, as ridiculous and comical. Imagine a well-meaning saint sickening the healthy, or a god whose lightning bolts shoot back into his hands, uncausing destruction. Imagine an army of 'terrifying' flying, bloviating robots sucking deadly laser beams into their eyes, seemingly causing their own stupidity. These silly examples, off the top of my abnormally enlarged head, paint a picture of a profoundly different world. It could be that one's nature, one's aesthetic, would be so confused, so damaged by this reality that avoidance and blindness might become a necessity, circuitous paths a form of self-defense. This is how I imagine my multiplying rabic children as they rush headlong toward the beginning of time. Perhaps it is actual weather they became or some heretofore unknown analog, swirling and howling and spitting and destroying their way backward, unseen by a forward-plodding world, hiding in plain sight, growing in scope, becoming, in the end, a dynamic system blanketing the entire world at its very beginning. This is all just conjecture, a simple-minded tale an old ant tells himself to pass the time. One can do no more than foolishly wonder about a thing one can never know. And yet wonder I do. As I move forward in time, further and further, with each passing moment, from the origin of Air Rabies, with each one of those moments doubled as Air Rabies moves that much further from me, in the opposite *katefthynsi tou chrónou*, I waste what is left of my small life speculating, constructing a possible scenario, one I can never verify, a theory I can never test. But what else is there for me here, now, alone in this world with no hope of communion with another of my kind? I am as a child playing with dolls, making up stories on a rainy afternoon for my own amusement.

"And, also, why did the ants turn into zombies?"

My memory of the Calcium scene is interrupted by a series of intrusive thoughts in my head, seemingly delivered by many different shouting people, only some of them Marjorie Morningstar:

> Do not trust the others!
> Do not allow yourself to be laughed at!
> Protect your own interests!
> No one has suffered as much as you!
> You don't have a right to complain, considering all the real suffering in the cave!
> Many people have it much worse than you!
> Enjoy Slammy's!
> Don't be anyone's fool!
> Impress the others!
> Don't forget to have a Slammy's burger!
> The others are trying to cheat you!
> Look how pretty she is!
> Look how handsome he is!
> Look how successful they are!
> Listen to this song now: "The cave is beautiful and love is the answer / you need to be dutiful and avoid getting cancer / You must remember—"
> *Eat at Slammy's!*

Dance!
Try this drug!
Don't do drugs!
Religion is a lie!
The group that isn't yours is trying to destroy you!
Mmmm! Taste this!
You are ugly!
Watch this Brainio!
Boy, that kid sure is a prodigy and you were not!
Don't you feel like crying now?
Watch this cute dog!
Everyone is laughing at you!

The barrage ends. The space around me is filled with Trunks and words and Rosenbergen and smoke and bad nonsensical ideas and reviews: Everything is reviewed, analyzed, hated, loved, puked back at us in endless iterations, multiplying, replicating, repeating itself, repeating patterns, echoing, but the voice in my head at least has quieted enough for me to get back to my memory of Ingo's film.

Someone knocks into me. Jesus. Is it Jesus? I can't see much in all this smoke, but someone has bumped into me hard and it feels like what I imagine it would feel like to be bumped hard by Jesus. It's a good thing, really. A compassionate bump. Someone or something with a beard and long hair. Of course, who knows what the historical Jesus looked like or if there even was a historical Jesus. Certainly we have contemporaneous mention of him in the writing of Josephus, but it doesn't tell us anything much about this so-called Jesus. Yet with this nudge, I felt a calmness, instantaneously blissful. Join us, he would plead, I imagine, and I would scoff.

Black wool, I want to ask him, is that how he achieves this smoke?

I try to ask him, but he is gone. Still, my calm remains. I'm happy to marvel at the billowing black noxious beauty of it, at the rib-cracking hacking, the caterwauling symphony of coughs and screams. Is it black wool? It doesn't matter; it is beautiful. I am reminded of the poem "A Drunk Man Looks at the Thistle" by the great Scot modernist Hugh MacDiarmid, in particular the stanza:

And Jesus and a nameless ape
Collide and share the selfsame shape
That nocht terrestrial can escape?

Is this the collision I just experienced? Is this perhaps every collision? Is every collision a collision that results, on some level, in the so-called God particle?

CHAPTER 81

ERE IN THE cave, I attempt to hide from the ever-present battle. It's almost impossible to focus on the Calcium memories
what with all the explosions, nightmarish screaming, and gnashing
of teeth. My boss, the editor of the *Slammy's Gazette*, appears, sus-
pendered, cigar-chomping, in my head and orders me back onto the
battlefield to report on the war. I don't think I have ever seen him in
person, only in my brain. I'm not certain he exists in person. In this
way, he is much like the historical Jesus. Still, he is terrifying, with
his sleeve garters and green eyeshade.

"Rosenberg, why the hell are you just sitting there like a sack of
shit?"

"Sorry, chief. I was just thinking about a movie I saw."

"Well, get off your goddamn ass! There's a war on, son! You want
the *Trunk Trumpet* to scoop us?"

"No, sir. I just—"

"I don't recall asking to hear your pansy excuses! The world
needs to know what's happening!"

"OK, chief. Sorry."

My editor steps back into his office, also in my brain, and slams
his brain door. A framed photo of Truman holding up a newspaper
saying Dewey beat him falls off the brain wall outside his office and
crashes to the floor of my brain. Broken brain glass everywhere.

"I'll be back," I whisper to my memory of Calcium and head to
the front.

All's quiet when I get there. I spot a soldier sitting against a stalagmite, having a smoke, staring up at the constellation of Gemini Pollux created by drilling holes into the ceiling of the cave.

"Hello, soldier," I say.

"Evening, mister."

"How was the fighting today?"

"Tough. I lost five buddies from my unit. But I ain't sad. They died fighting for the country they loved."

"Which country you fighting for, soldier? I can't tell from your French army *kepi* hat."

"Slammy's," he says. "One hundred percent pure beef, one hundred percent pure patriot!"

"You have any message for your loved ones at home, soldier?"

"I love you, Mary Lou. I'll be home to you soon and—"

His head gets blown off, and I reflexively jump behind the stalagmite for cover. I'm shaking and panicked and I can't remember the name of the woman he said he loved. It's especially bad because with his death, his quote would've been a great end to the piece. There wouldn't be a dry eye in the cave. I'm pretty sure he said Marilyn. It's really not the kind of thing I want to get wrong, because it could create bad feelings if his girlfriend (wife, daughter, boyfriend, thon) thinks his last words were to someone else. But I'm almost certain he said Madeline and that's what I will go with. I drop the piece and a photo of the soldier (pre–head explosion, of course!) on my editor's desk in my brain. He picks it up, looks at it.

"Good stuff, Rosenberg. Now get the fuck back out there."

I peek out from behind my stalagmite. Hundreds of Trunks hover, in sleep mode, charging their batteries with electrical cords plugged into outlets along the cave wall. They bob gently up and down like buoys. It's almost peaceful. The CEO of Slammy's, who it turns out is now Barassini in a ball cap that reads in braille, "Blind Faith Is True Faith," is projected on a gargantuan television screen, sound asleep in his office chair. His snores fill the cave through mounted speakers. I watch out for snipers, who, as any non-dead war correspondent will tell you, never sleep. Somewhere in the distance, a lone bugler plays a mournful rendition of reveille, which seems odd as I always thought reveille should be chipper. Maybe this is a reimagining of reveille, the way someone might take an up-tempo pop song and turn it into a sad song. I often enjoy this kind of reimagining, of course not when Kaufman tried it with "Girls Just Want to Have Fun" in that abysmal "sad white middle-aged man" movie *Anomalisa*. Then it was terrible, making a mockery of the very spirit of the original version of the song by Cynthia Looper, an anthem, of course, to female (trans woman) empowerment, a song that at its core states unequivocally that women (trans women) do not need men (trans men) in order to enjoy themselves (trans selves), a melodic version of the brilliant feminist rallying cry of the 1970s, "A woman needs a man like a fish needs a bicycle" (coined by the great 1930s American film actress Irene Dunn, no less!), because as everyone knows, a fish would have little to no use for a bicycle, a) because it lives in the ocean and can easily swim where it needs to go, and b) because a fish has no legs, so how would it even pedal? Barassini wakes up to the alarm on his Slammy's Phone playing "Hypnotised" by Coldplay. He groggily feels around, presses STOP, and looks eyelessly into the camera.

"Good morning, my fellow Americans, it is a good day for saving on all Slammy's merchandise—fifty percent off today only!—and a good day for saving civilization as well. Remember that our goal at Slammy's is to serve you, to provide you with top-quality goods and services, conveniently and at a reasonable cost. The same cannot be said of our competitors. The question you have to ask yourself is, how much are you willing to sacrifice for this convenience and value, or for the right of Americans like yourselves to have an idea for a product, to start a small business like we did, to work hard to build that business, to acquire wealth, honestly, through hard work and sacrifice? You have to ask yourselves this: Did all those Trunks work hard to acquire their wealth and lasers? Did they start their professional lives as humble hypnotists/Broadway actors, as did I? Or are they lazy, bloated robots, built by robots, whose very presence is an affront to our way of life? At Slammy's, we employ only people, not machines, to make your food, to ship your products, to build your water bicycles, your robots, to wash your—"

By this point, the Trunk robots have switched themselves off sleep mode, disengaged from their outlets, and are listening to Barassini's speech. As one, they begin to sing "The Girl From Ipanema" in a beautiful, relaxed, jazzy a cappella rendition. Doors open inside my brain (and I assume the brains of others out here on the battlefield), and a beautiful bikinied Trunk emerges, walking by me with hips a-swinging. He *is* the girl from Ipanema. Jesus, he's beautiful. I can no longer hear Barassini's voice at all. The perfume wafting toward me from Trunk's warm, meaty body is heady: vanilla, lavender, musk, old man sweat. He beckons me to him with a delicate finger. This unattainable goddess is beckoning me! The *me* in my brain, my homunculus, as it were, walks toward him. Suddenly Marjorie appears, floating above me in a diaphanous gown, a sexy angel Halloween costume. I look up; Trunk looks up.

"Curses," he says.

"B.," Marjorie coos, "at Slammy's, we care about you. We deliver ourselves to your doorstep, hot and juicy. And at Slammy's, we've got real junk in *our* trunk, not just massive, shit-stained, old white man KFC-fed ass."

Marjorie rotates in space, a sexy rotisserie chicken—much healthier than KFC—so I can see her buttocks, which are truly magnificent. I look again at the beckoning Trunk and find the illusion gone. He is once again, in my estimation, almost unfuckable. My allegiance now is to Slammy's, to Marjorie, to pussy, not cock. An exploding mortar shell shocks me from Marjorie to the real horrors of war. Not fifteen feet from me are a pile of maimed soldiers, dead and dying. Some are dressed as Star Wars stormtroopers, some as Batmans, others as Wonder Womans. There's even a skinny, sad-looking fellow dressed as Mandrake the Magician and a middle-aged Bob from *Bob's Burgers*, whose blood-soaked apron conceals what I assume is a soon-to-be-fatal evisceration. I take pictures of the wounded. I take pictures of the dead. It is my job; I am a chronicler of war. Later in the mess hall, unfortunately seated between Hawkeye and Trapper John trading TV-level quips, I attempt to clear my mind of the suffering I witnessed today and remember more about the end of the movie.

* * *

So, CALCIUM DIGS in a cave. Is it this cave? The very one I am in? I think I recognize that stalactite over there. His paleontological hobby staves off his loneliness, it seems, for there is something reassuring in the notion that life is a long, uninterrupted chain, that he is part of this chain, that it will continue after he is gone, that there is hope: that there is a future, not only a past. I feel thusly as well. This cave has been his most fruitful dig site, he explains in voice-over. We cut to a panning shot of all sorts of odd fossilized remains, reconstructed animals filling the ballroom of his mansion. Today is no different: He uncovers a skull, a new species, enormous, with an unprecedentedly large brain pan. We recognize it as the skull of a human being. Calcium speaks to it:

"What are you, my friend? Such an odd skull as this I have never before seen. Alas, poor creature, would that I had known you. I feel a sudden and profound kinship. Is it that we share a similar cranial design and that by this similarity I infer a similar intelligence, a similar Weltanschauung? Would we have been friends, my giant, my string bean? Would my own lonely soul find relief in our association? I like to think so."

Calcium continues to dig, finding more and more of this human skeleton. With his immense ant strength (ants are ten thousand times stronger than humans), he drags his haul back home, bone by bone. This takes a full five hours of screen time. Once there, he assembles the skeleton (seven hours of screen time), then goes about the painstaking task of forensic facial reconstruction (thirteen hours). I studied anatomy at Harvard and notice there is something amiss with the skeleton's clavichord. Has it been damaged? I also marvel at Calcium's technique, which is as remarkably skillful as it is highly accurate. In fact, once complete, the skeleton's face quite closely resembles my own.

"I will call this heretofore undiscovered species the Great Ache, from the Greek *akhos*, meaning grief."

My recovered memory of this part of the film is so startling as to be revelatory.

"I'm sorry," Calcium says to the head (my head?), "that I ran out of Pantone 489C clay and found it necessary to use the Pantone PMS 2583 clay on the southwest quadrant of your face and neck."

Oddly, perhaps coincidentally, perhaps not, the purplish clay falls precisely where lies my own aforementioned port-wine stain birthmark.

"It's fine," I remember myself saying during the screening, sitting in the hard wooden chair alone in Ingo's apartment, for it was after Ingo's death. I feel a shiver of recognition running up my spine now, as I felt it then. Or is it down?

"I do have some plant matter here I might use to cover up my pigmental inaccuracy. I call it old man's beard. Not that you are old, my giant, it is simply the informal name for this substance, which I know formally as *Usnea*."

With this, he pulls some hair-like lichen from a storage bin and adheres it to the lower third of the reconstructed face. This is when, in the screening, my jaw hung open. For it is me. Without a doubt, this is my skeleton, my skull that Calcium has dug up a million years in the future. That this all exists within my memory of Ingo's film adds to my confusion. Did Ingo shoot this scene after I moved in across the hall from him? Or did he, with otherworldly prescience, anticipate my arrival? Either way, I now understand why this film felt so very personal to me after my initial viewing, for I am in it. The film is about me.

"There," says a gentle Calcium. "Perhaps there was indeed such odd fringe hanging from your face. I have no way to know, but it seems feasible that a creature might evolve such a fringe for warmth or perhaps as a display of great reproductive health and virility, both of which I feel certain you had. I believe you were likely the most sexually healthy—"

I die! I realize. Here is the proof. I don't know exactly when, but at some point in the future, I die and am reconstructed, an exhibit in the natural history museum of a sentient ant.

"Of all my fossils, I love you best," says Calcium. "What did you think about when you were alive, sweet creature? What were your worries? Your joys?"

"Probably the same as yours, Calcium," I responded. "Art, mortality, Tsai."

"Likely the same as mine," Calcium muses. "Art, mortality, Betty. Oh, I do so like talking with you. . . . What shall I call you? Is B. for boron right for you? Or shall I call you Rosenberg after the desert rose gypsum formations above the site where I unearthed you? Or perhaps the two in tandem?"

Either! Both! And I shall call you Calcium, I thought.

"You can call me Calcium," he says. "You know, B. Rosenberg, my own kind, the ants, seem so happy in their lives. But I don't know how to fit in. At parties, everyone else knows exactly how to act, while I sit awkwardly in the corner. I have a strategy that never works: I attempt to look sad and deep. Sometimes I read a book to appear thoughtful. For some reason, I believe that'll attract someone. I guess because it would attract me. So there I sit, waiting for another ant to come over and say, 'You look deep and sorrowful. What are you reading?' But it has never happened. And of course the other ants don't speak at all, let alone know what a book is, so it never will. But still I continue with this 'pickup' technique, even though it is a dismal failure. I tell myself (for sadly there is no one else to tell) that this is perhaps the very definition of insanity."

"You can tell me!" I said to the screen.

"But I can tell *you*, Rosenberg, of course," says Calcium. "Even over eons and eons, I know you understand me."

"I do," I said.

And then for some reason, I start to cry. Now. Here.

"I am so lonely, Rosenberg," Calcium says once again. "So terribly lonely."

I recite some Tennyson for him: "So runs my dream, but what am I? / An infant crying in the night / An infant crying for the light / And with no language but a cry."

"Y'know, Rosenberg," Calcium continues, "I've developed this method of looking at the world, a sort of framing device, if you will. How do I explain this? Hmm. What I do, I attempt to cultivate a sort of distance, or rather detachment, from difficult events in my life and in the world. I allow a certain lightness to envelop them. I gently mock them and myself. I call it 'boking fun' or 'jokking,' and if performed properly, it transforms a painful experience into a tolerable one."

"We call that comedy or humor," I said to the screen that now lives in my memory. "And I for one question its effectiveness and even its value. Although, in my time, there is a genius we call Judd Apatow, who—"

CHAPTER 82

A BULLET PIERCES MY shoulder, shocking me from nostalgic memory to harsh reality, then immediately back into memory as I realize the injury to the skeleton's clavichord is precisely where I was just now hit. Is this how and where and when I die?

"Medic!" I call. "Medic!"

Two clowns in white coats, carrying a stretcher between them, barrel toward me from parts unseen. I am worried; I know this bit. I try to shoo them away, but it is pointless; this is going to happen. They arrive, lay the stretcher down next to me, and place me on it; then each grabs one end of the stretcher, lifts, and tries to run off with me. Except, of course, they are facing opposite directions, and when they run off, the stretcher with me on it falls hard to the ground. I hear laughter among the wailings of the maimed and look up to see that the entire scene is being played in real time on the giant Slammy's TV. I watch, too, as the clowns, unaware that they are no longer holding the stretcher, continue to run off in opposite directions to much continued laughter. I am hoping that they never realize their mistake and some actual medics appear and take me to a hospital. Even Hawkeye and Trapper John would be an improvement. I am, it seems, losing a lot of blood. The audience laughs again as the two clowns realize at the exact same moment (how do they coordinate that?) that they are no longer carrying me. After they play up their surprise with wide-eyed clownishness, they come back to get me, pick me up in the stretcher, mime an argument about who should face which way, work it out, and run off with me.

A third clown approaches and mimes asking them the time. They both simultaneously lift their right hands to check their watches, releasing one side of the stretcher and dropping me again to the ground. This to more laughter and applause. For the next fifteen minutes, I am dropped and thrown and "inadvertently" stepped on. I am stuffed into an ambulance so small my head hangs out the rear. When it hits a bump, I fly out and land in a hole in the cave floor.

Eventually I arrive in a clown hospital, where I am swathed like a mummy in bandages from head to toe, arms and legs elevated by those traction pulleys one sees only in old movies and single-panel *New Yorker* cartoons, attended now by a male clown dressed as a female nurse with giant inflated balloons as breasts. The wall-mounted television in my room shows me this very bit as it continues to play out. Being here, in this position, is not at all comfortable, and it is humiliating, but it gives me time to think about Calcium, who now, in my memory, wanders the empty, burning streets of the future in the town he will have built, past the power station, the cinema, the tailor shop. It's small, because he's an ant (the hat shop is almost normal-size), but also because there is no one else here with whom he can share it, so he really has had no reason to expand. The other ants can't be persuaded to join his community. They don't even seem to recognize it as anything other than a place to scrounge for crumbs, mostly in the kitchen of Delicieux, the five-star seafood restaurant where Calcium is both chef and sole patron (a pun?). He steps into the cinema, turns on the projector, and waits in the otherwise empty theater. Titles appear on the screen.

Calcium Presents
Calcium in
What a Sight!

The film begins with an ant (Calcium) walking down an empty street. He looks up to admire the natural world: the clouds in the sky, the trees, the distant snowcapped peaks of Oleara Debord. He is not watching his path, trips over a grain of sand, and goes flying.

When he lands on his chin with a *thunk*, his right eye pops out of his head and bounces away.

"Oh no!" says Calcium, as he chases after it.

It's a magnificently clever chase sequence, putting Friedkin's abysmal *The French Connection* (in which Gene Hackman's Popeye Doyle chases his own popped-out eyeball for five miles underneath the elevated train tracks in Brooklyn) to shame. It easily tops my "escaped" eyeball genre list, and it took only a million years to arrive in theaters. Calcium cleverly illustrates his character's now monocular POV by blacking out the right half of the frame. This deficiency in his field of vision leads to all sorts of mishaps: bumping into lampposts, tripping over waste receptacles, narrowly missing an ant (also Calcium, here in false eyelashes) pushing a larva carriage. The solid black eyeball finally bounces into the Fun-Zone Bowling Emporium and rolls down an alley causing a strike. Calcium waits patiently at the automatic ball return for his errant eyeball. When it reappears, he inserts it back in his head, then cries, "I still can't see!" His actual eyeball eventually makes its way into the ball return. Realizing his error, he pulls the bowling ball from his skull and replaces it with his eye.

"Seeing is bowl-ieving!" he says to the camera and winks.

Calcium then fist pumps into a triumphant freeze-frame, which I personally think is gilding the lily.

Calcium in the audience laughs and applauds, looks around for the reactions of others, remembers he is alone, and becomes strangely subdued. Oh, how I recognize that look. Calcium and I are the same in many ways. Both autodidacts (although I attended college, in the end, I had to teach myself so I could then teach my teachers), both isolated from our fellows due to our superior intelligences, both ever testing the boundaries of cinema.

AT THE ICE cream parlor after, Calcium wonders, "Would it be possible for me to meet my friend B. Rosenberg if I were to go back in time? Would we be friends in real life? Would this giant recognize me as a kindred spirit or see me only as something to be squashed underfoot? I would like to think we would be fast friends."

"We would, Calcium!" I shout through my ridiculous bandages. "You would ride on my shoulder!"

With my suddenly free arm, I scoop up some ants from the hospital floor and try to find one with an introspective expression. Alas, they all look the same. And let's face it, they all look stupid. I realize this is a form of bigotry or speciesism or just plain anti-antism on my part, and I am correctly ashamed, but for the life of me, I cannot tell one from the other of these idiotic-looking creatures. There's one that seems to have a dimple on his (her, thon) face, but I suspect it is only some sort of injury or birth defect. In any event, it makes him (her, thon) look kind of cute, especially when he, she, thon smiles, which makes me decide he, she, thon is even less intelligent than even the regular ants. Again, I realize this is looksist, and I am correctly further ashamed. I place the cute ant back on the floor and drift back into my memory of Calcium.

A volcano has erupted on Oleara Debord. The future sky is black with toxic smoke. The streets flow with lava. The camera scours the smoldering heap of ashes that is Calcium's mansion, eventually finding Calcium, unconscious and covered in blisters. After a long moment, he awakens and groggily looks around.

"What happened?" he says.

His eyes come to rest on the remains of his house.

Calcium cries out and limps to it. There he stumbles upon the charred remains of the remains of his dear Rosenberg, the only part intact a hunk of wine-colored clay. He falls to the ground and weeps.

"Now I am truly alone," he whispers bitterly.

Later, he wanders aimlessly, stomping out embers, at a loss. He finds his laptop computer, the cover melted, but miraculously still in working order. He types his thoughts.

It is entirely possible that my children, my Air Rabies, as they travel back in time, will one day meet this huthon (for that is the species name I have given his kind) B. Rosenberg, alive and struggling, for are not those two words synonymous? But here he is dust, and thus he will forevermore be. While I, trapped in this "forward" direction of time, will move ever further away from my long dead friend.

Calcium lies on the ground weeping for ten days and ten nights, the passage of which is marked by falling calendar leaves and yet still takes ten days of film time. Then he speaks out: to no one, to the heavens.

"My Nameless Ache is gone, crushed to dust and bits of clay. It was a friendship unlike any I have known, intellectually but also spiritually. I know he suffered. I can see from his fractured skull and broken bones, his pierced clavichord and missing fingers, that he suffered a great fall into a great hole or perhaps many lesser falls into many lesser holes, culminating in a fall into the pretty deep hole in which I discovered him, followed by (or perhaps preceded by) a pro-tracted period of self-toe-and-finger-eating. I have lost my only friend. There is nothing here for me anymore."

Calcium contemplates suicide. He keeps an ancient can of ant spray under his kitchen sink just in case. But when it comes to it, he finds himself unable to press the button. He wants to live! He wants to live in the past!

"Is there a way," he wonders, "that I, too, can travel backward in time so that on some future/past day, I might finally meet my long-dead friend still alive?"

"Yes, please," I weep. "Find me, Calcium. I will wait for you."

"I will find you," weeps Calcium, "if it is the last thing I do. Or would that be the first thing I do? But how?"

Calcium needs a distraction to help him think. He checks the paper; there's a movie starting in fifteen minutes. It's his film *Calcium Carbonate*, a comedy in which he stars as a soft-drink magnate who produces an artificially orange-flavored soda called *Anta*. He fills giant paper cups with the product, then spills them on the side-walk to attract ants, because even though he is a very wealthy busi-nessman with several mansions, he is lonely. On one such occasion, a beautiful female ant happens by, and Calcium is smitten. Betty (for this is what he's named her) doesn't even seem to know he exists. It reminds me of Godard's *Éloge de L'Amour*, the greatest film of the

2000s in its reversal of time as well as its usage of contrasting film stocks. The performance of Betty by Betty the Ant is as heartbreaking as that of Cécile Camp as Elle in Godard's masterwork. To say that Betty is so natural, so human (for lack of a better term; so *ant*?), that she seems completely unaware of the camera is perhaps the understatement of the decade, or, more accurately, the myr.

I watch along with Calcium, wishing I could really be there and not wrapped in gauze in a clown hospital, wishing he could know how much I admire, no, love his work. Forgetting for a long moment that there is no Calcium, that he is the somewhat confused creation of Ingo Cutbirth, that he has sprung forth, fully if inconsistently formed, from the mind of a sharecropper's (?) son, that he encompasses all of our fears and hopes as human beings: the hope of brilliance and the fear of never being understood, not in a million years, not in a million lifetimes, not in a myr, not in a million myrs, *et chetera*.

Suddenly, the film catches in the gate. A hole burns through the image of one of Calcium's mansions, and he scrambles to the booth to switch off the projector and contain the damage.

Later, in the booth editing bay, he snips out the ruined frame, edits the two remaining pieces together, restarts the film.

As Calcium and I once again watch the film, now from the booth, the projector passes smoothly over the missing twenty-fourth of a second. It occurs to me that perhaps we as humans have been thinking of time travel incorrectly. Maybe it is more like this: Each moment of existence is quantized. So if a house is burning in one moment and the moment is excised, the burning of the house does not carry over to the next moment. The house in all other moments would remain intact with, perhaps, the slightest of almost imperceptible glitches of nonexistence where the remaining time is spliced together. Of course Apatow explored this very notion in his film *The 40-Year-Old Virgin*. Is anyone ever in front of Judd Apatow? If one remembers the hair-waxing sequence (how could anyone ever forget such classic Apatow humordy?), this is the very thing he was teaching us, a thing I, for one, was not ready to learn. "I am now, Judd," I say to the cosmos. A single coarse black hair pulled from

Steve Carell's chest would do nothing to alter the thing we know as the "hair" on Carell's chest. The only way to change our perception of Carell's chest hair would be to pull out hair after hair after hair. Each individual hair contributes to the perception we understand as "Steve Carell's chest hair," but the removal of just one hair would go unnoticed by any but the most astute of electrologists. So it is with a film or a quantized reality.

It is no accident, of course, that Ingo named the ant Calcium. A quick anagrammatic exploration of the term *Calcium Ant* results in the telling *Lacuna Mict*, and a quick acronymatic exploration of MICT reveals it to be the abbreviated term for Multiple Image Computed Tomography. A quick dictionarial search for the word *tomography* reveals it to be the scanning of an object in sections. If just one of those "slices" was missing from the imagery, would it be missed? And if not, what does that say about the world in which we might very well and most certainly do live?

Is perhaps this missing million years nothing more than an incidental detail of the film, a single "Carell Hair," if we were to coin a term for it? Truly, I feel certain the only significance of this missing million years is that it is the wall that separates us, my friend Calcium and me.

And I wish I could, across the endless, meaningless myr, communicate this to Calcium. Perhaps it would help ease his burden. Then I remind myself once again that Calcium most likely does *not* exist in the future. In point of fact, he exists only in the past in a film Ingo long ago made, and not even there, for that film has been destroyed. By me. Therefore, Calcium exists only in my brain, in my imagination, in my memory; therefore I *can* communicate with him if I so desire. For we are both of us in my head.

CHAPTER 83

Tonight as the nurse changes my bandages, once again comically pressing "her" balloon breasts against my face to great laughter, I recall another scene (do I recall it or am I inventing it?) in which Calcium sits alone in his house and writes in his journal:

Let us say, for the sake of discussion, time functions just as a motion picture through a projector, in that it is made up of discrete moments, that true movement is an illusion of perception paired with the mechanism of a cosmic "projector." If this were so, then an element traveling in the converse timal direction would instantly disappear without a trace from the view of a so-called "forward traveling" observer. Perhaps my experimental compound embarked on such a route. There is no way to know with certainty, as any attempt to re-create the compound would again result in instantaneous disappearance of said compound and would allow no "time" for evaluation. And what if this element were somehow alive, or perhaps viral in nature? It was, after all, bullet-shaped, not unlike the rabies virus. How might it interact with the environment in which it finds itself? In other words, what might I have done to the past by creating it? What might I be doing this very moment to the past with my continued recklessness? Traveling forever away from this alien reality, I can never know. It haunts me.

A clown orderly bathes me by tossing a bucket of confetti on me. Laughter.

"What does any of this mean in my life, such as it is now?" I wonder from my hospital bed. "This is all just a movie. And I, in reality, am in bandages and confetti in a clown hospital in a cave at the end of the world. If I am a series of discrete images, then am I even alive in the conventional sense? Am I an illusion to myself? Are we all just a series of photos?"

Calcium, on his knees, pleads with an unseen force. His God? The universe? His own psyche?

"Why am I so alone? Why have I been left friendless? I ask so little. My life has been one of service, an attempt to better the circumstances of my species. And now the one thing I did for me— building B. Rosenberg, a prehistoric monument many times larger than my largest skyscraper, a symbol of inclusion that I posed with arm lifted high, holding a torch to light the way of lost and weary travelers, a gesture of great goodwill—is gone."

I feel an overwhelming affection—an abiding love, really—for Calcium, this stop-motion ant in a movie . . . no, not even . . . my *recovered memory* of a stop-motion ant in a movie, colored by all the inexact haziness of memory. Just as my distant memories of the animated birds Hegel and Schlegel bring me comfort, as my memories of those cartoon saints Willibald and Winibald warm me, remind me of the joys of siblinghood in these desolate "only child" times, as my memories of Groebli and Mauch, the animated ice-skating monkeys, remind me that sometimes the closest of ties can be between those not physically related. In the end, we *find* our families, don't we? I'm worried about my eyesight, though. There seems to be a tunneling, a degradation of the peripheral. It is difficult to assess its progress, especially swathed, as I am, in bandages, but I suspect, were there to be a time-lapse, I would be experiencing an irising similar to the technique ubiquitously employed in the end sequences of silent films. Perhaps it is glaucoma. Perhaps the movie is over.

Perhaps there's no more to remember. Yet there's so much still to worry about. The future is still coming, whether or not the movie continues, one frame at a time, one worry at a time. How will it go? Where will I go? I wish I had a friend in the world right now, not a million years hence, once I'm dead. What good is that? I wish I had my Calcium by my side here: together solving crimes, discussing philosophy, *et chetera*. I wish I had a Groebli. I have never in my life had a Groebli. Someone to call who would tell me it's going to be OK, someone with whom to ice-skate. Wouldn't that be a relief? I need a hobby. I've always needed a hobby. I never learned to skate. I never took the time. It was always about studying for young B. Where did that ambition come from, that desperate ambition?

The movie is over and I am unmoored. What can I spend my time thinking about now? What do I remember of my own life? Not Ingo's movie, but my own life? I can't bring myself to start again. I can't even enter the Slammyplex to do my film criticizings. Those movies are not for me. I don't know who they're for. They're not films anymore. They're . . . *bombardments*, mindless assaults on the senses. There is, I have heard, one film currently playing, quite well-reviewed, I am told, consisting entirely of a young person of inde-terminate gender screaming, "Look at me!" at the camera over and over for ninety minutes. The *Slammy's Gazette* called it "the quintes-sential coming-of-age story for our times," but I will not see it. They went on to say, "Borchard Melnoir delivers the performance of their career. Their yelling embodies the pain of all Hupersonity." Where is the nuance? I ask. Of course, I applaud its multiracial, multigen-dered cast—we've certainly come such a long way in that regard—but I fear we have as a culture foregone subtlety. I will not endorse this trend with my Slammy's Bucks. Movies for me have always been a way of understanding the world. It's all come to naught, though. Even Ingo's film, what does any of it matter? So I remember it. Who cares? It has changed nothing. My time has passed, and this is what I've done with it.

But wait.

There is still more to Ingo's film. It comes to me now, as if to save me from this emptiness, from my own failures. It is a blessing. There is, perhaps, a God.

CHAPTER 84

CALCIUM CALCULATES. HIS chalkboard filled with mathematical scribbles and chemical equations, he ponders. He paces. He stares out a still-standing window frame at his ruined town. He plays his burnt violin. Unearthly music. Modern Phrygian mode, I'm guessing. He goes back to the board. He practices rock climbing on what remains of his interior climbing wall. It doesn't seem like he would need the hand and foot holds, since he is an ant and I presume has arolia. Perhaps his various hand and foot mutations have rid him of those. He is, in any event, quite skilled. I was, for several years, an avid recreational climber and quite good at it. I had been told by my internist that my body type is well-suited to climbing, so I took it up, and in a very short time, I was teaching my teachers. If it weren't for an unfortunate and frankly inexplicable fall to the bottom of a sixty-foot sinkhole at the base of Mount Bald, I would still be at it. I wasn't seriously injured, but I spent four days down there before my outfitter realized I had not returned my equipment. It was a traumatic experience and put me off climbing. That I had to eat three of my toes to survive contributed mightily to my subsequent aversion to this sport. I cannot say why I felt compelled to eat the first of my toes within fifteen minutes of the fall. I attribute it to an irrationality that often accompanies panic.

"Eureka!" shrieks Calcium.

And I am ripped from my reverie.

"The compound I created does indeed travel back in time," says Calcium. "The question that remains is does this compound exist as a life-form and, if it does, does it ingest other life-forms and therefore affect the world through which it travels, therefore causing change in a reversed timeline? In other words . . . No, that's not correct. It would cause change in a forward-moving organism, but this energy would be utilized to propel itself further into the past. What if—and I'm just spitballing here, but hear me out—what if this new life-form ingests thoughts and memories and fantasies in the brains of forward-moving creatures, uses the resulting energy to multiply, leaving the brain of these creatures, finding other brains further into the past, where it does more of the same, depositing waste products in those brains, which are the digested thoughts, memories, and fantasies of the previous (future) brains?"

Calcium paces, wringing his hands.

"Now that I am attempting to predict the reverse chronology of my time rabies creatures, I need to consider its life cycle."

Once again, Calcium calculates. The chalkboard quickly fills with new equations. Now Calcium enters his workshop and uncovers a massive model of a barren landscape. He pulls a cardboard box marked ANTS off a shelf and shakes out what seem to be a thousand ant puppets. One needs to remind oneself that these ant puppets are probably one-sixth scale. Their actual size is impossible to determine on the screen, but if Calcium is ant-sized, his puppets are probably about one millimeter each. Since I believe it would prove nearly impossible for Ingo to have worked with such small puppets, one would have to assume that Calcium's ant puppets would have to be at the smallest, say, two inches long. There are approximately twenty-five and a half millimeters in an inch, so Calcium (a puppet himself, don't forget!) would have to be six times larger than that and would come in as a puppet himself at twelve inches, which would mean as a human, say I am five hundred times as tall as an ant, then the fossilized B. puppet would come in at five hundred times twelve, which equals six thousand inches or five hundred feet. I check my math. No, that is definitely correct. Ingo had built a five-hundred-foot fossilized skeleton of me. If he was indeed working on this part of the movie after he had met me, how could I never have seen such a monstrous thing? Where would he have shot the scenes?

His apartment ceiling was the same height as mine, nine feet. It's all mind-boggling. Even if, through some Herculean feat of manual dexterity, Ingo was able to construct and animate actual-size ant puppets, he would still have been required to build an actual-size puppet of me. Even then I feel certain I would have seen such a thing. I am not a tall man, but I would not fit in a box on his shelf, of this I am certain. Not yet, anyway, for, as of now, the shrinking has still left me generally human-sized.

In the film, Calcium is building Time Rabies (for that is what I have renamed it) puppets, puppets even smaller than the ant puppets, small enough to fit several into the head of an ant. I might have to go back to the size calculation drawing board, for these puppets are perhaps one-eighth the size of the ant heads. This would make the fossilized B. puppet close to two thousand feet tall. There is nowhere Ingo could've hidden this in all of St. Augustine where it would not be at least partially visible to me and everyone else. I check my math again. Twenty thousand feet? Two hundred feet? Two hundred thousand feet? My brain is not wrapping around this right now. Suffice to say, very large indeed.

The small Time Rabies puppets he now sculpts are transparent and amorphous. He works feverishly, the analog clock on his wall speeding up to indicate the passage of forty-eight hours. The time-lapse complete, Calcium has dark circles under his eyes and is in need of a shave. He looks exhausted, but he is on a mission and continues to work, setting up lights, setting up a line of ants, positioning his camera, and beginning the task of moving the ants forward frame by frame. We push in to the clock once again, this time watching it speed through a fourteen-day period. We pull out to reveal an even more exhausted-looking Calcium, now with a fairly substantial beard. He collapses into the chair at his desk, turns on his computer, and watches the result of his work. On the screen, the line of puppet ants marches toward an anthill while a second line marches away from it. There are the outliers as well, those ants who seem confused, bumping into things, going off at odd angles, finding their ways back. The animation is astounding; Calcium is Ingo's equal in terms of his artistry and skill. I remind myself once again that there is no Calcium; Ingo is the über-puppeteer here. I chuckle at my understandable mistake.

Suddenly in the film, there appears one of the amorphous creatures floating aimlessly in a backward timal trajectory. This creature, seemingly by happenstance, finds its way inside an ant's ear. Wait. Do ants have ears? I can no longer recall. I believe they do, just as birds and fish have them, although whereas the ears on birds and fish have no external presence, the ears on these ants look very much like human ears, which I'm almost certain is incorrect. Although I guess if anyone would know, Calcium would. Now I once more must remind myself that Calcium is a puppet and Ingo created him. Ingo was not an ant, so maybe he got that detail wrong. No matter.

We follow the creature into the mind of the ant. Do ants have minds? They do have brains, I believe. Obviously, Calcium's brain is much more sophisticated than the average ant's (more than most humans', too! Ha ha!), but they do have brains. Whether or not they have minds is something perhaps no human can answer. For according to Descartes, a brain is not a mind. And I am of a similar mind (brain?! Ha ha ha!). It is clear to me that Calcium has both, but does the average ant? Calcium (Ingo! Remember!) seems to think so, for the scene shifts to the mind of the aforementioned invaded ant. There we see his wants, his needs, his disappointments, his small triumphs, illustrated in the form of stop-motion sepia-tinted memories and fantasies, cinematic in their depiction, perhaps most closely resembling the work of the great female genius Maya Deren. The amorphous creature swims among these vignettes, gobbling them up, much like the protagonist of Toru Iwatani's *Pakkuman*, a popular electronic children's toy of the 1980s. As it eats, the creature splits into two identical creatures and they exit the ant, immediately entering the brain of a second ant, this one existing a moment earlier in time (for they are traveling backward through time, remember!). The two creatures eat some of this ant's thoughts (I must say, they are disappointingly similar to the previous ant's thoughts), but this time, they extrude waste products from the first ant's thoughts, leaving them in the brain of the second ant, which then become (in a somewhat degraded form) part of the second ant's consciousness. The two then divide into four, then exit into the recent past. Sometimes the Time Rabies reenter the same ants they've just fed on, but moments before their first visit, thus depositing the waste product thoughts of the ant into its own earlier incarnation. Perhaps this could explain déjà vu? Or maybe déjà rêvé? Or déjà entendu? Or, in any event, one of the myriad déjàs. It's difficult to parse this reverse movement through time. As a student of physics, I know the laws of time are symmetrical, and so it does not matter which way one moves through it, but of course as living human beings, none of us has that experience. If heartbreak has taught me anything, it is that things will not change back to what they were. And as healthy as I might be for my age, I know I will never again run a mile in just under four minutes (Bannister coached me while I was on Fulbright at Oxford. *You're better than I. Trimming your beard will cut the drag, and you'll break my record. Love, Rog*, he wrote in my yearbook). Today I'd be lucky to do it in just under five. That's what time does. Still, there is something exciting in Ingo's speculation. What does it say about time, but maybe more to the point, what does it say about everything that these future thoughts, digested and shit out into unsuspecting past brains, might do? Have the Time Rabies yet arrived here at my time? Have they infected all of life from its beginning on this planet? Where do they go once they have moved past the beginning of life and on to a cold dead Earth? Do they die there? Do they turn around and head back like someone on a road trip across the United States, who has to head back because of work?

CHAPTER 85

"WHAT IF I could use Time Rabies as fuel for my jet?" thinks Calcium in voiceover. "Would it work? Would my jet take me back so I could search for my Rosenberg?"

Calcium calculates.

"It would take a great deal of Time Rabies fuel to get back to B.," he mumbles to himself. "And there is, of course, the Great Nothing to factor in. The mysterious mass extinction. Part of me believes it was the result of an asteroid. Part of me believes it was a gamma ray burst. Some of me believes it was a flood. Then there is my clathrate gun hypothesis, which is about a fifth of me. Global warming, perhaps. Global cooling. I am of many minds. In any event, there was, it seems clear, a long period, perhaps a million years or myr, during which all life was extinguished with the exception of ants. Probably I should not have named it the Great Nothing because that is, of course, dismissive of my own kind. Perhaps the Great Very Little? This has two meanings, since we are small creatures and as such is clever. I must use that in something. Still, the Great Nothing packs a wallop, and since my kind does not seem to know the difference or care, I will stick with it until such time as I hear any objections, at which point I will happily change it. So according to my calculations, it was a million years of ants. And a million years of backward-traveling Time Rabies feeding on them. If I could invent some sort of net, some sort of vacuum device, to sweep Time Rabies from the air, I might be able to use them as fuel for my jet and travel back to the time of B. Rosenberg."

And so Calcium works on rigging his jet with such a sucking machine. When it is complete, he fills his plane with Time Rabies, points it backward, and watches through his windscreen as the present disappears forever.

I KNOW MY creator is finished with me. I know he has gotten me out of his system. He has reduced me to a punch line. He has abandoned me here in the clown hospital. I know he is tired, exhausted from the effort and the time it took. The jokes. The jokes. The fucking endless jokes. These take their toll, I am sure. I know he will move on from here, to something else, someone else, someone else on whom to seek revenge, and I will cease to be. I know that is coming. He is tired and I am mined. I will, however, continue to exert my existence, my opinions, which are the things that prove I exist in my own independent, autonomous, crippling reality. I have opinions. I must have opinions. The only way to be in relation to the world is to be in opposition to it, to stand firm, majestic, unbreakable, like Oleara Debord before me. Otherwise a person is nothing but weather, at the mercy of the breeze, the wind, the tides, the ideas of others. Ephemeral, billowing smoke, going this way and that, dissipating. No one watches the ocean and thinks, look at that amazing water molecule over there. No, that water molecule is one of trillions, going for a ride, unseen, anonymous. And, anyway, I am not contrary as an end in itself. My contrariness, when it occurs, is always the result of my refusal to submit to groupthink, my need to look beyond the hype, the spin, the faddish, the now. My opinions are born of painstaking analyses. But now I am tired, and there is very little I grasp about this new cave world. The young people have their slang: *pibbly*, *q-swipe*, *Michelle Trachtenberging*. I don't know what any of it means. I no longer care. They have their new celebrities: DeLazer Flypaper, Cappy Bint, The W, Nils Treak, Liddell Bopeep. Good-looking man-children and manic pixie dream girls. And I cannot bring myself to care. I have fought. I have fought a losing battle.

I have attempted to make myself relevant in this vacuous culture constructed by Slammy's and enforced by the Trunks. For it seems now they are in it together (were they always?). I despise the products of this insane marriage, but oh how I want them to love me. I long for them to adopt me as their William Burroughs, their Sam Fuller, their Hunter Thompson—their sagacious primogenitor to be trotted about, admired, raptly listened to. But I suspect it is not to be. That position has been filled by that monstrous and doddering Armond White, who has the distinct advantage, at this point in history, of being African Cavian.

It occurs to me that even my forgetting the movie seems almost to have been orchestrated by Ingo. Was it designed to be forgotten after viewing? Was my coma built into the film, just as was Molloy's? The world after watching the movie is different. Of that I am sure. I am changed by it, but the change is mysterious and impossible to pin down; the change is always changing, you see. People are different, angry sometimes, sometimes smiling for no reason. The weather has grown strange: stagnant, hot, cold. Often there is no weather at all. I feel weird. I am not me. I am me as a child and me as an adult, all at the same time. My head is soft. My neck is stiff. There's something that doesn't make sense right now. And it is always right now. I am so tired. That door won't open. Staying up this long to remember the film has left me confused. What door? There is no door. What did I mean?

"Everyone is miserable. Injured. In pain. Worried," comes an announcement from somewhere. This goes without saying, so why announce it?

And then it is over. The final reel has unspooled and I am stunned. This Nameless Ape viewing is like no other Nameless Ape viewing that has come before. I can only sit here, mute, as the projector continues to whir. I cannot speak. I do not want to speak. I am mute. I stare at the now-white rectangle before me. The film has left me broken. It has fixed me. I am reborn. My very DNA has been altered. I sit here for what feels like hours, days, before I am able to move, to walk, to step into the world.

CHAPTER 86

OUTSIDE, EVERYTHING LOOKS different, *is* different. The light is brighter, the sky bluer. Now the air breathes me. And I walk. A calm has enveloped me. The people I pass smile and nod. How strange and wonderful to be in this world. How strange and wonderful to smile and nod back. I am in on a secret. I am part of something larger. I am truly changed. But I do not look at my former self in judgment, in disdain. I have nothing but compassion and love for that person, for every person, for every dancing, spinning electron in the universe. I understand now that I do not need to show Ingo's film to anyone. Indeed, I cannot show Ingo's film to anyone. The film was meant for me alone. The only way to share the film with others is to share what I have become. I have been transformed by it, and my presence will transform others. The entire film itself is, of course, the Unseen, at least by others. That is so obvious now.

I will remember it again. And again. I will remember it for the rest of my life, but not as a critic. I will not attempt to master it, to own it, to teach it. Those days are over. The days of flag planting, of claiming ownership, are done. From here on in, I will submit to great art. It will do with me as it sees fit. I will go where it tells me. I will let it in, let it tear me limb from limb, eradicate me, rebuild me in its own image. I will dwell in it as does a subject in a heavenly kingdom. I will never again attempt to own anything: no film, no person, no idea.

I call my editor.

"Hello, Davis," I say.

"B., where are you? I've been trying to get in touch with you for months now."

"I'm sorry," I say. "I have been immersed in a life-altering experience."

"Are you OK? You sound different."

"I am different, wonderfully different." I chuckle warmly.

"Um, great. How's the *Enchantment* piece coming? We've been waiting to see pages."

"Davis, I love you and I am so appreciative of the opportunities you've provided for me."

"Great. My pleasure."

"I've arrived at a different place, and I can no longer live in judgment of the work of others. I am just so grateful to be alive, and I am grateful that the world is alive in all its magnificent complexity."

"What are you saying?"

"I can't write any more criticism."

"We've invested in this piece, B. We sent you down to Florida."

"And I'm so grateful. Thank you. Perhaps you can give it to Dinsmore? I'll send them my notes. As Dinsmore is a trans man, the piece is rightfully theirs."

"I don't really get what is happening here."

"For the first time in my life, I can honestly say I don't know what is happening, either. And it feels wonderful. Goodbye, Davis. I love you."

I hang up, but not in my typical angry way. I hang up gently. I hang up with gratitude, without guilt. I hang up because it is time to hang up. I then call to cancel the memorial slide I had ordered for Ingo's gravesite. I will lose the deposit, but I do not care. Then I order a new stone for Ingo. Just his name and dates. Simple and discreet. Maybe even that's too much. I don't know. I don't know anything right now. I am learning. I am a student. Always and forever a student. An absolute beginner, as they say. And that's good. That is the right thing to be. I can breathe. There is nothing to defend. I am free.

CHAPTER 87

OVER THE NEXT few days, I am happy. I have no expectations in my interactions with people and because of that everything is easier. I am kind and gentle with the world, and the world returns the favor. I am no longer . . . I stop. I don't know how to finish that thought until I recognize that is the thought in its entirety: I am no longer.

The plan, such as it is in my new life, is to pack the film, Ingo's notebooks, and all his props and sets into a large rental truck and haul it back to New York. Once there, I will find new employment, perhaps working for a charitable organization, perhaps running a community garden in some underserved food-desert community. Something like this is my dream now. I hope only to be of service. Then once a year, I will arrange for time off so I can watch Ingo's film again in order to learn more, to feel more, to become more present, to better serve. This is my plan, such as it is, understanding full well that, as Mr. J. Lennon taught us, life is what happens while you are busy making other plans.

On the road, driving the twenty-six-foot truck towing my car, I spot Slammy's up ahead. It is the Slammy's I stopped at on the way down here. So much has happened. So much has changed. I smile thinking back to the misadventures of that me. Was anyone ever so young? I decide to stop, perhaps pick up a Slammy's Original Board-walk Cola for the road, perhaps a Slammy's veggie burger, no cheese, since I am now an abolitionist vegan.

The lot is empty. Still I park my huge rig at the far end on the grass, so as not to take up multiple spaces (perhaps there will be a lunch rush!). I make my way across the lot. It's so hot I can feel the sunbaked asphalt through the soles of my shoes. It feels good. It also feels good to step into the air-conditioned interior. It also feels good to see my old friend again behind the counter. She probably doesn't remember me. Why would she? I smile and she returns it.

"Welcome to Slammy's," she says. "May I help you?"

"Yes, thank you," I say.

It's clear my face is not ringing any bells. That's OK. My old self would've been hurt. But I now know she probably sees hundreds of people a day. I'm just one more. It's fine.

"Yes, please, I'd like a Biggy Slammy's Original Boardwalk Cola, please."

"OK, baby," she says. "Anything else?"

She called me baby. I'm taken aback. I'm pleased. I need to fight old instincts.

"Yeah, I'd also like a Slammy's Veggie Burger. No cheese, please."

"Cheese come on it, baby," she says.

I fight the urge to tell her I'm a vegan and that I cannot in good conscience ingest any animal products.

"OK, that's fine," I say.

"Anything else?"

"No, that'll do it," I say. "Thank you."

"$5.37, baby."

It's nice that she keeps calling me baby. It doesn't mean anything other than she's being pleasant. It doesn't mean she's flirting with me. It is most likely a common term of endearment among African Americans in this region. Like a waitress in a coffee shop calling one "honey."

I pay her and take a seat. I try to make eye contact with her, to see if there might be anything else between us. Not that I expect anything more. But she just stares blankly past me, out the window. It takes a while for the food to come out, which is surprising as there are no customers here other than myself.

"That your big truck out there, baby?" she says to me, finally.

"Yeah," I say. I have a sudden urge to tell her about Ingo's film, about his African Americanness, his Swedishness, about how the film changed me. But I remember I made a vow to myself and to Ingo not to reveal its existence to anyone. This new attitude is rewarding me. I must remain constantly vigilant.

"Cause it's on fire," she says.

I whip my head around to see billowing smoke pouring from the truck.

CHAPTER 88

SMOKE GETS IN my eyes. And in its new, particulated form, I see the film again and for the last time. I know this smoke can never be put back into a movie. I know enough about entropy to know this. The universe is on a constant slope toward greater and greater disorganization.

And then in an instant, humanity is extinguished. Only ants now. And fungus. And some occasional strange mutated flowers, roses of an unearthly hue, colors without precedent or explanation. How is it possible that Ingo created a color never before imagined? It is the color of a scream, the color of paradox, the color of nothing. And for a million years, there is no sound, as ants and fungus and flowers have no ears. There is no comedy or tragedy in this world. For ants could not comprehend of it, have no need for it. Ants, you see, are perfect beings. They know who they are without knowing they know who they are. There is no shame or hubris. Their antness is unapologetic, clean. There is no need to tell themselves stories, create mythologies or gods. And this section of the movie, which is a month long, is not here to entertain me. I am simply a fly on the wall of antkind, and I can watch it or not. And I watch it.

There are entire days of film in which no ants appear at all. Just rocks. Just fungus. Just preternatural flowers. It is not about me. Of course, simply not being about me makes it about me. Everything is about me. Everything is understood in relation to me. There is no way around this. This is the imperfect mechanism of consciousness. I remember the experience of sitting through this month of the film as entering a new state of being. Everything slowed. There being no choice of focus by the director (other than camera placement, for you can't get completely away from subjectivity), I found my eyes free to wander the frame. It was frightening at first, as when a child is given a school assignment with no instructions. But over time—and there was much time—I began to find this freedom exhilarating and, just as in self-guided meditation, I became painfully aware of my own "monkey mind," then gradually started to gently quiet it.

By the second week, I watched the ants, the no ants, the rocks, the fungus, the flowers without judgment, without assigning human motivations to any of the goings-on, without anthropomorphism. In a word, I simply lived there. It's true that at the end of each day, while I tried to sleep, there were elaborate and manic masturbation sessions with fantasies I had never before entertained, but I understood those to, again, be the result of my "monkey" mind leaving my body, like so much semen in a spasm of surrender. I began to suspect that all that came before was presented only to clear the way for this essential transformative experience. And even after my epiphany, the million-year sequence persisted for another two weeks, during which nothing at all happened. Enough is enough, I finally thought. Really, I get it. And with that, everything changed. When the student is ready, the teacher appears.

CHAPTER 89

Lying in the clown hospital bed, I know I am different. Well, I think I am different, but can I know for certain? Perhaps my memory of how I was is inaccurate. But if my memory now is inaccurate and I am exactly as I was, then my memory before was inaccurate, and I don't remember having an inaccurate memory. It occurs to me that coming out of a long-term coma is the only opportunity a huthon has to see him or her or thonself after a long absence. The experience of seeing a friend or relative after a long absence is familiar to us all. They look older. They look taller. They look fatter. But as we are with ourselves every second of every day, we don't have that opportunity. Furthermore, our assessment of their changes is not necessarily objective. When I saw my childhood house after decades of being away, it looked smaller. Certainly it had not grown smaller. My memory was at fault. Or at the very least my subjectivity: I recalled the house as bigger because I was smaller, because my world was smaller then. So am I different now? Maybe when I get back to New York I can take a poll of those who knew me: Do I seem different? If so, how? Am I, as I believe, growing smaller?

Most who knew me seem to have abandoned me here. I've been told by staff that there have been no visitors. No calls. My ex-wife is not surprising. But my daughter? That is painful. My son? Certainly something is different. I can feel it. So even if they were to tell me it isn't so, I wouldn't believe them. They'd be lying. For whatever reason. Kindness. Meanness. Expediency. But something has been lost.

A certain spark. A lightness in my step (felt even while in traction). I was younger then, so maybe this is what it feels like to be three months older. I have never been this old before, so how would I know? How *can* I know? The only thing to do is move forward without ever knowing why I am different, only how. And not even that. I am confused. My memory is faulty. Perhaps my attractions have changed. I can't tell yet. My needs. My sexuality. I can't yet tell.

I AWAKEN TO find a puppet, swathed in gauze and in traction, in the hospital bed next to mine. She tells me, she, too, was injured in battle, a foreigner here, from the Unseen, who came to fight alongside the Diggers. She tells me the fight against corporatism, against fascism, is everyone's fight, that these things must be battled wherever they arise. So she came here, to the cave. But now she is wounded, she is broken, she is homesick. She misses her sister Molly. I ask her if by chance she has a penis under all those bandages, because it occurs to me she might.

"I do," she says.

I ask the puppet how she can get back to her world if it is irretrievably gone in time and fire. She says you can't go back to something that is gone. You can only go forward to where it is now.

"What does that mean?" I say.

"Nothing is lost in the universe. Things just shift. They reconfigure. The atoms are there. The chrontoms are there."

"Chrontoms?"

"Units of time that make up moments. Building blocks. They remain as well, just reconfigured into other moments, different moments. Elsewhere."

"So for all intents and purposes, one can't find those lost moments because the chrontoms are part of other moments now?"

"It's not physically impossible, of course. But the odds of the chrontoms happening to change back into the exact same configuration is as likely as all the dispersed atoms of a cremated dead person coming together again to re-create that person."

"Could that happen?"

"It could."

"A clone?"

"No. The same person. But at a different time."

"So the chrontoms could come together to create the same time but at a different time?"

"Yes. But you would have to move into the future to find this possible past."

"This feels nonsensical."

"Yet you're drawn to it."

"Yes. One is always looking for magic in the world. One never gets past that. One wonders why."

"One does," she says.

"I don't want to die."

"I know, sweetheart. I know."

CHAPTER 90

Is the record the same as the original? And what of an art form that exists only as a record (e.g., a moving picture film), which may be a representation of a series of still tableaux but is understood in the brain of the viewer as merged together through time, due to the viewer's brain being tricked by what amounts to nothing more than an optical illusion? In this very real sense, the film does not exist outside the brain of the viewer, and in the case of Ingo's film, this viewer alone. As Harry Rimmer expressed so eloquently in his defense of the veracity of the Bible: "The writers of the Bible are all dead and have been so for many generations. Their testimony was undisputed in the days when they were alive and could be called into question, and while other witnesses to these same facts were also living. *It is a fact recognized by the laws of evidence that when the testimony of an eyewitness is not disputed in his own lifetime, that testimony is fixed for all time and is not subject to challenge by those who come after him.* (emphasis mine) So the matter of the authenticity of the Bible is beyond the jurisdiction of the court." In a nutshell, I am the only witness to Ingo's film; what I say goes.

I feel certain now that I've remembered the film as much as is humanly possible. I should go about remembering it backward. I suspect this film, more than most, would greatly reward backward rememorying. There is, it seems, an interest on Ingo's part in this area of exploration. And, in truth, there comes a time in any person's life when there is not much to look forward to and the only direction to look is back. However, I would not jump back to memories to then play them forward but rather play the whole film in reverse, to study effect and cause, to suck all that Pandora has unleashed back into the box, to understand true backwardness. I think Ingo instinctively recognized this; the son of an illiterate Pullman porter (?), he witnessed a brutality few of us have.

The movie is over. I remember the ending. I believe I have gotten all I will out of this forward viewing, this Nameless Ape memory. Much is missing; much is confused. Perhaps in my reverse memory of it, I will discover those missing parts. Perhaps starting with effect will lead me to cause, and through this process I might learn more. But, of course, the experienced reality of the human animal is that time moves forward. So I must walk forward through time, while looking backward through memory. This is my plight, much as Dante's fortune-tellers are damned to walk forever forward with heads facing backward, much like Lot's wife, not even assigned her own name in that patriarchal text—let's call her Yvonne—looks backward and is punished by being transformed into a pillar of salt. One cannot either look forward as did the fortune-tellers or backward as did Yvonne, it seems, without being punished for it. I guess, then, one might as well look wherever one wants.

So I look back. And walk forward. And think about what might have happened to Calcium as he made his way into the past, watching the world fold instead of unfold. Did he ever find me? Wait. I am recalling a moment. I was driving down to Florida, my windshield spattered with—

I fall into a hole. It is dark and apparently deep, for I plummet a long time. I know—or believe I know, from precedent—that this fall will not result in death or even serious injury; it is simply a thing that happens to me. Some people have eczema; I fall into holes. This realization allows me to relax into my fall; it is said that drunks and babies don't get hurt in falls because they do not tense their bodies, having little ability to anticipate. I am neither a drunk nor am I a baby, but I have come to the place where I can say I am a Buddhist, having studied Insight Meditation with the great Jack Cornfeld, and Jack always told us, "You must live in the present moment. You must. Live in it, assholes!" and we did. So as I fall, I continue my work; I play the remembered film in reverse in my head. This changes everything, of course. It's what Jack called a "paradigm shift" in his now-famous lecture at the Naropa Institute, "Have a Fucking Paradigm Shift, Assholes!" Now I see my fall in reverse; I see myself ascending from the hole, a hero, a superhero, really, my effect leading to cause, my humiliation leading to a mastery over gravity. That is a true superpower. I am Reverseman. I see more of the film in this direction. I see Henrietta, Tsai, Barassini, Grace, all on their roads to birth, their scars erased, one by one. I see them unborn, splitting into sperm and egg, uninheriting the traits of their parents, becoming free. I see Trunk, too, getting smaller, unlearning his sadnesses. At each erased sadness, I see the path to which it led erased. I imagine the various lives he might have had. And if I can imagine them, they must be true somewhere. It occurs to me that as I recall the movie, I am also recalling myself, for the film doesn't exist without me. Well, that one version from B2 does, and that other version, the one in the rectangular film cans, but those are not the true versions. Rather, they are some sort of corruption, some sort of reconstitution, a parody, contemptuous and odious. I recognize now that remembering the movie is the movie, that even the pieces I can't remember are the movie. Memory is imperfect. It is imprecise, but it is the only tool we have to maintain contact with the world through time. Without it, life as we know it ceases to exist. I hit the bottom.

ACKNOWLEDGMENTS

Many thanks to Anna Kaufman, Ben Greenberg, Claudia Ballard, Deanna Storey, Denise Monaghan, Emma Balay-Wilson, Eva H.D., Helen Kaufman, Ken Richman, MacDowell Colony, Myron Kaufman, Riva Lehrer, Sharon Jackson, and Susan Kaufman.